Hobnail and Other Frontier Stories

HOBNAIL AND OTHER FRONTIER STORIES

A CENTURY OF THE AMERICAN FRONTIER

WITH A FOREWORD BY *NEW YORK TIMES* BESTSELLING AUTHOR TOM CLAVIN

EDITED BY HAZEL RUMNEY

THORNDIKE PRESS
A part of Gale, a Cengage Company

Copyright © 2019 by Five Star Publishing, a part of Gale, a Cengage Company.
Kanta-ke © 2019 by James D. Crownover
Rata Remembers © 2019 by Paul Colt
The Times of a Sign © 2019 by Rod Miller
Legend © 2019 by Johnny D. Boggs
Arley © 2019 by Wallace J. Swenson
Grogan's Choice © 2019 by Lonnie Whitaker
Boxcar Knights © 2019 by Steven Howell Wilson
The Bells of Juniper © 2019 by Vonn Mckee
Frank Rule and the Tascosans © 2019 by John Neely Davis
When Tully Came to Town © 2019 by Richard Prosch
The Caves of Vesper Mountain © 2019 by Greg Hunt
Hobnail © 2019 by Loren D. Estleman
The Assassin © 2019 by Patrick Dearen
Apaches Survive © 2019 by Harper Courtland
Spanish Dagger © 2019 by W. Michael Farmer
The Way of the West © 2019 by L. J. Martin
Return to Laurel © 2019 by John D. Nesbitt
Thorndike Press, a part of Gale, a Cengage Company.

ALL RIGHTS RESERVED

**LIBRARY OF CONGRESS CIP DATA ON FILE.
CATALOGUING IN PUBLICATION FOR THIS BOOK
IS AVAILABLE FROM THE LIBRARY OF CONGRESS**

ISBN-13: 978-1-4328-6436-1 (hardcover alk. paper)

Published in 2020 by arrangement with Five Star Non-Royalty

Printed in Mexico
Print Number: 03   Print Year: 2020

TABLE OF CONTENTS

5

FOREWORD

BY *NEW YORK TIMES*
BESTSELLING AUTHOR TOM CLAVIN

In the nineteenth century, as people moved west so too did the American frontier. Initially, to the European explorers and the settlers who soon followed in the 1500s and 1600s, North America was one big frontier. It was literally uncharted territory: to the Spanish on the West Coast the land appeared to spread east forever; to the English on the East Coast the frontier to the west seemed to have no end. The concept of "frontier" may not have been created by those first European visitors, but it did become an ideal to be passionately pursued and embraced in a land of seemingly infinite potential.

In the 1700s, the first frontier for those most keen on taming and settling on large swaths of land was what awaited on the other side of the Appalachian Mountains. When Daniel Boone and others cut their way through the Cumberland Gap, they found forests and fields teeming with game and fertile fields begging to be farmed. With Ohio, Kentucky, and Tennessee being settled, it was time to move on, the frontier now beckoning from the other side of the Mississippi River. Especially in the nineteenth century, that boundary separating "civilization" from the frontier kept shifting enticingly west, to the Missouri River, to Texas and Kansas and Nebraska, to Colorado and Utah, to New Mexico and Arizona, until finally, with the wagon trains and telegraph lines and railroad tracks, all of the Lower 48 was connected.

The Oklahoma Land Rush of 1889 was the last great burst of pent-up energy on a frontier waiting to be claimed. A year later, the U.S. Census showed that the "frontier line," a point beyond which the population density was less than two persons per square mile, no longer existed. With that Frederick Jackson Turner, director of the U.S. Census Bureau, announced that the American frontier was closed. From then on, we've just been filling in the gaps.

Of course, there had been a pesky problem for people looking to embrace the frontier and all its beauty and challenges — the presence of native inhabitants. It cannot truly be said the frontier was virgin or pristine if people already lived in it. And what strange, incomprehensible creatures, ones who looked and dressed differently, spoke any number of languages, performed bizarre rituals, were blithely unaware of land ownership, and who fought with savage brutality. As the frontier shrank throughout the nineteenth century, so too did the world and future of American Indians. The process of exploring and settling and civilizing the frontier was also one of conquest that bordered on — or perhaps simply was — genocide. For most white men and women, the frontier kept moving westward, but for America's original residents the frontier was a circle that kept getting smaller and tighter until only the reservations were left.

Sadly, there could not have been another way. The clash of cultures was too loud and harsh for all to survive and prosper and enjoy the opportunities the frontier offered. Increasing the pressure in the 1800s were the waves of immigrants arriving at the docks of major cities, especially on the East Coast. Some were welcomed by those who had come before; others aimed rickety wagons west, searching for the vast open spaces and big skies that would have been unthinkable options in their native Ireland, Germany, or Italy. America offered promise and the frontier was a promise within a promise. Helping to hammer together many of the communities that suddenly popped up out of the ground like prairie dogs west of the Missouri were people who also spoke different languages but shared that deeply American desire to forge a new life on the other side of the horizon. Perhaps a reason why the immigration issues of today are so intense is that we no longer have that seemingly limitless horizon because, as Turner declared in 1890, there is no more American frontier.

To understand where we were in the nineteenth century and then how we got here can be an academic exercise. Much more enjoyable, though, is to read stories set in that period. Writers' imaginations remain a limitless horizon. But while this may serve especially well practitioners of science fiction who write about worlds we do not (yet) know — a new frontier that may indeed be endless — stories about the American frontier must read and feel authentic. No longer is there a gullible public on the East and West Coasts who will swallow whole the exaggerations, embellishments, and outright fabrications of the dime-store novelist. Today's readers of fiction about the West want to be entertained, yes, but they also want the research, the facts, the authenticity that satisfies intellectually as well as emotionally.

That is why a collection such as this one is necessary as well as a welcome addition to bookshop and library shelves (and Kindles). Each story, from James D. Crownover's "Kanta-ke," set in the very early 1800s, to John D. Nesbitt's "Return to Laurel," taking place as the frontier was becoming history, portrays a piece of America, a specific time and place rendered clearly in addition to action and the beating hearts of characters. In Paul Colt's "Rata Remembers," we are given a unique perspective on the dawn of the Texas Revolution. In "Legend" by Johnny D. Boggs, we are offered a different view of the dime-store novel and its impact. The first sentence in Lonnie Whitaker's "Grogan's Choice" — "Jake hated to think about leaving the dog" — is such a gripper one has to keep reading.

Among other benefits, in Richard Prosch's "When Tully Came to Town" we learn about the inner workings of a mid-1870s newspaper office. In the story "Spanish Dagger" by W. Michael Farmer, we not only learn what Spanish dagger is, and its significance, but enjoy such appealing passages as, "Jordon's face was peaceful, close to smiling, eyes closed. He looked like he was taking a nap except for the black, half-inch diameter hole between his eyes." And of course, one feels all around better for having read anything by Loren D. Estleman, and "Hobnail" in this collection adds to his reputation as one of our finest writers in any genre.

Let's face it, the first goal of this collection is to satisfy the appetite of discerning readers of western fiction. The stories cited and the others in this gathering do that. But when the last sentence has been devoured, we have a sense of having spent a century on the American frontier, when it was still full of promise and an undiscovered country . . . and scary and dangerous and occasionally violent. Well-written and authentic stories give us that picture, full of colors and shades and big enough to cover the entire canvas.

Tom Clavin is the author or co-author of eighteen books, among them the best sellers *Dodge City, Halsey's Typhoon, The Last Stand of Fox Company,* and *The Heart of Everything That Is.* The forthcoming *Tomb-*

stone (February 2020) will complete a "frontier lawmen" trilogy that includes *Wild Bill* and *Dodge City.* Visit tomclavin.com for more info.

A Century of the American Frontier 1800–1855

■ ■ ■ ■

KANTA-KE

BY JAMES D. CROWNOVER

■ ■ ■ ■

I
THE BATTLE OF
THE SHAWNEE ARMADA

1800
In an unnamed tavern somewhere in old Pittsburgh sat two Dutchmen of Quaker ancestry . . .

The first time we noticed him, he was standing in the door to the tavern — more accurately, he filled the doorway, his head above the lintel and only glimpses of light indicated that the door was behind him. I admit to being well into my cups and only heard the noise of his first challenge, but understood it the second time, "I can whip any two o' ye lubbers wi' one hand an' never spill me ale," he roared, waving his tankard and sloshing beer here and there.

"Never thee mind the sailor, Jemmy Hall, play thy dice," Jobe Pike, my hunting partner, demanded. I shook the leather cup and dumped the dice on the table. Jobe chuckled. "Ye lost again, Jemmy, boy," and turning to the serving wench called, "Two more,

21

me girl, Jemmy is buying again."

"And that is the last I will buy tonight," I vowed.

The wench filled our tankards and leaned between us to set them on the table, pressing her ample bosom against Jobe's shoulder and revealing a goodly amount of cleavage for his appreciation.

A tankard slammed down on the table and the sailor grabbed the woman's arm, "Gie me thy pitcher, wench." Holding her by the arm, he grabbed the pitcher and turned it up, spilling ale down his beard and shirt while the woman struggled to be free.

Jobe stood and faced the giant. He could have walked under the sailor's outstretched arm with room to spare. "Turn the woman loose," he demanded.

The sailor looked down at the little man and grinned. "That I will, mate." He loosed the woman and with the same motion, slammed Jobe beside his ear with the back of his fist, sending him flying across the table, wiping out two tankards and upsetting the table.

There I sat, holding my mug and no place to set it, so I stood and slammed it into the face of the giant, spoiling his foolish grin. He staggered back a step or two and his eyes widened when he noted that I was fully as tall as he and maybe a stone heavier.

"Thee must not pick on wenches and little men," I said. The pewter mug had collapsed and trapped my fingers against the handle. It would not shake off.

My opponent grunted and sprang at me, arms flailing. I ducked his first swing and met his other fist with my trapped hand. His fist hit the mug and dislodged it from my fingers. It felt like my little finger had stayed with the mug. The way my other three fingers stung when the ale sloshed on them, they must have lost some skin too, but there was not time to look.

Our Sinbad charged, his lowered head striking my chest; arms about my waist pulled me to him and we fell to the floor. I kneed him in the groin and grabbed both his ears to keep his teeth away from mine. He was not as light as other men I had fought, but I was still able to throw him off and rise to my knees. As he came to his knees, I hit him with my injured fist. The blow hurt me more than him.

He grinned when his huge fist connected to my jaw and the world turned blurry. Just before it faded completely out, a pitcher crashed down on my opponent's head.

I awoke lying across the back of the sailor and hearing a low humming in my ear. Sitting up at last, I found the wench sitting on the floor with Jobe's head cradled to her bosom, softly humming and rocking. *They always go for the little man, and here I sit, hurt just as bad — bleeding even — and no one cares.*

I stood, and immediately looked for a chair. As my knees folded, someone slipped a chair under me and stayed my return to the floor.

Someone clapped me on the shoulder, "Great fight, friend."

"Never seen nothing like it," another voice said.

"Ah-h-h, two giants and a midget go at it and a woman saves the day," a third disappointed patron said.

My little finger was still attached, but with a new crook in it. There was not much skin from my knuckles to my nails and blood dripped from my fingertips. I wrapped the hand in as clean a cloth as could be found.

The sailor stirred and groaned and the crowd grew quiet, watching the big man return to the land of the living. "Wha' 'appen?" Sinbad's lips were swelling and it was beginning to affect his speech.

I nodded at the battered pitcher on the floor beside him, "That pitcher fell on your head." It lay on its side in a pool of ale. The big man picked it up and took a long pull from it. I declined his offer and he drained it. "Hafa go." He lunged up and teetered in the general direction of the door.

Jobe was showing little improvement in his condition, and it looked like it would be a long recovery for him. I stood and he winked.

"I am going to bed," I said and caught the door when next it spun by.

Outside, the cold fresh night air revived me somewhat and by feeling my way along the wall, found the corner of the building. My first step around the corner brought my foot against an obstacle and I fell across somebody. From his smell, I knew it was not the first time tonight I had fallen on him.

"Wake up, sailor, and go to your ship." He was lying facedown and I shook his shoulder. No response. When I tried to turn him over, my hand brushed the hilt of a knife. The blade was buried between his ribs and there had been little bleeding. I began shouting, "Murder!" It was a long time before a lantern came from the tavern and shone on the scene. The sailor was dead and I was the primary suspect.

Jobe had recovered enough to come see and when the constable arrested me, whispered, "I will have horses ready behind the livery."

The constable shackled me hand and foot and led me to the gaol. "Hold this lantern, prisoner, while I find the right key." He fumbled with the large key ring until he had the right key and unlocked the door, pulling it open. I shoved him in hard and slammed the door, turning the key to lock it. The key ring came apart, scattering keys everywhere. No time to look for the shackle key, I shuffled off down the alley to the back lots and the horses.

"Can thee not get thy shackles off?" Jobe asked.

"No, not in the dark and without making a lot of noise." My horse looked back at me when I sat down sidesaddle. "Shut up and get going before I crack thee one." I'm daft if she did not snicker.

They would expect us to ride south and west, so Jobe led us north beyond the farms and into the Pennsylvania woods. We stopped in the midst of a windfall about midmorning.

"A fine fix this is, no food, no guns, no tools to break thy shackles. What are we going to do? I tell thee now, Jemmy Hall, I will never come to Pittsburgh again. Zanesburg is as much civilization as I will ever want," Jobe vowed.

I laughed. "Mayhap it will be Holderby's Landing if the ale is good and the fur prices fair." With my head and fingers aching and my ankles and wrists chafing, I had to agree with him. "Is not tomorrow the Sabbath? Then the good people will surely go to meeting and stay the day. We shall borrow farmer Fleming's forge and tools and remove these shackles like the angels did Paul and Silas."

Jobe grunted his disgust, "Then we will gather our horses at Holderby's and gear and take the path to Kanta-ke with our silver in our purses."

It would be the first time we returned to the hunt with money in our pockets. There was no place in the wilderness to spend it, so when we came and sold our pelts, we stayed until the money was spent, then returned to the hunt without a shilling to our names. Two hungry men lay on their horse blankets and nursed aching heads. My chafed ankles and wrists and skinned fingers added to my discomfort.

Midafternoon, we moved back toward the settled country and found a farm likely to have a forge and waited for the dawning of the Sabbath. Just before dawn, the farmer came out and turned the calf out with his milch cow, hitched up the buggy, and returned to the house to put on his Sabbath clothes. Soon, they departed; husband, wife, and covey of kids, two boys dangling bare feet off the tailgate.

Hardly had their dust settled before we were in the shed starting the forge. The hinge pins on the ankle cuffs were easy to punch out, but the wrist cuffs were a problem. The farmer would be puzzled when he came back to find his forge warm, but he would understand the next spring when he plowed up the shackles we buried in his field. We took the smallest ham from the smokehouse and left silver for payment. Hard cash in a farmer's hand was as rare as ice in Hades in those days, so we knew he would be happy with it.

"Sneaking about like a murderer chafes as much as those cuffs did," I said to Jobe.

"It is the *truth* of the matter that is important, not what some sheriff *thinks,*" Jobe replied. "Ye could hire some barrister to plead thy case and he would take thy silver and horses and traps and guns and present thy case to the judge and shrug when the judge pronounces thee guilty withal. And when thou art hung and dead, he will demand thy clothes for final payment and thou wouldst go before thy maker naked as the day thee were born. Let us return these horses, get our gear, and go."

Two days gone, and the innkeeper had our gear for sale, though we were paid up on our rents. The remorse he showed was for getting caught, not his sins. We left him with the hope that the thrashing he got showed him the error of his ways.

We stole a boat and set it adrift where the young Ohio River turns north in a great loop before it dips south and west in the hope the good sheriff would pursue it while we tramped west through the woods to the river where we had cached our canoe. We thought it prudent to pass Zanesburg with its lovely Betty Zane and its Fort Fincastle in the dark and go on to Holderby's Landing where our horses waited.

Several times in our journey, we were saluted by Indians on the northern shore. They were mostly Shawnee with a few Wyandot and Mingo thrown in. Their bows were not powerful enough for their arrows to reach us, and we taunted them until in one group, a white man in British costume stepped out and shot at us with his musket. The shot fell fifty yards short.

It was surprising how much more accurate our guns were after we changed to rifled barrels and Jobe scrambled to return the

Lobster's salute. "Hold steady, Jemmy, while I aim," Jobe said. He scooted down and propped his gun on the gunnel while I back-paddled to hold the canoe steady.

The soldier fired again, cutting the short-fall by half.

The crack-bang of Jobe's shot made me jump and we watched a moment as the shot flew. The Lobster threw his hands up and fell and a second later we heard his cry.

The greatly disturbed Indians gathered around the fallen man and he must have said something about being exposed to the fire, for they suddenly looked our way and ran for the woods, leaving the wounded man to fend for himself. He rolled to his knees, sat up, and climbed his rifle. Crimson stained the back of his white pants from mid-thigh down.

Jobe grunted, "Damme, through and through, it missed the bone."

"He must have moved after you fired," I said sarcastically. We moved on and the Indians came out yelling and gesturing until Jobe scooted down and aimed again.

"Just like magic, they are gone," Jobe said, and we laughed.

We had to go with the river, and the afternoon after our encounter with the British officer, we were again accosted by a larger band of Indians, mostly women and children and a few old warriors. They showed more respect for our guns than before. The river here flowed south, then looped in a big bend and flowed north before again bending south. Before we were out of sight, the Indians were running into the woods, intent on cutting across the neck to greet us again.

"Why do they not get a canoe and come out to meet us?" Jobe asked.

"Who says they do not have one? And do thou really want them to?"

"Just one boat at a time, I mind." We rounded the bend and could see where the river swept on around to the north.

"That is thy idea of a good fight, not the red man's. Their idea of a good fight would be a half-dozen boats converging on us from all directions, which they would gladly do . . ." I stopped mid-thought and turned the canoe sharply for the shore, "Dig deep, Jobe."

In the wilderness if one does not react instantly to an urgent call, he could find real trouble. Jobe dug deep with his paddle and we shot under the overhanging limbs of a willow thicket at the end of the tongue of land. When we were well hidden, he asked, "What is it, Jemmy?"

"How many warriors were in that crowd?"

"Not many . . . thou thinks mayhap the warriors are in an armada!"

"Let us wait and see." We held the drooping willow wands and waited. Our wait was frightfully short, for racing around the bend from behind us came two large canoes with six painted warriors in one and eight in the other. The only weapons they carried were their knives and tomahawks.

Jobe stared. "Damme, Jemmy, damme."

"Shoot the near boat at the waterline," I whispered, "I'll sink the other." They were beyond us before we were ready and both shots were hurried.

"Ready on three," Jobe said, "one . . . two . . . three."

The two shots sounded as one loud bang and we were enveloped in a cloud of smoke trapped under the thick trees.

Cries from the river told us our shots had been on target. Both boats were sinking and the bullets had taken effect on three of the passengers. Jobe's shot had broken some of the frame and we heard the gunwale snap and the boat spilt its occupants into the waters. My target was still afloat, but the confusion on the boat had caused it to turn broadside to the current. The bow pointed straight at us and I took another shot along the near side, hoping to open a long gash in the birchbark skin at the waterline. It must have worked, for the canoe listed to that side and turned over, spilling its occupants, who were swimming in all directions to get to a shore. We had little time to watch them, for two more canoes loaded with men swept into the scene of the fight from downstream, a British soldier in the middle of each boat, with a musket.

"You get the far Lobster this time, the near one is mine," I said. We both aimed and Jobe counted down again, and again the shots sounded as one. Jobe's target slumped forward and the musket tilted overboard before anyone could catch it. My target, alas, was unaffected, though the Indian just behind him fell over and began his long journey to the Happy Hunting Ground.

The smoke was thick and choking around us, and it was a wonder that we had not been discovered because of it. I reloaded quickly and searched for my target. He must have been lying on the bottom of the boat, for I could not see him, though his space in the canoe was not occupied. "Laying down, art thou? Well, we will see about that," and I aimed at the waterline below where he had sat. When Jobe was loaded, I fired. A hole appeared just above the waterline and crimson flowed from it.

"Thou got him," Jobe said.

A splash drew our attention and we saw the last of the other dead soldier as he sank into the river. There were shouts from the lead boat and the front man was pointing at something to our left. Apparently, the wind had released smoke from the willows and the boat was going straight into it. The second boat nosed into the willows downstream from us and we shot out of our cover into the open water. There was no need to urge haste.

Without taking time to turn the boat around, the downstream canoe backed out of the willows. Jobe fired his pistol into the bottom of the boat. As they spun around to parallel our course, I stuck the muzzle of my rifle against the side of the canoe and fired. It blew a large hole and struck the legs of the warrior kneeling there. Hands grappled for our gunnel and Jobe slashed at them with his dirk while I tried to paddle us away from their grip. Abruptly, we were free of the sinking canoe and warriors were swimming for the shore. Jobe began reloading his weapons.

The fourth canoe was flying across the water, closing the gap between us too rapidly for escape. "Hurry, Jobe," I called and spun the canoe crossways of their path. My pistol shot struck the front man in the boat and he fell back against the man behind him, the resulting upheaval rippling the length of the boat. It lost way but remained moving enough to strike us amidships. The bow of the light canoe crumpled just as Jobe fired a load of birdshot into their midst. I heard our boat gunwale crack and saw water flowing to my feet.

Several of the enemy had eaten their last meal as a result of Jobe's shot, and the remaining were too injured to do us damage. We pulled away as the enemy canoe sank.

"Head for the south shore, Jobe, before we sink also," I called. By the time we got to the shore, water was above my ankles and the bow was entirely out of the water. Jobe jumped out and pulled the boat up on the shingle. I hopped out to lighten the load and push the boat as far up on the shore as we could. A hatchet blow on the back end of the canoe allowed the water to escape, hopefully before it ruined anything. We reloaded as fast as we could with an eye out for unwelcome visitors.

The forest was quiet in the gathering gloom of twilight and far across the waters we heard echoes of the wailing of widows, mothers, and sisters for their lost warriors. It was a haunting sound.

II
THE CACHE

"What do we do now?" Jobe asked as he shouldered his pack.

"I do not know, but we better do it fast, or we will be the favored guests at a Dutch roasting. One battle we have won, but it is sure we will not win the war."

"Better cache this gear and run," Jobe said. "I figure we are twenty leagues to Holderby's by land and forty by the river."

Looking over our supplies, I could see little we could afford to leave behind. Our one bow to personal comfort would be the keg of fine rum, but that was all that was easily dispensable. "We cannot carry these packs and outrun any pursuit. Our canoe is useless and here we stand on the horns of the dilemma when we should be moving."

"Here is an idea," Jobe said. "Why not leave them the rum?"

I laughed. "Then our journey would be a pleasant walk through the forest."

"Better would be a cruise down the river," he said. He emptied a pack and, opening the powder keg, poured its contents into the pack.

Perceiving his intent, I opened the rum keg as he filled the powder keg half full of water. It took only a moment or two to pour half the rum into it. "Rum, water, and gunpowder," Jobe said with a chuckle, "A deadly combination if the powder stays dry."

Before we refilled the rum keg with water, Jobe said, "Hold there, Jemmy," and handed me our canteens. When both were filled, as solemn as a wake, we each took a swallow of as fine a rum as money could buy in Pittsburgh, and each picked up a keg and plunged into the brush. Jobe was leading and stepped into a hole up to his chest, left by a rotted stump. It turned out to be fortuitous for us.

"How did thou dig a hole so fast?" I asked.

"Fie on thee, hand me up."

"Is there room for thee to set thy keg down in the hole?"

It took a lot of grunting and scooting, but he finally managed to get the keg on the ground. "Can thee set this keg down too?"

"No, and I be on me way out." He stood on the keg and climbed out of the hole. I lay on my stomach and lowered my keg into the hole. It would not slide down beside the first keg, so it sat on top.

Already, Jobe was pushing soil into the hole and soon the hole was filled and in the midst of a bowl-like depression. From other places, we gathered armloads of leaves and twigs and laid them over the bowl. As a last incentive, we sprinkled a cup of rum around on the leaves over the hole. To find the cache would be as child's play to the Shawnee.

Our efforts to cover our tracks in the dark were clumsy at the best, but we had to make it look as genuine as possible. We gathered our packs and started our trek to Holderby's Landing, the cries of the mourners fading away.

"When do ye think they will come?" Jobe asked.

"About sunrise. That is when we will turn around." When it was light enough, we made our passage as invisible as possible and made a wide circle to come back to where our boat lay. From the brush, we could see three canoes pulled up on the shingle, with three people guarding them. The one nearest us was a woman.

"Must have been a bad squaw," I whispered. "Look at the rope around her neck." We were preparing to rush the two men when a call and shouting from the woods drew their attention and they trotted off.

"Now!" Jobe grunted and we ran to the near boat. The woman saw us and ran to the other canoes and pushed them into the river. We heaved our packs into the canoe and pushed it into the water. Jobe was about to cut the tether that tied the woman to the bow when she rushed by him and climbed into the boat amidship, forcing Jobe on the other side to hold the boat level to keep it from swamping. He looked at me with a grin and hopped into the bow. No two men ever paddled as we did. We cruised between the two freed canoes and Jobe secured the tether rope from one while the woman grabbed the other and tied it to the gunwale, rocking us precariously.

"Be still," I demanded.

There was the cry of a small voice and the woman picked up a bundle from between her feet. "We have a passenger and a stow-away, Jobe."

"Do not bother, keep paddling."

The woman sat with her back to me, nursing her child. In polite company, she would have been shamed as naked, for the cloth she wore would not cover her body. It was an unfortunate thing I sat behind her, for she stank — *worse* than an Indian. The thought jolted me, she could be diseased and affect us both. The bottoms of her bare feet were black and crusted. Her thin frock did not hide the welts on her back. Indeed, there were smatterings of blood on the cloth. Her dark hair was a tangle and even from my seat a few feet away, I could see lice crawling, and nits.

Jobe caught a moment and turned to the woman and spoke the Shawnee greeting, to which the woman looked up at him, but did not respond. Jobe blanched, and asked, "Dost thou speak the King's language?"

"What is the matter, Jobe?"

"Her eyes are blue."

It actually took my breath away; we had heard of white captives and seen some who had grown up Indian and happy to stay that way, but this was our first contact with a captive white woman, and it took a few minutes to digest the facts.

"Dost thou speak the King's language?" Jobe repeated. Again to no response.

"Dost thou speak Dutch?" I asked in the language.

After a moment, she nodded her head, but still did not speak. Jobe had turned around to paddle and did not note the nod. "She nodded her head, Jobe, guess she speaks the Mother Tongue." I spoke in Dutch so she could understand and we spoke that language from then on. We were going north in one of those eternal loops this river makes and as we approached the head of the loop, our passenger became agitated and we saw a village. It was set so the villagers had a long view both upstream and downstream.

"That must be the village of her captivity, Jobe. Lie down, woman, and hide thyself." I said it three times before she seemed to comprehend and lay in the bottom of the canoe.

We stayed midstream and very few people came out to watch. There were only two canoes on the bank and I noted there were no warriors in sight. This was a small village.

"All the warriors must have gone upriver to do battle with us," I said. "Little do these people know that all thoughts of war have left their warriors and that they are drunk and stranded across the river. We will get to the Kanawha before midafternoon, Jobe. This woman needs some attention, so let us go up that river to our old camp."

"I think thou art right," Jobe answered in English. "I would hate to be downwind very long." He must have gotten a whiff or two.

"Do thou suppose it is a disease?"

"A disease of squalor," he replied.

We paddled well into midafternoon before

the mouth of the Kanawha River came into view.

I spoke to the woman, "We are going up that river over there and camp where thou can wash and eat."

She nodded. It was the first time we thought she understood what we were saying. We turned up the Kanawha River and hid the two empty canoes. About a mile up that stream was a small stream that came in from the left. Its mouth was hidden by the willow thicket around it and the only way it could be found was by tracing it from the land. Jobe and I had used it several times and never been bothered by the natives. We found our lean-to intact and unmolested and the long pool in front of the camp looked very inviting.

Jobe and the woman jumped out, and while Jobe pulled the boat to the bank, the woman disappeared into the woods.

"She is not running, is she?" I asked.

"No-o," Jobe said, and pointed to the bundle still in the boat.

We unloaded our gear and began looking through it for things we needed for the woman. It was a good thing, for once, that Jobe was fastidious and wanted to stay clean. He had even bought soap for his weekly baths and I sat out a bar of it with our new shears (we had traded off our old pair for lead) and two new blankets. There was also the buckskin we had brought along. She could make herself some moccasins.

Jobe took up his bow and disappeared into the woods while I lit the fire.

The woman returned and began gathering wood to stock the firepit. The baby gave a little cry and she retrieved it from the canoe and sat on a stump near the firepit nursing the child. I wondered if she was giving enough in her condition.

"I need to cut your hair," I said, picking up the shears.

She nodded and looked at me with those blue eyes. "All," she said.

"All of it?"

"All of it, *all of it.*" Her anger took me aback, but I was glad she agreed with me, and I began snipping and throwing the clippings into the fire. When I paused, she felt of the one-inch long hair that was left and demanded, *"All of it."*

I looked at her and smiled, "Very well, milady." More rummaging in our packs produced my cup and razor and I lathered her head and shaved it to the skin. When I finished, she lay the child down, ripped off her ragged garment, and slammed it into the fire.

Her paps were pink where the baby had suckled, but the rest of her body was incredibly dirty. She was so thin. Her ribs and shoulder blades stood out. How she could still nurse her baby, I will never know. It was obvious the child was hungry most of the time. She grabbed up the soap and a cloth and walked into the creek. Amidst the welts from her knees to her neck were old scars that had healed in some fashion. She had been a captive for a long time. Her nudity in my presence was not untoward under her circumstances; indeed, she needed help in order to get clean and doctored.

When she began washing, I busied myself and set a kettle of water on the fire to warm for the baby's bath. I set a kettle of dried beans cooking for the morrow and turned my attention to the baby. His clothes were not nearly as dirty as his mother's and he was reasonably clean also. His thick black hair showed positive parasite infection and would have to be removed when his mother returned. *Another half-breed. Lord help us and help this child.*

She was still scrubbing her body. "I could wash thy back." My call startled her as if

44

she had forgotten anyone else was around. She almost smiled and almost blushed and then nodded. When I waded out to her, she stood up, her back to me, and handed me the soap and cloth over her shoulder. I began where she had washed her shoulders and very carefully washed away as much of the dirt and old blood as I could. She still had pain when around the fresh wounds. She took the cloth when I had cleaned down to her waist and indicated she could take care of the rest. She still spoke very little, but did tell me her name was Arabella Big Horn and her baby was Curly Big Horn. We called her Belle. She fit into one of Jobe's new shirts and fashioned a skirt from one of the blankets.

Jobe got a fat doe and we stayed there three days, the woman alternating between baths and feasting. We could tell she was stronger and the baby was more content.

"Damme, Jemmy, another half-breed," Jobe whispered once when the child was nursing.

Canoes leave no tracks nor spoor and we do not know how Belle's Shawnee husband found us. I knew of him when he struck me between my shoulder blades with the blunt end of his tomahawk. I fell with the man on my back pulling my head up by the scalp lock he was intent on taking. His knife had just begun its cut when Belle screamed in anger and plunged a long knife into his lung. My world went black.

I awoke and sat up in time to see Belle heave the man into the canoe. She tried to shove it into the creek and collapsed, sobbing. I stumbled to the boat and saw the naked man lying there on his back, a horrified expression on his face and the bloody end of his phallus protruding from his mouth. I retrieved one of the spare canoes after I had pushed the bier into the current of the river and vowed never to provoke that woman to anger.

We had paddled all night and reached Holderby's near noon the next day — and lo and behold, we had no more than stepped ashore than Jobe was engulfed by the wench from the tavern. Belle peeked from under her scarf in surprise. I could not help but laugh.

We had left Pittsburgh hastily, not waiting on our friends, Jake and Drewery Moss, another hunting outfit, to join us. They had originally come through Cumberland Gap with the rest of the Tar Boilers and lived at Boonesborough for a while, then moved off on their own. Dicey Vincent had run away from her husband and convinced the two of her love for Jobe and they gleefully agreed to take her to him. They passed us while we camped on the Kanawha.

Jobe's enthusiastic welcome must have dampened their fun. Parson Holderby pronounced the wedding vows, whereby Dicey gained a second husband.

It was our intention to leave Belle at Holderby's to return to the towns, but she would have nothing of it because of her shame of having a child. We had to buy two horses for the women to ride.

III
KANTA-KE

Holderby's love for silver was fortunate for us for we got bargains on the few items we needed before returning to our hunting grounds. He should have paid *us* to take that sorry keg of rum he sold us. We only stayed a day before moving on out of reach of the constabulary that would have me hanged for murder.

There was a decided coolness between Dicey and Belle at first, but the sight of Belle's scars and the wiles of the baby soon warmed Dicey's heart and they became friends. Belle's modesty returned and we saw her bathe no more. As time passed, she became more at ease with us and talked more.

Our adventure in Pittsburgh had caused us to return to the wilderness midsummer instead of the late fall just before prime fur time. As a result, we had much idle time on our hands. Our "home" was in a walled-up shelter cave on a ledge above the valley floor of a creek that fed into the Licking River. On our first hunt, we had built a cabin and we returned from running our traps one day to find it burned to the ground and our furs carried off on the backs of our horses. That was when we moved up the bluff to the cave. It was large enough to house us on one side and our horses on the other. Dicey was put off by the cave and betook herself to campaign for a cabin. We showed her the ruins of our cabin and Belle convinced her the cave was much safer.

Our quarters were walled up to the ceiling with a stacked rock wall, and Jobe and Dicey decided to plaster it with mud. They got dirty as pigs and we suspect they took more pleasure in washing off in the creek than anything. When they finished, the wall looked like a part of the earth, effectively hiding our home.

A lot of time was spent in gathering

firewood, for it would be sure that we would need much more of it with the women and child. We had built a fireplace and chimney in the back of the shelter when we discovered that the smoke was drawn through a crack high on the wall instead of finding its way out the mouth of the shelter. We never found where it emerged from the ground, but were thankful it was not nearby.

The discovery of a beehive in a red oak some distance from the cave moved me to harvest some honey and beeswax. The women were to send Jobe with containers when he returned from his hunt. Meanwhile, I took my axe and began chopping the tree down.

A sixth sense develops in the wilderness that tells you when danger is near and after half an hour, I got that feeling of being watched.

"Jobe, over here." There was no answer, so I resumed chopping only to have a stronger feeling of eyes on me. With my pistol in my belt, I searched unsuccessfully for a visitor. When I returned to my axe, there not twenty feet away sat a mountain lion, tail twitching and mouth watering. It was plain to see he had a hunger for honey. Keeping one eye on my visitor, I resumed chopping on the tree. Just before the last few chops brought the tree down, I stopped to rest and contemplate my visitor's intentions. Would he share the honey, or was he going to demand the whole crop? There he sat, tail still twitching and a little drool in the corner of his mouth. It was a curious thing and I sailed a wood chip at him just to see what would happen.

The chip had not stopped bouncing when that lion sprang at me. I had no time for defense with axe or gun, but threw up my fist at his face and rammed it down his throat. The force of his leap bowled me over and I plowed a trench with my head and shoulders with that cat on my chest, gagging and choking on my arm. Blood oozed from his mouth. It was mine. The axe had flown away with the force of his leap and my pistol was gone. The lion stood on my chest, his hind paws clawing for traction to remove himself from me. If he got free, I would be dead, so I kept my fist balled up. His struggles became feeble and he fell over and died with my arm still in his gullet. I passed out.

"... and that is how I found him, laying there asleep with that lion sleeping beside him, his head on Jem's arm," Jobe was telling the women. "Only the lion was not resting his head, he had Jemmy's whole arm in his mouth, all the way to his elbow.

"That horse almost had a runaway when he smelled blood and cat, but I held him long enough to get a rope on that lion's hind legs and hold Jem while the horse pulled until the lion spit that arm out. He wanted to keep going, but I caught him and laid Jemmy across the saddle. A breeze must have stirred the trees, for that honey tree gave a groan and fell almost on us. Those bees swarmed us and me and horse needed no more incentive to leave the area."

I looked up from the tabletop and grinned at them, "I got ye some honey, miladies." Their pallor puzzled me, until I remembered my arm. It must not look so good. I tried to raise it and the pain caused me to faint again.

When next I opened my eyes, it was to find out what that snip-snipping was and why it was stinging my arm. There was a strong smell of rum in the room, and a pale and determined Dicey was trimming ragged skin from my arm.

Belle was holding my arm still and patted my shoulder, "Hold still, Jemmy, we will be through in a moment."

"Here, Jem, suck on this." Jobe stuck a rum-soaked rag in my mouth.

The snipping stopped and Dicey said, "We

have four long cuts to sew up, Jem, and it is going to take some time. Jobe, give him a strong drink and hand me a cup."

The rum was fiery, but not near as fiery as the rum she poured in one of those cuts, returning me to my dreams of lions and honey and pain. When next I heard their voices, Jobe was saying, "One down and three to go, Jemmy, me boy." I bit hard on the cloth.

It was a relief to wake in the night on my pallet. The room was quiet and dark save for a glow from the fire. Soft breathing told me someone was lying behind me, but I neither knew whom nor did I care. The fire drifted away into darkness.

Cool hands touched my brow and Belle was saying, "He has no fever."

"But he does have a hunger," I said.

"We are cooking thy meal as ye speak, Jemmy," Dicey replied.

Curly cooed and kicked on the pallet next to me. There was a sleeping space between us.

"How do thee feel?" Belle asked.

I took stock of myself. "My arm hurts and my mouth has died."

Dicey laughed. "Warm saltwater will help, Belle — or hair of the hound that bit him."

"I shall give him saltwater, the rum is

52

low." Belle smiled at some secret they shared.

"How much rum did I drink?" I asked.

"One cup per cut," Dicey said. She and Belle giggled.

"O-o-oh? And how much did *thou* drink?"

"Only one cup . . ." Belle began.

". . . per stitch," Dicey said and both of them laughed and laughed.

I groaned. "Is there any rum left?" My question only made them laugh harder. Nobody relished a trip to Boonesborough for that rotten whiskey those Tar Boilers brewed.

"There is half a keg left," Jobe said as he entered. "I had to take it away from them before they were out on the floor and I would have had to finish their sewing," he added. "The stress on them was such that they were stone sober when they finished. Indians could have carried all of us away that night, we were so tired."

"That night? Thee means last night, do thou not?"

"Night before last, Jemmy."

I had slept through a whole day and two nights and not even known it. On the third night after, I awoke with a burning fever and one of the cuts on my arm was hot and tender to the touch. It was infected and nothing could improve my condition. Belle and Dicey conferred and Belle disappeared for a while. When she returned, the two conferred again and came to me. "We have another cure, but it will be uncomfortable for thee."

"Something has to be done or I will lose my arm or worse," I said. "Go ahead and try."

They stretched my arm out and Dicey leaned on my upper arm, "Mostly so thou wilt not see," she said.

They cut the first stitch at my elbow and wiped the flux and gore away. After working with it awhile, they reapplied the stitch and wrapped the place up. Other than a little pressure relief nothing changed with my arm. Belle still cooled me with wet cloths to keep the fever down. Late in the night, something stirred in my arm and it felt like something between an itch and a tickle. I stirred, with the intention to scratch only to find that a string restrained my good arm. Immediately, Belle awoke and asked, "What is it, Jemmy?"

"My arm —"

"Do not scratch, it is the cure working. As long as it tickles, it is curing thee. If it stops, we will have to open the wound again." Thus began a time of torment, but the arm began improving and my fever subsided little by little. Belle and Dicey monitored my arm closely and when the tickling stopped, they opened the wound a little bit and took out two dark elongated eggs. We put them in a cup and watched them turn into — for me — beautiful blue-tail flies. From that time on, the arm healed up nicely.

Jobe and Dicey harvested much honey and wax and we had the luxury of candles. Belle had watched over and cared for me that whole time. When I was well enough, she made to move back to her bed, but I asked her to stay and she has. I know little of love, but much of a brave and true heart.

IV
AUX ARCS

1803

The Great Warrior Path is a trail between the Shawnee and Cherokee lands. It is used by the two tribes to raid upon each other, for they were ever enemies. In the fall of the second year of the women, a large force of Cherokee warriors bent on raiding the Shawnee was accidentally met on the Great Warrior Path by a large force of Shawnee warriors hunting Cherokee scalps. The woods were full of Indians hunting Indians and both sides killing whites when they found them. Hunting was impossible. In the middle of all that fighting, a small Shawnee party found our cave.

Jobe finished reloading and licked his front sight. "Did not take them long to discover our rifled guns covered more ground, did it?" We allowed the Indians to drag away a fallen warrior — one less for us to bury.

"It will not be long before the rest of the tribe gets here and our goose will be cooked," I said. "We need to leave now."

"We are nearly ready," Belle called. They had loaded the packs while we held off the Indians. The last thing we wanted was to be cornered in this shelter, and we found that a long passage could be made from the stable along the cliff face and behind huge boulders. The first thing we did with a new horse was to train him to use the passage.

"We leave at sunset," I said. Meantime, we fashioned a bomb out of gunpowder and gravels and hung it in the chimney with a trip-string attached to a partial keg of rum. It would drop the bomb into the fire.

"Sure hate to use up that powder," Jobe said.

"We have enough left and it will serve us well." We sent the women to the stable to wait on us.

"Here they come, Jemmy." There were eight of them spread in an arc, and if we stayed too long, the fight would be hand-to-hand. We shot the two Indians closest to the stable with our pistols, leaving the rifles loaded and ready.

"Run, Jobe." We both rushed to the stable and moments later watched as the savages entered the cave. Two entered our living rooms and shortly gave a shout that brought the rest of the warriors. Their happy chatter was cut off by a terrific explosion that blew out the wall of the house. The interior wall leaned, rumbled, and collapsed inward, burying the victims.

"Rest in peace, vermin." Jobe did not care for Indians. "Where to now?" Jobe asked, though he well knew.

"West," I answered. And thus began a trek of several months across the wilderness. We crossed many frozen rivers that winter, including the Mississippi, and followed a trail we found going southwest until it came to a small white settlement on the banks of a clear-running river and at the eastern foot of a range of hills. Several men came out to meet us while women stood in doorways, little eyes peeking from behind their skirts.

"Welcome, strangers," one man said in the

King's tongue.

"Thank you," I answered. "What is this place?"

"We call it Flee's Settlement after the man that greeted us when we got here," another man said. He extended his hand and we shook. "Come on to the settlement, you can use old Flee's cabin, he'll never use it again." They turned and led us into the midst of the cabins.

"Tar Boilers — and away out here," Jobe whispered in Dutch.

As if in answer, one of the men said, "We left Boonesborough when it got too crowded there. Game's a lot more plentiful here."

"In those hills?" I asked pointing to the mountains west of the settlement.

"Yes, the Ohs Arcs Mountains, home of the Osage Long Hunt — and the white men of Flee's, if we do not get caught."

"Just like Kanta-ke?" Jobe asked.

"Ju-ust like it," another man answered. "Say, would you have any tobacco on you? Our crop froze out."

"Because he was too damme lazy to pick it, and his wife did not have time," Jobe hissed under his breath.

"Say, what year is this?" one of the men asked.

"Nought three a couple of months ago,"

Jobe replied.

"Is Adams still president?" another asked.

"Lost to Jefferson in nought one," I said.

"Jefferson, huh? Partial to Washington, meself,"

"Me too," I agreed. They plied us with questions about things in the east, but none of it seemed to be very important to them. None of it affected their lives. It was even doubtful that they knew they were in Spanish territory and not the United States.

We arose a few days later aware that some sort of disturbance was going on in the settlement. Several of the men were facing a man on horseback in a strange uniform. He was backed by several foot soldiers with long muskets and bayonets. Jobe and I stood behind the corner of a cabin and listened. The officer was speaking English with an accent so heavy as to be unintelligible. I understood part of it the third time he said, "You are all trespassers and I place you under arrest in the name of His Imperial and Royal Majesty, Napoleon Bonaparte, of France. Surrender your arms and prepare to leave this place."

"Damme Frogs." Jobe hated Frenchmen.

If the grins on the frontiersmen faces did not mean anything to the officer, they said volumes to the two of us.

The officer turned and rode aside and called an order to his men, who brought their guns to the ready. As they prepared to aim at the next order, Jobe shot the officer off his horse and the frontiersmen greeters charged the soldiers. I shot the sergeant standing beside the squad, but that was the last chance to use a gun in that mix-up.

Our two women took our rifles and began reloading them while we joined our comrades, dirk against bayonet. It was a bloody fight, but the French soldiers held no advantage over hardened frontiersmen, and soon the battlefield was quiet.

Dicey and Belle handed us our guns, looked us over, and declared our wounds paltry. They hurried past us with bandages and hot water to help the wounded. Not a Frog was standing, nor did any need bandages.

"Great fight, Jemmy Hall," Jobe shouted and threw his hat in the air. We looked around, but there was nothing more to do except bind the wounded. One man in the settlement died from his wounds.

It seemed we had gone as far as was practical. South of Flee's were vast empty lowlands full of swamps and forests, and west was the Osage hunting ground of Aux Arcs.

Hunting was good in and out of the hills, and the hide harvest was generous. Our neighbors proved to be good people we could share our lives with, even though they spoke a strange English tongue. Jake and Drewery Moss joined us two years later.

Belle and Dicey both proved fruitful and it was not long before two Dutch cabins were brimming with children. We continued the Long Hunts every winter, contending with every manner of Indian, the Osage being most numerous and bothersome. Every year or two we hauled our furs to St. Louis, always taking enough men that no one bothered us. We never lost a fur.

AUTHOR'S NOTE

There were at least three regions all tribes set aside as holy and hunting grounds; He Sápa (Black Hills), Aux Arcs, and Kantake. No tribe, clan, or individuals were allowed to live permanently within these areas. As a result, they became dark and bloody battlegrounds.

Frontiersmen in the northern colonies were not contained by a mountain barrier, but traveled west on the Ohio River before the pioneers of the southern colonies discovered the Cumberland Gap.

Flee's Settlement, at the falls of the White

River, continued to grow. It was in the territory of three nations, Spain, France, and United States, and part of three territories, Louisiana, Missouri, and Arkansas. The Ozark Mountains remained an isolated, almost trackless wilderness into the twentieth century.

Inside every major event in history are hundreds of smaller events performed by men and women with little notice from the historian. **James Crownover** believes that these unnoticed people and the aggregate of their labors are the essence of any great event in history. These are the people he wants to recognize and write about.

■ ■ ■ ■

RATA REMEMBERS

BY PAUL COLT

■ ■ ■ ■

Me llamo Rata. I know no other name. As you know, we rata keep our tales to our own kind. We take our daily comings and goings, feedings, mating, and sleeping with no need to remember them in stories we repeat among ourselves or recite for the benefit of others. We live on the fringes of other societies, scavenging for scraps, foraging where we are not welcome. This is our lot in the larger order of life. I come forward with this tale for it is an extraordinary remembering. I am gifted among rata, though the events I observed in these days are beyond even my understanding. Still I observed them. They ring loud in the passage of many seasons. I remember the old mission. I cannot escape the memories witnessed there. I tell them here that perhaps you may hear, remember, and understand. Not many of your kind survived to tell this tale. None witnessed these events as I did.

I came to the mission in the time of the sandal-feet friars. Here our days passed in peace, so long as we kept to the dark places when the two feet were about. The mission afforded many places we took refuge. Corners under the sinks in the scullery, between and under casks in the wine cellar, and dark recesses of the stable with its loft. I favored the wine cellar and stable. I preferred the soothing scents of white oak barrels and straw to the harsh wet scent of lye soap under the sinks. Still, all these places afforded safety and refuge.

Caught in the open by day, one might be forced to scuttle away from some two feet with a broom. These risks, however, were small for one such as I, gifted in guile and craft. I easily avoided them, by simply abiding the rhythm of the bells. Bells called the friars to a place they call chapel for morning prayers and evening vespers. I ventured there once. A golden place, colored in light, scented in beeswax and the long past presence of some perfumed smoke. There they prayed and sang their hymns, announcing times safe for foraging. Safe from the sandal feet, not so from *El Gato.*

El Gato roamed the mission day and night

between naps. Big and black with yellow eyes, the cat moved with stealth on padded paws. Padded yes, but armed with sharp claws and long pointed teeth. The cat regarded us as natural prey to stalk and pounce upon at any moment. We foraged with ears and noses alert. Always we hewed to our defenses, a nearby safe haven and knowledge of El Gato's habits. Did I mention he sleeps? He does. He prowls from one nap to the next at various times and places. Knowing his habits freed us to forage when the bells proclaimed the proper times.

That is not to say our feedings never encountered the cat. The monster was quick and cunning. We lost more than a few of our number to his prowling. Still, in the natural order of things, it thinned the colony, making the food supply more plentiful for those of us clever enough to survive. Did I mention I live by guile and craft? I do. And so I minded El Gato's habits. His presence merely added spice to my foraging adventures.

Adventure we did. Feeding in the refectory where we found scraps from the table. Table scraps could be most tasty, though their presence uncertain. One day the refectory might yield a bountiful banquet. The next swept spotless to famine. Thankfully the stable was certain to be stocked with grain for the livestock. There could be found burlap sacks. These we opened by gnawing a small hole in the threads, releasing a feast. If one chose his sack wisely, many days might pass before his sack was selected to feed the stock. Did I mention clever begets wisdom? It does. My sack always made the choicest selection.

At various times, barefoot *peones* came to the mission. Here they were greeted by the friars with gracious hospitality and generous feedings. Peones squat in the dusty plaza to eat their fill of frijoles and tortillas. By night we foraged the scraps they dropped. These were as tasty as refectory fare and never swept clean. What is a little dust to such splendid repast? *De nada.* So passed halcyon days in comfort and plenty little troubled by small risks. All in peace and serenity until the day of the coming.

The coming arrived on winter chill. Winter was expected. This one intruded with unfamiliar sights, sounds, and scents. It came with many two feet in blue coats and fine leather boots. They called themselves Texians. They brought with them heavy iron trees, felled on wooden caissons. These they hoisted to the top of the mission walls with heavy ropes accompanied by much shouting and grunting. Sacks of round iron fruit were carried and stacked in their place along with wooden kegs handled with much care. The kegs reminded me of the wine casks in the cellar. They smelled not of sweet grapes and white oak. These smelled of bitter salt, offering no temptation to feed. In days, the mission walls bristled with iron trees the two feet called cannon.

I thought all this curious. I might even have welcomed the change for the foraging that fell from the plates of so many new feeding two feet, except for the air. The restful peace of the friars given way to groans, curses, and sweat. Unlike the gentle friars, these two feet were rough and coarse with sweat scented of something unknown to me. A sour odor flavored the air with promise of some grim tension. I turned this unfamiliar taste on my tongue. In coming days, I would learn to know it more and well.

More Texians arrived with the two feet I called Big Knife. In the days that followed, I heard him called Bowie. He carried his blade as one in authority. The motley rabble who came with him wore moccasins, shabby boots, buckskins, and ragged sweat-stained filthy clothing. Big Knife Bowie climbed the mission walls and walked among the cannon trees, nodding some silent approval. These two feet too smelled strange. The scent of some impending danger grew stronger with these new arrivals.

El Gato is a danger I understand. Two feet danger too is well known to me. I rely on guile and craft to serve me well. I am confident in the face of these dangers. This new danger I did not understand. This danger visited on the two feet. Could cannon, knives, and fire-sticks of every length and size make a craft to protect them? I sensed no confidence in these, only strange sour scent. I sniffed more change in the hot dusty wind. Change with foreboding known to your kind.

Twelve nights foraging passed. With so many mouths to feed, victuals grew scarce. We noticed the paucity of droppings and scraps we found to quench our hunger. A young long knife arrived with still more two feet in blue coats and fine boots this time mounted on horses. These horses filled the stable and ate into the grain supply. It would not be long before even your humble Rata would feel the pinch of hunger.

The young long knife Texians called Travis carried his blade with the air of one in authority. Big Knife Bowie regarded Long Knife Travis with suspicion. I sensed tension between them. I puzzled over it, searching for something in my experience to explain it. Two male rata might come to such feelings over mating rights to a female in season. Little got in the way of such feelings, little save for a danger such as El Gato. Would these two put aside their mating fits for the danger gathering like clouds building before a storm beyond the mission walls?

Five forages later I encountered a new threat. A raccoon sat brazenly on a table in the plaza. These creatures possess voracious appetites. It would consume still more of what little was left to us to eat. I watched for a time, curious the raccoon did not forage in the night as was their custom. It slept. At the coming of day, I took refuge in the stable loft where I could observe the intruder. It did not forage. It did not take shelter. I grew suspicious. Could the raccoon be dead? A tall two feet I had not seen before rolled out of his sleeping blankets nearby. He approached the coon, carrying a long fire-stick. I brightened at the prospect he might shoot it. They are voracious foragers, you know. Such was not to be. This two feet picked up the coon and placed it on his head. I twittered with laughter, quickly catching myself lest I give away my presence to El Gato. This coon would not challenge us for food. This coon gave his skin for two feet's cap.

Fifteen forages passed amid the bustle and commotion of much preparation. The blue coat two feet marched and drilled with their fire-sticks. They took turns climbing the walls to tend the cannon trees and watch. Big Knife Bowie's two feet watched and waited. Watching, searching, always on the lookout. Somewhat more must be coming. But what?

The sixteenth night I foraged in the stable at a discarded grain sack. The sack, empty for the purpose of feeding horses, contained kernels caught in the seams and spilled where the stable boy tossed it. It made a meager meal; but in these days, a meal was a meal and all to be taken for it. As I licked up the last lap, I noticed quiet. Quiet sounded alarm, sending my instincts a twitter. Somewhere in the darkness a horse stomped. Straw rustled some response. *El Gato?* One never knows in such cases, but one so gifted as I never takes chances. I scampered through a chink in a stall door just as the monster struck. Dare I say my tail slipped through outstretched claws? Did I mention I am quick? I should. I ducked between a horse's hooves and I scuttled up a beam to refuge in the loft. Had El Gato anticipated my hiding place, he might have cut me off before I could reach it. As it happened, I knew where I was going. The cat did not.

As morning broke, I settled into my hole in the stable loft. I caught my breath, heart pounding in my breast. The encounter closer than I cared where the cat might be concerned. It was then I noticed two feet scrambling in every direction bent to some grim purpose. No laughter, little talking, some shouting. Blue coats and Bowie's ruffians took positions on the walls; some with fire-sticks, others near the cannon trees. It was only then I observed in the gray light of dawn, two feet in red-breasted coats, more than your humble rata could count, massed in the distance beyond the walls. This must be the reason for all the preparation, watching, and the source of the strange scent given off by the two feet. But why?

A rider wearing gleaming black boots and much gold braid across his red-breasted coat approached the gates on a great white horse, carrying a white flag. He exchanged words I could not hear with Long Knife Travis. The rider wheeled his horse and galloped off to rejoin the red-breasted line in the distance. Word murmured along the walls in hushed tones. I strained to hear.

Santa Anna. What means this Santa Anna? Soon enough I would know.

Long Knife Travis turned to the nearest cannon. The two feet there touched a smoking taper to it. A fearsome roar of fire and smoke made my heart stop. A blast force of sound washed over me, blinding me with an acrid flash of terror. The cat, the cannon, my poor heart; the beat scarce contained in my breast. Bitter smoke scent hung in the air cleared on the breeze, leaving something behind. A scent that did not wash away in the wind. I sniffed. I tasted. The scent I did not recognize mingled with my own terror. I now knew it for fear. Fear only grew stronger with waiting and watching through the long days of preparation.

That night I foraged in the refectory. I found precious little to feed on. Crumbs of bread and cheese. Scared and hungry, I took shelter in the wine cellar. What followed fairly frightened the life out of me. For days and nights smoking thunder rained out from the mission cannon. More thunder rumbled in the distance as a summer storm gathering force. The air above whined in great screaming rushes. Powerful thumps shook the earth, rattling hollows in the pit of my stomach. I judged these the fruit from Santa Anna cannon called ball and grape. Grape.

These grape made no wine. They sloshed wine in the casks above me. Thick adobe walls trembled and cracked. Dust fell from the rafters and hung in the air as a fog. The smell of fear tasted bitter and strong. Soon other scents flavored the fetid air. Choking powder smoke, iron blood-smell mingled with sweet, putrid death.

Starved after days of constant bombardment, I ventured out. The refectory yielded no food. Massive holes gaped in the roof. I took a chance on the stable. There I found a little grain and made way to my hole in the gray light before dawn. As I scampered across the loft I came upon a lump of shattered remains. The hackles at the back of my coat stood on end. El Gato lay twisted, barely recognizable, a grotesque mask in death. I remembered the fearsome threat he once posed. No more. Fighting two feet show no mercy to the living, even those who have no part in their fight. I cannot say I mourned my former adversary, though I noted but for the trickery of fate, the dead might have been me. Guile and craft gave no quarter to the forces unleashed in this fight. I hurried to my hole.

By the first light of dawn, I looked over the plaza and along the walls. Everywhere death lay by destruction. The plaza pocked in craters. Walls cracked and breached. Two feet bodies lay where they fell. Wounded huddled bandaged and bleeding. Still two feet stood at their stations. I recognized Long Knife Travis and the Coonskin called Crockett. I did not see Big Knife Bowie. Beyond the walls, storm clouds of Mexican black boots moved about as shadows covered over by rising dust; they drew up a great line on all sides.

I sensed more fighting to come. Why? Why do these two feet kill each other? Why? Are they not the same kind? Rata do not kill our own kind. Oh, we males may fight over breeding rights. Such things improve the species. But here there are no breeding rights. El Gato was our natural enemy. He would kill us for food. That we understood. But here there is no food worth fighting over. Here there is only blood and gore and horror visited upon one's own kind. As I ruminated over these disturbing imponderables, a clarion call split the morning stillness. A guttural roar rose from the ranks of the red-breasted line in the distance as it surged forward.

Thunder smoke spewed a storm of ball and grape on the Mexican advance, throwing great gouts of dirt against pink and blue morning sky. Coonskin Crockett and two feet on the wall fired their long-sticks and reloaded at a fevered pace. Smoke hung a blue haze over the walls. The Mexican advance faltered. The Texians rallied their cries, pouring still more fire and thunder on the assault. I sensed a sweet hint of hope.

The Long Knife Santa Anna mounted on his great white horse rode to the fore of his line. Gold braid flashed on his red-breasted coat. He circled his horse, brandishing his knife gleaming in sunlight. The Mexican line stiffened. Raising a primordial roar, they rushed forward. Texian cannon and fire-sticks rained shot and charge on the Mexican line, ripping gaping holes in their ranks. Still the Mexicans came, more filling holes for the fallen. Texian thunder could not blunt the attack spurred on by this willed force Santa Anna.

Attackers battered barred mission doors. Red-breasted coats threw ladders against the walls, cracked and breached by days of bombardment. They climbed faster in number than the fire-sticks could reload. Coonskin Crockett used his fire-stick to push a ladder off the wall, sending those climbing screaming their fall. Climbers on other ladders made it over the wall. More red breasts followed with a roar. Long Knife Travis drew his blade to meet attackers breasting the walls. He impaled one at the top of the wall and pushed his ladder away. Those climbing the ladder behind howled as they fell. Black boots clamored over the wall at Long Knife's back. The first red breast leveled a pistol. It spit fire and smoke. Long Knife Travis fell, his blade clattering off the wall, broke in the fall.

I sensed peril in the harsh scents of powder smoke fog. Day or no, I scurried down from the loft and raced for the only safety I could think of, the chapel. There the light was no longer golden, no longer colored in hues. Colorless gray cast a pall over the once warm restful setting. Beeswax and any remembrance of perfumed smoke too were gone. Here I smelled more dread, blood tasting death, and bitter smoke. Battle sounds raged in the plaza beyond the adobe. I hid beneath a bench near the place where friars prayed. I have no understanding for the meaning of their prayers, but from what little I knew of them, it seemed some were needful that day.

I heard running feet. Desperate Texians poured through the chapel doors. They stacked heavy wooden benches against the doors and took cover behind other benches, bracing for further attack. Fire-sticks and long knives leveled at the chapel doors.

Boots sounded beyond. A heavy ram battered iron bound doors. Stout doors held, bowed, splintered. Red breasts poured into the breach. Texian fire-sticks erupted, deafening roar filled the chapel. The first Mexicans fell. Others filled the doors in their place. Long knives and fire-sticks turned clubs met the rush. Mexicans fired pistols and thrust fire-sticks bright with blades fixed. Texians fell. Blood-splattered death flowed all around.

Smoke burned my eyes, sulphuring the air, resting bitter harsh on my tongue. The chapel filled with blood scent and death. No safety here, my guile screamed. I scampered through a hole behind the altar before the black boots could do me harm. I ran to a sewer drain under the wall. Dark and wet, I welcomed human stench that did not kill. The sewer emptied beyond the walls. I raced to refuge, hollowed out in the roots of a nearby cottonwood tree. There I listened to the waning sounds of battle.

Cannon fell silent. Assault ladders stood here and there, stark sentinels now to mission doors thrown open to receive the conqueror's quest. Smoke spread a pall over the battle-scarred mission. Dust clouds churned by storms of black boots colored the smoky underside dun gray. Two feet shouts mingled triumph with death throes. Fire-sticks, pistols, and knives finished the grisly work of total defeat. Battle sounds faded away to the moaning and wailing of the wounded and dying.

Presently a new sound thrummed from within. Drums. I peeked my nose above my hole to a curious sight. Heavily armed red breasts marched by twos behind the drummer. These were followed by the Coonskin Crockett and a few other Texians. All these were accompanied by still more armed black boots. Last the gold-braided Santa Anna mounted on his white horse followed them out to the mission wall. There Crockett and the other Texians were lined up with their backs to a still-standing section of mission wall. Mexican black boots drew up in rank. Santa Anna ordered aim. The drum rolled. The Texians stood firm. Santa Anna raised his long knife. The blade flashed. Black boot fire-sticks charged. The Texians fell, Coonskin no more.

I let go a breath I'd forgotten I held and wondered at what I witnessed. These Texians fought and fell bravely, no chance against so many. Why did they fight? Even your humble rata knew when to run. Why did they die? Why? It must be something for your kind to know. Clever that I am, I confess I cannot know. I do know such a fight must be remembered. I tell you this tale so you may know; and remember the old mission they call . . . Alamo.

Paul Colt takes a fanciful departure from his critically acclaimed, award-winning historical dramatizations and western fiction to offer a unique remembrance of the Alamo. Inspired by his wife, Trish, "Rata Remembers" is Paul's first short story.

■　■　■　■

The Times
of a Sign

BY ROD MILLER

■　■　■　■

The truth of it is, that advertising sign on my place of business ain't nothin' but bullshit. It says:

FOR SALE
MULES & OXEN
BREEDING STOCK

Now, anybody with a lick of sense knows mules can't breed. Leastways not so's it amounts to anything. Besides, most all of them that needs it is gelded, anyhow. And the only ox worth a damn is a steer, which as everybody knows can't breed neither — they just plain ain't got the tools for the job.

It all comes down to that fool sign painter I hired way back when to make the sign. Had he put a little flourish or fancy or some such between them last two lines it would've worked out fine. But when I complained, he said he was too busy for such nonsense and

85

wouldn't do it 'less I paid to have the whole thing done over.

But with things the way they is in Independence, and as they have been since I first hung up that sign, I been sellin' every mule and ox I can get growed up enough to pull a wagon as quick as, well, I can get them growed up enough to pull a wagon. So, I guess it don't make no never mind about that sign.

You see, it's like this. Independence is the place where most folks wantin' to set out for the western territories — Oregon and California and whatnot — gets outfitted. Then there's all them freight trains wheelin' down the Santa Fe Road like they been doin' for years. Fact is, that Santa Fe Road is why I'm in the mule business in the first place. I got into the ox business later, but that don't matter for now. What you want to know is how I came to be doin' what it says on that sign I'm doin', so that's what I'm a-goin' to tell you.

Before I go on, I reckon I had best clear up that sign business. See, we do sell breeding stock — brood mares that will birth baby mules if bred to a jack — but we don't sell jacks no how, no way, them bein' the very lifeblood of my business — and we sell cows that'll produce passable calves that might make an ox one day. And we don't sell no bulls, neither. Good Durham bulls that throw sizable calves ain't that easy to come by, so when we get a good one, he ain't goin' nowhere.

'Course I don't let on that the mares and cows we do sell is the ones that ain't quite up to snuff, but that's just horse tradin'.

I already told you my name is Daniel Boone Trewick. No relation to ol' Daniel Boone his own self, but my daddy thought him a hero and thus hung the name on me. Most everybody calls me Boone, save my wife, who calls me Danny — which I don't prefer, but it's what she called me back when we was young and I guess she can't get over the habit.

What I ain't told you is that I got a partner in this here business, his name bein' Juan Medina. Now, Juan, he's a Mexican from out in California I hooked up with, but that was before . . . Aw, hell, I guess I had best quit ramblin' and just start at the beginning of this here story.

What happened was, me and a girl name of Mary Elizabeth Thatcher was sweet on each other back when we was young — me bein' about sixteen at the time, and her bein' fourteen or maybe fifteen. This bein' back about '39. Her daddy was Reverend

Thatcher, and he had no use for me — or any other boys, of which there were plenty — sniffin' around young Mary Elizabeth. One day up in Liberty, where we all lived, we was in the reverend's carriage house sittin' in a buggy gettin' to know one another, you might say, when the reverend caught us at it.

Well, he yanked me out of that buggy and went to wailin' on me, which was not to my likin'. So, with me havin' got my growth up to where I was of a size where I didn't have to take such from anybody, I returned the favor.

Hangin' there on a peg on the wall was a singletree, which sort of fell right into my hand, and I walloped Reverend Thatcher upside the head with it. He went down like a poleaxed steer in the slaughter yard and Mary Elizabeth started in to yowlin' like a scared cat and the reverend was layin' there with blood pourin' out of his head like used grass and water out of the back end of an incontinent cow and me seein' nothin' but trouble to come from it all, I lit out of there and hit the road for Independence and never looked back. Never even slowed down to say goodbye to my ma and pa nor nothin', which didn't matter much on account of them havin' so many other kids scratchin' around the place that they might not even notice I was gone anyhow.

'Course, I didn't stay around Independence long, on account of it bein' near enough to Liberty that the Clay County law would certain sure come there lookin' for a murderer. Perchance, there was a freight outfit ready to pull out for Santa Fe and they hired me on as a herder. So it was that I come to spend day after day a-horseback on an old high-withered swaybacked nag of theirs, chafin' my backside on a worn-out Mexican saddle they found for me somewheres, followin' a bunch of oxen that they took along to take over for them that lamed up or tired out and needed a rest from them big freight wagons they pulled.

I had no notion at the time of my leavin' what I was to do with myself once I got to Santa Fe — my only purpose was to avoid gettin' strung up for killin' Mary Elizabeth's daddy. But somewhere along the way, I took up thinkin' about them mountain men and free trappers that I'd read about and had seen from time to time in Missouri on their way to someplace or another, and thought to look into becomin' one of them. When we got to Bent's Fort out on the Arkansas, there was some of them mountain men hangin' around, and listenin' to their stories made me want to try that way of livin' for sure. 'Course bein' young and dumb and all I had no idea how to go about doin' such a thing, but it was in my mind.

Anyhow, after makin' it on out to Santa Fe and collectin' my pay — which amounted to more money than I ever held in my hand at one time before — I heard tell there was mountain men livin' up at a place called Taos, on account of them bein' up there and out of the way, the Mexican government left them alone.

So it was off to Taos I went. Once I got there, I met up with a fellow with a wooden leg named Pegleg Smith, who, I was told, was one of the best of the trappers ever there was. Him and some others let me know right off that the times when a man could make decent livin' trappin' fur in the mountains was gone. Pegleg his own self was lookin' to keep his belly full in other ways, one of which was goin' partners with a man makin' whiskey that come to be called Taos Lightnin' by them that got struck by it.

But at present, Pegleg and Old Bill Williams and some others was outfittin' for a trip out to California to steal horses and mules and bring 'em back to Santa Fe and sell 'em at a handsome profit. They asked me along with the promise of a share in the takin's, and me havin' nowhere else to go and nothin' else to do at the time, seein's as my becomin' a trapper wasn't in the offing, I did so.

Even bein' in Mexico as I was, there was too many Mexicans in on that horse-stealin' deal to suit me. I could see right off it weren't so, but I could not get rid of the notion that those people was by nature lazy and shiftless. And then when we got to this place called Abiquiu, there was this black man name of Jim Beckwourth came along. Me and him ended up in a dispute when he told me to do some thing or another and I let him know that where I come from, white folks *give* orders to his kind, not *take* 'em. Near as soon as I said it, I found myself on my back with his foot planted in my middle. But it turned out all right on account of he was one of them — a mountain man and trapper, I mean — and he was one of them that cooked up this here foray to California we was settin' out on.

And if it weren't bad enough to be in cahoots with Mexicans and a black man, a ways up the trail we hooked up with a bunch of Indians — Utes they was — and one of 'em, called Wakara, was as much in charge of things as was Pegleg or Old Bill or that black fellow Beckwourth.

I'll tell you, they got a whole different way of doin' things out there than what I growed up with here in Missouri.

Well, anyway, we went on out to California followin' a wandering road that Mexican traders used. That path has since come to be called the Old Spanish Trail, even if it ain't that old and it ain't Spanish. We stole thousands of horses and mules and jackasses from California ranches and brung 'em back, just as planned — save for leavin' what must've been a thousand dead horses layin' out in the desert from pushin' 'em too hard, so as to avoid bein' overtaken by a posse of them Californios. I'll tell you, I seen things on that trip I never even knew to dream about, and was involved in all manner of adventures.

But all that's a story for another time.

There is one part I got to tell, and that's how Juan Medina came to be here in Missouri in this business enterprise of ours.

See, Juan is a Mexican from California and he worked on one of them ranches we stole horses from back then. 'Cept he wasn't there at the time we did it on account of him bein' in jail owin' to a dispute he had with the brother of a girl he was sweet on, which ended up with him bein' locked up 'til they sprung him to ride with the posse that was chasin' after us.

For reasons he'd rather I not talk about, he left off with that posse when it give up the chase and he followed us and throwed in with our outfit. Him and me spent a heap of time together on the trail and he learned enough white-man talk from me to where we could palaver some. Him bein' a hand with horses and mules the like of which you ain't never seen gave me an idea — I took a notion to take my pay for that horse-thievin' trip in mares and jacks — *yeguas y machos,* Juan celled 'em — and drive 'em back here to Missouri and raise mules.

There was always plenty of plowin' and whatnot to be done on Missouri farms, and some of the outfits headin' out the Santa Fe Road used mules, so I figured sellin' off what mules we could raise would be easy enough and make us a right smart of money besides. And I had seen right off that them California mules we stole was a hell of a lot better than what was raised here in Missouri back then, and it was all on account of them California *machos.* They was big, strong jackasses and they throwed big, strong mules.

Juan, he had nothin' else to do and nowhere else to go so he allowed as how he'd come in on the deal. I wasn't all that sure about throwin' in with a Mexican, but I seen how good he was handlin' critters, and he knowed a hell of a lot more 'bout *machos* and mares and mules than what I did, so I reckoned it was worth the risk.

What I didn't know at the time was what was 'bout to happen back in the States. I'll tell you more on that later on.

Anyhow, by the time we got that herd back to Santa Fe, I had talked it all over with Pegleg Smith and Old Bill Williams and them, and we had come to terms on my share of the takin's. Juan, meantime, had picked us out a nice string of mares and *machos* — some of 'em he'd had a hand in raisin' back on that California ranch he come from. I ain't sayin' how many head I got for my share, as that ain't no man's business but my own. Juan, he didn't get nothin' as he wasn't part of the outfit, but I took him on as equal partner anyhow.

You will recollect that I had gone out west with a freight outfit on the road to Santa Fe. But, fact is, I spent the whole trip in a cloud of dust followin' the spare oxen and, besides, I wasn't payin' all that much attention. So, I didn't have but a smidgen of knowledge about the road, and sure as hell could not pass myself off as an expert. But I knowed it took them ox trains two, two-and-a-half months to make it out from Missouri and I figured it would take them about as long to get back here. But we had no oxen and wasn't pullin' any wagons, and horses that ain't under harness or saddle can travel at a quicker pace, so I figured me and Juan ought to be able to get our herd back here to Independence in somethin' less than two months. We sold off some of our stock to buy supplies and pack outfits to haul 'em. We sure as hell didn't buy no pack animals, as we had horses and jacks enough to carry what we needed and then some.

We strung the critters carryin' packsaddles together head to tail and let the rest run loose, as we knowed they would stay in a bunch and not wander off 'less somethin' spooked 'em. Headin' southeast out of Santa Fe, the road winds through the mountains and over Glorieta Pass 'til strikin' the Pecos River and some fords called somethin' like *San Jose del Vado* and *San Miguel del Vado.* Don't know what them Mexican names mean, but I recall Juan sayin' it was somethin' about them namin' them crossings after some Mexican saints.

Juan and me decided to lay over in Las Vegas for an extra day, that bein' about the only town that amounted to much between where we was and where we was goin'. We fed up good in them bean parlors there, not knowin' when we'd again have occasion to eat food cooked by someone who knew what they was doin'. See, neither of us was much of a hand at the cookfire. Oh, we could put the scorch to enough provisions to keep ourselves alive, but it ain't like what we fixed was worth eatin' otherwise.

Whilst we was havin' dinner the day before pullin' out, a trail-worn old man — I say old, but lookin' back, he likely hadn't more'n forty years on him — stepped inside the door and looked around in the dim light in the place 'til seein' us.

He wandered over to our table. "You the young fellers got that bunch of horses and jackasses out yonder?"

I nodded.

He stood, waiting for more, shifting his weight from one foot to the other. I sliced off another forkful of meat and went to work chewin' it. He watched me, looked at Juan, and back at me. He shifted his weight again and cleared his throat. "Mind my askin' where you-all are takin' them?"

I watched him as I chewed and swallowed. "Why might that be of interest to you?"

The man shuffled for another moment. "Mind if I sit down?"

I nodded toward the empty chair he stood behind and set my knife and fork down. It didn't look as if he was goin' away anytime soon, so I figured I might as well pay him some attention. "Well?"

Again, he cleared his throat. "I'm lookin' to get back to the States."

"There's plenty of freighters on the road most anytime," I said.

"I know it. Thing is, I been a bullwhacker and mule skinner on them trains more times than I care to remember, and I've had my fill of 'em."

I could see how that could happen. It's a hell of a long road and the monotony and drudgery of it all can wear on a man. And that ain't even takin' into account the risk of mishaps of one kind or another, or a run-in with Indians.

Turned out the man had family up in St. Joseph and wanted to get back to 'em. Leastways that's what he said.

"You ever drove any loose stock?"

"Oh, hell yes. I was a herder on a couple trips out and back years ago, 'fore I got a place on a wagon. I can pack a mule or horse and throw a passable hitch. Ain't no expert at it, but I get by."

"Me and Juan, we can handle all that. The

drovin', too. It ain't like we need any hired help."

"I ain't askin' for no job. All I'm after is a way to get home. Travelin' that road alone ain't smart. You-all take me along, I'm more'n willin' to pull my weight with the work to be done. Keep me mounted and fed is all I'm askin' you to do. I'll even do the cookin' if you-all want."

After talkin' it over with Juan, we decided to take him on. Come the morning, we rustled up an old saddle and bridle at a wagon yard and added some extra supplies in the way of foodstuff. After a last café breakfast, we readied to leave. Our new man was leanin' against a tree out where the herd waited when me and Juan rode up leadin' a packhorse. I led it over to where he sat, untied a knot, and tipped the saddle off to where it landed at his feet.

"Pick yourself out somethin' with four legs to cinch that onto," I said.

He had already made his choice, as he walked right over to a leggy sorrel mare and slipped the bit into her mouth and slid the headstall over her ears. After getting her saddled, he helped us finish packing and loading.

We pulled the last diamond hitch snug and strung out the pack animals and swung aboard our mounts, with Juan holdin' the lead rope for the string.

The new man squirmed into his saddle, lookin' for a comfortable seat. Then, "You boys decided where you-all are goin'?"

"What do you mean?"

" 'Fore long — I'd make it about twenty miles — we'll come to a place called *La Junta de los Ríos*. Get there, you got a choice to make. The road branches there and you-all can take what's called the mountain route, or the Cimarron route."

I pulled off my hat and scratched my head. "I don't know nothin' about that. Only thing I know is when I come out here, we followed the Arkansas River and went by a place called Bent's Fort."

"That'd be the mountain route."

"What's the difference 'tween that and the other'n — what'd you call it, Cimarron?"

"That's right. Cimarron route. It's a good ways shorter, save you some time. Cuts off a big loop up through the mountains. Meets back up with the Arkansas not too far from where the road leaves that river."

I thought it over. I looked to Juan, but he only shrugged. Could be he didn't savvy all what the man said, or could be he had no more idea than what I did.

"What would you do?"

The man slid his greasy hat up his fore-head 'til it perched on the back of head. " 'Twas me, I'd go the mountain way. It be longer, but there's good graze and water most all the way. They call the Cimarron the 'dry route' and it's for a reason. Plenty of times out that way there ain't no more water than what a man could spit."

That decided it for me. "We take the mountain road, then. These critters has already had more'n their share of goin' without enough to drink. I thank you for the information." I nodded at Juan and he set out with the pack string in tow. "By the way," I said to the man as we waited to push the loose stock onto the trail, "that boy's name is Juan. I go by Boone. What's your name?"

He looked at me and pulled his hat back down over his forehead. "You can call me Conley."

So that's what we called the man from then on. Don't know to this day if that was his first name or his last, or if it was his name at all, but it's the only name I know.

Things went along without much of any-thing happening. We just plodded along the road up through Raton Pass and on down onto the plains. Looking to the east, there wasn't a thing to see but empty. Now, I wasn't raised in no mountain country, but for the past many months I hadn't never been out of sight of mountains, and bein' mostly in amongst 'em. Even them big ol' dry lakes out in the desert that the Mexicans call *playas*, which was the flattest places I ever seen, was surrounded by mountains. Anyway, the emptiness of bein' in a country without no mountains again was a mite strange.

We passed freight trains on the road to Santa Fe now and again, and overtook some on the way to the States. We'd share a camp on occasion with the freighters and there was a few men among them that seemed to know Conley. But no one of them ever went out of his way to act friendly to the man. I had no notion of why that was and did not ask.

Conley, he turned out to be the kind of man who didn't do a thing 'less he was told to. Oh, he would do pretty much anything he was told, and do a passable job at it, and whilst his cooking wasn't anything to brag on, it was way ahead of what me or Juan could've done. So, while havin' him along was a help in some ways, he wasn't the kind of a man you'd want to be in harness with any longer than need be.

I came to think that even more so when

we laid over at Bent's Fort to let the horses rest for a time. And I came to know why none of the bullwhackers that knowed him wanted anything to do with him. One day I was sittin' in the plaza there at the fort listenin' to men tellin' stories — some of them the same old mountain men and same old tales that put me in mind to take up fur trapping — when a man who looked to be from a freight outfit squatted down beside me.

"You're the one herdin' horses, ain't you."

It wasn't really a question, so I didn't say nothin' to him. He knowed who I was, so I just waited to see what he wanted of me. He waited a bit as I looked him over, then invited me to find someplace quiet to talk. We walked over to where the powder house was, as there wasn't anyone hangin' around there, and I leaned against the wall listenin' to what he had to say. He allowed as how he was wagon master on a bull train, and had run several such outfits out and back on the Santa Fe Road.

"You got a man name of Conley with you, ain't you."

Again, it was not a question, so I waited.

"Was I you, I'd keep an eye on that one. See, I've had him in my employ before, so I know him."

"What might it be that I should watch out for?"

The wagon master glanced around to make sure no one was near enough to overhear. "Conley's a thief."

"A thief? What's he steal?"

"That's the thing. He ain't like no other thief I ever seen. It's like he can't help himself. He'll steal anything. Even trinkets and such that won't do him no good at all."

I thought over what he said. Then he said more.

"He stole money and such, like you might expect. And we caught him pilfering out of the stores on the wagons. But he'd steal about anything. Take little keepsakes and doodads out of another's man's baggage. We booted him out first chance we got, soon as we could run him off where he wouldn't starve to death." He scratched his beard and kneaded his chin. "Like I said, sometimes it's like he can't help it. So was I you, I'd watch him, for it is my notion that a man who'll steal when he don't even have to will steal for sure when he sees it to his advantage."

I extended a hand to the wagon master and, as we shook, thanked him for the information. I allowed as how we would watch Conley extra careful. Then I looked up Juan and passed along the caution.

Things went along just fine for weeks as we trailed them mares and *machos* along the Arkansas. We come to several places where Conley said there was crossings for them that took the Cimarron way, and after that there was more freighters on the road. We chose to stay clear of them most times, and kept a close watch on our man Conley whenever we camped with them.

After a time, we reached the Great Bend, where the Arkansas takes a more southerly course and the road leaves the river and goes on east towards Independence. The country was startin' to look more like home, what with more and more trees a-growin'. We laid over at Council Grove, where I was told there'd been a treaty of some kind made with the Indians there. There was one big, old tree folks called the Post Office Oak on account of there bein' a hollow place at its bottom where you could find letters and messages and such left in there. Some had names wrote on them and was undisturbed by others, and some was just messages of a general sort meant for anyone who cared to read them. Some told about bein' on the lookout for someone who run off, children that got carried off from their folks, news about weddings on the trail, Indian troubles, and all manner of things.

I pawed through the stack of letters there and was nearly surprised right out of my boots to find a folded-up page sealed with wax that had wrote on it in a fine hand, if faded some, *Daniel Boone Trewick.*

It took some time to catch my breath and gather my wits about me. I could not fathom any reason why there should be a letter for me there, or who might have wrote it. I broke the wax seal and unfolded the crisp sheet. The writing inside filled a portion of the page. My eye went first to the name at the bottom, and again I was discombobulated to read *Mary Elizabeth Thatcher.* I went on to read what she wrote.

Danny,
I do not know what has become of you. It crossed my mind that you might have taken the Santa Fe Road in your haste to be gone from Liberty after the unfortunate circumstances of our parting. I hasten to tell you, should this missive find its way to your hand, that there was not then, nor is there now, any reason for your continued absence from Clay County. No doubt you were concerned for the well-being of the Reverend Thatcher, but I can assure you that Father is well. Any lingering difficulties

*between the two of you can, I am confi-
dent, be settled satisfactorily and I pledge
my heart to see it so. If you hold any feelings for me, please return at first opportunity and with haste to me in Liberty.*

Yours,
Mary Elizabeth Thatcher

That whole deal rattled my brain so that I
ain't got much recollection of what went on
the next few days. All I remember is that we
kept trailin' them mares and jacks along the
way to Independence. I had no firm notion
of how to proceed with my plans once I got
there, and that letter from Mary Elizabeth
only addled my brain more. I reckon that's
part of the reason why what happened next
happened.

We was camped along the trail within sight
of Blue Mound when things took a turn for
the worse. We was all three rolled in our
blankets sleepin' — or so I thought. We
never posted a guard on account of the
horses bein' content to graze and rest
through the nights and us havin' no notion
of any danger of any kind in that part of the
country.

But when I rolled out of my blankets in
the morning, it was a mite later than usual,
there bein' no smells in the air of Conley

cookin' breakfast or makin' coffee. I sat up and scoured out my eyes with my knuckles and looked around. The campfire had gone cold, without even a wisp of smoke risin' from the ashes. There weren't no sign of Conley. I stood up and hollered for Juan to wake up. We walked out to where the horses was pastured and there weren't but about a third of them there. There wasn't no other way to think about it, save that that sonofa-bitch Conley had made off with them in the night.

We talked over some what to do. We found the track where he took them out of there, and it appeared he was settin' a northern course toward St. Joe, but there was no tellin' how long he'd hold to that direction or if he'd only talked about St. Joseph now and then as a way to throw us off. What with Juan bein' a whole lot better tracker than me, we thought to put him on Conley's trail whilst I pushed on to Independence with what horses and jacks we had left. That was one thing — Conley hadn't stole a single one of them jacks — he only took the mares.

Then we thought better of sendin' Juan off in pursuit. What with him bein' Mexican and all, and his English bein' somewhat lacking, we decided he might find himself in more trouble than he could handle should he be accused — by Conley or on general principles — of bein' the thief.

Which brings up somethin' that might matter in the circumstances. Them horses was stolen by me and them others way back in California. But that was Mexico, and this is America, so it likely wouldn't matter. But I had tucked away a bill of sale wrote up and signed by Thomas L. "Pegleg" Smith, declaring me the rightful owner of them animals. He even had it attested to by some make-believe official of the government in Santa Fe. Still, even with that paper in hand, folks might not be inclined to believe Juan, him bein' Mexican and all.

So I set off after Conley and my mares and left Juan to wait where we was. Well, not exactly where we was — we determined to push a ways farther off the trail, where him and them horses would be less likely to be found by anybody. If he was found, well, all we could do was hope for the best.

It turned out Conley held true on a course towards St. Joe and he made no effort to throw me off the trail. But he was movin' fast, so I was glad to have brought along a spare horse on a lead, which allowed me to move at a good pace over the prairie, stopping only for a few hours' sleep in the dark of the night.

By the time I hit Fort Leavenworth, Conley wasn't but a couple of hours ahead. There was men at the fort — soldiers and civilians both — who had seen him with my horses, and said he could yet be gettin' them across the Missouri River on the ferry. With promise of a reward, I hired on two men who looked like they knew their way around a scrape. When we got to the river, the man who kept the ferry — name of Cain, as I recall — said Conley and the horses couldn't be more than half an hour gone, as he had just tied up after returnin' from the last trip haulin' him over. I don't know where Conley came up with the money to pay the man, but he had it from somewheres.

We caught up with Conley pretty quick. One man wrangling a herd of horses ain't no match for three men horseback. My two men stayed out of sight behind the herd and I hurried off through the woods to get ahead of the thief. His look of surprise when he saw me sitting horseback on the trail turned to fear before despair overcame him.

"Boone, I —"

"— Shut up, Conley. I don't want to hear it."

He looked around and I could see he was mulling over making a run for it. But then the men from Fort Leavenworth rode up and I could see he was resigned to his situation.

One of the men said, "This him?"

I nodded.

The other said, "Well, hell, we might just as well get on with it."

It sickened me to hang a man, but we left Conley dangling from a red oak tree and rode away. Hanging from his neck by a loop of whang leather was a piece cut from a saddle skirt with the words HORSE THIEF scratched on it.

We got the horses ferried back across the river and those two men offered to help me get the horses back to the Santa Fe Road.

"No, gentlemen. I reckon if that sorry sonofabitch Conley got them up here, I can get them back."

What cash I had been carrying was now in the hands of the ferry man, so I allowed my helpers to take a mare each from the herd. Pretty good pay for a day's work, I thought. Even if the job required stringing up a horse thief.

I found Juan without no trouble and we set off for Independence, which I figured to be two, maybe three days away. We made it in two.

Me and Juan spent a few days riding

around the country and located suitable pasture that was there for the taking. It was a different deal in town, where I had to put the horse herd up as security for a bank loan to buy land in town for a barn and pens and an office.

As you might imagine, most all them mares had already been serviced by them big jacks on the trail somewhere between here and California, and was carrying foals, so our first crop of mules was already on the way. Them *machos* did their job that year, and every year since. So did that herd of mares, as have them we've added since.

By the time we got that first bunch of mules raised up and Juan got them broke to drive, things had changed in Independence. What we figured to be a ready market among freighters was still there. But in the meantime, all kinds of folks from the east was headin' west, most bound for Oregon and some for California. We couldn't raise mules fast enough, and every team that left our barn left behind a hefty profit. That's when we got in the ox business, bringin' in some big Durham bulls from back East and breedin' them to lanky longhorn cows brought up from Texas, and whatever other cows of a suitable size we could find hereabouts. We been at it ever since, sellin' every

111

mule and ox we can get raised up to a proper size for work.

Which brings us to that damn sign. I confess that slab of wood daubed with paint is right handsome, even though it's showin' its age all these years later. And it has sure done its job. But, like I said, the way it looks makes it look like we're sellin' mules and oxen for breeding and there sure as hell ain't no such thing. Sticks in my craw. I could have had a new sign made over the years but never did. Fact is, as much as the damn thing bothers me, I like the look of it. And plenty of folks stop in to ask about it, just like you did.

So that's the story about that sign, and I don't know what else I can tell you. Well, there is one more thing. After we got settled in and doin' business, I made my way across the river to Clay County and on up to Liberty, where I made my peace with the Reverend Thatcher. It took some talkin', but I done it. It didn't take much talkin' at all to convince Mary Elizabeth to marry me. The reverend allowed as how she was too young for it, but she was past sixteen and as stubborn as one of my mules, so he finally gave in. Hell, he even read out the rites for us. The passel of kids that's come along since has been to his likin' as well.

As for me, I've been content and have not ever once been tempted to take another trip on the road to Santa Fe. And, no matter how much I admire the horses and mules and *machos* out that way, I sure as hell ain't been back to California.

Four-time winner of the Western Writers of America Spur Award, **Rod Miller** writes fiction, history, and poetry about the American West. His writing has also been honored by Western Fictioneers, Westerners International, and the Academy of Western Artists. Find him online at writerRodMiller.com, RawhideRobinson.com, and writerRod Miller.blogspot.com.

LEGEND

BY JOHNNY D. BOGGS

"Kit, look what we got." The pockmarked Dragoon waves the penny dreadful over his head, motioning for the small man to step closer to the fire.

"You ain't gonna believe it." The sergeant also beckons the scout. "Alyicious found it in a grip over yonder."

Lowering his coffee cup, the St. Louis Frenchman whispers to the soldiers, *"Mes amis,* this is a mistake you make. He will not wish to see these . . ." — and sighs — *"mensonges."*

"You're just jealous, Leroux," the sergeant says. "On account nobody's never writ nothin' 'bout you."

"C'est la vie." With a shrug, Leroux focuses on his coffee. It is not his place to argue with Dragoons or imbeciles. He is paid as a scout and guide, just like the small man who turns his gaze from this never-ending country of red rocks, harsh winds,

and a river, more mud than water.

Leroux stares at his cup, empty now, and waits, hearing no footsteps, but even if dead twigs carpeted the ground, no sound would be heard. Kit Carson walks like a ghost. The Dragoons grow excited, alerting Leroux that Carson approaches the fire.

"See what we found," the pockmarked one says again.

Carson remains quiet.

"It's a book," the sergeant says.

"I ain't that ignorant," Carson says.

"But it's about you," the one holding the book says.

Now, Antoine Leroux raises his eyes.

In front of the fire, but not too close, for he has learned to stay in the shadows, Carson cocks his head.

The sergeant points at this gaudy, cheap . . . book? No, Leroux could tell them that a book is *Le Père Goriot*. A book is *Les Trois Mousquetaires*. A book is not . . .

"*Kit Carson, The Prince of the Gold Hunters,*" the sergeant reads aloud, as best as he can. "*Or, The Adventures of the Sacramento: A Tale of the New Eldorado, Founded on Actual Facts.*"

Out of the growing darkness, Carson — short but solid, with long, stringy hair and grizzled face — moves closer, incredulous at the slender volume the sergeant shoves forward, like a scalp or a jug of Taos Lightning. Carson's gray eyes bore through the bold letters and brassy illustration before he stares at the soldiers.

"Somebody writ a book 'bout me?"

"That's right," the pockmarked Dragoon says. He bends his head to make sure of the name and says, "Charles E. Averill."

"Chargin' two bits for it," the sergeant adds.

"Charles E. Averill," Carson says. "Don't recollect meetin' no Charles E. Averill." He stares at Leroux. "Do you?"

Leroux smiles gently. "Names rarely stay with me. And *Capitaine* Averill did not write about me."

"He's a capt'n?" Carson asks.

"They are all *capitaines*. Unless they are *colonels*." A joke, which no one understands.

Squatting, Carson rubs the stubble on his chin. Leroux can read the hesitation in Carson's face. The small man turns back into the gloaming, wets his lips, and stares once more at the book, before finding Leroux. That look passes quickly, and Carson's Adam's apple bobs; he draws in a deep breath, and asks the question Leroux dreads.

119

"Would one of you boys mind readin' that thing . . . ?" Carson sticks a gnarled finger at the twenty-five-cent piece of garbage.

A man like Kit Carson knows of many dangers, but not this kind, Leroux thinks sadly, *but you would have made the same request were you illiterate.*

The sergeant stares at the novel. "Well, it's a thick book." Which it isn't. "And . . . dark is coming fast . . ."

"And," another young Dragoon adds, "won't we be moving out? Keep after those savages?"

"We got what we came after," Major Grier says. He points his flask toward the grave. "We return tomorrow."

Leroux whirls toward the commander. "The baby remains missing," he says.

"I know that," Grier snaps. "But we have no forage for our horses, not enough rations for our men, and winter is fast approaching. We will deal with the Jicarillas later and avenge . . ." The sight of Carson's glare silences him.

Grier has lost his nerve, has no taste for pursing Indians in a cold, barren Hell, yet Leroux finds no fault in Grier. The major had been shot during the attack on the Jicarillas' camp. If that ball had not struck a suspender button, Grier could lie dying in

120

his bedroll or already be buried beside the woman they had been ordered to rescue.

"Read the story, Sergeant," another soldier says, and Leroux realizes others have gathered around the fire. Even the New Mexico Volunteers, who speak passable English if at all, want to hear.

"Well . . ." The big man wets his lips, turns the cover. The dreadful shakes in his hands. He says, "Chapter One," and starts stuttering over something before a German immigrant who has joined the Dragoons tells him what he's attempting to read isn't important and to get to the story.

" 'From the Old South clock,' " the sergeant begins, too soft, too uncertain. He's goaded to read like a man. After clearing his throat, he continues. " '. . . and the State House bell chimed the hour of nine.' " No interruptions. The sergeant gains confidence. " 'The living word of Boston's — ' "

"Boston?" Carson says, not quite a bark, for Carson rarely raises his voice. "I ain't never been to Boston. Been to Washington City . . . taken a train . . . but didn't get to Boston."

The sergeant blinks repeatedly. He stares at the page, and scans down and up the columns, moves to the next page, turns a page, focuses again on the cover to make

121

sure he's reading the right book, flips another page, skimming now, another, another, swallows and says, "I think this fellow's name is Harry." He thumbs through more pages. "There's a Eugene here." He digs deeper inside the novel.

Leroux holds up his tin cup. A jug is being passed around, and the German, leaning on a rock, has the rum. He splashes some in the Frenchman's cup. The sergeant is halfway through *Kit Carson, The Prince of the Gold Hunters.* Leroux does not yet sip the liquor, but offers an explanation.

"They are Easterners. Young. They will leave Boston eventually and strike out for California. After many adventures, they will meet Kit Carson, befriend him, and he will save many lives."

Even Grier studies Leroux. "You have read this?"

Leroux laughs. "No, Major." How could he explain to these men? Charles Averill is no Balzac, no Dumas. No Dickens or Thackeray. Certainly no Hugo. "It is a blood-and-thunder. They are all pretty much the same."

"I ain't no prince," Carson says. "And never hunted no gold. Iffen I ever found any, I sure wouldn't let nobody know 'bout it . . . not from all the mess 'em emigrants has caused of late in Californy, and just get-tin' there."

"Read the story," Grier orders. "From the beginning."

He says this to appease Carson. The sergeant flips back to the beginning. He reads.

Leroux remembers.

II

Sitting in the inn, sipping brandy, enjoying the fire and the song the raven-haired señorita sings in Spanish.

The door opens, and Major William Grier enters, lets his eyes adjust to the darkness, and spies Leroux.

"Antoine." The major speaks brusquely. "Trouble. I need your services."

The song has ended, and a *ranchero* begins talking to the singer, showering her with Spanish praises, and she smiles, a most charming sight. Sighing, Leroux sips his brandy and nods at Grier.

"Indians raided a train near Point of Rocks," the major says. "Part of Aubry's caravan."

Leroux knows Francois X. Aubry. Who doesn't in New Mexico Territory? A wiry, young, fearless man with French ancestry, too, only his from Canada, not Leroux's St. Louis.

"Aubry wasn't with them," the major says. "At least, not from what we've learned." Grier looks around, as though hoping someone will bring him a drink, but few pay attention. "This man White — I cannot recall his Christian name — had a dozen or more wagons he was bringing to Santa Fe to open up a mercantile. Aubry sent Calloway ahead to fetch fresh mules."

Another familiar name. William Calloway, Aubry's wagon master.

"This White, he didn't want to wait," Grier continues. "So he and his party rode out with Calloway."

"Aubry let them?"

"I'm sure Aubry told White it was a damned fool idea. They're east of Point of Rocks when Jicarillas hit them. One boy lived, must have played dead. After the Indians rode off, he crawled to Point of Rocks. Hugh Smith, who happened to be on his way to Washington City, found the boy. They all hightailed it back to Santa Fe."

"When did this happen?" Leroux asks.

"Best we can figure from what the boy said, the twenty-fourth."

Leroux smiles his saddest smile. "*Mon ami,* there is nothing to be done but . . ." He

124

makes the sign of the cross.

"The boy says the Jicarillas took women with them," Grier says. "And a kid: White's wife, her baby daughter, and a colored woman who must've been the girl's nanny."

The brandy sours on Leroux's tongue. He rises from his chair, turns to find his coat and hat, as Grier keeps talking.

"I have a company ready to march. Captain Valdez of the Volunteers has forty men with him, and a battery of six-pounders. A courier rode in from Santa Fe this morning saying that the Indian agent and Aubry have put up a thousand dollars each to ransom the women or pay for their return, at least Mrs. White and her kid."

Leroux cares not about the reward, or even the pittance he will collect from the Dragoons. With such a head start, the Jicarillas will be hard to find, and he already knows who has led this raid. Lobo Blanco. The Llaneros band of the Jicarillas has been raiding since the Americans arrived in the territory. Ferreting out Lobo Blanco will be a challenge. And finding the women and child?

"Point of Rocks," he says, absently finding the St. Christopher dangling from his neck. "That means we must ride through Rayado."

III

Kit Carson has arrived.

Not in person, not yet, not the way Charles Averill tells his story, but the heroic young aristocrat from Boston is gazing upon a portrait of, in Averill's words, "the famous hunter and adventurer of the Great West" . . . "hardy explorer" . . . "daring guide" . . . "hero of prairie and forest" . . . "prince of backwoodsmen."

The sergeant's voice has turned hoarse, even though noncommissioned officers in the 1st U.S. Dragoons are supposed to be able to yell for weeks on end. He pauses to wash down the dryness in his throat with rum.

Averill is nothing but a hackney writer, Leroux can imagine his father saying, yet Averill has pretty much described Kit Carson to perfection.

The soldiers begin cheering. One even dares to slap Carson's tough shoulders. Carson smokes his pipe, stares at the fire.

"You're famous, ol' hoss," the pockmarked one says. "I knew you were legend, but, to have a book writ about you, now that's somethin'." He waits for the sergeant to pass the jug along.

The jug does come into the Dragoon's

126

hands, and *Kit Carson, The Prince of the Gold Hunters,* rises to the sergeant's bloodshot eyes. He has trouble finding his place in what's more pamphlet than book.

"It is said that there is a steamboat on the Mississippi and Missouri," Leroux says, "that is called the *Kit Carson.*" Which makes him realize that someday there will likely be towns, marble and bronze monuments, and perhaps other ships, plus parks, mountains, rivers, and forests named after this Kentucky-born, Missouri-bred legend.

"A steamboat is not a book," the German says.

"Oui," Leroux says. He thinks: *But a steamboat never speaks.* He wishes he had never suggested that Grier stop at Rayado.

IV

Josefa holding the baby under the portal of the adobe home in Rayado. What a beautiful woman.

By the corrals, Major Grier and Captain Valdez speak with Carson while Leroux, holding the reins to his horse in one hand, removes his hat and bows to Carson's wife.

"For what reason have you come for my husband this time?" Josefa asks in Spanish. Barely out of her teens, she appears to be

127

with child again, but though married to Carson for perhaps six years, life has not aged her. Her hair is glossy black, parted down the middle. An oval face, unblemished by the sun and dry winds, perfect eyebrows, aquiline nose, rounded lips, she could have had any of Taos's finest, but she, and her father, chose Kit Carson. Her dress is blue. Her eyes are sad.

With a shrug, Leroux answers, *"¿Qué más . . . ?"*

The baby squirms. Josefa looks at her husband, then back at Leroux. *"Vaya con Dios."*

"Desde siempre," he says as she disappears inside the dark adobe home. But there is no God where he is about to ride.

By the time he leads his gelding back to the soldiers, Carson is lugging blanket and saddle toward a mule.

One of the Dragoons snorts and spits tobacco juice onto the ground. "He don't look like much to me, Alyicious. A slight breeze'll blow him away."

As Leroux swings into the saddle, he remembers Carson telling a story once, so he uses the last line on the foolish soldiers, trying to effect Carson's own drawl.

"I reckon he ain't the Kit Carson you was lookin' for."

128

V

If they let the sergeant keep reading, they will be thawing out in the spring before they reach the end of *The Prince of the Gold Hunters*. Besides, his slurs of Averill's words and his monotone has sent some Dragoons and Volunteers to their bedrolls. The sergeant has no objections to relinquishing command of the dreadful. The major shakes his head when his troops seek him to narrate. The German points and says, "What about him?"

Leroux starts to decline, but Carson speaks.

"Go on, Antoine. Read it." He laughs bitterly. "Ain't like I can."

The book moves through the blackness. Leroux lets the novel hang there as he peers across the fire. Carson tamps the pipe, which he has not smoked for better than an hour. "Go on," Carson says again. "Get 'er done."

VI

The land looks flat, but is not. The grass looks dead, and is. The bodies, what's left of them, leave soldiers puking.

Carson has been here at least an hour

129

before Leroux guides the major's command ten miles beyond Point of Rocks.

Captain Valdez's Volunteers cross themselves, mouth prayers. A few even cry.

Wolves have dug up the dead from shallow graves covered hurriedly, scattering carnage from that feast more than a hundred yards.

Leroux hobbles his gelding and moves through the bones and litter — bridles and harnesses that have been cut, clothes and other items carried by the wind into cactus, chests and crates broken open, wagons burned or reduced to kindling. Behind him, the major and the Mexican captain order burial details.

Carson squats and stares off to the southeast.

"You see the stone wall?" Carson asks without looking back at Leroux.

"I did."

"Indians built it, hid behind it, then ambushed 'em."

"Lobo Blanco gets smarter all the time."

Carson spits between his teeth. He has pulled a weed and twists it around absently with his fingers.

"Who buried these men?" Leroux asks.

"Barclay be my guess," Carson answers. "Wagons, oxen, mules come down the

130

Cutoff, found what happened." He points. "Kept movin' toward Mora Creek."

Alexander Barclay, decent enough for an Englishman, runs a way station on that creek. They would have found the bodies, buried them quickly. Who could blame them? Fearing Lobo Blanco's Jicarillas might still be around, few men would have even made an attempt at covering the dead.

"They have made finding the Jicarillas' trail harder," Leroux says.

"Lobo Blanco didn't leave much for Barclay and his boys to mess up," Carson says.

Leroux breathes deeply, slowly lets it out. "The women? The child?"

Carson tosses the twisted stem of grass to the ground. With a sigh of weariness and age — though he has not quite reached forty years — Carson stands. "I don't know," he concedes.

VII

The naïve young wayfarers from Boston, now in a rugged land east of Sacramento filled with "pesky" redskins and treacherous barbarians, have found Kit Carson, whom they all know as "the prairie-ranger, the scout, the gold-discoverer . . . whose name the Union rings," Averill writes.

131

" 'Yes and no, stranger!' " Leroux reads. " 'You *do* see Kit Carson, *plain Kit Carson,* mind you.' "

He reads to the chapter's end. "My God," Carson whispers.

Leroux folds the book, keeping his place with his forefinger.

The pockmarked Dragoon laughs. "You do have a 'lynx-eye,' Kit."

The German says: "But you don't talk like that."

" 'Cause he don't talk at all," the sergeant says.

"Keep reading," Major Grier orders.

Carson shrugs. "Might as well."

The book is opened again, but as he finds his place, Leroux considers that this Averill must have interviewed someone who knows Carson.

Leroux corrects himself. *Nobody knows Kit Carson.*

Yet Carson's smile is always "good humored," his countenance is typically "calm and quiet," and while the dialogue is overblown, the descriptions trite, the story convoluted and often crass, much truth can be found in Averill's prose — not that Leroux will seek out *Secrets of the High Seas, Pirates of Cape Ann's Secret Service Ship* or anything else by Averill.

132

VIII

At the edge of the first Jicarilla camp they discover, Carson breaks open horse apples, then curses. They are still days behind.

The major, who has lost his patience, yells, but a biting gale drowns out those words.

Carson inches his way off to the southeast; Leroux moves from the northwest. Scouts Dick Wootton and Tom Tobin, who have joined the command, read the ground two hundred yards from camp.

Carson is legend, but Tobin, Wootton, and Leroux know this country well and have earned deserved respect as trackers. Yet this brutal land refuses to give up its secrets.

"How many directions?" Leroux asks Carson when they meet.

"South, southeast, southwest."

Leroux tilts his head toward the opposite directions. "North, northeast, northwest."

"At least they ain't goin' up or down." Carson walks to the approaching major, who reins in his horse.

"They split up here, Major." To be heard above the wind, Carson must yell. "Two, sometimes three, headin' ever' which way."

The major's mouth opens, and his lips try to form words, but nothing comes out.

"They will, most likely, circle around at

some point, join together," Leroux explains.

"But figurin' out which way they wanna go will take some doin'," Carson says.

"By Jehovah, we could be wandering around this godforsaken land forever," Grier roars. "We don't even know if that damned woman is with them."

Carson opens his hand to reveal a piece of torn calico, yellow with green and white polka dots. "She's with 'em."

"And the child?"

Carson shrugs. "Maybe so." He moves to his mule. Leroux finds his gelding. They mount and ride, one north, one south, knowing that Lobo Blanco will continue to gain ground while they search for the right trail.

"Eventually," Carson tells Leroux, Wootton, and Tobin, "Lobo Blanco'll figure we quit the chase. It'll be hard-doin', but it's gotta get done, boys. We gots to get 'er done. For the women, and the little girl."

Sometimes, it feels pointless. Find a chip in the rock that might have been cut by an unshod pony's hoof. The droppings of a horse. The tiny ditch that could have been caused by an Indian urinating. A strand of blond hair on a cactus. Another piece of calico. Until the train turns, and they know that the Jicarillas are not traveling north. Unless they turn around again. Until they find where the Indians have rejoined and made another camp.

And then? Pony tracks leading in myriad directions. Another trail lost. Hours wasted. The trail found, only to disappear inside some canyon, vanish at a mesa, or be blown away by the wind that grows icier with each passing mile.

"Never," Carson says, "in all my years have I found a trail this hard to follow."

"The soldiers want to turn back," Leroux says.

"Let 'em. I ain't."

IX

A prairie fire has sent panicking buffalo into a deadly charge, and the heroes face certain death under the hooves of those big shaggies, but Kit Carson, that prince of gold hunters, uses flint and tinder to start another fire. The backfire stops the raging inferno, and turns the stampede. Again, Kit Carson has saved the day, and as Averill's hero begins speaking to those young adventurers from Boston, the Dragoons still awake, still sober enough, to be listening, cheer the Kit Carson who sits away from the others, away from the fire.

"By grab, Kit," says the pockmarked kid. "Did that really happen? Did you save 'em from gettin' trampled?"

Leroux stops reading to rest his voice. Carson says nothing. Over the past hour, he has not even grunted.

Carson stares at the fire, never acknowledges the questions.

"Maybe I should stop for the night," Leroux says. "We have a long way back home tomorrow."

"Go on," Carson says. "Ain't but a little more left."

After wetting his lips, Leroux finds his place, and reads.

X

Fording the Canadian River and following the trail southeast. Only to find the Jicarillas have turned back to the river, forcing scouts and soldiers to cross the frigid waters again — fifteen miles from where they crossed earlier. Damning Lobo Blanco. Damning themselves. Damning the days lost.

A week . . . ten days . . . twelve. Exhaustion and boredom leave Dragoons and Volunteers irritable, dirty, discouraged.

Nothing but bread to eat. No fires at night, no coffee, just a thin bedroll to keep warm. Horses and mules feel no better. Nor do Leroux, Wootton, or Tobin. Only Carson seems more alive than dead.

On the outside, Leroux begins to think.

"Buzzards!" The pockmarked Dragoon reins in and points.

Dick Wootton sees the black birds taking flight. "Ravens," he corrects.

Already, Carson lopes his mule to where the ravens have been roosting.

"What is it?" Grier demands, and hearing no reply, turns his horse toward the cotton-woods.

"Rest easy, Major," Leroux says, but does not face the officer. His eyes follow the *caw-ing* ravens' flight.

Grumbling, Grier slackens the reins. A few minutes later, Carson emerges from the trees and rides to the soldiers.

"Camped here," Carson tells the major. "Ashes still hot."

"Mrs. White?" Grier asks.

Carson holds up another ripped piece of calico.

"The kid?" Leroux asks.

Carson nods. "But no sign of the Ne-gress."

"Well . . ." Grier doesn't know what to say.

Leroux points. "Ravens."

"Yeah," Carson says. "They're camp followers, Major. Eat what they can, what the Jicarillas toss away. Follow 'em black birds, we find what we been huntin'."

By the end of the day, after forty bone-jarring miles, they camp in another cottonwood grove, the leaves long fallen, but hope returning to sleeping men.

At dawn, they set out at a hard trot toward the Canadian. In the distance, Tucumcari Butte beckons them. Carson is too far ahead to be seen.

Leroux smells smoke. Carson gallops back toward the soldiers, slides the mule to a stop, and waves. "It's Lobo Blanco's bunch, boys. We've found 'em. Give 'em hell. Follow me." The mule has already been jerked around. Carson holds a Hawken rifle in his right hand.

Wootton and Tobin charge after the scout.

Yes, yes, Leroux spots the Indians. No woman. No child. One old Jicarilla waves arms over his head.

Major Grier's voice is lost. His mouth opens, but it is Leroux who speaks.

138

"They might want to parley," Leroux says. "Ransom the woman and her little girl."

"I . . ."

A heavily bearded Dragoon rides forward. "Major, we can't just sit here."

Carson gallops back. "Come on, you sons of bitches. Come on." Without waiting, he tears back toward the camp.

The bearded Dragoon throws his saber into the dirt. "For God's sake!" he yells.

"Hell." Leroux realizes his mistake. The Indian waving his arms is a decoy. Touching the gelding's ribs, Leroux says, "Quickly, Major. Attack. Attack."

The bullet almost knocks Grier out of the saddle.

XI

All's well that ends well. Villains conquered. Kit Carson's vow fulfilled. The stolen child recovered. A wedding to be planned. Enough gold to satisfy everyone. And a sequel, *Life in California; or, The Treasure Seekers' Expedition,* to be published — probably already in mercantiles across the United States and her territories — in pamphlet form.

"Well," the German says after Leroux closes *Kit Carson, The Prince of the Gold*

Hunters. "That was something."

"Was any of it true?" the pockmarked Dragoon asks.

Carson stares without blinking.

Once Leroux stands, he stamps his right foot to get the blood circulating again. As he looks around, he realizes that most of the men have retired. The major walks away. A few Dragoons and two Volunteers sleep on the ground, no pillows, no blankets, but it has been an exhausting day. Tobin and Wootton remain on guard duty, having not heard one word of Averill's blood-and-thunder.

Slowly, Carson rises, steps out of the shadows toward Leroux.

XII

Leroux sees the hole in the major's coat, hears the panicked gasps. Grier's face loses all color. Wheeling in the saddle, the major slaps his chest.

But there is no blood.

Grier's fingers enter the breast pocket, withdrawing the gauntlets. A flattened lead ball topples into the sand.

"Charge, Major," Leroux pleads. "Charge." He can wait no longer. He is as much to blame for the delay as Grier. The gelding explodes into a gallop.

Behind him, Leroux hears the trumpeter's call.

Jicarillas have crossed the Canadian. One floats in the reddish-brown water. Fires still burn. A few horses and stolen livestock from Aubry's wagon train wander about. Carson stands over the body.

Sickened, Leroux slides out of his saddle and moves toward Ann White. He does not need to try to find a pulse, but he does anyway.

"She was a brave woman," Tobin says. "Tearing up her dress and all, trying to leave sign for us to follow."

Carson bites his bottom lip.

"Imagine the hell she went through," Wootton says. "By thunder, just look at her."

She lies on her side, the bloody point of an arrow protruding from her chest, the yellow, green, and white calico dress hardly recognizable. A month ago, she must have been pretty. Now . . . her open eyes reveal misery. Hardships line her sunburned face. Death is supposed to bring peace, but her features exhibit eternal agony. But none wants to think of everything Ann White has endured these past weeks.

Leroux closes her eyes, and curses himself.

Some Dragoons and Volunteers swim their

horses after the Jicarillas. Muskets fire. Men yell.

"Search for the baby," Captain Valdez orders in Spanish. Yet Leroux knows the girl will never be found.

Their mission is a failure. There is nothing to do but bury the dead.

XIII

Crackling wood and popping coals are the only sounds. The wind has stopped completely, and no snores can be heard, no rippling of water from the river. Eyes around the campfire stare at the small scout as he stops in front of the Frenchman. Carson extends his hand.

Leroux passes the novel to the scout, who glares at the cover, and that artist's fancy interpretation of a gallant knight, part Homer, part Hercules, all legend. In the darkness — dawn is but a few hours away — Leroux sees the flames reflecting in Carson's eyes. He can also see the tears.

Perhaps Carson will talk later, but not here, not in front of the Dragoons. Yet Leroux knows the thoughts troubling Carson. He can hear the scout's words in his head.

Do you think that woman read this, Antoine? And that she knowed I was around these parts, and that she prayed I'd come to her rescue? And I did come. But . . .

The gray eyes fall to *Kit Carson, The Prince of the Gold Hunters,* and then the twenty-five-cent dreadful drops into the fire. At first, it smolders. The illustration of Kit Carson darkens, pages curl and with sudden violence, flames dance across the cheap pamphlet, devouring the words of Charles E. Averill.

Carson does not witness the funeral pyre. He has vanished in the darkness.

"Damnation, Leroux, I don't get that at all." The pockmarked Dragoon stares at the mass of ashes that once was *Kit Carson, The Prince of the Gold Hunters.* "He gets a book writ up about him, and he burns it. Don't make a lick of sense. By grab, that's Kit Carson. He's a livin' legend."

"Oui." Leroux speaks in French, but the Dragoon would not have understood even had he used English. "But even a legend can be cursed with something called humanity."

Johnny D. Boggs is an eight-time Spur Award winner from Western Writers of America. He lives in Santa Fe, New Mexico,

143

with his wife and son. His website is Johnny DBoggs.com.

■ ■ ■ ■

ARLEY

BY WALLACE J. SWENSON

■ ■ ■ ■

The rough-knuckled fist hit Arley's ear without warning, and the blaze of light behind his eyes flared as hotly as the anger he felt for not anticipating the blow. His brother, seven-year-old Jacob, crashed to the floor with him as the bench they sat on fell over. To Arley's relief, Jake scuttled on hands and knees to temporary safety under the table.

"Squintin' at me'll get you one of them . . . ever' goddamned time," his father shouted, the words slurred. The gaunt man, sallow and rheumy-eyed, slammed his whiskey jug down on the table and rose unsteadily to his feet. "Now get the hell outta here ya worthless whelp . . . 'fore I stomp yer guts out yer scrawny ass."

Experience drove Arley toward the door, but he chanced one backward glance: his mother, disheveled hair bound in a rag, stared back, her brimming eyes gleaming yellow in the light of the single lamp. Jake's hand appeared above the table's edge and snatched the corn cake he'd been savoring; an instant later, the hand reappeared and grabbed Arley's cake as well. Arley barged out the door and shoved it shut behind him.

The smell of river mud came to him on a chill breeze as he hurried toward the gray, weather-beaten barn. This day had gotten off to a bad start and had steadily gotten worse. But now, sixteen hours later, he was too tired to care, and all he felt was gnawing hunger and fear. The best he could hope for tonight would be his father passing out, or being too drunk to cause any damage if he came looking. Or worse — Arley's fists clenched and his heart raced — the drunken pig would turn his attentions to his mother. Jake would hide — he was good at that — but the youngster would then have to listen to what went on and wonder.

That morning, a mid-April Saturday in 1855, had dawned clear and calm on his thirteenth birthday, but he hadn't expected the date to make the slightest difference in his day. Even with good equipment and a stronger back, young Arley would've been hard-pressed to grow much of anything on such a hardscrabble farm — to say nothing of producing enough to feed a family of four. They lived on nine poor acres; all that remained of the original seventy his grandfather had wrested from the wilderness along the Illinois River starting in 1820. The higher, more productive ground now belonged to their neighbor, Axel Holverson, sold to him piecemeal for money, then wasted by Arley's father on whiskey and gambling.

Before the sun cracked the horizon, Arley had risen from his nest in the barn to milk the cow and turn her into the pasture. For some reason, the normally placid beast put a foot in the half-full bucket and tipped it over, soaking his trouser leg and filling his brogan for good measure. He was relieved his father had already left for work in town.

With the milking finished, after a fashion, he headed for the corncrib while two hungry sows and their thirteen shoats grunted impatiently in their pens. Their beady eyes tracked his steps across the yard, and he smiled to himself despite his sticky-wet pant leg and squishy foot. He enjoyed feeding the pigs and had once said as much. His father's ridicule of such a notion only made the rowdy swine more appealing to him. Arley knew whose company he preferred. The pigs lived downhill toward the river and fifty-eight paces from the house. He knew the exact number because counting them helped focus his mind when weariness fuddled his brain; house to barn took forty-five. He reckoned today might be just such a day. Besides daily chores, the garden needed work, and he had to finish planting the field corn — or else. He'd been warned.

Two separate, plank-sided, half-covered pens provided shelter for the two sows while their offspring, weaned weeks ago and each weighing over two hundred pounds, ran free inside a rail-fenced area next to them. They ate a lot and he was glad they'd soon go to slaughter. The older sow grunted her impatience and tossed her enormous head back and forth as he approached the three-foot fence; the two full buckets of shelled corn banged his legs. He dumped the first into her trough while the younger sow in the next pen assaulted a split-log partition that separated the four-hundred-pound animals. Watching her out the corner of his eye, Arley hurried to get the agitated beast her ration. Last year's harvest had been poorer than usual so he held back on their feed. He and his mother had worked the sums and decided to feed more to the weaned piglets. For his diligence, his father had given him a hot-tempered warning not to lose any and an emphatic punch to the chest that still pained him.

After another trip to the crib, he stood outside the larger pen. There the troughs lay at right angles to him so he couldn't simply dump the feed over the fence. Leaving one bucket on the ground, he climbed the planks and shoved his way through the rambunctious animals. They followed his every move, snouts jostling the bucket of corn as he struggled through them. He knew to keep moving lest one of the feistier beasts took a nip, or worse, knocked him down. He'd overheard his father tell his mother about some hogs upriver eating a man; they'd gobbled up everything but his skull. Arley had halfway believed the story despite his father's tendency to stretch the truth; maybe more than half — the story still haunted him once in a while. He dumped the corn along the trough in one sweeping motion and made for the rail. Six or seven of the larger pigs butted and bit their way to the food, their smaller brothers and sisters squealing in protest.

Just then, a barefooted and smiling Jake appeared carrying a wicker egg-basket. Arley pointed at the second bucket of corn. "Hey, Jake, put them cackleberries on top the corner post and hand me that bucket."

Stretching, Jake carefully placed the basket, and then grabbed the bucket handle with both hands. For a few seconds the boy's perpetual smile changed into a determined grimace as he heisted the bucket into Arley's grasp.

"Heavy," Jake said and grinned. With his bony elbows poking through a ragged shirt, and his charity trousers reaching only halfway down his clothes-peg shins, he had no more reason to be cheerful than did Arley, but he always seemed to be.

Mr. Holverson had once used the word *enigma* to describe Jake. Arley had sounded out every "in" word listed under "I" in his mother's *Webster's* before finding it in the "E's." A riddle it said. It still didn't make much sense. He dumped the corn, and then scrambled out of the way to climb the fence and face Jake. "Do you think you could carry half a bucket from the crib?"

"Long as I don't have to put it in there." Jake glanced warily at the black-spotted animals.

Arley had warned Jake away from the pigs, the youngster's skinny body a guarantee he'd lose any contest for control of the bucket. "Nope. Just get it here and I'll do it. I've got to haul water."

"Okay." Jake picked up the bucket and

152

sauntered away.

The sows needed about ten gallons of water each: four trips from the well with two, three-gallon buckets swinging at the ends of his neck yoke. The hogs would get what they needed when he turned them into the rough riverside pasture in the afternoon. Next year Jake might be big enough to carry water — half-buckets to start. At least that's what Arley hoped. He dumped the first two buckets about the time the sows had each finished bolting six gallons of corn, and their eagerness to get a drink made the drudgery of packing it a bit more tolerable. It wasn't hard to imagine a smile on their faces.

Trudging across the ground on the second trip, his gaze wandered over the hard-packed farmyard. Their house, such as it was, stood midway between a two-story barn on the right and a tangled mass of charred wood surrounded by a scorched stone foundation to his left. A tall chimney stood tombstone-like at one end of the mostly burned remains of his grandparents' house. Burned down in the night, they'd both died inside, and Arley had heard whispers that the fire had been set on purpose; hushed conversations that ceased whenever he came close enough to hear. He remembered moving from Bittsburg, the town a mile east where his father worked in the clay pits. His father had promised to rebuild the burned-out shell, and they'd moved into the hovel the black field-hands had once lived in.

The shack, squat, square, and sad-looking, had been built by the field workers using whatever they could find, mostly refuse and driftwood washed up on the riverbank. The flat roof leaked. Centered in the front wall, a rough-hewn plank door hung slightly askew on three leather straps, and the two small windows on either side — the only ones in the house — didn't have glass, instead filtering the light through sheets of mica. Attached on the left side, a lean-to clung desperately to the wall; storage for firewood and coal, plus a few tools and a place for Arley to sleep during the hot summer months. The two-story barn had been built with more care, as had all the other outbuildings: chicken coop, pigsty, corncrib, and smokehouse, but neglect showed everywhere. The Negro workers' shanties in town looked better.

Back at the well again, he twice lowered the bucket into the musty darkness, the windlass squeaking wood-on-wood. Then he shouldered the yoke and walked back to the pigs. The sows now lay in the morning sun on the clean cornstalks he'd put down the night before. They'd seek cover in the roofed section come afternoon. The covered part stayed warm in winter, and he'd once tried sleeping there instead of in the cold barn. The nose-burning stench of ammonia, and the cloying air made it a one-time experience. But it wasn't just the warmth that had drawn him to spend the night; the pigs seemed to appreciate what he did for them: cold, clean well-water, scoops of corn — hard-won using a hand-cranked shelling machine, pitchers of skim milk and whey, and clean, dry stalks to root around in and sleep on. Last year they'd gotten three and a half cents a pound for the eleven hogs they sold, over six dollars apiece, and he knew how important they were. He poured the water into the trough.

On his way back to the well, two dozen chickens followed, all scolding him as he walked. Jake must have opened the coop. They'd been fed yesterday, so today they got nothing, but they didn't know that. At the well, they clucked to each other for a minute or so, and then wandered off. Back at the pen, a beaming Jake stood waiting with the corn bucket. Arley glanced at it; three quarters full. "Ain't you the mule?"

He ruffled the boy's sandy hair. "Good job. Now go find a hoe and get after the garden." Jake took a deep breath, widened his smile, and ambled away.

Arley hated to work his little brother so hard, but there was only so much one person could do. He fed the corn to the voracious pigs and then took the empty buckets back to the crib. He winced at the meager amount of corn in the catch box; two days' worth maybe, certainly no more than three. Then he'd have to spend three or four grueling hours turning the crank on the hungry red corn-sheller while Jake or his mom fed it cobs. His shoulders started to ache just thinking about it. That would have to wait; the last acre and a half of feed corn had to be planted, and there was only one way to do it: one hole at a time. He headed for the house to get something to eat and tell his mother he was ready to pull the board.

Liesl Dachauer punched the pan of dough down again and breathed the sour smell of starter that wafted up. She then covered it with a piece of dingy linen. Two large loaves of sourdough bread would go into the oven in an hour and a half. She hated the thought of telling Arley he'd have to go to town today for more flour, but she'd used almost the last of it. If her husband demanded pancakes in the morning, she'd be in for it if she couldn't make them. The thought had no sooner formed than Arley walked through the open door. "Did you see Jacob?" she asked.

"Yup. He's pestering some weeds out back."

"He does a pretty good job for a seven-year-old." Her heart felt it when Arley slumped onto the rickety bench across from her and folded his arms on the uneven tabletop. He looked at her with old-man eyes. "I can pull a piece of dough off this batch and fry it if you'd like. A spoonful of treacle on top?"

Arley nodded. "And maybe a small piece of ham? We have to finish that corn today. Pa said —"

"I know what he said. Nothing would come of it if that last acre waited until Monday." The look in his eyes spoke to her folly, and she sighed as she lifted the cloth and pulled off a fist-sized lump of dough. "Cut a little off the side of that ham. The fat will do you better than the lean today." She put a skillet on the hot stove and dropped a dollop of lard into it before working the wad of bread dough into a flat cake.

The smoked meat hung in a corner of the cramped room, and Arley soon returned with a small piece of meat. "I hate to tell you," she said, "but we're out of flour, and you'd better go to Stringham's first thing. I don't want your father to catch you."

"He knows I go to town."

"But it irritates him if you're not working." She dropped the flattened piece of dough into the hot grease. "No sense offering him an excuse — he finds plenty."

Over the strenuous objections of her Irish Catholic father, Leisl had married a rowdy braggart, Klaus Dachauer, convinced she could settle him down. At first her constant attention to his slightest whim had worked well: Klaus's skill earned him a promotion at the pottery, affording them a decent place to live, and Arley was born. Soon after his birth, Leisl became pregnant again. Maybe it was too soon, because the child was stillborn, and then she lost yet another one. Klaus blamed her and bolstered his insulted ego with a whiskey jug, and punished Leisl by keeping her pregnant. That led to her father dealing Klaus a severe and public beating, and the die was cast. She couldn't know for sure, but in her heart, she believed Klaus had gotten the last fiery word. His drunken misbehavior eventually relegated him to working with the Negroes in the clay pits for a dollar and a half a day.

After Arley finished his meal, she took two dimes out of an old soda tin and laid them on the table. "Get three pounds of flour and a box of salt. Tell Mr. Stringham I don't need cake flour." Arley looked at the two coins and then up at her. "I know it's too much," she said, "but for your birthday, I want you to get two sticks of candy each for you and Jake." Arley grimaced. "Don't worry," she said. "We'll keep it a secret."

"But Jake can't keep secrets."

"He will if his second piece of candy depends on it." She put her hand on his shoulder and squeezed. "Now go."

The road to town went close by the Holversons' farmhouse, and as Arley had hoped, Mr. Holverson was out in the barnyard. Klaus hired Arley out to the friendly Swede in exchange for the use of a boar every June, and they used Holverson's mules to plow in the fall. "Off to town, we are?" the farmer called in his melodic Swedish accent as Arley approached.

"There and right back," Arley said. "I've got a bit more corn to plant."

Holverson hustled across the yard to the front gate. "I tell your father he was welcome to my planter."

They'd lost their two-wheeled cart and one of a matched pair of mules to the sheriff for debts, and one animal trying to do the work of a team took its toll; the remaining beast now struggled just to pull an empty, wobbly-wheeled wagon. "I know," Arley said with a sigh. "He says we can do it by hand."

"We?"

Arley shrugged. "Yeah."

Holverson shook his head. "Sometimes it is a wonder."

Just then, Mrs. Holverson came out of the house, her apron a-flutter, and hurried to join her husband. Though Arley really liked the farmer, he was truly fond of his wife. "Hello to you, Arley," she said. "How is your mother?"

"Baking bread this morning." He grimaced. "Then we're going to plant corn."

"That is not woman's work," she said, and scowled at her husband before looking back at Arley. "You can stop for a few minutes?"

"Better not." Arley nodded towards the gathering clouds to the west. "If we could get it planted, it just might rain on it."

"Then tomorrow. Today is special day so I bake you a cake." Her husband raised his eyebrows. "He is thirteen years today," she said.

"Aw, no longer the boy."

Mrs. Holverson snorted. "Foolishness." Then she touched Arley on the arm. "Sneak along in the afternoon. And bring sweet Jacob."

"I'll try. It depends . . ." He shrugged.

"I know," she said, her eyes misting. "I know."

"Better git." Arley raised his hand and hurried away.

Mrs. Holverson didn't wait long enough to speak to her husband because her words reached Arley clearly. "I take both those boys, and I hurry," she said to her husband.

"Yaw, that's for sure," Mr. Holverson replied.

Arley made the trip to town and back in less than half an hour.

Jacob stood beside his mother at the table, his eyes gleaming with expectation. "I *can* keep a secret, Arley," he said firmly as soon as Arley reached the table. "Lemme see what ya got us."

Arley tousled Jake's hair, and handed the string-tied package to his mother. "Nineteen cents." He put a penny on the table.

She carefully untied the knot, took a six-inch ball of string off a shelf, and added the day's prize to it. Then she folded the dirt-brown paper open. Jake's eyes opened wide and his jaw dropped as she picked up several pieces of stick-candy. Arley caught the spicy scent of mint. "Nine?" she asked.

"A man at the store paid the extra half-dime," Arley said. "I think he works at the pottery. He had chalk on his shoes like Pa." He paused a moment. "What's a *dickensurchan*?"

"Dickens's urchin. Two words. Where'd you hear that?"

"That's what the man said to Mr. Stringham. 'Give the boy five more. He looks like a dickensurchan.' "

"A boy in a story written by Charles Dickens, an Englishman. A very hardworking and smart boy."

"Was it all right to take them?"

"Of course. That man thought you were worth it." She turned to Jake. "Now I want you to tell me what we talked about while Arley was gone."

Jake furrowed his brow and bit the inside of his lip, his smile gone. "This is our favor and Pa will be mad if he doesn't get one but he has his own favors so it's fair and we won't tell." He took a deep breath and his smile returned.

"I'm impressed." His mother pinched his cheek. "But I wasn't expecting so many.

And just so you can enjoy a sweet another day we'll put five back until then. Okay?"

Jake's smile struggled to hang on.

"No later than Monday," his mother said and held out two sticks. Jake brightened again and reached for them.

Just then a high-pitched squeal reached them from outside, followed immediately by several spine-rippling screams. Fighting pigs! Arley bolted through the door, and raced down the hill to the pens — his father's warning echoed clearly in his mind. The rail fence rattled alarmingly, and he reached it to find all thirteen hogs crowded against the planks. He'd seen squabbles erupt over a share of corn or a bucket of turnips, but this seemed different somehow, more frenzied. Blood smeared the faces of several pigs.

His mother arrived with Jake. "What's wrong?"

"They've got something in the corner," Arley said helplessly, then held onto the top rail and leaned over.

She grabbed his arm. "You can't go in there. Nothing to do but let them fight."

"I know, but . . ."

"Is that my egg basket?" She pointed at some mangled, yolk-smeared wicker.

Just then, one pig broke out of the pack

and scampered to the back of the pen, hotly pursued by another. The second hog charged past on the right, and the first one turned left, its eyes rolling, wild and crazy-looking. From the pig's mouth hung the rear half of an animal with blood-smeared tawny-brown fur. "They've got a raccoon," Arley shouted when he saw a flailing ring-tail. Three more pigs took off after the two at the back, squealing so loud it hurt his ears. He shook his head and pointed at the corner post. "Jake left the basket there this morning to give me a hand."

"And the raccoon smelled it," his mother said. "Egg-robber."

Two more pigs broke off, running side-by-side; one with intestines trailing from its mouth, the guts still attached to the raccoon's front half clamped in the jaws of the other hog. The remaining pigs, all smaller, packed the corner, shoving, biting, and butting, the noise now a series of grunts and the occasional angry squeal.

"I forgot," Jake said, looking sadly at his mother.

"Not your fault, I told you to," Arley said. "An accident."

"Just that," his mother said and pulled Jake to her side. "And it's over and done. How many eggs?"

"Four." Then Jake's eyes opened wide. "But I only looked in the coop," he said hopefully.

"Then there'll be more, and those four won't be missed." She studied the milling swine. "I don't see anything too bad. Pigs *will* bite each other."

"You think that's good enough?" Arley asked.

"You can slosh a bucket of water over a couple of them. The blood will wash off and no one need be wiser. Besides, how often does he come down here to look?"

Arley raised his eyebrows and shrugged.

"Exactly. It's done. Let's go enjoy the candy, and then we'll plant corn."

Arley glanced up at the gathering clouds, and then took up the strain on a rope looped around his chest. He pulled until the tail end of the ten-foot-long dibber board drew even with his mother's foot and she stopped him with a word: "Hit." Seven, two-inch round holes, eighteen inches apart, penetrated the centerline of the heavy plank. His mother, walking down the left side, poked through each opening with a blunt wooden rod, and Jake, on the other side, then dropped three kernels of corn into each hole she made. When she said "Go,"

Arley advanced the plank again, the weight of the board dragging dirt into the cavities. To the end of the field and back, his legs trembling with exertion, Arley concentrated on keeping the rows straight, crooked ones were a beating offense. "Hit." "Go." "Hit." The time between his mother's calls got longer and longer as Jake tired, and Arley cursed his father for not allowing them to use the mule. "Got you, no need wear out the damned mule." Arley visualized his father's sneering face. They finished with about an hour of daylight left. Jake and his mother hurried to the house, both hugging their chests against the cold; Jake's smile long gone.

Arley put the board and dibber pole in the corncrib, and then went to look at the pigs. His bucket of water earlier had done the trick, and he saw no flowing blood, nor any trace of the clumsy raccoon; nothing of the morning's carnage except for scattered remnants of the wicker egg-basket. He breathed a sigh and walked up to the well. When the sky had clouded over, he'd decided to leave the pigs penned for the day. Now he wasn't so sure that had been a good decision. Which was worse, chasing pigs or toting water?

After watering the hogs, he carried a

bucket of coal and some wood into the house, and then got the cow from the pasture and milked her. Counting the forty-five paces to the house, he went inside, slumped down on the floor by the black iron stove, and leaned back against the crudely daubed wall to wait.

He wanted to quit, but the family's survival depended on him and his strong back. That it ached chronically from the hard work and regular beatings had to be put aside. Fleeting memories of a better life used to help him a little, but those thoughts came less frequently, and now he simply wanted to sit still. Nobody ate until his father came home; another brutally enforced rule.

Home by dark meant his father might be almost sober, but after that his state of drunkenness increased with each passing minute. Arley's stomach had been cramping for hours when his father, carrying a jug, stumbled into the house at ten o'clock. He sagged onto his kitchen chair, and Arley's mother scrambled to her feet, then took a pan of corn cakes and five small slices of fried ham from the warmer oven and put them on the table. From atop the stove she got a covered pot of red-eye gravy, gave it a stir, and put it by his plate. She then stepped away from him. He speared the ham slices with his fork, dropped all of them on his plate, and then arranged five of the eight cakes around the outside. After pouring gravy over the lot, he put the pot down beside his plate again and looked directly at Arley, his eyes mean, his brow lowered.

"Come to the table, boys," his mother said quietly.

Arley got up, his hunger overwhelming his caution, and sat down on the tableside bench. Jake sat beside him and his mother took a seat opposite his father. Jake, head lowered, eyed the three cakes as his mother picked one up and put it on his plate. He grabbed it with both hands and nipped a tiny bite before putting it back down. She gave one to Arley and took one herself. "Is there any gravy left, Klaus?" she asked.

Arley's nape hair bristled, and he stole a sideways glance at his mother.

"Who needs it?" Klaus grumbled and sniffed a snotty nose.

"The boys. They finished planting the corn today, just as you wanted."

"Damn . . . good thing." He picked up the pot and half-threw it across the table. "None for bright-eyes." Arley sensed his father's gaze. "Heard he was foolin' 'round in town."

"I needed flour, in case you wanted pancakes in the morning."

"That don't take all day."

"He was only gone half an hour. And we all worked hard today — all day." She picked up the pan and glanced inside. "You've left nothing."

Arley cringed.

"Goddamn right. I take what I want," Klaus paused, "when I want it."

"Arley can't work as hard as he does without eating. You treat that mule better than him."

Arley glanced at his father, swallowed hard, and then stared at his mother, horror-stricken. *He'll kill you.* The rough-knuckled fist crashed into the side of his head without warning and he flew backwards, taking Jake and the bench with him. Jake scuttled under the table on hands and knees as Arley scrambled to his feet.

"Squintin' at me'll get you one of them . . . ever' goddamned time," his father hollered, his words slurred.

Arley ran for the door and looked back as he grabbed the latch. Terror etched his mother's face, and helplessness swarmed over him as his father picked up the whiskey jug and slammed it onto the table.

The man struggled to stand, gripping the

table's edge. "Now get the hell outta here ya worthless whelp . . . 'fore I stomp yer guts out yer scrawny ass."

Arley darted out and pushed the door shut, his mind in chaos. This had all happened before so why did he feel such a panic? Why did this time feel so different? In the barn, he kicked some inferior grass-hay into a loose pile, burrowed into it, and pulled a mildewed piece of canvas over his head. The cold, clammy, and unyielding ground met his bony butt, and he pulled his knees to his chest. The vision of his mother's face denied him exhaustion's numbing solace and he trembled in his isolation.

His baby brother Percy had died the day after Christmas; he'd watched him die of starvation: wasting away slowly, surely, and silently. He knew about two tiny ones before that; and three or four that he'd never seen, born long before they were ready and taken away by Mrs. Holverson, who came over to help. Was his father doing the same thing to him as he'd done to Percy? The storm-chilled darkness sent shivers through his body, and his stomach cramped again.

He could have run away, and his mother had told him many times to do just that. But what then for her and Jake? Tears stung his eyes. *What then?* His exhausted brain searched for something, anything that made sense. And then he heard the door drag across the dirt. He turned back the canvas and peered over the edge.

His father, raised lantern in hand, stood just inside the door, leaning on the frame, his bleary eyes fixed on Arley's. "Took care . . . of the hag," he said with a sneer, and wiped one eye with the back of his hand. "Jake run off . . . I'll find 'im." His gaze shifted around the barn for a few seconds, and then he hung the lantern on a wall bracket. Arley's breath caught as his eyes followed his father's to a three-foot-long, three-inch-thick oak singletree leaning against the wall by the door. On each end, iron bands held harness rings, and in the middle, a heavier band for the chain ring all added weight to the heavy wood. He clambered to his feet still clutching the canvas, barely able to breathe.

His father reached down and grasped one end of the rigging, his eyes never leaving Arley's face. *Took care of the hag.* His father's words screamed in his head, and he released his pent breath with a gasp. The image of the wild-eyed pig that morning appeared, and the icy fingers of fear seized his heart — it was the *same* look. The singletree rose shoulder-high as his father staggered forward, and then it swung in a wide, looping arc toward Arley's head. He threw the canvas and ducked. The heavy implement crashed into a stall post and the rings clanged against the bands. His father stumbled sideways and fell facedown in the dirt, losing his grip on what Arley now saw as a weapon — a murder weapon.

Arley snatched it up, and then faced his father, who pushed himself to his knees, both hands tightly clenched. Narrowed eyes looked back, unblinking, and yellowed teeth showed behind snarling lips. "Time to go see Percy," his father growled, and started to get up.

Arley could not remember the first blow, nor the second, or third. Only after his arms would no longer lift the heavy oaken bar did he see what he'd done. He dropped the bloody tool alongside the misshapen head and battered, blood-soaked body at his feet. Bile rose to the back of his throat and brought him to his knees as his stomach rebelled. The powerful stench of unleashed bowel forced what little he had in his stomach to gush onto the dirt. *What have I done?* He stared at his bloodied hands and clothes and shuddered as his fingers stuck together.

His heart slammed hard against his chest

when his piece of canvas floated past him and settled shroud-like over the dead-still body. A hand gently touched his shoulder.

"Get up, Arley," his mother said.

He took a shuddering breath.

"Come out of here." She pulled on his arm. "Come out."

He stood up, legs numb and unsteady, and she laid his hand on her shoulder. "Hold on to me." She paused to grab the lantern, and then led him outside and into the cool fresh air; living air. He stopped, then slowly and completely filled his lungs. "What have I done?" Swallowing hard, he choked back a sob. "I'll burn for this."

"You did what you had to do," she said softly. "And nobody here will judge you."

For the first time he looked at her. Blood seeped from her left ear and flowed freely from a two-inch cut over her swollen left eye. She carried her largest butcher knife in one hand. "Jake?" he asked.

"In the corncrib."

"What are we going to do?"

"*You're* going to do nothing more here."

"We have to tell the constable."

"I'll take care of that. You're going to take Jacob to Mrs. Holverson. She and I have talked before so she knows what to do. And then I want you to go south — Tennessee maybe, or Georgia. Find work and stay there."

"But I don't know anything."

"You wouldn't be here today if you weren't smart and strong, Arley."

"But I killed my —"

"Because of *my* weakness he was your father, and because of his own, he turned into an animal. He meant to kill all of us tonight."

"But —"

"You saved your brother's life, and mine. I will not see you punished for that. And please, please don't make yourself pay for it either." She stared at him a moment with her one seeing eye. "It was not your fault. You had no choice. Do you hear me?"

Arley nodded, and then looked down at his bloody hands. "I've got —"

"That will wash off. Everything will, and no one's the wiser. Go to the well and do that, then go change into your other clothes before you get Jake. I'll be along in a minute."

He started to speak.

"I'll take care of this. Now go!" She shoved him towards the house.

Less than an hour later, with seven dollars and thirty-eight cents in his pocket and a bewildered Jake in tow, Arley stopped at the end of the cornfield and looked back at his home. He could not think of it any other way even though his mother had told him to forget it existed.

"Will Gramma Holverson be awake?" Jake asked.

"Yes."

"I know Ma said she'd be happy to keep me awhile, but I'm not sure."

"I am. She told me so only yesterday."

"No fib?"

"No fib." Arley turned and had taken one step when Jake grabbed his hand.

"Is that Ma?" He pointed back toward the house.

The yellow light of a lantern bobbed across the farmyard, away from the barn and towards the river. There it stopped for a few seconds and then moved back to the barn and disappeared.

"Well, is it?"

"I don't know, Jake. Maybe she's got belly business."

"Oh."

Arley stood a bit longer. *Why'd she go to the river?* Then the light reappeared at the barn door. There it stopped for several seconds before moving towards the river again. Move, stop, move, it stuttered across the ground towards the water for another couple minutes. And then, well short of the river, it stopped again. Arley squinted into the darkness, waiting for it to continue, and then his scalp clutched when the high-pitched screams of several hogs ripped the night. His heart stumbled when Jake grabbed his leg and hung on tight. "Another raccoon," Jake whispered, "or something else?"

At that instant, lightning defined the western horizon, and a blast of cold air whipped their clothes. *The knife. The river. They'll eat everything but the head.* The image of the savaged egg-robber swarmed his mind and then vanished as quickly as it had appeared, leaving nothing but black. "Could be that," Arley said as he pulled Jake off his leg, "or the storm we got coming." Thunder muttered as the two boys turned away and hurried before the wind.

Wallace J. Swenson was an award-winning Idaho native who lived in the Upper Snake River Valley. He is the author of ten novels.

176

A Century of the
American Frontier
1855–1875

■ ■ ■ ■

GROGAN'S CHOICE

BY LONNIE WHITAKER

■ ■ ■ ■

Jake hated to think about leaving the dog. Goddamned copperhead, anyway. Shep's head had swelled up like a dead hog in the sun. Only minutes ago, he had bolted after a cottontail at the edge of the river and stuck his head into the brush, wagging his tail. Then came the hurt yelp. Next thing Jake Grogan saw was Shep shaking the snake like a rag.

In seconds the venom hit. Shep dropped the snake and began pawing at his muzzle. Instantly, Jake pulled his pistol from the pommel holster. The injured serpent tried to slither back into the weeds, but one shot from the Colt Dragoon left the twisting snake's body in search of its missing head.

Jake shoved the pistol in the holster, sprang from the saddle, and rushed to Shep. He stomped the snake's head with his bootheel and kicked it into the weeds.

"Easy, boy." Jake wrapped his arms around

the shepherd-mix and carried him a few yards to the river and laid him at the water's edge. Shep lapped hard at the water but threw it up.

Jake cut incisions across the fang marks with his Barlow and sucked out what poison he could. He cupped river water in his hands and dripped it over the inside of Shep's lips, which had turned from pink to white. His glassy eyes were beginning to swell shut.

He knew dogs had a lot of fat in their heads that would absorb the poison and slow down the effects, but if Shep didn't drink water he would die of thirst in the August Missouri sun.

In 1868, Jake was the only dentist between Lexington and Kansas City, that is, the only one who had actually graduated from dental college. And on this afternoon, he was headed to an emergency call for someone who was very dear to him.

Earlier that morning, a cowhand from Sam Chilton's cattle spread had ridden into town with news that Sam's daughter, Esther, had a swollen jaw. "Doc, she's got a knot big as a pawpaw, and she's in considerable pain."

It was the same girl with the yellow hair that Jake had seen with her parents in

Lexington just weeks after General Price's troops had forged west after the second battle there. They were riding in a horse-drawn wagon when Jake straggled into town still wearing Confederate gray.

"Mr. Chilton says if you're not there by tomorrow, he's going to let Sledge pull her tooth," the cowhand told him.

The image chilled Jake. A few months before, Chilton's young blacksmith, Sledge, had pulled a tooth and broken the jaw of a cowhand in the process. The man would never speak right again.

"Tell Chilton I'll be there tomorrow and not to let that blacksmith near her." It was twenty-five miles to Chilton's and even if Jake rode until dark, camped along the way, and was back in the saddle by first light, it would be late morning before he arrived. And Jake still had two patients in his office that he couldn't abandon.

The cowboy traded horses at the livery stable, and Jake gave him a small bottle of laudanum, with written instructions on how to dose it.

After Jake had finished with his patients, he packed his medical satchel with dental instruments and supplies: rubbing alcohol, clove oil, alum, cotton, ether, and laudanum. He also wrapped up some biscuits and sausages left over from breakfast, ground coffee, and lucifers, and stowed them in a bailed boiling pot. By late afternoon, he mounted up, whistled for Shep, and they left Lexington.

Back on that day, four years ago in Lexington, Sam Chilton had seen Jake, too, and his stare wasn't charitable. When his yellow-haired daughter gazed back at Jake, he heard Chilton say as he snapped the horse reins, "He's deserter-scum, Esther. An unworthy coward. Pay no attention to the likes of him."

A deserter, yes, but after the battle at Pilot Knob, Jake had seen all the killing and maiming he could stand and vowed to escape at the first opportunity, even if it meant being branded a coward. It wasn't his skill as a dentist the Confederate States of America wanted when he was drafted — he was assigned the worst head wounds, and he stood side by side with the surgeons as they sawed off limbs. One night he just slipped out of camp and disappeared into the darkness.

Months passed but he never forgot the girl's face. How she looked at him. Her blue eyes and her yellow hair. She was sixteen — too young for him, at twenty-one. But things had changed a year later, at a pie supper to celebrate the end of the war.

Most of an hour had passed since Shep was bitten. Shep was too sick to travel, but Jake couldn't bear the thought of abandoning him, unable to defend himself from coyotes or even buzzards. He had heard buzzards would attack helpless animals that weren't yet dead.

The sun was low in the sky, so the buzzards would be roosting, but not the coyotes. The vision he imagined gnawed at his gut: Shep alone and stalked by snarling, circling coyotes. A plaintive sigh slipped out as he gazed toward the western sky. "Lord, I don't ask for myself, but I pray that You be with Esther until I can figure what to do with Shep. And please don't let that blacksmith get near her before I get there. Amen."

Something on the river caught his attention. Shafts of sunlight filtered through river willows and sycamores casting shadows and a golden glimmer on the water. Upstream, a canoe emerged from the shadows — with an Indian paddling.

Thoughts swirled through Jake's mind. An Indian in these parts? The Missouria and Otoe tribes had all but vanished in the Indian Wars or were moved onto reservations years before. But sure as hell, here was one.

Brown as a nut, the Indian paddled from a kneeling position. He steered the canoe toward Jake and stopped at the shore a few yards away. He stepped out, pulled the canoe onto the bank, and stood erect — tall and sinewy. His hair was dark and fell from the middle in a natural part to just past his ears, and his eyes were black as midnight in a cave. His age was difficult to discern — thirties, perhaps.

Jake thought of his Colt in the holster on his horse, but as the Indian approached wearing only moccasins, a breechcloth, and leggings, Jake could see he was not armed.

"Aho," Jake called out, using one of the few Chiwere words he knew.

The Indian smiled broadly, and in perfect high diction said, "You use the common language, but do not worry, my friend. I speak English, and I mean you no harm." The resonance and tone of his voice echoed confidence. His smile seemed almost indulgent.

The Indian gestured toward Shep. "Your dog has been bitten by a serpent." Without waiting for a reply, he knelt next to Shep.

Jake stiffened. "Be careful, now, Indian."

"Nature teaches beasts to know their

friends."

Jake considered the Indian's response and then said, "Only two kinds of folks around here quote the Bard — cardsharps and shysters. Which are you?"

"Neither, friend. My Christian name is Jonah Smith, and I can help your dog. What may I call you?"

"I'm Dr. Jake Grogan."

The Indian raised an eyebrow. "A medical doctor?"

"I'm a dentist. I was on my way to an emergency call when Shep was bitten."

Jonah Smith nodded in response as he gently touched the dog's snout. A shaman divining an evil spirit. Without looking at Jake, he said, "I think the copperhead did not deliver a full bite."

"How do you know it was a copperhead?" Jake's tone was skeptical.

"The copperheads come to the river at dusk to hunt and drink water." Jonah Smith smiled, looked up, and held his gaze on Jake, seemingly assessing his worth or intelligence. "You have cut the bite, that is good. I will make a poultice out of thorn apple leaves to draw out the poison."

"Thorn apple?"

"Jimson weed." Jonah Smith patted Shep's head. "I will be back shortly, my dog friend."

He turned and strode past his canoe, a brown shadow disappearing in the river underbrush. It was eerie how silently he moved.

Twenty minutes later the Indian returned with a fistful of green plants in one hand and two round river stones in the other. Looking at Jake, he said, "I will crush the Jimson weed for the poultice with these stones. I will need your bandanna."

"Jonah Smith, why are you doing this act of kindness?"

"Because I hate to see an animal suffer . . . and I heard your prayer."

Jake started to respond, but hesitated. Words failed him. He looked down and began untying his neckerchief. When he looked up, the Indian was smiling — that same all-knowing smile. Jake handed him the neckerchief and said, "Jonah Smith, I would be obliged if you would fix that poultice."

Jake backed away and watched as Jonah Smith gently applied crushed leaves to Shep's snout. Shep raised his head several times, but each time the Indian soothed it back down with soft-spoken native words Jake did not understand.

After Jonah Smith had secured the poultice with the bandanna, Jake said, "I'm going to camp here tonight and figure out how to transport Shep. I'm fixing to brew a pot of coffee if you would care for a cup."

With the mention of coffee, Jonah Smith showed the first sign of emotion. His eyes widened and a smile appeared, but it was different. To Jake it seemed to be a sociable, friendly smile.

"Thank you, I would like some coffee. It is well that you are staying here tonight. Your dog will be improved tomorrow, but he should not try to walk a long distance. I can show you how to make a travois so you can travel with him."

"Again, I am obliged to you."

"You are not in my debt. I could, perhaps, find a rabbit to go with that coffee, if you would not mind company."

After a meal of roasted rabbit and biscuits, the Indian and the dentist sat in silence staring at the campfire and savoring the last of the coffee. Jake puffed on a cheroot. In the distance a couple of owls were calling and frogs croaked along the river. Shep labored in his sleep, twitching a paw and making muted yelps, as if exacting revenge on the snake.

In the reflection of the firelight, the Indian had a mystical air. It seemed to Jake that he might begin chanting some strange incantation — like the words he uttered while ministering to Shep. Jake exhaled smoke from his cigar and then broke the silence.

"Now, I am really curious, Jonah Smith. Just where in the hell do you come from? You speak English like a professor, yet you dress like your ancestors, and you suddenly appear on the river to help my dog."

Several moments passed, and Jake wondered if the Indian would respond, when he said, "My ancestors are from Missouri. My father died when I was young, and my mother and I traveled west with Mormons. She became one of many wives to a cruel man who spoke of a god I did not understand. I ran away but was taken to a reservation. There I was taught by Jesuits." After a short pause, he added, "It is time to sleep now."

Jonah Smith wrapped himself in his blanket and said no more.

The next morning Jonah Smith was gone. But next to Jake's mare were two long poles cut from saplings, lashed together with cross limbs and rawhide strips. And covered with Jonah Smith's blanket. He had left his blanket to transport Shep. Jake shook his head and said, "Thank you, Lord, for sending Jonah Smith."

Miraculously, Shep was able to stand and

walk. He drank some water but turned his nose when offered some rabbit scraps.

On the trail, thoughts of the strange Indian and concern for Shep faded into the task ahead. Jake worried that Esther was suffering and hoped the laudanum was making her pain tolerable. If not, he feared Chilton would allow the blacksmith to intervene.

It was midday when Chilton's large barn and two-story frame house came into view a half-mile away. The place was far enough off the main road that it had avoided damage during the war, and Chilton had been mercenary enough to supply beef to both sides. The war had all but ruined agriculture in Missouri, but now Chilton was prospering from increased prices and access to a railway spur to Sedalia.

A couple of hounds barked but kept their distance as Jake neared the house. He dismounted and assisted Shep off the travois and coaxed him to walk. Wobbly at first, Shep padded several yards to the shade of a post oak and lay down. "You stay here, boy."

Hearing footsteps, Jake looked up and saw Sledge, the blacksmith, striding toward him. Sledge's gate had a swagger, and his face was fixed in a confident sneer. His black hair looked as if he had dunked his head in a watering trough and slicked it back with his fingers. Perhaps nineteen or twenty years old, and a half-foot shy of six feet, he stopped arm's length from Jake. Too close. The boy's odor drifted aggressively through his sweat-soaked chambray shirt.

Jake offered his hand, but the blacksmith crossed both arms over his chest. His arms, huge from pounding out horseshoes with a sledgehammer, bulged against the shirt-sleeves rolled above his elbows.

Jake took a step back. "You got something on your mind, Sledge? If you do, be quick about it because I have a patient inside waiting on me."

The sneer still on his face, Sledge said, "It took you long enough to get here. I could have had that tooth out yesterday." He nodded toward Shep. "If you hadn't been dragging that dog you might have gotten here sooner."

Jake's jaw tightened, and he met Sledge's eyes with a glare. "And broken her jaw, too."

Sledge dropped his arms and clenched his fists just above his waist. The sneer was now an angry stare. "You better tread lightly, tooth doctor."

"What are you saying, Sledge?"

"I don't chew my cabbage twice."

Jake turned his back to the blacksmith and

retrieved his medical bag from his horse. He saw Sam Chilton open the door to the porch. From behind Jake, Sledge said, just loudly enough for Jake to hear, "And don't be getting any ideas about you and Esther." Jake kept walking without looking back. "Did you hear me, tooth doctor?"

Chilton met Jake at the door. "Thanks for coming, Doc."

Inside, Chilton led Jake to the parlor where Esther was sitting in a chair wearing a dress that would have been suitable for a church social. Her golden hair, which looked as if it had been recently washed and brushed, covered her shoulders in a cascade of shiny waves. She would have been the picture of health, but her eyes were red, no doubt from tears and lack of sleep. And her right jaw, which she cradled with her hand, was horribly swollen.

She attempted a smile as Jake entered. "Thank you for coming, Dr. Jake." Her voice was weak.

"That's okay, I just wish I had gotten here sooner. Did the medicine I sent help?"

"At first, but now it doesn't seem to help much. I took the last dose a couple hours ago."

"Mr. Chilton, would you please assist me by getting a small pan and a towel?"

"I'll tell my wife. She's in the kitchen making dinner."

"Thank you, sir."

When Sam left the room, Jake took both of Esther's hands. "I am sorry we have to meet like this, darling, but I'm going to help you get well."

He gently touched her swollen jaw and could feel the heat of infection, and that slightest touch made her wince. "Sorry, Esther. I'll be as gentle as I can."

He unrolled the cloth wrap that held his dental instruments onto a nearby table. "Esther, open your mouth as wide as you can and lean your head toward the window so I have some light."

He dabbed the inside of her mouth with clove oil, and with a probe he tapped on the surrounding teeth to make sure he had found the offending tooth. When he tapped the most likely suspect, Esther groaned.

"Sorry, Esther. You have infection from a lower molar abscess that appears to be coming to a head. It has to be drained. If Sledge had pulled that tooth, you likely would have ended up with blood poisoning that could have killed you."

Esther's eyes widened, and she uttered a fearful moan.

"But don't worry, I'm here and you are

going to be all right."

Sam returned with the towels and dishpan in time to hear Jake's dire prediction.

With the probe, Jake applied light pressure to the swelling, and pus erupted into her mouth.

Esther screamed and gagged and began spitting and hacking the corruption from her mouth. Jake grabbed the pan and held it in front of her. Between gasps, Esther blurted, "This is so foul."

"Mr. Chilton, if you would assist again, a glass of water with a half teaspoon of salt in it."

"Now, Esther, this is gonna be painful, but it will make you feel much better." He told her to hold the pan and then made a small incision with a lancet to enlarge the opening in the abscess. He pressed on the swollen jaw. Esther moaned and began spitting more blood and pus.

After she rinsed her mouth with the saltwater, Jake placed an alum pad on the incision to stop the bleeding

"Dr. Jake, the pain is much improved."

"It was the pressure that was causing most of the pain. The tooth may have to be extracted, but I want the infection to subside first. You'll need to come to the office for the rest."

Sam, who had been observing from a distance, said, "I'll get your mother."

"Jake," Esther said, "I can't thank you enough."

"You can thank me by letting me speak to your father about us."

As he spoke, Jake noticed Esther's eyes begin to glisten, almost dreamlike. He suspected it was mostly lack of sleep and the lingering effect of the laudanum . . . but perhaps not completely.

"Oh, yes, Jake."

A dog's howl from outside snapped Jake back to earth. "That was Shep. And he's hurt!"

Jake bolted to the yard. The smell of burnt flesh hit his nose and smoke was rising from Shep's hide where his fur had been scorched. And Sledge strolling toward the barn carrying a branding iron and a pistol — Jake's Colt. Without another thought, he charged toward the blacksmith. As Sledge turned around, Jake tackled him to the ground. The gun and the iron fell from Sledge's hands.

The two men wrestled on the ground each trying to gain the upper position. Jake landed a glancing blow to the jaw with little effect. Sledge wrangled his legs around Jake's waist and clutched Jake's throat in a viselike grip. "Now, you're done for, tooth doctor."

From the porch, Chilton yelled, "Let him go, Sledge."

"Daddy, help him! He's going to be killed."

"Get my shotgun, Esther," Chilton said, and rushed to the fight.

Jake pried and scratched against the death grip, but Sledge's hands were like a steel trap. He was on the cusp of blacking out when he saw a brown blur lunging at the blacksmith. Sledge screamed in agony and released his grip. Shep had locked on Sledge's ear and was shaking his head, the same as he had shaken the copperhead.

Sledge knocked Shep away and screamed, "Goddammit, he chewed off my ear." Blood spewed from the side of Sledge's head where only ragged gristle remained. Enraged, he grabbed Jake by the throat again.

Esther came to a running stop and pointed a double-barrel ten-gauge shotgun inches from the blacksmith's face and pulled back both hammers. "Let him up, Sledge, or so help me God, I'll blow your head off." Sledge released his grip.

Chilton took the shotgun from his daughter but kept it cocked and pointed at Sledge. "Now, get up, get your things, and get off

197

my property."

Esther dropped to her knees in tears next to Jake. "Please be all right."

Jake, still struggling for breath, said, "I'll be okay, but I need to check on Shep."

Sledge yanked off his shirt and pressed it to his wound. He glared at Jake. "This isn't the last of it, tooth doctor."

Chilton motioned toward the barn with his shotgun. "I said I want you off my property. And if you are still in the county by tomorrow, I will swear out a warrant for your arrest for attempted murder."

"He attacked me — it was self-defense."

"That's your side of the story. We have three witnesses here who see it differently."

Sledge spit on the ground and headed to the barn holding the shirt to his ear.

Shep was lying under the post oak tree licking his wound as Jake and Esther checked to make sure he wasn't too badly injured. While Esther was patting Shep's head, Jake untied the blanket from the travois and laid it next to Shep. Maybe some of Jonah Smith's healing power remained in it.

After Sledge rode off on his only possession, Chilton convinced Jake to spend the night to tend to his daughter's tooth and not chance being ambushed by Sledge.

Although Chilton had come to respect him as a dentist, it had taken longer to accept his daughter's fondness for Jake. After supper, he allowed that it would be permissible for Jake and Esther to sit together on the porch swing, with Shep as the only chaperone.

In the quiet moonlight, Esther kissed Jake on the cheek and nestled her head on his shoulder. She sighed and said, "I have dreamed of a night like this."

Jake touched her hand and said, "but not a *day* like this."

Esther didn't respond. She had fallen asleep leaving Jake with his thoughts. *It had been a lifetime in a day.*

Lonnie Whitaker, a retired federal attorney, works as a freelance writer. His novel, *Geese to a Poor Market,* won the Ozark Writers League Best Book of the Year award. His stories have appeared in magazines, anthologies, and *Chicken Soup for the Soul.* His children's picture book, *Mulligan Meets the Poodlums,* was published by Little Hands Press.

■ ■ ■ ■

Boxcar Knights

BY STEVEN HOWELL WILSON

■ ■ ■ ■

This story takes place in the years following the American Civil War, c. 1868

"Now, Marshall! Grab the damn rung!"

"Don't swear!"

"I'll stop damn swearing when you damn grab the damn rung!"

They had practiced this. They had watched for days, hiding in the fence row just north of Danville Station, watching the cars go by, learning the different types, memorizing the location of ladders, footholds, hatches, and access doors. They had climbed cars on the siding by the light of the moon, to get a feel for it. Two weeks they had studied. Marshall had insisted they know everything there was to know before they made their first attempt at hopping a freight.

Two weeks, and now the cussed little sumbitch was going to lose his nerve and leave

Carl alone on a train to Indiana.

The train was gaining speed, and Marshall, running, still hadn't worked up the nerve to take hold of a ladder rung and haul himself up. Carl, having gone first, had seized hold, found his footing, and scrabbled up to the top rung, where he now glared with disdain at his best and only friend. Was he going to have to jump, and possibly break his own neck, just so he could convince Marshall to try again?

He held out his hand. "Grab the rung and grab my hand. It's now or never!"

Chestnut eyes wide with fear, Marshall took a deep breath, shot out a trembling arm, grabbed the rung, and swung himself onto the ladder, a hand reaching to clasp Carl's. Marshall yelped as the train's momentum seized and wrenched him, but he was on the car.

"Hold onto my belt," instructed Carl, and he swung down and began to inch along a narrow, treacherous lip of steel, towards the open door.

Ordinarily, Carl didn't give orders. Marshall was the planner. He was the one who knew things. He read books. He listened attentively when old Sister Hapgood taught lessons. He organized the other boys and girls in activities to keep them busy, out of her hair, and unpunished.

But Marshall was at a loss when it came to physical activities, dangerous activities, like climbing a rock face, or swinging into the lake from a rope . . . or hopping a freight. Carl tried not to make too much fun of his friend's lack of physical courage, against the day he would have to confess to Marshall that he, Carl, couldn't read. He knew it was going to be on Marshall to teach him.

Someday.

The door loomed open in the fading October sunlight, a black hole amidst the cool red and gold splashes painting the car. The climb was easier once they reached the door, its ribbed surface providing hand-holds, or at least fingerholds. Carl inched his feet, a hip's width at a time, sideways toward his goal. Marshall's knuckles dug into his spine.

"Ease up on my belt!" he shouted against the wind.

"If I ease up, I'll fall!" Marshall yelled back into his ear.

Great, the kid's probably afraid of falling, along with everything else. He's probably all froze up and can't move a muscle.

"Okay, here's the door," he called out. "You go in first."

"I can't!" said Marshall.

"You have to. If I get inside, and you're hanging out here, I can't help you. Climb behind me, then take hold of the door-frame."

Marshall grabbed too hard onto Carl's belt, pulling him back and almost making him lose his hold on the open door. As Carl's body jolted and recovered his balance, Marshall's hand, making for the door, missed and grabbed his shoulder. Fingernails dug hard into Carl's flesh.

"You're doing good," Carl winced, promising himself that, if Marshall corrected him and said he was doing *well,* he would pitch them both to their deaths on the tracks.

Marshall was too distracted to correct him.

"Now take hold of the door. I'm going to move us both over."

Struggling with the weight of an extra boy on his back, albeit a scrawny one, Carl dug toes in against a rib of the door and levered them both toward the opening. Marshall, hanging on, was lined up with it.

"Now, let go of me! Drop to the floor!"

"But —"

"Drop!"

And don't roll out the other side of the damned car!

But Marshall did not drop. He snaked an arm around Carl's waist, holding Carl in a stranglehold, and fell onto his butt on the floor of the car. Carl's butt landed on Marshall, his spine wrenched by the fall, and he called out three of his favorite words at the air.

The boys spent the next half minute recovering their breath, taking stock of their body parts, cataloging their injuries, and assuring themselves they were still alive.

After that work was complete, Carl asked, "Ya got anything to say for yerself?"

"Those words you said aren't Christian."

"Neither is pulling a feller down on his ass when he told you to let go!"

"I was scared!" protested Marshall. "And please stop saying those words."

"Ass!" bellowed Carl in Marshall's face. "Ass, ass, ass!"

Marshall dropped his eyes and swallowed. "I hope Jesus's grace will keep you out of the flames."

"Fer now, maybe some of Jesus's grace will find us a comfortable place to sleep."

"That's blasphemy," protested Marshall. "Don't take His name in vain."

Carl sighed out loud and stood, not enjoying the process. His wounded back complained in language that might have given

Marshall a stroke. He surveyed the dark space about them, wishing they had had the chance to steal some candles. His eyes made out the wooden slats of crates, stacked three high and tied to the walls of the car. A narrow passageway between two rows seemed the only form of shelter they would manage. He wondered idly if any of the crates contained something that could be used for bedding, but then they had no way to open them anyway.

"We'll have to just hide out as best we can at the end of the car," he said to Marshall. They had deliberately selected a car near the front of the train, as they tended to be loaded first, and fuller. They were less likely to be entered by rail hands soon.

Marshall dropped to a cross-legged position on the dusty floor and settled himself against a crate where he could look out at the thin sliver of moon peeking through the clouds. "Well," he sighed, "at least we got away from Sister Hapgood. I think we were gonna get a lot worse than locked in the basement this time."

Yesterday evening, Marshall had lost his temper and shouted at Sister Hapgood, right in front of the other orphans in the Baptist Home. She had promised to "wear the flesh off" Marshall's body with a switch.

"And you'll be taking your punishment next to him," she had promised Carl. Carl hadn't complained or asked any questions. Of course, he would be punished too. They were always punished together, usually because Carl had committed the infraction, and Marshall had tried to stand up for him. The usual punishment — for stealing, for lying, for falling asleep during lessons — was to miss dinner and be locked in the basement for the night, to sleep if one could sleep. The basement of the old farmhouse, which the church had adopted as an orphan asylum, had a low ceiling — Carl's head brushed its beams, and he was not full-grown. It was dank and filthy, with a dirt floor. Mice and rats were often spotted, and, where there were rodents, there were snakes, hungry for a meal. Carl didn't mind snakes. Marshall was deathly afraid of them.

If a child had a history of escaping the basement in search of better sleeping arrangements, then he was chained by the wrist to the wall, fastened to hooks. No one knew if the hooks were original to the farmhouse — used to restrain slaves, perhaps? — or if Sister Hapgood had ordered them installed.

Corporal punishment was not exactly rare, but it was saved for extreme cases. Sister

Hapgood would have used it more often, but the church pastor, an older man named Brooks, valued moderation. Indeed, it was Pastor Brooks's influence that had reduced Sister Hapgood's promise of immediate violence to a threat to be carried out the next morning — after Marshall and Carl had spent another night in the basement.

Marshall and Carl had left the orphanage that night.

"Why ya always mouthin' off at that old bitch anyway?" Carl asked as he took a seat opposite his companion.

"You're family."

Marshall said it with a shrug, as though it were obvious.

"I ain't yer family!"

Marshall's face did not fall, but it settled into that look of quiet, patient suffering that told Carl he could heap as much pain as he wanted on his friend. There would be no anger, and no retribution, only profound sadness.

Damn Marshall's sadness anyway!

But Carl softened his tone and continued, "I mean ya only met me a few months ago. I can't replace the family ya lost. I'll never be enough."

"That's plain. You're a pretty poor replacement."

Carl reared back and let his foot fly into Marshall's knee, eliciting a yelp.

"But you're all I've got," said Marshall as he rubbed his wound.

Marshall's parents and younger sister had died in the War Between the States, which had ended just three short years ago now. His daddy had been a Confederate soldier . . . for a little while. He had died of measles before seeing any action and was buried in a mass grave . . . somewhere. His mama had got sick and died before she could collect his pension. The Confederacy had died not long after. She still would have had a pension from the U.S. Army, but now she was dead. A lot of people had died during and after the war. There was no food. They were burned out of their homes. Soldiers had torched the Marshall's family's cabin the night they learned his daddy was dead.

All of this history, Marshall had confessed to Carl during sleepless nights, either in the cramped boys' room upstairs, or in the basement. Well, sleep had evaded Marshall. Carl had been cheated of sleep by Marshall's never-ending personal history lessons.

Now, Marshall looked to be ready to launch into another one.

"Before Mama died, she told me —"

"Oh, not another dad-blamed story!" moaned Carl.

"She told me there's nothing more important than family, to go and find mine," finished Marshall, undeterred.

"And all ya found was me."

"She meant to find my uncle in Evansville."

"And we're on our way to find him," said Carl, "courtesy of the Christian charity of the Tennessee Railroad."

Marshall snorted. "How can it be Christian charity when they don't know we're here?"

"The Lord moves in mysterious ways."

"Not that mysterious, he doesn't."

Carl felt around in his pockets, hoping to find a scrap of tobacco left to smoke. Coming up empty-handed, he swore under his breath and then asked, "You sure that uncle o' yours is gonna help us?"

"He's my mama's elder brother, and I've got no one else. He pretty much has to."

"He don't have to take me."

"I told you, you're my family now. He'll take you in. Besides, he'd be getting two anyway, if —"

Marshall choked on the end of his sentence, but he didn't have to finish. Carl knew that his sister had died within minutes of his mother, of the same illness. Their bodies had been too starved to fight it off, there being little food to spare in the refugee camp they had landed in, outside Danville. From there, the orphaned Marshall, a boy not yet tall, with no beard, had been shipped off to the state-funded, church-run orphanage.

Six months ago, Carl had been brought to the same orphanage, a wild boy with fiery hair and coal-black eyes. Nobody knew where he had come from, or who his parents had been. He had just been found wandering on the road. If he remembered a home and a family, he wasn't talking about them. He didn't know his own age, and he might have been old enough to go to work, had there been work. Someone had decided that he was young enough for the church's care.

When Marshall pressed Carl for his story, he was told to mind his own business. He had come to learn that, if he wanted to be friends with the only boy his age in the asylum, he'd best do just that. And so he did. He didn't like it, but he did it.

"It don't help to think about the past," Carl said now.

Marshall nodded, blinking away tears. "You're right."

"Guess we should get to the back of the car and try to sleep."

"Reckon so."

Marshall did not know how long he had been asleep when the weight of the world landed on his chest.

Awakening, breathless and in pain, he quickly realized that it was not the weight of the whole world, but rather the weight of one of its occupants, a wiry figure, smaller than himself, dressed in a ragged but heavy coat. Muscular, canvas-clad legs squeezed Marshall's middle until he feared his ribs might crack, and something cold and sharp pressed the exposed flesh of his throat.

"Best you make yer peace with the good Lord, white boy," croaked the voice of the figure.

Marshall held his breath, wondering if he would ever draw another. He was pinned. There was no option for resistance. He tried to whisper, "What do you want?" but his voice was apparently still asleep. Only a squeak came out. He said a silent prayer that such an undignified sound might not be his last, swallowed carefully, and was making to speak again when what he now realized was a well-used Bowie knife was yanked from his throat. A familiar hand had seized the wrist of the attacker. Marshall looked up to see Carl's arm wrapped around the stranger's throat.

Struggling under the weight of the new arrival, Marshall pulled away until he saw an angry, brown face, teeth clenched, mouth curled into a snarl. The black boy pulled his knife hand close, dragging Carl's arm with it, and sunk his teeth into Carl's flesh. Carl recoiled but brought his unbitten arm forward to knock the knife from the attacker's hand. Before he could get in close enough to restrain his opponent, however, the black boy drove a knee into Carl's groin, then shoved his doubled-over form backward.

Marshall cried out in alarm as his friend came dangerously close to the open door of the moving car. Carl steered his fall enough to avoid ejection, but his head struck the door frame with a sickening crack. He collapsed and did not move.

"Carl!" Marshall shouted again, coming to his feet. He did not have time to examine Carl's injuries, however, for the new arrival was moving to reclaim his knife. Marshall was not as accustomed to fighting as Carl apparently was. There had only been much younger boys at the orphanage with him, and fighting was not Christian anyway. In this case, however, with both their lives in danger, he had little choice in the matter. He flung himself at the black boy, impacting him low, and wrapping arms around muscular legs, bringing him down hard.

His opponent, apparently more familiar with close combat, quickly used leverage to throw Marshall onto his back, landing once again on top of him. He raised a fist to strike. Marshall raised one arm to block the punch, and grabbed at the boy's chest with the other, hoping to get hold of his coat or shirt and gain the upper hand. His hand thrust under the coat and seized something soft and warm, like —

"Good Lord!" Marshall snatched his hand away and stared aghast at his opponent, who seemed suddenly amused.

"What's the matter? Don't got any fight left?"

"I can't fight you, you're a girl!"

"Ain't stopping me," said the girl, and brought her fist down hard against Marshall's jaw.

He tasted blood, and wriggled, trying to get away. "Stop that!" he barked. "I'm not going to fight you."

"Real gentleman, huh? Well they bleed red like everyone else, I hear." She drew back to strike again.

216

Marshall heaved his hips up hard and threw her off him. As the girl scrambled for her knife, he held up two placating hands. "Stop! Why are you doing this?"

"This is my place," she hissed.

"We didn't know," Marshall said, looking sideways at the still-unmoving Carl. "We just got on the first open car."

The girl's eyes narrowed. "A open door usual means they's somebody already here. And what you doin', gettin' on a car full o' crates? Don't you know you could get smashed if they fall? Yer s'posed to get in a empty car."

"But you're here."

"Ain't no empty cars."

"Well then —"

"Shut up!" snapped the girl.

"We didn't know to look for an empty car," said Marshall quickly. "We don't know anything much about riding the rails, except what a friend who'd done it told us."

She appeared to relax ever so slightly. "Reckon ya don't look like reg'lar hoboes."

Marshall attempted to look disarming. "First time. I promise." He nodded at Carl. "We're just a couple of orphans on the run."

"Couple o' dumb orphans," replied the girl.

"A couple of dumb orphans, yes," agreed

Marshall. "But we're not here to hurt you or try to take your space. Now, could you put down the knife, so I can check on my friend."

The girl considered it, then nodded.

Marshall crossed carefully to Carl's prone form and knelt. The other boy was breathing, thank God, and stirred with a groan when Marshall shook him.

"Carl, can you hear me?" Marshall asked.

"Uhnh," said Carl.

"Do you know who I am?" Marshall asked this because his only experience with a person who had been knocked unconscious had happened when little Sonny Lacy had slipped on a rock and hit his head at the swimming hole. Pastor Brooks had asked the boy if he knew the names of people around him, by way, Marshall supposed, of making sure his brains weren't all smashed up inside his skull.

"Yer a pain in my ass," muttered Carl, and rolled over to his side, facing away from Marshall.

"I guess he's okay," Marshall concluded. He looked back to the girl. "What's your name?"

"Venus."

"Venus? Nice name. She was a Roman goddess, in mythology."

"It's a boy's name," said Venus, gesturing with her still-raised knife.

"If you say so." Marshall leaned back against a crate next to Carl and settled down to sit, legs outstretched. "You're tough for a girl."

"I'm tough for a boy, too."

"I would agree with that. How did you get here?"

"I run away from a plantation."

"You were a slave? But they outlawed slavery."

"Not 'fore I run away they didn't. And outlawin' slavery don't make a lot o' difference to a colored girl on the rails. I might as well be a deer for 'em to shoot and eat."

"Why did you try to kill me?" asked Marshall.

Venus rolled her eyes. "Weren't gonna kill you. Just wanted t' scare ya."

"Why?"

"Get rid of ya. So ya won't turn me in."

"We don't want to turn in anyone. We just want to get to Indiana. Besides," he added, "turning you in would mean letting someone know we're here. That would be kind of stupid of us, don't you think?"

"Guess maybe. But ya don't look too smart, so I ain't bettin' my life on you."

Marshall ignored the insult. Girls insulted

boys. It was the way of the world. He didn't know why and hadn't asked in many years. "Why are you dressed as a boy?"

" 'Cause on the rails, ya don't wanna be a girl. Ya keep yer head down and yer knees together." She paused and looked him over, finally taking a seat opposite him as she did. She situated herself cross-legged with perfect balance. Once she was comfortable, she asked abruptly, "Ya got money?"

"No. We weren't allowed to have money in the orphanage."

"Well, I ain't gonna give you nothin' if you don't have money."

"I haven't asked you for anything."

"Every boy asks every girl for somethin', sooner or later."

For a moment, Marshall was confused. Then her meaning overtook him. He spluttered, "I — are you talking about . . . ? — I would never presume to ask you for that!"

Now she looked at him in disbelief, head cocked to one side. "What's wrong with you? Ain't you a proper boy?"

He had no idea what she meant by "proper," but he answered, "I — I think I am. It's just . . . well, it isn't right for a gentleman to ask a young lady —"

Venus threw back her head and laughed out loud. "I don't know about you, Mistah

Gentleman, but I ain't no lady."

"Well . . . well, I'm not asking for . . . that. Do you really take money for — ?"

"I take money however I can get it. Sometimes men gives it to me for lettin' 'em get between my legs for a few minutes."

"That's awful!"

She shook her head. "You ain't no kinda hobo, gettin' all flustered talkin' about a little brush."

"I'm not a hobo. I'm . . . I don't know what I am. But I won't take liberties with you."

"What about your friend?" She looked over at the sleeping Carl. "He got any money?"

"No."

Lips pursed, she said, "Too bad. He's pretty, like a pony or a li'l puppy."

"Boys aren't pretty."

"Sure they is. You are too, kinda. If ya do get hold of any money, I won't say no."

"Um . . ." Marshall felt his face grow hot. He could think of nothing to say but didn't want to be rude to a young lady. "That's a very kind offer."

Venus swore quietly and shook her head, then she rolled easily onto her side. "I'm gonna get back to sleep now." She held up the knife. "But don't get any ideas."

"Not a one," agreed Marshall. He scooted closer to Carl, verified that his friend's skin was warm, and that his breathing was still even, and then he lay his head down on his elbow.

Marshall was awakened before dawn by the sound of Carl groaning unhappily. He lifted up on one elbow to see the silhouette of his friend in the faint light from the door. Carl sat with his knees raised, his head resting on them. His hands were knotted at the back of his neck. He was still in pain.

"Headache?" asked Marshall.

"No thanks, I've got one."

"I kept an eye on you overnight."

"Good, it's comforting to know was somebody here to wake me up and tell me if I died." He looked at Marshall, clearly aware of his friend's displeasure at the remark. "Thanks. Don't mind me. I'm cranky on account of this hole in my head."

"I checked. You don't have a hole in your head. At least not any new ones."

Carl looked across to the sleeping form of Venus. "Did you kill him?"

"No. And he's not —"

"Did you get his knife away?"

"No, but you should know —"

"Jesus!" hissed Carl, and he was on his

222

feet, jumping to where Venus was, grabbing for the knife clutched at her breast. She awoke as he touched her and, with the thrust of one hand, knocked Carl flat on his backside.

"Get his knife!" shouted Carl.

Venus leapt to her feet and, brandishing the knife, made to carve Carl some new openings from which to blow hot air.

Marshall jumped between them, grabbing Venus's arm. "Don't," he said. "He's not going to hurt you. He just woke up and he's confused."

"He ain't confused," said Venus.

"I ain't confused," said Carl.

Defeated, Marshall threw up his hands. "Well, then, by all means, let me step out of the way, and you two fight it out. I'll continue on to Indiana with the survivor."

Both seemed to consider this seriously.

"Or," Marshall went on, "you could both realize that nobody here wants to hurt anybody, and maybe we can help each other."

"Tell that to the boy with the knife," said Carl.

"He's not —"

"I only got my knife up on account o' you tried to steal it!"

"I only tried to steal it on account o' you

tried to slit my friend's throat!"

"All right," shouted Marshall, "*stop!* Carl, this is Venus. Venus, this is Carl. Venus is a runaway slave and a professional hobo. Carl is a runaway orphan and a professional troublemaker."

Carl sighed. "Hello."

"Hey," said Venus, who still did not put the knife away.

"Where were you a slave?"

"Kentucky. Ran away and wound up in a contraband camp."

"Contraband camp?" asked Marshall.

Carl, no doubt pleased to know something Marshall did not (for a change) explained. "Places where escaped slaves and freed men could go to live, and some white folks would look out for them."

"Ours was at Camp Nelson," said Venus. "Union camp. We thought we was safe, but the Union soldiers turned us out. Most folks died. I learnt to hop freights."

"Among other things," said Marshall.

"Don't go gettin' high and mighty with me, boy," said Venus. "You two don't look like nothin' to me but poor white trash. You ain't no better than me."

" 'Than I,' " corrected Marshall.

"Oh, good, Marshall. Torment the boy with the knife," said Carl.

"He's not —"

"Hey!" Venus cried, leaping to her feet. In two steps, she had her hand on Carl's shoulder and was pulling him back, away from the door where he had moved to sit.

"Get off me!" barked Carl as he fell onto his back.

"I'm savin' your damn life! What did you think you were doin', hangin' your legs out like that?"

"I was just getting some air."

"Gettin' your damn legs cut off, more like, if we come upon a hillside, or if the door rattled shut. Don't you know nuthin'?"

"I think we've established that we don't," said Marshall.

"And don't go puttin' yer face in the door, ya scenery bum," Venus went on to Carl. "Somebody sees ya, they'll come toss all of us off the train, and they ain't gonna slow down first!"

"Sorry," said Marshall. Carl just looked angry.

"What you goin' to Indiana for, anyway?" asked Venus.

"My uncle lives there."

"He got money?"

"I don't know. A little, I guess."

"Make you a deal. I'll look out for you two, teach you how to get around on the tracks. You give me money when we find your uncle."

"Maybe we don't need you," said Carl.

"You still got yer legs 'cause o' me. You two'll be picked up by bulls before the day's out if I don't help you."

Carl looked at Marshall. "What are bulls?"

"See?" asked Venus. "Bulls is railway police. You keep out of their sight."

"You're right," said Marshall. "We really could use some help."

"Glad one of you got the brains to see it." Venus glared daggers at Carl.

"When we get to Indiana, I'll see what my uncle can give you. A meal at least."

"Speaking of which," said Carl, "where do you find food around here? I'm starving."

Venus shook her head. " 'Less you knows somebody on the crew that's got a lunch pail, we ain't eatin' till this train stops."

"How soon is that?"

"Dunno. Never rode this spur before." She said irritably, "Just settle back and see what you can see."

They were silent for a while. Venus, staring out at the racing scenery, began to sing. She had a clear, melting soprano, and her song was about the joys of meeting Jesus in Heaven.

"That's pretty," said Marshall. "Where'd

226

you learn to sing?"

"Got to learn to do somethin' when you're riding. Hoboes don't set idle."

"I thought that's what hoboes done best," said Carl.

"Proves you don't know nothin'. Tramps set idle. Hoboes work. And when they ain't a job in front of us, we do somethin' useful. I sing. People like it."

"I like it," said Marshall. "Please don't stop."

Venus looked to Carl, as if for a second opinion.

"Do what you want," he muttered. "I don't care none."

Marshall's muscles had internalized the rhythm of the tracks, so much so that he barely noticed the vibrations of the floor beneath him. What motion he did register had become comforting to him, soothing his tired limbs and tortured mind.

It was evening again, and he relaxed, alone, against the stack of crates near the open door, mindful of Venus's warning to keep out of sight.

In the darkness, there was not a lot to see outside — dark shapes flying by, like giant bats, or midnight storm clouds, hulks of old houses and barns, dying trees — or were

227

they dying? Everything looked dead in the darkness of this night. But then there were the houses whose windows were warmed with the glow of lamplight, pale orange and radiating heat into the evening. Marshall was almost warmed by it as well, and by the thought of being in a home again, after years in camps and the drafty old orphan house, where Sister Hapgood allowed a coal fire only first thing in the morning. Nights, she said, should be cold to encourage sleep and godly quiet.

Marshall wondered what it must be like to sit at the dinner tables of those houses, to eat warm, buttered biscuits and salted ham, pickled green beans put away by a grandmother who smelled like smoke and pine oil, later to stroll the town main street, lit by gas lamps, its dust held down by the evening dew.

What were the people in those houses like? Was there a father, upright but tired from a day's labor in the field, or angry, drunken, and stumbling? A mother with hands reddened by chores, warm and ready with a comforting arm, or shrewish, criticizing, ready to complain? Were there children? Were they well-behaved, with maybe just a hint of mischief in their eyes as they plotted an adventure? Or were they spoiled and brattish? Or bullies with hateful gazes? Did they have dreams of greatness and riches, or were they defeated from the start, aware that the world had nothing to offer and would take any meager portion they chanced to have?

From the far end of the car drifted moaning sounds. Marshall recognized Carl's voice from nights when dreams were not pleasant, and sleep did not come back after they visited, and from nights when dreams were pleasant and . . . well, it wasn't proper to think on such things.

Not long after, Carl returned to Marshall's side, his red hair ruffled, still buttoning his shirt as he sat down.

"What were you doing?" asked Marshall.

"Talkin' to Venus."

"Must have been quite a talk. I didn't hear any words."

"We said what we needed to."

"Guess she told you she's a girl."

Carl snickered. "She didn't have to."

Marshall looked away, not wanting Carl to see the look on his face, not sure of his own feelings.

After what may have been thirty seconds, Carl said, "What?"

"I didn't say anything."

"That's why I asked. When you don't say

nothin', I know there's trouble. What's itchin' you?"

"You . . . you acted on your lustful impulses — with that innocent girl."

Carl snorted. "She ain't innocent, trust me."

"It's not Christian."

"See, that's why I need you here — when she spread her legs, I forgot to ask if it was Christian to put my —"

"Shut *up*! I don't want to know what you put where! You should be more godly."

"Like you?"

"Like Jesus."

"If I run into him, I'll ask his advice on what to do in that situation."

"You'll only run into him if you pray."

"Then I guess I'm on my own."

Evansville, Indiana, was the most despair-ridden place on Earth. There seemed to be dust on everything, as if the owners of the town had gone out one day, expected to return that evening, and been instead ambushed or — more likely, given the territory — scalped and left to die in the blazing sun. In their absence, everything had accumulated dust — even the people they had left behind — and now, Evansville was just the corpse of a town that used to be lived in

and cared about. The people remaining —
dusty shadows — were merely abandoned
playthings.

"Your uncle lives here?" Venus asked
Marshall as they shuffled, hungry and sore,
down the town's main thoroughfare.

"If you call being in this place 'living,' "
muttered Carl.

"Beggars can't be choosers," said Marshall.

Venus returned the suspicious glance of a
man sitting on his unclean front porch. "I
ain't a beggar. I work for a living."

Carl answered with an irreverent smirk
that would have got him slapped by Sister
Hapgood.

"It's not much," said Marshall, "but if my
uncle will put us up, I guess it's home."

"Y'all damn near broke your necks to get
here," wondered Venus. "Which o' you fools
—"

"The Bible says not to call a man a fool,
Venus."

"Okay, Reverend Marshall, which one o'
you mush-headed *idiots* came up with the
idea to hop a freight to come here?"

"We got the idea from Phil," explained
Carl. "He was a, I guess you'd call him a
kind of a stray, come to church one Sunday
and asked if there was work. Pastor Brooks

gave him a job trimmin' back the blackberry brambles out back, so's we could have a proper Sunday School picnic someday."

"We helped him," said Marshall. "He told us he had been a Confederate soldier."

"Pretty much all o' them lookin' for a job now, if they're able to stand up straight," said Venus. "Fair number of 'em hoboes."

"Phil had been with General Jo Shelby's division in Texas," Marshall went on. "Seems the general and his men decided, when the war ended, that they were going to just keep going south — to Mexico — to avoid capture by the Union."

"They make it?" asked Venus. "Did they get away?"

"Doesn't sound like it. Phil wasn't a hundred percent sure. But he broke away. He wanted to try and make it home to Maryland."

"Virginia's as far as he got," said Carl. "They found out who he was, the Army did, and they took him away from our place in chains. But not before he told us all about ridin' the rails from Texas."

Venus laughed under her breath, low and caustic. "God musta handed you a extra dose o' luck, that he got took away. You damn fools done fell for a jocker!"

"A what?" asked Marshall.

"Listen, they ain't many women on the rails, right?"

"Present company excepted," said Marshall.

"Huh?"

"He means 'ceptin you."

"Right. So, hoboes bein' mostly men, well, they get horny —"

Marshall went pale.

"You okay?" asked Venus.

"He cain't hear words like that," put in Carl. "It aches his Jesus bone."

"Well that's how they gets, reverend. Ya can't change men." She looked ruefully at Carl. "Or boys. Anyway, jockers needs some company, so they go for the next best thing to a woman, a fresh, smooth, boy."

"That's disgusting!" said Marshall.

Carl was silent.

"They sees a boy who ain't on the rails," said Venus, "but maybe's a little unhappy. They tells him tales of mountains made o' candy and places where gold grows on trees."

"And boys go with them?"

"You come."

"By ourselves."

"Ya still fell fer the pitch."

"I don't think Phil was a pervert," said Marshall.

"For his sake, hope he weren't. Hoboes, most of 'em, don't like to see a young'un took advantage of. So they takes care of any jocker they catch at it. Y'all would do best to stay away from anyone who seems a little too friendly."

"How do you stay safe?" asked Carl.

"I sticks to the young ones what decides to take up the life on their own."

"He decided," said Carl, pointing to Marshall. "I just followed him."

"You just follows him everywhere?"

Carl shrugged. "Till I get a better offer."

"Well, we made it here, didn't we?" asked Marshall. Before she could say it, he added, "Thanks to you, Venus." He stopped and pointed. "There's the post office. Let's go find out where my uncle lives."

The man in the post office had no good news for them. When Marshall gave his uncle's name, he shook his head. "Sorry, son. You're a few months too late." He seemed a kindly man, middle-aged, eyes warm behind small, wire-framed reading glasses, a neat, gray beard decorating his chin. "We had the smallpox."

"He's dead?" asked Marshall, his face blank, almost as if it didn't know the word.

The postmaster nodded. "The whole family. Too many families. It's hardest on the children."

Marshall just stared at the floor.

"What about his house?" asked Carl bluntly. Venus had waited outside, not wanting to attract attention.

Marshall looked at Carl in surprise, but Carl said reasonably, "If the whole family's dead, their property would be yours."

"Oh, were you family?" asked the postmaster.

"He was my uncle."

"I'm so sorry. And I'm sorry to tell you that the house went to the bank. He owed on it. Most people do, 'round here. I reckon no one knew he had a nephew. Any personal effects likely went to the church. You could ask —"

"No," interrupted Marshall. "Thank you for your . . . time. There's nothing we need."

Carl followed him out of the small building and into the street where Venus waited.

"Sorry about your uncle, Marshall," Venus said as they walked back to the train station.

"Thanks. I never knew him. It's hard to mourn a stranger." He stopped and looked at the sky aimlessly. "But now I suppose I'm really an orphan." He turned to Venus. "And there's no money. I don't know what I can do for you, after all your help."

Venus chewed her lower lip. "Mama always said never to feed a stray kitten. You feed 'em, you stuck with 'em, she said."

"What's that even mean?" demanded Carl.

"Means let's get on the train, orphans, 'fore I makes up my mind to drown you like the pair o' strays you is."

"Stop right there!"

"Shit," muttered Venus, who was halfway up into the empty boxcar when the voice rang out across the yard. Marshall and Carl were still on the ground behind her. "Bulls," she observed.

Two men in dusty overcoats and mismatched caps strode toward them. The taller one had a long face decorated by a handlebar mustache that obscured a protrusive lower lip. He looked like he'd been belted in the mouth and the swelling had stuck. He had his hand on his belt, drawing his coat back. There was a glint of metal in the sun.

"They have guns," whispered Marshall.

"Always do," said Venus.

Drawing near, Belted Mouth stopped, kicking gravel as his boots dug in. "Lookin' for a free ride?" he asked.

"Naw," said Venus, "we was —"

"Ain't talkin' to you, boy. Talking to your

236

masters here."

"There are no masters, sir," said Marshall.

For his trouble, Marshall received a cuff in the mouth. His lower lip, cut against his teeth, began to bleed.

"Wrong, boy," said the tall man. "I'm the master here, and you all do as you're told."

"We just wanted to see the train," said Carl. "Ain't never seen one before."

"Ain't never gonna see one again, ya don't stop yammerin'," said the second, shorter bull. He was older, grayer, and even his face was short, appearing to be a size too small for his skull. His chin was too close to his nose.

"Now you boys gonna get out o' here right now. You come back," he leveled the gun at Carl's forehead, "you gonna meet my pistol here, up close an' personal." He looked Venus up and down. "Might shoot yer colored friend anyhow, make sure today's lesson sticks."

"No," said Marshall, stepping protectively in front of Venus. "We understand. You don't have to hurt her."

"Her?" Both bulls' eyes went wide. Belted Mouth pressed his gun against the seam of Venus's ragged jacket and pushed it aside. As the barrel pressed soft flesh beneath, he nodded knowingly and said again, "Her."

He wrapped an arm around Venus's waist, pulled her close against him, and grabbed her breast hard. He pushed her back against the boxcar's edge, into the door's opening. "You boys go on get out of here. I'll send your friend your way if there's anything left when we're done."

"No!" cried Marshall.

The little gray bull began to advance, but his cohort had frozen at Marshall's outburst. As Carl pulled his friend by the shoulder, trying to encourage him to run, Belted Mouth sighed, "Weren't plannin' on killin' no damn fool boy today, but —"

With his free hand, he raised his pistol, pointed at Marshall's heart.

"Run!" screamed Carl, pulling Marshall again.

There was a loud screech from the front of the train, the whistle of impending motion. The boxcar lurched, and Venus took advantage of the moment to thrust her knee into the groin of her assailant. He doubled over in pain, dropping the gun. Carl, abandoning thoughts of escape, rushed forward to kick him in the back of the head before he could rise again. Venus scooped up the fallen weapon.

The second bull tackled Marshall, pinning the skinny boy easily to the ground and raising a fist that, in two or three punches, would probably pulp Marshall's face, or crush his windpipe. Marshall closed his eyes and turned away, but the blow never landed. There was a crack, like a whip being unfurled, and Marshall's would-be killer fell backwards and off of him. Getting to his feet, Marshall saw a red spot, slick and growing, on the front of his shirt.

"Sweet Jesus," Marshall muttered. "Have mercy."

"Marshall, come on!" called Carl.

Marshall looked up from the dying man at his feet to see Carl scrambling onto the now-moving boxcar, his hand extended. Venus was already onboard and safe. Marshall ran, saying uselessly over his shoulder, "I'm sorry," to the corpse behind him. He extended his arm, grabbed Carl's hand, and used his knees to propel himself into the air and onto the moving car. As he landed on the hard, wooden floor, something grabbed his foot. With Carl's hands firmly gripping his shoulders now, Marshall looked to see the surviving bull, his face twisted in rage, holding onto the iron step of the car with one hand and Marshall's ankle with the other. His feet moved comically, trying to keep up as the car gained speed.

Venus, kneeling, reached out with the gun

she still held and drove the butt of the grip into the bull's forehead. He screamed but did not release. He tightened his grip and yanked, trying to pull Marshall out of the car.

Venus struck again, harder this time. The pistol connected with a sickening crunch, and blood spurted from the impact point. The bull tried to say something, then gasped. His hand on Marshall's ankle relaxed, pulled free, and he fell backward into empty air, off the train. Marshall looked away.

"Sissy," muttered Venus, her breath still ragged. "Can't watch a man die when he done tried t' kill you?"

"Reckon he ain't as bloodthirsty as you," said Carl defensively.

Venus glared momentarily at Carl, then, as if she could contain herself no longer, burst into laughter. "He done all right for a uppity white boy." She placed a hand on Marshall's head and mussed his hair. "Thanks for standin' up for me." She looked at Carl and added, "Both of ya."

Carl helped Marshall to his feet, and the three moved away from the open door.

"What now?" asked Marshall.

"Now we head to the jungle," said Venus.

"No!" insisted Carl. "I ain't doin' it!"

"But —" Marshall began.

Carl threw himself down on the floor resolutely, arms crossed, as if daring the other two to move him. "I ain't goin' to no jungle."

"It's not a real jungle, fool," said Venus. "Ain't no lions or nothin'!"

"It's a hobo jungle, like Venus said," Marshall explained again. "A safe place where we can —"

"A safe place is California, where Phil said there's work! And there's orange trees, and open space. It never rains, and it's never cold."

"An' the mountains is made of candy!" jibed Venus.

Carl ignored her, speaking only to Marshall. "Even if we didn't have a place to live, we could just sleep out under the stars nights. You and me, Marshall, we could —"

"And what about Venus?" Marshall demanded. "Sure, you and me, we could just fade into the background all the way to the coast. Maybe even steal tickets and pretend we're passengers." He looked at the girl. "But a black girl with two white boys? We'd stick out like a sore thumb. And they'll be looking for us! We probably killed both of those policemen!"

"Thugs," said Carl. "We probably killed two thugs who was gonna kill us."

"Dammit, Carl — !"

"Whoa!" Carl's eyes, which had been closing as if in preparation for sleep, flew open. "Did you just swear?"

"You damned well drove me to it!"

"Past it, I'd say," said Venus.

Carl looked at her. "You promised to get us to Indiana. You done that and thank you. But now —"

"We promised to pay her," Marshall reminded him.

"But we couldn't. Circumstances beyond our control. Act o' God. If she wants to come to California, we'll make some money and —"

"I just said, if she tries to go with us, we'll all get caught."

"Then she better go hide in her jungle. Me, I'm goin' to California."

"Without me, you won't last a day," said Venus.

"We'll take our chances," said Carl.

Marshall shook his head. "No. We won't. I'm going with Venus."

For just a moment, Carl's mouth dropped

242

open. He looked as though Marshall had punched him in the chest. His eyes looked moist. For just a moment. When the moment was gone, he said, "Fine. Safe travels."

"Carl!"

"What?" the boy asked irritably.

"You — you're no gentleman!"

Carl closed his eyes and settled his head back against the wall of the car. "Reckon I'm not."

At a stop whose name Marshall never learned, he and Venus climbed out of the car, fell down in a gully by the tracks until the train passed, and he followed her into the woods.

"River's this way," she said, beckoning. "I ain't been to this camp, but I know it's near the river, and not far from the tracks. They all are."

Marshall stopped, watching the receding train, moving off into the afternoon sun.

"What you lookin' at?" asked Venus.

"Nothing, I guess."

"You gonna cry, sissy?"

"No, I am not going to cry," he snapped at her. "I just — Carl was my family. I can't believe he just . . . left."

"Look to me like he stayed in one place, 'far as that went. You was the one got off the train."

Marshall swallowed. "It was the right thing to do."

"If you say so. Me, I never had time t' think about what'uz the right thing and what'uz the wrong thing. I just always does what I got to t' get through to the next stop."

"I suppose that's all Carl's doing too."

"Families doesn't always stay together, does they?"

Marshall laughed harshly. "Not mine."

"Do you reckon maybe a black girl and a white boy could be . . . ." She stopped suddenly and looked away.

"What?" asked Marshall.

"Nothin'."

"But —"

"Drop it, sissy!" Her voice was cold. Marshall knew the subject was closed.

She tugged at his shoulder. "C'mon, it's gettin' dark. They'll put out the fire soon, and we won't get nothin' t' eat."

Indeed, shadows were lengthening in the woods. Sundown would be in an hour or so. Marshall followed the girl dressed as a boy, his feet crunching through old, dried leaves, and occasionally sticking in wet muck beneath them. "Why would they put the fire out at dark? Don't they want to keep warm?"

244

"Fool, the bulls can see a fire. So can the locals. And they loves to blame every little thing on us hoboes. You want to be safe, you don't attract no attention."

"Are you sure they'll feed us?"

"Of course they'll feed us. Hoboes feed each other. That's part of the life."

She stopped at a tree, traced her finger in its bark.

"What is it?" Marshall asked.

"Says it's safe to camp."

"I don't see any writing."

She seized his wrist, brought it to the tree, and traced his finger in a deep, carved groove. It went down, angled, went parallel with the ground, then angled back up again, forming a square with no top.

"That's a hobo mark."

"How do you — ?"

"Shhh! Listen!"

Marshall obeyed, and heard a vague rumble of voices, very quiet, as if the speakers did not wish to be overheard. Their speech was occasionally punctuated with metallic clinks, and the pops of wood on a fire. As he heard them, he smelled smoke on the breeze.

He started toward the sounds, but Venus pulled him back. "Can't go empty-handed."

"But we don't have anything!"

She nodded at the ground. "Find some wood for the fire. I'm gonna hunt around."

Marshall, baffled, searched the surrounding ground for broken limbs. Most were too spindly to be of any real use, and many were wet and pulpy — no good for burning. He did not know much about the hobo life — he did not know anything! — but he knew how to gather firewood. He had learned at home — his real home — and learned well enough to avoid extra punishment at the asylum. A boy or girl bringing a too-spindly stick for the fire would find said stick applied to his or her backside in quick time.

As he was using his foot as a pry to break up a medium-sized, dry branch, Venus returned, two armloads of greens caught in her elbows. "Wild onions," she said. "Ain't much, but they's good in soup."

They started again toward the sound of voices and the smell of a campfire. "Are you sure they won't rob us?" Marshall asked.

"Don't nobody rob nobody in the jungle," said Venus. "If'n they tried, they'd get beat good and proper."

"By whom?"

"By everybody else there. Hoboes don't tolerate no foolishness. The camp is a safe place."

Laden with their offerings, they came

upon a clearing in which a fire burned. Three ragged men sat around it, while others lay on bedrolls nearby. One man stood, shirtless, by a tree, glancing into a mirror mounted to the trunk, shaving with a straight razor and a bowl of water that steamed.

The men by the fire were sipping from tin cans and smacking their lips. Their makeshift cups obviously contained whatever was simmering in the kettle that hung on a rustic hanger over the fire. It smelled wonderful to Marshall. He knew that, in fact, it might smell like the outhouse the morning after a midnight storm, but he had not eaten in some time.

The old man stirring the kettle looked up. "You boys lost?"

"No," said Venus. "We come to stay the night." She held out the onions, and gestured to Marshall's supply of wood. "Looks like we in time to clean up after supper."

The man nodded thoughtfully. "You look awfully young."

Marshall began, "I'm fif—"

"We old enough," Venus interrupted him.

"You in trouble?"

"Maybe a little. Maybe some bulls didn't like the look o' my friend."

"Runaways?" pressed the hobo. "Left your

folks to have an adventure?"

Venus shook her head. "Ain't got no folks. Him neither."

" 'Cause runaways get took home," the man went on.

"And you'd be welcome, if'n either of us had homes." She looked at Marshall. "My friend, he's kinda new. I'm teachin' him, on accounta he lost his people in the war." She slapped Marshall's shoulder. "He's green, but I'll whip 'im inta shape."

Again, the man nodded. A slow smile grew on his lips. "Kinda like you, boy. You'll do all right." He raised a pointed finger. "If you does the cleanup."

"We certainly will, sir," said Marshall.

The man narrowed his eyes once more and looked at Marshall as he might have at a traveling circus freak.

"My friend, he talks a little funny. I'm workin' on that."

"Well," said the old man, "let's get them onions cut up, and some o' that wood on the fire before we gotta put it out. You're just in time. I sent the other new boy to the river to get the water t' douse it."

"There's another new boy?" asked Marshall.

The old man nodded. "Scruffy boy," he observed. "Wild look in his eyes. Hair as red as hot coals, and eyes as black as cold ones. Didn't have a good feeling about him, but thought I should give him a break, after what he said."

Marshall's voice trembled as he asked, "What did he say?"

"Said he just needed a place to stay while he looked for his family."

Steven Howell Wilson has written science fiction and fantasy for DC Comics and mythological adventure for Crazy 8 Press's *ReDeus* series. His original science fiction audio drama, *The Arbiter Chronicles,* has earned the Mark Time Silver Medal and the Parsec Award. Prose adventures of the Arbiters are available from Firebringer Press. "The Colonel's Plan," Steve's weekly blog about the joys and sorrows of completing the fifty-year-old house his late father designed, is available at www.stevenhwilson .com.

■ ■ ■ ■

THE BELLS OF JUNIPER

BY VONN MCKEE

■ ■ ■ ■

Folks, the name's Ralph Carlisle and my sweet wife here says I need to set this little story down on paper before I go forgetting it. For posterity, she says. But I'm here to tell you that me losing track of this particular memory ain't likely to happen. No sir, not in this lifetime.

You see, that was the day — July the 12th, it was — in eighteen and sixty-nine, that I both killed a man and fell in love with a woman. To be honest, I couldn't tell you which one I done first. Didn't mean to do neither one. Well, I'm already getting ahead of myself.

Anyway, it started like this. I was in the store filling an order. Yep, I'm the proprietor of Carlisle's Mercantile and I reckon I shoulda done told you that. It was shaping up to be a regular old same-as-usual day when, about midmorning, I swore I heard the church bell ringing. Well, I found that curious so I stopped weighing Mrs. Lynch's coffee and cocked my head to listen. There was so much going on outside — wagons rolling by and folks walking on the board-walks — that I decided I must've been hearing things. I knew for sure it wasn't Sunday.

You see, there ain't but two bells in Juniper, Wyoming, and after a year of working there on Front Street, I guess you could say my ear had got tuned to 'em both. The first bell is down at the train station and we hear it twice a week now that the last spike was drove in at Promontory last May. That opened up the rails all the way to California and turned Juniper into a right bustling little town.

Now, the other bell hangs up there on top of the First Methodist Church and that's the one I was thinking I heard. Preacher Crane's boy, Willie, rings it at ten o'clock every Sunday morning, and on special oc-casions. The ladies was some proud when that bell came in on the train all the way from Richmond. But I ain't here to tell you about that.

Anyhow, when I got up to the counter to write up Mrs. Lynch's bill, I heard the bell again and I knew something was sore amiss. Weren't no wedding or funeral going on or I would have known it. I saw through the window that people was looking up the street towards the sound. I made my apologies to Mrs. Lynch and excused myself. I yanked off my apron and charged out the door.

There was probably a dozen men running along with me. I didn't see or smell any smoke. Clifford Meeks, the undertaker, passed me like I was a lame mule. I might mention here that Clifford gets more excited about tragic events than is fitting and proper. I said, "What do you reckon is going on, Clifford?" But he was done out of earshot.

When we got to the church, what we saw stopped us all cold there at the front steps. The door was standing open and inside there was a woman slouched down on the floor crying and a big man standing over her pointing a revolver towards the top of her head. I realized that the woman had her arms wrapped tight around the bell rope that hung down inside the door. Every time the man would reach down and try to grab her arm, she would rock her head and shoulders back and forth and moan something — maybe no, no, no — and that would make the bell ring a couple of times.

Daniel Willingham was the first one of us to say anything since I guess all the rest of the men was dumbfounded like me. He hollered out, "You let her go, mister. No need to be a-pointin' a gun at nobody. Let her go, hear me?" But the man just looked at us, real crazy and mean-eyed, and said he'd shoot her if he wanted to, weren't none of our damn business. He said it right there standing in the church house. Well, the woman started wailing like a lamb with no mama and the bell started ringing again from her pulling on it.

"What'll we do?" I asked Daniel since he had kind of put hisself in charge by being the first one to speak out. But Daniel didn't look like he knew what our next move might be.

He said he didn't think we ought to shoot somebody inside the church and, besides that, he didn't have his gun on him. Daniel was still wearing his smithy apron.

That's when I said, "Well, it looks to me like *he's* about to shoot somebody inside the church so we'd best do something quick," and all of the men nodded.

The man with the gun looked nervous and called out, "This here's my wife. I caught her with another man."

The woman shook her head no and looked out towards us. Her face was all red and wet with crying but I noticed she was a pretty girl, maybe a lot younger than the man. It seemed like she put her eyes dead-center on me. "No, no," she was saying but it didn't make any sound. I figured right then the man was lying.

Matter of fact, now that I looked at him, I remembered him coming in the store about once a month to buy a bill of groceries. Nothing fancy, some tobacco and flour and such and, once, a few sewing notions and bolt of calico. I knew that calico wasn't likely for him so I figured he must have him a woman. But I never seen her come in, not even one time. Thought it strange. The man didn't like small talk either. Just paid his bill and left. Kind of man that looked like a mule eating briars, as my ma used to say. Well, he was worse than eating briars there in the church house that day.

Well, back to the story. That big man was a sight — his hair was all mussed up and he was breathing heavy — and he shook hisself sudden-like and turned away from us with a big roaring sound, grabbed the girl by the hair of the head, and twisted her face up towards him. I swear she turned whiter'n a china plate. Then he brought that revolver down slow and careful and pressed the barrel to her lips — almost like a kiss, now that I think about it.

I can't say that I remember just what happened next. All I know is that, in the space of a rattler strike, I was up there tackling that man down like he was a runaway calf. I know I had to have got up those steps somehow but I can't tell you how I did. Must've jumped 'em all in one bound.

Well, that fellow was a beefy one and had a good forty pounds on me but I somehow got a hold of his gun arm and was trying to back him away from that girl. I have thought many a time how lunk-headed I was to run up there with him holding a gun to her face. I can't hardly think about how bad that might have turned out.

Anyhow, I was just durn lucky, I guess, and caught him off his mark. But it wasn't two seconds before he bear-wrapped both arms around me and wrestled me down. Had me on one knee and was trying hard to work that revolver up to my skull.

I didn't think, I just did. Kinda like jumping the church steps. I threw my weight forwards to get my feet under me. Then I jumped up and twisted backwards all at the same time, kinda like a whirligig. He still had me but at least the bulk of him was behind me. I grabbed his wrist — he had big bear-paw hands too — and I was aiming to squeeze it hard enough to make him drop that iron. What an ox he was!

I squeezed and pushed but that barrel kept easing towards me. I could see the muzzle and I was thinking I'd never seen one up that close before and that I might not again.

I was in sore need of a miracle and durned if it didn't show up. Ole Daniel come charging in like a bull through the church door. He was being as fool-headed as me about breaking in on somebody with a gun almost to their head. But I was sure glad to see his homely mug anyhow. His surprise visit was just enough to throw the grizzly man off. His arm loosened up but I forgot to stop pulling and the gun kicked towards us both.

I heard a *boom* . . . and a bell ring!

I was on the floor and when my eyes could look straight, I saw the big man lying maybe a foot away from me. His eyes was open but there was a round hole just under his chin that was beginning to bleed. What I couldn't see until later was the top of his head. Or what there was left of it.

"Ralph, Ralph, are you hearin' me?" Daniel was shaking me.

"Daniel, of course I'm hearin' you and seein' you too, sorry to say. I know that can't be the face of St. Peter. Wouldn't nobody walk past that through them pearly gates."

Daniel pulled me up and started laughing and slapping me on the back. Guess he thought I could have been dead about then. I tell you he wasn't the only one.

We both remembered the girl and saw that she was standing back in the corner quiet and pale. She looked to me like one of them statues of Mary you see in them old missions. I said, "Let's get you outside," and I went over and put my hand on her shoulder. She was a little thing. I led her out the door trying to stay between her and the man's body but I reckoned she'd already seen. When we got out in the daylight, I saw there was a bruise where he'd been holding her wrist. Not only that but there was other dark places further up her arm that looked like they was healing up. Made me sick to my gut.

Well, that's the story — of that day anyhow. Preacher Crane's wife insisted on taking the girl in until things settled down. Some of us offered to escort her back home, which was only a mile from town but hid back in a draw. She got all big-eyed and scared and said she didn't want to ever set foot back in that place again so we went out and got what belongings she said she'd like to have.

I got in a habit of dropping in to check on her now and then. The Cranes began inviting me for supper once a week. I started going to church for the first time since I was a youngster.

Though it wasn't my finger that pulled the trigger, I'll always feel like it was my doing that took a man's life. But I reckon it saved somebody else's too. I leave all the reconciling to the Good Lord.

And it wasn't just the girl's life that was saved neither. It didn't take the Cranes and everybody else long to figure out I was falling for her like a schoolboy. She was the gentlest, nicest human being I had ever met and it riled me to think that someone could ever raise a hand to her.

Sometimes when she's standing by the window, I still think she looks like a pretty church statue. Even prettier now that she smiles. Her name isn't Mary though. It's Emmeline. And I was one happy storekeeper the day the Juniper church bell rang for us on our wedding day — happy in spite of the fact that I had that blockheaded Daniel Willingham for a best man. I reckon he'll do though.

Oh, and what we figured out later was that

the bullet (the one that lead-poisoned her stinking excuse for a husband) went straight on up into the belfry. Willie Crane saw the hole in the ceiling and climbed up to investigate. He said there was a skint mark up the side of the bell. I knew I wasn't hearing things!

If you want to hear more than that, you'll have to come on by the mercantile and get it from Miz Emmeline. My story writin' ends here, folks. You all have a fine day now.

Regards,
Ralph Carlisle

Vonn McKee, Louisiana-born and descended from "horse traders and southern belles," is a two-time Western Writers of America Spur finalist for short fiction. Now based in Nashville, she enjoys antiquing, destination-less driving, and writing stories of the West. Her website is vonnmckee.com.

■ ■ ■ ■

FRANK RULE AND THE TASCOSANS

BY JOHN NEELY DAVIS

■ ■ ■ ■

Frank Rule had pushed the insanity down into the depths of his being for so long, the craziness was feeling natural. He would not admit it to anyone — not that he had many opportunities up here in the desolation of the High Plains — but it was almost comforting.

Oh, Ellen still came to him in the stillness that permeated his house just before dawn, and her voice remained soft and almost musical. She talked of their future and her love for him, and he found solace in her words. However, as the horizon lightened with the rising sun, she went away and little fringes of madness accumulated at the outer edges of his thinking.

The Devil was a frequent, uninvited visitor into Frank's world, giving advice, taunting, goading. Recently, the rancher had succeeded in turning the demon away, but he knew the power of his adversary and that,

in time, he would surrender to the relent-
less attacks of the beast.

Perhaps a more philosophical man could
rationalize what was happening, but that
was far beyond Frank's ability.

This morning Frank was doing one of his
least favorite ranching duties, arm deep up
in a brindle cow that seemed to insist on
doing everything opposite from the rest of
the herd. The lanky animal was unsuccessfully trying to give an out-of-season birth to
a jug-headed calf fathered by a neighbor's
fence-busting bull. Pulling a calf was exhausting under the best of circumstances.
However, the cow had tired of her fruitless
activity and, ignoring the fading labor pains,
was munching contently on an armload of
hay.

Frank tightened the cord around the calf's
front feet and gave a final tug. The animal
squirted out onto the ground and lay there
for an instant, large eyes staring at the
brightness of its new surroundings. The
rancher wiped the newborn with a burlap
bag and helped it stand. Holding the calf by
the flanks, he helped the wobbly-legged
animal toward its mother, who seemed to
have little interest in her offspring.

Shirtless, Frank sat at the tack room door

and, using the same burlap bag, cleaned afterbirth from his arms and hands.

Hey, will you look at what's comin' down the road. You got company. And here you are all dressed up. Old Scratch thinks you're gonna make a helluva bad impression.

Clenching his teeth, Frank shook his head. It had been a week since the Devil had talked to him.

Whoa! Fancy. That man's got on a white shirt and is wearing a tie. And here you are, lookin' like something that has fallen outta a cow's innards.

Frank walked across the stock lot and waited at the gate as a spic-and-span buggy pulled by a gray horse came down the rutted lane toward his homestead. The horse came to a stop, and a light swirl of red dust rose around the buggy, then settled on the driver.

"Good afternoon, sir," the nattily attired man said. "I believe you are the man I'm seeking. You are Frank Rule, aren't you?"

Oh, he knows damn well who you are. He turned you down for a twenty-dollar loan last winter. Said you were a poor credit risk. Unsatisfactory collateral he said.

"Yes, sir, I'm Frank Rule. And who would you be?"

Atta boy. Put him in his place. He is riding in

your territory now. Mr. High-Hat-Banker.

The man stepped down from the buggy and shook the red grit from his calf-length duster. "You probably do not recall meeting with me last winter. It was about a loan. I'm Harald Donovan. Longsought Bank?"

"Yes, sir. I remember."

"Yes. Well, I want you to understand I've regretted the decision to not make the loan ever since I made it. I . . . I acted in haste. I've come out to make the loan. Today. Right now. No strings." The banker raised the buggy seat and withdrew a small canvas bag. "I can let you have it in fives or tens. Your choice."

Whoa. Watch the sumbitch. He's fixin' to pee on your leg. Betting he's not come all the way out here just 'cause he's had a change of heart. He's after somethin'.

"Mighty kind of you, Mr. Donovan. But I don't need the money now. I needed it last winter. Needed it to buy feed. Had a couple of cows starve. But, I'll get over that. Pastures are starting to come around now, and I reckon I'm in pretty good shape."

"Well, I'm glad things are working out for you. Just wanted you to know that anytime in the future I can be of service, Longsought Bank will more than welcome you."

268

Get on with it. Quit beatin' around the damn bush.

Donovan cleared his throat and then looked at Frank's barn and house. "Mighty nice little place you've got here." He removed his hat and revealed a bald scalp that might never have experienced unshaded sunlight. "Yes, sir, mighty nice."

Okay. Enough of this. He needs to quit wasting our time. We've still got that wobbly calf in the barn.

Using a thumbnail, Frank scraped dried afterbirth off his forearm. "Harald, I don't 'spect you come all the way out here just to talk about my little spread. What you got on your mind?"

Yeah. What's goin' on under that bald head of hair?

". . . and I never heard anything else," the banker concluded.

Frank leaned against a buggy wheel and studied the banker. "You never went over there?"

"Oh, heavens, no. There have been better men than me who rode into Tascosa horseback and were carried out flat on their back in a wagon. I wrote Sheriff Siringo. Waited and waited. Found out he was looking for that McCarty kid and his buddy Tom

269

O'Folliard somewhere down in New Mexico Territory. I hired a couple of . . . couple of men who were supposed to be good at . . . getting young men out of trouble. They took my hundred dollars and — *poof* — never heard from them again."

You see where he is going with this, don't you? Come out here, sugar-wouldn't-melt-in-his-mouth banker man.

"So, your boy, believe you said his name was Cal, been goin' over to Tascosa looking to buy a ranch or sheep from some of them *pastores.* Didn't come back. That right?"

"Yes. He was on his third trip. Had no trouble before. Early on, I'd sent a couple of pretty tough fellows with him. I figured everything would be all right after he kinda got his feet on the ground. Figured he'd learned his way around."

Helluva lot different figuring in a bank than figuring in a place like Tascosa. Gotta use a different instrument. Something that can do a whole lot more subtracting than adding. Like a gun!

"So, why are you telling me all this?"

The banker clasped his hands and drew them in against his chest. "Yes. Well. I understand that you traced preacher Clark's wife down."

"Then you know I never brought her

270

back. Preacher tell you that?"

"Yes. Yes, I'm aware of that. But you found her. I hear she ran off on her own. Cal's not like that. He is being held against his will. His mother thinks that, and I do, too. She . . . we want him back."

"And you want me to go get him?"

"Yes."

"What if he's dead?"

"Please don't say that. Even if he is, we still want him back."

"You willing to pay me?"

Damn. Thought you would never get around to that. This old banker has more money than God. He has been sucking money outta poor ranchers like a skeeter drawing blood from a baby lying on a summertime pallet.

"Yes. I will pay you."

"Whatever I ask?"

"Well, within reason. I'm not gonna be held up like I was some . . . Yes, I'll pay whatever you ask."

"I want a hundred dollars 'fore I leave." Frank thought about his past dealings with the banker. "Want it today. Hundred dollars when I get back if I've got your son." The rancher dragged his boot toe through the dirt and made two straight lines. "And I want fifty for every man I have to kill, and if I have to kill a woman, it'll be an extra twenty-five dollars." Frank smudged the lines with his boot. "If I don't bring your boy back alive, I'll still keep the hundred and you'll have to pay me for any killin' I had to do. Won't owe me nothing else."

The banker climbed back up into the buggy, raised the seat again, and removed a packet of bills wrapped in a piece of wagon sheet. He stepped to the ground and counted the bills out on the floor of the buggy. "There," he said. "In my business we always draw up a contract . . . something saying what each party is obligated to do when money changes hands."

Frank Rule glared at the banker, and the man looked away, avoiding the icy stare of the rancher.

Harald Donovan's voice was ragged like a man who needed to swallow, a man whose voice was weak and crippled with stress and anxiety and fear. "But, I don't suppose under these . . . these circumstances . . ."

Frank almost felt pity, not quite, but almost. "I don't know 'zactly what the word circum . . . whatever you said means, but I'll shake your hand, and that's a lot better than my name on a piece of paper."

"Yes, certainly. Of course it is," the banker said after shaking Frank's hand. He fumbled in his duster pocket and withdrew two photographs. "Mrs. Donovan sent these two pictures of Cal. They are a couple of years old. Had them made on a trip down to Oneida. She thought it would aid you in your search. He's our only child, and we miss him. You will be careful and bring him back, won't you?"

Rule nodded. Somewhere out there in the vastness of the Llano Estacado, his own son was a captive. Or perhaps, after these ten years, he had become a Comanchero and adopted the ways of those fierce renegades. Ellen talked about him last night — he was seldom far from Frank's thoughts.

Banker Donovan climbed back into the buggy, pulled his gloves tight, and looked down at the bespectacled, rotund man he had just bargained with to find Cal. He opened his mouth to say something, but then thought better of it — anyway, Frank had stopped listening. The banker turned the buggy around in the scrubby pasture, slapped the reins across the horse's back, and, trailed by a veil-thin cloud of red dust, traveled west.

You could have got a damned sight more money out of him. A whole lot more.

It had taken three miserable days, and he had faced the swirling southwest wind as it ferried sand and tumbleweeds toward lands of the Cherokee Nation. On the second night after the gust settled, twice he imagined he saw a faint twinkling of scattered lights. But he could not be sure because the flatness of the country made estimating distance a fool's game. He squatted before a miserly fire, splurging with a second cup of coffee. Unless his bearings had wandered from the teaching of the army compass, he would reach the confluence of Atascosa Creek and the Canadian River tomorrow. He thought of the wind again and took comfort in knowing, at least, going home it would be at his back. If he got to go home.

He had been to Tascosa two years ago. It was a dusty Panhandle, cattle-trail village, two hundred forty-miles south of Dodge City, a thirty-four-hour, bone-jarring stagecoach trip. *Pastores,* sheepherders from overgrazed New Mexico, brought their herds here to forage in the broad *vegas* and take advantage of the well-watered springs. But the XIT and other large ranches were tiring of sheep and their habit of shearing the grass to ground level and spreading mange. Joseph Glidden's newly perfected barbed wire was spreading like locoweeds across the open range. It took no wise man to forecast that hostilities were imminent.

Tascosa was only three dozen houses strung out on either side of Spring Street, a dirt road that became a loblolly during the infrequent rains. On the east side of town, Charley Patton ran a blacksmith shop and livery stable next door to a laundry and barbershop run by a Negress, Lucy Williams. Across the street, Otis Taylor operated a combined grocery store and mortuary, and just past that, Homer Martin ran a boardinghouse. West of town, the Equity Bar and the Jenkins Saloon, usually inhabited by down-at-the-heels drifters and overnight freighters, sat side by side on the bank of the Canadian River. North of town, a small but growing cemetery squatted on a low hill — Tascosans called it Silent City. A quarter of a mile past that, two houses of ill repute, Jolene's and Bitsy's, were staffed with two dozen women whose looks ranged from kinda ugly to spectacularly ugly. Cowboys without the wherewithal to spend a few minutes savoring the female delights lounged on the whorehouse front porches, playing dominos and telling tales so preposterous that even the most gullible and green cowboy quickly discarded them.

Outside of town and scattered along Atascosa Creek, Mexican shepherds lived in plazas, small collections of native sandstone houses held together with adobe mortar.

An average day in Tascosa was dull; an average night, hair-raising.

To the southwest, the sun faded behind the never-ending horizon. Frank made good time today, mostly because he had gotten an early start. Just before dark last night, he had hobbled Red and the other mule and pitched his bedroll on the bank of a narrow arroyo. He enjoyed sleeping under the stars; it reminded him of the trip up from the New Mexico Territory. He and his wife had slept outside most nights — "communicating with God," Ellen said — while their son and daughter slept in the wagon.

Those good times were gone. Forever. The Indians took those times by killing Ellen and their daughter and kidnapping their son.

In the darkness, Frank fidgeted in his bedroll. He wanted Ellen to come and talk with him. Tell him of their plans, about having neighbors, sending their children to school, monthly trips into town to buy supplies.

But she didn't come. It frightened Frank. What if she never came again?

Restless, he had gotten up before dawn lightened the eastern sky, collected his mules, and headed west.

". . . four bits a night for the mules seems about right," Frank agreed with Charley Patton. "Reckon, you'll throw in free lodging for me in the hayloft?"

"Long as you don't eat no hay," the liveryman said.

Frank laughed. "No, I ain't much on victuals. Hay or any other kind. Gimme a cup of coffee and some bread, I'm good for fifty miles."

Charley opened the lot gate and waited for Frank to lead his mules inside. "You ought to fit right in around here," he said. "You can get food, such as it is, down at Homer Martin's place. But I wouldn't make a habit of it. It'll stunt your growth, I've been told. Some say it'll make your toenails turn black and fall off."

"Don't think I'll be around long enough for that. I've just come down here to get a feller. His daddy got worried about him. Wanted me to bring him back home."

"What's his name?"

Frank took the two photographs from his coat pocket and handed them to Charley. "Name's Donovan. Cal Donovan. You familiar with him?"

"Seen him. Been a while. That's his rig

right over there. His pacing horse threw a shoe. I couldn't get to it right then, so he rented a saddle horse from me. I never saw him again."

"You reckon he skipped out with your horse?"

"No, wadn't that. I still got his rig and horse, lessen, of course, he stole it off somebody and it ain't really his. Anyway, my horse come back. Donovan feller didn't."

"He pay you when he left with your horse?"

"Yep. In advance. And he paid me for shoeing his horse, too. I think he meant to come back."

Don't believe I've ever been hungry enough to eat something that looks like this. You'd be a whole lot better off goin' out on the creek bank and doing your own damn cookin'. Eatin' crawdads and the such.

Frank looked at the stew and mentally agreed. In a way, he had missed Old Scratch. Sometimes, the Devil could be downright funny.

". . . then, I told him, 'sure I'll keep your room a couple of nights.' " Homer Martin was raking crumbs from the table onto the floor, much to the delight of two mice and a half-grown rat obviously getting their share of daily bread.

Frank tried to ignore the rodents now in a wrestling match over a half-eaten sourdough biscuit. "Then . . . he . . . he didn't show up?"

"No, sir. Weekend come and I needed the room. There were a couple of Dodge City freighters wanting a place to sleep. I took Donovan's stuff outta his room and piled it in a shed in the back. Didn't throw 'em out in the street, like most folks would have done."

Frank moved the stew around in the bowl, looking for something he might recognize. "Yeah. I get through eating supper I'll have a look if you don't care."

A pair of custom-made boots, two shirts, leather braces, broad-striped trousers. Two hand-drawn maps, three unsigned deeds, and a half-dozen blank bills of sale for sheep. No gun. No knife. Folded and stuffed down in one leg of the trousers, Frank found a pair of woman's drawers — didn't look like they had ever been worn, but definitely red and definitely silk. He unfolded the underwear and a note fell to the floor: Fifi from Cal.

Whoa. Froggie went a-courtin' and he did

ride. Mhmm. A sword and pistol by his side. Mhmm.

Frank slept well that night as a light rain pattered on the tin roof of the hayloft. The pack of coyotes rejoicing at the edge of the river did not interfere with his rest, nor did the five-shot gunfight at the Equity Bar. At daylight, a screech owl broke out in a quavering call and caused the rancher to leap from the hay burrow and wildly claw for his shotgun.

After rubbing the rheum from the corners of his eyes, Frank climbed down from the loft on a rickety ladder and interrupted Charley Patton's early morning routine of watering the livestock.

"Enough rain last night to settle the dust," the liveryman said.

Frank cleaned his glasses with his shirt-tail. "And I had enough roof to keep me dry. Sure beats sleeping in a bedroll under a mesquite bush. I was young, didn't mind it too much. Gets old pretty quick now."

"You have any luck last night down at Homer's?"

"Not really. Found Cal's clothes. Found out he'd paid two days ahead for a room, then never used it."

Hey, tell him about them fancy drawers. That

280

ought to get the old goat goin'.

"Ain't surprised. Money didn't seem to mean much to him." Charley put a pinch of snuff behind his lower lip. "If I was you, I'd go down to the Equity Bar and the Jenkins Saloon. Show the man's picture around. Jenkins gets most of the cowboys; Equity gets folks that don't talk English. Somebody at one of them two places might have seen him. Getting anything past a bartender is like sneaking daylight past a rooster."

Rusty Jenkins stood behind the long wooden bar reading a two-month-old newspaper. He leaned forward to look at the photos Frank spread before him. "Don't know. Maybe. We get a lot of fellers in here. Some I see only once. He's right ordinary looking, 'cept he is dressed terrible fancy. Wish I could help you, but I can't recollect him right off. Might try over at the Equity. Talk with Badlegs Watson if I was you."

Frank crossed the alley and stepped onto the porch of the Equity Bar. A man in a wheelchair, wearing a dirty apron and a week-old salt-and-pepper beard, sat, arms resting on an overly ample belly. He watched a Mexican scrubbing the floor with soapy water and a stiff brush. He acknowledged Frank, *"Buenos días."*

281

Frank didn't respond.

The wheelchair-man grinned. *"¡Hola! ¿Cómo te va todo?"*

Frank shook his head and extended his hands, palms up.

"Said, good morning." Wheelchair-man smiled and revealed a mouth of picket-fence teeth. "Wouldn't you just know it, sumbitch got shot out here last night? Bled like a stuck hog. If you don't get that blood up 'fore it plumb dries, it'll stain just like oil. Every time it rains and the wood gets wet, blood will show up again. I've seen puke do the same thing."

"Knew that about blood; never heard that 'bout vomit," Frank said.

"Yeah, you run a saloon long as I have, you learn a bunch of stuff like that. Ain't worth nothing, but you learn it anyway. I'd whole lot druther a sumbitch get shot out in the street as inside or even out here on the porch. Not near as messy. You needin' a drink? Little hair of the dog what bit you?"

"No. Too early in the day for me. You Mr. Watson?"

"No, I'm Badlegs. Mr. Watson was my father." After Badlegs finished the joke, he went into a coughing spasm that ended with his face as red as a fall apple.

Frank introduced himself and showed Badlegs the photographs of Cal Donovan. "You seen this man?"

"Can't say as I have. Shore don't look like any customer I can recall. What's he done? Beat you outta money?"

"No, nothing like that. I was just trying to help his daddy out."

Badlegs nudged the Mexican with the wheelchair's footrest. *"Diego, obtenga un balde de agua y enjuague el piso."*

The Mexican nodded and jumped from the porch down onto the packed street.

"Mr. Watson, I'll be around town for a couple of days. You see this man, let me know. I'd sure appreciate it."

The water pump down near the river stopped squeaking, and Diego rounded the corner of the saloon with a wooden bucket. He threw the water across the porch and watched the suds drain onto the red clay.

Badlegs held the photos out for Diego to look at them, *"Sacuda su cabeza."*

The Mexican shook his head, and the saloonkeeper handed the pictures back to Frank. "Mexican ain't seen him either. 'Bout the best I can do for you. Where you stayin'?"

"Down at Charley Patton's."

"You sleeping in the barn?"

Frank nodded.

"Dang!" Badlegs turned the wheelchair and rolled through the swinging doors into the darkness of the saloon.

So, how about that Badlegs Watson feller! Reckon if he'd known we lived on the Rio Grande for twenty-five years, he'd have thought we might speak Spanish just about as well as Diego. Telling that Mexican to deny he'd ever seen Cal Donovan. Humph. We gonna put old Badlegs right at the top of our lying list. He's liable to wind up with something a whole lot worse than blood on his damn porch.

Charley Patton wasn't around the livery. Frank saddled Red and rode northward toward the low hills and the cemetery. Some caring soul had built a picket fence around the graveyard, not to keep the inhabitants in but the sheep and cows out.

Frank tied his mule to the gatepost and then walked through the cemetery. Most graves were unmarked, just low, narrow six-foot-long mounds of dirt covering the remnants of people betrayed by nature or their own carelessness. Judging by the new growth of buffalo grass, he figured that the newest grave was over two months old and wondered if the man shot at the Equity last night might show up later today.

Whoa, let's get outta here. Dead folks give me the willies. I like 'em alive so they can hop around when the fire gets hot. Fact is, I believe I recognized that name on the wood cross at the back of the damn graveyard.

Frank stepped back up into the saddle and followed the dusty road as it cut across the hill toward the whorehouses.

All right! This is more like it.

Perched on sandstone piers, there was little to distinguish the two unpainted houses. Frank chose the one on the left, the one with a bedraggled cowboy sitting on the front steps.

"They ain't open yet," the cowboy said after identifying himself as Cletus from the Lazy Eight ranch. "Women stay up pretty late. Sometimes, Bitsy lets them sleep 'til after dinner. You'll have to come back, or you can sit here with me. Or you can try that 'un over there, Jolene's." Cletus lazily pointed to the house a little higher on the hill. "I'm kinda partial to this 'un. Little redheaded woman, ain't been here more'n six months works here. When I got the money, I see her. She's plumb rowdy, all right. Name's Fifi or something like that. Claims she is a French woman."

285

The cowboy shook his head when Frank showed him the photographs of Cal Donovan.

The front door was open at Jolene's as if welcoming a breeze to come inside and freshen things up a bit. No one waited on the porch. Inside, a tousled blonde-haired woman stood behind a makeshift bar constructed of three rough planks nailed across two wooden sawhorses. She was smoking a cigarette and eating a sandwich constructed of cornbread and fatback.

"Won't be open for another hour," the woman said. "But if you can't wait that long, I might . . ." her words trailed away, but Frank knew what she was saying.

She did not recognize Donovan's likeness.

Hey, not too shabby. Not been in one of these places for a couple of weeks. What say we have a drink and see who else shows up? Don't never hurt to look.

Two women, both dull-eyed and tired, came from behind a bead-curtained doorway, vigorously scratching beneath their wrinkled gowns. No, they hadn't seen him either.

Sit down, Frank. We're not in a hurry. Or, at least, I'm not.

The whore that seemed to have the great-

286

est need to continue scratching followed Frank out onto the porch. "I could get in trouble for this, but . . ." she paused and pried something foreign from under the fingernails of her scratching hand, "but you might want to talk with that feller that chucks the rowdies out over at . . ." She looked toward Bitsy's but did not finish her sentence.

Dang! Looks like we got outta there just in time. I'd have hated to see the next bunch of women that come out from behind that door. Believe, longer they come, worse they was gonna look.

Frank rode past Bitsy's. Nothing had changed: doors still closed, Cletus still sat on the steps — by himself. Frank waved and the cowboy nodded, then touched thumb and forefinger to the front of his wide-brimmed hat.

"So, you finally got around to me." Lucy Williams moved to the single window of her one-room barbershop-laundry and examined the photographs. "You figured a black woman ain't gonna know doodly-squat 'bout what's happening here in Tascosa."

"No. No. It's not that. You was just the last person I come to."

"Um-hum. Yeah, see if you can make me

287

believe that."

Frank took the photos from Lucy. "Not gonna try to make you believe nothing. That's the way it is. You was the last person. You'd been open this morning, you might have been the first person. Look at it this way. Somebody's got to be last. And today, it was you."

"Where you from, mister?"

"Longsought. On further up in the Panhandle."

"I know where that is. Got some kin that lives over there. You know any of the Manesses?"

Frank wrinkled his brow. "No, can't say as I do."

"That's a good answer." Lucy laughed, laced her large fingers together, rotated her hands, extended her arms, and cracked eight knuckles. "All my kin lives up in the Indian Territory, and they named Kizer, not Maness." She laughed again, cheeks billowing like summer clouds and forcing her eyes into slits. "Good to find out you don't lie 'bout little things. Man that'll lie 'bout little things will shorely lie about big things."

Hey, old girl is pretty smart. Might make a good range detective.

"I ain't known for lying," Frank said.

"No, I suppose you ain't. I know your"

young man — man in those pictures — or leastways I've seen him. Did his shirts a couple of times. Even give him a haircut and a shave once."

"How long ago?"

"Um. Twenty-three days ago. It was on a Tuesday."

"How can you remember that?"

Lucy snorted. "Well, I ain't dumb. I got a calendar and I can read. You read?"

Frank nodded. "Enough to get by."

The woman laughed. She was starting to understand the deadpan rancher. "He always paid me a little extra. And he was a clean man. Underwears wadn't never very dirty. Didn't hardly have to boil his shirts none. Just drag 'em over the rubboard couple of times, starch and iron them."

"When was the last time you saw him?"

"Nineteen days ago."

Frank counted the days on his fingers. "That would be a Saturday. I know. You got a calendar and you can read."

"You learn kinda quick for a cowboy from Longsought."

"Reckon I ought to say thank you for that compliment."

Lucy laughed again. "Don't be thanking me too quick."

Frank removed his glasses and huffed

moisture on the lenses. Lucy handed him a clean cloth, and he wiped the dampness away. "You got such a good memory and all, anything happen about that time that was out of the ordinary?"

"Yeah. That big ugly man what keeps order up at Bitsy's brought a shirt in to be mended up and washed. Had couple of right bad-burned places in one sleeve and soot all over it. Liked to have never got it clean."

Frank thought about the whore at Jolene's, what she'd said or almost said. "I'm gonna bet the shirt was bloody, too."

"Dang, mister. For a white man, you're pretty smart."

Frank roused. He was getting accustomed to sleeping in Charley Patton's loft. Somewhere around midnight, gunfire woke him. But he turned in the hay, much like a dog making a bed on a buffalo robe, and went back to sleep. Near dawn, Ellen came and whispered to him. When this first happened, he struggled to wake because he wanted to talk with her — touch her — smell her. But, of course, she wasn't there, and it took days for the sadness to leave. He was smarter now. He enjoyed the dreams and did not try to leave the happiness of sleep when his wife visited.

After checking for scorpions and spiders, he pulled his boots on, then climbed down the shaky ladder to the open hallway of the barn. His mules pricked their ears forward and then watched as he forked hay and took it to their feed rack.

Yesterday, he had left his shotguns and the Henry in the loft wrapped in his bedroll; today he would carry the sawed-off .10-gauge, L.C. Smith double-barrel shotgun. Probably wouldn't need it, but a man can never tell.

In his shop, Charley was stirring the coals of his forge, leather apron already cinched around his narrow shanks. "You up and moving around, Frank Rule? Must have a pure heart to be able to sleep this late. Sun's just about to come up. Figured I'd not start hammering on these horseshoes 'til you come awake. But I was about to get tired of waitin' on you."

" 'Preciate you doing that. Letting me sleep. I'll try to return the favor someday."

"Betcha four-bits that'll never happen." Charley raised his farrier's hammer and struck the anvil; the clean *whannnng* sound rolled out into the freshness of the morning air. "Heard you spent most of yesterday snooping around, visiting whorehouses and the such."

Frank shook his head. "Not what you're thinking — the whorehouse part, I mean."

Charley pulled a cherry-red horseshoe from the forge and eyed its curvature. "Yep. That's what I used to tell my wife when she was alive. 'It ain't what you think, honey, me stopping by the whorehouse and all.' Never made much progress with that kinda tale. She was a hard woman to fool." He waited for that to sink in, then said, "Most of the time."

Frank saddled Red and led him out into the hallway. "What do you know about the man that works up at Bitsy's? Man that keeps things under control."

"His name is Kermit Bricknell. Folks call him Brick. Tough old boy. Throwed a rowdy halfway down the hill the other night. Broke his collarbone and a bunch of ribs. If I had my druthers, I druther be kicked by a mule than hit by Bricknell."

"You think he would kill a man?"

"If the need come about, I believe he would. Quicker 'an a hiccup."

Frank grasped the saddle horn and put his left foot in the stirrup, "Going down to Homer Martin's to get a little bite of breakfast. I'd buy yours."

Charley shoved the horseshoe back in the

coals before looking at Frank. "Not just no but hell no. I ain't gonna eat down there. Rather rassle with Brick than Homer's food."

Frank studied the watery scrambled eggs while Homer Martin rolled a cigarette one-handed and sat on the bench across the table from him. "Guess you heard what happen last night?" Homer said, after he got his cigarette going.

Frank tilted the plate so the liquid drained away from the eggs. "I heard shooting. That's all. Didn't know where or who."

"Over at the Equity. I hear tell, cowboy and a freighter got into it. Freighter died. And to top that, man got stabbed up at Bitsy's. Two dyin' in one night, 'bout average, I reckon."

Frank moved the eggs around on his plate, and they continued draining. "Was they local?"

"No. Freighter was outta Dodge. Man who got killed up at Bitsy's was from the Lazy Eight, big spread over on the New Mexico Territory border."

"Man from the Lazy Eight, was his name Cletus?"

"Dang," Homer said. "How did you know that?"

■ ■ ■ ■

"Just wanted you to understand that you are the second stop I've made today. Didn't want to hurt your tender feelings." Frank stood in the backyard of Lucy's laundry and barbershop and watched the proprietress stir a black pot of sudsy water and clothes with a battling stick. "Reckon you ought to drag a little more fire around the pot, make that water hotter?"

Lucy stopped her stirring, looked at Frank, and mopped the sweat from her brow. "Reckon you ought to go help somebody that be needin' it. I've washed more clothes than you've ever seen."

"I thought everybody washed on Monday."

"Thought wrong. On Mondays, I wash everything that needs washing from Jolene's; Wednesdays everything from Bitsy's; Saturdays, just townfolks' clothes."

Frank moved across the backyard and sat on a wash bench beside a galvanized tub of clean water. "So, this being Wednesday, those clothes are from . . ."

". . . Bitsy's. Maybe you ain't as smart as I thought you was."

"Uh-uh, don't sell me short. I know

there's eight days in a week."

Lucy went back to stirring the clothes. "You full of foolishness this morning, ain't you?"

"Well, let me try this. I'm guessing there's nothing in that pot but sheets and pillowcases — maybe a few washcloths and that many towels. Maybe some women's drawers."

"Yeah, you be pretty right. 'Cept there was something rolled up in the sheets this morning that ain't in the pot."

Frank laughed. "You want me to ask what, don't you?"

Using the battling stick, Lucy lifted a sheet from the boiling pot and dropped it into the tub of fresh water. "Up to you."

"I give up, what was it?"

"Man's shirt. It's soaking in a bucket of cold water in the house."

"And the reason you are soaking it is . . . ?"

"It was bloody."

"It's Bricknell's shirt, isn't it?"

"I believe it is pretty safe to say that, since ain't no man 'cept Brick what lives up there with all them women. One other thing you might ought to know. He carries a nine-inch Bowie knife in a leather sheath cradled against his backbone. Just thought you might want to be acquainted with that."

■ ■ ■ ■

"We ain't open." The voice was distant.

Frank knocked on the door again.

"Told you, dammit, we ain't open." The voice was closer, threatening.

Frank made a fist and pounded on the door, the hammering booming down the hall of the whorehouse like a spring thunderstorm.

The door was violently yanked inward. Brick stood in the entry, pantless, gut hanging over dingy drawers, barefoot, shirtless, hair tousled.

"I told you, dammit, we —" Brick stopped in mid-sentence. Initially, he was surprised that a Tascosan or any other man living in the Panhandle would have the nerve to cause such a disturbance at Bitsy's. The man standing before him wore spectacles and a parson's hat, and would not reach his shoulder in height, but he was broad and thick in his chest and his arms were oversized. And a sawed-off shotgun was clutched in his right hand.

Frank looked up at the man standing in the doorway. "I reckon I need to talk to the person what runs this place."

Brick eyed the shotgun. "Well, I reckon

that would be me."

"No. I don't believe that's right. You're not the owner. You are just a flunky that tries to scare people. Maybe even bust up a still-wet-behind-the-ears cowboy named Cletus."

"You calling me a liar?"

"Yep, 'cause that's what you're doing right here to my very face. Now, I reckon you ought to let me talk with Bitsy. If there is really a woman by that name."

"You are not talking to anybody, 'cept me."

Frank raised the L.C. Smith, cocked both hammers, and jammed the gun barrel into Brick's navel.

"You're not scaring me," Brick said, his sentence ending on a note high as a teen-aged girl.

"Not intending to scare you. Just want you to understand that I'm gonna talk with the woman that owns this place. Now, you may be dead first, but I'm still gonna do it."

Way to go, Frank. Put a charge of buckshot in him. See how tough he is with his guts draggin' on the ground.

Raising his hands to ear level, Brick took a half step backward, and slowly turned his head to the side, "Bits, man here to see you."

■ ■ ■ ■

Unwavering, Frank stared into the woman's face, his eyes reluctant to explore other regions.

Bitsy might have been an attractive woman forty years ago. But most likely, not. In the dim light of the bordello's parlor, she sat on a four-person, stained sofa, smoking a long-stemmed pipe, and drinking from an over-sized cup. Her dingy-red housecoat was featureless except for one pocket bulging with a Remington .41 double-barrel derringer. Buttonholes had expanded to a point they no longer served their intended purpose, so the robe gaped open, revealing tired breasts resting on an ungirded midsection laced with stretch marks.

Damn, Frank. Wished you'd warned me. I'd have stayed outside. If I can't get this outta my mind, I'll not sleep a wink tonight.

"You ain't some kind of preacher, are you?" she said, her voice raspy as the first-of-morning caw of a crow. "Aim to come in here and save souls? Disrupt my business? Cost me money?"

"No. Come trying to find this fellow," Frank said, pulling the two photographs from his coat pocket. He turned so Brick remained in his peripheral vision and extended the pictures toward the woman.

She took the pictures in her arthritic hands and shifted so that the light shown more favorably on Cal's likeness. "Sit down," she nodded toward the end of the sofa, "I don't bite." She did a half-moon grin and revealed pale, toothless gums.

Frank sat and leaned back against the arm of the sofa — he would have liked more distance.

Whoa, reckon how long it's been since she seen a washrag?

Bitsy studied the photos. "Brick, you ever see this fellow?"

Bricknell came from the shadows, briefly looked at the pictures, shook his head, and retreated to wherever he'd been.

Bitsy handed the photos back to Frank. "May have seen him. May not. What's he done?"

"Nothing. I've been employed by his daddy, Harald Donovan, over in Long-sought. I've come to find the young man and take him home."

Bitsy showed Frank the toothless half-moon again. "What does this Harald Donovan do, pray tell, so that he goes about hiring men to hunt other men?"

Frank put the double-barrel shotgun

across his lap and rested his hat over the stock. "I reckon banking, mostly."

"Banking! Well! I don't recall doing business with a banker. Not in a bank, I mean. Had plenty of bankers stop by, stayed an hour or two. Most was customers. One paid to just hide in a closet and peek through a part open door and watch the goings-on. Always found them to be mighty tight with a dollar. This Harald feller, he pay you on the front end?"

"Yeah, some."

"Good. Always a good idea to get the money first. I had a banker try to crawl outta a window one night. Wanted to play, didn't want to pay."

Dang, that's pretty good — Wanted to play, didn't want to pay — I'm gonna remember that.

Bitsy raised the coffee mug over her head, a crooked index finger through the ear of the dangling cup. "Brick, I'm ready for 'nother 'un. Mayhap you hit it a little harder with whiskey this time."

Frowning and staring at Frank, the bouncer crossed the floor with a large, blue enamel coffee pot and refilled Bitsy's cup. He upended a pint of whiskey over the cup, and the bottle gurgled three times before he turned it right-side up.

Bitsy took a drink and shuddered. "This banker, this Harald feller, you think he'd pay to get his son back?"

"No. I don't expect he would. That's my job to get the son back. And I don't pay for what I can do myself."

"Then, I think you might have a problem finding young Mr. Donovan."

Frank stood and placed the flat-brimmed parson's hat on his bald head. "Might be right. But I'll tell you one thing. If I find out that somebody knew where the boy is and didn't tell me — or that something has happened to him — I'm gonna be mighty aggravated. Folks generally pay to see that I'm not aggravated."

Bitsy looked at Frank. "My. My. Do we — Brick and me — take that as a threat?"

"No, ma'am. I don't hold in threatening. Found it to be a waste of everybody's time. Just letting you in on the way things are with me."

The woman ran a finger across the top of her smooth lower gum as if searching for something. "Brick, do you believe this man is trying to scare us?" The investigation was fruitless, so she traced the same route with her tongue.

Frank checked his coat pocket to see if it still contained the photographs. "Not my job to scare folks. I'll be leaving now."

Bitsy hobbled alongside Frank to the door, then watched as he climbed into the saddle and set out down the dusty road toward Tascosa. "Gotta bad feeling we ain't done with him. A bad feeling."

Two hours past midnight, Diego walked from the Equity Bar, a still-dripping mop in one hand and a kerosene lantern in the other. He stood on the porch and waited while Badlegs Watson padlocked the large wooden outer door.

"No later than nine," Badlegs shouted to Diego, although the Mexican was only six feet away. "You better be hearing me. None of this 'My wife was not feeling well' crap. That's getting old."

The dim lantern barely lit the narrow path the Mexican followed along the river. Once it entered a grove of cottonwood trees, the path became almost obscure. It had been a long day, and Diego dreaded the three-mile walk to the shepherd's camp.

"¡Hola!"

Diego had only heard the voice once, but he knew it was the man with the glasses, the man who questioned *el jefe* about the photographs. And he understood the two cold circles pressed against his neck were the business end of a double-barrel shotgun.

"*¿Hablas inglés?*"

"*Sí. Un poco,*" Diego whispered.

"*Bueno.* I'll bet your little bit of English is probably better than my Spanish. I have questions for you, and it is important that you be truthful with me. *¿Entender?*"

"*Sí.* Yes, I understand."

"The man in the picture I showed Watson. You know him, don't you?"

"*Sí,* I mean, yes."

"How?"

"He was *el jugador.*"

"I see. He was a gambler. Will you speak only English if I take the shotgun away from your neck?"

"Yes, it will be easier. I can think more better."

"The man's name is Cal. He gambled at Watson's?"

Diego nodded. "Yes. Many times."

Frank lowered the shotgun and continued, "Poker. Did he play poker?"

"*Sí.* But not very well. He lost his money."

"How much?"

Diego struggled with the answer. "Don't know how much. But it was all. And more."

"Who did he play poker with?"

303

"Señor Watson and sometimes, Señor Brick."

"Brick, that the man who works at Bitsy's?"

"Yes. That one. The big man."

"Is Brick a good player?"

"About the same as . . . the man, Señor Cal."

"Did Brick owe Watson money?"

"Yes. But . . . the man . . . Señor Cal, he owed more."

A light skift of clouds slid across the sky, temporarily shielding the two men from the moon's light.

"Do you know how much he owed?" Frank asked.

"No, but it was many dollars. Señor Watson became very angry. Pointed gun at Señor Cal."

"He shot him?"

The clouds moved on and the moon shown again on Diego's face. "No. But another day he told Señor Brick to take him . . . the man you call Cal . . . away. Kill him."

"Kill him? Watson paid Brick to do this?"

"No. He told Señor Brick that he would not owe him any money if he did this."

"So, Watson cancelled Brick's gambling debt if he would kill Cal?"

"Yes. I think that is the way for you to say it."

On the opposite riverbank, something thirstily lapped water, stopped, then moved almost noiselessly back into the cane thicket.

"Did you see him do it? Kill Cal?"

"No. But they left together one night, and I did not see the man . . . Señor Cal . . . again."

"Ever?"

"No. Never again."

"So, if he killed him, he had to bury him somewhere. You know where his grave is?"

Diego's voice was little more than a whisper. "I do not want your question."

"Oh, you'll answer me. I've got to know. The man who hired me will need to know. Will want to see his son's grave."

"Señor Brick didn't bury him. He took this man, Señor Cal, out to a *barranco* and burned him."

"Burned him in a ravine! What do you mean, he burned him?"

Diego put his hands across his eyes and shuddered. "My brother saw it. He had been to see his *novia* on the other side of the river. He was walking home. Saw Señor Brick wrap a sheep's *cuerpo* around Señor Cal, poured kerosene over them. Set them on fire."

"You've seen the bones?" Frank asked.

"No. The coyote and lobos carried them off."

"Nothing left?"

"Nada. No."

"Diego, do you have a family? Mother? Father? Children?"

"Yes, I have all this."

"Do you swear what you've told me on the heads of your family? And if I find that you have been untruthful, I will kill all your family. But I will let you live so you can be in sorrow for the rest of your days."

The Mexican knelt before Frank Rule and crossed himself. "I swear this on my faith and my *familia.*"

Frank raised the shotgun and placed it against the kneeling man's forehead. "Have you told anyone else about this?"

Diego crossed himself again. "No, señor. Only you."

Frank removed a thin oilskin packet from his pocket. "I want you to have this money. But for you to keep it, you forget that we ever talked. Do you understand what I'm telling you?"

"Yes, I understand."

Frank moved the gun from the Mexican's forehead. "Remember your oath. Don't force me to come back to Tascosa and find you."

I don't know 'bout this. Old Scratch thinks, maybe you should have killed him. Can't trust a Mexican far as you can kick him. You are turning into a namby-pamby, if you ask me, course you haven't asked me anything lately.

The men who ate breakfast at Homer Martin's sat at the table until almost noon, drinking coffee, smoking, and discussing the happenings.

"Two in one night!"

"Yeah. Heard it happens in big towns, Dallas, Fort Worth, Dodge. But, hellfire, for it to happen here in Tascosa, I just don't get it."

"Could have been worse. Good thing for us, Bitsy and her girls all got out."

The oldest man at the table grinned. "Speak for yourself. I ain't had no use for the such in ten years. That kind of women, I mean."

"Hear tell that Fifi got to Brick, but she couldn't rouse 'im. She told the sheriff that Brick's throat might have been cut. Said there was blood, but in all that smoke and runnin' and screamin' and hollerin', she just couldn't be sure."

"Um-hum, I'll bet it was hell among the

307

yearlings. All them whores tryin' to get outta there at the same time. Charley Patton said the roof caved in about two minutes after the building caught on fire."

"Otis Taylor tells that the Equity was roaring like a wintertime fireplace when he got there. Said him and Rusty Jenkins tried to get in but it was just too damn hot. They could see Badlegs, crawling around on the floor, bellowing like a calf that was gettin' pulled down by a pack of wolves. Said his face looked like somebody had beat it with a two-by-four. Then this morning, they found his wheelchair out in the river behind the saloon."

"His wheelchair out in the river! Why, I never saw the man outta that thing. He couldn't walk a step."

"Yeah, strange goings-on. Never had a building burn down, and then have two in one night. But reckon it ain't all bad, we got rid of Badlegs and Brick."

Frank Rule tied the pacing horse and Cal's rig in front of the two-story bank. Inside, Harald Donovan sat at a plain desk in the corner of the lobby. When Frank came in, the banker stood and crossed the wooden floor with long strides, his face expectant as a child anticipating a birthday gift. "You've found Cal!" The banker continued past Frank, opened the door, and stood staring at his son's horse and rig.

Frank shouldered past the banker and stood in the street. "It was . . . it didn't turn out like I'd hoped."

"But you brought him back?"

"No. No, I didn't."

Harald looked in the back of the rig. "This is his rig. That's his clothes."

"Yes, he left the rig with a blacksmith and the clothes at a boardinghouse in Tascosa."

The banker held onto the top of the rig's back wheel, his body slumped, and he stared down at the dusty street. "But you found him, and he'll be coming along later. That's it, be coming along later. Or you carried him by the house, and he is with his mama right now." His words were hopeful, but his voice was not.

"No. Sorry to tell you, your boy is dead."

Donovan moved to Frank and placed his hands on the rancher's shoulders. "Did you see the body?"

Frank pulled away from the banker's grasp and shook his head. "No. I didn't."

"Then you're not sure?"

Frank shook his head again and, this time, looked across the prairie at the buffalo grass swaying from an unseen force. "I'm sure.

You don't need to question me no more. It'll be easier on you if you just take what I'm saying. Let it go at that."

"But his mother will want to —"

"No. Not from me. Make up whatever you want to. Tell her what you think might give her peace. But, you will never have no more proof than my word."

"Then if there's nothing else you will tell me, I guess our business is finished." Harald's lips were tight, thin, and little more than a slash across his face. He turned, gathered his son's clothing from the buggy, and moved toward the bank's door.

"Wait." Frank's voice was so low that Harald was not even sure the rancher had spoken. "You owe me money. A hundred dollars more."

The banker placed his son's clothing back in the buggy. "That's not our deal. You didn't bring our son back. So I don't owe you anything else."

"Yes, you do. Our deal was that if I had to kill a man, I'd get fifty dollars more. I killed two men that needed killin'. That comes to a hundred dollars."

Harald shook his head. "You don't have a contract saying that. This is robbery. I'll not pay it."

Frank stared at the banker. "We shook

hands on the deal. You either pay me the hundred dollars, or I take your lying hand — the one what shook mine — with me."

Panic and fear, the kind a pack rat has just before the rattler strikes, ignited in the banker's eyes. "I would have to make arrangements."

Rule pointed to the bank. "Lots of money in there."

Harald shook his head. "But it's not mine; it's the bank's. I can't just walk in there and scoop up a hundred dollars."

Liar, liar, pants on fire. What's good for a liar? Brimstone and fire. Watch him, Frank. You know how he is with money. Old-man banker is tighter than Dick's hatband.

"Might be true. But you can do it, and you better do it. I'll sit out here on this bench for an hour, 'spect you to come back out with the money. You don't, I'll come inside. I'll have what you owe me. A deal's a deal."

Harald gathered his son's clothes again and, without looking at Frank, went inside the bank, passing no closer to the rancher than necessary. He sat at his desk, opened a drawer, and made notations in a thin leather-bound book. Occasionally he looked through the window, hoping the sturdy, bespectacled man wearing the parson's hat was gone.

I'm keeping my eyes on him. Remember what Bitsy said. "Want to play but don't want to pay." He's just the kind that will try to crawl out through the back window. I'll tell you if he tries that. You can head him off, fill his sorry ass full of buckshot. Make the world a better place and make getting loans a lot easier. Why, I might even be able to get a loan myself.

A teller came from the bank, barely glanced at Frank, and continued his way through the twilight along the wooden sidewalk. One by one, lights in the bank faded and, minutes later, Harald came out, masking his anger by making a great pretense of locking the bank's front door. "Here's your damned money." He shoved a sealed envelope at Frank. "You don't have to count it. It's all there. Don't ever come near me again."

Frank folded the envelope and put it in his coat pocket. "I'll not worry about counting the dollars. It'll all be there or I'll be back. You don't want that. And don't forget, this last time I didn't come to you, you came to me."

Frank stepped up into the saddle and, leading his other mule, turned northward. The wind had shifted and skeletons of dead tumbleweeds came bounding past him. It would be near midnight when he got home and looked after his livestock.

After that, there would be only the empty house filled with memories of Ellen. She had died years ago; it seemed like only yesterday.

He rode through the dusk wondering how much the banker loved his son or even if he loved him at all. He thought about his own son, captive, dead, or perhaps wandering somewhere out on the High Plains. He'd sell his soul for the return of his boy.

You'd sell your soul, would you? What makes you think I don't already own it. Or at least, most of it.

Frank slumped in the saddle, and his eyelids hooded against the blowing sand.

Maybe Ellen would come tonight.

John Neely Davis, a writer of western and Appalachian fiction, lives in Franklin, Tennessee, with his wife, Jayne. His most recent western novel, *The Chapman Legacy,* was released by Five Star in June of 2018.

A Century of the
American Frontier
1875–1885

■ ■ ■ ■

WHEN TULLY CAME
TO TOWN

BY RICHARD PROSCH

■ ■ ■ ■

The sight of Rex Tully standing in the rain-soaked street of Randolph City, his heavy boots and slick denim trousers caked with rust-colored mud, made Smith Oberlin's stomach lurch.

And his heart raced the tick of his pocket watch.

Tully!

Roughneck and loudmouth.

Sneak-thief and womanizer!

The last time Smith had seen him — back in Wyoming — Tully had promised to fill Smith's guts with lead.

What could he want in Randolph City?

Was he looking for Smith?

And why now of all times? With the press broke down and the newspaper facing a deadline.

Smith ducked back into the shadow of Gerty's General Store, tasting the bacon and beans he'd had for lunch across the

319

street at the Stockman's Café, clutching the paper-wrapped package he carried tight to his chest.

Maybe Tully hadn't seen him.

"You okay, Smith?" said Matt Gerty coming around the store's counter behind him.

No.

"Y-yes," said Smith. "Yes, I'm fine."

Smith closed his eyes and breathed deep, letting the familiar smells of the shop slow his pulse. Rich, oiled leather, spicy sawdust and dried fruit — raisins and dates — mixed with the woody smell of assorted nuts in an oak barrel. Over all came the full, warm scent of a spring rain wafting in from the street through windows propped open with cedar dowel sticks.

Smith exhaled, pushing away the fear. Opened his eyes.

The image of Tully, raw-boned and lanky, pockmarked and soaked to the skin, his long mustache drooling over a fat upper lip, was still there.

Eyes squeezed shut, Smith took another few breaths.

His watch clicked away a lazy half-minute, then another.

When he looked again, Smith saw sunshine breaking through the clouds and Gerty hovering at his side.

Outside, the street was empty.

Tully had moved on.

"Good old Gerty," said Smith, clucking his tongue. He put a hand on the older man's shoulder. "I'm quite all right."

"You weren't all right just a minute ago."

"A momentary, ah . . . indigestion."

"Indigestion? Got just the thing." And even as Smith opened his mouth to object, the proprietor slipped behind the tall square counter with its bins of beans and seeds toward a row of brown bottled liniments and glittering cure-alls.

"I'd rather not," said Smith. "I do have a printing press to repair." He held up the just-purchased package. "Mustn't keep old Brownstown waiting."

Smith poked his head out the door once more, eyes darting this way and that. "At least not any more than I have to," he said.

North Street, running east and west in front of Gerty's General, was clear with only a single old-timer tottering out of the café, moving toward the livery stable in the opposite direction of Tully's march.

"If you're sure . . . ?"

Smith made another quick scan and nodded obediently. "Sure as an April shower," he said, half to himself.

Certain that the street was clear, or at least

free of Rex Tully, he squared his shoulders and put a boot to the saturated boardwalk. With a fast wave goodbye, he turned to the left, and, after another quick left, scurried down a row of busy emporiums, watching his reflection in the store windows. Heavy package in hand, his lanky frame, sandy brown crop of hair, and schoolmaster's physique slid past the busy hitching posts and street full of bustling customers.

A pleasant spring Saturday surely brought folks to town.

But why — thought Smith — oh, why did it have to bring Rex Tully?

A man who'd shoot Smith Oberlin on sight.

Smith recalled the last time they'd been together.

A ranch in Wyoming.

There had been a fight. Smith had made a remark about a girl. Tully took offense.

In memory, he heard Tully's warning: "I ever see you again, I'll dump so much lead into your guts you'll sink on dry land."

Two years and a thousand miles ago.

Now here was Rex Tully in Smith's Nebraska hometown.

And today of all days — with the added strain of a broken press crippling the next edition of the *Randolph City Monitor* and

Smith under a deadline to finish his newest story.

Just two steps from Ben Brownstown's two-story frame building, home of Randolph City's only newspaper, Smith's stomach lurched again.

Striding up the street, sloshing through a swirling gray puddle directly toward him, came Rex Tully.

Wearing a gun.

Smith ducked into the *Monitor* office with only seconds to spare.

Through a front window, Smith watched his nemesis pound up the street toward the general store.

"Cowardice?" said Smith. "No, I wouldn't exactly call it that."

He handed Brownstown the iron wrench, now unwrapped, that he'd procured at Gerty's store.

"I'd call it . . . a prudent reluctance to engage the man without all of the facts in hand," he added.

Twisting around the frame of the big printing press, the old publisher snorted as he fit the wrench to a stuck lug nut on a heavy support beam for the middle paper roller. The roller's main bearing was a tangle of metal filings. "Fancy way of sayin' you're

323

scared," said Brownstone.

He gave the wrench a tug with no result.

"I simply want to know why he's in town before engaging him," said Smith.

"You think he's looking for you?"

"I don't know," Smith said. "But it's awfully odd, don't you think? Why here? Why now?"

Brownstown grunted, pulled on the wrench until his face turned the color of fresh beets, then let it fall to the hard wood floor of the office with a clank.

He kicked the machine.

"You'll be the death of me," he told it.

The nut, bent frame, and frozen roller remained stoic and noncommittal.

Brownstown uncurled himself from the monstrosity, stood straight, and wiped his forehead with a grease-covered rag. He kicked the wrench over to Smith.

"You give it a try."

"What? Me?"

"You got your mind too much on this Tully. Not enough on work."

Smith shrugged, retrieved the wrench.

"I mean it," Brownstone continued, "Even if we get this press up and running, you've got that wagon train story to write. How's it coming along?"

"I've done some general research on the

families involved with the Floran wagon train. Traipsed around the prairie some, even followed the trail for some miles across the plains."

"But have you got anything down on paper?"

"Let me give it a go."

Smith snaked through a pair of iron rods and smacked the wrench onto the nut and the clank echoed back from the high ornamental tin ceiling through three lazy belt-driven ceiling fans.

"We don't get this roller spinning, there's no paper this week," said Brownstown, reminding Smith of their predicament.

"Or next week, or the week after," Smith recited in harmony as Brownstown continued on.

"What we really need is a machinist."

"Call Angus Wegner," said Smith.

"Wegner's a blacksmith. I need somebody who knows gears and levers. Somebody who can take this thing apart and put it back together better than we can."

"Funny," said Smith, fumbling again with the wrench. "The best machinist I know is Rex Tully."

"Again with this man? You're obsessed, son."

"I mean it," said Smith, pulling away from

325

the press. "Back in Wyoming, I saw Tully fix everything from wagon wheels to pipe organs. For all his bad habits, the man's got a real knack with tools."

"Would he do it? Would he fix the press?"

"I expect that if the price was right, Rex Tully would try just about anything. And he'd deliver. In that sense he was a fair man."

Brownstown nodded, his mind made up. He handed Smith a blue shop cloth.

"Go find him."

Smith handed back the cloth. "Like hell."

"This machine won't fix itself. And apparently neither can we."

"Ben, please understand."

Brownstown put both hands on Smith's shoulders. "We need to get the press fixed, Smith. Both our livelihoods depend on it."

Smith cleared his throat.

"I understand your fear," said Brownstown. "But if this man can help us, isn't it worth a try?"

The older man's level gaze was unwavering.

Smith answered. "I'll need to arm myself." Then he wagged a finger. "And I'll have you responsible for all of my doctor bills."

"I doubt this fellow would draw on you in broad daylight."

"You don't know Tully."

Smith tossed the cloth aside and walked to his desk where he retrieved a heavy pepperbox pistol.

"Most foolhardy thing I've ever done for this paper," he said. "And mark my words, I've done some foolish things."

Brownstown waved him away with a dismissive left hand. He was already back to studying the broken press.

Pushing the gun into the waistband of his trousers, Smith turned and left the building.

"Rude fella, this man you described," said Bill Carpenter. "Didn't say two words to me." The livery owner adjusted his bent spectacles and straightened his big felt hat, quietly working a plug of tobacco in his cheek. "Can't say I cared for his looks, but his horse is in good shape. Seems well cared for. Just muddy." Carpenter shrugged. "With the rain last night, what can you expect?"

"He didn't say why he was here?"

Carpenter spit into the hay-covered dirt of the livery floor. "Nope."

Smith leaned on the rough oak station next to Carpenter. The livery barn was wide open, with only two equestrian residents in a pair of rear stalls. A black horse that Smith recognized as belonging to the stable.

"The buckskin must be Tully's," he said.

"Yeah, that's the one your stranger rode in on," said Bill, retrieving a broom from its place near the doorframe. "Like I said, he's in good shape. Covered with mud. They both were."

"Any word where he came in from?"

"He didn't tell me. I'd say west. Mud covering him and the horse was red. Wish I could tell you more. He came in with a single canvas bag. Paid me cash for a stall."

Smith toed the dust, drew a question mark, kicked it away.

"For how long?"

"No more than a week. That's just how he put it."

In Smith Oberlin's mind, fear was giving way to curiosity.

"Tell me this," he said. "Did he take the money from a pocket or from the bag?"

"Bag," said Carpenter.

That fit with the man Smith remembered. Tully never carried money on his person.

Carpenter swept a path away from Smith toward a gutter dug into the livery floor. "Paid more than he needed to. Gave me a twenty-dollar piece."

"Did you get the impression he had more where that came from? Did it seem he was carrying much money?"

Carpenter leaned on the broom. "I'd reckon that's a good bet. Heard some jingling when he reached inside the bag."

"A man with a bag full of money might not want to carry it around," said Smith.

"Hotel would be your next obvious stop." Carpenter chuckled. "But, hell. If I had that much money, I'd take it to the bank."

Smith grinned and reached out to shake Carpenter's hand. "Thanks, Bill," he said. "I owe you one."

Back on the street, Smith followed Bill Carpenter's suggestion.

From the general store, Smith had seen Tully muddy and wet from his ride. Not at all a man who'd checked into a hotel and had a chance to dry off.

Neither had he carried a canvas bag like Carpenter had described.

Maybe he *had* stopped at the bank.

Keeping an eye over his shoulder, he made it to the Randolph City Savings and Loan.

Inside the clean room with its white-washed walls and walnut trim, Melvin Russell invited Smith to join him at the rear of the bank beside his desk.

"I really shouldn't," said Smith. "I've just been to the livery and my shoes are rather dirty. No sense me tracking up the place."

Russell rose from behind his desk, and stroked his bushy white mustache.

"You're a considerate man, Mr. Oberlin, quite considerate. Why, I was just telling Mr. Brownstown the other day how fortunate we are to have you in Randolph City."

"Thanks, I —"

"No, no," said Russell. "The thanks are mine. And ours — all of us that call this little oasis on the prairie home. Now," he said with both hands on the counter. "How can we help you?"

"I'm looking for a gentleman who may have been in here today. Drooping mustache, muddy attire —"

"Looking for a gentleman? Why didn't you say so?" Russell winked. "Of course, I can't divulge anything confidential, but we'll do our best to help out one of Randolph City's favorite sons."

"That's dandy," said Smith, cocking an eyebrow. "I think."

"Oh, think nothing of it. Nothing indeed. Can I get you a coffee? Perhaps a cookie? Mrs. McCallum recently brought in a tin, and well — I believe she's still in back." Russell turned and called through a rear door. "Meg? Bring Smith Oberlin one of your cookies and some coffee from the stove."

330

Smith chewed his bottom lip. Russell had always been friendly enough when crossing paths with Smith, but the two weren't exactly friends. Since this was the most words they had ever traded, Smith couldn't help wondering why the banker was treating him so well.

From a back room, rolled the widow McCallum as though on wheels. Dressed in her Sunday best and carrying a pink parasol against the rain, the woman had nothing better to do than pass the time of day wherever gossip led, the bank, post office or *Monitor* building.

So Smith wasn't surprised to see her.

Wherever the laundry was aired, Meg McCallum was there.

"Sweets for the sweet," she sang, dumping two penny-size cookies onto the counter.

"Oops, I forgot the coffee." She returned to the back room.

Smith glanced at the clock on the wall above the counter, then took in Russell's smiling gaze.

A notepad, inkwell, and pen lay at odd angles to one another on the counter.

"This man, Tully, you see —"

"Let's wait for that coffee," said Russell.

"You have an admirable commitment to hospitality," said Smith.

"Anything for our good citizens, Mr. Oberlin. May I call you Smith?"

He nudged the pen and pad, lining them up with the inkwell.

When Meg McCallum returned, two tin cups in hand, she gave one to Russell and the other she placed carefully on the counter before Smith.

"You boys just go about your business," she said.

"How can I help you?" said Russell.

Before he could be again interrupted, Smith gave them Tully's description, then told them about Bill Carpenter's twenty-dollar coin and the warbag. "Sound familiar?" he asked.

Russell cleared his throat.

"Well, naturally, sir," he said. "Naturally."

Smith drummed his fingers on the counter.

"So you admit he's a customer?"

"I admit a man matching your description was here just before lunch, opened an account, and that he seemed amiable in nature."

"He was wearing a gun, wasn't he?" said Smith. "Did that seem amiable to you?"

"A lot of good men wear guns, Mr. Oberlin." Russell leaned over the counter, peering down at Smith's waistband where the

332

butt of the pepperbox was plainly visible.

Smith drummed his fingers some more.

"So he didn't give his name?"

"I'm sure you know his name." Russell slurped from his cup and set it down.

"You seem to think I know more than I do about the man's business."

"And why not?" said Russell. "He gave your name as a reference for his deposit."

Smith sat back on his heels.

"He didn't seem so amiable to me," said Meg.

"Why don't you get us some more cookies, Meg," said Russell.

"And of course, you know about the girl," said Meg.

"I don't think that's relevant to Mr. Oberlin's interests," said Russell with a stern voice.

"Why not? This stranger, whatever his name is, asked us directly about the girl. I wouldn't consider that part confidential."

Smith knew there wasn't much Meg McCallum considered truly confidential.

He took the bait and ran with it.

"What did he say, Mrs. McCallum?"

"He asked if we had the acquaintance of a young woman named Lynn."

"No last name?"

"Lynn Bertrand," said Mrs. McCallum.

"And do we?" said Smith.

"We most definitely do not," said Russell. For some reason, the subject seemed to be making the banker more nervous by the minute. "If you won't get those cookies, I will," he said, leaving the counter.

Meg McCallum leaned over into the space Russell vacated. Cupping her hand to her mouth, her words came to Smith in a knowing hiss.

"We got the impression that young Lynn Bertrand is a girl in trouble," she said.

"Ooohh," Smith whispered back. That explained the banker's attack of the nerves. "But why is the old man being so nice to me?"

"Like we said, the stranger used your name as a reference when he opened the account," said Meg, still whispering. "Why, he deposited nearly twenty-five-thousand dollars!"

Smith returned to the street, determination nipping his heels.

The newspaper man shoved aside the fearful boy.

There was a story here, and Smith wanted to get to the bottom of it.

Rex Tully was driven by money and women.

Twenty-five-thousand dollars was a lot of money.

The other element seemed to be this girl, Lynn Bertrand.

No, Smith corrected himself. This *troubled* girl.

He followed a hunch and walked straight to Betty Fischer's Boarding House.

As it turned out, the madame was in.

Dressed in a cool blue satin dress that hugged every curve, Betty Fischer's greeting was a breath of evening shadow. Her long, ebony hair a nighttime contrast to its resting place of sunlit bare shoulders.

Betty always tried to fluster young Smith, but he gave as good as he got.

"You changed the color of your hair?" he said.

"I don't think so."

Smith snapped his fingers. "Must've been a different girl."

"Probably those naughty tintypes you boys pass around on poker night."

"Betty, I need your help," said Smith, abruptly all business.

"I've waited weeks for you to realize it."

"I'm looking for a man."

Betty rolled her eyes. "That could be arranged. But I must say, I'm surprised."

Smith stepped in close enough to smell

335

Betty's heady lavender perfume.

"Betty," he whispered. "A man who might've been here. A stranger asking questions."

"No men here today except the usual."

"Big fellow," said Smith. "Long, unkempt mustache. Wearing a gun."

Betty smiled. "A dream walking."

"Melvin Russell gave me the impression he left a large sum of cash with the bank today."

"How large?"

"Pretty big."

"When it comes to size, Melvin tends to exaggerate. Believe me." Betty wrapped a lock of hair around her index finger.

"He's not exaggerating, Betty."

"I don't think — Wait!"

"Yes?"

"This big money man, was he covered in mud? Like he just came in off the prairie?"

"He was," said Smith.

"Then he *was* here," said Betty. "I barely noticed because I was doing some cleanup in back, but he came in and I overheard him ask one of the girls about somebody named Lynn."

"He asked about Lynn?"

"I thought that's what I heard?" said

Betty. "Does the name mean anything to you?"

"It might."

"The way he said it was like he was real eager to find her." Betty lowered her voice. "Like he was desperate."

"Did you hear anything else?"

"Apparently this Lynn was . . . well . . ."

Her words trailed off, and Smith cocked his head.

"What, Betty?"

"He said it like she was more than a friend, and he made it pretty clear that's the case."

"How so?"

"Apparently Lynn is . . . in a family way." Betty smiled with mischief. "If you get my meaning."

"I get your meaning, indeed," said Smith. "And it's silly for you of all people to be coy."

"He left in a real hurry," said Betty.

"Did he say where he was going?"

She shook her head. "No."

"And you don't know where Miss Lynn might be?"

Betty shook her head. "I don't know anybody named Lynn. Neither do the girls. I wish I could be more help."

For a brief moment Smith questioned her

with his eyes. He'd come to Betty's boarding house because of her reputation for helping lost souls.

But he sensed she was telling the truth about Lynn Bertrand.

Smith bent and kissed Betty's cheek.

"You've been a great deal of help," said Smith.

"Come back," Betty whispered, "when you're not looking for a man."

On the street again, moving back in the direction of the newspaper office, Smith reviewed the situation.

It wasn't unlike a news story, or even one of the many wild western tales he'd read in the periodicals published back east.

Of course, such sordid details as had obviously befallen Tully were usually smoothed over for the readers' delicate tastes.

Apparently, Big Rex Tully, the boasting philanderer, had made one conquest too many.

The poor recipient of trouble, this girl called Lynn, had fled the region as so many are forced to do. She could have traveled in any direction, but perhaps with summer coming on, she came to Nebraska where there'd be plenty of seasonal kitchen and garden work.

Now Tully was on her trail . . . with

twenty-five-thousand dollars.

Smith wondered why.

To help or to hinder?

To redeem the girl's honor, and perhaps salvage his own?

Or to force her into final silence?

As in any narrative, he needed to take the next step.

He marched straight to the courthouse, halfway hoping now that he'd meet Tully head-on.

But it didn't happen.

He did, however, get all the answers he needed.

And it left him feeling like a heel.

Out of breath from an all-out run up the boardwalk, Smith pushed open the *Monitor* office door with a fast shove and almost tripped on the threshold.

"Brownstown," he cried. "We've got to find Rex Tully."

But before he could finish, a crusty rasp of a voice cut him off.

"Smith Oberlin?"

Instinctively, Smith reached for the pepperbox, pulled it from his waistband, and swung it around in the direction of Rex Tully.

The man was crouched beside the printing press, surrounded by tools and miscellaneous parts. His fist clamped around a polished Colt revolver, he issued a stern warning.

"Drop the peashooter, Smith."

Smith's eyes held Tully's gaze; he didn't lower his gun.

Tully had aged in the two years since Smith had seen him last. Or maybe it was just that he was still covered in drying mud.

But no, Smith thought, the eyes were tired, the beard and mustache more unkempt than ever.

"I know why you're here," said Smith.

"Back in Wyoming," said Tully, "I gave you a warning. Do you remember?"

"You said the next time we met, you'd fill my guts with lead."

"I meant it."

"What's it about, this beef between the two of you?" said Brownstown.

"I've got the information you want," said Smith.

Tully blinked.

"Isn't that why you're here at the newspaper office? After covering half of Randolph City asking about Lynn Bertrand? Isn't there still something you're looking for?"

"Lower your guns, both of you," Brownstown said.

"Smith and me used to work on a ranch together," said Tully. "He was always making the smart remark. The know-it-all comment."

Smith smiled. "I can't exactly deny it."

"One day he made a comment about my family. My sister."

"In fairness, I never met the girl." Smith rolled his eyes. "It was a general insult leveled at the man's family."

"At the women in my family."

"All right, yes, fine." Smith shrugged. "I was angry. We both were."

"I'm asking you both — for the last time — to put down your weapons."

"You shoot me," said Smith, "and you'll never find what you're looking for."

"I'll take my chances."

But even as Tully began to squeeze the trigger, Brownstown brought the wrench down hard on the man's wrist.

The six-shooter clattered across the floor.

"Doggone, it! You sonnuva —" Tully rolled ahead, holding his arm and whining,

Smith walked forward, keeping the pepperbox straight out in front of him.

"Now," said Smith. "Let's make another deal."

"That's enough, Smith," said Brownstown. "He's no danger to you now."

Tully rolled onto his knees, sat back rubbing his wrist. "I'd rather deal with the devil."

"What makes you think you aren't?" said Smith, lowering his gun. He tossed the pepperbox onto his desk and placed both hands on his hips while he examined the printing press.

For once, Tully kept quiet.

"You were always quite the machinist, Tully. Back in Wyoming, you could fix anything. I want you to fix Mr. Brownstown's press."

Tully cursed under his breath, then said. "What's in it for me?"

"I told you. I know why you're here in Randolph City. I know about Lynn Bertrand. Fix the press, and I'll take you to her."

Wide eyed, Tully stammered. "Y-you know about Lynn. How?"

"Who's this Lynn?" said Brownstown.

Smith picked up Tully's gun and tossed it onto his desk where it landed beside his pepperbox.

"Lynn is Mr. Tully's sister," said Smith, putting his hand out to Tully. "And in the past half hour, I've gotten to know her quite well."

"I don't understand," said Tully.

"I'm sorry," said Smith. "For my slur back in Wyoming. For my terrible, terrible words. I apologize."

Tully let Smith help him up.

"I was wrong, Tully. Your sister was the best of us all."

After Tully got the press working, Ben Brownstown stayed at the *Monitor* office while Smith and Tully rode the black gelding and the buckskin stallion five miles northeast of town.

Smith followed the signs he'd left during his study of the Floran wagon train, bringing them through wet creeks and sharp hedgerows of multiflora rose and Russian thistles.

On a high hill under a clear blue sky, he reined in his horse and invited Tully to dismount.

They walked a few yards to the summit where several yards of spring grass were fenced off with wood pickets.

They walked through the cemetery gate.

Among several squares of flint embedded into the topsoil, one was of interest to the men.

Madelynn Bertrand. Born 1853 Died 1873

Tully's eyes were red and his jaw clenched

and unclenched.

He looked at Smith.

Smith nodded and Tully knelt down, brushing the marker with his fingers.

"She came to town with the Floran wagon train," said Smith.

"I knew that much myself," said Tully. "I just didn't know where she was."

"The money you brought along," said Smith. "It was for her?"

Tully nodded. "An inheritance. Our old dad died back in Illinois. It was up to me to divvy things up. Last letter I got from Lynn said her and her husband, Jan, was here, near the little settlement of Randolph City."

"Not so little now. It's growing."

"I thought I'd find her alive."

"The Floran train passed through here in late August on their way west — woefully behind schedule. Lynn was with child, having a rough go of it. She and her husband, Jan Bertrand, made camp here with a local settler and his wife, hoping that bed rest would cure all. Sadly, she and the child both passed."

"How did you know where she was?"

"Once I saw her name in the locals records of the deceased, with you listed as her brother, I made the connection with the burial place."

Tully stood.

"One question," said Smith. "Why did you give banker Russell my name as a reference?"

Tully chuckled. "Better the devil you know," he said. "When I said the account was for the family of Jan Bertrand, the banker didn't recognize the name."

"There's nobody in Randolph City with that name now."

"So after Lynn passed, Jan went back to the wagon party?"

"Or just simply left town. No way to know where he is now."

"Anyhow, Smith, I knew you were in Randolph City," said Tully. "Some of the boys at the ranch still read that crap you write for the story magazines. They sort of keep up with you."

"Tell them I appreciate that," said Smith.

"Send 'em a wire if you want." Tully slapped Smith on the back. "I can't tell 'em."

"You can't?"

"Hell, Smith. What little I been in Randolph City, I like it here."

"You do?"

For the first time in two years, Smith saw Tully smile the big, obnoxious tooth-filled smile he'd learned to be wary of.

"I'll be putting down roots here," he said. "I'm staying."

Smith swallowed hard.

At least we'll have a reliable press man, he thought.

"Now," said Tully, turning away from the grave. "Tell me more about this Betty Fischer and her boarding house."

Or, thought Smith, maybe we won't.

After growing up on a Nebraska farm, **Richard Prosch** worked as a professional writer and artist in Wyoming and South Carolina. In 2016, Richard won the Spur Award for short fiction given by Western Writers of America. He lives in Missouri with his family. Visit him online at Richard Prosch.com.

■ ■ ■ ■

THE CAVES OF VESPER MOUNTAIN

BY GREG HUNT

■ ■ ■ ■

It was dusk now, and the thick ominous clouds above promised more bad weather on its way. Ridge Parkman knew he would soon have to find someplace to hunker down overnight, whether or not his companion returned from his latest scouting excursion or not. But surely, they would at least be able to find each other in the morning.

Making up his mind at last, he turned his horse off the road and up the cut of a shallow, half-frozen creek. General Grant was a husky, sure-footed animal, and found purchase on the stony ground even though the light was nearly gone. A couple of hundred yards into the forest, he found a spot where a wide slab of rock extended out over a flat patch of dry ground. It was tall enough to shelter the General and promised some protection from the stiff wind blowing in from the west. It would have to do.

He gathered a couple of armloads of

deadfall to build a small fire, then unsaddled General Grant and laid out his bedroll in a niche toward the back of the overhang. The fire might be a bad idea, but he had been yearning for a hot cup of coffee for the past few frigid hours, and decided it was worth the risk.

Since midday yesterday when this escapade started, not a dang thing had gone his way. He had been up in Springfield at the time, testifying against a woman-stealer he had chased to ground, and was looking forward to a hot meal and a warm hotel bed before heading back north. But then the telegram from Captain Wooten in Kansas City arrived, dispatching him south to Cable Springs, where a rowdy gang of heathens had raided the town. The captain had made it clear that he didn't want to set eyes on Marshal Ridge Parkman again until the leader of the gang, Jethro Swope, was swinging from a rope or otherwise out of business permanently.

Parkman made the twenty-mile ride south that same day.

Everything continued to run foul when he reached Cable Springs, starting with a past-his-prime town marshal named Tom Brigance in Cable Springs who wasn't about to round up a posse and take out after the gang who had just robbed their bank, ravaged several other businesses in town, and left five corpses in their wake — four citizens and one yellow dog. Still, Parkman understood the marshal's take on things. The last time Jethro Swope's outfit raided the town two years before, Brigance had mustered what manpower he could, and lit out on their trail. But they never did come close to catching a single outlaw because of the shoot-and-run ambushes that Swope had strung out behind to discourage any pursuit. Even two or three men with rifles could slow down a posse several times their number, then dissolve into the woods before anything could be done about it.

After that chase, Brigance had returned to town three days later with two of his men dead across their saddles, and two more bloodied. This time, chances were slim that anyone would be eager to saddle up and ride out again, even if the town marshal had wanted to, which he didn't. By the time a U.S. marshal showed up, Ridge Parkman in particular, Brigance was relieved to back away and let a federal lawman carry the water.

When Parkman realized that he would be riding out alone this time, the plan he came up with was simple enough. Cut off the head. He'd do his best to quietly track Swope until he went to ground with few or none of his men still around, then kill or capture him, as circumstances allowed. Afterward, local lawmen could deal with the remaining members of Swope's gang, or not, as they saw fit. And that would have to satisfy the captain's orders.

At the last minute, a man named Mel Carroll, a lean, somber character, a local farmer with a hard, determined look but little to say, had volunteered to come along, explaining that he intended to hound Jethro Swope to the grave whether or not Parkman wanted to partner up with him. Carroll knew the territory here in the mountains of southwest Missouri well, whereas Parkman did not, and Carroll's brother-in-law had been shot dead during the raid. Parkman welcomed the help. He offered to swear Carroll in as a deputy, but Carroll said that a badge on his chest wouldn't make any difference to him.

When they left Cable Springs, the day was pleasant enough for early February, but Carroll was already talking about worse weather on the way. Later in the day, as they probed deeper into the remote, hilly territory south of the town, thick gray clouds began to roll in and the storm hit. It started with a steady rain that froze on everything it touched and kept the forested hills filled with the brittle noise of crackling tree branches. Next came the hail, big round chunks that hurt when they whacked a man and kept the horses spooked. The snow came finally, blowing and swirling in from the west, not stopping until it layered several inches on top of the ice and hail.

Mel Carroll had spent most of the time scouting ahead, knowing that any men that Swope left behind weren't likely to ambush a single rider when they were expecting a full-out posse to come riding down the road at any time. But there had been no ambushes so far. Parkman figured that by now, three days after the raid, Swope was probably feeling secure in the knowledge that even if there had been a posse behind him, they were already on their way back home. But Parkman and Carroll were still cautious.

The iron pot of beans and jerky was nearly ready to eat when Parkman heard the distant crunch of horse's hooves breaking through the ice of the creek, coming from the same direction he had ridden. He was pretty sure of who it was, but still slipped into a cluster of brush, beyond the light of the fire.

"That fire sure is a welcome sight, Marshal," Mel Carroll called out from the darkness nearby.

"And so are you, Mel," Parkman said. He uncocked the hammer of his Colt and holstered it as he returned to the fire. "The coffee's boiled, and there's beans a'plenty if you can stomach my cooking."

Over supper, Carroll began to tell Parkman what he had discovered farther down the road. "The snow had pretty much covered up all the tracks on the road, but I did find a place a mile or two down where it looked like six or eight horses had cut off into the forest."

"There was twelve or fifteen of them back in Cable Springs, so the town marshal said. If there's only half that many left, Swope must be splitting up his gang," Parkman said. "He's an old bushwhacker from back in the war, and that's how Quantrill used to do it when the Bluecoats were after him. Sometimes he'd even peel away on his own and let the Yankees ride on after the rest of his band."

"They seem to be heading southeast into some rugged territory that stretches all the way down into Arkansas. Those mountains would be a good place to hole up 'til they see if anybody's still after them."

354

"Maybe Swope will get cocky and careless if he decided he got away clean."

"And then comes our turn," Carroll said, spitting into the fire.

It was late afternoon the next day when all hell broke loose for the first time.

The tracks they had been following since they left the road that morning became clearer as they rode along on a game trail deep into the foothills of the mountains ahead. These Ozark Mountains weren't as tall and ragged as the Rockies and the other high-country ranges Parkman had traveled through out west, but they sure were as rugged, and the trails were just as steep and twisting.

When they heard voices ahead, on the other side of a jumble of ragged boulders, both halted their horses, dismounted, and readied their weapons. The voices continued, indicating that their preparations hadn't been heard. One of the men up ahead was moaning and cursing, obviously in pain, and another one seemed to be trying to convince him that he'd be okay.

Parkman and Carroll talked in whispers. "Just two of them, you figure?" Carroll asked.

"Just two talking," Parkman answered in a

low voice. "But there could be others. With all of that yowling, one of them must be hurt for sure. Let's go at them from two sides, and maybe we'll be lucky enough to take at least one of them alive."

"Suits me."

"Do you want one of these?" Parkman asked, raising his Colt. "I've got an extra in my saddlebag."

"I'm used to this scattergun. It clears a wide swath, and I can reload faster than you'd think."

As Carroll slipped around the edge of the jumble of rocks to the right, Parkman eased forward along the trail as far as he dared go without being seen. Then, when he figured he had given his companion time enough to get in place, he leaned his head and his revolver far enough around a boulder to cover the small clearing where the men were.

The man who had been cussing and complaining lay on his back, with one leg twisted unnaturally. Another man knelt beside him, and a third one remained mounted on the far side of the clearing. Two horses waited nearby, one favoring a front leg.

"We can do it the easy way, fellows," Parkman called out gruffly, "as long as you don't try to fill your hands."

But there was no easy way for men like these. They knew that if they were taken alive, nothing but a dancing loop of rope waited for them back in Cable Springs. The kneeling man was the first to take a chance, but a blast from Carroll's shotgun and a .45 slug from Parkman both found him about the same time. The mounted man slapped his heels into his horse's flanks, and the animal bolted away into the brush. Parkman slung a couple of wild shots in that general direction, but it wasn't until Carroll emptied his second barrel that the escaping man let out with a surprised yip. Jittery by then, the other two horses galloped away behind the escapee.

The remaining outlaw, still prostrate on the ground, had been fumbling around trying to lay a hand on his pistol, but it must have fallen out of his holster when he went down. Parkman saw it a few feet away, then walked over and kicked it a little farther.

"Damned if you don't look familiar. Your name's Parkman, ain't it?" the injured man said, ignoring his pain for a moment. "I knew you and your kinfolk too up north of Independence. I rode with some of them in Quantrill's bunch, back during the rebellion."

357

Parkman stepped closer to get a better look. "Gillum, isn't it? Something Gillum? I recall we did meet a couple of times."

"Claude Gillum," the man said, seeming to see a sliver of hope in the middle of this mess. "I rode with your cousins, John and Daniel, for two years, right up to the last hurrah outside Westport, and then for a little while after with the James brothers."

"I remember," Parkman said coldly. "But all that doesn't buy you any favors, Gillum. Not after what you and the rest of Swope's bunch did up there in Cable Springs."

"I didn't hurt nobody," Gillum said. "I was guarding the far end of town while all the shooting was going on, and I never broke leather."

"You're a lying dog," Carroll growled, feeding two fresh loads into his shotgun as he walked over to them. "I seen you out front of the bank. I can't say you're the one who shot my brother-in-law, but I can testify that I saw you with a smoking gun in your hand."

"There's not much we can do for you, Claude," Parkman said. "But if you'll tell us where Jethro Swope is heading, we'll build you a fire and leave you some food before we ride on."

"I ain't the kind to do something lowdown

like that to a compadre like Jethro Swope," the injured man said defiantly. "And anyway, I don't fancy hobbling around the rest of my life on only one good leg. I'd druther wait in hell for a hunnert years for the two of you to show up than . . ."

The blast of Carroll's shotgun interrupted whatever solemn vow Gillum was about to make. Parkman snapped his head around to his companion, hardly prepared for such a sudden execution.

"There's a druther for you," Carroll said, sending a squirt of tobacco juice down on the dead man's face. He stepped forward and pulled the dead man's hand from under his side, revealing to Parkman the small hideout gun Gillum had been trying to put into play. Then, without saying more, he turned and crossed the clearing to the spot where the third man had escaped. Carroll disappeared into the brush for a couple of minutes, then came back to report as they mounted up.

"There's a few drops of blood on the leaves alongside the trail, so I guess we stung him at least."

"But not bad enough to knock him out of the saddle."

"Nope. But maybe if his horse caught some of that buckshot, it'll slow them down

359

a bit."

like that to a comrade like Jethro Swope," the injured man said defiantly. "And any-

Jethro Swope had put together a comfortable little nest for himself a dozen steps back into the cave, and was looking forward to the best night's sleep he'd had since before the raid. With a fire nearby to keep him almost warm, he was leaning back against his saddle, and had his blanket spread across his legs. He held a revolver in one hand, and a half-full wine bottle in the other. Most of his men had gone for the whiskey when they raided the saloon in Cable Springs, but Swope favored the luxury of wine when he could get his hands on some.

He raised his pistol when he heard voices outside the cave entrance where the sentries were posted, then rested it back down on the blanket when he realized there was no excitement or any hint of danger in the conversation. It was probably just Gillum and his bunch coming back to report, he thought. And he felt confident that the news would be good. Between the snow that covered their backtrail, the misery of the cold, harsh nights, and the rugged country they were heading into, he figured that any posse that came after them was already on their way back to town. But then, maybe there never had been a posse, he thought with a crooked grin, not after the lesson his gang had taught them the last time.

Swope lifted the wine bottle to his mouth and took a swallow as he watched two figures enter the cave and walk toward him. He was disappointed to see that neither of them was Claude Gillum, his longtime friend. The man on the right was Abel Branch, his second in command, and the other was one of the three men he had sent out that morning to scout the trail behind them. It couldn't be a good sign that Gillum was nowhere in sight.

The man approaching with Abel Branch had a pronounced limp, and his right arm dangled at his side like a worthless appendage. His shoulders sagged and his hat was missing.

"Spankler's got some bad news to deliver," Branch announced. "Seems like Gillum and Kane both got shot up a few hours ago back down the trail. Spankler here caught a scattering of buckshot, but he got away."

"And the buckshot hit you in the backside?" Swope asked gruffly. "Why not in the front?"

"After I emptied my gun, I had to hightail it out of there or I'd have gone down too," Spankler explained. "There was just too many of them. Six or eight, maybe, and prob'ly more back down the trail. They caught us plumb off guard."

"Wasn't it supposed to be the other way around, peabrain? Didn't I tell the three of you that if you saw a posse coming up the trail, you were supposed to pick off a few of them with your rifles, and then scatter into the woods? So how in hell did they manage to ambush you instead?"

"We would've done like you said, Mister Swope. But things was already going bad even before they jumped us." Spankler was so jittery that his hands were shaking and his high-strung voice was a sure sign that he was lying his way through this whole tale. "Claude's horse twisted a hoof on the rocks, and when he went down, he fell right on top of Claude's leg. That leg was mashed like a fritter, and Claude took to squalling 'cause of the pain. The posse was not far back, and I guess that's how they knew we were there. They came in shooting, and we fought them off for a while, but there was just too many of them."

"And that's how you caught that buckshot in your hind end? By fighting them off?" By then, Swope was so aggravated and frustrated that he considered just dropping this inbred moron where he stood. He felt like it might almost be an act of mercy but he knew the rest of the men in his gang would frown on it. Bloody Bill used to get away with such things once in a while . . . but that was then, and he wasn't Bloody Bill Anderson.

"So, when you hightailed it, the first thing you did was head straight here so that posse would have a fresh trail to follow in the morning?"

"I figured you might want to know," Spankler mumbled, seeming to realize his own mistake even as he spoke.

As Spankler stumbled away Swope noticed the bloody scattering of buckshot wounds across his back and right arm. Branch sat down on the ground near Swope and pulled a small brown bottle out of his coat pocket. He was a rotgut man.

"I guess we'll have to hightail it," Branch said.

"Looks like it," Swope agreed. "At first light for sure, or maybe even earlier if the moon comes up and the clouds don't hide it. I'll pay the other men off in a while, and tell them to scatter in the winds. That might keep the posse confused long enough for us to get lost deeper into the mountains."

"Yeah, maybe." There was no confidence in Branch's voice.

After a while, Jethro Swope wandered to the edge of the rock-strewn clearing outside the mouth of the cave to settle his nerves. An uneasy feeling plagued him, the kind of feeling that experience had taught him to heed. Maybe it was finally time to get out of this business and head out to California, like he'd been thinking about doing for years. All it took was just to do it, but there was always that nagging thought that he needed to put together just a little bigger stake to make a good start out west.

This wasn't like the old days. He could still put together a big enough crew to take over a remote little berg like Cable Springs for a short time, but it wasn't like it once had been, back during the war when the bushwhackers rode out by the hundreds. He had been at Lawrence and Centralia when they thundered into town like avenging devils, taking what they wanted, killing who they wanted, and leaving only chaos, corpses, and towering blazes in their wake. He was just a common thief and a hunted criminal now, with no claim to a higher cause behind what he did.

Everything seemed wrong about how the Cable Springs raid unfolded, starting with the caliber of the men he rounded up for the job. The best never showed up anymore, men he could trust, men who knew what it was like to live by the way of the gun. Now it was the weasels and scalawags and morons who answered his call, men like that cowardly fool Spankler, who wouldn't have lasted a week riding under the black flag of Bill Quantrill or Bloody Bill Anderson.

Then there was the nearly empty vault in the Cable Springs Savings and Investor's Bank, which he had counted on for ten thousand dollars or more to make this whole enterprise worth the time and effort it took to put together. Once he paid off his motley band, there would scarcely be enough left to cover his expenses and keep him fed for the next few months.

He was almost embarrassed by the pointless savagery of a few of his men. It was one thing to shoot it out with other armed men, but there had been no resistance in Cable Springs this go-around. So why had there been a scattering of dead and wounded in the bank and in the streets when they rode away? He thought bitterly that if he could have found out who shot that poor old yellow dog, he might have gladly gunned the bastard down himself. What kind of man shot a dog just for running alongside them and barking?

Now there was the matter of whoever was

on their backtrail. If Spankler's report was even close to the truth, there might be a lot of them, scattered out like buckshot through the forests and mountains nearby, and it worried him that there was no good way to tell. All he knew at this point was that whoever was back there must be good, a lot craftier and more determined than the backwoods trash that he had riding with him.

Swope heard footsteps behind him and turned to see Abel Branch approaching. "So, what do you think, Abel?"

"I admit, it sure ain't like the other time when we hit Cable Springs," Branch said.

"Remember how we hit that posse three times in two days, and the third time they turned and scattered like a sack of rats?" Swope said. "Just like Bloody Bill would have done it. Aren't there any of the good ones still left from the old days?" He took a gulp of wine from the bottle, then passed it over to his companion.

"Mayhaps, it's only you and me now, Jethro."

"When Ham came back after the war, there wasn't much left of their family place but ashes and bare ground and fields full of unmarked graves. There'd been a big fight there, just like at my place. It took his daddy's life, and after, I brought his mama and two sisters back to what was left of my farm. I married the older girl, Rochelle."

It was the most Mel Carroll had talked since they partnered up three days before, and Ridge Parkman just stayed quiet and listened.

"He was a good man, God fearing, hardworking, and always patient and kind to his addle-brained mother. Within five years he had the place shaped up again, even though he was still turning up bones in his cornfields, just like me. He married one of the Butterfield girls. They had three little ones running around, and another in the oven. If I ever had a best friend besides a dog or a mule or my woman, I guess Ham would have been it."

Parkman glanced over to see if he might be joking, but saw no sign of it. There was scarcely any humor in Mel Carroll's makeup, especially on this bitter mission. Carroll rearranged a log at the edge of the fire so it would burn better, then spit a cord of tobacco juice expertly into the flames.

"We was in Cable Springs for the stock auction. Ham had a fine young Angus bull to sell, and I brought along a brace of two-year-old mules I was ready to part with.

Soon as we made our sales, Ham walked down to the bank to turn our vouchers into cash money, and that's where he was when Swope's outfit rode in. His guns was in the wagon. I'm sure he'd of given them what-for if he'd been armed, but he must have tried even unarmed, and got himself killed for it."

"Sorry to hear that, Mel," Parkman said. "Sometimes life just don't seem fair, does it? To survive all through the war and start up a new life. And then this . . ."

"The Bible says vengeance belongs to God," Mel said, "but in this part of the country, we figure sometimes we have to help Him out a bit."

"I suppose that's not much different than how we feel in my line of work. We just call it justice instead."

They had stopped for the night when it got too hard to track the lone survivor of the shootout, but Carroll had risen well before dawn, eager to get going again.

They both drained the dregs of their morning coffee from their metal cups, knowing it was the last, and wrapped the remains of last night's pone in cloth for later. They had provisioned themselves for four or five days when they left Cable Springs, and they were about to run out of everything. Pretty soon they'd be living off the land. Parkman wiped the skillet, coffee pot, and cups clean with handfuls of snow, then stowed them away in a canvas pack. Carroll went over to the horses and checked their cinches.

"We've got a clear trail to follow, and we'll need to make the best of it while we can," Carroll said. "We could get more snow after dinnertime."

As they mounted and started up the steep game trail once more, Parkman scanned what lay ahead. A stark winter landscape of rolling forested hills, daunting stone cliffs, and occasional peaks loomed on all sides.

"We should have gone west, Jethro," Abel Branch mumbled sullenly. "Or south on the post road down into Arkansas."

"With a posse on our trail?" Swope scoffed.

"There's just two of us now, and we could lose them easy enough."

"They've stayed with us this long, and I want to get lost out there someplace where they never could follow us. You know this country, Abel, and I'm counting on you to lead us plumb to the far side of nowhere."

"I know it all right." There was an odd tone to Branch's voice that Swope couldn't remember hearing before. "Maybe I know it too well. That there's Vesper Mountain up ahead."

"So?"

"It's some of the roughest country you ever imagined. No trails in and none out. Cracks in the rock that go straight down to hell, and caves that can swallow a man up whole. The talk I heard all my life goes way back to Indian tales, about men that went in there and never come back out again."

"Sounds like a perfect hideout," Swope said, trying to lighten things up. "Maybe we should build a cabin back in there someplace."

"Laugh if you want . . ."

Parkman unloaded and unsaddled the horses while Carroll scouted around and read the sign near the gaping mouth of the cave. When he came back from a short jaunt into the surrounding woods, he was carrying an armload of deadfall for the evening fire.

"They must have spent a night here. There's a little clearing down the hill a piece where they kept their horses, and we might as well do the same. There's a patch of dead grass the wind swept clear that they can nibble on, and a little stream running too fast to freeze over."

As Parkman scraped together the remnants of the fire the outlaws had built and blew up a small flame from the smoldering coals, Carroll turned and stared off into the distance. "Looks like they rode due east from here," he noted. "I was hoping they'd go just about any other direction instead."

"Why's that?"

"It's rough country over there. Rough and dangerous. You can't see it from here, but there's a place over there called Vesper Mountain that folks in these parts know to stay clear of." His voice trailed off, and he seemed caught up in his own thoughts.

"Maybe Swope's got a hideout back in there someplace," Parkman suggested.

"Not likely. If he'd ever gone in there once and made it back out, he wouldn't be wanting to go in again."

"That bad, huh? Have you ever been there, Mel?"

"Just into the edge of it. Some horse soldiers chased me in there back during the war, and I hid out there for a night. But I think if I had to do it again, I'd take my chances with the soldiers."

"But if Swope goes in there . . ."

"I know. I s'pose we'll have to go after him, won't we?"

Later as Parkman was frying up the last of the bacon and keeping an eye on the biscuits baking in a cast-iron pot next to the fire, he told his companion, "This is it for me, the last of the food I brought along. You got anything left?"

"Some jerky, and a sack of beans. In the morning I'll put the beans in my canteen to soak, and then we can cook them at suppertime."

"And after that?"

"The Lord will provide, I suppose."

Parkman lifted the lid on the pot and checked the biscuits. They were charred on the bottom and doughy on top, but edible, more or less. Carroll didn't complain. It would be good to sleep in the cave tonight. They could build the fire up to stay warm, and if any snow fell overnight, at least they wouldn't wake up buried in it. After they finished eating, Parkman rolled a smoke for himself, then handed the makings over to Mel Carroll, who packed some of the tobacco in his cob pipe.

Finally, the marshal decided to broach the topic that had been on his mind all through supper. "You know, Mel, you're a puzzling man."

"When Rochelle says something like that, I know it means trouble," Carroll said.

"It's like this. Back in Cable Springs, you're the only man that stepped up when you saw I was going out after Swope and his bunch, even with all the odds against us. You're a courageous man, no doubt about it." Carroll sat across the fire, leaning against a boulder, looking at Parkman and waiting for him to make his point. "But a while ago, when you were talking about Vesper Mountain, there was some kind of look in your eyes. It's hard to explain what I saw."

"Every man carries around fears inside of himself that he don't know are there unless a particular thing happens to him. And then, just knowing that's inside of you is like having it chained to your leg. You'll never be free of it again."

"I guess I don't know what you're talking about. I've been afraid lots of time in my life, but not that kind of afraid."

Carroll turned his gaze away, out into the night, the forest, and probably the past. "I don't never talk about it to anybody, not even to my wife when I used to wake up at night once in a while, wet as an otter, yelling out all kinds of nonsense. But I will tell you this. I think I went mostly crazy that night out toward Vesper Mountain, and I ain't sure I ever came all the way back.

There's dangers that you understand, and those you don't, and it's the last ones that keep a man tossing on the tick at night."

Parkman waited a moment, still feeling like he didn't completely believe or understand what his companion was talking about. It sounded like sheer superstition to him. "And yet you're still willing to ride with me tomorrow to the place that did that to you."

Mel Carroll cocked his head, and a crooked almost-grin reshaped his features for an instant. "They killed my kin," he said, as if that explained it all.

Now, with only Abel Branch remaining, the deeper they forged into this rugged country, the more confident Swope felt that he could quickly leave the posse behind. Surely, they'd lose the trail in this raw, rugged wilderness.

"We've rode together for a long time, haven't we, Jethro? Been through plenty of bad scrapes together." Abel Branch was riding ahead, carefully picking his way uphill through a tangle of boulders, fallen rocks, and jagged fissures.

"Many a mile, and many a fight," Swope agreed.

"And you know I ain't a cowardly man.

I've always been loyal to you, haven't I? But there comes a time . . ." He fell silent for a moment, as if he didn't quite know how to turn his thoughts into words.

"Get to it, Abel. If you want to part ways, just come right out with it."

Ahead was a grade so steep that Abel's horse threatened to balk at climbing it. "I've never been to the cave up there myself," he said. "But I heard another man speak of it, and we seen it ourselves from back down the trail. If your mind's still set on it, you can make it up there alone. But I swear on my daddy's grave, I can't bring myself to go along. The whole idea of it's got me so worked up I'm about to wet my britches."

"We wouldn't want that. Cut loose and head on home, Abel," Swope said.

"And you won't hold it against me? I still get my share?"

They paused for a moment while Swope loosened the straps on a saddlebag and pulled out the canvas satchel from the bank. He counted out the money he owed his companion and handed it over. Abel Branch stuffed it inside his coat without counting it.

"Keep one eye open even when you're sleeping, Jethro, and keep your guns cocked. Don't stay around these parts any longer than you have to."

"You know I will."

The two men shook hands, and Branch turned his horse toward their backtrail. Swope watched him go, haunted by some strange feeling that this was the last that they would ever see of one another.

Sundown was approaching, and it would be dark in an hour or less. A wind was blowing steadily from the west, bringing the serious nighttime cold with it. Mel Carroll turned up the collar of his coat and held the front together to keep the wind from blowing in.

The circling buzzards high in the sky alerted them that there was carrion up ahead. With each patient pass, the smoothly gliding creatures descended a little more. They were in no hurry. The larger animals below on the ground would have to eat their fill before the broad-winged, crook-necked birds got their turn.

Carroll and Parkman heard the wild hogs up ahead before they actually saw them. Their frenzied grunting and squealing were familiar to Carroll, and he knew they were feeding. It would be smarter to backtrack and cut a wide trail around them, but that wasn't possible on this bewildering, stone-strewn mountainside. There was no guarantee that there was another way around, and even if they found one, there was a good chance they would lose the faint trail they were following.

"Check your loads and let's have at 'em," Carroll said to the marshal. "It don't sound like more than three or four." As Mel cocked the hammers on his double-barrel, Parkman drew his Colt from its holster and pulled a second handgun from inside his coat. "Keep shooting 'til they're all stone dead. They're thick-skulled and they don't go down easy."

The hogs were feeding in their own rambunctious way on the fresh carcass of a horse, crowding and squalling and slashing at one another with their long, curved tusks as they greedily tore away chunks of meat and swallowed them down. They didn't seem to notice the appearance of the two riders until the shooting started. Mel downed one with both loads of buckshot and quickly began to reload. Parkman finished another one off with a succession of shots across its skull and shoulder. But the third, also wounded but not yet ready to die, spun and charged. The marshal killed it within feet of the horses, but not before Mel's horse reared in panic, pawing the air with its front hooves. Mel Carroll tumbled backward in a disheveled heap on the ground.

Parkman was already reloading. "You all right, Mel?"

"Not sure yet." The hip he had landed on hurt like blazes, and he noticed that one of his arms was no help as he struggled clumsily to his feet. Sharp pain was beginning to shoot up his arm and shoulder.

"That must be the fellow who was riding the horse," Parkman said. He pointed at a body several feet away, bent awkwardly across a fallen tree. He lay face up, his backbone clearly snapped. They both went over to take a look.

"I know this man," Mel said. "Name's Abel Branch. He settled a few miles east of my place after the war. I didn't know he rode with Swope, though." To his and Parkman's surprise, the corpse's eyes fluttered, then opened. He looked around for a moment, then his gaze settled on the two men looking down at him.

"Who's that?" the man asked.

"It's Mel Carroll," Mel said. "We thought you was dead already, Abel."

"Not quite yet, Mel. You riding with the posse?"

"Tom Brigance wouldn't put together a posse because of what Swope did to them last time, so it's just me and the marshal here."

"You mean it's only been the two of you all along? Well I'll be damned."

"I had to come along because yours and Swope's bunch killed Ham Adderly in the bank holdup. He's my brother-in-law, and he didn't even have a gun on him. No sense in it, and I had to avenge him for Rochelle's sake, and her family's."

"Yep, I was there when he got shot, and I felt bad about it right off. I was sorry about him, and sorry for that poor ol' dog too. Ham smart-mouthed the wrong man, and got a bullet for it."

"Are you hurting bad, Abel?"

"Nope. I don't feel nothin'. Can't move nothin'. I heard the hogs over there eating my horse, and I figured I was next."

"Yep, and there's buzzards that'll be along shortly." Carroll knelt beside the paralyzed man, his gaze cold. "For my money, you ain't getting no worse than you deserve, you son of a bitch. Ham had a wife and three little ones, and now they'll have it hard for a long time to come."

Branch's eyes sagged closed, and for a moment Carroll thought he had died. He scanned the man's mutilated body. Branch's back was curved across the log like the blade of a scythe, and his neck was twisted awkwardly.

"I knew it warn't right what we was fixin' to do," Branch said at last, his eyes opening slowly like a man just waking. "But my family was most near starving, and it was my own fault. Folks told me we was too far north and it wasn't hot enough to grow cotton, but I set my mind to give it a try. I had that good bottomland and it seemed to make sense at the time. But the whole crop failed."

"Yep. Corn's the thing in these hills. Corn, and maybe some wheat if the soil's right for it."

"I know that now." Branch's eyes fluttered and rolled back like he was dizzy. His breathing was shallow and seemed to stop briefly, but then he gained control again. "I ain't got the right to ask, Mel," he said, "but I always heard you was a good man. They's a roll of money in my jacket, three hundred dollars, and I'm hoping you might have the charity to take it to Delilah. She and the children might starve without it."

Carroll scoffed at the notion. "If I was to give the money to anyone, it would be Ham Adderly's wife and children, not yours. If your brood was in need, you should have been there yourself to see to them, not riding off with the likes of Jethro Swope to steal and murder. The Good Book's got something to say about the children paying for the sins of the fathers."

For the first time, Parkman intervened. He knelt on the other side of the man's broken remains and reached inside his coat for the money. "This goes back to the bank in Cable Springs," he said. "And I agree with Mr. Carroll. You can start your trip to hell knowing that whatever hardship your family goes through is on you." His voice was hard, bereft of sympathy. "But I will make you one bargain. You tell me what you can about where Swope is, and where he's heading, and I'll make sure you don't have to lay here helpless when the wild animals hereabouts make a meal of you. The buzzards start with the eyes. I've seen it."

Carroll watched Branch's eyes as they shifted from Parkman to him, and then back to the marshal. Even though the muscles of his face were still, his eyes seemed filled with terror at the thought of it.

"He was bound for a cave up yonder on the side of Vesper Mountain," Branch said at last. "I can't say where exactly 'cause I never been there and wouldn't go now. Folks I knew and trusted always said it's best to stay out of these parts."

"I've heard the same my whole life," Carroll said.

"So what were his plans after he got to the cave?" the marshal asked.

"He said he'd hole up there 'til the posse gave up and turned back, and then he'd head south. He's got kin down in Arkansas someplace."

Parkman nodded his head, then he and Carroll rose to their feet. They both backed up a few feet so the blood wouldn't splatter on them when the marshal kept his bargain with Abel Branch.

"I can feel the break up under your skin," Parkman said. Carroll gritted his teeth against the pain as the marshal probed the flesh of his arm one last time. The growing pain in his right arm was convincing him that his injury was worse than he first thought, but he hadn't mentioned it to his companion until they were settled in for the night.

Neither of them wanted to make camp in a spot where a dead man, a dead horse, and three dead hogs were lying close around, so they had ridden a short piece back down the trail to a spot where there was some deadfall for a fire and a protruding slab of rock that would serve as scant shelter when the weather turned bad again. Tonight, they kept the horses in close so they wouldn't suffer the same fate as Abel Branch's animal had.

The two men sat side by side near the fire, and Carroll's injured arm lay across Parkman's legs. One end of the broken bone pushed up against the skin of his forearm like a huge boil, and it was twisted unnaturally.

"Can you set it?" Carroll asked.

"I wouldn't even try," Parkman said. "It feels all splintery inside and turned wrong." The broken bones had not punctured the skin, but his arm was already swelling and turning red. It was bleeding in there, and no way to stop it. "Lucky for you I thought to check that man's saddlebags," he added, handing a small dark whiskey bottle over to Carroll. "I've got a feeling you're going to want plenty of that before we get you back to Cable Springs."

"But first we go up the mountain and finish off that skunk, Jethro Swope. Right?"

Parkman was silent.

"Right?" Carroll repeated.

"You need a doctor who can cut that arm open and put the bones back together like they belong, and then sew you up. You could lose that arm, Mel. Or something even worse."

Mel Carroll gritted his teeth again, this time out of frustration instead of pain. He stared out into the night at the moonlit slopes of Vesper Mountain. "But he's just right up there," he said, his voice filled with frustration and defeat.

"I know," Parkman said. "But this is an easy call for me. Jethro Swope will get his when the right time comes. My worst problem will be trying to explain all this to the captain when I get back."

His life was reduced to darkness, and pain, and terror.

He was deep into the cave now, too deep for light or cold or any outside sound to penetrate. Those things had quit looking for him, seeming to know that if they roved beyond the dim glow of outside light behind them, they might end up as lost as he was. His eyes ached from staring into the impenetrable darkness, desperate for any hint of light, but all he saw was an occasional fleeting pinprick glow, created by his own mind, perhaps to give him an instant of hope where there was none.

The only sound was a distant gurgling ripple of flowing water, like the noise of an energetic stream trickling down a mountain-side. He would have liked to locate it and get a drink, imagining how good the cold water would taste. But it mocked his efforts to find it, sometimes over here, sometimes over there, seeming to move around like a malicious sprite. The last time he tried to find it, his leg had slipped down into a slash in the rock and he fell forward. He heard the bone snap, and felt the pain lance up the length of his leg. After that he could barely crawl, and he gave up on getting himself a drink of water.

Cable Springs would be his last robbery. A man like him never had as much money as he wanted, but this experience was surely a sign. He had enough. His slowing brain skipped right on past how he would get out of here, straight on to the part about traveling west across the open plains and towering mountains, not stopping until the waves of an endless ocean lapped at his feet.

The pain wasn't quite as bad when he sat very still with his back against the smooth stone wall. With every breath his chest felt like drying strips of leather were tightening around him, and odd sounds came out of him, like a man asleep and snoring. He understood that things were busted inside, and he could feel warm trickles of blood flowing down his back and into his pants. The back of his head was sticky with blood, and when he probed with his fingers across a small protruding bone, everything inside of his skull caught fire.

Women, and good food, and good wine. He'd heard it never got cold out there in California.

No man, not even a carnival show giant, ever grew that tall, nor had the strength to pick a man up with one arm and throw him against a rock wall ten feet away. But that huge, brutish thing did. It had all happened quicker than a man could blink, just as he passed around a little turn in the cave entrance. He remembered the stink and the yellow-gray hair and the petrifying growls and snarls in the shadowy chamber. He remembered tumbling through the air like a leaf in the wind and slamming into pain worse than anything he could have ever imagined. And he remembered the mind-less terror.

It all got fuzzy and confusing after that, staggering into the dark away from the grunts and growls behind him, tripping and falling and stumbling blindly into unseen rocky hazards. And finally, when he fell one last time and was too spent and damaged to get up again, all he heard were his own moans and gasps.

Buy a little saloon. Maybe get married again, or else just keep a clean, decent whore handy. Make a baby, a son to replace the one they took away up in Liberty . . .

At first, resting there on the stone floor, full of relief in knowing that no one, or nothing, was still after him, it took him a moment to understand the full meaning of it all. Those sounds behind him had been his last connection to any notion of direction. There was no forward or back, no understanding of which way would lead him out of the cave, and which would take him deeper into the belly of the mountain.

The howling was the worst. The loud, shrill shrieks didn't come close to anything he had ever heard before. There was no relation to the varied cries of the big cats he was familiar with, nor did it sound anything like the grunts and growls of bears or hogs. There was something hauntingly human about it, although he could not imagine any human throat ever issuing those soul-racking sounds. All he was sure of was that when those noises echoed back from time to time through the coal-dark recesses of the cave, it was like hearing Satan bawl out his name.

The money he had hidden away was right

there waiting, buried behind the foundation rocks at his uncle's abandoned cabin near Fayetteville. All gold, because paper rotted. Just waiting. The kind of woman that smiled when she looked at you. Maybe a back room for gambling. A train huffing and smoking beside a station ramp, ready to carry a man away out west. He'd remember his name again by the time he got out there.

A bloody yellow dog lying in a mud puddle. Dead just for doing what dogs do.

There was no real thing called time anymore.

Greg Hunt has published over twenty Western, frontier, and historical novels. A lifelong writer, he has also worked as a newspaper reporter and editor, a technical and freelance writer, and a marketing analyst. He also served in Vietnam as an intelligence agent and Vietnamese linguist. Greg now lives in the Memphis area with his wife, Vernice.

■ ■ ■ ■

HOBNAIL

BY LOREN D. ESTLEMAN

■ ■ ■ ■

The town of Hobnail boomed.

Not, like so many cities of frontier legend, because of precious metals or cattle or, later, oil, but on the basis of something far more precious in that burned-out country. Despite the wisdom of the ancient philosophers, it was not lead that could be transmuted into gold. An entire population could survive without ever laying eyes on a double eagle or a pocket watch ringed in the yellow stuff of legend, but it could not last ten days without that thing that covers nine-tenths of our spinning planet.

Josephus Gannon was a swamper. He scoured wagon trails for bottles, sticks of furniture, and other nonessential items shed by pioneers when the going got rugged, trading them for victuals or drink or a night's lodging in town. One day in this pursuit, he got a skullful of sun and wandered off the rutted road into uncharted desert. Groping around for his bearings, he stepped into a soft plot of ground and turned his ankle.

Had the reason been what he suspected, a prairie dog town undermined by verminous rodents, he'd have perished there for lack of transport and thirst, and gone unrecorded by history. But when he sat down to assess the damage and saw that his boot was plastered with mud, he knew his future was assured, and with it, his fortune.

The boot's sole was studded with hobnails. Gannon was a simple man and staked his claim to that previously worthless plot of earth under that name.

It got better: The water was warm, almost piping hot.

It was potable, of course, once it was allowed to cool. But the heat and effervescence of its geologic origins promised at least a century of tourists desperate to partake of the healing waters.

In those days when "The Great American Desert" was accepted as gospel, whole civilizations sprang up wherever a man spat, like cottonwoods. What began as a rude dugout, suitably provisioned with water from the underground spring and prairie hens ripe for the taking, grew swiftly into a metropolis: Investors poured in, hired horse-drawn dredges, and transformed Gannon's Sink into Olympia Hot Springs almost overnight.

But the real secret of Hobnail's first flush of glory had only partly to do with slaking one's thirst or soaking away one's inflictions. We can grant that particular burst of genius to Henry Ward Beecher Pruitt, its first chief constable.

The date is disputed, even the year; but most accounts favor 1881, when the name of Jorge Castillo rivaled General Lew Wallace's epic novel *Ben-Hur,* if not in bookstalls and general mercantiles throughout the U.S., then certainly by way of wanted readers posted on telegraph poles and the walls of barns from San Antonio to Sacramento. A reward of $10,000 — back then a life's lease on the pleasures of the flesh — was offered for the Mexican Devil's capture, dead or alive. The enterprises of the Wells and Fargo and Butterfield stagecoach lines and the Union Pacific Railroad had pooled their interests to make good on the pledge, as Castillo and his gang had been looting their treasuries for the better part of a decade.

For years, the gang had prospered by raiding targets in Texas and New Mexico Territory, then fleeing back to old Mexico. There they dispersed among scattered villages whose residents favored well-behaved visitors over sworn authority. Questions from strangers met only with blank stares and the local incomprehensible dialect; machetes, if the interrogation grew irksome. But the Castillistas became victims of their own success. The Texas Rangers, dormant since the conquest of the Comanche Nation in 1875, reconvened with the specific purpose of apprehending the road agent and his cohorts, and a treaty was struck between Washington, D.C., and Mexico City calling for the federales to root out the brigands "by means best left to these authorities." In time, real and suspected accomplices decorated so many cottonwoods on both sides of the border that the waggish press dubbed the gang "the Christmas ball bandits."

The survivors cast themselves in all directions; some east to the Atlantic seaboard, some north to Canada, others sailing as far away as Europe and (it was rumored) Japan. There an Occidental referred to as "the Yankee Samurai" badgered the ancient trade roads for silks and spices for months until he was overtaken by mounted forces commanded by a former shogun and hacked to pieces.

Much of this is unsubstantiated, but it's a

matter of record that a gaunt and exhausted Jorge Castillo straggled into Hobnail astride a broken-winded mule not long after H. W. B. Pruitt was sworn in as peace officer, and laid down a handful of pennies — likely all that remained of his swag — to share a flea-infested attic with a half-dozen other vagabonds already in residence.

He was recognized from his well-advertised likeness by one of his fellow wayfarers, who promptly put in to Pruitt's office with the intention of collecting the reward. Instead, the man was charged with vagrancy and handed over to a prison road gang.

Pruitt was a visionary. Rather than settle for ten thousand in one lump sum, he saw the opportunity to rake in many times that by offering the hospitality and shelter of Hobnail to fleeing felons in return for a cut of their take and the pledge that they would commit no crimes within a hundred miles of the town. He dispatched two deputies to conduct the half-starving bandido from his filthy bunk to his office and put the matter to him.

Castillo shrugged. "But, *el jefe, es imposible*! I was forced to trade my guns in El Paso for that miserable beast I rode to this place; and I doubt very much it will carry me another mile, much less one hundred!"

"Ask for Campbell, the manager of the Olympia Hotel, on Gannon Street; he's my brother-in-law." Pruitt scribbled on a writing-block, tore off the sheet, and handed it to him. "This instructs him to advance you two hundred dollars. Buy a good rifle and pistol, a sound horse, and a decent set of clothes; no one would take you seriously in those rags. This is a loan, which I'll add to what I expect you to share with me from your first — let's call it a transaction."

He waggled a finger. "Mind you, if you are not back here with the proceeds in ten days, you will be tracked down and dealt with on the spot. Dick Running Horse, who runs the livery, scouted for General Crook. He can read sign across a field of polished granite and will be only too happy to split the ten thousand with me in return for delivering your head in a jar to Austin."

The thief pulled his forelock. "You have my word, señor."

"I'll accept that when I have eighty percent of your take."

"*Ochenta!* But that is highway robbery!"

The constable grinned behind his moustaches. "Right you are, partner."

Castillo came through, of course; with

fifteen hundred dollars in gold seized from an Overland strongbox in Palo Pinto. If he retained reservations about the inequity of the cut, he was reassured by his stay in the Olympia Hotel, Hobnail's first and most luxurious place of lodging, with room service and the most skilled sporting women the thriving resort town had to offer. It all came at the price of his twenty percent, but he was undisturbed by lawmen who came from outside to inquire after the marauder's whereabouts. It was the first time in many months he felt at ease remaining in one spot for more than a few days.

Unfortunately for him, his pioneering status came to an abrupt end when the money ran out and he exited a bank in Sweetwater square into a field of fire belonging to the local committee of public vigilance. His bullet-torn corpse was packed in ice and shipped to the capital. Back in Sweetwater, men came to blows over how the reward should be split among thirteen armed citizens.

By this time, events in Hobnail were going swimmingly under what became known (to those who were aware of it) as "the Pruitt System." Communications along the Outlaw Trail traveled swifter than Western Union. Others came in to take advantage of the opportunity. Floyd Donegan, a former Confederate guerrilla who'd extended his war on the Union long past Appomattox, carried the fifteen thousand dollars' bounty on his hide into a standing reservation on the second floor of the Olympia. In between visits he would launch a personal crime wave in such far-flung places as Brownwood, Lampasas, and Comanche Creek. Soon after, he vanished into history — slain, most likely, in some undiscovered stretch of desert for what was in his possession by commonplace cutthroats, ignorant of their victim's identity and the value of his lifeless shell.

Parades of lesser fugitives came to "take the cure"; these enjoyed their freedom in the more modest surroundings of the Railroad Arms and various boardinghouses until they, too, passed into obscurity, the state prison at Huntsville, or the noose.

As might have been expected from men of low character, there were some who took unfair advantage. Cherokee Jack Swanson shook Pruitt's hand and at the first opportunity stuck up the local train station for several hundred dollars' worth of federal securities, and returned downtown, under the impression that his flour-sack hood would shield him from discovery. Within hours, Pruitt's deputies entered the Celestial Gardens spa and shot him in the head as he was soaking up the waters in a complete state of nature. The constable, always magnanimous with his men, shared equally with them the five thousand dollars paid for Jack's capture dead or alive. Other cheats, upon whom the reward wasn't worth the expense of ammunition and the effort of disposing the bodies, were apprehended, bound, and dumped in the desert, either to succumb to heat and thirst or to wander into the hands of their pursuers. The combination of theirs and Cherokee Jack's fates was sufficient to keep others in line.

But career criminals weren't the only ones to stray from the program. In the fall of 1884, a rookie deputy named Logan was overheard, over his fifth whiskey in the Lucky Boot Saloon, boasting of his plan to kick open Bass Ballenger's door in the Olympia, shoot him in the foot, and haul him in his buckboard to San Angelo, where he was wanted for robbery-murder, then decamp to New Orleans with five thousand dollars in cash. He passed out soon after divulging his intentions, to awake with a gunnysack over his head and his wrists bound behind him. In that condition he was transported in his own buckboard across the county line and off-loaded into a patch of mescal. How he fared after that — survived, dead of thirst, or slaughtered by Comancheros for his goods — brightened many a conversation among his former fellow deputies for months. Any other inside outrages against the System guttered out at the start whenever Logan's name came up.

Needless to detail, Henry Ward Beecher Pruitt grew fat in his job; and his job was secure. Those citizens who suspected, or were even fully aware of, Pruitt's methods, gloried in Hobnail's reputation as the city with the lowest crime rate west of the Mississippi; or so it was reported in *Harper's Weekly* and *The New York Herald.* Tourists, and especially settlers hoping for a safe place to raise their families, arrived by the trainload, contributing to the wealth of merchants and the treasury. The constable was re-elected automatically, with none foolhardy enough to waste money and time bothering to oppose him.

All things, however, are finite, and good ones the most perishable. In 1890, with the West settled, the forces of law and order trading the hit-and-miss methods of hot lead and breakneck horsemanship for solid detective work, and the seats of justice established within mere miles of one another, the days of wild outlawry neared an end. The gangs had failed to move with the times and had paid dearly for their lack of vision. Some hung from proper scaffolds, others broke rocks in Huntsville. The flood of fugitives seeking asylum slowed to a trickle.

One day in this season of change, a canvas-clad, cheroot-smoking hoyden going by the name Bess Browder galloped into town. She was preceded by a flurry of gaudy popular novels celebrating her daylight assaults on banks, trains, and freight offices across the Southwest. Circulars came by the bale, pledging a whopping $25,000 for her delivery to justice.

True to her reputation, she marched boldly into Pruitt's office, deposited a jingling sack stenciled BANK OF ALBU-QUERQUE on his desk, and demanded sanctuary until the trail cooled sufficiently to allow her to decamp to old Mexico. The constable was as impressed with her appearance as he was with the cascade of double eagles that spilled onto his blotter when he upended the sack. She was even prettier than the illustrations in her fanciful biographies, with chestnut locks spilling to her shoulders from under her sweat-stained slouch hat, an oval face, robin's-egg-blue eyes, skin burnt but clear, and a trim athletic figure that even the sack coat and leathern breeches could not dissemble.

He stood to proffer his hand — a courtesy he'd never extended his male guests — and said he'd make arrangements for the bridal suite at the Olympia.

"I'm no man's bride," she said. "A hot bath, a warm meal, and a proper bed will suit me down to the ground. I've had my life's portion of rat-filled barns and cold sowbelly."

Still, he installed her in the hotel's finest accommodations, with an adjoining bath and limitless privileges in the dining room, where ham was served in champagne sauce with ice cream for dessert and a different French wine with every course. Both Pruitt and the manager were relieved when each time she appeared in public she was outfitted in the latest eastern fashions, unpacked from her worn valise and set right by the laundry and valet. In feathered hats, silk skirts, patent-leather shoes, and corsets, she could keep company with the finest ladies in New York, Chicago, and San Francisco.

At the end of six weeks — considering the number of people sharing in the largesse and the constable's own elevated tastes — the contribution she'd made to the Pruitt

System began to run low. It was time for a fresh infusion.

To broach this delicate matter, he brushed and put on his dress uniform — dove gray, with bright silver buttons and Napoleonic epaulets, topped by a fore-and-aft admiral's cap crested with an ostrich plume — and presented himself at her door. She admitted him, attired in a comely dressing gown that matched her eyes and paper slippers. Over piping-hot tea and fresh warm scones, they discussed the proposition.

"Naturally," she said, "I won't burden you with my plans. I will require a good mount, as the one I came in on has seen his best days, a box of .44 cartridges, and an advance of five hundred dollars to cover incidentals and the unexpected. I assure you the good citizens of Hobnail will be more than satisfied with the return on this investment."

"Of that I have no doubt. Er, would you do me the honor — ?" He presented her with the latest panegyric to appear in print, a red-and-yellow-bound copy of *Bold Bess, the Pirate Princess,* attributed to one J. Shoemaker and published by the Parker Press of St. Louis, Missouri. Laughing throatily, she rose from the settee they shared, sat down at an elegant writing desk, dipped a pen, and on the title page wrote, in an elegant hand: "To Henry Ward Beecher Pruitt, with pleasurable anticipation of things to come. Bess Browder."

The details were worked out. Expressing reservations about the possibility of another duplicitous Deputy Logan rearing his head (How, he wondered, had *that* bit of information found its way out of town?), Bess insisted that Pruitt share their agreement with no one. They would meet, alone, behind Dick Running Horse's livery just before sunup, when all the businesses were closed. The constable would be leading the promised horse, saddled and provisioned, and deliver the five hundred in cartwheel dollars, whereupon she would ride out, to return in not more than two weeks with the proceeds.

To all this he had no objections. For some time, he'd bridled against the increasing demands from his deputies, Campbell the Olympia manager, Running Horse, and others who had to be let in on what was surely no longer a secret. The spread of civilization would continue to dwindle the System's profits, and the notion of retiring East with what he'd socked away had been with him since the official closing of the frontier. A fresh injection, courtesy of the Pirate Princess, was just what was needed to turn the thought into reality. Once again, the pair shook hands; once again, he was surprised by the tensile strength of his lovely partner's grip. He bowed. She curtsied. What strange twist of frontier fate, he mused on his way back to his office, had turned so refined a young lady into bandit royalty? A drunken brute of a father, a wastrel of a husband, forcing her into the twilight life to make ends meet? He shook his head. "Ah, 'tis an imperfect world, populated with such shiftless men."

Shortly before dark, he collected his own mount, a sleek blue roan, from the livery, and placed upon it his own blanket and fine saddle. Dick Running Horse's seamed face showed nothing of what was behind it. "I'll be closing up in an hour. Won't hang round waiting on you to return it."

"It won't be tonight." Pruitt slapped his great round belly. "I'm getting fat as a hog; so's Old Mike here. Camp in the desert overnight, shoot a jackrabbit for my supper, race some coyotes for an hour or so come morning, and burn some of the suet off us both."

"Mike's fit already. Take more than a scrawny meal and a gallop to turn you into a greyhound."

Disgruntled, he led the roan away. The liveryman's insult made him feel better about deceiving him. To have asked for a strange horse would have invited more questions and suspicion. Better Dick think him an old fool than a cheat. You never knew what unscrupulous behavior a half-breed was capable of.

Darkness crept toward dawn. It was November. The desert heat had long since drained away into the sand, making him grateful for the fleece that lined his old leather coat and the woolen lumberjack's cap with the flaps down over his ears and tied under his chin. His breath crawled in the chill air. He was early: The back wall of the livery, untouched by the sun's first glow, cut a blank square out of the spray of stars. He tethered the roan and inspected the saddlebags containing canned goods and salt pork, the five hundred in their plain sacks, and the water bags slung from the horn. Satisfied, he dug his fists deep in his pockets and stamped his feet to keep them from turning into inert sledges. The soft life had made him impatient with discomfort. Before sunup! What did so unspecific a time mean to a woman, a breed well known for its disregard of the clock?

Just then a light step displaced gravel. Turning toward the sound, he saw a figure approaching from the corner. Immediately his humor lifted. The newcomer's dark attire contrasted against the spreading tails of a white linen duster that reflected starlight. The silhouette was indisputably feminine. As she drew near enough for him to make out details, he was struck once again by her beauty. In a man's worn slouch hat and the shapeless garments of trail riding, she was quite as comely as when decked out in feathers and silk. Could it be he was falling in love? After twelve years a widower, he'd thought he was past all that.

He was moved to impress her. Slapping the roan's strong neck, he said, "Best in the stable; in Texas, if you'll forgive the boast. It's my own, along with provisions sufficient and *three* boxes of .44s in the boot. Nothing too good for our association."

"I'll be the judge; if you'll forgive the impertinence. Strike a match so I can inspect its teeth."

He reached inside his coat, taking his eyes off her as he did so. Something swished. Before he could react, a bright blue light burst in his skull. His knees gave way. He was out before he hit the ground.

When he awoke, his brain athrob, he was

lying on his stomach. He tried to push himself up. He lacked the use of his hands, bound as they were behind his back. Blinking away tears, he saw Bess Browder standing over him, holstering a long-barreled Colt, the polished wooden butt of which he was painfully familiar.

"Wha-what's this then?" His voice was hoarse, as if it hadn't had use in days. He was sure he hadn't been senseless more than a few minutes. "The money's here, just as arranged."

"The Agency will see what it can do about returning it to its lawful owners." Even in the present circumstances, one could not fail to notice the refined quality of her voice.

Bewilderment turned to indignation. He struggled against his fetters, cold steel against his wrists. Then what she'd said registered. He lay still. "Agency?"

She produced something shiny from inside her rough coat. His vision had cleared enough to make out the wide-open eye embossed upon the shield and the word PINKERTON NATIONAL DETECTIVE AGENCY.

"I'm a beginner," she said. "The office in San Francisco put me into the field after a crash training course, in light of my special circumstances." Her voice deepened.

"Henry Ward Beecher Pruitt, I'm placing you under arrest for malfeasance in office and as an accomplice after the fact to forty-six counts of armed robbery and murder, and one count of murder in the first degree."

"I never did murder!" In his confusion, he failed to take note of the fact that he had implicitly confessed to the other crimes.

"You directed your deputies to do it for you, but Cherokee Jack Swanson's dead just the same. I imagine at least one of them will be only too eager to testify against you in return for a life's sentence in Huntsville instead of a short rope and a long drop."

"Who in thunder is Cherokee Jack Swanson?"

"No one. He took the name to protect his family, or what's left of it. He was born Jacob Shoemaker. I felt it fitting to use it for a *nom de plume* when I wrote all those dime dreadfuls about Bess Browder. My publishers were so caught with the sales potential they agreed to print up a few dozen wanted readers bearing my likeness. I have the Messrs. Pinkerton to thank for the money I brought as bait."

While he was laboring his hellish head to sort this out, she placed two fingers in her mouth and blew a shrill whistle. A brace of broad-shouldered men materialized at her side from the darkness. He recognized them as local teamsters.

"Volunteers," she said. "Not everyone in town approves of the Pruitt System." To them: "I'll hold the horse. Throw this sack of offal aboard his fine mount and we'll start for the U.S. marshal's office in Dallas." She favored the prisoner with a saintly smile. "It's a hard ride, I admit, facedown across the saddle; but no less arduous than the poor souls you pitched into the desert, on foot and without supplies or provisions."

"What are they to you?"

"Them? Not much, apart from Christian sympathy. You can mark time in your death cell considering the folly of killing the brother of a woman who matched him in ruthless intelligence. Elizabeth Shoemaker, your escort." She touched the brim of her greasy slouch. "This is all I have to remind me of Jacob. It found its way to me through one of your disgraced deputies — you remember Logan? — along with all the information I needed to apply for a position with the Agency."

Loren D. Estleman has published more

410

than eighty novels and two hundred short stories in the areas of mystery, western, and mainstream. He has received more than twenty national honors, including four lifetime achievement awards.

■ ■ ■ ■

THE ASSASSIN

BY PATRICK DEAREN

■ ■ ■ ■

The assassin crouched in the shadows of brushy mesquites and surveyed the sagging house ahead. Through a mist falling from a black sky, he noted the large covered porch with skirting, as well as the screened windows that cast muted light across a series of flat rocks leading from the weathered steps.

Thunder roared and shook the tinseled leaves above him, causing a beaded spray to sprinkle his coat. A sudden gust tossed the pliant limbs, but he held his position on the soggy ground even as thorns raked his face.

He was very cold and tired, but it didn't matter. His eyes narrowed as he measured the width of the little clearing. From the brush line to the drip of the porch eaves, it was about twenty paces, maybe twenty-five.

He couldn't see anyone through the twin windows, but he knew they were there. He didn't know their names nor did he care.

Lightning flashed, illuminating the scene

for an instant. It was a white, box-and-strip house with cracked paint and warped cedar shingles, an isolated home nestled in the mesquite-covered hills of rugged West Texas rangeland.

His blood ran hot in his forehead. He hated them — them and their home and the horses in the adjacent pen and everything they touched. The smell of them seemed to choke the night, just like the ozone stirred by the storm.

He watched the rain fall through the lamplight and ripple the puddles of water outside the pen where the small bay and big Appaloosa stirred. He had first seen the two horses many miles away, right after it had happened. He had chased after the animals as long as the dust plume had been in sight. Even afterward, when there had been nothing but craggy rangeland ahead, he had followed the tracks down the pitted wagon road.

And now he crouched there quietly, watching . . . waiting. The riders would come out sometime. Sooner or later they would push open that door and step out on the porch.

And he would be ready.

His eyes wandered past the muddy yard and small house, even beyond the dark hills in the distance. He would give them no more chance than they had given her. The mist blurred his vision as he remembered how they had ruthlessly attacked her and left her to die in a pool of blood beneath the swollen sun.

Hate and vengeance clouded his eyes. They would pay.

He padded stealthily out of the shadows and approached the house. A bolt of sky fire lighted the yard for an instant, and he grew still on the ground, almost as if he were a part of it.

The roar of thunder passed, and he continued on, a low shadow slinking through the night. The assassin had never killed a man before, but he knew he would this time. He was sure he would, because of the terrible, terrible thing they had done to her.

As his angle to a window changed, he caught sight of a young woman inside the house. She sat slowly rocking as she clutched something small and white to her breast.

Theirs, he thought. The child of the man who had taken so much from him.

His gaze shifted to the elevated porch only yards ahead. He stopped for a moment, studying the black shadows at one end — shadows that lurked within reach of the rotting plank floor. He crept on across the puddles until the dark veil crawled over him. He huddled there, intuitively assessing the porch and measuring distance. It wasn't far to the screen door that banged in the wind — he could be at it in moments when the time came.

He licked his lips in anticipation, the quiet fury in his eyes burning deeper.

The tin skirting of the porch crowded him, and as he shifted position, he bumped it hard, the clatter like counterpoint to the crack of thunder and whistle of wind. He checked the door, piercing it with a stare as he waited and wondered. Suddenly it screeched open, and he crouched lower in the shadows, but not so low that he couldn't see the screen as it framed a silhouette that included a long object that must have been a lever-action carbine.

The man stood alone in the threshold for long seconds, facing night and storm. All the while, the assassin stayed frozen with the patience he had long nurtured. Then another form appeared in the doorway, a slender one that exuded strong perfume that wafted into his nostrils. He hated it, for he had caught that same fragrance over the bloody pool. In the young woman's arms was a small, blanketed form that must have smelled like its mother, and he hated the tiny figure also.

A tentative, girlish voice broke the whisper of wind and patter of rain. "What's wrong, Johnny? How come you got the gun?"

The man in the screen turned. The lamp-light fell on his face, and the assassin noted the browned skin and dark hair and jutting chin he had seen once before on that day. It was a cruel face, indeed — fiendish and yet so very human.

The man nodded to the darkness. "Some-thin's out there."

The girl shrank a step and hugged the baby to her breast. "Don't scare me that way! Not after what you — not after today, the —"

"I heard somebody. I know I did." He looked back into the storm and gripped the carbine tighter.

The girl shuddered and moved closer, begging for the arm that he slipped about her. "Come on in. May-maybe it was just the wind, darlin'. Shut the door and come on in!"

Still, he surveyed the blackness, but now with his forearm against the screen door. "Who in the . . . ? I'm gonna have a look-see."

"No, Johnny! Stay inside!" she implored. "Don't be lookin' for trouble!"

"Be back in a minute. Stay put."

The woman continued to plead, but the man pushed open the screen and stepped out, the Winchester carbine ready at his hip. Now the assassin hugged the shadows at the porch base even closer, especially as the planks creaked with footsteps that ended almost above his head.

He knew the man scanned the stormy night, ready to wield that potent weapon at any quick movement, any sudden noise. But the assassin made no such mistake; he stayed motionless, allowing no greater sound than the pounding of his blood.

Finally, he heard the footsteps resume, the creaks growing fainter, but only after they ceased entirely did he risk a look. The man now stood at the porch's far end, the light from the window bathing his back.

With anxious eyes, the assassin saw the young woman push open the screen and step indecisively onto the porch, the baby still sleeping in her arms. On spring-loaded legs, the assassin tensed.

"Come on in, Johnny!" she begged. "Please! I'm scared!"

The man looked over his shoulder at her, and then turned again to the darkness. He took a deep breath. "I'd've sworn I heard

somebody. I'd've sworn somethin' was out
h—"

The assassin sprang for the porch. The
woman started at the sound and whirled. In
a split second her eyes widened as if witness-
ing hell, but the scream on her lips died in
a muffled cry as he fell upon her.

Yes, they would pay.

The woman went down. The one she
called Johnny spun and cried the terrified
cry that she had been unable to voice.
Brandishing the Winchester, the man lunged
across the porch as the assassin tore the
infant from the woman's grasp. The carbine
boomed, a wild shot that creased the assassin's shoulder and ricocheted into the night.

The searing bullet was unlike any pain the
assassin had ever felt, but he didn't care.
For with a great bound, the puma was off
the porch and dashing through the shadows,
in his mouth the grisly mass of flesh that
had been the child of the man who had
killed his mate.

Winner of the Spur Award for his novel *The
Big Drift,* **Patrick Dearen** is the author of
fourteen novels and ten nonfiction books.
His new novel, *Apache Lament,* is based on

the events surrounding the last free-ranging Mescalero Apaches in Texas, an era that ended with an 1881 fight with Texas Rangers. See patrickdearen.com for more information.

*   *   *   *   *   *

A Century of the American Frontier 1885–1900

■ ■ ■ ■

APACHES SURVIVE

BY HARPER COURTLAND

■ ■ ■ ■

Rose awakened at noon to pounding on the door to her crib — just a tiny room with a bed, the sort where the cheapest whores stayed, those who were older or broken down to the point where they couldn't command higher fees. Hoping to find a daytime customer, she dragged a comb through her hair and pinched her cheeks before opening the door to find the potbellied crib owner scowling at her. "It's time to move on, Rose," he said. "You aren't making enough money to stay here." Behind him, a stringy-haired brunette in a soiled red dress stood smirking at her.

"But you said I could stay through the winter," Rose said, taken aback. "What am I supposed to do when the cold sets in?"

"Not my problem," he said, hooking a thumb under his suspenders. "I meant you could stay if you brought in enough money. Now, hurry up and get out because this young lady's ready to move in." Having no choice, Rose gathered her few belongings and vacated the space.

Not knowing what else to do, she set up a makeshift camp in a piñon thicket outside of town.

Near midnight, Rose hadn't eaten all day. She pulled her shawl tighter around her shoulders. It had been a hot late September day in Kingston, New Mexico, but the desert night air was chilly. Standing in the alley between the Three-Legged Dog Saloon and a hardware store, she heard a man's boots approaching on the wooden sidewalk. When he reached the place where the sidewalk ended, she called out, "Hello, dearie. Could I offer you some entertainment this evening?" She stepped out of the alley, keeping to the shadows to make it harder for him to see her face. The man, tall and stout, maybe fifty years old, kept moving toward her without saying anything. When he reached her, thinking she had a customer, she touched his arm, but he shoved her and said, "Get away from me, you hag."

She would have fallen but her shoulder slammed into the rough corner of the hardware store. "You could have just said no," she hissed. She wished she could cut him with the knife strapped to her leg. When he was gone, she rubbed her shoulder, which would surely bruise, and sat down on an old crate in the moonlight.

Maybe that was just what I needed, a bit of pain to take my mind off my hunger. A fresh round of laughter rose inside the Three-Legged Dog and spilled into the street. Rose stood when a lanky man left the saloon, but she sat back down when she saw the chubby whore in a blue dress at his side. Her motion drew his attention, though. "Well, hello, darling — have a round on me," he called, tossing a coin over near her feet.

"Why'd you do that, Walter?" the whore asked. "Do you think she has nothing to steal?"

The man stopped for a moment and rubbed his chin. "It's good practice," he said. "Haven't you heard the saying, 'Do unto others as — ' "

"But it isn't fair," she whined. "You make *me* work for my money."

"Ah, yes," he said. "That's tragic." He reached into his pocket and handed the greasy-faced woman some cash.

Rose waited until they moved on to pick up the half-dollar the man had thrown to her. She wanted a whiskey, as the man had suggested, but she took it into the saloon and ordered a beer, a bowl of hot chili, and two biscuits to tuck into her pockets for later. Upon leaving the saloon, she slipped back into the alley, passed through it, and headed out of town, moving like the mist after a rain.

Upon arriving at the piñon thicket, she checked to see that everything was still there — her blanket, a comb, a small mirror, a tin cup, a gunny sack, a whetstone, a box of matches, a cooking pot, a bowl, and a spoon. She wrapped herself in the thin blanket, got settled, and ran her hands along her threadbare dress. It frightened her to think of the oncoming winter.

Rose didn't know why she'd kept the mirror. She didn't want to follow the progression of lines in her face or see the gaps where two teeth were missing. She wanted to forget that her honey-colored hair was almost half-gray. The only thing on her face that reminded her of her childhood was the red, berry-shaped birthmark on her left cheek. She was thirty-four years old, but her youth and good looks were spent.

But she could take pride in simply being alive. She knew many whores never survived into their thirties. Whores died of diseases, at the hands of violent men, from drinking too much, from drug use, and, often, by their own hands. She knew exposure could also kill working girls when they were thrown outdoors, but she thought, *I'm an Apache. Apaches survive.*

She wasn't an Apache, of course. In truth, her life had been stolen from her twice: first, when a band of Apaches had taken her during a raid on a wagon train when she was four years old and, second, when she was fourteen and the U.S. Army had taken her from that Apache band's encampment. The Apache woman she'd been given to as a slave had named her *Alch-ísé,* which means "the little one." She had beaten her until she learned to do her chores properly, but eventually she softened to her and treated her more like a daughter than a slave. So Rose had learned how to be silent, how to gather nuts, roots, and berries, how to trap and skin a rabbit, how to make stew with deer meat, and how to make fry bread. And she had grown content with her life among the Apaches.

One morning, she'd awakened to gunfire, horses' hooves pounding the earth, and the smells of blood and death. She had run from a wickiup into the confusion outside, and a soldier had snatched her up onto his saddle and taken her out of the carnage.

Later, she'd been placed in an orphanage where the keepers forced her to relearn English and beat her for crying and begging to return to the Apaches. But why shouldn't she cry? The Apaches considered her a woman after she had started her menstrual cycles, and she had been promised to Dark Wolf, a young warrior. A few more weeks in their camp, and she would have been an Apache wife with all the honor and respect of her position as such. Her white rescuers only saw her as a foolish and ungrateful child.

Looking back, she couldn't understand why it had taken her more than a year to find the courage to steal a butcher's knife and slip away from that orphanage to search for her Apache family. A couple of miners found her, and she soon learned that white people expected the worst of her since she'd lived among Indians, but it hadn't been Apaches that took her virginity forcibly. Upon losing it, she knew she would be considered "soiled goods" in either culture and took up the one profession she saw fit for herself.

Rose sighed and tried to shake off the memories. Her life had become a mess she couldn't fix. Even so, she had once known how to live off the land. She could do it again.

The next morning, Rose found a stream, bathed, and ate one of her biscuits before heading for the Black Range Mountains. Reaching the base of the mountains, she wound her way up a narrow pass, enjoying the songs of little canyon wrens until she was startled by a light brown, mongrel dog, which stepped out from behind a rock and growled at her. She stopped and retrieved the knife she kept strapped to her leg because, even though the dog was very thin, it was large and probably weighed almost as much as she did. She and the dog sized each other up for a moment before the dog came nearer to her and sniffed the air.

Rose sighed, took the remaining biscuit from her pocket, and said, "Come here, girl." She broke the biscuit in pieces and fed it to the dog until it was gone. It seemed crazy to feed a dog when she had so little, but as the man who'd tossed her a half-dollar the night before had said, giving was good practice. Addressing the dog, she said, "I'm going to name you Misty because your hair is colored just like that of a girl I knew in my younger days." Misty nudged her hand, apparently wanting to be petted, and gave her a doggy smile.

As they walked along, Rose gathered whatever she found along the wayside, including a few wild onions and some wild carrots. It was well past noon when Rose left the canyon trail and followed deer paths under the cover of trees. She was glad she had fed the dog because Misty moved with her more silently than she would have expected, and she felt safer with the dog at her side. They came to a place where the ground was covered with acorns, so Rose decided to rest there for a while, thinking she'd gather some later. As Rose drowsed, she felt Misty lunge forward without barking first or making any sound. When the dog returned, she laid a gray squirrel at Rose's feet.

"Good girl," Rose whispered. "Let's be quiet and see if you can do that again." In less than an hour, they had two squirrels, and Rose gathered some acorns and decided they must move on. Soon, she found a good place to camp by a natural spring and set about dressing the squirrels and stewing them in her pot with the acorns, wild carrots, and wild onions. The site was excellent for camping, especially for travelers with horses because there was a huge clearing on one side covered with grama grass. She sat about gathering grass to sleep on, but then she heard Misty growling at the other side of the clearing and went to see why.

An Apache warrior sat up in the grass, knife in hand. "Stop!" she yelled in Apache. "I'll kill you if you kill my dog!"

Drawing closer, she realized she had threatened her old Apache band's great leader, Goyahkla, "the one who yawns," better known among whites as Geronimo. She could tell he was very weak and sick because he was sweating and the hand holding his knife trembled slightly. Though she expected a sharp rebuke, Goyahkla wheezed a laugh and fell back into a horizontal position. She ran to get her cup and filled it with cold water for him.

He tried to pull himself up again when she came with the water, but she shook her head and lifted him, wedging her knee behind his back. He was burning with fever, so she laid him back after he drank, cut some cloth from her skirt, and wet it with spring water.

As she smoothed the cold, wet cloth over his face and neck, he touched the birthmark on her cheek and said, "I had not thought to see you again, Alch-ísé. Do things go well with you?"

Tears came to her eyes because she was overwhelmed that this heroic man remembered her name after so many years had passed. For a moment, she couldn't speak, and then she said, "The white man's world isn't kind to me."

"It isn't kind to me, either," he said. "But the spirit world is good. I performed a sing for my healing a little while ago, and soon I'll be better." He closed his eyes and drifted into sleep.

Rose hurried to cut more grass for herself and for Goyahkla. Before the sun began to set, she filled her bowl with stew and took it to him with another cup of water. This time, he was able to sit on his own to eat and drink. A troubled look came over him, and he asked, "I left my pony hidden before approaching the water supply, thinking I might ambush anyone here, but I found no one. Being feverish, I thought to rest a few minutes and awakened in this state hours later. Will you water my pony and bring him here where he can eat grass?"

"Of course, where is he?"

"About five stone throws up that ridge," he said, pointing to an area beyond the spring. Though Rose was hungry, too, she left to find the pony before it became too dark. On the way back, she found a creosote bush and cut some of it to make a tincture for Goyahkla's fever. She let the pony drink

436

at the spring, but she did not let it overdrink because she didn't know how long it had been without water.

Once she had the pony hobbled in the grass, she returned to her cooking pot. Of what was left of the stew, she poured a portion on a flat stone for Misty, and she ate the rest straight from the pot. After washing the pot, she began boiling the creosote. Darkness had fallen when she took a bundle of grass, rolled Goyahkla onto his side, and stuffed it under him. Then she applied some of the tincture to his chest and wrapped her blanket around him. "I'll check on you during the night. Call for me if you need anything," she said.

She settled onto a bundle of grama grass and cuddled with Misty to keep warm. Around midnight, she took another cup of water to Goyahkla, bathed him, and applied more creosote tincture to his chest. Well before dawn, she awakened and found Goyahkla moving about the camp, preparing to leave. Getting up, she said, "You should rest."

Goyahkla shook his head. "Sickness has already delayed me too long. My sing and your stew and your care have broken the fever. I have important business. I must go." He handed her the blanket and said, "I was going to put it over you before I left, but I see you are too much of an Apache for that to happen without waking you. You say the white man's world isn't kind to you. You're welcome to come back to us, though you must know the bluecoats continue to hound us. If you stay near this spring, I'll send someone for you within a matter of days. Will you do it?"

"I will. I wish to come home." She stood there a moment with a question on her lips, afraid to ask it. As a holy man in their tribe, she supposed he sensed it, for he turned and asked, "What is it?"

"The warrior Dark Wolf. Did he survive the attack on our encampment?"

"He did. He has a wife and three fine sons."

She felt tears stream down her face, but she made no sound. "I'm glad for him," she said after a moment passed.

Goyahkla replied, "Perhaps he would welcome a second wife now." Rose nodded and turned her face away from him. "Why do you turn from me?"

"Because I'm old and ugly."

Goyahkla touched her hand and said, "No need to turn from me or any man. You're a fine woman. Dark Wolf will likely see you as that beautiful girl he knew — and he has

438

changed, too. He still speaks of you at times." Goyahkla mounted his pony and repeated their plan, "Wait here. I'll send for you and your dog."

It felt good to be living as an Apache again, but within three days, a fever came on Rose. By midafternoon, she was burning hot and weak. She knew she'd be unable to protect herself if hostile travelers came to the spring, so with the last of her strength, she dragged her gunny sack over to where Goyahkla had lain hidden in the grass and prepared for the hard time to come. She filled her cooking pot with drinking water and covered it with its lid, placing it by her bed of grass. For a while, she lay there dreaming and clinging to her dog through periods of light and dark, for how long, she did not know. She was dimly aware that Misty left her at times, but she always returned.

Once she heard wheezing and thought Misty had gotten sick, so she held her more tightly and dreamed she was a young girl again, waiting in a wickiup for Dark Wolf to come to her for the first time. Another time, she heard a gurgling sound and assumed her dog was worse. "Let me rest just a bit longer, and I'll get up and find something for you to eat," she whispered before drifting into the depths of dreams again where she was strong and healthy. It seemed she could be anything in the dream world. Soon, she found a fierce desire to become a shape-shifter, so she sat on the edge of a broad overlook and scanned the valley below as her body changed to that of an eagle.

Beside her, Misty growled and Alch-íse thought she heard voices near her as she spread her wings. She felt her body being lifted from the ground effortlessly, and then she was flying out over the valley, thinking, *Apaches Survive.*

Melissa Watkins Starr, writing as **Harper Courtland**, is a native of Eden, North Carolina. She is a former news reporter and a cancer survivor. She works as a writer/editor from her home in Virginia. Her first novel, *Indiscretions Along Virtue Avenue,* was released by Five Star Publishing in December 2019.

■ ■ ■ ■

Spanish Dagger

BY W. MICHAEL FARMER

■ ■ ■ ■

The sun straight overhead, a dust devil appeared out of nowhere to rattle and twist the mesquites and creosotes. Soon disappearing, its intensity left Oats with a sense of foreboding that grew as he saw the distant dust streamer from a horseman heading for him. He pulled Old Joe to a stop. Checking his revolver's load, he threw a leg around his saddle horn, and waited. He soon recognized Tomás Bonito spurring Blackie and slapping him with the reins as lather flew from his neck and withers. Uncurling his leg, Oats sent Old Joe off at a run toward them.

Their horses hung their heads in exhaustion as they walked up the canyon toward the spring and past the neat little house by the corral. Cattle, enjoying the good grass, paid them little attention. Oats saw Jordon stretched out in the shade of an overhang at the spring. His hat was pulled down low over his forehead, a large rounded rock his pillow. His legs were crossed at the ankles; a horsehair quirt he was braiding rested on his chest; his gun was holstered; his gun hand with its fingers partly curled rested on the ground.

Oats tied Old Joe to a piñon and climbed down. Jordon's face was peaceful, close to smiling, eyes closed. He looked like he was taking a nap except for the black, half-inch diameter hole between his eyes.

Nausea burned in Oats's throat; water crept to the edge of his eyes. He dropped down by Jordon and leaned forward to stare at the ground while he swallowed down the bile. The nausea and tears gave way to howls of anger filling his soul. The chaos in his mind ended with a vow that his best friend since they were little boys was going to have justice.

Oats and Tomás circled the body, studying every square inch of ground until they found a place fifty feet away where the grass was bent and bruised. Close by was a pair of boot tracks in the crusty sand, damp from the spring's water. Ten feet from the tracks, a horse had stamped around while tied to a piñon. Another ten yards up the canyon, the tracks showed the horse already in a full run.

They followed the tracks up the canyon until they crossed the ridge into the next canyon and disappeared — a clean getaway. It was Tomás who first saw the little string of hide and blood on the Spanish dagger point fifty yards down the trail from the body. The shooter had run his horse by the sharp, pointed blade of the cactus. There was just enough hair on the hide to make Oats think the horse was white or gray. He ran his fingers over the little piece of hide and dried blood trying to remember who in the basin had a white or gray horse. There were at least twenty, maybe more. He didn't care. He'd check them all.

Tomás helped him wrap Jordon in a blanket. Oats found the slug that killed Jordon pancaked against the bloodstained rock he had used for a pillow. It was three quarters of an inch in diameter with rough splayed edges and grit from the rock smashed into the back surface. He washed it off in the spring and put it in his pocket, and wore it on his watch fob for the next fifty years.

On the way home, they stopped in Canto. Oats sent a telegram to his little sister and mother shopping for a wedding dress in El Paso. He agonized over the words, but found no easy way to tell them to come

445

home right away and that the wedding dress wasn't needed.

The next day, he met Clemmy and Mary at the train. Clemmy's eyes were red and swollen, Mary grim and quiet. They buried Jordon the next day after sitting with his coffin all night. Clemmy wept in soft sobs until the spring in her soul ran dry. Mary stared at the coffin box in the flickering candlelight, her heart lower than a stone falling in a black well. She remembered all the men she had buried in her life. Men who were killed accidently by animals, the land, or weather, but none had been murdered.

The minister gave a fine sermon; everyone in town turned out for the burial service. Jordon had been an iron-nerved young man they all liked and respected. Even as the minister spoke, Oats was looking out the church window at the five gray and white horses ridden to the funeral. None of them were cut — he didn't really expect them to be.

Gloom settled over the Oats ranch house. They all did their work but said little, each immersed in thoughts of Jordon and what might have been. Oats struggled to keep his anger from boiling over and filling his guts with dynamite ready to explode as he tried

446

to get his mind around how to find who had filled his life with such misery.

He expected the sheriff to come investigate. When Asante hadn't put in an appearance, Oats saddled Old Joe and rode the fifty miles into Felicidad. Asante had his boots upon his big rolltop desk ready for his afternoon siesta when Oats appeared in the doorway. Holding his palm out and flexing his fingers to motion him in, the sheriff tilted his hat back. "Howdy Oats. Just gittin' ready for my siesta. Yuh lookin' for me?"

"Afternoon, Sheriff. I came to ask what you planned to do about Jordon's murder. I expected you or a deputy to be doin' an investigation by now."

Asante folded his hands, shook his head, and put on his solemn face. "Decided against one — waste of time." He saw Oats's scowl and held up his hands palms out. "Don't get me wrong, it ain't like Jordon don't deserve to have his murderer caught. But there weren't no witnesses, no suspects at all, nothin' to give us a clue. There just ain't anything I can do. Yuh wanta convict in court, yuh gotta have a charge clearly proved. Yuh got it — a charge clearly proved? Ain't a chance in hell we'd prove anybody done it with what we know." Asante shrugged and turned his ear toward him listening for an answer. "Is there?"

Oats's jaw muscles rippled. "No, Sheriff, I guess there ain't." He turned back to the street leaving Asante staring after him.

On the ride home, Oats recalled that a body had been found two years earlier. An owner of a trading post on the reservation had been killed — shot between the eyes while he slept. The shooter had not been caught. Word among the cowboys around their cooking fires was that José Serna had been the killer. Oats, Jordon, and Serna got along well — there was no apparent reason why Serna would murder Jordon. Besides, Serna rode a sorrel. But Serna was now very friendly with Nate Wells. Nate Wells, six-three, mean, no-good. He was the middle son of Charlie Wells, operator of the biggest ranch in the basin. Charlie had tried to run the little ranchers off their homesteads and block their access to the free range. Many of them left rather than stand up to him. Charlie and his backers took over the deserted homesteads giving them more water with which to control thousands of acres of free range.

Jordon didn't blink when the Wells clan — Charlie, his three sons, a son-in-law, and Charlie's brother, Israel, and his four sons — tried to run him off. At the fall roundup,

Jordon faced down Nate over who owned what cattle and he enforced the branding rules when the mavericks were branded. Nate didn't like it a bit. He swore he'd get even. When Jordon and Charlie Wells crossed paths in Canto, Charlie tried to bully Jordon into giving him compensation for the mavericks Nate had lost in the branding argument. Jordon wouldn't have it and backed Charlie down when their hands settled on revolvers. Nate's favorite horse was a black and white pinto. Killing someone while they slept was just Nate's style; he settled into Oats's mind as the prime suspect for Jordon's murderer.

A week passed. Oats took the wagon and drove into Canto to get supplies. Tying the team at Torrey Lofton's Mercantile, he saw Nate's pinto tied to the hitching rail stomping at flies in front of the saloon a couple of doors down. Casually walking down the street, he stopped and looked the pinto over. There was a cut in a white patch of hide. The horse snorted and its muscles quivered as Oats gently ran his hand by the cut. It was tender, just beginning to heal. The cut was about the right height for the bloody Spanish dagger at Jordon's place. Hearing Nate's loud, raucous laughter in the saloon, Oats stared toward the saloon doors before turning back to Lofton's.

The next day, Oats and Tomás rode over to the Wells ranch. They found Nate's pinto in a pasture far from the ranch house and borrowed it for the afternoon. The return to the little ranch in the canyon, filled with bittersweet memories, and the corpses of a thousand plans, was as hard as anything Oats ever did. Asking Tomás to lead the pinto by the Spanish dagger, he dismounted and stood to one side to watch how the bloody tip matched against the cut. At first, Tomás had a hard time coaxing the pinto close enough to the dagger point for Oats to tell; it kept shying away each time it was led near the cactus. Finally, they put Oats's shirt over its eyes and were able to lead it close enough to almost touch the offending spike. The match of spike height and cut on the pinto was flawless. There was little doubt the horse's rider had murdered Jordon. Still, Oats didn't have enough evidence to take to the district attorney for a charge clearly proved.

Nate Wells was a blowhard. He bragged about everything he did or owned. Oats decided that if Wells had murdered Jordon, then he probably bragged about it to the men who worked for Charlie.

Oats began stopping off at the night fires of the Wells's free-range cowboys to have a little coffee, talk water supplies and grazing, and swap stories. At first the men didn't say much when he was around, but after a visit or two, they took Oats as a friend and began loosening up.

One night while finishing a cup of Arbuckle's, he listened to an argument over how good a man needed to be with a revolver to survive on the free range. Pete Cowans maintained that a man needed to be fast, but accuracy was far more important; he was instantly rebutted by Jeb Fortis who said it didn't do you any good to carry a gun at all if you were shot in your sleep by your enemies. The silence that fell around the fire was instant. Heads turned toward Oats who sat with his coffee listening and saying nothing. In a couple of minutes, the argument had regained full steam. Fortis, saying nothing else, kept glancing at Oats who showed no emotion over what was being discussed.

The next day Oats found Fortis trying to get a calf out of a mudhole while the mother stood at the edge bawling for the life of her baby. After struggling in the wet goo that sucked strength out of hard muscles and made getting a hold on the calf like trying to catch a greased pig, Oats and Fortis managed to pull it free and return it to the side of its mother.

Sitting down in the shade of a mesquite to rest, they shared a canteen and Fortis rolled a smoke.

"I shore appreciate yuh helpin' me out with that calf, Mr. Oats. I'd been in that mudhole for near to an hour and hadn't made much progress."

Oats grinned. "Glad I came along. Sometimes the littlest ones can give you the most trouble. Besides I wanted to talk to you about what you said yesterday evenin' about being shot in your sleep. I'm sure you know about Jordon bein' shot when he was asleep. Just wonderin' if you knew any more about it."

Fortis looked at the ground and shook his head. "I don't want no trouble, Mr. Oats."

"You ain't gonna get in no trouble if I have anything to do with it. I want to know who did it. You ain't got to do anything that'll get you in trouble with anybody."

Fortis sighed and stared off down the cattle path. "You promise this ain't goin' no further than me and yuh?"

Oats held up his right hand as if to swear he was speaking the truth. "You ain't gonna git in trouble with nobody."

Fortis nodded, but wouldn't look at him. Staring at the ground between his boots, he said, "When we was playing cards in the bunkhouse, Nate bragged that he killed Jordon. He said somethin' like, 'By damn I caught that son of a bitch sleepin' and plugged his ass. He ain't gonna bother my daddy no more, that's for shore.' "

Oats clenched his teeth and looked Fortis in the eye. "Who else was at that card game?"

"Well, sir, let me think . . . Pete Cowans was there, Jack Quade, Brownie Newman, Nate Wells, and Ty Hulst. I think that was all."

Oats nodded and stared out toward the mountains in the brown haze. "Cowans seems like a pretty good man, smart in an argument. Do you like him? Has he got spine?"

Fortis took a draw and blew the smoke into the whispering breeze. "Yes, sir, I'd say he's a pretty fair hand. Ain't got a fast gun, but like he was sayin' last evenin', he's accurate and all the years I've knowed him, he ain't never backed away from a threat."

Oats lay back in the shade resting on his elbow, thinking. After a while he said, "You know, I've been trying to find me a couple of top hands for a while now. You and Cowans look like you might fill the bill. Tell you what I'll do. I'll give you five dollars a month more than what old Wells is payin' if you'll come work for me. What d' you say?"

Fortis's jaw dropped. "Five dollars a month more than Wells pays! Mr. Oats, yuh can count me in and yuh can bet I'll work my tail off for yuh too. I don't like old man Wells and those hard-assed sons of his at all, especially Nate. They treat their hands like they's dirt. I can't speak for Cowans, but I'm sure he'd be interested. When do yuh want me to start?"

Oats smiled. "Wait until next payday. Doesn't Wells pay at the end of the month? That's next Friday. You tell Cowans the deal and to think about it. I'll drop by your fire in a day or two and discuss it with him privately."

Fortis grinned and nodded as he stubbed his cigarette.

Cowans was eager to accept Oats's offer when they talked. He didn't like the Wellses and was already thinking about leaving.

A couple of weeks after Fortis and Cowans moved into his bunkhouse, Oats had a come-to-Jesus meeting with them.

"Boys, I'm worried about you stayin' alive."

They frowned, looked at each other and then him. Cowans spoke up. "Just 'xactly what do yuh mean, Mr. Oats?"

"Everybody in this basin knows that Jordon and me was best friends and that I'm lookin' for his murderer. Everybody thinks I plan to shoot it out with who done it. But, I ain't. I'm lettin' the law hang who done it. Sheriff says I got to have a 'charge clearly proved.' That means witnesses. Both you boys heard Nate Wells say he shot Jordon when he was asleep."

Cowans, his teeth clenched in rage, turned to Fortis. "Yuh stupid idiot! Why in hell couldn't yuh keep yore damned mouth shut? Now we're in it for shore!"

Fortis was shaking his head. "But Mr. Oats said what I told him weren't goin' no further than me or him. Didn't yuh say that, Mr. Oats?"

Oats looked at them with hooded eyes. "What I said was you ain't gonna get in trouble with nobody. I want to keep you boys alive and Nate Wells hanged. It ain't me that's spreadin' stories about you boys talkin'. Nate and Charlie ain't fools. Soon as you boys came to work for me they started askin' themselves why I'd hire you two over some other good hands. Then Nate is gonna remember that poker game you was both in and him running his mouth. He's gonna add it up and figure he'll put you down the first chance he gits. Now, boys, I'm swearin' on my mama's good name that ain't gonna happen if you'll promise me you'll give evidence to the grand jury in a couple of months and in a trial if he's indicted. What do you say?"

Cowans and Fortis looked at each other and then stared at Oats in the deepening silence. Cowans slowly nodded. "Reckon we ain't got much choice if we want to go on livin' do we, Mr. Oats?"

"No, you ain't."

For the next two months, Cowans and Fortis worked around the corral and barn doing chores and keeping watch for threatening riders. None ever came. The night before the grand jury was to meet, they along with Oats saddled their horses in the gathering dusk and rode all night along desert trails, avoiding the main road, to reach Felicidad before sunrise.

Oats, Cowans, and Fortis met with the district attorney early that morning. He asked many questions, often asking them to repeat themselves to be sure he understood what they were saying, and he took copious notes. When time drew near for the grand jury proceedings to begin, he asked them to stay around town and be available when he needed to call them.

As the hours waiting passed into days, Oats began to wonder what was taking so long. Why hadn't they been called? The hope for justice that burned in his soul began to dim.

The grand jury adjourned about noon the last day they met. Sheriff Asante was the first man out the door. He smiled and nodded as he walked past Oats and his witnesses. The district attorney was the last one to leave. He saw Oats and shook his head. "Your case wasn't called this session. Maybe next time."

Oats knew the case was never going to be called. He didn't say a word on the ride home.

A rider from Toby Stewart's ranch found Nate Wells in the big ranch house and handed him a note. It read:

Mr. Wells,
    Four days ago, your black and white pinto showed up in our pasture. I'm tired of feeding it. Please pick him up in

the next day or two.

Thanks,
Mrs. Toby Stewart

Nate thanked the rider and said, "Tell Mrs. Stewart I'll be over to pick up that damned troublesome jarhead before dinnertime tomorrow and that I apologize for not getting him sooner. I didn't even know he was gone."

The next morning, Nate saddled up after breakfast and told his wife he'd be back before dinner. When she told him she was worried that he was riding into a lion's den, after all Toby Stewart was Oats's half-brother, Nate laughed. "Oats and Stewart? I ain't afraid of nobody, much less them little desert rats. I'll be back by dinner. Have it ready."

Nate didn't return home by dinner, as he promised. Being young and newly married, Nate's wife was pacing the floor late in the afternoon when Charlie Wells came through the front door after a business trip to El Paso. He saw her puffy, tear-streaked face. "What's the matter, daughter? You look like you lost yore washin' in a dust storm."

Snuffling, she said, "Nate went over to Toby Stewart's place to get his horse. He was supposed to have been back hours ago.

It ain't like him to miss his dinner. Paw, I'm scared somethin' has happened to him."

Charlie flew into a rage. "That fool idiot! Don't he know Stewart and Oats are half-brothers! That gang of thieves and outlaws will kill him if he's alone." He stuck his head out the front door and bellowed for his foreman.

The sun had turned the sky to a brilliant orange glow that painted puffy clouds on the horizon a dark fire red. Toby Stewart was enjoying the peaceful evening sitting with his wife on the porch steps of their ranch house. They were watching Nate Wells's black and white pinto cavort in their corral where they'd put him in expectation that Nate would pick him up earlier that day. Toby was disgusted. Good neighbors kept their word.

At first, they thought the low rumble was thunder in the distance, but the falling light was bright enough to show a dust cloud rolling toward them, hard riding horsemen.

"Toby, do you want me to get your rifle?"

"Naw, it's probably Nate come to claim his horse in grand style. Stay here with me."

Charlie Wells thundered up to Toby's front steps at the head of twenty-five men, their rifles at the ready. His face twisted in rage, he roared, "Where the hell is Nate?"

Toby frowned and looked at his wife. "He ain't been here. We were expectin' him before dinner. That's his horse over there. I don't know where he is."

Charlie turned to his foreman. "Take that son of a bitch inside. He's gonna tell me where Nate is or he ain't gonna see the light of another day."

Charlie spent most of the night "interrogating" Toby. All night Toby swore he didn't have any idea where Nate was. The grandfather clock in the corner was striking four when Charlie growled, "Hang the son of a bitch."

Charlie's son-in-law stepped between Toby and the men with a noose they'd just finished. "Wait a minute, Charlie! What if he ain't lying? What if you hang an innocent man? Your friends and Asante will have to do something and at the very least that's gonna mean jail time. If this man's guilty, we'll find it out and hang him then. You can't do this now. Use your head and think about what you're doin'."

Charlie did think about it as he glared at his son-in-law and then paced the floor for a while before he spoke. "All right, Stewart, you ain't gonna get hanged this night. I can wait. But just look at this here floor. It's got my son's blood all over it. You burned your own house to get rid of the evidence. Get this murderin' bastard and his wife out in the yard and then burn it, boys."

The son-in-law started to speak, but Charlie held up his hand palm out and shook his head.

Charlie and his men spent two weeks searching the range and every ranch in the basin for some sign of Nate. On the third week, an old prospector told Charlie he thought he saw buzzards picking at something buried in the sands.

They found the bones exactly where the prospector said they might be. The skeleton was from a tall man; his boots, fancy and practically new, a gold watch chain and Navajo silver and turquoise bracelet, and a revolver and holster were all that were left. The revolver had been fired twice; the remaining chambers were still loaded. The skull had two bullet holes an inch apart in the left temple.

When Charlie saw the watch chain and bracelet, he knew he had found Nate. As his anger came to a rolling boil, he directed his men to collect his son's remains and swore he would wipe out Oats, Toby Stewart, and any man that stood with them.

Charlie Wells spent the next two months chasing Oats, Toby Stewart, and their friends with a warrant he had gotten from the judge in Felicidad. He never caught them. Oats's trail would disappear up canyons. When Charlie's riders turned back to try and pick it up again, the Oats riders would be sitting their horses not far behind the posse on its back trail. Oats's ability to disappear off a trail and then reappear in a position where he could easily murder the entire posse spooked Charlie's men. They began wondering when Oats would stop running and start shooting. Soon the posse began to lose members as the riders decided discretion was the better part of valor and quit, but all the family men refused to leave the posse. Without riders or bosses to maintain and oversee Charlie's ranching operation, it suffered from neglect and steadily lost money for the businessmen with whom Charlie had herds on shares. As Charlie's riders dwindled down to a small handful, so did his investors. It finally dawned on Charlie that he was never going to catch Oats and that his focus on the chase had led to the ruin of his ranch. It was time to move on to greener pastures and let the law hang Oats and his friends.

When he learned that Charlie Wells's ranch was up for sale and he was leaving the country, Oats rode into Felicidad, turned himself into Asante, and posted bond until the trial. Wells's backers paid a prominent attorney, Allison Tenet, one of the best in the territory, to assist the district attorney in Oats's prosecution for murder.

Tenet conducted a thorough investigation and claimed to have found an old Mexican who had worked for Toby Stewart at the time of Nate's disappearance. The Mexican said he had seen Oats, Tomás Bonito, Toby Stewart, and two men he did not know tie Nate to a post behind Stewart's barn and shoot him to death. Tenet even claimed to have the bullet-riddled post the old man claimed Oats and the others tied Nate Wells to while they filled him full of lead.

Oats hired his own attorney, a young man who had fire in his belly and was not intimidated by the reputation of Allison Tenet.

The courtroom was packed when the old Mexican took the stand. To Tenet's surprise and disgust, the old man eyed the defendant and shook his head at all questions. He denied he'd ever seen anyone tied to a post and shot to death by Señor Oats and the others. Tenet went after the old man for more than three hours but could not make him change his story. Oats's attorney didn't even cross-examine him. The rest of the prosecution witnesses established that Oats had motive for killing Nate Wells, but that was true for half the men living in the basin.

The defense established that on the day Nate disappeared, Oats was in El Paso on business. It took the jury less than ten minutes to declare Oats not guilty.

After the verdict, two crowds formed. One was around Oats surrounded by his neighbors to offer congratulations, and one was around Sheriff Asante surrounded by Charlie Wells and his investors. They were quick to let the sheriff know how angry they were. It was obvious that that verdict was due to the sorry evidence he provided the prosecuting attorneys, and he wasn't getting their support in the next election.

Red in the face and still smarting from the verbal abuse from Charlie and his backers, Asante came up to Oats outside the courtroom, thrust out his chin, and said through clenched teeth, "Yuh got away with it this time, Oats. But next time, by God, yuh'll hang!"

Oats looked Asante in the eye. He nodded and carefully measured his words, a smile flickering at the edges of his lips. "I reckon I will sheriff, when you have a charge clearly proved."

Asante's face became brighter red. He said nothing before he turned and stomped off toward his office.

W. Michael Farmer has published short stories in anthologies, and award-winning essays. His historical fiction novels have won Will Rogers Medallion Awards and New Mexico–Arizona Book Awards for Adventure–Drama, Historical Fiction, and History.

■ ■ ■ ■

THE WAY OF THE WEST

BY L. J. MARTIN

■ ■ ■ ■

"Aye, Mr. Hogart, I hear you perfectly well, and I understand you, but I still think it's about as good an idea as ticklin' a mule's heel to cure your toothache." Big John Newcomber spat a stream of tobacco juice in the dust to punctuate his point.

"Come on inside and let's gnaw a cup of coffee," Hogart said, trying his best to sound like the men who worked for him.

The owner of the recently renamed Bar H, Harold L. Hogart, reared back in his chair, stuffed his fat banker's cigar in his mouth, and narrowed his eyes. He wasn't a banker, but he was the next thing to it; he was an investor. And he had invested in the Bar H a year ago after old man Wells lost it to the Merchant's and Farmer's Bank — but then, old man Wells wasn't the only one to lose a ranch in 1886. All hoped this year would be a lot better.

The two men took a seat at the plank table

that served the bunkhouse. And Hogart did his best to sound the empire builder. "You and I have gotten along fine so far, Newcomber, I hope to continue the relationship. . . . But you've got to abide by my wishes, and his mother and I wish to have our son accompany you on this drive."

"I've already got a half-dozen whelps green as gourds, Mr. Hogart —"

"Then another won't matter much. Wilbur will be ready and waiting at sunup. He's eighteen, older than some of your hands, and perfectly capable. We want him to have this experience before he leaves for college in the East."

So it was settled. John Newcomber had his back up over the whole affair, but he said nothing knowing from long experience as a *segundo,* foreman, that it was hard to put a foot in a shut mouth, and besides, it's usually your own throat you slice with a sharp tongue — and he wasn't about to walk away from a good job when even a poor one was nigh impossible to find. Still and all if he could change the man's mind, he'd give it a go, but he knew that trying to make a point when Hogart thought otherwise was like trying to measure water with a sieve. He'd end up all wet with nothing to show for it. Hogart was slick as calf slobber, but he was the boss.

Ah Choo, the cook, who was nicknamed Sneezy for obvious reasons, filled the two men's coffee cups, but was thinking of his honorable ancestors as he did so — which he had a tendency to do when he had to face unpleasant tasks. He was the bunkhouse cook at the Bar H, not the main house cook. That was Mrs. O'Malior's job. The two of them spatted like a pair of cats whose tails had been tied together before they were tossed over a clothesline. And this afternoon, Sneezy had to go to the main house to round out his chuck for the month-long trip ahead. He did not look forward to the afternoon's chore, nor to having John Newcomber, who he had to be as close to for the next month as a tick in a lamb's tail, start on a long drive with a burr already festerin' under his saddle.

Mr. Hogart finished the varnish Sneezy called coffee, acted as if he enjoyed it, then rose and extended his hand to Newcomber. "You know how important this trip is to the Bar H, John. These cattle have to be in Mojave by the 16th of September in order to fulfill the contract with Harley Brothers' Packing. A day late and those robber barons will want to renegotiate, and the price I have now will just barely cover this year's costs.

Be there on time."

"God willin' and the creek don't rise . . . and some tenderfoot don't stampede the stock, we'll make it. Dry year or no." He couldn't help putting the dig in to the boss's withers like a cocklebur, but it rolled off Hogart like rain off an oiled slicker, not that there'd been enough rain this year to test the theory.

Hogart left the bunkhouse, and John Newcomber stood at a window staring out through the dirty glass, shaking his head. "This is gonna be like startin' a long trip with a sore-backed horse and hole in yer boot sole," he mumbled, more to himself than to Sneezy.

"Pardon, Mr. Maycom'er?" the little cook asked.

"Nothin', Sneezy. Pack a lot o' liniment and bandages, an' a Bible if you own one. I got a bad feelin' about this go."

"Yes, sir, Mr. Maycom'er, sir. Renament and ban'ages and the Christian book, snap snap."

Morning dawned fresh and breezy; with the Sierras at the ranch's back and the Whites — also the better part of fourteen-thousand feet above sea level — between it and the rising sun, it took a while before the sun touched the Owen's Valley bottom

472

with its warmth. It was the better part of two-hundred-fifty miles down the valley and across a piece of the Mojave Desert to reach the rail station at Mojave, and to be comfortable, they'd have to average ten miles a day to keep the schedule. Ten miles should be easy, all things being equal. But John Newcomber had driven stock long enough to know that all things never stayed equal for long.

Sneezy had rung the chuck bell at 3:30 a.m., a half hour earlier than usual, so he could feed the men the last of the eggs and milk they'd see for a good while, and still get a jump on the herd. He wanted to stay ahead of them if he could, at least on this first day — or he'd be eating dust the rest of the drive. And the four-up of mules he had pulling the chuckwagon would keep ahead of the herd, given no major trouble.

True to his father's word, just as Sneezy whipped up the chuckwagon team to get a jump on the drovers, Wilbur Hogart pranced up on one of the Hogarts' blooded thoroughbreds, a dun-colored horse with fine long bones that stood sixteen hands. It was a pleasurable animal to look at, but . . . He carried a quirt and wore a fine new Palo Alto fawn-colored hat, twill pants, a starched city shirt, and English riding boots

473

— on his hip gleamed a new Smith and Wesson chrome-plated .38 in a polished black holster. The bedroll he had tied behind the saddle couldn't have carried more than one blanket and one change of clothes. John Newcomber stood cinching up his sorrel quarter horse as Wilbur's animal proudly single-stepped over to the hitching rail.

"John," the young man said, "I'm ready —"

"You'll call me Mr. Newcomber while you're working for me," the Bar H *segundo* said quietly, his voice matching the cold-granite of his chiseled face — but Wilbur heard him clearly enough. The young man's eyes and nostrils flared a little, but he said nothing in reply. "Understood?" Newcomber asked, unsatisfied with the boy's silence, his own voice a trifle louder.

"As you wish, Mr. Newcomber," the boy replied, stressing the *mister* in a manner that rang of sarcasm. John left it at that, knowing it would be a long trip and that time and the trail would work out most of Wilbur Hogart's kinks. Hard work had a way of doing that to a man, or breaking him, if he wasn't much of one to start with. John really had no way of knowing if Wilbur Hogart had any sand, but time and the trail would tell.

"Dad said I was to ride point," Wilbur added, rubbing salt in the spot Harold L. Hogart had already galled on John's back.

"You'll ride drag, like all new hands do, Mr. Hogart." John Newcomber swung up in the saddle, forking the sorrel and waiting for him to kick up his heels with the first saddle pressure of the morning — he didn't, but John knew the sorrel was saving it for later. He took the time to switch his attention and give Wilbur a hard look.

The boy glared at him. "Dad said —"

"Wilbur, let's get something straight right up-front. Your daddy's not going on this trip, and if I hear you say one more time, 'daddy said,' I'll not take kindly to it and I might lose my temper. I've got a deep well of temper, Wilbur, and I can lose it every hour of every day and not run out. It's been tested. That's the kind of trip this might be, Wilbur, if you say 'daddy said' ever ag'in."

"But —"

"There ain't no buts about it, Wilbur."

"Yes, sir," Wilbur said, to his credit, and reined the tall dun-colored horse away.

Sally Fishbine had ridden for the Bar H for fourteen years, the first thirteen when it was the Lazy Loop, and the last one under

John Newcomber. He reined his bandy-legged gray over beside John and paced him out to what they called the creek pasture, where the eight hundred fifty seven head, by yesterday's count, of Hereford mix — with Mexican Brahma — were gathered. The rest of the hands, a dozen of them, were holding the cattle and getting their minds right for the drive.

"Salvatore," John said quietly as they gigged the horses toward the creek pasture, "is the weather a'gonna hold?"

"Bones say it is," he said, stretching. About that time John's sorrel decided he was awake enough to shake loose, and began a bone-jarring humpbacked dance. "Step lively!" John shouted, giving the big horse his spurs and whipping him across the ears with the rein tails at the same time. The sorrel settled, and John knew from long experience that that was it for the rest of the day.

"I swear, you two are like an old married couple . . . got to have yer spat or you can't get the blood to pumpin'," Sally said, rolling a smoke with one hand as his own mount plodded along.

"Both of us got to show how young we still are," John said, reaching forward and patting the big horse on the neck. "If'n I didn't pop 'is ears ever' morning, he'd think I didn't care for 'im."

They picked the pace up to a cantor, with Wilbur Hogart keeping a respectful twenty paces behind. Wilbur had learned to ride English, in Oakland at the Hogarts' breeding ranch, across the bay from their home in San Francisco, and he could sit a saddle with the best of them by the time he was sixteen, and rode jumpers, but it was different from western riding — considerably different in that you handed the horse to a groom when finished for the day, and you finished for the day whenever you tired of the animal and the exercise. Still, he knew he was equal to anything the country and John Newcomber could throw at him — at least he was quite sure he was.

They crested a rise and looked down into creek canyon, and close to a thousand bald-faced and mixed-breed cattle lowed and grazed while a dozen cowhands waited the chance to earn their dollar a day and found.

Stub Jefferson had ridden in the year before, and John Newcomber had hired him on without so much as a second glance. His rig, and the way the black cowboy sat the saddle and kept his own council, was enough of a resume for John.

Sergio and Hector Sanchez, a pair of

young brothers up from San Diego, were hired on just for the drive. John knew nothing about them, other than they rode fine stock and carried the woven leather reatas of the vaquero, and theirs were well tallowed and stretched to seventy feet with the weight of many a cow.

Old Tuck Holland had been working cattle on the east side of the Sierras for as long as John could remember. He had tales both older and taller than the Sierras and would tell 'em until they chopped ice in Death Valley, if you'd listen. His age was indeterminable but he had to be on the shady side of seventy. He looked so puny he'd have to lean against a post to spit to keep from blowing himself down; but he was tough as whang leather, had a face carved and etched like a peach pit by sun, sand, and wind, and spent most of his time looking back to see if the younger hands were keepin' up. And they were struggling along wondering why he made it all look so plumb easy.

Colorado, which was the only name he gave and consequently was the only name used for him, was redheaded befittin' his name, bow-legged enough that a pig could charge twixt his knees while he was clickin' his heels, and loud; but he pulled his own weight. He too had been hired on just for

478

the duration of the drive.

Pudgy Dickerson was the last of the hands hired on, and John had to bail him out of the Bishop jail in order to do so, but he needed a hand and the rest of the able-bodied men in the valley had run off to another silver strike in the high country — another whiff of bull dung as far as John Newcomber was concerned. But particularly when times were tough men seemed to jump at the chance for easy money. It normally turned out to be grit and grime and beans and backache, but still they chased the will o' the wisp.

The remuda man was Enrico Torres, as good a man with horses as John had ever seen. He pushed three dozen head of rank half-broke stock so the cowhands could trade off a couple of times a day. It was hard country between the north end of the Owen's Valley and Mojave. Some spots of good grass and sweet water, but more than enough hard-as-the-hubs-of-hell ancient lava flows and flash floods, cactus and snakes, and heat if the weather decided it wanted to run late, or snow if it ran early. And it usually decided to do one or the other — and sometimes both — when a herd was being shoved to market. It was hard on horses and men, and hard as hell on a good attitude.

They pushed the herd out, jittery, but then all of them were when a drive began and before they settled into the routine. The men found their positions, all unassigned except for Stub Jefferson, the black cowhand who was riding point, and the Sanchez brothers, who were assigned drag with Wilbur Hogart and quickly took up positions flanking and staying out of the dust. The Sanchez boys had ridden enough drag to know they could stay out of most of it on the flanks, and still do their job. So they gave Wilbur the position of honor . . . or so they told him . . . dead center trailing the herd.

John Newcomber floated from position to position, judging the men he didn't know, watching the herd, eyeballing the weather, and worrying — that was his job.

They hadn't gone three miles before Wilbur Hogart let his horse drift over close enough to Hector Sanchez so he could call out to him. "I'm Wil Hogart," he called.

Hector looked over and nodded, and touched the brim of his sweat-solied sombrero.

"What's a fella to do about the privy?" he shouted again.

Hector looked at him, a little confused.

"I need to pee," Wilbur said.

"Sí," Hector repeated, "the señor needs to 'pee.' " He reined over closer to the fancy-looking gringo, who didn't look quite so fancy now that he was covered with a half-inch of dust. "Well, señor, you ride sidesaddle to accomplish that task."

"Sidesaddle?" Wilbur questioned. "You're funnin' me, *amigo.* I meant do you take the drag while I drop out, or just what?"

"Señor Newcomber will be very angry if you stop to water the sagebrush, señor. It is the tried and trusted sidesaddle method —"

"Fill in for me, señor," Wilbur said, and reined away to find a bush, which was no problem as the country was chaparral covered.

"Sidesaddle," Hector said to himself, then laughed aloud. He couldn't wait to tell his brother.

"Sidesaddle," Wilbur repeated to himself, pleased that he had not fallen for the obvious prank of the other rider. He knew he would be the butt of many attempts, but was wise to them.

He dismounted and unbuttoned his trousers and began to relieve himself, just as the grass under his attacking stream came alive in the most terrible buzzing and thrashing Wilbur had ever heard. He stumbled back

481

and pawed at the Smith and Wesson when he realized it was a four-foot rattler he had the misfortune to awaken from his repose in the sun.

Wilbur emptied the six-shooter, managing to scare the snake into retreating even faster than he already was, but not managing to kill it.

Still, Wilbur was satisfied with himself — until he heard the men begin to yell, and felt the vibration of nearly four thousand hooves begin to beat in rhythmic stampede.

"My God," Wilbur said aloud to himself. "Did I . . . ?"

He raced for the thoroughbred, mounted, and rode after the advancing wave of cattle and men, and into a wall of dust as he had never seen.

The cattle ran for three miles, then the heat and the sun dissuaded them and they slowed, and finally, no longer hearing the explosions that had set them off, stilled and grazed.

John Newcomber sent Stub and Sally back along the flanks to pick up any strays, and checked with each of his men to make sure they were present and accounted for.

Wilbur Hogart, who sat at the rear of the herd, catching his breath as the thoroughbred stood and hung his head sucking in

482

wind, was the last man he approached.

"You managed to keep from getting ground up," Newcomber greeted him.

"Yes, sir."

"Let me see that firearm," Newcomber said, his face turning to granite.

"It was a snake, Mr. Newco—"

"You shot at some poor ol' snake who was trying his best to get the hell out of the way!"

"He was only a couple of feet away, makin' a terrible noise."

"Give me that weapon."

"Dad said —"

"What did I tell you about that 'dad said,'" Newcomber snapped.

Wilbur looked red faced, but quieted and reached down and slipped the Smith and Wesson out of its holster and handed it over. Newcomber slipped it into his saddlebag. He eyed the boy up and down shaking his head. "Don't make any more trouble, Wilbur. You just cost the Bar H about a thousand dollars in lost weight. At a dollar and a half a day, not that you're worth that, it'd take you some time to pay it back should Mr. Hogart want his due."

"A thousand dollars?"

"A thousand dollars . . . that is if we get all the steers back."

John reined the sorrel away.

Wilbur sat chewing on that for a while, when Stub and Sally approached, pushing a half-dozen head that had strayed during the stampede. They reined over next to him as the strays rejoined the herd, kicking up their heels like a reunion of old friends.

"You the *jefe's* pup?" Sally asked.

Wil gigged his horse over and extended his hand. "I'm Wil Hogart." Sally shook with him, but Stub just touched his hat brim, and Wil said "Howdy."

"Did the boss tell you about Oscar?" Sally asked.

"Oscar?" Wilbur said.

"Oscar, the new hand with the six kids and the crippled wife."

"He didn't say —"

"Oscar got stomped under." Sally said, keeping a straight face. Stub eyed him but, as always, kept his own council.

"Stomped under?" Wilbur asked.

"Ain't enough of 'im left to bury," Sally said, shaking his head sadly.

"You mean —"

"Oscar's cold as a mother-in-law's kiss, boy." Sally looked as if he was about to break into tears.

"It's all my fault," Wilbur said, his face fallen.

"Don't know about that," Sally said. "It's the Lord's place to judge reckless behavior . . . the kind what causes the good to die young. Yer misbegotten ways will be laid out a'fore St. Peter soon enough. You may not even survive this drive. Many won't. Maybe you'll meet Oscar in heaven and can explain to him why you got him stomped into salsa. Well, it's nice to make yer acquaintance." He reined away. Both he and Stub were doing their best not to break into uproarious laughter, and in doing so, their shoulders quaked. Wilbur thought they were both in the throes of grief.

"Aren't we going to bury him?" Wilbur called after them.

Stub turned back, wiping the tears of laughter from his eyes. "He's already stomped so deep he'll take root and sprout." He turned away, and the shoulders shook again.

Wilbur Hogart had never felt so terrible. What kind of a man was John Newcomber to worry about running off a thousand dollars' worth of fat, and not even mention a man who had been stomped to death?

The word traveled quickly among the men, and all stayed away from Wilbur for the rest of the afternoon — knowing they would break into laughter if they rode up beside the dejected boy, and give it away. Wilbur clomped along behind the herd, his eyes and ears filled with dust, his mind filled with remorse.

They caught up with where Sneezy had made camp, an agreed spot ten miles from the home place on the edge of Bar H property and on the bank of a fair cold creek, lined with willows, a couple of spreading sycamores, and a few Jeffery pines.

Wilbur was the last to the camp, and the men parted from a group as he rode in — Wilbur presumed it was because he was approaching, and that they didn't want to have anything to do with the man who'd caused Oscar's death. Not that he knew who Oscar was. He'd only met a couple of the men, and Oscar had not been one of them.

Wilbur dropped the saddle from the thoroughbred and turned him out with the remuda, then walked straight over to John Newcomber.

"They told me about Oscar," he said, his weight shifting from foot to foot. "I want to go back and pick up his body. A Christian —"

John Newcomber gave him a dubious look and started to say something, but was interrupted.

Sally stood nearby and offered quickly,

"Oscar wanted the coyotes and other critters to have him, boy." Sally removed his hat and placed it across his heart. "It was his last wish. He always was a kind soul to the little critters. And it's the way of the west. We'll say a few words about him after we bean up."

Wilbur was still unsatisfied, but didn't know what to say. It was a custom he'd never heard off, but little would surprise him with what he knew of cattle drives and drovers.

"The coyotes?" he finally managed to mumble in amazement. His gaze wandered from man to man, but none would meet his and none offered to disagree with what he thought was a pagan practice.

"Oscar was a religious soul, but he was the outdoors type . . . thought these here mountains was his . . . what do ya call them fancy churches . . . his cathedral. He wanted to be spread all over these mountains," Sally added. "Nothing like a band of the Lord's scavengers to spread a body about. Crows and buzzards and such fly for miles doing their business and the coyotes and skunks and wolves'll deposit him in all the places he loved — not in exactly the way I'd personally favor it, but he'll get spread. Ashes to ashes, dirt to dirt, dung to dung, so to speak."

Wilbur thought he was going to be sick to his stomach. All the men turned away, and some were obviously overtaken with grief. They held hands to face and shook, or turned away. He walked away from the camp and into a clump of river willows and found a rock by the creek and sat, watching the water tumble by, wondering what would happen to "Oscar's" six starving children. He sat there until he heard Sneezy bang the bottom of an iron skillet, and hurried to get his beans — grief and remorse was one thing, hunger was another.

The men ate in relative silence. Once in a while, one would mention one or another of Oscar's children, or his crippled wife.

The men cleaned up the biscuits, bacon, and beans, and hauled their tins to Sneezy. Darkness was creeping over the camp, and chill setting in. The drive would take them from fifty-five-hundred feet elevation on the slopes of the Sierra, which rose to fourteen-thousand feet behind them, down to less than two-thousand feet at the railroad corrals at the town of Mojave.

"Time for the ceremony," Sally said. "Gather round, boys."

All the men gathered in a circle, standing, drinking their coffee, gnawin' chaw, smoking roll-your-owns. "Now, what do you remember about Oscar?" Sally said. "You start, Stub."

Stub removed his hat and scratched his woolly head. "Well, I ain't much on reminiscence, so to speak, but I might remember something, given as how Oscar was such a fine fella." He took a long draw on the tin cup, then began. "You know that ol' Oscar used to run the Rocking W down near San Berdo. He was countin' cattle there for a buyer from San Francisco, and knew the W didn't have enough cattle to meet the contract, so ol' Oscar set his countin' chute up against a small hill. The buyer set up on the top rail and went to markin' off the stock. Ol' Oscar had the boys drive those heifers and steers round and round that hill till the buyer counted what he needed, then drove the herd off to the yards. The W got paid for nigh five-hundred head . . . twice. Oscar saved the Rocking W, which the bank was sure to grab."

The boys laughed at that, but Wilbur found it to be down right dishonest. He smiled tightly.

"How 'bout you, Tuck?" Sally encouraged the old cowhand.

"Well, Oscar was a tough ol' bird." Tuck scratched his wrinkled chin and its stubble of a day's growth of beard. "One time the foreman of the Three Rivers Ranch bet him a season's pay that he couldn't make love to an Indian squaw, kill a grizzly bear, and drink a fifth of whiskey in one day . . . and the foreman knew where the bear's den was and knew an ol' squaw who was a mite friendly to all the Three River's hands, were they to bring her a bag o' beans or sugar. Well Oscar took that bet, but the thing was, he drank the fifth a' rye first, then . . . a little confused with the firewater an' all . . . he shot the ol' squaw dead as a stone. The hard part was holdin' that griz down . . . but he did an' that's why some bears here about is such sonsa'bitches."

The boys laughed and slapped their thighs.

Wilbur began to get a little suspicious.

"How about you, Colorado?" Sally asked the pock-faced redheaded cowhand. He sat away from the others, sharpening a ten-inch knife on an Arkansas whetstone.

"I never much cared about tellin' tales," he said, and spit a mouthful of tobacco juice, then went back to his work on the blade.

"You, Pudgy," Sally asked the man John Newcomber had bailed out of the Bishop jail to join the drive.

"Nobody," Pudgy began, "could ever find his way home, good as old Oscar. One time over at the Whiskey Holler' saloon in Virginia City, old Oscar went up to the bar with a bunch of hands he'd just finished a drive with, and they got to drinkin' and drinkin'. A couple of the boys, realizing how drunk ol' Oscar was, went out to his nag and turned the saddle around — they didn't want him riding into trouble. Oscar, hanging onto that poor ol' nag's tail, rode clean to Sacramento before he sobered up and realized he was facing backward. He never could find his way to Sacramento after that, unless he reversed his saddle. But he was always real good at knowin' where he'd been."

By this time Wilbur was red in the face.

"We need to cheer up," Hector Sanchez said, after he quit holding his sides from laughing. "A little friendly competition. Who's the newest hombre to sign on?" Hector asked.

"Must be ol' snake killer," Sally said, putting an arm around Wilbur's shoulders. "You get to go first."

"Wait a minute," Wilbur said. "Did any of you fellas even know this Oscar fella? In fact, was there even any Oscar at all?"

"I've knowed a few Oscars in my day,"

491

Sally said. "How about you, Stub?"

"Cain't say as how I ever knowed an Oscar."

All the men broke into laughter, slapping their thighs. Wilbur reddened again, and he felt the heat on the back of his neck. He didn't know whether to get angry and stomp away or offer to fight, so he just stood and got a silly grin on his face.

"Ain't you proud you didn't cause nobody to get hurt with that fool stunt?" Sally said, more serious than not.

Tuck cut in before Wilbur could answer. "Give the boy a chance to show he's as good as the rest a' ya." Old Tuck looked serious. "Ya'll been funnin' him enough."

Hector stepped over in front of Wilbur. "Can you swing an axe, Señor Hogart?"

"I imagine."

"Good, then we have the notch cutting contest."

"Notch cutting?"

"Sure, every drive has the notch cuttin' contest."

John Newcomber walked away shaking his head, but was unseen by Wilbur who was anxious to redeem himself for being stupid enough to be taken in with the stomped-in rider story.

"Notch cutting," Hector said. "You go

492

first, so the rest of us know what we have to beat."

Sneezy had already fetched the double bladed axe out of the chuckwagon and offered it to Hector. "Come on, over here." He led Wilbur to a fallen log, two foot in diameter.

"This is a good log for notch cutting," Hector said, and the other men agreed with him. He lined Wilbur up in front of the log. "Get your distance, *amigo*," he suggested, and Hector adjusted his distance from the log.

"Now, here is the rub, *amigo*." Hector stepped behind Wilbur and encircled his head with his red-checkered bandanna.

"Hold on, now," Wilbur tried to protest.

"This is how it is done, *amigo*. Blindfolded. You can do it."

Wilbur allowed himself to have the blindfold put on.

"Wait until I give the signal," Hector said. "Your hat, *amigo*," he said, and removed Wilbur's new fawn-colored, now dusty, wide-brimmed hat. "You will do better without the hat."

"One, two, three, go," Hector called and, and the men yelled their encouragement.

Wilbur, with vigor born of embarrassment and a desire to show these men he was equal to any of them, swung the axe five times before Hector yelled for him to stop. "Time is up, *amigo.*"

Wilbur reached up and removed the blind-fold, anxious to see how much of a notch he'd cut. And he'd cut three fine ones . . . in his hat. His new Palo Alto lay in front of the log, its crown split, its brim with two wide splits.

"Carambra," Hector said, a sorrowful look on his face, "you have cut the notch right where I put your *sombrero* for safe keeping."

The men roared with laughter.

"You win the contest, Wilber," Tuck said. "The prize is a free millinery redesign. That's now what's known as an Owen's Valley special."

Wilbur's mother had bought him that hat, just for this trip. The anger began to crawl up Wilbur's backbone, and to the men's surprise, he cast the axe aside and went after Hector Sanchez with his fists. Hector was quick as a snake, and backpedaled as Wilbur took four or five healthy swings, then Hector charged in low and tackled him and drove him to his back. He got astride him and pinned him down. Wilbur was red in the face and spittin' mad, but he couldn't move.

"Hey, *amigo,* you can't take a joke?" Hector asked.

"Let me up and I'll show you."

"I think I hold you here awhile until the pot she don't boil so much," Hector said.

"Let him up," John Newcomber said, crossing the clearing from where he'd been leaning against a log, taking it all in. "And Mr. Hogart, you will find your bedroll and a place to bed down. The fun is over."

"You might think it's fun."

"I notched my hat, as did most every man here. It'll pass and you'll see the humor in it."

"The hell I will."

Hector unloaded off of him, and Wilbur regained his feet, spun on his heel, and stomped away.

"Remember the Alamo," he said under his breath, but no one heard.

He found a spot away from the others for his bedroll, and ignored the feigned compliments to his hat the next morning as the men ate beans and cornbread by the dawning light. He turned in his tin and got a handful of jerky and hard biscuits for his noon meal, and was the first to saddle up for the day's work.

The wrangler, Enrico Torres, cut out a new horse for him — ignoring Wilbur's suggestions that he ride his own thoroughbred with a terse, "Horse has to last the trip, and you will get a new *caballo* at least twice a day, sometimes thrice, from here on."

The ragged-looking buckskin selected by Torres stood and allowed the currycomb, then the saddle and bridle, but went into a stiff-legged bounce as soon as Wilbur forked him. As much as the boy fought to control the animal, he turned and bounced right through the middle of Sneezy's camp, kicking fire, and ash, and dust in every direction. The Chinese cook scattered for cover, cursing in Oriental jabber, then sailed a pot lid after the boy and high-jumping horse as they moved on into the chaparral.

But to the surprise of all who watched in amusement, Wilbur stuck in the saddle.

He tipped his hat after he got control of the animal, yelled, "Sorry, Sneezy," then gigged away the snorting horse, keeping the animal's chin pulled to its chest, to take up his position riding drag.

"Not bad for a stall-fed tenderfoot," Enrico said to Sally and Stub, who were currying their animals nearby. "His ridin' ability is a bit better than his sense of humor."

"Spent his first day admiring his shadow, cause there was no mirror handy," Stub said. "I thought at first he might be studyin'

496

to be a half-wit, but I believe he might just end this trip knowin' dung from wild honey. He's game enough, and has more sand than I figgered."

"I donno," Sally offered. "It seems to me he's taken too much of a liking to thick tablecloths and thin soup, but we'll see . . . we will see. My bones is goin' to achin', weather's a' comin'."

Before noon, the sky turned from deep bright blue to flat pewter and the temperature plunged forty degrees. The wind whipped down out of the Sierras, and men pulled coats from rolls behind their saddles.

Wilbur Hogart had a coat, but a light one that served as little more than a wind-breaker, and the gloves he pulled from his saddlebag were kid leather — not working gloves, nor warm. Before long, he was cold to the bone, hunkered over like a ninety-year-old man, and shivering in the saddle. To add injury to insult, the hole in the crown of his hat leaked water, and his head was soaked.

Hector Sanchez had kept his distance and the two young men had no more than exchanged glances.

By midmorning, flakes of snow began to drift. Both Enrico and Hector Sanchez had pulled heavy *serapes* from the rolls at the back of their saddles, and their wide sombreros kept the snow from their shoulders. A steer began to fade back from a position between Hector and Wilbur, and both men moved to haze it back into the herd.

As they did so, Hector spoke for the first time that day. "You do not have a heavy coat?"

"I'm not cold," Wilbur managed through teeth gritted to keep them from chattering.

"I see that, *amigo,*" Hector said, and smiled and reined away.

"Greaser," Wilbur said under his breath, and pulled the light jacket closer as he moved back to his position. At least the dust had stopped.

After a moment, Hector again moved closer and yelled to Wilbur. "I must leave for a *momentito.* Cover the flank."

Wilbur said nothing, even though he heard. He watched the Mexican gig his horse and lope away, then laughed to himself. If the herd did fade and stray on Hector's side, Hector would get a dressing down from Newcomber. He ignored the herd on Hector's flank and tended only those cattle directly ahead of him.

But as fate and the cold would have it, the herd did not stray but rather bunched closer, and Hector soon returned. He drifted over to Wilbur and tossed him a bundle. "It was Oscar's *serape.*" He laughed and slapped his thighs. "He needs it no longer so he left it to me. It is not because I am generous, *amigo.* If you continue to knock your teeth together like the castanets, you will cause another stampede. And more work for us all."

Wilbur held the wool *serape* in his hands and stared at the young Mexican, saying nothing.

"Ayee! You stick your *cabeza* . . . your head through the slit, tenderfeets."

"Though the slit," Wilbur repeated. And without hesitation, learned the use of the *serape.* The same one he had seen Hector use as a blanket the night before.

"*Sí, amigo,*" Hector said, and spun his horse to return to his position.

"*Gracias, amigo,*" Wilbur called after him.

"*Da nada,* Wil," Hector said, and gave the spurs to his horse. "You have mastered the *serape,* a difficult task. Tomorrow, if the weather is better, I will teach you the use of the reata . . . it should be nothing for a man who can chop a notch as you can."

"Tomorrow, if the weather is better," Wil called after him, and wondered what new trick Hector had up his sleeve and he knew that if Hector was fresh out, the others weren't. He wondered if he could borrow a needle and thread from Sneezy to sew up his hat — if Sneezy wasn't still wanting to sail pot lids at him for riding through the middle of camp.

But he was sure Sneezy had long forgotten the incident.

The wind picked up again. But he didn't care. He was warm, for the first time that day.

He removed his hat, eyed it skeptically, and began to chuckle.

L. J. Martin is the bestselling author of over fifty western, crime, and thriller novels. He lives in Montana and winters in California. Check out more from his website: www.ljmartin.com.

■ ■ ■ ■

RETURN TO LAUREL

BY JOHN D. NESBITT

■ ■ ■ ■

The print shop I was looking for lay on a side street a few blocks from downtown North Platte. My route took me past a row of meat markets and green grocers. At a little before eight in the morning, a row of delivery wagons stood in the street, each one backed up to the sidewalk with a team of horses turned at an angle. When I walked down the same sidewalk the evening before, to make sure of the location, the street was calm and quiet. Now the area was bustling, with men and boys unloading sacks of potatoes, crates of melons, and bushel baskets of fresh corn in pale green husks. One wagon had a box of dressed chickens, white and yellow, on a bed of crushed ice. I paused at the last wagon, where two men in newsboy caps and shirtsleeves were grappling with a block of ice the size of a coffin. They slid it onto a cart that had small wheels with wide iron rims, then hauled the cart into the dark interior of a shop that sold fish.

Down the street a ways, I found Empire Printing and went inside. The clock on the wall showed a few minutes before eight. A man wearing a gray apron was working at a stack of burlap bags, brushing black ink across a tin stencil. As he set aside a printed bag, I saw the word "BEANS" in capital letters, with "50 Lbs. Net Weight" below the word. Along the walls I saw bills and posters on display, advertising horse sales, theatrical productions, and a traveling wax museum.

The man set his brush in an inkpot and turned to me. He had long, straight hair and thick spectacles, and he had a few dots of ink spatter on his face.

"Yessir. Help you?"

"My name's Henry Tresh. I have an appointment with Mr. Haines."

"He's in his office. Come on back."

He led me to an office with a window looking out onto the work area. Inside, a man sat behind an oak desk. Off to his side, a woman dressed all in gray sat with her hands in her lap.

The man rose. He was in later middle age, with weight showing in his face and his upper body. He had thinning brown hair, a

504

trimmed mustache, and a pale complexion. As he reached across the desk, he said, "Mr. Tresh. I'm Edwin Haines, and this is my wife." We shook hands.

I took off my hat, nodded to the woman, and said. "Pleased to meet you both."

"Have a seat," said Mr. Haines.

I took one of the two wooden chairs on my side.

"We appreciate your traveling this far to visit with us." He settled into his seat and picked up a polished steel letter knife. Looking at it as much as at me, he said, "It's very difficult for us to get away. My business has me tied down."

"I understand. Travel is part of my business, at times."

"I'm sure you're wondering why we wrote to you all the way out in Cheyenne, Wyoming."

I shrugged. "I assume people have their reasons."

"You could say we have two. One is that we understand you have had some success at finding missing persons. We read the story of how you found the girl in Laramie City. Alive."

"I consider myself very lucky. And in her case, thankful as well."

"And the second reason is that the work

505

we would like you to do is in Wyoming. Close to the center of the state."

"I see." I glanced at Mrs. Haines and back at him.

He stared at the letter knife, frowned, and looked up at me. "Mr. Tresh, it's our son. His name is Arthur. He went missing quite a while back."

"I'm sorry to hear that." I nodded toward Mrs. Haines to include her. She continued to sit with her hands folded and her mouth firm.

Mr. Haines let out a heavy breath. "It's been almost twenty years, and there's never been a day without anxiety for us."

"Have you tried looking for him before now?"

He spoke in a weary voice. "It's so far away, and Wyoming is such a vast area. And to tell you the truth, we didn't know where to begin until just recently. We didn't know the name of the town where he was last seen."

I let him speak. I assumed that if he wanted me to do this piece of work, he would tell me the name of the town without my asking.

"You see, he got into trouble because of a girl. Don't get me wrong. He didn't get the girl into trouble in that sense. But he took off with her."

"They did not elope," said Mrs. Haines.

"No, they didn't," said her husband. "They didn't get married or anything like that. They just ran off together, on a kind of adventure. Something happened, we don't know what, but the girl showed up again, and Arthur didn't."

"She must have given you some explanation."

"She has never cooperated with us. Any time we've tracked her down, she goes somewhere else. And she won't talk."

"It's all her fault from the beginning," said Mrs. Haines. "Arthur would not have gotten into any kind of trouble if it weren't for her."

"Very well," I said. "I have an idea of the case. Perhaps we should determine whether I'm going to work for you."

"Of course," said Mr. Haines. "We need to tend to the business details." He held the letter opener by the point as he tapped the back of his other hand. "We'd like to know your fees."

"Not to be too blunt, but I need a hundred dollars minimum for my time, plus my travel expenses. If my work goes beyond two weeks, my fee continues at three dollars a day."

"I see. When does your time begin?"

"It already did. When I left Cheyenne."

Mr. Haines took a long breath, glanced at his wife, and said, "I suppose we should."

"Very good," I said. "If the girl lives anywhere near, I can begin by talking to her. What's her name, by the way?"

"Bella Collingsworth. But I don't know where you can find her."

"How old is she now? You say this was about twenty years ago?"

"Yes. Arthur would be thirty-eight now, and this girl, who is no longer a girl, would be about thirty-seven."

"And her last known address?"

"It was in Broken Bow, but that was years ago. She's moved around. We thought you might make more efficient use of your time if you went to the town where Arthur disappeared. As I said, it's been but recently that we learned the name of the place, and that's why we wrote to you."

I saw that I was going to have to ask after all. "Very well. If you could tell me the name of the town, I'll have a place to start."

Mr. Haines looked at his wife and back at me. "This is a very important undertaking for us."

"I understand. And I'll do the best I can."

"Laurel," he said, turning again to his

wife. For a moment I thought he was speaking to her, until he met my eyes and said, "The name of the town is Laurel."

I found the town named Laurel, first on the map and then on the rolling plains, a day's ride north of Douglas on Walker Creek, not far from Thunder Basin. Like many such towns, it sat on a main trail and drew most of its business from the surrounding ranch country. I took a room at the Blue Star Hotel and lingered a few minutes to visit with the person at the desk.

She was an attractive woman, with dark brown hair, brown eyes, and a clear complexion. She wore a woman's business suit consisting of a dark blue wool jacket and skirt with a white blouse. I guessed her to be about my age, somewhere around thirty-five.

"I hope you enjoy your stay in our town," she said as she handed me the key. "If there's a way I can help, please let me know."

"I appreciate it. You might be able to recommend someone. I'm interested in the possibility of doing a little hunting. Perhaps antelope but more interested in deer."

"You don't have to go far for antelope. As for deer, there are some breaks and pine ridges over to the east, and from what I understand, that's where they find deer. If you want someone to take you out, I know of one young fellow who does that sort of thing. His name is Clay Cooper."

"Good to know. I'll tell you, I've heard a story of a huge buck deer, with a great set of antlers, that someone killed in this area about twenty years ago."

"Clay would be too young to know much about that, and he didn't grow up here."

"I'm sure there are some old-timers. Someone might even have a photograph."

"No telling. But if you want to talk to someone who's been here a long time, there's Mr. Boynton, the druggist. He's rather knowledgeable on a variety of subjects, and he's something of a town historian, though he hasn't written it down, as far as I know."

"Mr. Boynton."

"Yes. Hugh Boynton. They call him the old bachelor."

I met her eyes and gave her my best smile. "Thank you. You've been very helpful."

"And the young man's name is Clay Cooper."

"Right. I caught that."

"You'll find him at the blacksmith shop. If you need a horse shoed, he's good at that."

"Thank you again."

I found Clay Cooper by following the sound of metal on metal. I came to a low wooden building with most of the white paint worn off. Inside, a slender young man of about twenty-five was beating a short-handled sledgehammer on an iron rod. He wore a leather apron and a cloth skullcap, both grimy. He looked up from his work and smiled.

"Howdy."

"Good afternoon. The lady at the hotel says you're a man who knows his business."

"That's nice of her." He looked past me. "What do you need done?"

"Nothing at the moment. But with fall in the air, I'm thinking of doing some hunting."

"There's some of that around. Deer, I guess?"

"I could try for an antelope, but what drew me here was the deer. I heard a story about a legendary deer that someone killed in this area about twenty years ago."

Clay shook his head. "Haven't heard of it. But there's some big ones out there in the breaks. Hard to git. That's how they come to be so big."

"I believe it. The lady at the hotel —"

"Miss Glover."

"Yes. She told me that the one person in town who knew all the old stories was a Mr. Boynton."

"Oh, the old bachelor." Clay gave a short laugh. "They say he knows just about everything."

"If he's anything like Miss Glover, he might be able to —"

"Ha. He's nothing like Miss Glover. Though they know each other."

"Being an old bachelor, he's probably not her gentleman caller."

"Ha-ha. Far from it. But he's got the biggest house in town, and she's got the best business." Clay gave me a sly look. "Got an eye for her?"

"Nothing more than normal. And she seems pretty reserved."

"Oh, she's all right. She's just a little above most people here. She's been out in the world, had some kind of an upset, and came back here to run the hotel when her father died. If she doesn't keep a distance — well, even as it is, she has to cool off every teamster or cowpuncher who's got four bits for a room. She's not your common kind of heifer."

"All for the best, I'm sure."

"So when do you want to hunt?"

"What do you think? You know more about this country than I do."

"Cottonwood leaves are just beginnin' to turn yellow. I'd say in another week or two. If you kill a nice buck, you want to be sure his horns are out of velvet."

"Oh, yes." I glanced around the shop and came back to the smith. "And what about Mr. Boynton? Miss Glover said he's a druggist."

"He's only in his shop when someone needs him. You can usually find him at home."

"In the biggest house in town."

"That's right." Clay pointed with his thumb over his shoulder. "You can't miss it. Big wooden house on a stone foundation. Gray with white trim."

Clay Cooper was right about not missing the house. I saw it from a block away, stately with two dormer windows, scrolled white woodwork, and a stone foundation painted white. I guessed that the house had a cellar or basement, which with the main floor and then the attic made for a large house for an old bachelor.

The front yard on either side of the walkway had a series of flower beds, with taller plants like daisies and zinnias growing

513

in the plots closer to the house, while lower plants of the pansy and petunia variety grew in front. Closest to the street, the earth had been worked up in a strip about six feet wide and twenty feet long. A man was jabbing at the dirt with the tip of a garden spade, breaking the clods into smaller pieces. As I approached, he looked up and paused in his work.

He was an older man, about sixty, above average in height, with a not very firm physique. He was wearing a drab work shirt with a low collar and three buttons. It fit him close, so that his sagging chest muscles showed like breasts. His shoulders sloped, and his waist spread, like that of a man who spent most of his time in a stout chair, yet here he was, working on a sunny fall afternoon.

He wore lightweight leather gloves. Holding the shovel handle with one hand, he rubbed his forehead with the other. "Good afternoon," he said.

"How do you do?"

"Well enough for an old man."

"Getting some exercise. That's good." I stopped at about twelve feet from him. His short-brimmed hat cast a light shadow on his face, but I could see him now.

His face was thick with age, full and not

wrinkled. He had pale eyes with heavy brows above and bags beneath. His blond hair had gone not to gray but to the colorless hue of dead grass in winter. He was clean-shaven, and his small, yellowing teeth showed when he spoke.

"It's that time of year to plant the tulip bulbs."

I looked at the ground and nodded.

"Visitor?"

"Yes. For me, it's that time of year to think about hunting."

"This is a place for it, though I haven't ever taken an interest in it myself."

A strange, cawing sound drew my attention toward the front steps of the house. Sitting in the shade in front of the door was a large wicker cage, with a dark form shifting inside.

"Is that a crow?" I asked.

"Yes, that's Henry. I named him after a cockatiel that belonged to a lady friend of mine, many years ago. He would whistle and say, 'Henry is a pretty boy.' "

"This bird doesn't talk, does he?"

"No. They say that if you split a crow's tongue, you can get him to say a few things. But I wouldn't know how to go about it."

I recalled a house in Cheyenne where the owners set a parrot and its cage in the shade of the house on warm afternoons. I said, "He's good company, though."

"Of sorts." The man looked me over. "So you're here to hunt?"

"Here to see about it. By the way, my name's Henry Tresh." I stepped forward and offered my hand.

He had a firm handshake. "My name's Hugh. Hugh Boynton. I'm the old man in this town."

"You don't look so old to me."

"Nice of you to say so. But I don't fool anyone."

"Well, it's a pleasure to meet you. I suppose I should be on my way. Not interfere with your work anymore."

"I'm done for today."

"Oh. And what's next?"

"Daffodils. No rest for the wicked." He stepped back and laid his hand on a short-handled manure fork that I had not noticed. It was stuck in the ground at the edge of the tulip bed. He pulled the fork loose with a quick jerk, rested it on the ground, and rubbed with his shoe to clean the tines. With a placid expression he smiled and said, "It's good to meet you as well, Henry. Enjoy your stay in our town. And good luck with your hunting."

"Thank you, and good luck to you, Mr.

Boynton."

"Hugh. Call me Hugh."

I found my way to the Shanty, the one saloon in town, that evening. If the barkeep had thicker spectacles, he could have passed for the twin brother of the printer's devil in North Platte. As he poured me a glass of whiskey, he told me his name was Mike.

I told him my name was Henry. He asked what brought me to town, and I told my usual story about looking into the prospects of hunting. He left me alone, and I fell into my own thoughts. I wondered about Hugh Boynton and the restraint he showed in conversation. Nine people out of ten would have said something about my name being the same as a pet crow's. It seemed to me that he hadn't missed the opportunity to mention that he had a lady friend. I thought of his tulip bulbs, nestled in their bed, waiting for the first snow.

Movement at my right caused me to turn and look. A fellow about my age, wearing a short-billed cap that was ridged up in front, tapped on the bar with the edge of a silver dollar.

"Gimme a whiskey," he said. He stretched out his arm and drew it back, in a restless sort of way. He raised his hand and pulled on the back of his neck, then pushed up his cap so that it sat cockeyed on his head. He had whitish blond hair, cropped close, so that the lumps on his cranium were visible. The shortness of his hair reminded me of what they call a jail dock, and I recalled reading about phrenologists and their interest in measuring criminals' heads.

"Have you got the makin's?" he asked.

"No," I answered. "I don't smoke."

"Just as well." He stretched out his arm again. "Son of a bitch. What does a fella have to do to get a drink?"

Mike appeared with a relaxed smile and his eyes half-closed. "You say you want a drink?"

"I guess I do. Seems like I been here an hour."

"You'll be all right. Whiskey?"

"That's what I said earlier."

Mike set a glass on the bar and poured enough for a lumberjack. "Passin' through?" he asked.

"Maybe."

Mike pointed at me with his thumb. "He's here to hunt."

The newcomer tipped his head and looked at me sideways. "What do you hunt?"

"Nothing yet. But I'm thinking about deer."

He drank a slug of whiskey. "I used to hunt. Then I got smart. Found out I could stay in bed on cold mornings." He rotated his glass. "What do you do for a living?"

"I delivered groceries for several years. I'd like to go into business for myself. I'm thinking about the printing business."

"That's what I should do. Print money."

"I think there are some restrictions on that."

"There's restrictions on everything. That is, on things you like."

Mike wiped the bar top with his cloth. "I'm Mike, and this is Henry. We're all easygoing here. What's your name?"

"Ned." He had large blue eyes with puffy lower eyelids, and he rolled his head to gaze at me. "So you delivered groceries."

"That's right. I delivered ice for a while, also, but I didn't like carrying the heavy blocks."

"You remind me of a guy named Deadwood Dick."

I had heard the word "guy" before, and it struck me as the kind of slang that people used in poolrooms. "I don't know anything about him," I said.

"There's not much to know."

"What kind of work do you do?" asked Mike.

"I've worked as a stone mason."

"That's good work." Mike smiled. "You know, they're planning to build a new prison in Rawlins."

"They can have it. I'd rather work on a bank."

"It'll be a while till they build a bank in this town."

Ned snorted. "I'd say so."

"Are you here for the scenery, then?" Mike polished the same spot on the bar as before.

"You ask a lot of questions." Ned rotated his glass a quarter of a turn and knocked off the rest of his drink.

"Care for another splash of firewater?"

Ned pushed his glass forward. "Rawlins. I wouldn't live there if they paid my rent."

Mike kept his eyes on the whiskey as he poured. "What's your idea of a good town?"

"Ogallala."

"Isn't that the one that the drovers used to call the Gomorrah of the Plains?"

"Six whorehouses for every saloon. And no one asks questions."

I sat by the window at breakfast the next morning and stared at the street, which among other things was a main trail running north and south. I thought about Ned

520

from the night before, and I wondered if he came from the north or the south. One might assume the south, as the two towns he claimed to know about lay quite a distance to the southwest and the southeast — both railroad towns, for that matter, which went along with his hard manner. But he could have come from the north on this trip. One thing I had learned in my line of work was not to make assumptions and not to make details fit an idea I had already formed. Keep the idea open.

Along with that rule came another I also had to remind myself of. I did not have to like someone in order to do my work. In the Haines case so far, the only people I had liked were Miss Glover and the young blacksmith. Bartender Mike did not cipher very much one way or the other. As for Mr. and Mrs. Haines, Hugh Boynton, and Ned of the close-cropped hair, I did not think so much about whether I liked or disliked any of them. I grouped them according to another principle, the extent to which I thought they told the truth. I seemed to have met them in descending order.

In addition, the town of Laurel gave me an uncertain feeling. For as much as it seemed like a place where people followed normal tasks such as beating on hot metal, planting tulip bulbs, and serving fried potatoes, it also seemed like a place where something dark could have happened.

I turned my thoughts to a brighter topic, Miss Glover. I did not expect to see her until later in the day, as the reception desk was attended by a clerk with high cheekbones and an upturned nose. I had given him my key when I came to breakfast.

When I finished my meal, I asked for the key and went back to my room to while away some time reading a book.

The sun warmed the day, and the afternoon was a replica of the one before. I went out for a stroll, walking on the east side of town first, then crossing the thoroughfare and ambling toward the gray house with dormer windows, white trim, and a painted stone foundation.

Out front, on the other side of the walkway from the tulip bed, the old bachelor was digging up another plot. He was dressed in the same clothes as the day before, showing his soft form. He was wearing his light work gloves, and I recalled his firm handshake.

As he put his weight on the shovel head, it sank into the ground. He lifted a spadeful of dirt, turned it over, and cut it twice with the blade. He kept at his work until I drew near, although I suspected he saw me coming. Nearby, the manure fork with thick tines was stuck in the ground, and next to it sat a basket full of yellowish-brown flower bulbs.

"Good afternoon," he said. "Out for a walk, I see."

"Wonderful day for it. Good to see you back at your work."

"Today's the day for daffodils."

"Have you had the first frost here?"

"Yes, but not a very heavy one. My zinnias are still hanging on." He waved his arm toward the house.

At a distance, I could see tinges where the frost had nipped the leaves and outer petals. I said, "Zinnias bring hummingbirds, don't they?"

"That they do. And it's a pleasure. Of course at my age, those are the pleasures that are left. The small ones. A glass of wine, a hummingbird on an August afternoon."

"When do you get your first snow?"

"There's no set date, of course, but usually after the first of October."

"That must be a source of pleasure, too, to look out the window and think of all those little fellows slumbering beneath a blanket of snow."

"I don't know if I'm that poetic. Or deep."

"Maybe it's the book I was reading this morning."

"Do you stay at the Blue Star?"

"Yes, I do."

"Very good establishment. Excellent hostess, Miss Glover. I'm glad to count her among my friends — not that I have many to count."

I expected him to mention his age again, but he didn't.

"Have you met Clay Cooper?" he asked.

"Yes, I have. Miss Glover recommended him."

"He's a good lad. If anyone can help you find a deer, it's him."

"It's still up to me to pull the trigger, of course."

"I don't know anything about that. When I was in school, studying to be an apothecary, we took a couple of science courses where we had to collect our own specimens. Something like a pill bug didn't bother me, but I didn't like killing the higher forms, like butterflies."

"Some of the great ornithologists brought down beautiful birds — hawks, eagles, owls — all in the interests of science, of course."

"I'll stick to my mortar and pestle."

"Let Audubon and Burroughs kill the herons and the chicken hawks."

"Put it as you may." He stabbed at a clod with his shovel.

"I can tell I'm keeping you from your work. And I should be moving along. I need my exercise, too."

"Oh, don't take me too seriously. Sometimes I'm an irritable old coot. But it's good to talk to people with ideas from the outside."

"I doubt that any of my ideas are that new." I took a step. "Good luck with your gardening."

"And good luck to you in your hunting, Henry."

"Thanks." I went on my way in the warm afternoon.

I found Miss Glover at the reception desk when I returned to the hotel. She was wearing a lavender-colored dress with a neck scarf of a darker shade, and her dark brown hair was pinned up in neat coils.

"Good afternoon," she said. "I hope you're enjoying your stay."

"I am. I met young Mr. Cooper, at your recommendation, and I also met your friend Mr. Boynton."

"I suppose he's my friend. I don't know him that well. Was he familiar with the story of the big deer?"

"He doesn't care to talk very much about hunting. He seems to be more interested in butterflies, hummingbirds, and daffodils."

"You make him seem like a gentle old soul. I don't know that side of him."

"I can't say that I do, either. He's not the type you get to know right away. A bit brusque. But he's civil enough."

"I would agree."

"By the way, and this comes from an entirely different source, do you know of someone named Deadwood Dick?"

Miss Glover frowned. "That's the name of a dime novel character."

"Oh." My spirits sank a little. "I can't say that I look into that sort of literature."

"Neither do I, but I've heard of that character — maybe because we're not far from the Black Hills. Not that those stories are based very much in reality anyway."

"Well, right now I'm reading *The Portrait of a Lady,* and I can't say that it has much to do with daily life as I know it, but it does have a level of reality and seriousness."

"Oh, yes. James is good, even when he's so precious about life among the Europeans. There's still something in it for us."

I wondered if she had met her Gilbert Osmond, as Isabel Archer did in the story. "I agree," I said. "As for Deadwood Dick, I met a fellow who said I reminded him of someone by that name."

Miss Glover drew back her head and gave me an appraising look. "I'd think you'd need a more gaudy outfit, with two revolvers, an embroidered jacket, an ornate sombrero, and flowing mustachios."

"I had the impression he meant a real person."

"Oh. Maybe he did. A nickname." She flicked her eyebrows as if to brush away the topic. "And how does it go for the hunting itself?"

"As I said, I spoke with Clay Cooper. He says the time would be right in another week or so."

Miss Glover spoke in a lower tone. "That is what you came for, isn't it? Deer hunting?"

"Well, yes." I met her brown eyes, and I felt a level of confidence that did not include much romance. In a tone that matched hers, I said, "But I have other interests."

"Other kinds of hunting?"

I nodded one way and the other. "Not butterflies." I met her eyes again. "Maybe information."

"I had a sense of something like that."

I thought I must look like a duck out of

water in this town. But I was here, and I needed to follow through. "I'd be willing to hear anything you might have to share."

In an even lower voice, she said, "There's a woman staying in this hotel who's scared to death. Won't go out of her room. I don't know what she's waiting for. But in a small town like this, if one person's looking and one person's hiding, there might be a connection."

"I'm not looking for a woman, at least not in that sense, but you're right. There might be something. What's her name?"

"She goes by Sarah Ewing. If that's her real name, mine is Isabel Archer."

I nodded in recognition, then said, "What would be the best way for me to talk to her?"

"Well, she won't come down to the dining room, that's for sure. If I take you to her room, that's against hotel rules. Same as if she goes to yours. But there's a suite of rooms not in use on the second floor. You could meet in the sitting room part of it."

I sat in a wooden armchair for a long while, trying to keep still, until the door opened. I stood up as Miss Glover came in with another woman behind her. Miss Glover stepped aside and ushered the woman forward.

"Mr. Tresh, this is Miss Ewing. Miss Ewing, this is Mr. Tresh, the gentleman I mentioned."

The woman had a clouded face and squinting eyes. She made a tentative nod.

Miss Glover stepped back. "I'll leave you two to visit. If you need anything, just pull the bell." She turned and walked out, closing the door behind her.

I faced the woman again. She was of average height for a woman and neither thin nor stout. She looked as if she had had a good figure but had not won the battle against time and a hard life, for her shoulders, bosom, and waist all sagged. Her light brown hair had begun to turn gray. The clouded effect I had noticed was due to swelling and blotching, familiar signs among people who drank more than a glass of wine while appreciating the hummingbirds. She raised one hand to rub her nose as she sniffed, and then she spoke in a hoarse voice.

"The landlady said you wanted to talk to me."

"I appreciate your willingness to visit. You might know something that will help me. I might be able to help you in return. Miss Glover suggested that you might be in a predicament."

"I'm a decent woman, Mister —"

"Tresh. Henry Tresh. Though I don't think my name matters."

"I haven't heard it before."

"Have you heard of Deadwood Dick?"

Her face went motionless as her eyes opened.

"Don't be startled," I said. "Please sit down." When both of us were seated with the table between us, I continued. "I came here in the employment of an older couple in North Platte. I don't suppose that surprises you."

She shook her head.

"And just to be clear, I would guess your name is Bella Collingsworth."

"One name is as good as another in a place like this."

"Then who is Deadwood Dick?"

"I think you know."

"I assure you I don't."

"Well, he's like you, I guess. He was someone Arthur's parents hired to try to find him — or what happened to him."

I felt as if I had the wind knocked out of me. "They didn't tell me they hired someone else. Where is he?"

"We think he's dead."

I paused. "Then let's go back a couple of steps. How do you know about him?"

"Well, they hired him. They offered him a reward. He came and found me in Broken Bow. He asked a thousand questions, and he told me what he was up to. I thought he talked too much about what he was doing, but it must have worked, because he got out of me something I had never told anyone else, and that was the name of this town."

"And once he got it, he left?"

"That's right. I felt like a fool, but it wasn't the first time. Or the last."

"What was his name, by the way?"

"Dickerson. First name was Paul, I think, but I'm not sure."

"So he went on his way."

"Yes, and I went into hiding. I didn't know what to do. Then after a while I decided to mention it to a friend of mine. He thought we could beat Dickerson to the reward, but he had a head start on us."

"You say 'we.' Is the other person named Ned?"

"Yes, sir."

"Last name, just to be complete?"

"What does it matter?"

"I never know. But it would help, and it might even help me help you."

After a few seconds, she said, "It's Brower. Ned Brower."

531

"Thanks. Let's go ahead. Did the two of you travel here together?"

"No. He came first and laid low, and then I showed up."

"You've talked to him since you've been here?"

"Yes."

"And that's why you think Dickerson is dead?"

She hesitated. "Yes. He disappeared before Ned got here."

I brought out a pint bottle of whiskey from inside my jacket. "Do you care for any of this?"

Her eyebrows went up. "I don't like to drink it out of the bottle."

"It's all right. I won't contaminate it by drinking any of it myself."

"I didn't mean that."

"Nothing personal taken." I set the bottle on the table between us.

She unscrewed the cap and lifted the bottle to her lips. She did not seem like an altogether coarse woman, and I felt sympathy for her. That's a mistake in my line of work, but I can't get rid of the soft spot I have for women — most of all women who have had a fall.

When I thought she had braved herself with a swig, I said, "Let's go back again. To the first time you came to Laurel."

She shook her head. "I don't know if I can."

"Look," I said. "I'm not after a reward. These people are paying me a flat fee, so what I want is the truth. Incidental to that is justice for Arthur, if it can be found, and justice for you."

"For me?"

"His mother told me they blamed it all on you from the beginning."

"They did. And I can't ever hope to change that."

"So you just came for the reward."

"It was Ned's idea. I would never have come back on my own. Never."

I motioned with my hand. "Go ahead."

She took a second drink, and I thought I could see the warmth flowing through her.

"Let's give it another try," I said. "We're on the top floor of this hotel, and only one person in the world knows where we are. It's these four walls." I waved my hand.

She shook her head as before. "I've never wanted to tell anyone this story, but something tells me I should. I hope I don't hate myself for it, but it's no worse than how I've felt all this time."

"I'm not here to judge, and I'm not here to get an advantage over you. If you can tell the story, I'm here to listen."

Her chest went up and down as she took a deep breath. "All right. I think I'd better." Her hand moved toward the bottle, then stopped. "It happened like this. Arthur and I took off on a lark together. That's what he called it, a lark. I don't want to blame everything on him, but it was his idea, and he stole the money from his father. We took the train from North Platte, then another from Cheyenne up this way. By then, Arthur said he was tired of the train, so we ended up on this road, and we ran out of money when we came to this town." She reached for the bottle and laid her hand on it.

"Go ahead," I said.

She took a drink from the bottle, capped it, and set it aside. "We met an older man — old to us, at least. He invited us to go to his house, so we did. He served us a meal, which all seemed normal, and then he gave us some wine. I think he put something in the wine. As I recall, he was a druggist. It made me woozy with less than half a glass, and it made Arthur silly."

She paused, as if she had to get her nerve up. "The old man started playing with him, like sitting next to him on the couch and patting his leg. Instead of moving away, Arthur started giggling. Flirting, it seemed like. I asked him what he was doing, and he said they were just having fun. It didn't seem new to him. But it scared me. I didn't know what old men did to pretty boys — I still don't know what they do, but back then, I didn't even know they did it. So I got scared. I was afraid of the old man, afraid of what they were going to do, afraid of Arthur knowing I knew — afraid of everything. So I ran. Then I was afraid of what Arthur would do when he caught me, and when he didn't come back to North Platte, I was afraid of what the old man would do if I ever said anything. I never mentioned the name of this town, and I never wanted to come back."

I let out a breath and widened my eyes. "And here you are."

"Yes, like the biggest fool in the world."

"You came for the reward, you said."

"Ned wanted to, and I went along. But I don't want to have anything to do with any of this now."

I frowned. "Then what do you want?"

She leveled her gaze on me. "I want to get out of this town."

"Can't you just tell Ned?"

"I don't know if he wants to go, and I don't know if he would think I was going

535

back on him. I thought I could trust him, but I'm not so sure of that now." She breathed with her mouth open. "I wish I had twenty dollars. I'd leave on the stage, and no one would ever be troubled by me again."

I said, "I don't have twenty dollars on me, but I'll see if I can find it." After a second's thought, I said, "You don't think Ned would tell the old bachelor you're in town, do you?"

"I don't think so, but Dickerson might have mentioned my name, and the old man could do something to me sooner or later."

"Well, it's enough to be worried about. Ned could make a slip."

"Do you think you can find twenty dollars?"

"I'll try." I knew where it was in my bag. I didn't like the idea of having to pay out a considerable portion of my fee, but I could see I was headed in that direction.

"Mister, I'll —"

"Don't worry about the money. I'll ask Miss Glover to help me get in touch with you later tonight. The hard part will be getting you onto the stage without anyone seeing you, but that can be done. I assume you don't want Ned to know."

"Not at all. I just want to get away."

■ ■ ■ ■

I stood by myself at the bar in the Shanty. Night had fallen, and Mike had the company of two cowpunchers who had ridden in from the country north of Fort Fetterman. They were telling stories and laughing it up about the famous Hog Ranch down that way. The taller of the two punchers was doing card tricks.

I had plenty to think about, though I was not astonished by anything Bella had told me. I had her in the group of people I considered believable, and everything she told me confirmed my impressions of Arthur's parents, the old bachelor, and Ned Brower. What I needed to do was plan out a sequence of steps I should take, plus alternatives in case some part went wrong. At present, the first critical moment entailed getting Bella onto the southbound stagecoach when it came through at ten the next morning.

Mike drifted into my line of vision. "Ready for another?"

"One more."

As he poured the whiskey, Mike tipped his head. "They say one of Bill Cody's men is in the country, looking to buy horses for the show."

"They should be able to find some."

"You'd think." Mike tucked the cork into the bottle. "Where's your friend?"

"I didn't know I had any."

"That jailbird-lookin' fellow who came in here last night."

"Ned? I haven't seen him." I was hoping to sound out Ned that evening, but I didn't say so much to Mike. "Why do you call him my friend?"

"Just kidding. He came in right after you did, and he left not too far behind you."

"If he had any interest in me, he didn't learn much. I came here from the hotel and went straight back, which is what I plan to do this evening. Thanks for the word, though."

"Don't mention it." Mike drifted back to the two cowpunchers and their stories about the Hog Ranch.

I left the Shanty with two ideas in mind. One was not to look over my shoulder or seem too cautious, and the other was to give twenty dollars to Bella Collingsworth. When I walked into the hotel, Miss Glover was standing at her station, wearing a wine-colored jacket along with her lavender outfit. She looked up from reading the newspaper and folded it.

"Good evening," she said as she handed me my key.

"The same to you." Lowering my voice, I said, "I'd like to ask you to do me a favor. I would like to convey some money to Sarah Ewing so that she can leave on the stage in the morning."

"You want me to deliver it?"

"If you would." I set a stack of four five-dollar gold pieces on the counter and held my cupped hand above them.

She bit her lower lip. "I'd rather not be carrying money in that way. But I can take you to her door. As long as you don't go in, there shouldn't be anything wrong as far as rules go."

I settled my hand over the coins. "That should work well enough. Thank you." I recalled a humorous saying about a certain kind of hotel in which a man did not go into a lady's room, but if he did, he did not sit on her bed. And if he did sit on her bed, they each kept one foot on the floor. I appreciated Miss Glover's drawing the line at the door itself.

I followed her down the hallway. Halfway to my room, which was on the left, she stopped at a door on the right. She rapped with the backs of her fingernails on the panel.

After rapping a second time, she stood closer to the door and spoke through it. "Miss Ewing. Sarah."

Miss Glover looked at me, raised her eyebrows, and said, "Perhaps we should go in." She produced a key from her jacket pocket and opened the door.

Soft light from the hallway spilled into the dark room. "Let me light a lamp." Miss Glover moved to a bureau, found a match, and lit an oil lamp. As light spread in the room, she said, "Uh-oh."

Bella Collingsworth lay on the floor on the right side of the bed as I stood at the doorway looking in.

"Come in and close the door," said Miss Glover. She led the way with the lamp and stood by, lighting the scene, as I knelt by the body.

Bella lay slumped, with her head on her left shoulder and with her left arm stretched out. I touched her neck with the back of my fingers. I felt no pulse, no body warmth.

"I think she's been dead for a while," I said. "A couple of hours or more. Do you mind holding the lamp closer?"

The face did not tell me much. Even in death, her features looked blotched and swollen and troubled. But I did not see any bruises or lacerations. I leaned close. I could not pick up an odor of chloroform or ether, though I knew those substances did not linger for a long time. Then something caught my eye. On the inside of her forearm, just below the crook of the elbow, a dark red dot showed where a bead of blood had dried.

I stood up. "It's best not to move the body or anything in the room until someone from the law has been here."

"Do you have any idea of who might have done this?" She had a dead serious expression on her face, and I thought she showed good repose.

"Call me superstitious," I said, "but I'd rather not say anything out loud until the law arrives. How soon do you think that could be?"

"They would have to come from Douglas. I can send a wire first thing in the morning. The office here in town is closed by now."

"Well, if you can, in the meanwhile, try to let on as if nothing has happened."

"What are you going to do?"

"The first thing is to get a pistol out of my bag. Then I think I'll sit by the door in my room and keep an ear tuned for footsteps. How would they have gotten in?"

541

"I think someone could pick the lock on the back door. I can't say it hasn't been done before, but I haven't had any trouble. Until now."

"I'm sorry to see it. Sorry for her."

We left the room, and Miss Glover locked the door behind us. We shared a wordless glance, then went our separate ways.

I tried to walk with as little noise as possible. The hallway had a thin carpet that absorbed some of the sound. As I walked, I tried to keep my thoughts in a straight line. Everything went back to Arthur. He was the source of this trouble, from the time he stole his father's money until now. Everyone wanted to find him — his parents, the ineffective Dickerson, Ned, Bella, and myself. I thought it remarkable that so many people wanted to find something that did not seem like much of a treasure. And at this point, I didn't care so much about finding him as I did about bringing the old perpetrator to justice. I did not think he should get away with whatever he did to Arthur, whatever he did to my predecessor, and what he did or had someone do to Bella Collingsworth. I did not even like him trading on the good image of having lady friends. I caught myself on that thought. I needed to keep my eye on the object, and that was to help bring this criminal to justice.

I reached my room with little noise. I unlocked the door and left it ajar as I found a match and struck it. As I lit the lamp and turned up the flame, the door closed.

The glow of the lamplight fell on the hard features and billed cap of Ned Brower. He stood with his thumbs in his belt and a pistol on his hip.

"Hello, Jack," I said.

"The name's Ned."

"What brings you here?"

"I thought you might like to know how to find Deadwood Dick."

His comment struck me as being off center. "I can't say that I'm interested. I don't even know who he is."

"Do you think anyone is fooled by your story of coming here to hunt deer?"

"There's only one person in this town whose opinion I care about."

"Well, aren't you sweet?" In a smooth motion, he pulled his six-gun and held it on me. "Don't take off your hat, partner. We're going for a walk."

"I tell you, I don't have an idea about Deadwood Dick."

"Never mind him. There's a man who wants to talk to you."

The night was dark and the streets were deserted as he marched me to the house with the dormer windows. I could see them with their white trim, like two eyes looking out into the night.

I had a hunch that Ned did not know what had happened to Bella, and I thought it best not to say anything until I knew how things stood between him and his new boss. I said, "You're just helping this guy get away with what he did to Arthur."

"Arthur," he said, in the same tone he had use to mention Rawlins. "He was as useless as tits on a boar. Bella says his own father said so."

"Still," I said.

"Yeah, yeah." He poked me with the gun, so I didn't say anything more as we followed the walkway between the flower beds.

Ned gave a light rap on the door, and the old bachelor let us in. He was not dressed in his work clothes but in what I took to be his evening attire. He was wearing a pink silk shirt, untucked with square tails. It fit him like a tent, falling from his flabby chest to his spreading girth.

He closed the door behind us. "This way."

He crossed the room and led us down a hallway. He stopped to light a lantern, then opened a door. Dark steps disappeared into the cellar. Holding the lantern forward, Boynton went down the stairs first. I followed, with Ned Brower's gun barrel poking me in the ribs.

The cellar had a packed dirt floor and a low ceiling. Boynton was not wearing a hat, and the joists cleared his head by an inch.

He led the way to a front corner of the cellar and held the lantern up. The light fell upon a wooden cage, a stout structure with a board floor and with vertical two-by-three studs about four inches apart.

"In here." He held the door open, followed us in, and reached out to slide the latch. He hung the lantern on a nail on one of the uprights, and I saw that he had a couple of items on the floor. One was a jar with a cork stopper, and the other was a small, cylindrical steel object I did not recognize at the moment.

Boynton reached down and picked up the jar along with a white cloth that lay behind it. He twisted out the stopper and put it in the waist pocket of his shirt. He tipped the jar to soak the cloth.

"Get your arms around him," he said. "This won't take a minute."

My heart was beating in my throat. I thought, *Chloroform. Then the needle.*

"You'll have to hold this." Ned motioned with the gun.

Boynton set the jar on the floor, and with the clean white cloth in his right hand, he took the pistol in his left.

As Ned began to lock his arms around me, I stomped on his toe. He yelped and jerked, and I dropped like dead weight with my feet out in front of me. It broke his hold on me, and I rolled free. As I came up, he lunged and hooked his arm around my head. I shoved, and the wall of the cage shook. Boynton fired the pistol.

Ned let out another yelp and grabbed his midsection with both hands. I turned toward Boynton, who did not seem very adept with the gun in his left hand. I punched him in the jaw as hard as I could, and he dropped the gun. I kicked it, and it slid across the wooden floor and rattled its way out between two studs.

Ned was on all fours, with blood dripping on the floorboards.

"Help me, you dolt," said Boynton, but Ned did not stir. Boynton came at me, large as a bear, with his arms reaching out.

I jumped to one side and then another until I had a chance to hit him again. His head went back, but he didn't stop. He backed me into a corner, got his arms around me, and tightened his grip.

He was stronger than I would ever have imagined, and I knew that he was driven to subdue me. I had to summon up just as strong a will not to let him. I thrashed and kicked. He lifted me from the floor, and I kept struggling. Then I drove my knee into his groin, and he lost his hold.

I ducked down and scrambled out of the way. I saw Ned, stupefied, still on all fours, but now he had a sheath knife in his right hand. I stepped on his hand, broke his grasp, and pulled the knife away.

I straightened up and looked for Boynton. I had lost track of him. Now I found him. He had crossed the cage and picked up the steel object, a four-inch cylinder with a two-inch needle sticking out of it. He had the white cloth in his left hand.

He came at me steady, not rushing and not feinting. He had his left arm out to catch me, and he held his right arm cocked and ready to plunge the needle. His mouth was open, and I could see his little yellow teeth.

He moved forward, and I jumped away, but he cut off my space. He was working me into a corner again. I shuffled to my right, then back to my left, and struck with the knife. A streak of blood appeared on the heel of his hand, and he dropped the syringe. I kicked it, and he clubbed me with his left hand. Then he moved in on me and got me in his grip again.

He hung on to me, hugging, and moved the cloth up to the side of my face. I tried to push away. He swung me to one side, off my feet, and we crashed into the wall of the cage. The lantern fell and smashed. I felt my feet touch the floor again as he began to tighten his squeeze.

I pushed the knife upward between us. His abdomen felt soft, like the dugs of an old bitch dog, and warm fluid spilled on my hand. He fell away, and I saw my hand as red as if I had gutted a deer.

He lay on his back, and both the syringe and the cloth were out of his reach. Flames were rising from the wooden floor. I turned my attention to Ned again.

He had his head turned to the side, toward Boynton, and his voice was coarser than usual. "You stupid son of a bitch," he rasped. "A soft-petered, clumsy old toad."

"Save your breath," I said. "If he's not dead, he will be in a minute."

"Good. Now nobody gets the reward."

"I doubt there's a reward anymore, but it

probably doesn't matter." I knelt next to him. "Why in the hell did you turn on us?"

"I didn't turn on anyone. He said he had Bella, and he would tell me where she was if I brought you."

"Who picked the lock on my room?"

"He did, though I could have done it myself."

"You're the fool," I said. "The old bachelor put her on ice, and then he played you like a fish on the line. Now this place is on fire, and I don't know if I can get you up those steps."

"I don't think I can make it." He sank to his elbows and made a deep, heaving cough. "Tell Jemmy goodbye."

I imagined Jemmy was a name, but I thought he might have meant either Jimmy or Jenny. "I'll do that," I said.

Ned Brower spilled over onto his side, and his cap slipped off his head.

The flames were spreading, and the low cellar was beginning to fill with smoke. Crouching, I moved over to check on Boynton. The old bachelor was dead.

I found the latch on the door and opened it, then went back, left the knife on the floor, and picked up my hat. I did not look for the pistol. I hurried up the wooden steps to the kitchen, where I washed my hands.

Smoke was billowing up the stairwell, and the main floor was in a haze. I ran out into the street and took deep breaths of fresh air. Before long, firelight was dancing behind the curtained windows.

Let it burn, I thought. *Let the son of a bitch burn.*

In the light of day, the townspeople found four graves in the back part of the cellar. Mike the bartender was able to identify the most recent remains as those of a man named Dickerson, who had been in town for a short while.

"He asked a lot of questions," Mike said.

The other remains were too old to identify. The townsfolk went on, recalling one time and another when someone came through looking for a missing person — way more than the two that I thought were unaccounted for. As for which set was Arthur's, I would have guessed the one on the left, as Dickerson was on the right. But then I told myself that I was making an assumption, for I did not know at what point in the old bachelor's career Arthur made his appearance.

It was not until someone asked about Boynton's crow that I became less theoretical. I had run right past poor Henry in the smoke. His was one life I could have saved.

I took leave of Miss Glover on my last day in town. She was wearing a tan dress, and she had a red ribbon in her hair.

I said, "Goodbye, Miss Glover. It's been good to know you."

"You know my name," she said.

In the course of giving our statements to the sheriff, I had learned that Miss Glover's name was Angela. "Yes," I said, "and it's not Isabel Archer."

"It seems like an unfeeling thing to have said, in light of what happened later. I don't think she was such a bad woman."

"Neither do I. And I don't think she deserved what he did to her. But at least there was some justice after all."

"And where do you go now?"

"I told Arthur's parents I would report to them in person. They pay for my travel, so it's not a loss on my part. I just have to work on the wording. After that, I suppose I go back to Cheyenne and keep on trying to make a living."

"Don't be afraid to come back this way sometime. We could play a game of backgammon."

The uncertain feeling I had had about the

town seemed to have gone away, thanks in part, perhaps, to the burning of the old bachelor's house. Here we were, talking about normal things.

"I've never played the game," I said, "but I could learn. That in itself could be a reason for me to return."

John D. Nesbitt lives in the plains country of Wyoming, where he teaches English and Spanish at Eastern Wyoming College. He writes western, contemporary, mystery, and retro/noir fiction as well as nonfiction and poetry. John has won many awards for his work, including two awards from the Wyoming State Historical Society (for fiction), two awards from Wyoming Writers for encouragement of other writers and service to the organization, two Wyoming Arts Council literary fellowships (one for fiction, one for nonfiction), four Will Rogers Medallion Awards, and four Spur awards from Western Writers of America. His recent books include *Dark Prairie* and *Death in Cantera,* frontier mysteries with Five Star.

ABOUT THE EDITOR

Hazel Rumney has lived most of her life in Maine, although she also spent a number of years in Spain and California while her husband was in the military. She has worked in the publishing business for almost thirty years. Retiring in 2011, she and her husband traveled throughout the United States visiting many famous and not-so-famous western sites before returning to Thorndike, Maine, where they now live. In 2012, Hazel reentered the publishing world as an editor for Five Star Publishing, a part of Cengage Learning. During her tenure with Five Star, she has developed and delivered titles that have won Western Fictioneers Peacemaker Awards, Will Rogers Medallion Awards, and Western Writers of America Spur Awards, including the double Spur Award–winning novel *Wild Ran the Rivers* by James D. Crownover. Western fiction is Hazel's favorite genre to enjoy. She has been reading the genre for more than five decades.

The employees of Thorndike Press hope you have enjoyed this Large Print book. All our Thorndike, Wheeler, and Kennebec Large Print titles are designed for easy reading, and all our books are made to last. Other Thorndike Press Large Print books are available at your library, through selected bookstores, or directly from us.

For information about titles, please call:
    (800) 223-1244

or visit our Web site at:
    http://gale.com/thorndike

To share your comments, please write:
    Publisher
    Thorndike Press
    10 Water St., Suite 310
    Waterville, ME 04901

BREAKING GLASS— BROKEN BARRIERS

Voyage of an Entrepreneurial Spirit

A MEMOIR

JOYCE VERPLANK HATTON

ARCHWAY
PUBLISHING

Archway Publishing books may be ordered through booksellers or by contacting:

Archway Publishing
1663 Liberty Drive
Bloomington, IN 47403
www.archwaypublishing.com
1 (888) 242-5904

Because of the dynamic nature of the Internet, any web addresses or links contained in
this book may have changed since publication and may no longer be valid. The views
expressed in this work are solely those of the author and do not necessarily reflect the
views of the publisher, and the publisher hereby disclaims any responsibility for them.

Any people depicted in stock imagery provided by Thinkstock are models,
and such images are being used for illustrative purposes only.
Certain stock imagery © Thinkstock.

ISBN: 978-1-4808-5584-7 (sc)
ISBN: 978-1-4808-5583-0 (hc)
ISBN: 978-1-4808-5585-4 (e)

Library of Congress Control Number: 2017919508

Printed in the United States of America

Archway Publishing rev. date: 07/09/2018

Nearly everything I did would have started anyway. In fact, people have said that Einstein was only about five years ahead with relativity, that other people were getting close, or maybe even three years. I think that the present environment, when there's so many well-trained, smart people in science, that if you're a year or two ahead of everybody else, that you're doing something original. If you're twenty years ahead, you don't have a chance ...

The Bubble Chamber, Bioengineering, Business Consulting, and Neurobiology, Donald Glaser Oral History BANC MSS 2008/168. Courtesy of The Bancroft Library, Oral History Center, University of California, Berkeley.

CONTENTS

Chapter One

THE ENTREPRENEURS

The story is, I fear, suffocatingly subjective ...

C. S. Lewis
Preface to *Surprised by Joy*, 1956

Joos Verplank and his nine sons

Patriarchal they all were. The original Bill of Rights included legal protection for landowning white males only. It would be our law for generations. And it was easy to enforce when my great-grandfather Joos Verplank's family produced ten boys and no girls, and my grandpa Tony's, five boys and no girls. Dad's generation proved different when I appeared on the scene in 1932. I was able to embrace our constitutional amendments and the positive Supreme Court case decisions that changed the embedded structure. I could follow in the footsteps of my energetic and entrepreneurial forefathers.

Great-Grandpa Joos Verplank lived to be ninety-nine years old. When

1

he died in 1943, he was the oldest living Civil War veteran in western Michigan. Joos wrote his memoir in 1921, at age seventy-six.

Joos's courageous story begins in August 1848. His mother and youngest brother had died of Asiatic cholera in Albany, New York, while en route from the Netherlands to the Dutch colonies in western Michigan. Joos describes the scene on the beach in Grand Haven, Michigan, when carried ashore by his Dad:

> It was dark when we arrived, and the crew pitched our luggage onto the shore. Father carried the four children one by one from the boat to the shore. Looking about, he found some tanbark, which he set up as a sort of shelter. However, as it soon began to thunder and lightning, he found an old barn to shelter us from the rain.
>
> The next morning old man Nicholas Vyn walked over to where we were. He had come to Grand Haven from the Netherlands in 1847.
>
> He said, *"Ben je ook een Hollander?"*
>
> *"Ja,"* answered Father.
>
> You can imagine his joy in meeting and talking with someone from home. After hearing the story of Father's trouble, he promised to find work for him. The next morning, he came with a big basket of food, and we had all we wanted to eat. He moved us into a shack of a house, where sister Jane, who was eight years old, cared for the others, while father worked at rafting lumber. He earned a dollar a day, and we would have gotten on fine, but father was not used to heavy work, and in a short time was very ill with bloody dysentery.

The family was again destitute, but soon a Dutch settler from Holland, Michigan, twenty miles south of Grand Haven, learned that Joos's father was a shoemaker, and he urged them to go to Holland. The colony of Holland was the family's original destination, but they had no money to get there.

Great-Grandpa Joos tells of their good fortune once more:

> Well, finally, Mr. Vyn of Grand Haven heard how badly father wished to move to Holland, and one night, at prayer meeting, he collected four dollars, which he brought over, and told us we could go. ...
>
> Our condition could scarcely have been worse. Father and four poorly nourished children, in need of everything, you might say. No bedding, no clothing, no furniture—just a big box that held all we owned.

The family arrived in Holland in the latter part of July 1849. Joos's father found work with a local shoemaker and then quickly branched out on his own. He had the entrepreneurial instinct—the new proprietor who owned and managed, and assumed responsibility for not only the results but also the larger community that had supported him and his family.

Soon Joos's largest community was about to ask for his help. In his eighteenth year, the Civil War broke out. Many of the Holland boys enlisted in 1861, and there was another call in 1862. Joos describes the scene:

> [T]he town was all stirred up. I tried to stick to my shoe bench; but, with people running up and down, shouting and singing, this was no easy thing for a young fellow to do. Finally, I threw down my tools, pulled off my apron, and ran away to the Town Hall, where men were speaking. Dr. A. C. Van Raalte, I remember, made a good speech. He said, "There are my two sons. If they wish to go, I give them free leave." Forty boys, myself among the number, enlisted that night.
>
> I did not go home until midnight.
>
> Father called out, "Is that you, Joos?"
>
> I answered, "Yes, I have enlisted."
>
> I heard him moan. I felt very uneasy, stayed in bed until he had gone to work the next morning, and tried to keep away from him.

After celebrating and training for two weeks in Holland, Joos reports how hard it was to leave home: "I shall never forget the weeping and moaning of the crowd of relatives and friends that met to see us off. I was eighteen that spring, tall and very thin. They all said, 'Joos will never come back; if he doesn't die in battle, he will die in the hospital.'"

But Joos did come back. He arrived in Jackson, Michigan, on July 2, 1865. After loafing all through the following winter, Joos sailed on Lake Michigan during the summer of 1866, first as a cook, and then he "took the mast."

When a vacancy opened up in 1872 for the office of town marshal in Holland, Joos was nominated on both the Republican and Democratic tickets in the spring of 1873:

> I was town marshal until the close of the year 1876. Since the year 1876 was a presidential year, the Democrats wished me to run for Sheriff of Ottawa County. I knew there was not much use, as Ottawa was so strongly Republican. As my friends urged so strongly, I consented.

I was well acquainted in all the towns south of the river. They were largely Republican, and this helped me get the nomination.

I put a mortgage on my home for all it was worth and went out electioneering. I was elected by a small majority, the only one elected on the Democratic ticket.

After Joos's two busy years as sheriff, the new Greenback party asked him to run:

The Democrats were depending on me for their ticket. There I was; thought of it day and night. I knew if I accepted the Greenback nomination I was almost certain of victory; on the other hand, I did not like to disappoint my friends. Finally, I made up my mind that my closest friends would stand by me regardless of party, so I accepted for the Greenbackers. Mr. Vanderhoef was put up by the Democrats and Woltman by the Republicans. I was elected by a majority of five or six hundred. I needed it badly, as I had spent so much money in electioneering.

When Joos lost the next election in 1880, he had a family of five boys, including my grandfather, Tony Verplank, who was born in 1877. Joos could have gone back to Holland as town marshal, but he felt that he had quite a family by this time and not enough education for business, so he decided to buy a farm.

Unfortunately, Joos had bought an inexpensive farm on the Crockery Township border, a few miles east of the village of Spring Lake; Joos complains about the farm "full of pine stumps and the land poor after they were out." Nevertheless, he insists:

By hard work, we made a good living. But soon four of the boys were married, leaving five younger ones who were in school most of the time. Then, too, there was so much work in the house, I decided that if I could sell I would go back to town.

The following spring, Joos built a house in Spring Lake. Joos thus concludes his autobiography:

We see you all married, and in your own homes, and making your own living. As parents, we are very proud of the family. You have no reason to complain, but should be thankful to your Lord and Creator. ...

My father, Vernon Verplank, was born in 1907. He didn't write a memoir, but he did give me an extended interview in 1995, when I moved back to Michigan. Dad had such a prodigious memory, especially of his childhood, that the interviews lasted all summer and, when transcribed, produced 450 pages.

Most of Grandpa Tony's brothers were lured to Gary, Indiana, to seek work in the high-paying steel-mill town—just not in the steel mills. Uncles Gerrit, George, and Albert spent the first part of their business careers in the automobile business. They were automobile dealers and taxi and gas station owners.

There was no slowing down Uncle George (nicknamed "Pipi"), in business or in life. Uncle George founded the hugely successful Calumet Paving Company in Gary, and moved the company to the state capital, Indianapolis, after receiving large state contracts to build part of the new Indiana-Ohio toll road and other interstate systems.

Uncle Joe, two years older than Grandpa Tony, pursued a demanding architectural career in Gary, designing some of the biggest buildings, including the Gary Theater. In middle age, he moved to Santa Monica, California, and found a second career in astronomy that he followed passionately. When our family visited Uncle Joe in 1946, he would escort me outside every night to describe the celestial bodies. I was only thirteen, and I remember finding it rather boring, because Uncle Joe assumed I knew something about the positions of the stars, but I was totally lost. All the sailors in our family could have used his knowledge of celestial navigation as we stared down the horizons on our sextants.

Uncle Grover was the ninth boy, twenty years younger than the eldest, Abe, and ten years younger than Grandpa. When Uncle Grover needed funds to complete medical school at the University of Michigan, all of his older brothers chipped in to help pay the tuition. Grandpa Tony, with his eighth-grade education, was only thirty years old and already the father of four boys, but he gave Grover $3,000. After medical school, Dr. Grover Verplank returned to Gary and became a busy obstetrician during the booming 1920s. By the time my brother Midge was born in 1931, Uncle Grover would brag that he had delivered more than forty-five hundred babies.

After the turn of the twentieth century, when Grandpa Tony was still in his early twenties, he went into the ice business in Spring Lake, with John Brongersma. Grandpa could see the business was growing, so he borrowed some money from Frank Scholten, president of the Spring Lake Bank, and bought out John Brongersma in1908.

Grandpa knew how to leverage his business. After borrowing $3,000 from the bank, Grandpa never paid it back; he just kept buying the local ice companies. In 1912, he bought the Frank Fox Ice Company, which had a big icehouse that "took up practically a city block" on Barber Street in Spring Lake—where Dad remembered circus people renting the icehouse in summer months to set up their trapezes and practice their routines.

Dad had become part owner of the Spring Lake Ice Company in 1926, when he was nineteen years old. When they had an open winter (no ice because of warmer-than-average winter temperatures) in 1930, Dad became very upset and called Grandpa Tony in Florida.

Grandpa said, "We're going to build an ice plant. Start looking around for a building. I'll head for home immediately."

I asked Dad why he wasn't worried about electric refrigerators in 1930. Dad explained, "After we started to build the ice plant, we lacked about $5,000 to handle the whole deal, and the bankers tried to discourage us from building. Their thought was that General Electric had a refrigerator with a big dome top on it, and Frigidaire had four-cubic-foot refrigerators."

Dad emphasized, "This was right in the middle of the Depression. A four-cubic-foot refrigerator was about $250 to $300. People making a quarter an hour could always find a dime to buy a twenty-five-pound block of ice, or two bits for a fifty-pound block, but they couldn't buy a refrigerator. When the bank meeting was over, within thirty minutes, George Christman, (a Spring Lake lumber titan on the board), called and declared, 'Tony, forget about the bank … you've got whatever you need.' So George Christman financed the $5,000 for that. And a few years later, when I was about to build a new house, I went to George Christman and got the money as I needed it, at 6 percent interest."

Because the ice business was seasonal, Grandpa Tony began selling coal in 1910. But it wasn't until the mid-1920s that the name was changed to Spring Lake Ice and Coal Company.

Grandpa Tony made a real estate purchase that turned out to be very propitious for his growing business. The purchase is described by Dr. David Seibold, with the editing help of his wife, Dorothe, in their marvelously detailed thousand-page history, *In the Path of Destiny*, subtitled, *Grand Haven, Spring Lake, Ferrysburg, and Adjoining Townships*, as follows:

In the days following the First World War, the only bridge from Spring Lake to Grand Haven was the Interurban Bridge, which had been built originally in 1866 and then reinforced in 1903 for the Interurban cars. It was used for pedestrian and vehicular traffic as well as the Interurban trains. Most teams of horses, including the ice wagon teams, had no trouble, but occasionally the Interurban cars would cause a horse or a team to balk, which made for an eventful crossing.

Tony Verplank conjectured that a new bridge might be built to replace the Interurban Bridge, not so much to separate the horse traffic from the rail traffic but because of the ever increasing number of automobiles using the West Michigan Pike after WW I. Playing his hunch, Tony bought the riverfront property in Ferrysburg between the railroad tracks and the Spring Lake Channel speculating where the new bridge might be built. As it turned out, Tony's hunch was correct. In 1923 a swing bridge was built over the Grand River with the north approach squarely on Verplank's property in Ferrysburg.

Dad reports a second purchase:

We always were in the coal business with the rail yard. It was 1930 when we bought the first piece of land on the river ... 407 feet ... and then a few years later, we bought another few hundred feet on the west end of the dock ... and then back in later years after Construction Ag[gregates] quit the gravel business we ended up buying all of that so we had all of the property from the Grand Trunk Bridge clear to the Sag—more than 3,000 feet of prime riverfront property. Good deep water the whole distance. And all the Construction Ag property was sealed breakwater, and all of our property was riprap. Big pieces of broken concrete—riprap.

Both ice and coal were dropped in the 1950s to concentrate on trucking from the Verplank docks, but the name wasn't changed to Verplank Trucking Company until 1984.

What attributes contributed to Grandpa Tony's success as an entrepreneur? Dad's simple answer: "He was hardworking, always worked himself, right up until the end."

What about Dad's mother, Grandma Jessie? She, too, must have been hardworking. As a young bride, Grandma ran the boardinghouse in Fruitport while nursing the first two of her five boys. During the years that Sherman, Merle, Russell (Whitey), Vernon (Tooter), and Raymond were growing up, Grandma Jessie took care of the books and collected the money for the family company. Grandma worked first from a makeshift front office in their home, and then from an actual office. In 1920, in her forty-second year, Grandma Jessie was working in her new Grand Haven office when the pen fell out of her hand, and she was rushed to the hospital. Her ability to carry on with any family role was cut short by a severe stroke.

Dad was barely thirteen, and Raymond was nine or ten, when Grandma Jessie had her stroke. Raymond lived at home, but Dad spent his time after school with his best friend, Pie Lawton, and eventually moved in with the Lawton family until he finished eighth grade. With no one to guide Dad at home, Dad dropped out of ninth grade for a month, before a friend of the family talked him into coming back to school, which literally was next door.

Dad was the only one of Tony and Jessie's five sons to continue past eighth grade. For Dad's graduation from tenth grade, the final grade in the Spring Lake school system, Grandma Jessie gave Dad a coveted ruby ring, which he treasured so highly that he never took it off until his dying day.

Fortunately, Dad kept the matriculation going and attended eleventh grade at Grand Haven High School in the fall of 1924. That was where he met Mom; they shared the same desk in bookkeeping class. Mom was only fourteen but already a sophomore.

By February 1925, Dad was restless and quit school again—this time to ship out on the *General Meade*, a 200-foot sand sucker. At seventeen, he was one of the youngest on the ship, signing on for seventy-five dollars a month as a coal passer in the boiler room. He stayed out of trouble, loaned the rough-and-ready gamblers on the ship money after they ran out of cash before paydays, and left in the late spring to haul ice for Grandpa Tony, at fifty cents an hour.

Did he like working on a ship? "Oh yeah, I always liked that. When we were bringing coal ... [from] Toledo, I remember you came along for the ride back through the straits to the Verplank Docks in Grand Haven. Was that freighter the *John J. Boland?*"

(It was a coincidence that I rode back as a teenager at about the same age that Dad shipped out on the *General Meade*. I told Dad that I remembered steering a huge freighter more than 400 feet long through the Straits of Mackinac, and the captain made me look around to see my path, and, of course, it looked like a snake weaving back and forth. The captain's comment: "Think how much coal you cost us!")

Dad then recalled, "I remember that John J. Boland Jr., was on that. He said you were up on the A-frame and all over the ship." (Yes, Dad, I found it very interesting ... lots of fun ... I took after you. I never got seasick, so that made it easier.)

After getting off the *General Meade,* Dad was ready to spread his wings ... but he needed his father's help. "I didn't have five cents to buy anything with—except I was working on the ice truck at that time."

Grandpa cautioned Dad, telling him motorcycles were too dangerous. When he found out that Dad was going to buy a clunker of a motorcycle anyway, Grandpa drove Dad to the Harley-Davidson dealership in Muskegon.

With Grandpa's check for $374 ("payment in full"), Dad rode away with his spanking-new Harley-Davidson motorcycle.

Hardly a week had passed before Dad took a direct hit—took it on the chin—from an elderly driver who ran a red light. After spending part of the summer in the hospital, with cuts, bruises, chipped teeth, and a broken arm, Dad was ready to get back on his dearly repaired Harley.

By late fall, Dad was ready to travel again. "I probably had fifty dollars in my pocket, and we [Dad and Preston Bilz] put the tent on the back of the motorbike, with a few changes of clothes, and took off for Niagara Falls. Then we rode down to Washington, DC. After we left Washington, that was where our trouble started."

First, Pres slid off a loose gravel road and injured his knee, and then, about an hour later, things got worse:

[W]e hit about an eight-foot-[wide] strip of blacktop on this gravel road. We were riding along there, probably forty to forty-five miles an hour, and the tobacco was about three-feet high on each side of the road and came right up to the gravel. This old beagle hound came just angling out of the tobacco, just leisurely, right out in front of me. I just zoomed around him like that. Next thing, I could hear steel crashing on the pavement. Pres hit the dog and blew out his back tire. I had a .38 revolver in my saddlebag, and I took my revolver and I had it on my side walking around the dog. I was going to put it right up to the dog's head because he was lying there badly injured. Just as I was walking around there, someone hollered, "You shoot that dog, and I'll shoot you."

A black man was standing at a little old cabin with a step to get into the cabin. He was standing on the step there with his double-barreled shotgun. The dog was down alongside him. Everybody just stood there like that. I never opened my mouth. I just went back, put my revolver back in the saddlebag, and asked Pres, "What do we do now?"

Pres returned home to Spring Lake, and Dad continued on to Daytona Beach. While trying to sleep in his new pup tent, he was invaded by "baby lizards" crawling all over him and his tent, and he headed home fast. With no rain in sight, Dad hit the hard clay roads on the westerly route through Georgia and Tennessee. Dad said clay roads were slippery when wet—so slick no one could ride a bike on them until they dried out; maybe use a horse and wagon, but never a bike.

Dad was greeted at home by Fred Nienhouse, who announced, "I'm leaving for California tonight. How about going along?"

"Fred, I'm flat broke. I just got back from Florida."

Fred pressed Dad. "Well, how much money have you got?"

Dad replied that he had thirty-five to forty dollars, and Fred said, "Well, forget about that. I have $300. I have a brand-new car."

"If you want to foot the bill, why, I'm ready to go."

And so, after a week of sad good-byes, they took off. "We just drove night and day."

Until they got to Texas, that is. First, they had to be pulled through mud up to their tire hubs by a team of horses. Next, they had to use their jackets to cover the radiator after it froze overnight.

They found Tucson quite a city, but after arriving at 4:00 a.m., they left at 9:00 a.m. They were eager to get to Los Angeles. "When we got down there and found out the number of people lined up to be employed, and not ever having any experience on the ocean, or maritime cards, or anything to show, it just was hopeless to try to ship out of there. So we decided we would head for San Francisco, a bigger seaport."

After an overnight visit with Uncle Joe in Santa Monica, Dad and Fred left for Frisco. When they stopped in Santa Barbara on Christmas Eve, they were invited to a roaring party at a transient boardinghouse. They looked around and realized that the city was still a mess from the 1923 earthquake, so they offered to be laborers on a construction site.

After a few days of scary earthquake tremors, Dad received a letter from Whitey's wife, Aunt Minnie, saying that she had a proposition for him. Aunt Minnie ran the office for Grandpa Tony, and she told Dad that Grandpa Tony wanted him and Uncle Sherm and Uncle Whitey to come back home to work, and if they did, Grandpa would make the three of them equal partners in the business. Dad knew that Uncle Merle was never coming back, and he knew that Uncle Raymond was too young to become an equal partner at that time.

I asked Dad if he was bummed out about coming home right away.

No, there was no bummed out about it," he said. "I'd been on the lam long enough to know that if you didn't have five cents in your pocket, well, you were just out of luck wherever you were. The opportunity there was to get my feet on the ground someplace where I could make a few nickels. This looked like the best chance I would ever get. So, naturally, it didn't take me long to make up my mind to get back home. Get home and get right on the ice truck and continue right on from there."

There seemed to be quite a few young guys who went to sea from Grand Haven and Spring Lake. Dad affirmed this: "Oh, practically all of them. ... My brother Sherm got off to come to the ice company after the war [World War I] was over. Les Hannah and Sherm got on the car ferries because, after the war started, they were both going to be in the draft, for sure. Both of them stuck right to the car ferries all during the war. ..."

Dad came back from California in the spring of 1926. He would turn nineteen in July. I asked Dad if Grandpa brought him into the business then or if he had to work for a few years.

Dad replied, "No, no, when I came back, we organized the partnership between Sherm, Whitey, Dad, and me. I think our deal was completed in '26, or somewhere along there. ... Anyway, first thing we decided to do was to tear down the old icehouse on the bayou and build a new, modern icehouse."

I was curious as to how they divvied up who did what and who ran the place.

Dad explained, "We punched a clock just like the rest of the men. We worked for fifty cents an hour. Sometimes, in the early part of the season, we hauled coal. We delivered coal, along with the rest of the drivers and some of the other drivers we paid on a tonnage basis. They made more than fifty cents an hour. It was not ... reasonable that we weren't paid on a tonnage basis too. So, if we delivered an extra few tons of coal during the day, we made more than fifty cents an hour. We worked by the time clock ... until the day we started to build our ice plant. Our wages were reduced to forty cents an hour to conserve our capital investment. We worked at forty cents an hour all during the season the ice plant was being built."

I asked Dad where he got this drive, this work ethic. "I got that when

I was off on trips to California and Florida. When you were on your own, and you didn't have money, your name was mud."

After a full decade exploring life on his own, Dad found his anchor to windward; Mom would keep him in good shape ... for many, many decades.

Now to Mom's side of this history. ... Mom was not as loquacious as Dad when I interviewed her in 1995. I had to ask specific questions about her childhood in Minnesota and Michigan, and I was happy I did.

When Grandma Bessie Jirele Secory, an only child, inherited her family's farm in southern Minnesota, Grandpa Louis Secory left bartending and bricklaying work in Mason City, Iowa, sold the Jirele family farm, and bought a new farm five miles outside of Brainerd, Minnesota. Now Grandpa Louie could be his own boss, make his own decisions, and produce what he wanted, when he wanted.

According to Mom, Grandpa Louie made all the decisions for the family too—*all* of them: "There was nowhere that Mom [Bessie] ruled the roost. ... Whatever Dad [Louie] said, was law. Men at that time didn't pay any attention to children. He [Grandpa Louie] was just like your dad, who never changed a diaper on you children."

If Grandpa Louie wanted to farm in the godforsaken cold of Brainerd,

Minnesota (home of Paul Bunyan)—where average January temperatures were five degrees Fahrenheit and average July temperatures only sixty-eight degrees—then that was what his family had to endure. Mom—born Lydia Secory—was the next to youngest of nine children, but only the four youngest were still living at home in 1915 when the family moved north to central Minnesota from Iowa.

Grandpa Louie had to have an English-language newspaper delivered every day, and a Bohemian-language newspaper at least once a week. Grandpa was well educated, having gone to college to study for the priesthood. After matriculating for a year and a half, Grandpa decided the celibate life was not for him. Grandma Bessie only finished eighth grade before being whisked off to marry Grandpa, four years her senior. And by the year 1912, before celebrating her fortieth birthday, Grandma Bessie had given birth to twelve children. Only nine would live to adulthood.

Education was important to Grandpa Louie. Pretty little five-year-old Lydia Frances Secory, nicknamed "Toots," walked with her older siblings a long way to their one-room schoolhouse in Minnesota. In the winter, she climbed over drifts that were three times taller than she was; in the spring and fall, she walked near bulls that she thought were coming after her. Mom confessed, "You never could trust a bull; they could be mean sometimes."

Mom and her two brothers and older sister were so scared of the howling wolves at night that they never dared leave the house. They couldn't go into town, except to buy groceries, because it was too far, and in the winter, they were forced to go by sleigh.

There were advantages to living on the farm. For one thing, there was healthy food. With no electricity, no refrigeration, and no ice cream, there were no cavities. Mom reported that she never experienced being hungry when she was growing up on the farm. A typical supper that Mom just loved was homemade bread soaked in fresh milk.

I asked Mom if she thought her family was rich or poor. She replied, "Well, they weren't rich, and they weren't poor. They were mediocre, I guess."

If accidents happened in Minnesota—teenage Al with a broken leg, or six-year-old Frank with a rupture—Grandpa had no way to communicate for help. They had no telephone, no electricity, and no automobiles. Grandpa would pile the boys into a cart or sleigh, hitch up a horse, and drive them into the hospital in Brainerd. Mom's analysis: "Grandpa must have had money somewhere to pay for that."

Grandpa Louie decided to buy a fruit farm in western Michigan in 1920. After the family moved to the farm in Robinson Township, it took only a year or two for Mom's older sister, Martha, (Aunt Mart) to earn enough money to buy a car—the only car in their country neighborhood. Aunt Mart would become the saving grace of her little sister and brother, eight and ten years younger, respectively.

The Robinson Township single-room elementary schoolhouse was located on a corner of Grandpa's farm. Mom loved the school and the teacher and preferred the classroom to the long summers in the field, where she was forced to work all day, every day, from the age of ten until graduation from high school in 1927. Grandma Bessie made Mom's dresses out of old flour and grain bags when she worked in the field, but once Mom started high school, Grandma made her dresses from patterns and fabric chosen by Mom.

Mom and her younger brother, Frank, felt very lucky. They were probably the only students in their one-room school who would continue past eighth grade. None of the others even contemplated it. How could they? The high school was almost ten miles away. There were no buses, no public transportation. The students would have to take the Interurban from Grand Haven to Spring Lake after eighth-grade graduation just to take a test to see if they qualified for study at the nearest high school. If they passed, they would have to pay twenty-five dollars per year to attend Grand Haven High School, because they lived in Robinson Township and not the city. Mom, whose birthday is March 9, was only thirteen when she started high school in 1923.

With all the requirements for entering high school, it was no wonder that Grandma Bessie didn't want Mom to bother with it, declaring that Mom was just going to get married anyway.

Grandpa was different. Mom explained, "My dad liked reading and stuff because he had more of an education than

Frank Secory, Bronco
Hall of Fame, 1970s

my mother did. He was the one who inspired us to go to high school. Mom didn't think that we needed to go to high school, but Dad said, 'Oh yes!'"

Mom emphasized, "If it hadn't been for Mart! … Of course, Dad knew that we could go in with her."

Grandpa Louie had a tough career playing baseball in a minor league in the nineteenth century. They had no gloves. They had to catch everything with their bare hands. Both Mom and Uncle Frank inherited Grandpa's athleticism and love of baseball. They played baseball every summer in the township. Uncle Frank played football too, but Mom said the girls didn't play. Mom was a star basketball player in high school and continued her career in a Spring Lake basketball league after she was married.

Uncle Frank was noticed as a "really good" baseball and football player as soon as he started high school. He was offered a scholarship in football and baseball at Western Michigan University ("Western"), but he first needed to work for a few years and also supplement the scholarship with additional summer work for Kellogg's, the giant cereal company located in Battle Creek, just a few miles from Western in Kalamazoo. For his ten-year career in the major league and twenty years umpiring in the National League, Uncle Frank was often recognized by Michigan sports enthusiasts, Western Michigan University, and the Grand Haven School Foundation's Hall of Fame.

Mom did not think about attending college. She knew she couldn't afford it; she was happy to get through high school.

When I asked Mom, in 1995, if she thought about the feminism of today, she answered, "No. Because we all were in the same boat. Not any of us even thought about going to work. It was just a way of life at that time in our lives."

It was a way of life if you were married and had children. Mom worked for almost three years as a telephone operator in Grand Haven and Grand Rapids before tying the knot in South Bend, Indiana, in February 1930. A year later, Lurelle Jay, nicknamed "Midge," was born. Two years later, I, named Beverly Joyce but called Joyce, was born. The caboose, Gary Lee, was born in 1940.

Aunt Minnie, who was married to Dad's older brother, Whitey, never was able to have children. Aunt Minnie helped Grandma Jessie Wills Verplank run the office of the Spring Lake Ice and Coal Company until Grandma Jessie suffered her stroke in 1920. Then Aunt Minnie took over and "practically ran the company for about thirty years," according to Mom.

Although Mom and Dad were married during the worst of the Depression, Mom said she never knew what the Depression really was. They were in the ice and coal business, "and that was what people needed." Especially several years later, during World War II! The huge Verplank coal dock supplied most of the coal to the war industries in Muskegon, and those industries, in turn, stole many of the best coal-truck drivers, with sky-high wages. Even Mom drove a truck, hauling a conveyor behind it, when called upon by Dad. Other women would help drive coal trucks too. Mom remembered a young mother who would strap her fifteen-month-old baby to the front seat of the coal truck so that she could help her husband fill his small coal yard in a rural northern Michigan town.

I reminded Mom that I had been very active in politics; where did that interest come from?

"No doubt from your Dad, because he was always interested in every-thing in the newspapers and on the radio."

When I asked Mom if Dad was like that since they were married, she laughed. "I would say so. Always, even when we lived up on the lake, if we were going out for dinner or anything, Dad would say, 'Oh, I've got to read the paper first before we can go.' We were always late because of that."

But did Dad pursue anything political, like his grandfather? "No, he said he just didn't have the time to do it. ..."

Mom learned discipline and responsibility from Grandpa Louie, and organization and respect and care for the products of their farm labor from Grandma Bessie. And the coeducational team sports in which Mom partic-ipated at a very young age sharpened her competitive skills. She excelled on and off the field, winning top honors in card games, especially duplicate bridge.

I consider Mom's most remarkable trait her innate politeness—to ev-eryone. She was not guileless, but gossip and witchery were never part of her modus vivendi. That may have been the result of a semisolitary early childhood in the harsh north country of Minnesota. Or, perhaps, it was be-cause of her appreciation of a rewarding life with her anchor to windward.

Chapter Two

CULTURE SHOCK

*Life is not what one lived, but what one remembers
and how one remembers it in order to recount it.*

Gabriel García Márquez
Living to Tell the Tale, 2003

Great-Grandpa Joos (in his ninety-ninth year), Joyce, Grandpa Tony, Vern. 1943

I don't remember much about my early childhood around our houses in Spring Lake, Michigan.

But school was different. I loved it. Hated summers because I couldn't go to school. *Bo-o-o-oring* I was always a good student and better at math than all the boys. For four of the six elementary grades I had straight As. I was salutatorian of our high school class of 150 students (yes, I did have two Bs).

And I loved politics. After being elected president of my class from grades one through six, I envisioned greater things. ...

And then, *wham!* In high school, the entire landscape changed, and I was not prepared for it. My competitive spirit did not like being "subbed" (subordinated, suppressed, submerged, or submissive), especially to guys I'd bested in school.

Initially, I was furious with Dad. During my entire twelve years of school, he had cajoled, goaded, and teased me: "You have an A-minus?"

"Stop teasing her!" Mom would shout.

During my senior year, Grandpa Tony stopped by the house, pulled Dad into the garage, and inquired, "Are you spending money to send her to college?"

No answer.

"She's just going to get married. Save the money for your two boys."

With that attitude floating around our tight-knit patriarchal Dutch community, I decided to look for a girl's college. Without consulting Mom or Dad, I applied to Smith College. As a backup, I applied to the University of Michigan as well.

Smith's tuition was three times the University of Michigan's. What an incredulous proposal for Dad this would become. Dad hadn't finished high school, although he was obviously very bright.

I begged, "Just see if I can get accepted."

He liked the challenge.

But not the next one. On a clear, cold January afternoon in 1950, I was driving to my piano lesson when I was hit broadside by a speeding furniture truck in the outskirts of Grand Haven. I was fortunate to be driving Dad's new huge Cadillac Coupe de Ville.

("Less than three months old!" Dad would remind me.)

SATURDAY, JANUARY 28, 1950   Price, Five Cents

Grand Rapids Youth Killed In Crash at Grant, Griffin

Truck Crushes John Wierenga

Joyce Verplank, Driver of Other Car, Escapes from under Overturned Coupe

John Wierenga, 16, of Grand Rapids, was killed in an auto-truck collision at the corner of Grant and Griffin street at 8:08 p.m. Friday. He was a passenger in a truck that collided with a new Cadillac driven by Miss Joyce Verplank, 17, Spring Lake.

Miss Verplank, the daughter of Mr. and Mrs. Vernon Verplank was released from Municipal hospital after being treated for facial cuts and body bruises.

Oscar Dewey, 22, also of Grand Rapids, who was riding in the truck, was thrown out of the truck, escaping with only an injured leg and ankle, while his companion, Wierenga, fell under the truck and was fatally crushed, dying instantly.

Dewey and Robert Tysman, 51 Wallace street, of this city, assisted in removing Miss Verplank from the demolished car, which had completely overturned. They found it necessary to break open a door of the car to extricate her. She was somewhat dazed and rushed to the hospital in Tysman's car.

No Witnesses

There apparently were no witnesses to the actual collision, police reported today. The truck and car both came to rest on the southeast side of Grant near the intersection. The truck was on its side and the auto, in rolling over, crashed into a light pole, breaking it off at the base.

Dewey, who reported the accident to police headquarters, said that he had come to Grand Haven to deliver some furniture for the West Leonard Upholstery Co., or Grand Rapids, of which Wierenga's father is a part owner. Young Wierenga, who was a junior student at Creston high school, had come along for the ride, Dewey said, and the two were on their way home.

Miss Verplank, a Grand Haven High school senior, was driving south on Griffin street, Dewey told the officers. Dewey was driving east on Grant street.

Continue Investigation

Officers Robert Phillips and Curtis Baldus were called to the...

FATAL CRASH—Joyce Verplank of Spring Lake was pulled from under this Cadillac five-passenger coupe after a car-truck collision at Grant and Griffin streets Friday afternoon in which John Wierenga of Grand Rapids, who was riding in the truck, was killed. (Photo by Sherm Robbins)

The force of the impact rolled the truck on its side and the car over twice. During the second roll, the car smashed a city light pole, breaking the pole and squashing the car in the middle, like an accordion. I was thrown back and forth across the front seat and ended up under the steering wheel column, where the police discovered me fifteen minutes later. I woke up in the emergency operating room at our local hospital.

Poor Dad. When he rushed into the hospital, the attendant stopped him and asked, "Is yours a boy or a girl?" The boy was in the hallway, fully covered by a white sheet. He was my age, the son of the owner of the furniture company, riding shotgun in the truck. He flew under the truck when it rolled.

Dad said he would never forget the scream of the boy's mother when she entered the hospital. I would never forget I couldn't stop in time. The other driver may have been speeding, but I couldn't stop. And another fact I have to live with—had we been wearing seat belts, that accident would have left the boy alive and me dead.

Our high school had a college prep course, but an Ivy League school like Smith had requirements totally out of our school's purview. I had some Latin, but no other language or other classical studies. Fortunately for me, half of our SAT test was math, and science teacher Frank Sanders (in his habitual chalk-covered maroon jacket) had prepared us all very well during our junior and senior year math and physics classes.

I was accepted at Smith College—with a small caveat: I would have to make up the requirements that were missing from my transcript. No problem.

My problem was Dad. He controlled the purse strings and worried about the college tuition for my two brothers, especially Midge, who was just completing his sophomore year at Kalamazoo College, a small, well-respected private institution about seventy miles away. How could Dad justify paying more for my education? I pleaded for just one year at Smith.

Dad finally caved. "Okay ... one year only. Then, back to the University of Michigan. I'm sure it's just as good at one-third the cost."

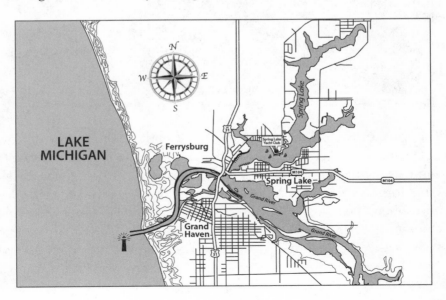

The beaches and sand dunes that line the western shore of Michigan's Lower Peninsula have provided a summer playground for tourists from Chicago and St. Louis since the turn of the twentieth century. I never wanted to travel or work elsewhere during summer vacations.

After World War II, veterans were eager to return to fun summers racing sailboats on Spring Lake. Our neighborhood gang hung out on the public swimming dock at the end of our block and watched longingly as veteran Chet Vink cruised up and down Spring Lake in his huge A boat—a thirty-eight-foot inland racing scow—always hoping he would stop at the dock and give us a ride. And when he did, we were hooked.

Mom and six-month-old Midge on Mackinac Island ferry

Dad was the authentic old man and the sea, fishing until the age of ninety-four. And his love of boating and fishing was quickly transferred to us. Midge and I were comfortable around the water from the time we were born. I can't remember Dad, Midge, or me ever seasick (just poor Mom), no matter how long we rocked around in a small boat, fishing in Lake Michigan and Lake Superior or canoeing in the wilds of Canada.

Boathouse

Just across the lake from our house in Spring Lake was a historic ramshackle boathouse that belonged to the Spring Lake Yacht Club. It became my second home. Midge and I paid our dues learning how to sail on boats that were smaller than the racing scows found at the Yacht Club. We owned an old Crescent, a small keel boat with a main and a jib. It was not part of the Spring Lake Yacht Club's one design racing fleet, which in the 1940s and '50s were mainly scows.

By the summer of 1948, Midge and I could race every weekend on an old Palmer design twenty-foot cat rigged C scow. We were forced to take turns at the helm, which resulted in constant shouting at the skipper from the designated crew. The poor third mate on board suffered through our bickering, commenting that we spent most of our time arguing instead of following the course. (That poor crew member, Paul Eggert, would become a trophy-laden E scow sailor and part of our family.)

The Western Michigan Yachting Association (WMYA) had been organized in 1930 to sponsor sailing regattas during the month of August on lakes bordering Lake Michigan. We often towed our sailboats up or down the coast from Spring Lake, which flowed first into the Grand River and then entered Lake Michigan. Four road and train bridges had to open before our flotilla of small boats with high masts could leave Grand Haven harbor. There were no fixed bridges. Waterways were still important for commerce as well as yachting.

Joyce, left; Al Jacobson, on knee; Ham Berry, striped shirt; Nancy Moriarty, hoop earrings; Carol Berry, standing; Albie Gibson, straw hat; Jack Batts, mask; Nancy Batts, big hat; Jule, bear rug; Pip Gignac, sitting on right. Spring Lake Yacht Club, circa early 1950s

The summer before college, I taught sailing at the yacht club during the day and partied into the night with much older guys, mainly the veterans of World War II who were still college students. Some attended Amherst; others went to Ivy League colleges near Smith. I looked forward to visiting their schools on fall weekends.

When I arrived in Northampton, Massachusetts, in September, wearing Mom's western jacket with leather fringe on the shoulders and sleeves, the new Smith freshmen from the East Coast wondered when I had left the Indian reservation. They really believed—in the middle of the twentieth century—western Michigan was the West. I couldn't believe their apparent naiveté. I traveled in my early teens with our family for an entire summer throughout the western states, camping at all of the large national parks. But then, I hadn't traveled *abroad.* ...

The majority of our freshman class had been educated in girls' prep schools. They seemed awkward and immature around the college boys who appeared early on to check us out. By comparison, I felt comfortable in a coeducational environment.

In elementary and junior high school, girls and boys played baseball, football, and basketball together. During the summer, we traveled together as a ragtag tennis team to tournaments in Kalamazoo; during the winter, we skied on snow-covered hilly sand dunes and skated on frozen Spring Lake.

My first semester at Smith College was culture shock—mentally, emotionally, and socially—especially French class. I took a double French course, six classes six days per week for six semester credits, to catch up on foreign language requirements. The teacher walked in the first morning and announced in a haughty, austere voice, *"Bonjour!"* sounding just like Julia Child (Smith class of 1932).

The class appeared to answer in unison, *"Bonjour!"*

I had no idea what was happening. I asked the girl on my right. She explained that she understood some French because she had spent the past summer in France. I turned to the girl on my left and touched her knee-socked leg. She screamed. The teacher glared. I blushed ... and got a D for the first marking period in French. I'd never had a D before.

And then there was English. The second week of class, the teacher asked us to write an essay comparing six Shakespearean plays. I complained that I had not read any plays by Shakespeare in high school.

"Too bad. Read six … before you write the essay."

Another fall weekend away from campus disappeared. That classwork earned me a C. I'd never had a C before.

Next came art. Studio Art was the course name. I thought it would be fun. It was a disaster. What did I know about drawing, or Picasso? (Was he French? Spanish?) At least I passed.

Finally, an easy subject: economics. I signed up for the most advanced course, a senior survey course that required much reading time—time I didn't have. I would be forced to rely on my street knowledge learned at the dinner table from Dad. (He was quite the energetic entrepreneur, especially during World War II, when he had to find and deliver coal from the Verplank docks to Muskegon industries that had switched from building trucks to tanks.) I got my best grade for the entire semester: a B-plus.

At Christmas break, I took a train home and stepped off the platform in Grand Rapids, looking rather ridiculous yet preppy, in new plaid Bermuda shorts, kneesocks, and a three-quarter-length muskrat fur coat. Although I hadn't quite figured out how to put that together, I had concerns that were more serious: I badly needed this vacation to catch up on schoolwork.

For the first time in my life, I worried about passing a course or two. Dad thought I was very industrious (my brothers weren't studying), but Mom thought I looked unkempt and unhealthy. She was right on both counts. With only females around day and night, none of us had any incentive to wash our hair, iron our clothes, or wear makeup. And I looked bloated: big swollen bosom and stomach, no doubt remnants of the terrible automobile accident almost a year before.

When I returned to Smith in January, I was determined to spend the rest of the year studying. No partying, no traveling. I kept asking myself: "How could I be so stupid? Why did I choose these courses my first year? Why did I talk my counselors into this program?"

I dug in the second semester and became quite the hermit: me, my books, my Sunday *New York Times* crossword puzzle—and, oh yes, my knitting. I tried to knit during lectures, but I couldn't concentrate. I've not perfected that skill yet. Or note taking. How could I write and listen at the same time? I found that, if I read the material in advance, I could follow the lecture and didn't need to take copious notes. I was becoming a scholar, and enjoying it. Next year was going to be different at Smith. I knew what I wanted, how to get it, and how to be good at it.

During spring vacation, Midge invited me to Florida. He had transferred his junior year from Kalamazoo College to a state school in Lakeland, Florida Southern College. He didn't care much about the merits of the school; he just wanted a bigger school far away from the Michigan winters. His friend, Dave Weeks, also from Michigan, was a pilot who gave me so-called flying lessons in his small plane so that we could tour the coastline while Midge attended classes. Neither one of them seemed worried about schoolwork, or the future … much less the Korean War, which consumed draftees Midge and Dave's age when they graduated from college. Dad must have known, because he insisted that Midge come back to Kalamazoo College to complete his senior year.

After carefully choosing sophomore courses and a serious but delightful Wilder House roommate, Durinda Purkiss, I hurried home in June to find work.

The previous summer at the Spring Lake Yacht Club, I met a handsome, debonair sailor, Julian ("Jule") Hatton Jr., who had an equally attractive wife and baby. He skippered an E scow with a novice crew, three classmates from Harvard Business School whom he had recruited to work at his father's tannery, Eagle Ottawa Leather Co.

This summer, Jule showed up alone at the Spring Lake Yacht Club, newly divorced. Now divorce, especially if there were children, was seldom contemplated in our seemingly idyllic environment, much less brought to completion with such dispatch. Although his situation was not openly discussed, gossipmongers hinted that his wealthy, Radcliffe-educated, bright, bohemian wife, baby in tow, ran off to Florida with an old beau from Milwaukee, her hometown.

Jule invited me to yacht club parties, beach roasts, and, finally, elegant dinners with the local high society. His friends were older, and they seemed much more sophisticated than my family or my contemporaries. I was enchanted.

About midway through the summer, Dad inquired, "Have you enrolled at the University of Michigan?"

"No."

"Why not? I told you that I was not paying for more than a year at Smith College."

I couldn't believe that he would enforce his year earlier admonition. I asked Smith College for scholarship information and then the University of Michigan for an enrollment application. After filling out both forms, I waited impatiently. By early August, Smith turned me down, explaining that Dad's income, by their standards, was sufficient to pay my tuition.

"How about work on Smith's campus?" I asked.

"That is not possible, either," was their curt reply. "Campus jobs are saved for scholarship students."

By mid-August, I was accepted as a transfer student at the University of Michigan. I would be living in a dorm for transfer students, Victor Vaughn House, which was located on the northern edge of campus. I became totally disgusted with the Smith College system that forced me into this new program. After all, they didn't understand Dad. His priorities weren't all that unusual—mine were.

After the first fall weekend in Ann Arbor, I recognized that only the male spectator sports, notably football and basketball, were important to a major university like Michigan. Since I liked to participate, not spectate, I found the library a refuge during Saturday afternoon football games.

However, that attitude toward male spectator sports was soon to change. My route to class passed by the Nu Sigma medical fraternity house, where I knew members like Dave Horning and Phil Frandsen from western Michigan sailing regattas. I took a particular liking to their classmate, Ralph Straffon, because he was an excellent medical student, a natural leader, and rather mild mannered through it all—quite different from my imperious summer boyfriend from Harvard. (Ralph also happened to be captain of the Michigan football team when they played Ohio State in the "snow bowl"—twenty-one inches of snow—in the fall of 1950. Winning that game gave Michigan the 1951 Rose Bowl invitation.)

Ralph was my first love at Michigan, but he was searching for a wife, and I wasn't ready to participate. After graduation from medical school in 1953, Ralph married a Kappa Kappa Gamma sorority sister, class of 1952. (Ralph was a leader all his life: he was the surgeon for one of the first cadaver kidney transplants in 1963. It was exciting to open that week's *Life* magazine and see a picture of Ralph rushing down the hall of the Cleveland Clinic during the operation. Ralph served as Chief of Staff of the Cleveland Clinic and also as president of the American College of Surgeons.)

My scholarly pursuits gave way to other extracurricular activities available on a coeducational campus. I pledged a sorority, Kappa Kappa Gamma. I joined weekend beer busts ... until a few girls were badly cut by broken beer bottles at a late fall afternoon country picnic hosted by a law fraternity.

Although I was frightened, my casual date, Bill Griffith, along with all of his fraternity pals, seemed to revel in their beer busts. (After graduation from Michigan Law School and a move to Denver, Bill calmed down enough to be elected to the Colorado State Legislature. He agreed to represent me when I needed a legal real estate broker for an FDIC bank sale in 1991, in Aspen—and collected half the commission. Full of fun, Bill would invite me to the Super Bowl when the Denver Broncos were playing in an interesting locale, like New Orleans. And he would show up on the Jerome Hotel ballroom dance floor at my daughter Lydia's wedding in Aspen—and in the hot tub with my boys after the reception.)

Surprisingly, none of my grades suffered from all the various distractions.

This school year, I had planned my class schedule methodically, picking out professors and even lab partners. But I was just plain lucky in physics: When our huge physics class of almost two hundred students (I was one of three girls) divided up into twenty students per discussion group, I was assigned to a young, exciting, very brilliant instructor. I got supercharged even thinking about his class. He made physics easy.

One of our final exam questions, five years before *Sputnik,* was this: "How would you send a satellite into orbit?"

My answer (as best I can remember) was "I would need a three-stage rocket to boost it through the earth's atmosphere."

With an A-plus for that marking period, I had a new major: physics. (Eight years later, my instructor, Dr. Donald Glaser, won the Nobel Prize in Physics for the development of the Bubble Chamber.)

The courses I chose so carefully paralleled my old high school interests in physics and economics, and the solid foundation in French, ground out during daily classes at Smith College my freshman year, allowed me to pursue other romance languages. Since my new summer beau, Jule Hatton, had a great love of classical music, especially opera, I studied Italian during the spring semester, and received my second A-plus.

I was a contented camper living at home in Spring Lake during the next summer break. A happy-go-lucky atmosphere pervaded beach parties at Holiday House, the Lake Michigan cottage built by Jule's parents after World War II. Jule's Harvard Business School classmates, all veterans (including Jule) and all married with children, would show up for late night swims in Lake Michigan. Their wives stayed at home with the kids. As Jule's new steady date, I became one of the guys (well … sort of.)

One of them, "Captain" Ed Meany, with three daughters under age three at home, sailed every weekend on Jule's E scow. That did not bother his wife, Betty. After surviving the bloody Battle of the Bulge in World War II as a triage nurse, her growing household never fazed Betty, even when three daughters grew to nine daughters.

Tom Newman's wife, Harriet, became my favorite girlfriend. She worked as a model and fashion buyer for the Jordan Marsh department store in Boston while Tom attended Harvard Business School. I marveled at her knowledge of music, art, and business, since she had never gone to college. She claimed she was too busy—working to put Tom through college and graduate school—to attend college herself. She seemed more energetic, more "with it," than any of her master's-degree cohorts. Quite pregnant that summer with their second child, Harriet, too, was enjoying full-time motherhood, her new "career."

And I had a favorite couple too: Libby and Jack Reichardt. Although fifteen years my senior, they swung with the wealthy aristocratic crowd that could be found inhabiting the summer cottages and estates of the lakeshore.

Libby Reichardt 1952

Libby made their friends her business. After working at Neiman Marcus in Dallas during World War II, Libby brought her southern drawl and sophisticated knowledge of retailing to the Tri-Cities and wowed the crowd with her European imports. (I can't look at George Jensen silver without remembering Libby. Not having pierced ears, I lost at least one of each pair of silver earrings given to me over a period of twenty years.) And she brought an uncanny ability to blend work with play.

Jack blended in beautifully with all the action. Cool, athletic, handsome, and tastefully dressed at all times—yes, all times—it was their business, and he never forgot it. They had two boys underfoot, but that never slowed Jack or Libby down. Help was a southern necessity in nice families, and someone would always appear at the appropriate time with food or child care.

Libby never entertained from the kitchen. Her guests could expect a repartee unequaled in western Michigan. And she never missed a copy of *The New Yorker* or the *New York Times* to help keep her worldly knowledge always on the cutting edge. It was a new world to me, still living at home— in a house located less than a block away from their entertainment center.

On a stormy Saturday afternoon in early August, Jule and I were attending a party at the Reichardts' house. Suddenly, Dad appeared at their door. A call had come from Jule's mother. She had been waiting at cousin Harriette Freeman's house in Grand Rapids to pick up Jule's dad, who was late. There had been an accident. They feared the worst. Dad drove Jule and me to Grand Rapids immediately.

Our seemingly carefree existence came to a crashing halt. Jule's father, Julian Hatton Sr., was killed at age fifty-two. His Detroit-based taxi collided head-on with a huge semitrailer truck on the rain-soaked highway, just thirty miles east of Grand Rapids.

Julian Sr., was the boss, the owner of their place of employ, a huge tannery bordering the Grand River, with almost a thousand workers, making it the largest business in our Tri-Cities area, which included Grand Haven, Spring Lake, and Ferrysburg. The only person trained to replace Julian Sr., or expected to replace him, was Julian Jr. At twenty-five years of age, Jule became the president and CEO of Eagle Ottawa Leather Co. His two uncles, almost ready to retire from the tannery, now reported directly to him. With no time left for fun or frolic, I was thrown into a new role: Jule needed a helpmate, and I fit the bill.

Campus life in September was bound to change. Jule wanted me by his side and, to that end, suggested I transfer to a school in a more convenient location. Ann Arbor was not a business destination. Jule picked the University of Chicago, noting that it had a three-year program for an advanced degree, skipping the bachelor's degree altogether. I loved the idea, but I couldn't afford it. Jule could, but we weren't married.

With mixed emotions, I moved into the Kappa Kappa Gamma sorority house in September. I wanted to pursue my studies, and I wanted a career—maybe in my new major, physics. I signed up for two math courses, along with the usual upper-level requirements for graduation. Although school was still interesting, if not exciting, sorority life presented a new twist: when Jule pulled me away from campus life with his mature interests, my joyous and fun-loving roommates would woo me back.

Finally, after a month of weekend visits to campus, Jule demanded, "Marry me now, or forget it."

Jule was too busy to be bothered with three-hour drives to Ann Arbor, a place he found boring when he did arrive for weekend visits. Humility was not his long suit, and he made his feelings abundantly clear to my sorority sisters.

In early October, I returned home to consult Mom and Dad, something I seldom did. They were wary of the Hatton family, wondering how the local aristocracy would accept them. Moreover, they were baffled, although impressed, by the Frank Lloyd Wright-type design of Jule's ultramodern, multilevel house being constructed on top of a sand dune that overlooked Lake Michigan to the west and the city of Grand Haven to the north. But they were thrilled for me, because they felt I would be able to afford whatever I desired.

A plan was decisively put together by Jule: We would become engaged in two weeks, and we would be married before the end of the year. Jule justified the timetable by telling Dad that he'd be able to afford the honeymoon from the income tax savings, a fact Jule knew Dad could appreciate.

Back at school, I visited the dean of women to explain that I would be getting married during our two-week Christmas holiday break and moving out of the sorority house. Nevertheless, I planned to return in January as a day student to finish the first semester studies. To everyone's surprise, the dean said no.

The dean said I would be setting a bad example for other students if I moved out of the Kappa house in December before the end of the semester and returned in January as a married day student. She said, "Leave now, or put off the wedding."

Appalled by her blunt decision, I continued my classes. I loved school. I wanted to graduate. I didn't want to lose my college credits for the fall semester, or be forced to return to Grand Haven, where I would be nothing more than a housewife for the remainder of the school year. I had no interest in domesticity, having watched Mom do dull chores day after day, year after year. (She did them dutifully but never with passion.) And I had no interest in decorating, not even a modern new house. (Mom had good taste, but Dad controlled every penny, so our house remained very practical.)

During our engagement party in October, I became immersed in the fun and games of the "Boy's Club," mostly local entrepreneurs and professionals: the owners of the fish market and the piano factory and the tool-and-die and stamping plants, dentists, salesmen—all men who spent a lot of time drinking and playing practical jokes on each other. Jule always seemed on the periphery, too aristocratic and full of hubris for their humbler upbringings. Not me. They didn't mind having someone half their age (not yet old enough to be served legally) around to decorate their informal nightly gatherings. The women were always bustling about, helping out but never instigating. It was a man's world. And the wives didn't mind at all, for they were part of the action. The Boy's Club planned parties and showers for us in December, only weeks before the wedding.

I knew I was mentally moving out of the college scene, pulled by the anticipation of new opportunities made possible by Jule's wealth. Over the past year, Jule teased me that he had to travel alone because of my college commitments. He would call me from the famous Swiss resort, Davos, where he was skiing, or from New York, where he was prowling art galleries or attending operas at the classic Metropolitan Opera House. Work never seemed to be part of those conversations.

George Cannon, Bill Lowry, Davos ski instructor, Julian Hatton, Al Jacobson, Davos, Switzerland, 1952

After leaving Ann Arbor the first week of December, I knew I would never go back. I planned a six-month sabbatical from school before enrolling at the University of Chicago.

While I was fighting with the University of Michigan, my older brother, Midge, was fighting the real war. Because of the continuous draft since World War II, Midge was drafted in October 1952 and sent to Fort Knox for basic training. He was not allowed to leave to attend any of my engagement or wedding festivities, muttering that he was left freezing in a pup tent, bivouacked for a week in winter field conditions while we were celebrating with champagne at the Spring Lake Country Club.

Midge knew we weren't worrying about him because Eisenhower had been elected in November and was going to end the war—the so-called Forgotten War that was never declared a war by Congress. When my cheerleading idol, Jack Mead, the son of our Grand Haven High School principal, was killed in 1950 during the most brutal fighting of the Korean War, everyone in our high school was stunned. Jack Mead died fighting that Forgotten War.

But it wasn't forgotten for Midge. When I received his letters in May and

June of 1953, I hid them from Mom and Dad. They were unlike anything I could have expected.

His combat battalion was encamped five miles behind the main line of resistance at the thirty-eighth parallel. The main line of resistance had become static because no one wanted to die during the last days of the war. More than fifty thousand soldiers had died already. Midge's main problem was the hundreds of Korean civilians who had been drafted as day laborers and assigned to him. They would steal anything. He kept his gun handy and slept on his wallet and watch.

Midge's war had become an artillery war. What he watched being blown up at night, he repaired during the day … and cleared minefields with rudimentary equipment.

At 6:00 p.m., July 26, 1953, Midge took a call from his battalion commander: "Break down everything, and be ready to move at 4:00 a.m."

They piled tents, bunks, and equipment into six-by-six-foot trucks and headed for the west coast of Korea. When they stopped for lunch, they heard, "The war is over … the truce is taking effect at 10:00 p.m. tonight."

At 5:00 p.m., Midge's battalion arrived in Seoul and found it was nothing but rubble. The streets were being bulldozed so that the troops could get through.

Finally, they arrived in the dark, at around 8:00 p.m., at a small valley on the thirty-eighth parallel. Midge compared the valley sky to "five hundred Coast Guard festival fireworks."

The first marine division artillerymen were pulling off lanyards and shooting artillery barrages at the Chinese (who Midge said took over the war in 1950). And the Chinese were firing back just as ferociously at the first marine division.

"The scene was unbelievable!" Midge wrote. "The whole valley was aflame. We had been up thirty-six hours straight … we were in complete awe … we thought the war would never end. It was bullshit what we heard. Suddenly, at 9:59 p.m., the valley went silent and dark. Not another round was fired. As abruptly as it started, the war ended."

While cruising Lake Michigan in early August 1953 on the *Galleon*, a large, old fifty-foot yawl owned by "Gloomy" Smith, one of the faithful members of the Boys Club, I commented to Dearie, his wife, "I think I'm coming down with the flu."

"Are you getting seasick?" she inquired politely.

"No. I've never been seasick, so it must be the flu."

Titters and knowing looks back and forth among the women.

"Do you think you are pregnant?"

No, I couldn't be; I had carefully followed the doctor's directions. Someone offered me a rum drink. I took one sip of it and knew something was different. Drinks had never made me sick before. I clenched my cramping abdomen.

Jule took the news with equanimity but insisted that we make immediate plans for a two-month tour of Europe. He had bicycled with his first wife throughout Europe on a long summer honeymoon before attending Harvard Business School in the fall of 1948, and he had skied in Switzerland and Austria the last two winters before we were married.

As a father of a four-year-old son, Jule knew there would be no extensive vacations for decades to come after the baby's birth. And Jule wanted at least a month on the continent to revisit all the iconic places he had discovered during his previous visits. He believed the exposure would help me appreciate his passionate and consuming interest in cultural Europe, especially all things French: cuisine, wine, museums, artists, fashions, and, needless to say to me, the French language. And to help excuse his long absence from Eagle Ottawa, Jule planned business meetings in Paris and a weekend with the inventor Madame Sark at her historic château in the French countryside.

We sailed on the majestic *Île de France* in early September. Blessed with Dad's tough stomach, I never got morning sickness or seasickness.

The *Île de France* was home to the rich and famous, and every night was a celebration. All the way to Europe! We would work our way down from first class to steerage as the evening wore on, accompanied by old movie star Nicholas Joy and young Steve McQueen. The best parties were in the bowels of the ship; the music and dances with native instruments were never planned but always lively, especially by early morning when no one worried anymore about their station or location, and no one had to get up until noon or afternoon.

Our first stop was Paris, where Jule contacted some physics and math professors for information about a new business venture called *Ionics*. Jule's illustrious professor and devoted personal friend from Harvard Business School, General Georges Frederic Doriot (who would become Frederic Crispin Hatton's godfather), founded the Association for Research and Development Corporation in 1946—the first institutional venture capital fund that "set the standard for venture capital forever," according to editors of recent venture capital books. Ionics was started by a Harvard chemist to make ion-exchange membranes that could make salt water potable, and, in 1948, the Association for Research and Development provided the seed money for the venture. (Think of the water makers on our ocean-voyaging sailboats.)

When the scientists invited us to dinner at a posh Parisian restaurant, I realized I needed something more formal than my black tartan plaid suit. I visited the designer dress shops in the morning and found out, to my dismay, that I would not be investing in any sleek size eights. Almost three months pregnant, my waistline had disappeared. The haughty clerks were on a tirade, insisting I buy something to replace my wool suit—a tunic, perhaps? But I refused. I had suffered sticker shock as soon as I entered their haute couture boutiques. No smock or fake maternity wear was worth those prices.

I walked back to the small, intimate bar of our historic Maurice Hotel to console myself and wait for Jule to return from his meeting. Sitting in a chair near the entrance, so small I hardly noticed her, was Elizabeth Taylor. She was dressed in an elegant black suit and seemed to be waiting for someone. I was twenty; she was twenty-one or twenty-two. Our figures were similar, except for my burgeoning waistline. Since she was alone, as was I now, I began to relax in my strange new environment.

Before dinner, I wandered into the hair salon. A dark-complected man, with long black hair drooping over one eye, was applying a heavy pasty-looking ooze on a toothbrush to strands of hair on a customer's hair-line. (What was it? Did I want it? My first highlighting? Yes!)

I loved it. My hair, usually a dirty dishwater blonde, had beautiful platinum streaks. Finally, I, too, felt elegantly prepared for the evening's events.

Jule promised me that I would be able to understand the scientific French discussion at the table because of my strong background in math and physics. I did comprehend quite a bit while the men were speaking, but I did not understand one word of the women's fast chatter. I sat and listened to the men, following with great interest their arguments, and the women chatted at the other end of our very large table. That experience was an exciting augury of things to come.

After the Champagne, the Bordeaux, the Burgundy, and the Cognac, I could not stay awake. My pregnancy and constant need to translate the French into English had taken its toll.

On to Madame Sark's country château. Tolstoy revisited. The château was dark, cold, and bare. We huddled around an immense stone fireplace. A large tray of iced vodka in tiny shot glasses was placed in front of us.

"Drink! ... Up! Throw the shot glass over your shoulder into the fireplace; the glass must break for good luck," instructed Madame Sark, our tiny, wrinkled, hook-nosed Russian hostess.

Next, we were ushered into the kitchen where the cooks were defeathering minute birds that had been shot that morning. I could see no meat on them.

"Watch for the shot when you eat them," warned Madame Sark, contemplating the immense pile of dead birds. Dinner would be late in coming. Back to the drawing room for more vodka.

There would be no serious business done the day of arrival. Only the celebratory feast.

I woke the next afternoon with a gargantuan thirst that couldn't be abated. I complained to Jule, and he asked Madame Sark for a pitcher of water.

"No! Not a drop of water! That will only make it worse; Russian tea—a large pot of Russian tea. And make sure that she drinks it all. No water!"

Miraculously, it worked.

Madame Sark had an ingenious contraption that screened complicated designs in a multitude of colors on silk and leather. Jule planned to use it on furniture leather. I did not understand the process, and Madame Sark did not bother to discuss it with me. She was concentrating on Jule.

I explored her château. It was fascinating, with its towers and turrets, yet depressing because of the lack of furniture. Only stone fireplaces and benches and tables. How did she find a château so quickly after World War II? And how did she get out of Russia with money and her curious invention? And why no husband or family? I will never know, and, if Jule knew, he didn't tell me.

When we left the château, Madame Sark handed me an emblematic scarf, a wheel with perhaps fifty spokes in hues of the rainbow.

*Congratulating Fritz's godfather, General Georges Frederic
Doriot, at Harvard Business School awards ceremony*

Our first child, Frederic, named after his godfather, General Georges Frederic Doriot, was born just fifteen months after we were married.

The physical and emotional strains of motherhood were overwhelming. My self-centered existence ended—*forever*. Jule insisted on full-time nurses immediately, so I should not have had much to worry about, as long as we could keep them in good supply. But Frederic ("Fritz") was very little and nursed every two hours for the first month, until my pediatrician surmised that my milk supply, although adequate, was not very nourishing. After four weeks, Fritz still had not gained back his birth weight, all of six pounds, so we resorted to the bottle. I could sleep, and he could eat. And I could travel again.

"Grammy" Hatton became a household institution, showering us with her staff, which included a full-time laundress and gardener-driver-handyman. Naturally, Grammy and I both wanted to run the show, so Jule was hard pressed every night to keep the peace. Our wine and her bourbon helped out, but getting out of the house became my best solution ... until I got pregnant again, six months later.

My first reaction to the second pregnancy was fear. I would (somehow) have to get through another delivery, and the first one, twenty-two hours of labor, was still fresh in my mind. Another concern, one that I was afraid to discuss openly at the time, was the amazing "vision" that I had when

Fritz was born. I was "let in" on how we earthlings integrate with the entire universe.

Yes, there was a supreme power—a supreme force that was forcing a magnetic planetary integration in my ethereal dream—but it didn't have anything to do with religious beliefs that I had experienced. Jule, with his strong Episcopalian upbringing, seemed so embarrassed when I brought up that subject, which I did every day for ten long days in the hospital, that I suppressed any further discussion of it. Now I wondered if the vision would reappear this time. My obstetrician promised there would be no gas or other dream-enhancing anesthetic, but Gregory Macauley arrived so quickly (a day early, on his Grandpa Verplank's forty-eighth birthday), the doctor flunked the test. A few whiffs of gas, and installment number two of my vision arrived along with Greg.

Michigan is fortunate to have three definite seasons, with the natural topography to enjoy them to the fullest. In between pregnancies, I could sail in the summer and ski in the winter. Bird hunting with the members of the Spoonville Gun Club or Kinney Creek Club was Jule's favorite fall sport, and fishing in Lake Michigan with Dad was mine.

Jule and I took turns skippering his E scow, *Andiamo,* in races at the Spring Lake Yacht Club and other WMYA clubs that hosted regattas for the E class boats. The E scow was twenty-eight feet, eight feet longer than our old C scow. Instead of the normal skipper and crew of one or two for the C, the E required a crew of three or four to handle all the sails: main, jib, and spinnaker, reacher, or chute.

With Jule on Andiamo, circa 1953   *Brett and Lydia and crew, circa 2016*

When I wasn't driving, Jule put me in charge of the light sails on the foredeck. Most of the time it worked out well, but there were a few scary moments in high winds when I, who weighed all of 105 pounds, would sail halfway up the mast holding a half-open spinnaker or chute.

Winter in Michigan means snow, and we can usually depend on lots of it from Christmas to Easter. I planned every weekend around ski trips to the northern part of the Lower Peninsula of Michigan.

We belonged to Hidden Valley, home of the Otsego Ski Club. Although the hills were not much by comparison to Boyne Mountain, which was less than an hour's drive from Hidden Valley, the setup was magnificent. The log cabins that housed our family were new and tastefully decorated by someone who didn't have to worry about meeting a budget. And money didn't seem to be a worry of the clientele, either. Most of the members were from Grosse Pointe or other wealthy suburbs around Detroit, with a small contingent from the rest of the state.

After skiing or sledding with the boys during the day, we hired babysitters for the evening. The main lodge was not casual dining. Clothes were important, and so were the cocktail hours ... and after hours.

One night, I sat at the small bar with Henry Ford, listening to him complain about some of the women in his life (who? which?). My favorite men, however, were the three Chapin brothers. Roy, the eldest and twenty years my senior, I admired the most. Probably because he was smart and serious, and the hardest for me to get to know.

And the women? Some I envied for their brashness and entertaining talents. Certainly not work. I soon realized that independent wealth also allowed independent spirit. Unfortunately, that didn't always include common sense. One ran off with our famous Norwegian ski instructor, Stein Erickson. Obviously, she didn't worry about who would support her or her children.

During the spring of 1956, Jule and I flew to Havana with Sherry and Jeanne Gay, an older couple from New Jersey who owned leather tanneries in the East. They were appropriately named Gay, for they loved the sportive life. They ferreted out hunting and fishing hot spots around the world, and they found one for us near the Isle of Pines along the desolate southern coast of Cuba. A dilapidated houseboat was to be our home for a week. And it was pure fun.

Jeanne was both classy and wild, the consummate party animal who could drink, hunt, or fish with the best of the men. She had two sons my age, but she definitely was not the motherly type—more like Auntie Mame.

And the men loved her. Jeanne did not spend time cooking, cleaning, or waiting on them. She relied on the same staff the men did, so our houseboat crew learned their role on board very quickly. It was a great lesson for me: I learned bonefish casting from Jeanne, and storing cases of beer in hot climates from the cook. And the captain had the daunting task of teaching us how to bathe in the shark- and barracuda-infested waters.

I learned something else on the Cuba trip. I was pregnant again. No wonder the fresh grapefruit and rum at lunch made me nauseated the last few days on board the houseboat.

And then, Grammy Hatton wanted me home early. Our two boys had colds. "You can go to Havana anytime," she explained.

Little did any of us realize that Batista and Castro were duking it out in the countryside, and the non-Communist tourists were about to disappear. Jule remained in Havana to meet with his Cuban tannery representative, and I flew home to the nest.

About two months later, I discovered a side of Jule that I felt could be devastating. We were driving to Chicago for a relaxing weekend at the Union League Club, a stuffy old boys club in the heart of downtown Chicago. Jule had just finished a leather company board meeting that had not gone well. Jule was depressed about the lack of sales for automobile and furniture leather.

When I tried to discuss his business problems, he tried to forget them. I wanted to talk. He wanted to drink. And drink he did. All weekend long. I became very upset; I was three months pregnant with our third child in the fourth year of our marriage. I felt caged, unable to fly on my own, stuck with a man refusing to think about work when the future of his company was at stake.

By the time we returned to Grand Haven, I harbored a slow burn. I was incensed by my own folly. Why hadn't I seen this side of him before? So unlike Dad or my grandfather or my great-grandfather, all of them competitive, hard workers when the chips were down. My childhood began during the Great Depression of the 1930s, and my parents never took anything for granted. I was a fervent believer in the old adage "When the going gets tough, the tough get going."

Jule was a child of the 1930s too, but his heritage was much different. With wealth going back many generations on his maternal side, Jule had access to all the cultural and educational pursuits that accompanied a rich tradition. His mother, Charline Leonard Hatton, was a gifted cello player who cofounded the Muskegon-based West Shore Symphony in 1938.

Always a brilliant student, Jule also became a very talented oboe and English horn player with the Harvard University Orchestra and the Boston Civic Symphony. His knowledge and love of classical music was legendary. Much greater than his love of business, I surmised.

Our third son, Julian Burroughs Hatton III ("Julio"), was born just six days before Christmas. It was not a difficult birth, and I didn't have much pain medication. Nevertheless, I had the same vision, or I should say the third installment, for it picked up where I left off from the last childbearing re-velatory experience. And it chided me, "Now ... don't you believe me (the vision)?"

This disclosure totally occupied my mind for the following week in the hospital. Nothing worldly seemed important. Budapest was on fire; people were dying in the streets; Russian bullies were everywhere. Yet my consciousness dealt with a different reality. Obviously, these minor confla-grations seemed of little consequence. I could see the distant world(s) all locking together in the cosmos. (I should have written the sci-fi 3-D movie, *Avatar*.)

After this third dream, I scribbled down what was bothering me, and, although I will quote it in full, it does not describe much of the content of the dreams:

> The problem seems to be how to relate (or equate) the two worlds—and which is the true real one, and which has just an appearance of reality. Or are they both equally real? But that cannot follow because there is no logical understanding of the one we know here on earth. Rather, there are so many unanswerable questions: Where do we come from? Where do we go—and why? This other world—which I seem able to get a fleeting glimpse of only at these special times—has never before this child had any relationship to what was going on here on earth when I "woke up"—but this time one led into the other—but *why* has my mind fabricated another—that it could never possibly experience in any way? Is imagination that wonderful and repetitive and logical?

(Bishop John Shelby Spong commented on becoming a mystic: "The deeper I experience the reality and presence of God, the less my words seem like adequate vehicles to express that truth. Then words cease and one enters the experience of wordless wonder. Perhaps that is the realization of the mystic.")

Instead of the mandatory ten days in the hospital, I was released on Christmas day. When Jule appeared in my room at Blodgett Hospital in the late morning, he looked awful. He admitted that the annual celebratory Christmas Eve Swedish grog at Tom Newman's house had taken its toll on all the guests, but he was the only one who had major responsibilities the next morning. After driving the fifty miles home and making sure that I climbed each step backward (doctor's orders) on the many flights of stairs to our living room, Jule was bushed.

Mom was ensconced in the kitchen, planning Christmas dinner, and Dad was running up and down all the stairs, carrying multitudes of packages to the living room and kitchen from the garage. And when I appeared and saw Dad, he looked worse than Jule! Dad was turning white as a sheet. I called Mom and she made him stop and sit down right away, warning him that she thought he was going to have a heart attack. Dad sat down and relaxed, but I was frightened too, and I hugged our six-day-old baby, not wanting to take part in any festivities.

It was my longest Christmas day in memory, but it would be dwarfed by what arrived the next week: chicken pox. Jule left for New York City on New Year 's Day. He claimed it was work related, and he knew I had daytime help. I pleaded with him to wait … to no avail. Jule was hardly out the door when both Fritz and Greg started crying all night. They had pox everywhere—even filling their mouths. Julian's crib and my cot had been placed in the library. I was nursing Julian, but he got little attention because of the screaming of his brothers, and I got no sleep. After three nights of hollering, I finally begged Dr. Hill, our Grand Rapids pediatrician, for help.

Dr. Hill's solution? I'll never forget it—from such a kindly, conservative, thoughtful pediatrician: "Drug them. I'm not worried about them. … I'm worried about you and Julian. You'll be sick, and Julian will be too, if you don't get some rest."

Fritz and Greg were prescribed single doses of sleep medicine every two hours until they fell asleep. It was a fretful sleep for me, concerned as I was about the location of our sleeping quarters far away from two drugged boys. Our house resembled a ship in design, and the library felt like the bowels of the ship. By the time Jule returned from New York City ten days later, all was quiet on the home front.

After bearing three children three years in a row, I was eager to get out of the house and "get going." But, this time, I would have to make it on my own. I needed skills, and I needed experience. After all, what did I know about running a business? Where were my credentials? Where was my Harvard MBA? I no longer felt I could look to Jule for guidance or future security.

My first business interest was realistically based. In the mid-1950s, no nursery schools or day care centers existed in western Michigan to educate my toddlers. Since I felt I needed a college degree to run a nursery school, I enrolled in the fall of 1957 at Hope College in Holland, a quick, twenty-two-minute drive from our house on the hill in Grand Haven. Again, I loved going to school. It was my vacation from home.

But I had an immediate problem: Fritz was already three years old, and Greg almost two, so time was of the essence for their preschool educations. I combed the Tri-Cities during the summer months of 1957, looking for someone qualified to teach early childhood education. I located Helen Arnold, an afternoon kindergarten teacher with a stellar reputation in the community—and soon found every bit of it well deserved. Helen used the piano creatively, emphasizing story lines, rhymes, and lessons. She agreed to teach two mornings a week beginning in September, if I could enroll fifteen children between the ages of three and five.

All the mothers I contacted seemed enthusiastic about the idea. And why not? They could have two hours free twice a week, and their children could have an educational experience at minimal cost. Church rent must be paid, so that I could get a serious commitment from the church authorities for space. Since their nursery classrooms were seldom used during the week, I didn't offer to pay much for their heat, light, and equipment. I expected the mothers, including me, to volunteer time on a regularly scheduled basis. The only paid staff member would be Mrs. Arnold. If the mothers worked outside the home (there were a few, mostly schoolteachers), they would be excluded from the volunteer list. The fathers would not be asked to volunteer.

By September, fifteen children enrolled. When the first day of school arrived, only nine appeared. I quickly contacted the mothers of the missing children. The women were apologetic but said they could not convince their husbands that preschool education was a worthwhile investment. In fact, some of the fathers argued that the mothers would be shirking their parental duty if they shipped their little offspring out of the house before kindergarten.

I pleaded with Mrs. Arnold to stay and teach only nine children, hoping I would be able to change some of the local parental mind-set. Mrs. Arnoid stayed, and Jule paid most of the bills.

During the first semester, it was a slow process: the class increased about one child each week; then half the class would be out with the flu, or the parents would take them out for vacations; then some of the fathers refused to pay tuition when their children were absent from school. It seemed the wealthier the fathers, the less likely they were to honor bills covering an entire semester. They would edit bills for missed classes, or for any other reason they could concoct, implying they really didn't think the school had much merit or made much of a contribution to their children's future educational experience. They considered this my toy, or my hobby, and I could afford it. They were older, and almost all of them had college or postgraduate degrees. Who was I to tell these fathers that their children needed a preschool experience?

I gave up on fathers and concentrated on mothers. What a battle it became for the women. They worried about being disloyal or secretive, but they began to send their children anyway. They were surprisingly tough—college-educated women on the cusp of the "feminine mystique." Gloria Steinem was only two years behind me at Smith College, but she would not be recognized as a leader of feminist causes until the mid-1960s.

After two years, the nursery school had a hundred students, many teachers, many paid assistants, and many more hours of existence. It was time to move on.

Shortly after Jule and I were married, but before I was old enough to vote, I was invited to a luncheon for my Michigan's Fifth District Republican congressman, Jerry Ford. Little did I realize then the lure of political life would define my career for almost two decades: politics was power, and

Congressman Gerald R. Ford, 1952 Courtesy of David LaClaire

political involvement provided a worldly mission that would move me out of the confines of our small town.

I joined the League of Women Voters in 1953, admiring the academic and infectious patriotic spirit of our Tri-Cities group. At the time, I was not cognizant of its ever-present, strong nonpartisan bent; the league didn't like its active members to have direct participation in a political party. Although I believed the league's raison d'être was to develop civic responsibility and leadership, I couldn't comfortably wear two hats, so we parted company in the summer of 1957 when Republican pro Jack Stiles (younger brother of Jule's future business partner, Fred Stiles) came calling with a surprising offer of membership on the Republican State Central Committee.

After my appointment, I left the county legislative campaigns and concentrated on the Michigan gubernatorial race. The GOP was sick of G. Mennen ("Soapy") Williams's long tenure as governor, and it needed a strong visible candidate who would appeal to Republicans and Democrats alike. George Romney was my choice. He rescued American Motors, so why not rescue the rest of the state from the union-controlled Democrats? And, of utmost importance to me, Romney was a moderate Republican. Ottawa County was very Republican, very Dutch, and very conservative south of Grand Haven. Keeping the right-wing ultraconservative John Birch Society at bay was crucial to my success as a moderate Republican leader in our county.

Why was I a "moderate" Republican? Better to ask, why was I not a conservative, for whom divorce and abortion were out of the question, and careers and higher education were suspect.

Yet my entrepreneurial spirit, so ingrained by Dad and his Dutch forbears, required loyalty to the Republican dream. At least leadership in the GOP was available to women if they could afford it. I could, and I embraced it eagerly.

Just as Madame Sark's multicolored silk screening techniques had intrigued Jule in 1953, Dorothy Liebes's award-winning colorful textile designs using unique materials like jute, bamboo, and leather strips, had piqued Jule's interest in the mid-1950s. Dorothy Liebes provided Jule new vibrant colors that she used in her textile designs, and she demanded the same colors be replicated in leather for her use. When Jule announced that he was going to New York City to visit Dorothy, I begged to go too. I had heard about her bi-level apartment with a Picasso rug dominating the entrance and an equally impressive Calder mobile dangling from the second-floor loft ceiling.

Dorothy wowed us the minute we opened her door. Modern designs everywhere … in very much the same theme as our house, except hers became a true modern museum of art—the originals, not just the reproductions. And then Dorothy presented her famous husband, Relman ("Pat") Morin. Pat was Dad's age, but Dorothy was ten years older. Pat was an award-winning journalist who started working for the Far Eastern bureau of the Associated Press (AP) in 1934 after studying and living in China and Japan. With my longtime interest in politics and government, I was eager to talk to him, and luckily, Dorothy whisked Jule off to her studio and left Pat to entertain me.

Pat asked if I would like to see his pictures of pre-World War II China. I couldn't believe my ears. China with Peking, the Forbidden City? We walked upstairs to his study, and he pulled out a large scrapbook filled with many small black-and-white photos. Yes, he wanted to show me Peking, the historic concentric ringed city with its walls and gates, and located inside the innermost circle, the Forbidden City's Imperial Palace. After viewing all the photos, I asked Pat about his work for AP in China and Japan before World War II.

Pat replied that he was head of the AP bureau in Tokyo in 1941. Where was he when the Japanese bombed Pearl Harbor on December 7? (I remember sitting on the carpeted living room floor in our new house on Jackson Street in Spring Lake listening to the radio with the entire family—even seventeen-month-old baby Gary—on Sunday afternoon, December 7, 1941.) Pat laughed and said, "We were told to vacate our Associated Press offices on Thursday, three days before the dawn raid on Pearl Harbor early Sunday morning."

Before we left, I asked Pat if we would ever have the opportunity to see Peking with him. Pat replied sadly that Peking, a beautiful city before the war, hopefully survived intact, but we, being white Americans, were definitely no longer welcome anywhere in China. We had just finished fighting the Chinese in the Korean conflict, a war that Pat knew firsthand, having won a Pulitzer Prize for the reporting of it.

Pat would continue to amaze us with his reports, and Dorothy with her beautiful pillows, but my further knowledge of China and Japan had to come from Pat's book, *East Wind Rising, A Long View of the Pacific Crisis*, which he published in 1960. I'm afraid Pat explained very thoroughly and factually in his book that the "white people" were getting what they long deserved from the raping of Chinese territories and trashing of personal dignity. And it would be another twenty years before I had the chance to find out firsthand.

While I was busy in the political arena, Jule was struggling with continuous problems at Eagle Ottawa. His uncle, Siegel Judd, one of the founders of the prestigious Grand Rapids law firm of Warner, Norcross, and Judd, was attempting to find consultants to work with Jule and all of his uncles and cousins who derived their livelihood from the business.

Dorothy Leonard Judd, 1960s
Courtesy of David LaClaire

When Jule and Uncle Siegel would go to New York on the family business, I often tagged along. If Jule was working with customers in New Jersey or elsewhere, Uncle Siegel would invite me to his private clubs for lunch or cocktails. Uncle Siegel had important European clients, including a famous Austro-Hungarian composer. I liked being a part of his world.

Aunt Dorothy Judd never accompanied Uncle Siegel on these trips. A 1920 graduate of Vassar College, she provided the prissy, austere demeanor that one learned to expect in the early twentieth century from those exposed to education at the Ivy League women's colleges. Now she was busy with her own civic career, which spanned more than a half century, first working with the League of Women Voters at the local, state, and national levels, while teaching and writing the history of Grand Rapids and then revising the local and state civil service. Through it all—and most important to Aunt Dorothy—campaigning for a new Michigan constitutional convention. She was a Leonard—she was Jule's mother's older and only sibling—and the Leonard Refrigerator Company was a well-known Grand Rapids institution dating back to the early nineteenth century. Great-Grandpa Leonard was very civic minded too, founding the first public utility in Grand Rapids.

The consultants to Eagle Ottawa seemed weak and ineffective to me, but I only heard about them from Jule's point of view. After struggling with Eagle Ottawa's financial difficulties for two or three years, Jule invited Albert Trostel Sr., owner of a large tannery in Milwaukee, to our house for cocktails. Albert flew across the lake in one of his company planes to explore a buyout of Eagle Ottawa.

I thought the sale of Eagle Ottawa would be beneficial to all, especially Grammy Hatton. Eagle Ottawa was her sole inheritance, and all her eggs were in that basket. Albert led me to believe it would be good for Jule too, because he would be part of a much larger company in the tanning business.

It soon became evident that Jule and Albert liked to conduct business at night. After drinks at our house, they would head downtown to Grand Haven's only full-service restaurant for the rest of the night.

Albert Trostel was huge. He could drink and eat all night long. He shouldn't have done either, because he was smart and knew what it was doing to his body. But he knew how to make a great deal for his inheritors. He bought Eagle Ottawa, but he didn't buy Jule. Instead, he brought in a young Swede who was forced to commute every week by company plane from Milwaukee ... because his swish Swedish wife would never move to Grand Haven.

Jule's troubles at Eagle Ottawa did not affect my lifestyle. With a Dutch housekeeper, a laundress, a handyman, and multiple babysitters for the three preschoolers—and, of course, Grammy Hatton in charge—I had plenty of time to play, work, politic, and go to college.

During my pregnancy (again) in 1960, I worked on the Republican campaign in the northern half of Ottawa County. Until five days before the November election, I sat on a small, hard folding chair in our rented downtown Grand Haven office and checked registration lists for every precinct in the area to identify reliable Republican voters. Our small dedicated staff called and reminded each one of them to vote. We wanted to keep Jerry Ford as the Republican congressman of our Fifth District (which, in 1960, encompassed only two counties: Kent and Ottawa). And we knew that Senator John Kennedy's popularity in more Democratic Kent County worried our Ottawa Republicans. We needed at least 80 percent of the Ottawa County vote on the GOP ticket to overcome any Democratic majority in the much-larger Kent County.

The voting on Election Day was viewed from my hospital bed. We were thrilled to have a beautiful daughter, Lydia Stansbury, named after her two attractive grandmothers.

And not thrilled with the presidential election result: Kennedy barely eking out a winning margin over Nixon. We were sure it was the result of massive fraudulent voting in Chicago's notorious Cook County.

Fortunately, the Fifth District Democrats couldn't touch Jerry Ford. He was reelected to Congress, thanks in large part to the 85 percent Republican vote from Ottawa County.

At Lydia's birth, I had the next installment of my vision of the cosmos. The universe fit together like the broken halves of an eggshell, or two hands interlocking. My obstetrician, Dr. Bill Jack, Grammy Hatton's stepbrother, was careful to monitor the anesthesia, hoping to find out why I had these revelatory dreams. He did not know if I had been given a "touch" of gas by the nurses before he arrived at the hospital, but he became very curious about my mystical description of life in the universe, which was so vivid, so worldly, so all encompassing.

I asked Dr. Jack if others had this experience when giving birth, and he replied, "No, never."

Dr. Jack was the head of the Department of Obstetrics and Gynecology at Blodgett Hospital in Grand Rapids, so I was deeply upset by his emphatic answer. My frustration with the visions was my inability to understand why I was chosen to have them. Again, it was difficult to talk with Jule. He was embarrassed by my openness and need to discuss the subject, an ethereal topic he considered much too personal for public discourse. I filed my new handwritten notes about the visions in a desk drawer in our library ... not knowing they would disappear forever.

I continued my Republican politicking at the county and state levels. And Aunt Dorothy Judd finally got her Michigan constitutional convention. I observed as a representative from Ottawa County. This was her nonpartisan show. Above politics—if that was possible. As a cochairman, George Romney worked side by side with Aunt Dorothy.

We needed a Republican governor elected in the fall of 1962, and I knew who would be well prepared for the job. Romney was being groomed by Aunt Dorothy to capture the independent vote, and Romney's success at American Motors was making him the logical choice for moderate as well as conservative Republicans.

Chapter Three

A CONFIDANT?

… We are nothing in and of ourselves. Our dignity and quality and stature and worth as a human being is to love and be loved, and to be a part of a loving and caring group…

Dr. Duncan E. Littlefair
Sermon at Fountain St. Church, 1960's

The paddle tennis team in the 1960s. In front: Allen Hunting; First row: Julian Hatton, Joyce Hatton, Bill Seidman, Nancy Van Domelen; Second row: Mary Pew, Jane Goodspeed, Mary Ford, Joan Rieger, Helen Hunting; Third row: Pete Van Domelen, Bob Pew, Phil Goodspeed, Charlie Rieger, Bil Ford

One cold wintry night in the late 1950s, I met Bill Seidman. He arrived unexpectedly for dinner at our house on the hill, having spent a long day consulting with Jule about Eagle Ottawa's accounting problems. Bill's brilliant father, Frank Seidman, a cofounder of the national accounting firm, Seidman & Seidman, had opened their Grand Rapids office in 1919.

Bill was immediately enthusiastic about topics of interest to me, which certainly piqued my interest in him, and I knew he was most curious about my work for the GOP. Bill appeared pragmatic, amazingly well organized, and goal oriented—quite the opposite of Jule. Nevertheless, he admired Jule's many artistic talents and enjoyed Jule's aristocratic lifestyle.

Jule and I soon found out that a large part of Bill's rich and varied life centered around his farm in Ada. Bill constructed rope tows on the ski hills behind the barn and built paddle tennis courts, the first in western Michigan. He blazed trails through the woods for horseback riding and fenced in fields for polo practice. And he attracted a wealthy, young, athletic crowd.

Bill's rambling country house on the Thornapple River, about a mile from the farm, became the hub of activity for our family on Sunday evenings in the fall and winter. The indoor swimming pool and sauna were a welcome relief after a full day of sports. Bill's artistic, beautiful, and soft-spoken wife, Sally, had a large kitchen with two refrigerators that she kept well stocked with hors d'oeuvres and steaks. These were the baby boom years, and we all were active participants: Sally and Bill would have five girls and a boy, and Jule and I five boys, including Jule's son, Mike, and a girl. And, to be expected, none of our kids played with each other.

Our house on the hill became a regular stop for Bill too. He wanted to discuss his political future, and he knew that I was impressed by his credentials for public office: Phi Beta Kappa from Dartmouth; distinguished naval career during World War II; law degree from Harvard; MBA from the University of Michigan; a job working for the family accounting firm, Seidman & Seidman, first in New York City, where he taught business courses at Wagner College, and then in Grand Rapids, where he managed their local office.

Romney had approached Bill to join his team for the upcoming gubernatorial race, even though Bill had never been seriously involved in Michigan Republican politics. I warned Bill that his first problem was Sally's sponsorship of afternoon teas for her Democratic cousin's various candidacies in Kent County. Bill admitted that he had not paid much attention to his wife's political activities, but he was well aware of the fact that western Michigan was a patriarchal society, and he would need to solve this problem quickly. After that was accomplished, I felt confident that he would be accepted readily by the state GOP.

No matter. By 1962, Romney was definitely in control of the Michigan Republican party. Romney got what Romney wanted, and he wanted Bill

Seidman to be the candidate for auditor general on his 1962 ticket. The two of them could not have had backgrounds more different: Romney, a strict Mormon and teetotaler, was born in Mexico to parents fleeing prosecution for practicing their Mormon faith ... and was totally devoted to his wife, Lenore, a former actress and also a Mormon. Seidman was a nonpracticing Russian Jew, married to Sally, a Presbyterian and former homecoming queen. But the two men got along well. Both were smart, energetic, and opportunistic. (To quote Romney: "Luck is where opportunity meets preparation.") And they learned from each other. What Romney lacked in formal education, Bill provided, and what Bill lacked in experience and exposure, Romney paved the way.

Our first vacation with the Seidmans, in the spring of 1962, was a quick trip to Mexico City and Acapulco. It was not a memorable vacation. Bill broke out with a sun rash in Acapulco and looked like he had a full-blown case of the measles. I suffered from Montezuma's revenge in Mexico City and ascertained that I was too sick to get pregnant. We couldn't wait to go home. Bill got out of the sun, and, yes, I got pregnant.

Consumed with events political in the early 1960s, I looked carefully at the professors teaching elective courses at Hope College. The slow-paced summer sessions allowed students full use of the college library. I could explore in depth whatever subjects I found of current interest, and, by noon, I could pull myself away from a cluster of books and hurry home. Our Dutch housekeeper, Gerritdena ("Dean") Korving, with five children waiting at her home, would leave as soon as I drove up the hill.

Hope College's overseas missionary educators were attracted to the summer sessions because of the balmy weather and lakeshore location of the college, and they offered courses in their fields of expertise. I found a political science course on East Asia, which included a retrospective history of French Indo-China, beginning with the fall of Dien Bien Phu in 1954. My professor was a retiring Reformed Church missionary who had grown up in China with his missionary parents. His most recent assignment had been a three-year stint in Indo-China, by then commonly referred to as Vietnam. He focused first on the French colonists, and then the American intervention.

He did not mince words. He saw the French as miserable failures, and he was exasperated with the Americans, who (he thought) had a flawed image of the priorities of both the North and South Vietnamese. This led to American foreign policy mistakes—mistakes he believed to be irreversible.

He contended that Kennedy and his cabinet not only misunderstood the mind-set of the North Vietnamese but also worried excessively about Communist influence in the region. Instead of sending more troops or diplomats to shore up the corrupt South Vietnamese regime, he simply wanted us out of there. Quickly and forever!

Romney won in November 1962, but Bill Seidman lost his bid for auditor general. That fact did not keep Romney from bringing Bill to Lansing to help draft new tax laws. And Bill's access to the legislators helped him win their approval for continual funding for Grand Valley State College, a new four-year college that Bill had recently established in western Michigan.

My opinion, especially in politics and education, was solicited often by Bill. But he always had the final word: I wanted a more dignified name than Grand Valley for the college, and I suggested the campus be located along the Grand River in downtown Grand Rapids, not in the cornfields near Allendale. It would be twenty years before the downtown campus was built, but at least Grand Valley State College soon became Grand Valley State University.

At the same time that Bill was developing Grand Valley, he was assembling a large diverse crowd of community leaders to apply for a new VHF television license that had become available from the Federal Communications Commission. I was convinced that Bill knew how to put all the pieces together better than anyone else. I begged Jule to let us be part of Bill's team, but Jule said we owed our loyalty to Uncle Siegel Judd, who was organizing a smaller assemblage of wealthy business titans from western Michigan. Since Uncle Siegel did not want my help, I worked with Bill once again ... and watched his enthusiastic band of young lawyers, bankers, and business and educational leaders steal the show. WZZM-13 went on the air in the fall of 1962, with a makeshift studio in an old Pantlind Hotel banquet room. I was determined to be a player in Bill's next FCC license application, especially for FM radio, which was still in its infancy.

After returning from Korea, Midge graduated with an MBA degree from the University of Michigan. He interned for a few months as a stockbroker for Merrill Lynch in Chicago before returning to Spring Lake to join Dad running the Verplank dock business—and to marry his college girlfriend, Mary Lou Landman.

By December 1962, Midge was the father of three-year-old Lynne and one-year-old Melissa. But my burgeoning tummy drew a sarcastic comment from him: "When are you going to figure out where all these kids come from?"

With my fifth child due in two weeks, I replied, "Well, Jule believes in Planned Parenthood, and someday we're going to plan one."

1962 Christmas card. Art by Aunt Betty Ellis

But I had made my own plan: Dr. Jack had watched the development of the Pill for years, and, in his protective and conservative approach, had refused to prescribe it for me until the government did further testing. Nevertheless, he agreed that five children were enough for one family and I could try the Pill. And he was tired of worrying about my Rh factor. Combining my Rh-negative with Jule's Rh-positive blood had cost me lots of bloody tests over nine years. Coombs tests (in both arms for safety of the sample) were done every month during all five pregnancies, and the labs on the delivery floors at Blodgett Hospital were ready in case my newborn baby needed blood transfusions.

Dr. Jack was going to be extremely careful with this very last delivery to ensure that I did not receive any drugs. He would order my first spinal anesthesia, and I liked the thought of no pain.

Two weeks after the baby's due date, there were no labor signs. When would this child appear? One would think that number five in less than one decade would slide out quickly. Dr. Jack ordered medicine to start labor pains. They started. Then they quit. Another week went by. Jule got tired of waiting and left the hospital for a meeting in Chicago, a four-hour drive away. More medicine. We were getting somewhere. Then the needle. Then the forceps to pull Brett out.

Then the vision. The last installment? Wow ... who was it? Who—or what—was I trying to fool with no enhancing gas? This force, like an immense wind, interlocking disparate parts of the universe and chiding me, "Don't you believe me now?!" Again, I understood that the universe fit together like the broken halves of an eggshell, or two hands meshing together.

I worried I was being punished for trying to trick my maker—or whatever "the force" was. Back in the recovery room, I promptly passed out. I felt I was dying. The nurses would prop me up; I would pass out again. Back down, then I couldn't breathe.

"Summon Dr. Jack. ... Summon the anesthesiologist."

Twenty-four hours passed. Still in the recovery room, up and down. Forty-eight hours passed.

"My God of the cosmos, have mercy!"

And he did.

Dr. Jack explained (I think) that the needle in the spine entered a little bit high, and, combined with my normally very low blood pressure, created this unfortunate result.

I still believe it was my special revelationist getting even with me for being a nonbeliever.

(During the Hope summer session in 1964, my English professor suggested I read C. S. Lewis's *Surprised by Joy*. When I finally got around to reading it, I decided that Lewis backed into Christianity. He ran out of options. Lewis used the word *compelled*, and my revelations have compelled me in the opposite direction. More like parallel universes, as described by Michio Kaku in his famous book.)

A few weeks after Brett's birth, an epidemic of Asian flu hit our neighborhood. First Fritz, then Julian, then Greg and Lydia, all with fevers of 104 degrees Fahrenheit at night. Brett, only one month old, had just finished a minor bout of pneumonia. Our neighbor, Barbara Steiner, the wife of Tom, our family druggist, offered to take Brett to their house. She kept him for three weeks.

I would drive the boys, one at a time, to Dr. Hill, our pediatrician, in Grand Rapids.

"Do they have pneumonia?"

"No."

I was frantic at night with all of the high temperatures, and Jule was not helpful. He had never taken care of the children when they were sick. But he was always willing to bring in more help. That was the start of our European nannies.

First, Françoise. Jule was such a Francophile that there was no hope for another country. But Françoise spoke no English. Great! Jule and I could practice our French. Jule was a renowned linguist who spoke five languages. The conversations with Françoise flowed when he appeared. My attempts at college French were kept to a minimum when Jule was around. He would laugh sardonically, and Françoise always knew where to turn for the translation.

From left: Fritz, Mike, Julian, Brett, Joyce, Greg, Lydia, Jule, Françoise

Jule's brilliant, aesthetic, and, to me, ascetic, Harvard classmate, Hispano-Filipino painter Fernando Zobel de Ayala y Montojo, had agreed to become Brett's godfather. He arrived in March 1963 at our house on the hill. Marking pens in hand, Fernando left no door or wall untouched in Brett's little nursery hidden under the stairs. Permanent cartoon drawings were everywhere.

By May, Fernando Zobel was in the process of moving from Manila back to Madrid, after six years working in the Ayala family conglomerate and four years teaching art at a Philippine university. His noble Spanish family had been nineteenth-century pioneers in banking, industry, and land development in the Philippines. And as the most prominent cultural and business leaders in the Philippines, the family expected all their progeny to spend an allotted time working in Manila before being released to pursue their personal passions in Spain.

Jule and I planned a quick trip to Spain, our first return to Europe in ten years, before I resumed Hope College summer classes.

Our tour of Fernando's neighborhood in Madrid was inspiring. I was introduced to cidre champagne, kitschy statuesque lamps (which we brought home), El Greco at the Prado Museum, and Spanish siestas. ("A siesta may last only twenty minutes, and one may not fall asleep—ever!" warned Fernando.)

Developing a museum for Spanish abstract art was Fernando's personal passion. And his selfless devotion and self-discipline would prevail. Three years after our visit, the Museum of Spanish Abstract Art would open its doors in a folk, Gothic-style cliff-hung dwelling in the picturesque rugged mountain town of Cuenca, a two-and-a-half-hour drive from Madrid.

Returning home to Michigan, my new "career" bloomed that summer. I had an appointment, courtesy of Bill Seidman and Aunt Dorothy Judd, to Governor Romney's Blue Ribbon Committee for Higher Education. With the passage of Aunt Dorothy's reconstituted Michigan Constitution, there would be an eight-member state board of education elected for staggered terms in the fall of 1964. Our Blue Ribbon Committee would determine the state board's role and its relationship to the other partisan-elected state university boards: Michigan State, Wayne State, and the University of Michigan. This would be my first experience dealing with a high-powered, mostly male committee. I felt I could contribute a unique perspective. My favorite lecture: "Attitudes, motivations, and healthy habits are set by the time our children enter grammar school. ... What makes you think good teaching at the college level is enough to change these traits?"

The Grand Rapids Press, *Tuesday, October 13, 1964*

I would present the importance of preschool educations, especially for welfare children, to the august members of this committee—importance which I believed was not recognized at all by them. They had professional degrees in business-oriented fields. My favorite member was Carl Gerstacker, the president and CEO of Dow Chemical, in Midland. There was a group of senior vice presidents representing the big three automotive companies from the Detroit area. They would arrive with their thin manila envelopes properly marked by their secretaries. But they all got involved. And they listened. And three of us agreed to run on the Republican ticket for the state board of education: Robert Briggs, sixty-one, president of Consumers Power Co., for a six-year term; Alvin Bentley, forty-five, of Mitchell-Bentley Corp., for an eight-year term; and I, "age not given, organizer and operator of a community-wide nursery school," for the four-year-term.

Bill Seidman called a weekday political meeting in July 1963, at his house on the banks of the Thornapple River. His family was vacationing at their cottage on the shores of Lake Michigan, south of Holland. After the other participants left, Bill asked me if I wanted to go canoeing on the river. I agreed. He seemed surprised by how well I knew how to handle a canoe. He didn't know I fished and portaged with Dad from canoes in the Canadian woods—and there were canoes always available on Spring Lake and the Grand River. When we climbed back up the riverbank, I got a short brush of a kiss on the cheek. He had become my best friend, my mentor… and now, my confidant? What was I to do? Realistically? Nothing.

Sally, nearing the age of forty, was about to have their sixth child. Neither one of us would be willing to give up family or community obligations. I drove the fifty miles home to Grand Haven. I was not depressed by my experience; quite the opposite. Being around Bill created a synergistic effect—on both of us.

By the summer of 1963, I, too, had six children; Mike, my stepson, had moved permanently into our household. Fritz was attending his first lengthy eight-week summer session at the academically esteemed Interlochen Music Camp, which Jule had attended and served as a board member. I was purchasing a newly designed twelve-foot racing scow called the Butterfly, which looked like a miniature twenty-foot C scow, except it had one centerboard and single rudder, instead of the C scow's two leeboards. The Butterfly seemed the perfect size for me to teach my kids how to sail and race. However, I had one potentially disastrous experience that year that haunts me to this day.

Western Michigan Yachting Association Regatta class C scow winner at Crystal Lake - 1963 From left: Harold McClure, Commodore; Craig Welch, Skipper; Joyce Hatton & Carl Reuterdahl, crew.

After Fritz returned from Interlochen, I took him and Greg sailing in our new Butterfly. It was early September, and the weather was windy and cold; we wore long pants and sweatshirts, and both boys wore life vests. We tipped over near the old duck farm, which was around the corner and out of sight of the yacht club and any sailors, and immediately "turtled" (with the mast straight down). Both boys got caught under the boat, tangled in the main sheet line, their life vests keeping them slammed against the upside-down boat deck. Fortunately, I was not wearing a life vest, and I dove to untangle the line and pull them out and away from the boat.

Dale Frank, our Butterfly dealer in Cedar Springs, quickly realized his company had a serious problem. They changed the construction materials in the heavy masts, so the masts would have some flotation before sinking. However, they still do turtle, albeit more slowly, so I continue to watch and worry. Some sailors think I am wrong to worry, commenting: "The kids have life vests on, so what can go wrong?" (Not my sailing instructor son Brett, however. He reminds me that as soon as his twenty-eight-foot E scow turtles—especially if they are flying a spinnaker—the first thing he does is take off his life vest. Young children do not always have that option.)

In early November, Bill and I flew to Traverse City in his small Cessna 310 with a professional pilot. Bill planned a morning meeting with Harry Calcott and other GOP bigwigs. After the meeting, Bill proposed another project: "Let's rent a four-wheel-drive vehicle and check out Tan Bark Lane."

Tan Bark Lane, about forty miles to the west of Traverse City, meant the group of ten or twelve tiny condominium cottages that lined Tan Bark Lane, a long, narrow walkway snuggled into the crest of the hill behind the Crystal Downs Country Club's main clubhouse. The condominiums tee-tered over a crumbling foundation built on a ledge above the escarpment. From the clubhouse on top of the hill, you could see pristine Crystal Lake to the south and Lake Michigan to the north. But Tan Bark Lane's views were only to the north, overlooking Lake Michigan and the famous Sleeping Bear National Park shoreline. Bill owned the western end unit, which had a side and front porch. I thought it the most desirable location on the lane.

Bill Seidman at Tan Bark Lane Crystal Downs Country Club, Frankfort, Michigan

As we snaked around the long drive to the clubhouse parking lot, I worried about getting back out to the main road, the only road which had been freshly plowed. Although the expensive homes that lined the Crystal Downs Country Club golf course were winterized, residents vacationed there only during the warm summer months.

It began snowing heavily. After Bill pushed the door open to his tiny unit, the interior felt frigid. The wind was howling, and the entire structure was swaying back and forth. I wanted to leave. Not Bill. He rounded up some wood piled in a corner and started a fire in the large stone fireplace. He had no intention of leaving; he had brought plenty of food and drink from the hotel restaurant. After I calmed down, we explored the lane. I was acclimatizing to the blizzard conditions and the perilous framework that surrounded us.

As we worked our way back to Traverse City, we were engulfed in a gigantic snowstorm. Yes, the weatherman had predicted a slowly approach-ing snowstorm. But within an hour, the entire landscape was covered with a heavy blanket of snow, and the drifts were amassing in every crevice of the roadways. By late afternoon, the police announced that they were closing the airport.

Bill immediately called the Park Place, the one full-service hotel in Traverse City, and procured three rooms. Then Bill called home and talked to his son, Tom, and, much to my dismay, commented: "I'm in my favorite city, at my favorite hotel, with my favorite girl. How lucky can one man be?"

Tom was fourteen. No way was I going to impart the same message at my house. My stepson, Mike, was a week younger than Tom, but always suspicious about my whereabouts. My brood of five, however, was used to my unscheduled absences from home, and they knew that Grammy Hatton would take charge whenever and wherever needed. And Jule would not like it one bit, even though he understood there was not much that he could do to change it.

I was nervous at the prospect of spending the night away from home —my first solo adventure in more than a decade of marriage.

By morning, the snow was still swirling outside the hotel windows. And the police reported the roadways closed. All of them heading south toward Grand Rapids. What to do? There was no way out. The roads were impassable and the flying impossible.

Now I was nervous for a different reason; my home obligations loomed large. Bill and I had twelve kids between us, but my six needed me. I was Mom to five very smart kids and one curious teenager. Fathers in the 1960s were not involved in nurturing the children—just bringing home the bacon.

With a sigh of relief, on the third day the airport opened. We picked up the pilot, who asked no questions of us. And Bill asked none of the pilot, guessing he'd probably enjoyed his three-day paid holiday.

"No! You can't go and accept that nomination. Absolutely no way. And, if you do, don't bother coming back to this house. ..."

Jule stood between me and the outer door leading down a long flight of stairs to our garage. I couldn't believe his words. He had said nothing for almost a year while I worked with the Blue Ribbon Committee. Now I was dressed, holding the papers for my acceptance speech, on my way to the spring meeting of the Ottawa County Republicans. They would be nominating me to be a candidate for a four-year-term on the new state board of education. I would be running on the Republican presidential ticket in November,1964. I hoped the ticket would be with Rockefeller for president, not Goldwater, but that decision had yet to be made.

I didn't believe Jule's words. I had to go, and quickly. Telegrams confirming my nomination would be sent that night to most of the other county convention chairmen in the state, and there were eighty-three counties. Our Ottawa County committee had worked for months to make my nomination possible. Jule's uncle, Ed Ellis, was still the county chairman. I couldn't disappoint them. I wouldn't. I had promised them ... and I had served seven years on the Republican State Central Committee to achieve this goal, this night.

I left. My head was spinning. Could I calm down enough to give this speech? Why did Jule put me in this position now? What did he hope to gain? He may have been worried about the time and money that I would have to commit to campaigning. But neither of us knew what this nomination entailed.

After the convention and nomination, I asked Bill for help with my campaign. Bill turned to his good friend, Harold Sawyer, a handsome, aggressive litigator at Uncle Siegel's firm, Warner, Norcross, and Judd. When I met Hal Sawyer casually in the 1950s, with my first look at him across the Spring Lake Country Club ballroom, and with his stare right back, I thought, *Here's the consummate lady's man.*

Hal was totally at ease leaning against the wall, standing solo, pipe in hand, observing the scene. A native of San Francisco, Hal had a distinguished naval record during World War II. After graduation from the elite University of California Hastings School of Law, Hal's wife, Marsha Steketee, a prominent member of our East Grand Rapids society, brought him to Grand Rapids.

Hal became interested in politics about the same time as Bill and showed up for working lunches with us. There were martinis all around, and excitement and energy provided by two of the smartest, most sanguine lawyers in west Michigan. We often met in small out-of-the-way cafés, yet quite in the public eye, for many local business and professional people knew them, but, fortunately, not me, their out-of-town guest.

I needed funds for my campaign, and Hal needed funds for his young associate at Warner, Norcross, and Judd, Guy Vander Jagt, who was seeking a Michigan State Senate seat. We raised money from the same sources and became close friends, but Hal always assumed Bill's association with me was more than politically motivated. When Bill found out I would be campaigning on the road for six long weeks leading up to the election, he vowed that he would not see or talk to me at all until after the election (and he kept that promise).

For Mrs. Hatton

GOP Gals' Caravan Visits Area

Mrs. Hatton Is Among Candidates

Republicans were out this morning to greet the GOP caravan which stopped here in their state tour.

Mrs. Robert Bareham and Mrs. David Jacobson had a special treat for their feminine visitors. They were delicious Ottawa County apples.

THE BUS had arrived from Muskegon where the ladies had breakfast. Other stops today are Grand Rapids, Holland, Benton Harbor, Kalamazoo and Battle Creek.

Women candidates and the wives of other state candidates are aboard the bus, which is making the 1,200-mile tour. The special bus for Mrs. Elly Peterson, candidate for the U. S. Senate, also stopped here.

The following were greeted by Mrs. Bareham and Mrs. Jacobson:

Mrs. William G. Milliken, wife of the candidate for lieutenant governor; Mrs. James G. Parker, candidate for state Board of Education; Mrs. Paul Bagwell, wife of candidate for MSU board of trustees; Mrs. Robert Briggs, wife of candidate for state Board of Education; Mrs. Meyer Warshawski, wife of candidate for attorney general; Mrs. Helen Miller, wife of candidate for judge of court of appeals; Mrs. Dorothy Pearl, representing Barry Goldwater; Mrs. John Fitzgerald, wife of candidate for judge of court of appeals; and Mrs. Hatton. (Tribune Photos.)

Mrs. Julian Hatton, candidate for the State Board of Education, was happy to stop here today and say "hello" to her children, including Lydia, 3, Julian, 7, Greg, 9, Fritz, 10, Brett, one, on shoulders of Mike, 15.

Grand Haven Tribune, October 8, 1964

The Republican State Campaign Committee had arranged a bus tour of the counties in the Lower Peninsula for women only. That meant the wife of the candidate for Lt. Governor, Helen Milliken, and the female GOP candidates for statewide office, especially our candidate for the United States Senate, Elly Peterson, who ran the show. Elly would become the first female Republican state chairman in the United States, and she was one tough cookie. And because I felt no special loyalty to her, Elly didn't like me much. Which was okay, because warm and wonderful Helen Milliken was always nearby. Governor Romney's wife, Lenore Romney, a strict Mormon who drank no coffee or alcohol, showed up infrequently during our long journey.

1964 campaign mail brochure

Once in campaign mode, speeches came easily; repetition of phrases, thoughts, and ideas made day after day were stored in memory and available at a moment's notice. When rudely awakened one morning as we approached Alpena, a far northeast town bordering on Lake Huron, I mumbled, "Where are we? ... Who is the audience? ... How long?"

We lined up on a small makeshift stage with a big microphone, which was dutifully passed to each one of us to say "a few words." I wore my standard gray wool plaid suit, with full pleated skirt, and black not-too-high heels ... trying to look like the schoolmarm candidate for our new state board of education.

My thirty-second birthday passed while on tour, but I looked ten years younger; blonde and petite, I knew no one took me seriously. No one wanted to hear or see me or the other minor candidates; they wanted to see Elly Peterson or Governor Romney's beautiful and vivacious wife, Lenore. Romney was at the height of his popularity in the fall of 1964—with conservative as well as moderate Republicans like Elly and me.

I would act like the cheerleader I used to be, exhorting them all to vote a straight Republican ticket. (After decades of hollering, my vocal cords were now permanently swollen, resulting in a very husky voice.) We were hoping Romney's popularity would carry us with him. Goldwater was not Romney's candidate at the GOP national convention in San Francisco, or mine. Our moderate Republican faction backed Rockefeller, but his messy personal life pushed all the conservatives into Goldwater's camp. None of us believed Goldwater had a chance to carry Michigan. President Johnson's so-called daisy commercial, depicting a young girl pulling petals out of a daisy while counting "ten, nine, eight ... three, two, one," followed by a mushroom cloud from a nuclear bomb, convinced most voters, including some conservatives from the Republican right wing, that Goldwater's militant anti-Communism could not be trusted.

By contrast, my speeches warned the voters that the war in Vietnam started by President Kennedy and supported by President Johnson was a disaster in the making. I repeated over and over that we needed to get out of Vietnam immediately and not get mired down in a war we couldn't win. Leave. I repeated my Hope College professor's complaint that our American leaders did not understand the mind-set of the North and South Vietnamese and worried excessively about Communist influence in the region. But I could get no traction with voters on the subject.

Finally, Jule took me aside, warning me that voters were going to think I was crazy if I didn't stop railing on the topic.

Romney won, and carried Lt. Governor Milliken with him. I received 400,000 more votes than Goldwater, but my opponent received 450,000. Goldwater won only six states and three of the eighty-three counties in Michigan, one being Ottawa.

My first duty after defeat was to thank everyone who helped in my campaign. Sitting in my library every afternoon, it became pure drudgery to write in longhand on personal stationery day after day, week after week. With six children demanding much-deserved attention, the job of writing seemed endless.

And now, as the newly elected Ottawa County Republican chairman, I had the burden of running the GOP for the next four years while stemming the rising tide of the conservative movement in the southeastern quadrant of the county. I had no idea what a burden it would become. I had to quickly learn Robert's Rules of Order because my John Birchers worked hard to stack the deck for every meeting. And they were not shy about their demands. The county chairmen nominated the board members for every state board—from hairdressers to hot rods, and the Birchers always had a candidate available. Fortunately, the county seat was located in Grand Haven, so many of the county officials living in our area maintained a serious interest in our geopolitics … and their jobs. They were older, but became great loyal friends and treated me respectfully; they didn't let me get lost in the quagmire of precinct politics. And I didn't leave them looking for money. The county GOP finance chairmen were my friends too, and I used our large house often for fund-raising activities—especially cocktails before a long chartered bus ride to Lincoln Day dinners.

*Reading message from Governor George Romney, Ottawa County
Lincoln Day Dinner* Grand Haven Tribune *photo*

Jule and I maintained our social friendships with the people I had met while campaigning, and during the spring of 1966, we planned a ten-day ski trip to the French-Canadian resort of Mont Tremblant, just northeast of Montreal. Our bon vivant, Creighton Holden, owner of the St. Clair Inn, was the trip organizer, Betty Parsons from Traverse City was the scribe, and Lt. Governor Bill Milliken, with his lovely wife Helen, were the guests of honor, along with a motley crew that had (according to scribe Betty) fifty-seven pieces of luggage piled on the train at Sarnia, Canada.

After a nightlong champagne cocktail hour, Betty reported that Jule, always the Francophile, would tell the "Citroën Story" (forty-five-minute version): " … To begeen wiss, we Franchmen are not vild, like you Americans sink …"; then, in Montreal, "a Hatton-led tour of Château de Ramezar and Eglise de Margerite de Bon Secour" and an introduction by Jule to "Framboise."

The best part of skiing at Mont Tremblant was the French cuisine. Betty reports, " …steak tartare for lunch and fondue bourguignonne for dinner and always croissants"—and fabulous French wines. Jule was in heaven—acting the sommelier.

And the weather? Sunshine and bitter cold.

And the slopes? Betty exclaims, " … exhilarating long sweeps alternating with bruising gos at icy walls, rocky moguls. Sun-drenched, sparkling frosted landscape, the beauty of skiing below timberline. Tilty single chair, comfy double one."

*Skiing with Lt. Governor
Bill and Helen Milliken*

The last day, I found a young tough local skier who led me down the mountain on her terms, which meant screaming over the tops of icy moguls at a pace where there was no turning back. I hung on for dear life, crouching so low in racing mode that my rear scraped the snowdrifts, hoping my guide really knew this mountain. I will never forget that run.

Helen Milliken later commented, "You had the young legs—you could do it!"

But I would never try it again. Or Mont Tremblant. It was just too cold, too icy, too far north. Sunshine and dry, powdery snow abounded in the west, as I found out years ago on our honeymoon trip to Aspen ... and that's where I would soon return.

1821 Doris Avenue, 1966

Construction on the final two-story, forty-foot-long living room wing of our house began in 1965—thanks to the will of "Aunt Fran" Hatton, Jule's scholarly stepgrandmother, who always treated me with quiet kindness while encouraging all of my political activities.

Aunt Fran's father, Justin Whiting, was an illustrious, boisterous three-term Fusion Congressman from Michigan's Seventh District and Fusion Party candidate for Governor of Michigan at the end of the nineteenth century.

And Aunt Fran's husband, Jule's grandfather, William Hatton, owner of Eagle Ottawa Leather Company, was chairman of the Ottawa County Republican Party for almost two decades and a three- or four-time delegate to the Republican National Conventions. Larger than life, looking and acting like his colorful president, "Teddy" Roosevelt, William Hatton was well remembered for his civic accomplishments too—from the founding of the Community Chest (forerunner of United Way) in Grand Haven, to the donation of Elizabeth Hatton Memorial Hospital (where I was born.) William Hatton was born in Dublin, Ireland, in 1864, and always accompanied my great-grandfather, Joos Verplank, a Civil War veteran, at the Grand Haven Memorial Day parades until Joos's death at age ninety-nine in 1943.

Our Ninth District congressman, Robert Griffin, was appointed as Republican senator from Michigan by Governor Romney in May 1966, to fill the vacancy created by the death of Democratic Senator Patrick McNamara. There was a scramble by our new Ninth District Republican county chairmen to find the right Republican to run in the August primary for Griffin's congressional seat. The new Ninth District which included Ottawa County, was considered a safe Republican district; therefore, the primary election was key to the aspiring congressional candidates.

Hal Sawyer showed up in my backyard, planning to groom his candidate, State Senator Guy Vander Jagt, for a run in our newly formed Ninth Congressional District. Guy would be the carpetbagger, having moved out of Kent County, which was no longer in our congressional district, back to his old family home in Cadillac. And his campaign would be managed and financed by his buddies, who didn't live or vote in the Ninth District.

Incensed by Hal invading "my" territory, I openly backed Irish Catholic Edward Meany, Jule's Harvard College and Business School compatriot, who lived and worked in our hometown. Ed had run for the US Senate seat in the 1964 Republican primary, traveling the byways and highways of the Upper and Lower peninsulas, with nine daughters in tow. Although Ed would lose in the '64 primary, no one took his candidacy seriously because of the popularity of the Democratic Senator, Philip Hart.

Bill was not about to get in the middle of our little squabble. He watched from the sidelines, busy with his own political battles in Lansing. But he knew county chairmen should never back a candidate before the primary, and he knew that Vander Jagt would win. Guy had all the requirements needed in western Michigan: he had a Dutch name; he was a graduate of the Reformed Church's Hope College in Holland—which was part of the Ninth District—Yale Divinity School, University of Michigan Law School (not one of those Harvard types); and he was a celebrated orator. (After Guy gave the keynote address at the 1980 Republican National Convention, he was briefly considered as a vice presidential candidate.)

When Guy won the congressional seat in November 1966, Hal called and woke me up at 4:00 a.m., not thinking about Jule and five sleeping kids at home. Hal was still celebrating their victory, and he wanted to be the gracious victor, knowing he had "the spoils." I couldn't get mad at him personally, because he was flattering and endearing—again, the wise litigator.

That, however, was the end of my influence at the congressional level. I couldn't ask Guy for favors, and I did not. And he was always polite to me, as he was with everyone. For me, his superb knowledge and skill at oration created an aura that oozed with insincerity. Words, words, words, but meaning or heartfelt emotion did not exist at my level. I could never take him seriously.

By the mid-1960s, my stepson, Mike, was sixteen, ready for prep school, and enrolled at the Leelanau School in northern Michigan. My interest in maintaining the nursery center was beginning to wane; Lydia was in elementary school, and Brett, the caboose, had only two more years of preschool. I looked for teachers with an interest in administering and owning the nursery center, and found two who wanted the job, both former elementary teachers with education degrees, which I still did not have. But I did have my Hope College BA. I remained responsible for hiring and firing, but my new administrators ran the school—with two to three hundred preschoolers enrolled—until they bought the school in 1968.

When Jule realized that his ties to the tanning business were over, he started a search for a company in which to invest his time and money. He traveled the country, leaving me at home alone with the children. We were between nannies, not yet ready for au pairs, waiting for customs to clear a young Dutch girl who was a relative of our faithful Dutch housekeeper, Dean Korving.

After long days of tax law negotiations in Lansing, Bill Seidman would stop by to report on the latest political schemes being hatched for Romney's bid for the White House. I couldn't believe Bill's energy, audacity, and tenacity. Whenever Jule was traveling, I knew Bill might show up. And I was happy to be part of the presidential quest, hoping to convince the paleo-conservative John Birchers and Phyllis Schlaflys to support a moderate Republican like Romney, who could appeal to a larger national audience.

"Sweeping the streets" at Holland Tulip Festival with Governor George Romney and Tom DePree, GOP Ottawa County vice chairman (on left).

After a three-year search, Jule found his new business. It would be called Stiles-Hatton, Inc. The modular housing factory was owned and operated by Fred Stiles, the older brother of my longtime political cohort, Jack Stiles. The concept of modular housing appealed to Jule, who was attracted to new techniques for doing business, much like his interest and early investment in Ionics.

The innovative prefabricated designs were originally developed by acclaimed builder, Donald Sholz, in Toledo, Ohio, in the early 1950s. The sections or panels of a 1,200-square-foot house could be delivered to a site quickly and efficiently, with bathrooms and kitchens fully finished and plumbed, and appliances installed. The offices and factory were not far from the residential district of the wealthy East Grand Rapids community where Jule's Leonard family relatives and many social friends lived, including Helen and Fred Stiles. And the Seidman farm in Ada was only twenty minutes away.

Our entire family was swept into Jule's new entrepreneurial circle. Musically inclined friends and relatives would join us at the Grand Rapids Symphony, a favorite charity endeavor of cousin Harriette (Hattie) Freeman, who studied voice in Philadelphia at the Curtis Institute of Music, a small, prestigious world conservatory.

Harriette and husband, Don, held soirees at their new, architecturally exciting, modern house, which had been featured in national magazines. The central atrium soared three stories high in a loose tepee mode, with a small pond in one corner, surrounded by giant potted plants, and a very grand piano in the other corner. A large, circular hand-hooked rug in rainbow colors, made by talented artist Harriette, dominated the white marble floors. Harriette was also a renowned chef—one who spent days planning and preparing an evening's repast.

"Don, Harriette, Judd and Mark Freeman home."
Courtesy of David LaClaire

That is where I met Dr. Duncan Littlefair. Duncan was sitting alone on a late Sunday afternoon in Harriette's library, which adjoined the atrium. He stared at me as I entered the atrium, and announced, "You are the most beautiful woman I have ever seen."

Flat statement. No frills around it. I was flustered and speechless; I had never met a man so confidently outspoken. And personally attractive. I turned to my host, Don Freeman, and asked, "Who is he?"

Don laughed and suggested I ask Aunt Dorothy Judd, his mother-in-law, who had invited Duncan to the party. Instead, I asked Harriette, who gave me a very engrossing reply. She confided that her flamboyantly dressed guest (still in morning coat, striped trousers, and fresh carnation in his buttonhole) was Dr. Duncan Littlefair, the minister of Fountain Street Church. Harriette's mother helped convince Duncan to leave the confines of the University of Chicago's liberal School of Divinity decades ago. Harriette urged me to join them on Sunday at Fountain Street Church to listen to Duncan.

I enjoyed and respected Duncan immediately. His intellect, his energy, and his humanistic insight were a refreshing alternative to the traditional religious dogma that plagued our Dutch heritage in West Michigan.

Still relevant today are Duncan's words from his sermons in the 1960s: "It will be in our children's growing days as a part of their consciousness that their life's sphere is this earth, that their hopes are here in this world, that if they mean to achieve any sense of glory and purpose and achievement, they will do it here or not at all."

And his comments on WOTV-NBC in Grand Rapids: "I haven't any question in my mind that the traditional Church is dead. It has totally outlived its philosophy. ... People who are attracted to this church come here because it's the one religious institution, the one philosophy they know, that makes sense."

Rev. Dr. Duncan Littlefair Courtesy of David LaClaire

Duncan often told me that I seemed very "ethereal," and I deduced that those comments emanated from our discussions of my revelations—my visions of our integration in the cosmos during childbirth. Unlike many of Duncan's friends, I was eager to talk about my agnosticism and include Bill Seidman in our intellectually stimulating lunch meetings, usually held in Duncan's favorite downtown haunt, the Peninsular Club. Duncan and Bill loved spending time together. Duncan reveled in any discussion of our relationship, commenting that he felt we were handling it in a very dignified manner. *Dignity* was the operative word for Duncan; he thought it crucial for long-term friendships. "... We are nothing in and of ourselves. Our dignity and quality and stature and worth as a human being is to love and be loved, and to be a part of a loving and caring group."

During a Detroit radio show in September 1967, Governor Romney made an irreversible gaffe by telling his audience that he had been "brainwashed" by American officials in Saigon while on a trip to war-torn South Vietnam. Up to that point, Romney had been ahead in the GOP presidential campaign polling. His popularity tumbled fast. People couldn't accept the fact that their candidate could be so easily flummoxed by the current administration. Especially when his chief rival for the Republican nomination, Richard Nixon, was known as a foreign affairs expert.

And our Grand Rapids-based contingent was devastated—having worked all spring to help arrange meetings in Europe for Romney. Jule was chosen as an advance man because of his linguistic talents. And since the advance team turned out to be for men only, I felt cheated. In our family, I was the one who had worked hard on these projects. At an elegant dinner and planning session at Bob Hooker's home in Grand Rapids, I became very irritated with the turn of events and, while gesturing in opposition to remarks at the table, knocked over a full bottle of red wine. Judy Hooker's beautiful antique Belgian linen tablecloth was awash in red. All the dinner guests started mopping up and treating the red-stained cloth. I knew it probably would never come out, having had many linen tablecloths permanently stained by red wine. I had never been so embarrassed—or so mad at a group of men. All that planning and all that work for George Romney, where my luck was not "where opportunity meets preparation," to quote his favorite saying.

Nevertheless, after much wobbling and seemingly numerous inconsistencies in the fall, Romney plunged ahead, campaigning for five days in New Hampshire in mid-January with a new and courageous alternative plan for getting out of Vietnam, but he got little traction with Republican voters. Nixon did not feel threatened in New Hampshire, and left the state open for Romney's forays. Romney supporters developed about five hundred private houses as local headquarters in all parts of the state—a unique technique used successfully by Romney in his 1966 run for governor in Michigan.

I flew to Boston in January with three boys, delighted to be buying only two full-priced tickets. The airlines offered cut-rate prices for children, so three boys flew for the price of one. My intentions were threefold.

First, I wanted Fritz to be interviewed by three top prep schools in the country: Phillips Exeter, Phillips Andover, and St. Paul's.

Second, I wanted to do a reality check on the progress of Romney's campaign.

Third, last but not least, was a treat for the boys: a long weekend of skiing on the steep and often icy slopes at Stowe, Vermont.

Romney's alternative plan for getting out of Vietnam received favorable national press and some positive local press in New Hampshire, but the damage had been done: the momentum was moving full speed ahead with Nixon, the perceived foreign policy guru, at the wheel.

Heading across New Hampshire to Stowe, Vermont, turned into a long, torturous drive. Stowe ski resort, with the highest peak for skiing in New England, was located in northern Vermont, about fifty miles south of the Canadian border. It had been ten years since I'd skied Stowe, and the boys had never seen slopes this long and narrow, with heavy wet snow that could freeze overnight, creating very dangerous conditions.

And that it did, the second day up the mountain. Mount Mansfield became a sheet of ice while we were riding up the double chairlift. With gale-force winds in our face, we had to be pulled off the chairs at the top of the lift, which was a platform of solid ice. The four of us slid into the warming hut next to the lift, and crowded around the fireplace. The building was wall-to-wall skiers, with no safe way down; the high winds forced the closing of all chairlifts.

The ski patrol decided that the four of us could help novice skiers down the mountain—but no one wanted to venture forth, and I didn't want the responsibility. Finally, the ski patrol said we all had to leave, so we planned our route next to the trees lining the slopes, hoping the trees could stop our icy slide before it got out of control. But the novice skiers were petrified when they watched us slide across the first slope into the trees. We coaxed them along, forcing them to stay near the trees. Some were screaming. Others were crying. But their fear kept them from venturing out into the middle of the icy terrain, and they crawled down the mountain. I was willing to help them, but I didn't want them taking the boys down with them.

Finally, the lower part of the mountain was safe enough for us to ski together, and we had fun reminiscing about our wild adventure. I told the boys that I didn't like Mont Tremblant because it was always cold, with hard-packed heavy snow, and now I knew that I didn't like northern New England either, for the same reasons. We were ready to head west.

When we returned to Michigan, Bill Seidman recommended that I take the Romney girls for the two-day weekend Wisconsin tour beginning Friday, February 2. During the fall campaign, I had outfitted Romney girls in straw hats and colorful paper dresses and capes with a Romney eagle logo imprinted on the front and back. The girls would be accompanying Romney as he moved from state to state. New Hampshire Republican women outfitted local Romney girls who met Governor Romney when he arrived in Concord for his January tour, and their picture appeared with the governor on top of the front page of the *New York Times*. The whole idea of teenage girls running around all winter in paper dresses carrying banners seemed frivolous, and, naturally, the job was assigned to me ... the former cheerleader.

After our Wisconsin trip, Romney's campaign sputtered. He was plagued by Rockefeller supporters, and although Rockefeller claimed he was not running, he was pushed by the moderate Republican faction back into the limelight. Romney withdrew from the race by early March, before the New Hampshire primary vote.

Mrs. Julian Hatton Jr.

"FIVE FOOT two, eyes of blue" is a fetching musical description of Mrs. Julian Hatton Jr., of Grand Haven. She is a gay and attractive woman who seems not to have a care in the world.

Mother of 6, the youngest 3 years old, Joyce Hatton also operates a nursery school that registered more than 100 pre-schoolers this term. She started the school with 15 youngsters 10 years ago. Now four teachers and two helpers carry on the school four mornings a week for children from the Grand Haven and Spring Lake area.

"Attitude and motivation are the most important aspects of education," she says, "and pre-school experience conditions youngsters to like school, like to compete with each other and like to study.

IN 1963 Mrs. Hatton was appointed by Gov. Romney to the Citizens Committee on Higher Education, created to make long range recommendations to the new State Board of Education established by the Constitutional Convention.

She was chosen in 1964 as Republican chairman of Ottawa County, one of few women county chairmen in state politics. Previously she had served on the Republican State Central Committee for seven years, and as chairman of its standing committee on research and education.

HER HOBBIES are all active sports. She was sailing instructor at Spring Lake Yacht Club before her marriage, and shares her love of sailing with her husband and family.

Mrs. Julian Hatton Jr.

Honored by the *Grand Rapids Press,* circa 1960's

As the Ottawa County Republican chairman from 1964 to 1968, I had many inquiries during my four years in office about the draft, our US Selective Service System. On March 21, 1966, I sent a five-point letter to Ottawa Republicans, warning them that "it is the responsibility of every young man to register with a local draft board within five days after he becomes eighteen," and "to keep the draft board informed immediately of changes in their individual situation."

In June 1967, amendments to the selective service system eliminated most deferments for postgraduate education, but retained I-S deferment for high school students and II-S deferment for undergraduate students under age twenty-four.

The rate of induction reached its peak of forty-two thousand per month in the spring of 1968. There were more than five hundred thousand US troops in South Vietnam. The Ottawa County draft board was drafting from the sixth and last category in my letter: "Nonvolunteers 18½ -19, with the oldest being selected first."

When my stepson, Mike Hatton, and Bill Seidman's son, Tom, turned nineteen in May, 1968, Tom was finishing his freshman year at Dartmouth College, and Mike was graduating from the Leelanau School. Mike would be attending college in the fall; both would be exempt for another year. ("No occupational deferment is for a period of more than *one* year …")

I was petrified of the draft. I had one stepson facing it head-on, but I had four more sons coming along who could be drafted in three or four years. And the Vietnam War had no appeal for the youth of the 1960s and '70s.

Great-Grandpa Joos Verplank may have rushed to join the North in the Civil War as soon as he turned eighteen in 1862; Uncle Ed Secory may have learned to hate the army only after fighting in France in World War I; cousin Sherm Verplank, after enlisting in the marines when the Japanese attacked in 1941, may have regretted his assignment to the tropically diseased Samoan Islands, where he contracted elephantitis; brother Midge, after the army drafted him the last year of the Korean War, may have wished he'd joined the navy—but no one was rushing to join the Armed Forces in this war. Quite the opposite: Michigan boys talked about heading to Canada. Mike Hatton worried constantly about staying in college, finally joining the navy in the summer of 1969, believing he would be drafted soon.

Our Ninth Congressional District Republicans elected two delegates and two alternates in the spring of 1968 to attend the Republican National Convention in Miami in early August.

—Grand Rapids Press Photograph

HAROLD CLOSZ JR. of North Muskegon and Mrs. Julian B. Hatton Jr. of Grand Haven, delegates at the Republican National Convention, represent the 9th Congressional District.

Nixon or Rocky? Michigan Delegation Still Undecided

GOP delegates Joyce Hatton and Harold Closz GOP Convention, Miami, 1968

I was eager to be a delegate, and, as the chairman of the largest GOP-populated county in the Ninth District, I won easily, as did Harold Closz, chairman of the second-most-populated GOP voting county, Muskegon. Neither of us liked Nixon.

We would be working for Rockefeller's candidacy for president, and we would be loyally casting our first votes for Romney, hoping to find him a vice presidential slot if Nixon was the presidential candidate.

With Governor Rockefeller, 1968

What we wanted foremost was a candidate who would get us out of the Vietnam War. And fast. We didn't care whether he called it a victory or defeat. As far as we were concerned, we were defeated … by the Viet Cong.

And the young Democrats felt the same way when they showed up for their hair-raising convention in downtown Chicago in late August. The demonstrations were fierce, even scary, with western Michigan family friends joining the Black Panthers parade. The democratic process was spinning out of control, and we knew that candidate Nixon would be the beneficiary of all the hullabaloo that the left wing of the Democratic party was fomenting. And because Vice President Hubert Humphrey was the Democratic candidate, he was stuck with the disastrous foreign policies that drove his president, Lyndon Johnson, from office.

Nixon promised to end the draft—and to end the war. He just didn't say how or when. Nixon did propose the creation of a lottery, which took effect in December 1969 (after Mike Hatton joined the Navy). The voters didn't know that Nixon would be invading Cambodia, and then Laos, and shelling Hanoi unmercifully until a truce was called.

flattered to be part of this small august committee that included Robert Pew II, CEO of Steelcase, the leading office furniture company in the country, as well as Bill, who was founder of GVSC and still chairman of the board.

Our committee would bring potential candidates to the GVSC board and faculty members for review. Not being fully employed, I could maintain a flexible travel schedule, but I didn't expect to be sent off alone to interview Arend Donselaar ("Don") Lubbers, the young president of Central College in Pella, Iowa. Sensing my distress, Bill Seidman and a faculty member jumped on Bill's small Cessna for the eventful trip.

Don Lubbers father, Dr. Irwin Lubbers, was president of Hope College during the early part of my long tenure there. But Don, unlike his father, did not have a PhD, a seeming prerequisite for a president of a college, especially one that would aspire to become a university. Don had already distinguished himself as the youngest college president in the nation when he took the position at Central College at the age of twenty-nine. Two years later, the "progressive young president" attracted national attention when *Life* magazine included him in its 1962 "Red-Hot Hundred" feature on the nation's one hundred outstanding young leaders.

Don had a previously planned trip to Europe in August, and he offered to stop first in Grand Rapids to meet the full search committee and GVSC board of trustees.

Our committee arranged a party at the Seidman's house in Ada, then a tour of campus, and finally some free time for golf.

I was given the task of escorting Don for his last day, which included a round of golf at the Grand Haven Golf Club and a visit to our house on the hill. When we drove up the driveway, I found none of the kids at home. I made Don a drink. When we entered our immense but sparsely furnished living room bathed in afternoon light through floor-to-ceiling windows, Don observed the Baldwin and Steinway grand pianos, placed back to back, which occupied almost half the room, commenting,

"You aren't much into knickknacks, are you?"

I was surprised by his comment; I was proud of the Robsjohn Gibbings ("Gibby") newly designed Widdicomb sofa, armchairs, and long, oval-shaped, upholstered bench—all covered in Gibby's richly colored Eagle Ottawa leather. And a large driftwood stump (hauled up from the beach by Jule and husky neighbors) had a thick pane of glass balanced on the inverted stump's sawed-off roots; it served as our coffee table.

Feeling the need to justify my décor, I explained that the modern furniture represented leather-based samples from the world-renowned furniture companies in Grand Rapids, and I pointed out the Baker dining room furniture with burnt-orange leather-covered chairs in our semicircular glass-walled dining room. Then I mentioned the Fernando Zobel paintings and the modern art provided by Fernando's friendly Spanish artists that covered the walls and hallways in the house. But that was it. I still had no interest in "decorating" a house. And obviously little talent.

I recalled a remark attributed to Robsjohn Gibbings, who had visited our home in the summer of 1956: "If Thomas Jefferson visited your home, he would judge it by its utility, not its antique charm."

A prescient event in 1968 was the arrival of our first professional nursemaid, big, burly, and very Dutch Anja. And just in time. Our longtime housekeeper, Dean Korving, had retired. It appeared to be Anja's duty to complain (to me only) that my two youngest children couldn't get used to my bizarre travel schedule; the lack of regularity was making them miserable. She had never worked in an American household like ours, where on a moment's notice, I would be called away for a political event or a business meeting. I ignored Anja's complaints (and the queasy feeling it left in my stomach), believing that the children missed their lifelong housekeeper. I assumed Anja's education emanated from European families who lived pedestrian lives. Yet I trusted her capabilities enough to pursue my passions away from the household.

It was time for me to go to work. Real work. My youngest was in kindergarten, Fritz at Exeter, Mike in college, and Jule in a new modular housing business. Now, I wanted to play the game.

I offered to work at Stiles-Hatton in sales. That decision was a disaster in the making. (Who would be my boss? Fred Stiles? Julian Hatton? Where would I sit? With the secretaries?) There weren't enough private offices to go around. And I needed to learn how to sweep the floor, not run the company. But my husband was running the company, along with his very knowledgeable partner, Fred Stiles, whose patriarchal nature would force him to conclude that this was nothing more than a dilettantish move on my part that must be tolerated. Fred would be the perfect gentleman—if I stayed out of his way.

With great enthusiasm for my first full-time employment, I plunged ahead. I was given lonely assignments with potential customers in far-flung corners of northern Michigan. Alpena, facing Lake Huron, was a favorite location for modular housing sales, although I never found out where these contacts originated. I just did the legwork.

If Bill Seidman or I weren't traveling, we would slip away for a picnic lunch on his Honey Creek property just north of Ada, not far from his farm. We took turns bringing food and wine. But not much of either one, because Bill was extremely busy in his new role as managing director of Seidman & Seidman, with headquarters in New York City.

Crystal Lake; Crystal Downs Golf Course; Point Betsie Lighthouse
Courtesy of Marge Beaver

Jule and Bill wanted to build a modular bi-level cottage overlooking Lake Michigan, in the highly esteemed Crystal Downs Country Club domain. We had become familiar with Bill's tiny condominium on Tan Bark Lane, located behind the clubhouse, and his valuable beachfront property, but Bill didn't want to build on his beach property, saying he wanted to save it for our beach access.

I was the overseer during the construction phase, driving north weekdays to check out the placement of the twelve-by-fifty-foot modular sections on the foundations. Jule's bi-level design was unique and novel—too novel, it seemed, for our stuffy banker neighbors. Because of our small lot, we placed part of the foundation perilously close to the steep wooded bank that was rapidly eroding from the new high water levels of Lake Michigan. The typical sand and Petoskey stone beaches were disappearing, and residents along the beach were building jetties to save their expensive cottages.

The cottage at Crystal Downs Country Club

We elevated two twelve-by-fifty-foot interlocking modular sections, tying them together on steel beams and posts that left open parking underneath the structure for autos and golf carts and bikes and boats. The other two sections were placed farther away from the bank at ground level, allowing for a huge twenty-four-by-fifty-foot open porch to be constructed on the roof. The ground-level sections were set up dorm style, with the boys occupying one section, and the girls, the other. With four bunk beds on each side, and a chaperone bedroom opening across the far end of the building, the Seidmans, with five girls and a boy, and the Hattons, with the opposite, were prepared for full family occupancy—which never happened.

Nevertheless, the new house parties for adults only were not to be missed! Jule brought a small spinet piano, and the guests brought the band, including full drums, horns, and just about anything else that made noise. Annie Lowry was the natural leader, playing the piano and singing a wide repertoire of popular music. Most of the talented players were devotees of New Orleans jazz. Bill loved it; Jule tolerated it; Sally and I just followed the crowd. It was the same athletic bunch that hung out at the Seidman farm—now transported to northern Michigan for long, exhausting weekends with little sleep in crowded dorm rooms.

If our friends or our kids suspected a special relationship existed between Bill and me at the cottage, they said nothing. Nor did Jule or Sally, even when Bill and I would leave early in the morning for a long jog down the beach road or over the sand dunes. They were always invited, but neither one found it an enjoyable endeavor. Sally liked to walk the beach, and Jule liked to play golf. With a magnificent golf course that overlooked Crystal Lake on one side, and Lake Michigan on the other, it was no wonder that the golfing crowd hurried out to play whenever possible. My golf game was more reliable than Bill's, and whenever Bill wasn't around, I would play golf.

Since Bill preferred tennis, he offered to build tennis courts on the edge of the golf course. He found just enough members to approve his project, and we all pitched in to pay for it. But Bill was resented forever by the avid golfers because they didn't like the high tennis court fences imposed on their manicured hilly landscapes ... and it was difficult for Jule to keep the peace with his golfing buddies. Bill never felt comfortable around the golfers or their clubhouse. Although I could forget that Bill carried a Jewish name, perhaps club members could not.

My job at Stiles-Hatton lasted just long enough for me to learn that Jule and Fred Stiles were kindred spirits—their long lunches away from the office, always at Sayfee's, which was five minutes from their office, guaranteed that the two of them would return, as they liked to say, "in time to sign the mail."

In the mid-1960s, WZZM-TV's owners acquired WKLW-FM and changed its call letters to WZZM-FM. It became one of the first FM Top 40 stations in Michigan to pose a serious challenge to its AM competition, especially at night, when its AM competition had poor or no signals. Since Bill Seidman was the major domo who put together a winning team in the early 1960s, acquiring the new VHF channel 13 license in Grand Rapids, which became the ABC affiliate WZZM TV-13, this FM acquisition and its impending success did not go unnoticed by him—or by me.

Or by Allen and Helen Hunting, who were entertaining us in the winter of 1967 at their elegant new Manor Vail ski condominium. As we were enjoying the hip AM radio music during après-ski hours, the music suddenly faded away ... gone for the night.

Our disgusted hosts complained, "What we need here is an FM radio station!"

Recreation Broadcasting" immediately became a concept, with six enthusiastic participants. Our discussions, supplemented, I'm sure, by plenty of liquid refreshments, swirled around the optimum locations for low-power FM applications. The best ski town was the first topic. Naturally, Allen and Helen liked Vail, with its immense possibilities.

Serious development of the ski terrain in the Vail Valley had begun in the early 1960s, and Allen and Helen were among the first buyers in Vail Village, along with Grand Rapids neighbors, Nancy and Ted Kindel, who built the first lodge, the Christiania-at-Vail, in 1963. When our then Grand Rapids Congressman, Jerry Ford, asked Allen where he should take his family skiing for their winter holiday, Allen naturally suggested Vail. And Vail would become famous as the winter White House of the 1970s, with Nancy and Ted Kindel entertaining some of President Ford's Kitchen Cabinet, including Dick Cheney and Allen Greenspan, during Ford's presidency.

Vail Mountain would become the largest ski resort in the United States and the second largest in North America, with seven bowls, boundless open terrain, and a fortunate geologic location that always produced some of the top powdery snow conditions in the state.

But unlike most ski towns in Colorado, which were former mining towns, Vail Village was designed and built only after the ski resort opened in 1962.

When Jule and I were asked which ski town we liked, we replied, "Aspen, of course!" Aspen had hosted the first FIS World Alpine Championships in North America in 1950, giving Aspen recognition as a world-class ski area. From our two-week honeymoon in December and January of 1953, we remembered Aspen's unique character: a raw, wild west former mining town combined with north-facing ski slopes that overlooked the town of Aspen and the Roaring Fork Valley. And it wasn't just the river that roared; the town was full of authentic characters who let it all hang out at night. At the Red Onion and the J-Bar in the Jerome Hotel, we found the locals mixing with the internationally famous skiers and our young wealthy adventurous ski crowd.

In the early 1950s, Alpine skiing was a tough sport; my wooden Head skis were long, stiff, and heavy, with strap bindings that bound my boots to the skis. And the Aspen Mountain slopes had no special grooming or snow-making equipment, leaving runs full of rocky patches surrounded by sparse areas of well-packed trails. The single chairlift was the longest in the world at that time, and we all bought lift coats to wear up the lifts and then discard at the top, with the chairlift operator piling our coat on the next chair for the trip down to the base area. I learned to forget about style and opted for comfort, exchanging my felt coat for an old fur parka that I found in a local used-clothing store.

All new skiers on the mountain were required to join ski classes, forcing us to be rated every morning for our improving skiing ability. I had a new instructor and class every day until I finally advanced to Jule's class of black diamond runners during the second week.

As much as we looked forward to returning to Aspen, family obligations ran the show for the next decade, and skiing vacations were limited to northern Michigan, with kids in tow, or long weekends, without kids, in New Hampshire, Vermont, Canada's chilly Mont Tremblant, and Vail.

We knew that our East Grand Rapids opera-loving friends, Bobbie and John Gilmore, were buying the Aspen Villas condominiums in the summer of 1967—and planning to buy the historic Jerome Hotel, built in 1889, when Aspen was a booming silver-mining town and new destination resort.

But it was Bill Seidman who convinced our enthusiastic group where we should apply for our first low-power FM license. Bill looked at the numbers—a natural job for him. And Bill knew that Jule and I preferred Aspen because of its historic authenticity as an old mining town, which attracted a sophisticated, wealthy summertime clientele.

Aspen won easily. Vail was too small and undeveloped to carry a year-round business. Aspen had both summer and winter attractions: the prestigious Aspen Music Festival and elitist Aspen Institute for Humanistic Studies in the summer, and four developing ski mountains—Aspen, Aspen Highlands, Buttermilk, and Snowmass—in the winter. However, our fledgling Recreation Broadcasting team would soon find out that the two off-seasons could be rather off ... even in the most prestigious ski resort in the country.

Our four older boys flew with me to California in June 1967. They were going to get a taste of their Uncle Gary's bachelor quarters on Manhattan Beach. While Gary hoped to keep the kids in line on the beach, I roamed off with Bill Seidman to interview local experts in the FM field. An important part of our not-so-well-hidden agenda was ferreting out Gary's interest in the new FM venture. We invited Gary to some of our exploratory meetings, knowing he could be the expert engineer needed on our team.

Gary was eight years behind me in school, and I paid little attention to his interests while he was growing up in Spring Lake. After he graduated from the University of Michigan's five-year engineering program in the early 1960s, he headed for Southern California. With an attractive, unassuming, and warm personality, Gary quickly obtained a sales position with Milwaukee-based Johnson Controls, and then surrounded himself with Manhattan Beach's ready supply of young bachelors looking for fun and games.

One of Gary's daring deeds, which I did not hear from him for decades, was his hilarious greased-pig episode at the University of Michigan's 1965 Rose Bowl football game. Entering the stadium with a greased pig stuffed snugly under his windbreaker and waiting for the opportune moment, Gary released the pig onto the playing field. All playing stopped while the baffled officials ran around the field, trying to catch the greasy pig, which amazingly eluded capture by racing back and forth across the field. The stadium was in an uproar! Mom and Dad were in the bleachers, scared into silence, knowing that Gary had stored the pig under their bed at his Manhattan Beach house. Finally, the dear little pig was put to rest, and the game continued. No one was arrested, and no one ever found the perpetrator.

By 1968, Midge needed Gary home to help with the family businesses. So-o-o ... after a two-month tour of the Far East, Gary bowed to his brother's wishes and returned to Michigan in the fall. Gary also agreed to become a full partner in our Recreation Broadcasting Company FM radio venture. Both decisions would turn out to have interesting consequences.

Shortly after Gary's return to Michigan, he applied for a private pilot's license—a goal of mine for the four previous years. My interest was kindled during my 1964 campaign for statewide office; a talented pilot and good friend, Mary Creason, ferried me all over the state in her small single-engine Cessna 182 for months, often waiting for me late into the evening before we could hurry home to the Grand Haven airport. One night, when we were about an hour away and cruising at low altitude, Mary turned to me and complained, "I think I'm getting the flu. I don't feel well."

How helpless I was, never having landed the plane. With six children at home (and Mary with four), Mary suggested I take flying lessons from her. It took four years and two ground-school sessions before I soloed on my birthday, on the very windy morning of October 6, 1968. (Yes, they cut off the tail of my shirt.) Ground school scared me, not because I couldn't understand the instructions, or the navigation, but because I never considered myself a mechanic, and I knew I must learn the perfect pitch of an engine—when it wasn't purring perfectly—and I must be able to figure out what was wrong, and what to do about it ... in seconds.

Midge's best sailing friend (who would become one of mine too), Paul Eggert, endured a tragic loss in the winter of 1966, when his younger brother crashed after takeoff in their private twin-engine plane loaded with Florida oranges, his brother's fiancée, and their dad. At first, the press reported that the crash was the fault of the pilot, because the Piper Twin Comanche exceeded the weight limits at takeoff, but after Paul and his mother sued Piper aircraft for malfunctions with the plane and won, the press retracted their article.

Nevertheless, there was always the concern that the pilot was too young, only twenty-two years old, and too inexperienced to handle emergency situations that often arise at takeoff. After that accident, I never got over that rush, that near-panic rush, that enveloped me at takeoff; I felt my hands were glued to the wheel and the throttle. Once the needle on the altimeter reached 400 feet, I calmed down immediately. And I accumulated enough hours in the copilot seat of Bill Seidman's twin-engine Cessna 310—and later, Cessna 411—to feel comfortable about landing a twin-engine plane in an emergency.

Gary was a much better student under Mary's tutelage, and soloed in a few months. His technical training, whether mechanical engineering or engine mechanics, far outpaced mine.

Photo Courtesy of Spectrum Health Beat

Mary Creason became a flying legend in Michigan: Mary's older sister, Mabel Rawlinson, was killed in March 1944, when she couldn't open the cockpit from the inside while flying on a training mission for the WASPs during World War II. Mary took over Mabel's shared interest in a private plane in Kalamazoo while she was a student at Western State University, and she has been flying ever since. Mary's career included owning and operating the local air training and transport service in the 1960s, managing the Grand Haven Air Park in the 1970s, joining the Michigan Aeronautics

Bureau in Lansing in 1977, and becoming the first woman pilot in state government.

(Mary and I shared an apartment in the capital in 1977 and 1978, when I was managing my child care businesses from headquarters in Lansing. Mary expanded aviation education in Michigan's public schools, developing the Come Fly with Me curriculum that earned her the FAA's Award for Excellence.)

With little or no opposition for our low-power license in Aspen, we were granted a permit and assigned the frequency of 97.7 FM in the summer of 1968. All four men in our group had full-time work obligations, so I was designated the president of our new sub-S corporation, Recreation Broadcasting Company. (An S corporation eliminates double taxation by allowing profits and losses to flow through to the individual stockholders.) I knew nothing about broadcasting, but Bill felt I knew something about business and dealing with the government bureaucracies. We would be working closely with Reed Miller of Arnold and Porter, a Washington, DC, law firm that specialized in leading neophytes like us through the complex web of rules and regulations that the Federal Communication Commission (FCC) prescribed for control of the airwaves, which included VHF and UHF television, AM and FM radio, and communication satellites.

Little did I realize the sweat equity that would be needed for future projects, from FM translators, to cable carriage, to microwave towers, to a low-power television station that required downlinks and uplinks. And little did brother Gary Verplank realize the sweat equity he would be putting into the project just to get us on the air. But Gary was single. And an

Bill Seidman and John Shepard, 1960's

engineer. And Gary was a great businessman—but that had yet to be shown.

My local expert in FM broadcasting was John Shepard of WLAV-FM in Grand Rapids. He was eager to guide us on our way, and he was so much fun and so spirited in his recommendations, that I knew my new career would be an exciting one. Our favorite meeting place with John was Sayfee's restaurant. It was only a few blocks from Jule's new business, Stiles-Hatton, and John liked the place so much that he became part owner. John was known as a risk taker; nevertheless, he thought our FM in this tiny community surrounded by mountains might be fun, but not much for business; our signal, no matter where we placed it, couldn't go out of the Roaring Fork valley.

John said we needed ABC radio news. We had no more than signed them up (or they agreed to sign us up), and we were off to the Olympics in Mexico City as guests of ABC. The 1968 Summer Olympics were being held in October, late for the typical summer Olympic schedule. But it was Mexico City; although 5,000 feet above sea level, it was still plenty warm. When Bill and I jogged across the downtown park near our hotel, the local workers just stared; not familiar with this relatively new morning form of exercise, they thought we were Olympians practicing before the field events. And when Helen Hunting roamed ABC's free food kiosks, Montezuma got his revenge, but not until Helen hurried home to Grand Rapids. Notwithstanding our rough initiation, the Hunting, Hatton, and Seidman troops thoroughly enjoyed their first taste of events via the press pass.

Jule and Brett (age five) with John Gilmore at Jerome Hotel, Aspen, Christmas, 1968

While we were gallivanting in Mexico, Gary was busy finding locations for our FM antenna and studio in Aspen. Gary approached John Gilmore, our friend and neighbor from Grand Rapids, who had just purchased the

Jerome Hotel. Gary wanted to place the antenna on the roof and the studio in the basement.

The basement was built in the nineteenth century; it looked and smelled like a cellar: low ceilings, with wires, cables, and pipes exposed in every direction, and wood, brick, and dirt floors that were damp from lack of ventilation.

We hired Dick Dorough, the owner of the hi-fi shop, to be manager, and Dick hired Jon Busch, a classical music devotee who worked part time for the Aspen Music Festival and part time for Dick Dorough, to be the carpenter constructing our studio in the Jerome basement.

Jon Busch reported, "After Dorough was fired, the station got on on a shoe-string. Ed Burzinski was the engineer whose specialty was to lean up against a wall looking dead-to-the-world only to be designing schematics in his mind. ..."

After Gary bought a transmitter and studio equipment at the National Association of Broadcasters convention, he and Ed Burzinski went to work putting it all together.

At Christmastime, Mike Hatton couldn't join the rest of the family heading west to check out the new Aspen venture. Mike had volunteered for the US Navy in the summer of 1969. He was assigned to the US naval base in San Juan, Puerto Rico, until President Nixon called a truce in the 1970s. Our family felt lucky to escape that desperate, helpless feeling that other families endured as they watched their drafted sons and husbands being shipped off to Vietnam ... to fight a war that just seemed to happen upon them—a funny thing that happened on the way to a CIA meeting, perhaps.

Michael Hatton's naval service, including the Vietnam War November 1969–October 1999

Before we left for Aspen, I located a young, wealthy bachelor's pad on the road to Snowmass, and hoped it would be large enough for our tribe of eight. The boys had fun checking it out, with the plush bear rugs, etc., on the beds—but little else of use to our ménage. We ended up at the Jerome Hotel, where our usual room choices were water, heat, or view.

Anja's assignment was to keep the tribe together when we weren't on the slopes. And when we were, Anja could take ski lessons at Buttermilk while our five experienced skiers could ski with me or their dad. It was fun exploring the new trails and mountain resorts. Snowmass was developing its immense terrain; Aspen Highlands was catering to the locals, and Buttermilk to the beginners.

Brett, not yet seven, and I rode the lifts to explore the top of Aspen Highlands. The very top. It looked manageable when I looked up to check where the single chairlift stopped on a cleared circular area. When we got off the lift, I was horrified. Why hadn't I checked this out alone?

We were surrounded by steep forested terrain on three sides, with a skinny path wide enough for only one skier at a time to descend to the packed and groomed slopes below. If Brett slid off the path, he would plunge down the mountain into the rocks. I let Brett watch some skiers make their way down. They were not expert skiers, so Brett knew he could do it. (But he never doubted he could; only Mom did.) I followed behind him but not closely. I wanted him to feel he was on his own. But I vowed to keep him away from the double diamonds for the rest of the week.

Jule and I were supposed to be working on the development of KSPN-FM, but our work consisted mainly of evening meetings with John and Bobby Gilmore in the iconic J-Bar of their Jerome Hotel.

Gary and I returned to Aspen in early February 1970, and Gary, Jon, and Ed worked all night on February 13. The official first song went out at 7:06 a.m., on Valentine's Day 1970.

Bragged Jon, "Nothing if not having pretentions, the first song was the Salzburg Music Festival opening fanfare."

My employment at Stiles-Hatton lasted one year. Bill Seidman again ferreted out a more appropriate role for me. He knew I should get out of a situation where I would be conflicted about my ability and willingness to change the direction of the enterprise, and he found a place where I could put my knowledge of child care to good use.

Bill was on the board of Care Corporation, a small nursing home conglomerate in Grand Rapids that he had just taken public. The company created a separate entity, Kiddie Care Corporation, believing that child care facilities on the expansive nursing home grounds would be beneficial to the company as well as their seniors and preschoolers. (An assumption that proved to have little merit.)

Care Corporation then hired James Hurst, a young, peppy former press aide in Romney's abortive campaign for president, to take Kiddie Care public. Jim had no children or background in child care, but he appeared knowledgeable around a balance sheet. By the time I arrived on the scene to become director of operations in December 1969, one large child care center had been built at Springbrook, Care Corporation's upscale nursing home in the wealthy East Grand Rapids suburb, and another facility had been purchased in Kalamazoo. More were planned for Grand Rapids and Muskegon.

Child care and physical facility design I understood, but I had no idea what was required to take a company public. I'm not sure Jim Hurst did, either. But Bill felt this was the appropriate time to work on my "balance sheet" education ... and the filing requirements of a public company. He would bring a bunch of balance sheets with him during lunch hour, prop them up on the steering wheel of his car, and quiz me over and over to see if I was learning what to look for—i.e., what was important in each balance sheet and the accompanying notes. I was very much the devoted student of a born pedagogue, and Bill loved teaching. When he kept pursuing my accounting education, I asked him why he was bothering to hammer home all this information for weeks on end. Bill replied, "You won't be happy with yourself if you don't know this."

He was so right! I was very proud of my ability to answer all of the accountant's questions about our prospectus. And Care Corporation's leaders were willing to move quickly to take Kiddie Care public on April 1, 1970. This was just in the nick of time—the market disintegrated that very day. I couldn't believe that we could raise $2 million so fast—and be the first child care company in the world to go public!

During the summer of 1970, I was so busy launching KSPN-FM and Kiddie Care that I found little time to enjoy our new cottage at Crystal Downs. One exception was the Chicago-Mackinac race weekend in mid-July. My kids were excited to see Paul Eggert's new entry in this legendary race, a world-class event that defined Great Lakes sailing races. (The annual 333-mile race from Chicago to Mackinac Island, starting in the nineteenth century, was the longest freshwater sailing race in history.)

Most of the 165 sailboats in this 1970 race were expected to pass close to shore near Point Betsie, which was just two miles south of our cottage. Crew members invited on the maiden voyage of Paul's forty-five-foot Whitby sloop, *Honey,* were brother Midge (the navigator) and six other Spring Lake Yacht Club scow sailors.

Paul Eggert and the *Honey,* circa 1970

Paul admitted that none of them knew much about seamanship before this race, nor did they know if crew members could get violently seasick. Trouble could be brewing. ... Chicago Yacht Club recorded that sailors experienced a gale, a northerly that knocked 45 on the nose for 16 hours, at night exceeded 60 miles per hour; out of 167 starters, 88 withdrew.

Where did they withdraw? When the northerly blast hit on Sunday afternoon, we saw many of them turning around and pulling into Frankfort, only six miles south of our cottage on Lake Michigan. Why withdraw then? Their next harbor or anchorage was Northport Bay, sixty miles north of Frankfort—a tough, close-hauled sail directly into the approaching storm.

Using binoculars, we searched for the *Honey* from the highest point at the Crystal Downs Country Club all Sunday afternoon and long into the evening. We could see the boats turning around and heading back to the Frankfort harbor, but none looked like the *Honey.*

With Michigan at the western edge of the eastern daylight time zone, it was light until ten o'clock at night in midsummer. But that Sunday didn't seem like summer; the northerly gale brought almost-freezing temperatures, along with sleeting rain. In the early evening, we headed downtown to check the boats that we knew were taking refuge in the harbor. It was a shocking sight: not a sailor was standing; a sea of yellow slickers lay prostrate, filling the small park at the foot of the marina. I ran up to sailors and asked about the *Honey*. They paid little attention to my inquiry. All they wanted to tell me was that they thought they were going to die. They were mostly young, scared, soaked, frozen, and exhausted. They felt lucky to make it to shore after enduring hours fighting the cold, the wind on the nose, and waves that amazed them with their intensity, building higher but shorter as the day progressed—"quick waves," Paul called them.

I knew those high but short waves coming into the Frankfort harbor, so typical of our Great Lakes, but not the ocean. A decade earlier, as a birthday present in early October, Dad took me fishing in Platte Bay, which was six miles northeast of our Crystal Downs property on the Sleeping Bear shoreline. As the day progressed, the wind was freshening from the southwest, the fish were biting, and Dad was in no hurry to leave. As we rounded Point Betsie on our return, the full fury of the Lake Michigan waves that were building from the Wisconsin shores eighty miles away increased to more than ten feet. Dad wanted me to take the wheel and learn how to handle the waves head-on, but when we reached the harbor, he took over. Before our turn into the harbor entrance, I could see that the pier heads were giving no protection to the crashing surf. Dad would have to power through it. I watched him. He looked at the wave patterns behind us. All of a sudden, we took off. … We surged ahead, riding one wave the entire distance into the harbor. Then it was suddenly calm. Dead calm. The relief. The exhilaration! To have battled the storm, and won.

Fishing in Lake Michigan with Dad Photo by Matt Young

But had the *Honey* won? Our family heard nothing for twenty-four hours. Where was the *Honey* when the storm hit? Off Pyramid Point, more than thirty miles north of the Frankfort harbor, it turned out. Most of the crew was out of commission—so seasick, cold, and exhausted that they lay in their own vomit on the carpeted cabin floorboards. As the waves increased in height and intensity, Paul reported the boat leaped out of the sea and dropped precipitously over waves, with a crashing sound—they could lose the mast! Paul admitted that he was too scared to be seasick; he thought the boat was going to sink and worried about the location of their eight-man life raft. It was pitch-dark at 4:00 a.m., when they reached Northport Harbor. None of the sailors wanted to continue racing to Mackinac Island. (They were not disqualified if they didn't go ashore.) After the race, Ted Turner, racing his twelve-meter America's Cup boat, *American Eagle,* publicly retracted calling Lake Michigan a "millpond."

My eagerness at Kiddie Care Corporation to combine government-subsidized AFDC (Aid to Families with Dependent Children) and private-pay children would create a mountain of problems for our infant company. On the dilapidated north side of Kalamazoo, we had a facility that would be housing mainly AFDC children, but our new Grand Rapids Leonard Street location would attract both AFDC and private-pay preschoolers. Mixing the groups did not appeal to private-pay parents, for obvious reasons: lack of cleanliness, reasonable physical and mental health, basic manners, and/ or rudimentary education. The runny noses streaming down the faces of three-year-olds could scare away the most tolerant of parents. And at that age, sickness was contagious and ever present.

Plus, the parents of the AFDC children, many of them unwed mothers who had to work to survive, left us with no alternative but to nurse their children back to health—both mental and physical. Yet I believed the melding together of these two disparate groups would be the fastest way to prepare these impoverished children for the public education they would be receiving—ready or not—when they reached school age.

I suggested we use Stiles-Hatton modular sections surrounding a central atrium for the facilities then on the drawing board. This design provided four private areas opening to a large central play area that could be licensed for more than a hundred preschoolers, ages two and a half to five. After we built three facilities with this open design, I recognized the lack of noise control. Our only solution was child control, and our best directors could handle it. But good directors with good preschool credentials were expensive, and we had a hard time keeping them employed in this demanding environment.

I'm not sure who at Kiddie Care Corporation started arguments with our parent company, Care Corporation, but I was the loser, and my position as director of operations was abolished, "effective December 22, 1970."

It was an eventful day. When I walked into what I thought was my office in downtown Grand Rapids, an office that was part of the larger Care Corporation offices, it was bare. Not even my pictures of the children survived. Nothing. I was appalled! Quickly, the new president of Care Corporation appeared and explained that they had stored my personal materials in a small box, which he handed to me. He said they were afraid I would steal (he didn't actually use that word) the proprietary information of the company if they didn't remove it first. Wow.

My office experiences were becoming more varied and more complex with each new business opportunity, but nothing seemed as vicious as the gossipy attitude that surrounded my day-to-day interactions with the top management of Care or Kiddie Care. The person responsible for the development of these companies, a brilliant local businessman and dentist, seemed resentful of my presence because it was foisted on him by Bill Seidman. After all, he knew that I had a wealthy husband, influential friends, and six children. Women in my position weren't given executive positions unless they had earned them by a professional route. And even then, not with five children still at home.

And then there was Kiddie Care's president, Jim Hurst. Jim was a favorite of Bill Seidman's, but again, not of Care Corporation's CEO. Jim and I got along fairly well, but Jim was young and new to the city of Grand Rapids, and therefore didn't have the resources or knowledge that I had developed.

Jim made a bad business supposition (that would eventually drive me from the child care business too): parents or government or charities would be willing to pay *good* money for *good* child care, thus enabling Kiddie Care to pay professional teachers or directors *good* wages—wages similar to the *good* wages and benefits paid to public-school teachers and administrators.

We couldn't find directors with preschool experience to work in the centers. This was a new business. Finding the right person was crucial to the success of each center—not like happened in public schools, where children showed up no matter what, regardless of the curriculum.

Our directors had to hire and fire all the teachers. With each center needing almost one hundred children enrolled before Kiddie Care reached profitability, directors were busy just keeping twenty teachers trained and disciplined.

And our directors had to do the interviews with parents as well. Our corporate office might do the marketing, but the personal contacts were made with the directors in the center. I quickly discovered that the personality of the director was key to each center's success. It had little to do with the director's educational training. (Besides, the person with a master's degree in education wanted more pay.)

My job competed with Jim's role at Kiddie Care, and there wasn't enough money to pay both of us. Yes, I was booted out—three days before Christmas 1970. I drove home and quickly signed up for unemployment benefits. I would be eligible for one year of benefits, and I wanted next summer free to play with my kids.

When I called Mom and Dad to tell them that I had been fired from Kiddie Care, they invited me and all five kids to go cruising in the North Channel the next summer. This waterway was a yachtsman's paradise of pristine cruising grounds northeast of the Straits of Mackinac, which separate Lake Michigan from Lake Huron. With the rugged Canadian shoreline on the north and the huge sprawling Manitoulin Island on the south, the North Channel is well protected from the fury of Lake Huron. In my youth, Dad took me fishing in the rustic Canadian port of Blind River, and in the remote town of Little Current on the northeast tip of Manitoulin Island.

Mom and Dad's cabin cruiser, heading north

Mom and Dad were part of a yearly entourage of small yachts, most ranging in size from forty-five-foot trawlers down to Mom and Dad's thirty-five-foot cabin cruiser. I was happy to tag along. Three of the boys were home for the summer from prep school. Mike was getting married and safely ensconced in the naval base in Puerto Rico. I was elated with my newfound freedom. As were the kids—all excellent sailors, even Lydia and Brett, who were only ten and eight years old.

Our voyage was scheduled to accommodate the older yachtsmen's interests. They liked to move north quickly. We left the Grand Haven pier at noon on July 14, 1971. The log reads, "Muskegon at 12:45 p.m., then White Lake, Little Sable Light, Pentwater, Ludington, Big Sable, Manistee, Portage, and Arcadia, arriving for the night in Frankfort at 5:27 p.m."

But then the pace slowed. After cocktails at our cottage on the Crystal Downs Country Club property only seven miles away, our fleet headed north on July 15 at 10:25 a.m. We toured the magnificent summer ports of Charlevoix, Petoskey, and Harbor Springs, before finally docking at every sailor's favorite watering hole, Mackinac Island, on Monday morning, July 19, 1971.

Mom and Dad biking around Mackinac Island

No motorized vehicles were permitted on Mackinac Island, but horses and bicycles were readily available in the early morning hours, and we rushed to find the best bikes at the best rentals. Everyone, including Mom and Dad, hopped on a bike for that initial eight-mile-ride along sandy and pebbly beaches on the broadly paved path that encircled the island. Then it was an exploration of Fort Mackinac, a tough ride or hike up a steep road to the entrance, which overlooked the busy marinas and docks below. (Mom and Dad opted out of that tour.) The boys loved the archaeological digs around the fort, especially Julio, who often came up with worthwhile finds, especially arrowheads.

No one was interested in the Grand Hotel, except to take pictures of it. The landscaping and flowers that lined the long, sweeping porches throughout the summer and fall were always spectacular, and the grandness of the size of this white structure was a beloved sight every time we approached the island. No wonder that the Chicago Yacht Club's race to Mackinac, along with the Port Huron-Mackinac race on alternate weekends every year in mid-July, was so popular. Since the races started on Saturday around noon and most finished on Monday (except in 1970!), all the marinas and harbor would soon be jammed with sailboats.

Dad was eager to leave for his fishing grounds, and pushed us on our way early Wednesday morning, with only a rich fudgy loot in the hold. The fish were so plentiful in Les Cheneaux Islands that Dad convinced his fellow travelers to anchor in the popular Government Bay anchorage for three days before heading east into the North Channel.

By the time we anchored and rafted our boats together, my fidgety five kids were ready to jump on the dinghy to explore the islands. With the adults happy on board during cocktail hour, I could follow the kids through the thick scrub and rocks that lined the coastline. Meals were always on board, because none of the adults were prepared to hike ashore—and all the women were experienced cooks in their respective galleys.

We cruised along the northern coast of Manitoulin Island, making only one stop to catch perch at Eagle Island.

It did not pay to get sick miles from a port or a hospital. When one of the boys announced that he was getting a migraine, I panicked. My usual solution, the emergency room at the nearest hospital, would be nonexistent. I needed space and medicine, neither one of which was in abundance. Coffee and aspirin were my only hope, along with some hiking trails on shore. Some of the older, stodgy yachtsmen were not sympathetic to my plight, commenting that I should not have brought children along who got sick. (If they only knew that I had another son who might get a migraine too, they would have been really upset.) We walked and walked for hours among the scrub and rocks, and, finally, at dusk, we walked off the worst of his migraine.

That experience was a sobering reminder that we might not be welcome with this tight-knit group much longer. When we pulled into the Canadian port of Little Current at the eastern end of the North Channel, I called home.

"Hurry back. Now. You may become the new president of Kiddie Care!"

Chartering a small single-engine plane, I crowded the kids in the back seats and climbed in the copilot's seat. I insisted we fly west over the island, not directly southwest across Lake Huron—which probably was illegal if we were to follow Michigan aviation regulations, because single-engine planes may not fly directly across Lake Michigan. Every time we crossed a smaller body of water, I bit my lip. To think that I was risking my children's lives in a strange plane with an unknown foreign pilot, was madness. Madness fueled by excitement and speculation.

What happened at Kiddie Care? Shortly after I left, Jim Hurst quit and joined Multico, a construction company in Flint that wanted to get into the day care business.

Philip Buchen, 1970 Courtesy of David LaClaire

Care Corporation formed a new board for Kiddie Care, with Philip Buchen as chairman of the board. A talented lawyer with an impeccable reputation, Philip Buchen was Congressman Jerry Ford's former law partner and a good friend of Bill Seidman's. With his legs crippled by polio at age sixteen, Phil was cerebral and slightly frail, often using two canes. And he was a loyal member of Fountain Street Church.

Phil wanted me to come back and run Kiddie Care, but he had a battle raging with the Care Corporation executives, so he asked me to set up my office at his law firm across the street from Care's office. The Old Kent Bank building became a second home: Bill Seidman's accounting firm was a floor above Phil's law offices, Buchen, Weathers, Richardson & Dutcher, and Uncle Siegel Judd's law firm, Warner, Norcross, and Judd, with Hal Sawyer as their top litigator, a floor above Seidman & Seidman.

By the time I took over the management of Kiddie Care, we had built two new centers utilizing the Stiles-Hatton modules, a third one in the southwest side of Grand Rapids and the first one in Muskegon. I still was not popular with Care Corporation owners because Kiddie Care wasn't making money. Muskegon was a drag because of its location next to the Muskegon Community College. It was too far from the AFDC inner-city population and too far from the wealthy North Muskegon set. One or two of the other centers were full, but the others needed to be locally marketed to attract parents wary of such big private day care centers. (Were these babysitting institutions or Montessori learning centers?) We were too new to be trusted by the educated parents, and the welfare community still did not comprehend that the federal government would actually pay for their children's all-day care.

After a year of struggling to fill the centers, I received a call from Jeff Poorman, a young broker representing Flint-based Multico, now bankrupt, and Provincial House, a Lansing-based publicly held health care company. Jeff had convinced Provincial House that day care centers would be an asset to their business, which included a real estate construction company and a computer company.

The bankrupt company, Multico, needed to sell its inner-city day care center in Flint and three substantially built new day care centers: two in Lansing and one in Kalamazoo. Jeff told Provincial House that they could "steal" the four Multico centers, but Provincial House needed someone to run the new company.

Bill Seidman and I drove to Flint to meet with Jeff and the corporate officers of Multico and Provincial House. As a current board member of Care Corporation, Bill surmised that Care would be eager to get out of the day care business.

What a highly charged meeting, and what interesting players: Multico's secretary of the board was Irv Nelson, a Harvard-trained lawyer and World War II tough CIA guerilla; Pat Callihan was the diminutive president of Provincial House, flush faced, right out of a fighting Irish script, ready to do battle; Bill Seidman was another Harvard-trained lawyer and World War II distinguished naval executive officer in the Pacific fleet; Jeff Poorman was the young, smart, stealthy broker who could smell a deal ready to be made.

I thought I got a great deal. But Jeff Poorman just laughed. He reminded me that I could have ended up with a much bigger deal if I were willing to take Irv Nelson's offer. Irv got a little tipsy; he offered to put $25,000 more into the deal if I would spend the night with him. I was flattered. Jeff roared, knowing Irv's background. Bill ignored it; he already had his deal.

I would be investing $25,000 of Jule's inheritance, and I would be moving my executive office to Provincial House's offices near the Lansing airport. I would be running nine day care centers, with plans to build at least two more. I would own 25 percent of a public day care company, a subsidiary of Provincial House. Our new company would be named Young World.

Lansing was one hundred miles from our house on the hill. It was an easy drive because we had a newly constructed empty I-96 for all but the first ten miles of it. One hour and twenty-two minutes at eighty miles an hour. When I exceeded eighty miles an hour, I got ticketed. Plenty of times. I had the maximum twelve points, but the police let me drive "to and from work," which could mean any time of day or night.

I begged Jule to consider moving to Grand Rapids, which was halfway to Lansing. He was in the process of selling Stiles-Hatton to Inland Steel and was looking for new businesses in which to invest. I felt that I had the only solid good-paying job, plus an ownership interest.

An adamant and angry Jule replied, "I built this house, and I do not intend to leave it … ever!"

Our Dutch nanny, Anja, had been replaced by Dominique, a twenty-year-old nanny from Paris who was way too smart and sophisticated for her role in our household. Her parents, although married, could afford to maintain separate apartments in Paris. Dominique knew what was going on the minute she met Bill Seidman at our cottage at Crystal Downs. She could have taught the boys perfect French, but she preferred to discuss my relationship with Bill. It was not long before Dominique found the demands of our country life boring and beneath her status, and she soon returned to Paris, much to my relief.

Janie and A. D. helping out on an eighteenth birthday celebration

To the rescue came Janie and "A. D." Howard. Grammy Hatton felt we needed a replacement, and located the only black couple in Grand Haven. Janie was plump, fun, and bossy. She ruled the roost in her house, with five peppy children and A. D.—and they all took directions from her. And so did we. I didn't fool Janie, but for some reason, she respected me. And all my children loved both Janie and A. D. They got into trouble together. A. D. would build a huge barbeque pit and cook the best spareribs in the neighborhood. The boys' parties in the summertime started getting out of hand once they turned eighteen. The house, inside and out, could handle hundreds of people during a long evening of A. D.'s ribs and beer and who knows what else. Yes, eighteen twenty-one (1821 Doris Avenue) was renamed eighteen twenty-*fun*.

How was the customer going to hear KSPN-FM in 1970? Peter Drucker liked to remind us that there was no business without a customer.

By 1970, there were few FM radios in the Roaring Fork valley households or hotels. The Recreation Broadcasting Company board quickly authorized the purchase of a thousand FM radios. At twelve dollars each, the vacationing skiers consumed them all immediately. Some autos did have FM receivers, but the Rocky Mountains were not conducive to FM's straight-line signal, and with our small 250-watt transmitter and antenna on the roof of the Jerome Hotel, there was no way for the signal to follow automobiles going west toward Glenwood Springs or, for a few summer months, east over Independence Pass.

According to a local reporter for the weekly newspaper, *The Aspen Times*, KSPN-FM had a successful launch on Valentine's Day, and Jon Busch "now was manager, DJ, engineer, janitor, and everything else."

Jon concurred with that analysis: "Those early days were the poor days, and I took more than one pay cut. I determined that the station would be twenty-four-hour from the start. All those Skully tape decks played 'elevator music,' but I started supplementing with more contemporary music tapes of my own until, eventually, the Muzak was gone entirely. Without the help of drugs, I worked myself down to my weight as a high school freshman, even often pulling the late night 'free form' shifts when the volunteer DJs failed to show up. That show went from 10:30 to 3:30. I'm sure a few FCC content rules were broken during those hours."

Jon laughed, adding, "One night, Hunter Thompson came down after the J-Bar closed, to 'liberate' the station. I let him have the mic [sic], but as his rant grew ever more incoherent, I realized that the only way I could get him out of the studio was to shut the station down—which I did."

And, finally, Jon complained that " ... those of my generation put up with a lot. There was a time when I literally lived in the studio's tool room, in a sleeping bag. One night, I felt something against my leg. Tossing the sleeping bag back, I found a little mouse there. I reached over the wall, took a handsaw down, and cut the poor little critter in two."

Jon Busch plowed bravely through our first year of start-up woes, but 1970 proved to be an exciting time for our local news sources in Aspen.

Hunter Thompson, with his new style of gonzo journalism, had decided to run for sheriff of Pitkin County, on the "Freak Power" ticket. And, conveniently for KSPN-FM, with studios now securely lodged in the basement of the Jerome Hotel, Hunter placed his headquarters in Parlor B, on the second floor of the hotel. John Gilmore complained that he lost the rental of the room, but admitted that Hunter and his Freak Power friends certainly entertained the customers at the now-crowded J-Bar every night. (It was off-season, so the election publicity was a godsend.) And the head bartender, Mike Solheim, was Hunter's campaign chairman.

Besides promoting the decriminalization of drugs, turning the streets into pedestrian malls, and renaming Aspen "Fat City" to deter investors, Hunter, having shaved his head, referred to the Republican candidate as "my long-haired opponent."

So ... with polls showing him with a slight lead in a three-way race, Hunter Thompson appeared at the *Rolling Stone* magazine headquarters in San Francisco, with a six-pack of beer in hand, and declared to editor Jann Wenner that he was about to be elected the next sheriff of Aspen, Colorado, and wished to write about the Freak Power movement. Thus, Hunter's very first article in *Rolling Stone* was published as the "Battle of Aspen," with the byline, "By Dr. Hunter S. Thompson (Candidate for Sheriff)." Well, Hunter Thompson carried the city of Aspen, but he garnered only 44 percent of the total county-wide vote.

During the first year, the Recreation Broadcasting board urged Gary and me to explore new low-power FM radio possibilities. We took a short trip to St. Croix in October, 1971, but we found the atmosphere so politically charged from recent tourist atrocities that we quickly left the island. Another trip was planned to Naples, Florida. We became worried that we couldn't stay ahead of the curve in these desirable vacation spots. When locals joined a group applying for the license, it was nearly impossible to compete, in the eyes of the FCC. All we could do was try to convince the interested locals to join with us, but once they found financing, they could send us on our way.

Helen and Allen Hunting had better luck in Winter Haven. They were able to buy the new low-power FM station already on the air, and Helen became president of Recreation Broadcasting of Winter Haven. She soon was approached by Joe Garagiola, the famous baseball sportscaster; Joe wanted to buy the station and apply for a full-power FM license, both of which he did very successfully.

Jon Busch felt that KSPN's first big move came when he hired away the very popular morning host from KSNO-AM, Dick Skidmore. The next big move came when Jerome Hotel owner John Gilmore found us a bean counter who was running an Aspen business. Steve Heater was smart and knowledgeable about the town, the mountains, and the local government. To entice Steve to leave his present business, brother Gary offered him different percentages of the company, depending on his ability to meet profitable forecasts.

After Gary and I left the tropics with no prospects of success, Gary and Steve started scouring the Rockies, hoping to find locations still available for FM radio applications. Steamboat had been taken by locals interested in applying for their own FM radio license, so Gary and Steve moved on to Crested Butte, where cousin Carl Verplank had a vacation home and his sons owned a successful bar business. I visited too, by taking a wild scary shortcut from Aspen, sliding down icy rocky paths hardly fit for our jeep. But, besides the difficult commute from Denver (and the impossible commute from Aspen most of the year), we knew the town was too small and would stay that way.

On to Vail, which had the best snow conditions on the best mountain, the best location on I-70, and the best future for development. We felt that our translator towers through Glenwood Springs would bring KSPN's signal to Vail and the newly developing resort of Beaver Creek. KSPN-FM radio's popular AOR (album oriented rock) format would be serving the same young, wealthy skiing audience at Vail as would be availing in Aspen. Vail valley news and sports would have to be accommodated with special local broadcasts.

Feeling bullish from recent financial successes at KSPN, Steve asked Gary to check out an FM station available in Pueblo. Steve knew I didn't like the idea. It was not a "recreation" location; it was a steel town. It provided no new FM business opportunity, because there were two or three other FMs already licensed to the city and already on the air. Steve insisted we buy it. He offered $160,000 for KVMN-FM, in September 1973, and that offer was quickly accepted. After a year or two of losses, we moved out fast, and KSPN again had to recoup "start-up" losses. We weren't prepared for the big time; none of the board members were ready or willing to fund new FM applications. Our broadcast interests had to change if we were going to stay ahead of the curve.

The KSPN board finally agreed to build the translators needed to cover the mountain towns down valley. Gary asked Steve Heater to locate a site on the western side of Red Mountain for our new FM tower. This transmitter location could bring both a clear signal into Snowmass Village and interface down valley with a broadcast translator tower that could retransmit our unaltered signal into Glenwood Springs on a different frequency.

I always knew it would be my job to lease the properties—which probably would be controlled by the BLM (the Bureau of Land Management), since the BLM owned most of the property in the Rocky Mountains west of Denver. I had better be ready to deal with government entities that needed to show their muscle. I had better be ready to spend hours preparing flawless paperwork that followed antiquated procedures. But we had hired a bean counter, and Steve Heater tackled my job with gusto.

Chapter Five

THE WHITE HOUSE

"...a short window of time."

BUSINESSWOMAN CONSIDERED

Child Care for Profit or Not?

BY JUDITH SERRIN
Free Press Staff Writer

For more than two years, the federal Office of Child Development, an agency that oversees government programs for children, has been operating without a permanent director.

The vacancy, critics charge, has hampered programs, including day care, and left the needs of children without an important advocate at the federal level.

Now a Michigan day-care businesswoman is being considered to head the OCD, but her candidacy is arousing protest from many national child care groups.

The candidate is Joyce Hatton, 42, of Grand Haven, who owns and operates 10 day care centers across the state under the name of Michigan Young World. The centers serve about 1,800 pre-schoolers.

Mrs. Hatton, an active Republican, was first mentioned for appointments as OCD director last April. When her candidacy became known, a number of groups sent protests to the Department of Health, Education and Welfare, of which OCD is a part.

Much of the criticism centers on the fact that Mrs. Hatton runs a for-profit chain of centers. In the OCD post, she would be working with public programs, like Head Start, and with non-profit child care groups.

(It is not unusual, however, for government appointees to come from businesses in the

Betroit Free Press
for and about Women

Wednesday, Nov. 13, 1974 1-C

Joyce Hatton: The news that she is under consideration to head the U.S. Office of Child Development brought protests.

Too many people talk about generalities, but "They don't know how to go about getting it done ... Priorities have to be set ... Perhaps what I could do ... is tell them what some of the options are, and what some of the costs are."
---

since Gerald Ford, a friend of her and her husband's, became president. Mrs. Hatton had lived in Ford's old congressional district has been an active party official and fund

GOP in Dem Stronghold

Noting that day care pro-

Child Welfare League, shared Ms. Bode's concerns.

"If the person in the Office of Child Development has to administer an extremely large Head Start program," he said, "they should have both the enthusiasm for and support of the Head Start constituency."

He said he was not sure that Mrs. Hatton had either. Further, he said, he would like to see someone in the office who "had been on the record for a while about being deeply concerned about the needs of children." He said, "I don't know whether she is more a child advocate or more a business person."

On the other hand, Wayne Smith, executive director of the National Association for Child Development and Education, a group of private day care operators, praised Mrs. Hatton as "the only person in the United States that has been able to mix successfully people from the ADC and the private sector. She has been able to show that you can make a profit by having a proper mix."

Mrs. Hatton said that about half of the children enrolled in her centers received Aid to Dependent Children, a total greater than that of any other private operator in the country.

Mrs. Hatton has owned Young World since 1972. For two years before that, she was president of Kiddie Care Corp., a public company she bought out. From 1957 to 1969,

tion Army, the Family Service Association of America, the Minnesota Children's Lobby, the American Institute of Family Relations and the children's section of the American

Detroit Free Press, Wednesday, November 13, 1974

During the summer of 1973, I sat in my new roomy but windowless offices in Lansing, listening every day as National Public Radio aired live all of the Watergate hearings. As much as I detested public broadcasting (for competing with our commercial radio stations for programming), I couldn't sufficiently thank WKAR-FM, the Michigan State University PBS station, for my summer entertainment. According to the *Washington Post*, "A summer of broadcast hearings ... produced a steady flow of testimony suggesting burglary, lies, duplicity and criminality at the highest levels."

I always thought Nixon was guilty, and I wanted him punished. (Nixon never convinced this delegate at our 1968 Republican convention that his

109

foreign policy experience—as vice president to President Eisenhower for eight years—made him more qualified to end the Vietnam War than my candidates, Governors Rockefeller and Romney.)

In mid-July 1973, Alexander Butterfield reluctantly admitted details of the tape system that monitored Nixon's conversations. Butterfield commented at the Senate hearing that he knew "it was the one thing that the President would not want revealed."

It was early Friday afternoon. I ran down the hall, telling everyone within earshot about the tapes. People looked at me, puzzled. Why was this fact so important? And why so important to me? I knew it would be the end of Nixon's presidency. I couldn't wait to tell Bill Seidman. He would understand better than anyone the implications of this revelation.

Nixon's vice president, Spiro Agnew, had his own battles with scandals in the summer of 1973, and he finally resigned on October 10.

I had no idea that Nixon would pick Gerald Ford for vice president. Who could know the perfidious mind of stressed-out Richard Nixon in the summer and fall of 1973? Everyone deduced that the mild-mannered Minority Leader of the House of Representatives would be easily confirmed by the Senate, but not be seen as a threat to Nixon's wobbling presidency. Ford's highest ambition was to be Speaker of the House, which required a Republican majority—a nigh impossibility in the 1970s.

On a warm fall weekend in 1973, Bill and Sally joined Jule and me at our cottage at Crystal Downs, along with any children still at home and willing to travel north with us. Most of our work and play schedules had changed in the last year: Bill had completed his six years as managing director of Seidman & Seidman, Jule had sold Stiles-Hatton, and I had a hundred-mile daily commute to Lansing. The older children were growing up and moving on to prep school or college, and beyond. And once school started, the Seidman's younger ones usually preferred to stay home and play with friends. I encouraged Lydia and Brett to bring friends with them because I couldn't participate in any after-school activities with them during the week.

About 7:30 p.m., the phone rang in the kitchen. I answered. It was a person-to-person call from Washington, DC, "for Bill Seidman." It was our old buddy, Phil Buchen, on the phone. We all hovered around, knowing that Phil was helping his former law partner, Congressman Jerry Ford, get settled in his new role as President Nixon's nominee for vice president.

We could tell that Phil was asking Bill to come to Washington right away. And, of course, Bill was excited too, knowing that his role in a vice president's office would lead to new opportunities.

After they hung up, Bill explained that Jerry was trying to organize his office and badly needed help; the mail was piling higher than the windows, and Phil said the organization needed the services of an experienced manager. Bill could move to Washington, with the secure knowledge of a promising new career.

What would this move mean to me? After the weekend, Bill called my office and explained very carefully that this was the time to create a new life together in a foreign environment—in a cosmopolitan city that understood divorce and the politics of power. And he hoped to have a powerful job, working directly for the vice president of the most powerful country in the world.

I couldn't believe Bill even suggested it. I commented sarcastically that he wasn't even divorced; he was hardly in a position to ask me to join him in Washington. And then I made the statement that probably bothered Bill the most: "I never intend to marry again."

I thought the institution of marriage had created a prison of regulations. I wasn't free to leave. My jobs couldn't go with me. My children wouldn't go with me. When I felt my youngest two were old enough, I could give them the choice of staying in their father's house.

I needed time. Time to develop my own career that could include Bill, not be consumed by Bill. And time to present options to my children. I respected them, I respected their decisions, and I wanted them to respect me in return. I would be the one walking out. Walking out of their house but not out of their lives.

Bill said there was only a short window of time. ... Sally would be ready to move at the end of the school year in June. He was heading to Washington alone. I knew my life with Bill would never be the same.

In early December, Jerry Ford was sworn in as vice president. To witness this historic event, Bill invited his old political buddies from Grand Rapids, including me, to fly to Washington in the Seidmans' slow-moving twin-engine Cessna. We drank martinis and played gin rummy all the way. By the time I got off the plane, I could hardly walk. I had about four hours to sober up, put on a long, elegant, black velvet gown with feather trim, and have my picture taken with Jerry—a picture that was destroyed the moment I saw it. I'm sure Jerry never noticed my glassy-eyed, cheesy smile. Shaking my hand would not have been one of his priorities in his new post.

I nevertheless was invited to Washington by Bill to testify before congressional committees about the private sector's role in public programs like Head Start and AFDC.

The reports to Congress were not fun. I was beat up by nonprofit child care organization leaders like Marian Wright Edelman, who had testified before Congress so often that she had her national numbers memorized—numbers representing preschool children "left behind" because the government was not taking care of them. I surmised that none of the leaders had ever been in the business of caring for these children, which led to my comments that it was the private sector that kept the public sector work honest. Our capital investment was not the national treasury. If we couldn't make ends meet, we were out of business. We knew what the costs were for the day care of AFDC children—because we provided it.

Bill would call my office in Lansing, with the latest gossip surrounding the White House. And the winter of President Nixon's discontent was full of it. Once again, I loved being part of the action ... and having the opportunity to play with their movers and shakers. My first tennis game was played in a magnificent setting near McLean, Virginia. Our hosts took their obligations to society very seriously. Noblesse oblige from birth was evident in their extracurricular activities, which included federal aid to education legislation, creation of the Public Broadcasting System, and memberships in organizations like the Aspen Institute.

Nixon thought "executive privilege" would save the day, but the independent prosecutor, Archibald Cox, insisted on unrestricted access to the White House tapes, which precipitated the infamous Saturday night massacre. Cox was fired on October 20, 1973. Finally, on October 23, Nixon was forced to release some of the White House tapes. The pressure was insurmountable. ... And then, a month later, Rose Mary Woods, Nixon's faithful secretary, "accidentally" erased eighteen minutes of tape. By now, Congress and the country were in an uproar, demanding the impeachment of the president.

Bill had to be very careful not to appear that he (or anyone else on the vice president's staff) was out to get Nixon dethroned. Since Bill was responsible for oversight of the vice president's press relations and speech writing, he felt particularly vulnerable. And I knew Bill's respect for the vice president's delicate position would carry the day. I envied Bill's legal training and common sense. Bill knew better than to talk to the press, whose members I am sure hounded his office for any of the juicy tidbits that might be available.

In the springtime, after the sale of Stiles-Hatton, Jule started looking around once more for a new business venture. He agreed to a meeting with John Shepard on his large cabin cruiser, which John docked at the Spring Lake Holiday Inn marina on the Grand River. John's success with WLAV-FM led to other wired interests, among them a new telephone interconnect company. John's partners included my childhood neighbor and a Grand Haven business titan. They wanted to sell Jule their struggling telephone interconnect business.

Jule and I were riding home together from Grand Rapids the day of the scheduled meeting. After parking the car, I joined the group on John's back deck. Although I definitely was not invited to this meeting, no one said anything when I arrived. But that didn't last long. My questions about national legislation that might be needed for this tiny interconnect company to thrive was not on their agenda. AT&T was being sued to divest its monopoly on local and long-distance lines. A new patent had been issued that allowed modems and telephone lines to interconnect. No one knew what the new legislative restrictions might be in this business. I told them this industry was in a state of flux, and advised Jule to stay clear of it.

"Don't you think your children need you right now? We'll give Jule a ride home after the meeting," ordered John.

That was it. I fumed, and stormed off his boat.

Yes, these salesmen convinced Jule to buy their business. I couldn't believe the difference between Bill's attitude about my business acumen and Jule's! Yes, other wives would not think of interfering. Who was I to intercede at this critical juncture? Jule, too, believed in them instead of me. If ever I wanted an excuse to get out of this marriage, this was the crowning blow. But I could do nothing. My children were too young.

On Friday, August 9, 1974, President Richard Nixon resigned, and Vice President Gerald Ford was sworn in as president of the United States. Bill Seidman called our house on the hill to report the exciting event. ... Bill said he was watching Nixon waving a tearful good-bye and entering the helicopter on the back lawn of the White House while the vice president's staff was assembling for the swearing in of Vice President Ford in the East Room of the White House. I was amazed that Bill was taking the time to share this momentous event with us as it happened. He was in a joyous mood.

We couldn't believe the drama—Ford occupying the White House the same hour that Nixon was leaving it. And Ford appointing another moderate

Republican, and one of my favorite candidates, Nelson Rockefeller, to be vice president.

Bill always joked about the fact that he wasn't Jerry Ford's best friend, but because he was from Grand Rapids and a good friend of Philip Buchen's, people in Washington assumed he had a very close relationship with the president. And those of us in the Michigan provinces had no idea that our soft-spoken friend and associate, Phil Buchen, now chief White House counsel, would be assigned a most difficult task.

After being hounded in late August by the White House press corps about a Nixon pardon, President Ford requested a pardon study from Chief Counsel Buchen. The Watergate special prosecutor assigned to the investigation, Leon Jaworski, had warned Buchen that the trial(s) could last years.

Phil quickly summoned our pastor from Grand Rapids, Dr. Duncan Littlefair, to Washington, seeking compassionate advice on the pardon of Nixon. Though himself a social liberal, Duncan felt this was a time to leave the past behind and allow Nixon and the country to move on: "Mercy and forgiveness cannot be weighed and measured, balanced and counted. It must always be free and unearned and undeserved. It is the foolish nature of mercy. Mercy doesn't preclude justice. Mercy precedes justice ... mercy is the context for justice."

And during a slow press time, Sunday morning after church services, September 8, 1974, President Ford said as much in his ten minutes of prepared remarks.

Now Duncan would defend the action publicly and praise the decision for its compassion. And to my surprise, so did right-wing industrialist O. W. (Bill) Lowry of Holland, Michigan, a social friend, but a critic of my moderate Republican beliefs in the 1960s.

The public was totally confused about this sudden action. As was the president's new press secretary, Jerald terHorst, a Grand Rapids native and former White House correspondent for the *Detroit News*. Jerry terHorst felt blindsided, after telling the press for a month that Nixon would not get a pardon. He resigned the same day the pardon was announced, writing the following in a letter to President Ford: " ... it is impossible to conclude that the former President is more deserving of mercy than persons of lesser station in life whose offenses have had far less effect on our national well-being."

I should have agreed with my former congressman and now president, Gerald Ford, and my moral compass and confidant, Duncan Littlefair, but I couldn't be that compassionate. I felt that Nixon was the leader of the pack, and, yes, the leader of our nation—pulling all the "persons of lesser station in life" into his whirlpool of quicksand.

But that's why Ford was the good politician, a compromiser. He did what he thought was best for the country as a whole. Unfortunately, my feelings were carrying the day, and if President Ford had hoped for any honeymoon, it was now gone in less than a month into his presidency ... and perhaps his presidency, too, would be gone in less than thirty months.

My work at Young World, Inc., was very productive in 1973, with the modular building of the last two planned day care centers: one on Linden Road in Flint and the second in Livonia, a middle-class suburb of Detroit. Both centers had indoor swimming pools, an easy construction addition accomplished by tying together two twelve-by-fifty-foot Stiles-Hatton modules and adding a peaked roof. The pools were a sensation the first few years because young mothers brought their babies to play in the pool while their older preschoolers enjoyed swimming lessons.

But like my problems with sound control in the open central atriums of the other modular centers, I soon realized the problems these pool areas would have from lack of adequate ventilation or use of solid, water-resistant materials. The basic wood construction quickly started to rot, allowing potentially dangerous molds to grow in the damp and humid environment. We finally covered the pools and converted the spaces to indoor play areas, which turned out to be a very positive use, since snowy and bitter-cold Michigan winters precluded much outdoor play for the preschool set.

I liked to work standing up, and my job required communicating with staff, either personally or by telephone, most of the time. I was a minor coffee drinker, but if I got past that second cup of coffee in the morning, I would stand there and "blank out"—and just admit that I couldn't think. And when I did, everyone knew what to do: set me down with head on desk, and wait at least five minutes.

The chairman of the board of Provincial House, Edward ("Otto") Solomon, was a tough Lebanese who had made his millions in the road construction business. My brothers knew him by reputation when they both were bidding for construction jobs with the state government. Otto Solomon would hold his meetings with me and other subsidiary leaders in Pat Callihan's presidential office. But I doubted other subsidiary presidents' meetings were like mine: Otto would listen carefully to my plans for expanding the day care centers in Flint and Livonia, and would surprise me with personal questions about my commitment to this job.

"You have five children at home," he would say. "How do I know you won't need to be there to take care of them? How can you do a full day's work every day when you may be needed by your family? Who's going to take care of them? And your husband too?"

Otto and Pat had me backed up against a wall, defending my ability to juggle two full-time commitments. I was angry and upset at this attack from a room filled with men. So I tried to turn the argument around on them.

I asked, "If you had a family member who needed to go to the hospital in an emergency situation, wouldn't you be there too?"

No response.

I said I was no different. My staff could take care of the two children who were still at home. The others were away at prep school or college. Otto was a little late carrying on these inquests, since my contract with Provincial House had been approved many months previous to our meetings.

Jeff Poorman, a decade my junior, always helped me out when he thought I was getting in over my head. He understood sale leasebacks so well that Michigan State University asked him to teach a course to their college students, and when he offered to teach me and other Provincial House staff members, I jumped at the chance. His class started at 6:00 a.m., and I was happy Jule was working in town because I needed to leave home at 4:30 a.m. Our helpers, Janie and A. D., had young kids at home, and they couldn't show up until 7:00 a.m. to prepare breakfast for mine.

Another Provincial House subsidiary, Compu-Link, had their offices and mainframe computers next to my office, and I felt comfortable visiting them whenever the occasion arose. Since I prided myself as a math whiz, I was fascinated by those huge six-foot cubes of metal that enclosed something totally mysterious—a world none of us understood if we weren't working with computer companies or manufacturers that produced the parts. Little did I know then that Compu-Link's location would prove to be very useful to my company in the very near future.

I was invited to Washington, DC, to testify on the Child and Family Services Bill, H.R. 2966, at the final hearings on June 20, 1975, before congressional subcommittees on Children and Youth and Select Education. I testified that I was serving on the Michigan State Advisory Committee for Day Care Services, the state Ad Hoc Committee for Child Care Center Rules, and a

Michigan Department of Education Referent Committee. And I stressed that half of our 1,600 day care enrollees were children of welfare families, making Young World, Inc., the largest private operator serving economically disadvantaged children in the United States. Further, I wrote:

> I hesitate to be critical of the bill because of the tremendous effort and concern that has been shown for helping young children by your committee members and your staff. ... But this is a very complex issue, and I would not be honest with you if I told you I thought this bill, as presently written, will accomplish its purposes. My reasons are:
>
> (1) It does not make economic sense for the public or private sector.
> (2) It does not provide leadership
> (3) It does not assure quality care
> (4) It does not protect freedom of choice for parents requesting services for their children.

I then tore into the "non-profit" status benefits of the bill:

> Nonprofits wear the halo and have many benefits the for-profits do not, courtesy of the federal government. ... Nonprofits are looked upon with favor by the press, radio and TV—for-profits are commercial and making money off of kids (no soliciting allowed). Foundation funds, HEW research grants, Model Cities programs, intern training programs with schools and colleges, community volunteers—all are available to the nonprofits. ... If there is a crying need for more quality child care, perhaps the Congress could encourage, not discourage, the private sector to invest in providing these important human services.

And leadership? I couldn't wait to complain:

> Parents cannot request something that doesn't exist, and the greatest need in this "infant" industry is management skills. Administering a large child care center is a difficult task, and not enough people have had the opportunity to improve their skills in this vital area. Administrators of programs with proven track records are not asked for in this bill, only community and parent representatives for policy committees and local program councils, and a child care specialist who more properly may belong in the classroom.

And quality? My entrepreneurial mettle was showing:

> Where in this bill is the motivation to provide quality, excitement, instill
> values to be accountable? Where is the opportunity for the market to
> work? For bad programs to fail? ... For a child care program—and the
> people in it—not to be stereotyped? No restrictions should be placed
> on enrollment.

I then quoted Gwen Morgan and Joan Bergstrom: "If poverty is a cri-
terion for participation in child development programs, the programs by
definition will perpetuate poverty."

Finally, I moved on to freedom of choice:

> According to William Raspberry, "Welfare parents should have the
> right to choose the day care center or home that provides the program
> and services they want, whether public or private, profit or non-profit.
> For them and especially for their children, if human equality has any
> pragmatic meaning, it is that people should have the opportunity to
> establish themselves as superior."

In his book, *Full Faith and Credit*, Bill Seidman recounted his experiences
during the transition to the White House from the Old Executive Office
Building in the fall of 1974. A noteworthy moment reported by Bill was his
getting sage advice from a former Nixon White House staffer, Tom Whitehead
(who would become my future business partner fifteen years later).

Tom Whitehead said, " ... the first thing you do at 1600 Pennsylvania
Avenue is get your name on the A list."

One of the perks on the A list was the right to play on the White House
tennis court. In early spring of 1975, Bill invited me to Washington to check
out his office in the West Wing—and suggested I bring along my tennis
racquet.

It was a beautiful day when I arrived. Bill grabbed his favorite new
assistant, Roger Porter, a former White House fellow, and Tom Brokaw, a
young White House correspondent for NBC news, and out we marched to
the tennis court. I wasn't nervous playing with Bill, but I didn't know the
capabilities of the others, and I didn't know who might be observing us
from on high. Bill teamed me up with Roger, a varsity tennis pro, and he
settled for Tom, a capable player, though not in Roger's league. It turned
out to be a very good match—so much so that I can't remember who won.

My trips to see Bill were few. Neither one of us had the time or the ability to get together. Bill's wife, Sally, moved to Washington in the summer of 1974 and quickly found a lovely Victorian in Georgetown near Dumbarton Oaks Park. With her knowledge and interest in art, Sally was enthusiastically welcomed by the docent crowd at the best art museums in Washington. In the summer of 1975, Sally invited Jule and me to a theme party at their house, and I dressed very inappropriately for the event: much too dressy, in a full-length Pucci silk gown. Sally wore a plain denim dress, which emphasized her theme of *Alice's Restaurant,* but did not enhance her very pretty features. Jule, as always, dressed preppy: a Brooks Brothers button-down oxford cloth shirt, summer suit, tie, and laced shoes. By comparison, Bill seldom dressed up—unless he was working in the White House, where he always wore a serious business suit. Usually, he wore old khakis, loafers or cowboy boots, and, when necessary, a blue blazer. The night of the party saw Bill in his customary attire.

The Seidmans' party made me very uncomfortable. I knew some of the guests, having met them with Bill in 1973 or 1974, before Sally moved to Washington. Yet I seemed to be the only one concerned, which was another lesson in Beltway politics. My favorite hotel, the Hay Adams, was only a stone's throw away from the White House. Everyone joked that the entire seventh floor of the Hay Adams had been reserved for President Kennedy's trysts when he lived at 1600 Pennsylvania Avenue.

In the spring of 1975, I gingerly brought up the subject of a divorce with Jule. He responded quickly and definitively: "It is not a topic for discussion"

When I told Bill about this experience, he cautioned me to think about what I was doing; he worried that my family and friends would desert me and I would not be prepared for the onslaught that would come my way if I physically moved out of the house. Bill knew that Jule would not leave the house he had built, and Bill doubted that any of the kids would move, either. Finally, Bill said that he thought I should not do this now.

Although I did not broach the subject again until fall, I rented an attractive modern house in Aspen for the summer season. When Fritz heard that I had rented a house in Pitkin Green on Red Mountain, he applied for the prestigious position of master-taping Aspen Music Festival summer concerts. Fritz was a devotee of classical music, so this opportunity was not to be missed. And it wasn't. We had been playing tapes of the festival concerts on Sunday mornings on KSPN-FM, and Fritz's job would make ours much easier to coordinate.

The freedom, the independence, the power to control my destiny—all slammed hard into my psyche that summer in Aspen.

When I returned to Michigan in September, I attempted to find out if Duncan Littlefair would talk to both Jule and me about our marriage. Surprisingly, Duncan agreed. A meeting was set up in Duncan's office at Fountain Street Church, but Jule was reluctant to go, knowing that Duncan had been my longtime friend.

Jule did go, and Duncan talked mostly with him. Neither one was very satisfied with the meeting. I asked Duncan for a meeting with me alone.

About a week later, I met Duncan in his Fountain Street Church office. It was late afternoon, and I got a phone call from Jule during our meeting. He said I needed to come home immediately because my son had a migraine. I gave Jule directions about handling the migraine until I returned. Jule demanded I leave immediately, reminding me that this was my responsibility.

Duncan was flabbergasted by the call. He asked why Jule couldn't handle this problem. I tried to explain that Jule didn't handle problems with any of the children's health.

The reply I received from Duncan changed forever the way I thought about our marriage. Duncan believed that Jule should have the opportunity to be his own person. Further, Duncan explained that the phone call was just an example of someone who has relied too long on his partner.

Duncan continued, "You have become mother and father to these children. Jule needs to go out and find a life on his own. You need to get a divorce *now*, so Jule can get on with his life."

I did not discuss divorce with Jule after that meeting with Duncan. Instead, I started looking for a place to lease in Grand Rapids, which would be halfway between my Lansing office and Grand Haven. A distant Leonard relative was a broker in the East Grand Rapids area where all Jule's Leonard family relatives lived, and she found me a dog-smelly bungalow in a wonderful setting on Reed's Lake, in the heart of East Grand Rapids. It was located on the swampy west end of the lake, which teemed with wildlife. I would have my own rickety dock, but it would need major repairs before the summer sailing season. The Grand Rapids Yacht Club was just around the corner on the lake, and I knew most of the sailors from twenty-five years of western Michigan sailing regattas. It was perfect for my needs, and I signed a three-year lease.

I had not contacted a lawyer because I did not want a court officer knocking on our front door with divorce papers—or any papers, for that matter. My most difficult decision was how to tell my children. Some were old enough, I believed, that my leaving would not be a challenge for them. I knew that if I discussed it first with Jule he might say something to them.

I talked to Jule and the kids the same day. I had packed two suitcases of clothing and toiletries earlier in the day. After I talked to Jule, I left. It was late at night.

The next evening, I drove directly from my Lansing office to Grand Haven. I was very nervous when I entered the house. Nothing was said by Jule, but he made himself scarce ... so much so that I didn't know if he was in the house or not.

The previous renter of my new home had three dogs, and all the carpets reeked of the smell of urine. I offered to pay for new carpeting if the owner would allow it. My landlady was so gracious and agreeable that I felt I could do anything I wanted. I just didn't know what I was getting into. Not only did the carpets have to be removed throughout the house, all the under padding had to be scrapped also, and the wooden floors had to be scrubbed. The smell was defiant, and I worried that the odor might have permeated the walls and draperies and furniture. It turned out to only be in the upholstered furniture, so out it went too. Now pacified, I felt my kids would not be embarrassed by my new digs and would bring their friends to visit. I did not expect my friends to come calling ... and they did not.

After I filed for divorce in 1975, Bill felt free to invite me to Washington with the slimmest of excuses. He planned a meeting in his West Wing offices with Felix Rohatyn in early January 1976, and wanted me to meet the man. Felix was famously known in the New York-to-Washington corridor because of his work as head of the Municipal Assistance Corporation (MAC). He had just saved New York City from bankruptcy, finally getting the help he needed from the White House with the passage of the New York Emergency Finance Act of 1975, which President Ford reluctantly agreed to sign in early December.

I arrived in Washington in the late afternoon and rushed to get through the White House gate security stops in order to arrive in Bill's outer office before his meeting with Felix ended. I was casually dressed for the White House (compared with the men in their striped banker suits), sporting a heavy, double-breasted tan suede pantsuit with matching turtleneck sweater. I'm not sure what Felix was expecting, but he stood up and greeted me warmly, suggesting that we move to the sofa and away from Bill's desk.

Bill just smiled and said, "I thought the two of you should meet because you both are newly divorced."

And then, while I was recovering from that comment, Bill regaled Felix with facts about "our business ventures": I was president and CEO of "our" new FM radio station in Aspen, and we were hoping to get "our" FM signal into Vail, which Bill knew was Felix's favorite ski resort. Felix added that his three teenage sons liked to ski Vail too. I said that I had five children who loved skiing out west.

I asked Felix the purpose of his mission at the White House, bragging that I had spent about twenty years in Republican politics, often working long election campaigns to keep President Ford in his congressional seat when I was a county Republican chairman in the president's old Fifth District in western Michigan.

Felix was very polite, but he was a Democrat, and he obviously had been very frustrated by President Ford's threats to veto any legislation that would help New York City. Felix explained that New York City almost went bankrupt, and MAC had been asking all year long for President Ford's help with federally guaranteed seasonal financing, which New York City finally received in December 1975—just in the nick of time. (And which was probably the reason Felix and Bill were celebrating in Bill's office in early January 1976.)

I returned to Michigan the next day and drove to Grand Haven to fix Brett's dinner. When I walked into the kitchen, the phone was ringing. No one was around, so I answered. It was Felix. I couldn't believe it. How did he find my phone number in Michigan? I'll never know because I never asked him—or Bill—ever.

Felix wanted me to fly to New York the following week. He was having dinner at "21" with Governor Carey and other friends of MAC and was eager for me to meet them.

I accepted quickly before anyone could walk into the kitchen and comment on my phone conversation. I was stunned. This was my first proper invitation for a date since I had moved out of the house, and it came via a telephone that I shouldn't have been answering. Yet the sense of freedom that accompanied my flustered acceptance was overwhelming. I was free! It was exhilarating to be able to make my very own decisions, openly and honestly, for the first time in almost twenty-five years.

Felix did not have the opportunity to offer to pay for any travel or hotel accommodations, but I was used to staying at the Westbury or the Hyde Park hotel—both small but acceptable Upper East Side hotels in the city, and I assumed Felix felt I was wealthy and sophisticated enough to make my own reservations, which I quickly did. And then I spent most of the weekend trying to figure out what to wear to "21," knowing that Felix' gang would be motivated to move up to Elaine's, a trendy Upper East Side restaurant described best by Felix as "an expensive hangout for movie and media stars, authors and reporters, moguls and models," and a place which was used by Felix and the governor to run the city, according to the local tabloids.

When I exited the gate at La Guardia Airport, Felix appeared, looking Scotland Yard diplomatic in his full-length double-breasted trench coat. Felix was nearer my age than Bill's, and his enthusiasm for this first date was evident in his demeanor. He announced that he was driving me into the city in his own car, a handsome, small BMW. It was the first—and only—time that anyone picked me up at a New York airport in his own vehicle. I was duly impressed!

And what I decided to wear that night at "21" seems crazy in retrospect, but I wanted to be Aspen chic, so I wore a quilted jacket with a matching long full skirt that my Grand Haven seamstress had designed and sewn from one of Grandma Secory's old beautiful quilts. I thought it worked. At least it was unique and probably admired for that reason alone.

I was surprised by Felix's slow and conservative consumption of alcohol at dinner. Not quite like our yacht club groupies—or Aspen's J-Bar aficionados. A glass of Kir, maybe two, all evening. I enjoyed Kir too, but, after a short time, I grew tired of the crème de cassis dominating the flavor of the white wine, and only drank Kir when I needed to mask the flavor of a bad white wine.

Governor Carey and the other guests at our table were ebullient, savoring their recent success in saving New York City from bankruptcy. We headed to Elaine's soon after dinner; the atmosphere was electric, almost rowdy, and the drinks flowed for all but Felix. Chaperoning me around had to be serious business. I was his guest from Michigan, from Detroit, and, finally, as the evening wore on, from Grosse Pointe. I believe that was the extent of his knowledge of the Midwest. And to my surprise, I knew a few of the patrons—friends of the Boorsteins or Seidmans who lived in the area. I loved the "in charge" steam that emanated from Elaine's, and I couldn't wait to return.

Felix suggested a skiing rendezvous in Vail with his three sons during their spring break from school. I hesitated. The timing wasn't good for my kids, and I was worried about exposing my boys to a new date on a long weekend's skiing vacation. When Allen and Helen Hunting's elegant Manor Vail condo became available to us that week, I agreed to go and hurried to find three teenage sons who could skip school.

I did not intend to tell Bill Seidman that Felix and his sons would also be in Vail for their skiing vacation. I felt he had put me up to this, introducing me to a "recently divorced" famous guy who liked to go skiing. And this time, it would be on my terrain. I didn't know Elaine's or "21" or the White House, but I knew the Rockies, and I knew how to ski extremely well and so did my kids. I knew what to wear and where to go on the vast slopes and trails of Vail Mountain, and I didn't need any guides. And, coincidentally, Steve Heater would be in Vail with the KSPN-FM radio team covering slalom races that weekend. I would have the excuse and the opportunity to check on our troops.

When I returned to Michigan from New York City, I found the application requirements for the USDA's new Child Care Food Program sitting on my desk. In the fall of 1975, Bill Seidman suggested that I look into the new USDA Child Care Food Program legislation that was specifically designed for preschool children enrolled in licensed day care centers or day care homes. I asked for a name of someone in the USDA who could explain the program and the application requirements, and Bill quickly complied, giving me the name of a minor bureaucrat who knew the importance of timing. I needed a statewide computerized program, especially for the multitudinous day care homes in the state, and I needed a nonprofit entity that could distribute the cash or food supplements to the homes and day care centers.

I thought I could write a computer program for the day care providers because I knew how much they could do and would do to earn the extra $1.50 per child per day that would be reimbursed by the USDA. And the providers would like receiving the free food too, when it was available. Compu-Link had to write their side of the program, and then we had to offer the statewide computerized program to a newly created nonprofit entity, which we named the Association for Child Development (ACD).

Only licensed day care homes and nonprofit licensed day care centers could qualify for the USDA reimbursement. Our eleven private for-profit centers would not qualify. But we were eager to move forward, nevertheless, before someone stole our idea or our customers.

The application needed immediate attention. I wished to be the first one approved in the United States; my plan was known to the bureaucrats in the USDA with whom I had conferred in the fall. I had no choice but to take the application with us to Vail.

As soon as we arrived at the Huntings' ski condo at Manor Vail, I tried to find Felix Rohatyn and his three sons, but I couldn't locate his rental house. The next morning, we skied over to check the schedule for the slalom races and found Steve Heater and KSPN radio announcers setting up for that day's race. I sent the boys off skiing by themselves and offered to help on the slalom course.

I found Felix in the afternoon. He showed up in a shiny purple vest. (Yes, he needed western training from Bill, with the requisite cowboy hat, muddy boots, and open truck or jeep with broom draped over the rear.) Felix explained that he and his three boys would have a busy schedule skiing the mountain with their two instructors all day, every day, but ... he wondered if I would I like to ski with them the next morning.

I told Felix I had three boys with me ... and asked if they could come along too.

His answer was a flat-out no.

Felix repeated that they only had two instructors (as if the boys and I needed any instructors), and the group would be too large, but ... he again offered to accommodate me, stressing "only in the mornings."

"Turkey? You want the dark meat or the light, Sam?" Cartoon
drawing by Julio, Vail, Colorado, March, 1976

I was furious. This trip was Felix's idea. He refused to let his boys ski with mine—or even meet them! Obviously, Felix had made other plans that didn't involve me. After I refused to ski with Felix without my boys, he offered to take me to dinner alone the next night, and I accepted.

The atmosphere was rather cool by the time we met at the restaurant. I hoped to hear about his latest political machinations and business forays—like I'd heard from him in New York City. Felix would have none of it. He just wasn't interested in discussing any business, mine or his. When we talked about our divorces, I told him that I would never marry again.

I don't think Felix had any idea of my very long relationship with Bill. But I knew Felix wasn't going to have a long relationship with me. Felix seemed interested in finding a wife who would play the New York socialite scene for him. I would want to learn his business, not run his house or his charities. And I probably wouldn't be able to appreciate his Democratic strategies after I'd fought for two decades to wrest political control from Michigan's powerful Democratic labor unions. Felix's ability to make deals with the unions and union bosses in New York City seemed crucial to MAC's success in rescuing the city from bankruptcy.

Too bad. I loved Felix's French background and his brilliant mind ... but he wasn't going to share either with me.

The next morning, I knew I had work to do for my USDA Child Care Food Program application. I set the alarm for 6:00 a.m. and turned the ample bathroom of Allen and Helen Hunting's condominium into my new office. I put a breadboard over the sink and dug in, knowing I would want to break at lunchtime to meet the boys on the slopes for an afternoon of skiing.

Fortunately, I now had the time to finish the application before we left Vail. Our application was approved by the USDA within a month. Young World became the manager of the nonprofit ACD and its new statewide computerized food program.

Invitations to join the Child Care Food Program were sent in March 1976, to every licensed day care home or group day care home (up to twelve preschoolers) in the state of Michigan. Because a majority of day care homes in Michigan were unlicensed, we advertised the attributes of the USDA Food Program in newspapers and on radio, hoping to encourage unlicensed day care homes to apply for licensing. By April 1, 1976, the opening day of the program in Michigan, ACD had signed up four hundred licensed day care home providers and most of the nonprofit day care centers. Our new statewide computerized Child Care Food Program—the first in the country—was a financial success from the day it started!

The Association for Child Development moved to larger offices on

Saginaw Street in East Lansing, and soon thereafter, the Young World day care centers converted to nonprofit status.

By the 1970s, Midge and Gary were testing their entrepreneurial mettle, following the long line of their tough, industrious, and oh-so-persevering progenitors.

After Midge joined the dock company in 1959, he switched the focus of the business from coal to aggregates. In 1961, Midge and Dad closed down the retail coal business. But it soon turned out to be a command performance on Midge's part: In May 1962, Dad got a pesky ailment that sidelined him from work for almost a year. And by 1963, Midge had opened their first dock on Muskegon Lake, the major industrial port in western Michigan.

Gary returned from California in the fall of 1968 to join Midge in the management of the dock company. Midge had recently added 600 feet of dock frontage west of the present Ferrysburg docks. They added new dock frontage on Lake Macatawa in Holland that year, and by the time they added 2,000 feet of dock frontage east of the Ferrysburg dock in 1978, the Verplank Dock Company had become the major dock operator on Michigan's western shoreline.

In the mid-1960s, Midge's nightly old-fashioned with a Spring Lake neighbor, Duffy Anderson, would lead to the creation of a major new family company. Duffy was a salesman for Welded Products, a rollforming company that was selling rollformed steel troughs for chicken and turkey feeders to the huge Bil Mar Foods Company in Zeeland, Michigan. Duffy wanted to use this relatively new technology of cold rolling steel through a series of roller dies to make frames for moveable office partitions.

The dock company had an unused warehouse behind the dock offices in Ferrysburg. With two other investors, Midge and Duffy formed the Coastal Rollform Company in 1966. It was too successful; Duffy was the salesman and needed Midge to manage the company, but Midge was swamped running the dock company. In 1969, Midge reluctantly sold Coastal Rollform, and Duffy too, back to the new owner of Welded Products, Technology, Inc., a Dayton, Ohio, rollform company. But the process haunted Midge and Technology's local managers. So...

In 1974, Shape Corporation was founded by original investor Stuart Pearson, the Verplank Dock Company—Midge and recent co-owner brother Gary, and three executives who moved from Technology, Inc.

They set up shop in the same warehouse building used in the 1960s.

Their first big order for rollformed office dividers came from Haworth Furniture Company in Holland. It was a great success, and soon Herman Miller and Westinghouse were using Shape. By 1976, Stuart Pearson wanted out; he was too busy and successful running his Chicago manufacturing company to be bothered with complaints from Shape's manager. Now Midge and Gary would own 85 percent of the ballooning Shape enterprise. Peter Sturrus, an innovative engineer and sales executive, joined Shape in 1977; his tool and die abilities were extraordinary and a great addition to the burgeoning rollform business.

Shape Corporation Founders: Gary Verplank, Midge Verplank, Robert Currier, Ron Kolkema Courtesy of David LaClaire

As soon as Gary took over Shape Corporation as president and CEO, the company broke ground in the mostly vacant Grand Haven Airport Industrial Park, erecting a 30,000-square-foot building. Within two years, increasing sales necessitated a 36,000-square-foot expansion. Shape was on its way, with Gary at the helm and Midge navigating, and they never turned back.

In June 1976, with the tall ships from fourteen countries heading for a stop in Bermuda on their way to celebrate the American bicentennial celebration in New York City on the Fourth of July, many local big boat sailors wanted to participate in the Newport-Bermuda race, a 635-nautical mile biennial race from Newport, Rhode Island, to Bermuda, held in late June in even-numbered years. Our crusty, old, wheelchair-bound Spring Lake Yacht Club C scow skipper, Craig Welch, enlisted all the best local sailors, including Midge, Paul Eggert, Chuck Jacobson, and Bobbie Currier Jr., to crew for him on his sixty-one-foot C & C sloop, *Brassy*.

Lydia was leaving for France in September, to study in the Andover-Exeter School Year Abroad program. I was eager to spend time with Lydia before she left, because this was her first summer living at home in Grand Haven without me around to care for her. I suggested we fly to Bermuda to meet the sailors and see the tall ships that would be anchored in the harbor. And Lydia knew she might be invited to sail the *Brassy* back to Newport if they could get enough responsible adults to accompany them. All our kids knew how to sail; only the parents knew how to chaperone.

The wind was very light for the entire Bermuda race, and the *Brassy* chugged along. *Brassy* did well in heavy air, not this light fluff. Midge said the race was very boring. That would be good news for Lydia and the other young sailors who could take their places on the return voyage to Newport. (Which they did.)

But it wasn't a boring time for me. Lydia and I met the first boat that finished. It was way ahead of the fleet, and the crew invited us to a celebratory dinner. I immediately accepted, but Lydia was wary. She was waiting for the *Brassy*. The crew told her the *Brassy* wouldn't be in for another twelve hours at least, so Lydia came with me but left immediately after dinner. A few crew members wanted to see our fancy digs on the beach; after a hot long race, they wanted to go swimming in the ocean. We had our pick of the motor scooters because so few boats had finished the race. We went swimming … we went cruising … checking the tall ships, checking the bars still open in the middle of the night, checking for *Brassy*… The freedom of it all! My kids said I was living my twenties in my forties, now that I was single. I thought these sailors were all younger than I, but the navigator, who was my favorite, was in his early forties. So was I, but I was used to being around people a decade older. I didn't feel comfortable in my new surroundings. And Lydia knew that; she appeared more mature than I that summer, and she probably was.

Midge liked the new Doug Peterson designed Williwaw that was winning light air SORC (Southern Ocean Racing Conference) races. He ordered a forty-two-foot Peterson-designed aluminum sloop to be built by Palmer Johnson in Sturgeon Bay, Wisconsin, and named it the *Sleeping Bear*.

Paul Eggert was part of the crew for the sloop's first race in June 1977. Paul reported the race in his humorous style:

> They (Midge and Doug Peterson) decided that, due to the light air in this area (Lake Michigan), they would put five feet of extra mast on the *Bear*.
>
> Well—that sounded fast! And the *Bear* had the best equipment that could be had at this point.
>
> So ... our first race, we went out to sail in Lake Michigan, but it was too foggy. We then decided to sail the race in Muskegon Lake. We had a # 2 up, I believe, and we seemed kind of tippy.
>
> *Bang!* The gun goes off. The whole crew looked down at Midge. He's underwater and the rudder is out of water. We have a complete knockdown at the starting line ... with a # 2 up! So we finally ease the jib out and off we go again. The *Bear* is faster than heck.
>
> We get up to the top buoy and set the spinnaker.
>
> *BANG!* Over we go again! *Why* are we having all this trouble? We're thinking maybe we put too much stick on. ('Stick' is the mast.)
>
> So ... the Queen's Cup, an 85-mile race from Milwaukee to Muskegon, is coming up in three days, and we don't know if anybody is going to be sailing with us after that experience.
>
> Anyway—we did sail the *Bear* in that race and in several other Queen's Cups and Mackinac races *and* won a Queen's Cup, a Chicago-Mackinac *and* a Port Huron-Mackinac race.

With Jack Reichardt on the epiphany porch

After graduating from Yale in June 1976, Fritz decided to take a year off before starting Yale's new master's degree program in public and private management. Fritz claims his interest in fine wines emanated from an "epiphanic" experience tasting a heavenly wine on his godmother Libby Reichardt's Spanish verandah overlooking Spring Lake. When he found out that Libby's son, Field, was opening a new boutique wine-and-cheese shop in the trendy East Grand Rapids shopping center just one block from my house on Reed's Lake, Fritz offered to help, although he worried that he had no experience as a "salesman." I watched, amused, as Fritz helped an elderly lady decide which wines to buy for each course of her dinner party, then open the door and take the packages to her car. I kidded Fritz, telling him that if he handled every sale that way, he would be considered the best wine salesman in western Michigan. And by the end of summer, his detailed knowledge of wine far outpaced my twenty years of buying the best French vintages from Chicago's top wine purveyors.

Fritz would drop in after work at my lakeside house, and if it was late, he would spend the night. One evening, I was entertaining a family friend, a bachelor, and I realized that this presented an awkward setting for Fritz, who was used to seeing me with one suitor only. And that one was working in the White House or running around the country trying to get President Ford reelected—not an easy task with Governor Reagan nipping at Ford's heels the entire primary season. After that painful episode with Fritz, I did not invite anyone other than Dr. Duncan Littlefair and his faithful followers to my cozy home.

It was a bumpy ride for me that summer, and I wasn't navigating around the buoys very well. ... But the freedom! It was exhilarating! It was exciting! Hold on ... and stay on board.

Nevertheless, Bill Seidman could not campaign that summer with me on board; as part of the White House team, he was too exposed. And now he was too busy chairing Ford's Economic Policy Board and campaigning against an unexpectedly strong primary foe. Reagan's primary fight was costing Ford conservative votes, and Ford barely won renomination, winning by a meager 117 out of 2,257 votes.

I watched from the sidelines with mixed emotions. Bill said that he could never divorce while working for President Ford. And I knew he wouldn't. He and Sally were now entrenched in the swirl of Washington politics and social life; they lived only a few short blocks from Katharine Graham, the powerhouse publisher and owner of the *Washington Post*. The *Post*'s exposé of Nixon's Watergate caper by reporters Woodward and Bernstein provided Graham with quick access to President Ford's table at the White House. And in later years, Bill would laugh about hitting her directly in the eye during a rough tennis game. ... How they both loved to play!

I paid little attention to the political scene in the fall. As soon as Lydia left for France in September, I ferreted out my best buddy, Harriet Newman, to convince her to leave her work in Detroit with the Michigan Heart Association and move to her old hometown, Chicago, to run our Child Care Food Program for the state of Illinois. Getting her organized and finding the right location in LaGrange took time. She knew no one from the Michigan organization who could help her in Chicago except me, and I didn't like to spend more than a day or two on any business visit.

Celebrating with best buddy Harriet Newman

But Harriet was successful early on. What a personality! A hug for everyone, and people loved her. And the day care home mothers loved their reimbursement checks. Free food distribution was haphazard, but their monthly checks were not. A computerized system was set up that mimicked our Michigan schedule. Harriet plowed into the depths of South Chicago and made friends quickly with the local community leaders, including Jesse Jackson.

Aspen, too, turned out to be a lucrative location for our Child Care Food Program. Our longtime friends, Peter and Nancy Van Domelen, had made a surprising move to Aspen in 1973. Peter was in his prime as a lawyer at Warner, Norcross, and Judd in Grand Rapids, and Nancy was working actively in the East Grand Rapids school system. Their four children were a little younger than our five. Nancy and Peter's talents were quickly recognized in the small Aspen community: Peter became KSPN's attorney; Nancy became intrigued by the Wildwood School, a fascinating innovative new facility that stressed the importance of environmental education for preschool children.

Nancy Van Domelen at Wildwood School, 1970s

The creator of the school was Robert B. Lewis, idealistic visionary, biologist, educator, inventor, filmmaker, and publisher. About the founding of Wildwood School, Bob wrote in 1973:

> The need today for environmental education is now accepted as unquestionable by more and more thoughtful people. ... Recently in the United States courses on ecology and environmental control have sprung up in secondary schools and universities in response to popular demand. ... Nearly all, however, lack the disciplinary coherence provided by a continuing organizational base. In contrast to these patchwork efforts, the Wildwood School in Aspen, Colorado, represents a sustained long-term approach to environmental education.
>
> Wildwood is a pre-school ... whose goal is to foster an environmental ethic during a person's earliest, most receptive years. ...

For those of us enamored of the Rockies lifestyle, this concept, this "environmentally ethical" curriculum, would be music to our ears, and that included Annie and John Denver. Annie was very actively participating with their children in Wildwood's activities in the 1970s. I couldn't wait to invite our city-bred preschool administrators and teachers to summer sessions in Aspen—or to invite Bob Lewis to come to Michigan to talk about his environmental preschool programs.

Nor could I wait to ask Nancy Van Domelen to develop a statewide computerized Child Care Food Program for Colorado. I knew no one in the field of education in Colorado. Nancy seemed to know everyone. And with her skill sets, she wouldn't need me once the program was initiated. Although Nancy knew Wildwood School, a not-for-profit child care center, could be included in the food program, she quickly broadened the scope of the program and opened a Denver office. She was off and running, and I could admire her work from our KSPN studios in the Jerome Hotel basement.

In 1977, when I made plans to rent a house along the Roaring Fork River in Aspen, our KSPN-FM manager, Steve Heater, started feeling the heat of my presence; he didn't like losing his power position. I might be the president of Recreation Broadcasting, but he was the boss of KSPN-FM, and I usually wasn't around.

Steve Heater discussing business with Peter and Nancy Van Domelen

Steve had built a strong FM team, with golden-voiced morning anchor Lee Duncan and young, chic Pat Miles, in her typical Aspen quilted vest, hard charging the news. And what news there was! When Claudine Longet (former wife of pop star Andy Williams) shot and killed her Olympic skier boyfriend, "Spider" Sabich, in March 1976, there was an uproar about her guilt and trial until she was convicted of misdemeanor negligent homicide in the winter of 1977. I remember CBS's *60 Minutes* demanding to televise our news people while they were reporting the story live "on air." CBS's *60 Minutes* had a nasty reputation for finding fault with just about anything they were covering, and I did not want them near our station. Our staff felt differently; they wanted the publicity. I don't remember seeing the result of their inquiries. But the publicity propelled Pat Miles out of KSPN radio news and into the top CBS TV station in Minnesota, where she was a star anchor for decades.

Chapter Six

MANY BASES OF OPERATIONS

From left: Lydia, Davy Seibold, Gary (holding Ashley),
Julio, Brett, Greg, Joyce, Fritz

Jerry Ford lost to Jimmy Carter in November 1976, but Bill Seidman didn't rush to leave Washington, DC. Ford made sure that all his faithful followers had the opportunity to travel far and wide with their families before January 20, 1977. I remember Bill saying that it would be foolish not to take advantage of this largesse. Besides, for three years, he had not taken a salary that was commensurate with his lifestyle. After travels abroad in December and New Year's celebrations down south with his family, Bill would have to figure out a way to move out and move on.

While Bill was traveling with his family, I celebrated the Christmas season alone in my Grand Rapids bungalow—and that experience turned out to be tougher on Mom and Dad than it was on me. They couldn't believe that Grammy Hatton would spirit off all of my children and Jule to Paris to join Lydia during Christmas break. Grammy Hatton knew everyone missed Lydia, who had been in Rennes, France, on the Andover-Exeter School Year Abroad program since September. And Grammy also knew how much Jule loved France and how much Fritz loved French wine. Greg reported that they all loved floating into Paris for two weeks of "material and cultural bliss."

Lydia sent me a letter in early January requesting that I put off my February trip to France and come in May instead, at the end of their school year. I was upset to hear how she regretted the two weeks with her family; she felt like a stranger back in her Rennes environment, claiming that she had lost both her French linguistic abilities and her closeness to her French family.

After Bill Seidman spotted an article in the *Wall Street Journal*, he suggested we look into the new UHF television station licenses that were being offered by the FCC on a competitive basis in smaller cities. The "public interest" requirements of the FCC were the same mixture that had been required for FM radio: community involvement with local ownership, including minorities; financial resources; and experience in the industry. Well ... I could do that. I'd worked for almost a decade on FM radio applications and all the translator requirements of the FCC that were needed to get an FM signal around the Rockies.

We started by putting together a list of the top fifty markets that were offering a low range of UHF signals—from UHF-14 to about UHF-35. (The higher the number, the weaker the UHF signal. VHF signals, by contrast, are all strong from 2 through 13). We picked three likely scenarios: UHF channel 23 in Albany, UHF-15 in Omaha, and UHF-16 in Little Rock. This was going to be fun, and it would give Bill and me an excuse to travel the country together.

Bill didn't consider this project a full-time occupation, and it wouldn't provide any immediate income. He joined the board of New York-based Phelps Dodge Corporation, a huge copper company that was being run by his friend from Dartmouth College, George Munroe. Bill soon became its chief financial officer.

I liked the fact that Bill still had his garden apartment in New York City, in a classic brownstone on 67th Street; I could have a base of operations from which to work on the Albany television application. And soak up all the culture of New York City with the peripatetic Priscilla Morgan. Larger than life, Priscilla occupied a grand first-floor apartment above Bill's, and she sniffed out talent in all directions—from the love of her life, famous sculptor Isamu Noguchi, to a prospective Albany UHF-TV board member, movie and television director, Arthur Penn. (We all knew *Bonnie and Clyde,* which had enjoyed great success at the box office.)

According to Arthur:

Priscilla Morgan, who had her own talent agency and later joined the William Morris Agency, represented a number of writers and directors— and, I am happy to say—me as a director. She was a most unusual agent. She was not concerned with "the deal." Priscilla ran a salon. Her instinct for introducing and encouraging talented people whom she perceived, in her magical way, would produce plays, musicals films, festivals and chamber concerts was astonishing. Painters, sculptors, matchless designers graced her dinners. Her gift for lasting friendships is very much present. An invitation to Priscilla's suggests an evening of good talk, sometimes heated, but always nourishing.

In the late 1950s, Priscilla embarked on a new project with composer Gian Carlo Menotti to recruit artists for his Festival of Two Worlds, in Spoleto, Italy. Saul Steinberg designed the cover for the 1969 Spoleto Festival book, and Priscilla gave me a huge signed poster of the cover, which hangs on my wall today. After the success of the Spoleto in Italy, Priscilla secured a grant from the National Endowment for the Arts to search for a site to house an American Spoleto Festival. In 1977, they chose Charleston, South Carolina, as the permanent home of Spoleto Festival, USA. My godchild, established artist Elizabeth Newman, Harriet and Tom Newman's daughter, would be invited more than a decade later to display her artistic work at the American Spoleto Festival.

The artist Christo has called Priscilla "the great connector" … and she soon would be showing us her magic.

I was working in my old Young World offices in April 1977, on a contract that would turn over the day-to-day management of ACD and Young World to Marge Langworthy, when, suddenly, a telegram was handed to me by my secretary. I could tell by the look on her face that it was bad news—bad news from the Andover-Exeter School Year Abroad office in Rennes, France. It was short, too short for this Mom: "An Andover female student has been killed on a moped in Rennes."

Everyone in the office kept reassuring me that it couldn't be Lydia; they rationalized that I would have received a personal phone call, instead of a telegram, from the school. I waited for word. … It seemed an eternity, but it probably was less than an hour. Then I received a telegram from Lydia: the student in question was her best friend, killed by a drunken driver who crossed the road onto the moped path. Lydia had to make plans for the funeral because the girl's parents were too old and upset to deal with arrangements for a service in Europe.

I wanted to go to France immediately. I was forty-four years old; I felt strong and healthy and free to move quickly. Lydia had been very sick that winter in her French household. I had not seen Lydia in nine months, and I no longer trusted their system to handle her needs.

But when I talked to Lydia, she did not want me to come right away. She would handle the funeral service. She wanted me to arrive at the end of her year abroad program, as planned, to take her and four or five of her favorite classmates to Paris. Lydia complained that they all were sick of being cooped up in the wet, cold, boring regional town of Rennes, and they were ready to see, feel, and enjoy "the material and cultural bliss" of Paris.

Now, if Lydia were true to Hatton tradition, she would be planning a blowout week in Paris. I asked where she would like to go after her classmates were scooped up or put on a plane by their parents. The Greek islands! A sunny island in a warm Mediterranean Sea surrounded by ancient archeological sites must have sounded heavenly to Lydia after suffering through a cold, blustery winter in northwestern France.

Rennes proved to be everything Lydia said it was: old, dark, bleak, and wet. And her French home? When Lydia opened the door, I thought I would pass out: the interior was a smoky haze. I asked if every resident in the house smoked. Yes, including the grown kids. Now I knew why she had bronchitis for half the winter. And she wasn't casually sick—flat in bed with fever and a cough, according to her letters. And she wasn't smoking, which seemed a miracle, too. But with a French family that spoke no English, Lydia spoke French fluently. Hoorah for School Year Abroad! But what a price to pay.

My red sedan with big open sunroof was jammed with suitcases and four classmates as we rushed to Paris from Rennes. The kids made sure I had a room, and they flopped everywhere ... I can't even remember exactly where. Nevertheless, there were two experiences I will never forget. First, the open sunroof gorged with all of them standing while I circled the Arc de Triomphe and sped down every main road around the city—it was the last week of May, and perfect weather for open-air sightseeing. Second, our dinner at the Ritz Hotel, with waiters passing around cigars after dinner;

all the boys took one, and I accepted one too—and smoked it, accompanied by a snifter of cognac. The boys thought it was hilarious. I don't remember what Lydia thought. Probably just as well.

What a delight Lydia's classmates were: bright, energetic, enthusiastic, creative students in the prime of their young lives. Matt Salinger's famous Dad was coming to pick him up early, and I hated to see him leave. All of Lydia's gang were *so* appreciative of the fact that I made this Paris adventure possible.

On to Athens, Greece. Buddy Melges, our famous inland racing scow sailor, designer, and builder, had sold Melges sailboats to a few wealthy Greeks, and he called one to find a place for Lydia and me to vacation for a week. They suggested Ayios Nikolaos, a very popular summer harbor on the northeastern coast of Crete. I thought it would be another party week, but Lydia was not in that kind of mood. She wanted to stay clear of the local touristy bars, knowing she would be accosted by Greek youths who were on the prowl. Instead, Lydia wanted to prowl the ruins of the ancient Minoan civilization, which was at its height in 2000 BCE. We toured the palace of Knossos and 8,000-foot Mount Ida, which Lydia remembered best for all its windmills.

Lydia said it was a good trip. But I recall our eleven-hour flight home from Athens; we were stuck in the last row of an old DC-10 with straight-up seats that would not recline, making it a miserably stiff homecoming for me.

By the spring of 1977, I started to worry that I had overstretched in my eagerness to have many bases of operation. After we moved the ACD offices to East Lansing, I agreed to share an apartment in East Lansing with Mary Creason. I still had my house in Grand Rapids … and soon a year-round house in Aspen.

Important groups coming to Aspen that summer were administrators of our Young World day care centers and some of our ACD administrative staff. I planned a two-week seminar based on the environmental curriculum developed by Bob Lewis for Wildwood School. The flora and fauna of the Rockies would be their laboratory to learn basic facts about the fragile ecological balance of life on our planet.

As soon as the group arrived, I realized that I had not anticipated their inability to acclimatize to the 8,000-foot altitude of the Roaring Fork valley floor. They would be hiking soon to 9,000 or 10,000 feet. Hardly any were athletically inclined, and none were in top physical shape; that wasn't in their job description. Our ACD leader, Marge Langworthy, had an altitude headache every day during her two-week sojourn in Aspen. After only a few days of hiking, my favorite bookkeeper, Mary Ruttan, slipped down a shallow path, hit a rock, and broke her arm. Part of Bob Lewis's protocol for Wildwood School required teachers to set an example for the preschoolers by their choice of activities. We had a long way to go, but this would be my last attempt in Aspen's rigorous terrain.

I did invite Bob Lewis to Michigan in the fall. He was eager to accept and lecture on the "environmental ethic" for preschoolers. I set up meetings and lectures for him, both with small groups of preschool teachers and a larger group of educators in northern Michigan. I thought nothing of traveling alone with Bob up north, but my staff thought otherwise. They believed we were more than friends, which we definitely were not, although Bob enjoyed giving that impression to everyone.

Back in Aspen, I put the heat on Steve Heater. His rather grim personality did not endear him to the staff, and his work at the Pueblo FM station for the past few years had not resulted in positive numbers there. It needed to be sold. Steve told the other board members that I just needed his job to justify my move to Aspen and that I was not equipped to handle the manager's post. I don't know what the board members thought about me, but I do know they were not very happy with Steve's Pueblo operation. The board knew I was shedding my day-to-day child care responsibilities in Lansing and spending more time on our three UHF television broadcast station applications, especially in New York.

The board paid Steve to sell the Pueblo FM station and help with an "orderly transition" of management. Steve kept his stock in Recreation Broadcasting Company, and I took control of KSPN-FM in July 1977.

It would be a rocky road ahead. The market was tiny, and my vision was grand. The only way to grow was by expanding the reach through microwave towers and translators. Satellite and Internet transmission were not on my horizon.

That was not the only rocky road that summer. Bill Seidman had been asked to join the Aspen Institute, and he graciously arranged for me to become a member too. He thought most of them a bunch of pompous faux intellectuals, but he knew I would love the Great Books classes, especially the ones with the well-known University of Chicago philosopher, Mortimer Adler.

The institute had the topic of Governance as the theme for their

Thought-Leading-to-Action seminars. John Gardner (founder of Common Cause) was their pedagogic leader. Although Bill did not seem much interested in the institute program—perhaps because he'd had enough "governance" for the past four years—he was always willing to take me, and sometimes my kids, to faraway events, the first one of which was on the big island of Hawaii, where we found the climate and the geology of Punalu'u less than inviting. It was the inaugural event for the Aspen Institute of Hawaii, but the cool, gale-force trade winds and blowing black sand kept us away from most of the outdoor activities. (The harsh climate must have negatively affected other institute visitors too. After a few years, the facility was abandoned because of deterioration.)

When Bill showed up for a week's visit at our Aspen house, he seemed very frustrated with my kids, bullying both of them around the house. I wrote in my diary:

> Bill was showing them his insecurity. If he were mellow, relaxed, and laid-back while he was here, he would have shown a comfortable and relaxed acceptance of the present situation. He can't accept it, because I find it untenable. Bill claims to be planning his divorce; therefore, he shouldn't come back to Aspen until his precarious position changes...

Mortimer Adler's seminars on Aristotle's *Ethics* didn't help my quandary. (Is the good that which is desirable? Or is the good that which we ought to desire?) How many of our decisions are truly ethical? Especially for the uninitiated? And who should make these choices? And if I make it, how do I know I finally have arrayed enough knowledge around me to make a right choice? Not a gallant decision, exuding confidence and courage in having done it. But right. For me. For my offspring.

I found the following notes about Bill and my travails jotted down in a marking pen across an old *New York Times* newspaper (probably written while listening to Adler's philosophical lectures at the institute):

> (We have) ... enjoyment and appreciation and respect for the value judgments made, and reciprocity of a commitment freely given, under tremendous pressures resulting from inherited social stigmas attached to such a commitment. ...

Why do we have such a long-standing interest in each other? Somewhat consuming? Wanting to be independent, yet together? A maddening, infuriating relationship. Frustrating.

But what in our childhoods made us attract? Achieving fathers? Attending mothers? Similar interests, such as sports, politics, outdoors? Not art, not music, not education, not parental interests. Disagreements abound, whether basic or tied to commitments previously made and already implemented, private schooling the obvious example.

My smart and stealthy Provincial House business associate, Jeff Poorman, took me out of the management tangle of profit versus nonprofit that had erupted with the surprising success of our nonprofit Child Care Food Program, now active in Michigan, Illinois, and Colorado. In August 1977, Jeff sent a memorandum to Pat Callihan, president of Provincial House, recommending a new agreement with me, Young World, and our nonprofit, the Association for Child Development.

Jeff knew I only wanted to work part time in the day care business. Provincial House cut my ownership of Young World by 20 percent and released me from my contract. Jeff felt the long-term health of the day care business was only in nonprofit centers because of the state and federal government's higher reimbursements for those centers; he suggested we lease our day care centers to the ACD. It was tough for me to keep up with Jeff's speedy yet subtle maneuvers. I became a consultant to both Young World and the ACD, with no direct line to management.

My fall schedule seemed more complicated than ever before. I needed to pursue the three UHF television licenses. The requirements for the UHF-TV application in Albany had to be tackled first, because the deadline for filing was January 30, 1979, less than eighteen months away. The two major time hurdles to be overcome were bank financing and land acquisition for tower placement. We needed an initial $2 million commitment from a reputable New York bank, and we needed to quickly hire a television tower engineer. Those were my specific assignments. I did not have money to invest, but I had the time and knowledge to earn my 10 percent share of the Albany station.

Bill Seidman picked out Manufacturers Hanover Trust Company and accompanied me to our first meeting. I would need to put together a portfolio of information that required weeks, if not months, of planning and review: decade-long cash flow projections, engineering costs for tower and studios, population coverage of a UHF-23 signal, programming costs for movie libraries, stockholder lists and personal financial statements, competition in the market place—all and more were required to satisfy "Mannie Hannie's" first-ever independent television station loan. And every time I went back to the bank, I did not know if they would make the commitment. Or if they would make it in time to meet our application deadline. I had all my eggs in one basket. Bill may have had backup that he wasn't telling me about. Better to have me scared for a year that my efforts would blow up at the last minute.

I wasn't worried about the land acquisition for the television tower because there was a tower farm in the Helderberg Mountains just southwest of town, which was home to most of the FM and TV communication towers. There had to be a piece of land available.

And now the fun part: the stockholders. We needed some board members from Albany, including women and minorities, some with the financial wherewithal to impress Mannie Hannie, and some with broadcasting experience. (Whew … I am finally included in the mix.)

Bill's first candidate was Richard (Dick) Dunham, who served with Bill in the Ford administration. Although Dick was still working in DC, he often returned home to Loudonville, a suburb of Albany. Dick brought us Ray Schuler of the Business Council of New York, and Carl Touhey. From Loudonville, Dick invited Norm Hurd, a PhD, and Laura Kirby-Nigro.

Priscilla Morgan found movie producer Arthur Penn, who owned a home in Stockbridge, Massachusetts, a small village just twenty miles east of Albany. And Priscilla convinced another western Massachusetts native, famous horse aficionado Judy Juhring, to join forces with us.

Now it was my turn. I couldn't wait to ask Allen and Jane Boorstein to become shareholders in our Albany venture. They were longtime personal friends of Jule's, Allen having graduated with Jule from the Harvard Business School in 1950. I worried about their reaction to finding Jule not part of our equation anymore. But Allen and Jane, sophisticated New Yorkers, knew Bill Seidman by reputation and respected his political and business judgment. They were happy to entertain Bill with me or Sally. (Jane would joke that she never knew whether Bill would show up at their Park Avenue doorstep with me or Sally. Ouch … that hurt, especially knowing that Allen and Jane could be entertaining my kids too, who were close friends with their artistic and talented entrepreneurial son, Jimmy.) Allen not only became an enthusiastic investor in Albany TV-23, he also bought a small share of Recreation Broadcasting Company stock.

During one of the boys' Doris Avenue summer bashes, a lovely, somewhat petite blonde perched on the living room steps. She was about my age, I surmised, and she looked vaguely familiar. The kids smiled knowingly. No one said anything. Finally, Jule walked in. How long was I to be tortured? None of my business, for sure. I should be happy that he found a girlfriend. A steady girlfriend. This was going someplace. But so soon? And to think I had taken nothing from the house. No pictures, no wedding gifts. Oh, oh. … Pretty stupid on my part not to think of that. I just assumed everything would be going to the kids. My kids, not someone else's. I asked my divorce lawyer (long since discharged) if I would be in trouble if I started to "lift" things from the house. He said no, but he suggested I take only pictures and a few wedding gifts that were special to me.

Jule said nothing to the family about a wedding. In February 1978, Jule and Nancy snuck off to Minneapolis to get married. The children seemed hurt that their Dad would get married without consulting them or inviting them. And to someone with three grown children, to boot. I was out of this picture, so I only heard the complaints. Thank goodness most of them were in school or not at home to vent openly to their dad.

My three-year lease in East Grand Rapids was up in 1978, and my apartment lease with Mary Creason in East Lansing had been terminated too. Now I needed a new place. Would Bill Seidman come to the rescue? We found a house on the low hills leading up to Independence Pass; it had a sunny corner porch facing Aspen Mountain to the south and west. And the price was right.

I was not too happy; this was not my Aspen dream house, nor was it in a classy locale like my past seasonal rental houses—two on the river and one on Pitkin Green. Bill wasn't bothered at all by the location; he urged me to buy it. I knew Bill would be unwilling to finance an authentic pricey Aspen Victorian or Red Mountain location. I finally agreed. Then Bill surprised me by suggesting that I borrow the 10 percent deposit from Dad. Bill said he would help me find a mortgage, which I assumed he would have to guarantee. Since it was going to be my house, Dad agreed to the loan.

The house was ample for my whole family: three bedrooms on the first floor, and down a narrow spiral staircase, two more bedrooms, a sitting room, a Pullman kitchen, and an outside separate entrance with a path up the hill to the parking lot. My kids loved it, and the KSPN staff eagerly eyed the lower level. They knew I would be renting it out. By 1978, the working locals were being pushed out of town and down valley by the rising costs for employee housing. Our beautiful bookkeeper, Kathy McEuen, was my first occupant.

My second foreign Aspen Institute seminar with Bill Seidman was a long weekend trip in the spring of 1978 to West Berlin. I promised my kids letters. Here are some excerpts:

> What a surprise Berlin is! I never thought the Germans so frivolous as to devote half of their city to greenery. Everywhere, Bill and I found forests, parks, flowers, lakes and rivers. All within the city limits of West Berlin. Perhaps I didn't realize the effect of my World War II upbringing on my attitude toward the city and the people. Certainly, viewing *Holocaust* for three nights prior to departure was no help.
>
> The director of the Aspen Institute of Berlin, Shepard Stone, served under John McCloy, US High Commissioner for Germany after World War II, and enjoyed a warm, personal friendship with the current chancellor of the Federal Republic of Germany, Helmut Schmidt. And when the chancellor arrived at 6:00 p.m. to lead the Friday seminar discussions, we knew this was going to be a very long evening. Cocktails were served outside while the chancellor was surrounded by a mixture of guests, security guards, police dogs, and spotlights. After all, East Germany was directly across the lake.
>
> To quote one of the guests, Zygmunt Nagorski (a Pole who walked from Warsaw to Paris via Hungary in 1940) in his East-West Report: "There is probably no place on earth where the inhumanity of man to man comes through in a more dramatic, more telling way, than in Berlin. The wall is still there. Erected many years ago, it has grown old, infamous and odious. It no longer stands alone. On the Eastern side it is hugged by barbed wire fences, anti-tank obstacles and a no-man's land that looks like huge parking lots without cars in them. ..."

We were happy to return to our lovely indoor restaurant setting (which had been quickly searched by police) and settle around small intimate tables for six. After an introductory toast by Shep Stone, Aspen Institute chairman Bob Anderson, who was also chairman of Atlantic Richfield Co., talked about energy and oil, and then, Chancellor Schmidt addressed our group. He spoke in a warm and relaxed manner; as an economist, he showed much candor and concern for our seminar topic, "Financing the Future," and he worried about financing the future of the East and West German industrial complex. According to Zyg Nagorski, arrangements between the two Germanys, based on the concept of one nation but two states, had allowed a flow of East German goods to the Common Market under the label of "Made in Germany."

Helmut Schmidt made me realize, for the first time, that our American currency was truly the world's currency—and our responsibility. I was thrilled and surprised at the chancellor's energetic participation in our Aspen Institute seminar ... and I stayed until our dynamic, chain-smoking, sixty-year-old chancellor left "reluctantly" at 2:00 a.m.

"Checkpoint Charlie" was awesome and infuriating! Finally, on Sunday afternoon, we were dropped off at the checkpoint. I took only my passport and forty marks. No sweater, film, etc. We were warned that newspapers would be confiscated. We had an eerie feeling that our passports, when handed over for examination, might not come back. We had to exchange 6.5 D marks for East German marks. We were determined to spend them, knowing they would do us no good elsewhere. We couldn't believe the empty feeling of the entire downtown area: hardly any cars on the streets; hardly any people. Stores were few but appeared well stocked. Trees were growing on roofs of bombed out buildings. But no graffiti anywhere. The soldiers at the peace memorial looked more warlike than peaceful. The groups of soldiers on streets made us feel unwelcome, but we were not hassled about our purchases, and they even accepted our West German marks.

By Monday morning, I had accomplished making one purchase: a new camera. And while taking pictures on our way to the airport, I wondered if the Aspen Institute's next long-weekend seminar shouldn't be about what we want to be "Financing *in* the Future."

I commented in my diary that it was difficult that spring to know where Bill Seidman was going: ahead of the curve in business, public or private, but back in the womb when it came to family. He cast himself in the image of his father when it came to fatherly duties, stating that he would be there when they needed him. I sensed Bill was too concerned about his community image; he didn't want to be seen as the bad guy leaving his marriage after thirty-five years. Hadn't he left twenty-five years before? But was I misplacing my values? I did not admire his dependence on others, but was I blind to my own? We both lived in the community and enjoyed others together;

but no one can be loyal to everyone, sitting on both sides at the same time. I saw him straddling the middle, teetering, unstable in new situations.

By July 1978, I was established comfortably in our Mountain Laurel Drive house. I had listened to Margaret Mead, the famous anthropologist , in her late seventies at the time, talk at a Sunday morning service in Snowmass about the future and the value of space exploration. *Quest* magazine had written an article the previous year about Margaret Mead's personal life. Every morning she would rise, be vibrantly alive, happy to be alive and have the opportunity to explore the world around her—no matter how small, insignificant, or mundane the subject matter might be—forever curious, thinking, exploring, synergizing, and so forth.

Since the article caught me at a time in my life where my morning activities were in a state of flux, I felt that I dwelled almost too much on what to do, what direction to take. I often physically felt like doing one thing but mentally rejected it, reminding myself that I would again regret that I had let one more day slip by without taking the time to think, to ruminate, hopefully write something down, to discipline myself to write it out completely, and also to let myself go, wander in the world of words, rely on my own ideas (my children criticized me for quoting others to make a point), have faith that what I think has value, if only to me.

I did wander that morning in the world of words, and wrote:

Create, for value? ... Read to write. Listen to speak. Look to draw—sculpt—photo—print.

Compete, fight, win—for what? What is "right"? Do I have the right to force my view (my "values") on my children, using a blood binding that ties up their minds? Only releasing them when I decide they are ripe, ready to receive other instruction (other values)? Otherwise, why are mine not different from me? And how could they be different? They sense the parent right from birth. They learn to walk, talk, and act like their parents. (What about adopted children? Less so, different structure, different chemistry—but more so than any other influence.)

Happiness—that elusive description of our finite pursuit—does not enter into the picture of child influencing.

God. Supreme Being, all knowledgeable, infinite, timeless, unable to be comprehended or explained or understood or rationalized. Still— invented? A necessary invention for the weak, the insecure? Why not an embarrassment to thinking men? To homo sapiens? To "civilized" people?

Prayers. Offered up at an innocent age … to train the impressionable minds in "right thinking."' Steer their course down a smooth path? Less dangerous than finding the answer for themselves? And how do they go about finding the answer? How nonprejudicial can child rearing be? Why not teachers with diverse values to influence, educate, train, lead, expose, demand, etc.?

What path? Right, wrong, maybe. Black, white, gray. Kind, cruel, honest. Love, hate, tolerate. Give, take, impregnate. Comprehend, idolize, rationalize. Barbarize, civilize, comprise. Grow, exist, live.

Well … I did not wander long in the world of words. Lydia was visiting, helping to paint the KSPN radio studios. Between old late-night movies in French and early morning tennis games and meetings with radio staff, we were running rather ragged around the edges. And I tried to fit in Aspen Institute activities, knowing their summer season was a short two months.

At the institute's panel discussion on energy—a rehash of our Berlin weekend—I ran into Libby and Doug Cater, friends from the Washington, DC, suburbs and now Aspen Institute regulars, who reported that they had just rented Bill and Sally's house in Georgetown for a year. Since Bill and I had played tennis with them in Washington in 1974 and again recently in Aspen, this announcement by them was quite a surprise. I knew I was not accepted in the rare atmosphere of the institute members—a "local" (working locally), divorced, traveling around the world to all their "in" meetings with a married man, and not joining the ladies' activities. (In Hawaii, I typed speeches for six to nine hours.) I was forever out of favor with the ladies in this older age group. Yet … I enjoyed being there alone, independent, and probably cocky. I didn't have to depend on someone else for a raison d'être. (Or did I?)

My new home was Aspen, but the pull of the Great Lakes in the summertime was still an overwhelming force. I managed to remain in Aspen over the Fourth of July holidays, knowing that KSPN had many civic obligations, whether they be parades or pedal races, but I was shocked and hurt to be told by Brett that he didn't want me to show up for the WMYA annual regatta at Muskegon Lake during the second week of August. Brett claimed that he had won most regattas on his new sixteen-foot MC scow with me as crew, and no one thought he could win a regatta without me as his crew.

I hadn't missed a WMYA regatta since my first regatta at Crystal Lake in 1949! Mom and Dad would be there. They never missed a regatta, either. My brother Midge was the WMYA resident agent. Brett would be sailing against mostly older sailors, like my brother Gary or "Happy" Fox or Larry Price, guys I had sailed with or against for twenty-five years.

So how did Brett sail while I sulked in Aspen? Proud Uncle Midge called me after handing Brett the huge first-place trophy. Brett got four firsts and a second over four days of racing. Midge hardly mentioned that the light air meant that Brett needed no crew—and the other sailors needed to shed a few pounds to keep even with Brett, who, at fifteen years of age, was little and slight. But Brett made no mistakes: no recalls, no fouls, no buoys or boats hit. Our sailing family was so proud of him, especially Grandma and Grandpa Verplank. I was so sad to miss it all.

Brett accepting first-place MC Scow trophy
from Uncle Midge Verplank, August 1978

The fall of 1978 brought a flurry of activity on the UHF television front. Bill Seidman called "Woody" Varner in Lincoln, Nebraska. Bill had known Woody from his work at MSU's Oakland campus, which Woody developed in 1959—about the same year that Bill started GVSC. Bill hoped Woody could bring together a group of citizens who would satisfy the FCC requirements for the Omaha UHF TV-15 application.

After serving as president of the University of Nebraska (NU) from 1970 to 1977, D. B. "Woody" Varner became chairman of the University of Nebraska Foundation. Woody turned out to be the perfect choice. He was known for his diplomacy, kindness, trust, and integrity. Bill Fitzgerald from Commercial Federal Savings & Loan and Gene Conley from Guarantee Mutual were two of his first candidates. Dr. Bernice Stephens Dodd, the young executive director of the Omaha Opportunities Industrial Center

(OIC), had recently mounted a successful fund-raising drive to build a new center and was interested in our television project. Bill and Woody set up an October meeting in Omaha, and I organized the details ... like the "advance man" in our political campaigns.

Bill and I stopped in Michigan before heading east to New York City and then back to Omaha. While Bill had to deal with an angry public hearing over the condemned roof on the new Grand Valley State University (GVSU) field house, Duncan Littlefair and I ducked into a cozy corner of the Peninsular Club, where he was surrounded by adoring friends and lunchtime waitresses. Duncan, now sixty-five, was looking forward to retirement as minister of Fountain Street Church, but his popularity was at its peak. His majestic sermons were delivered to a packed congregation in a " ... piercing theatrical voice that brings it all together, giving meaning to the experience of simply being there"—as described by Michael William Grass in his book *Littlefair.*

..."In a piercing theatrical voice that brings it all together, giving meaning to the experience of simply being there." Description and photo by Michael William Grass

Duncan's godless liberal theology still appealed to me. Nevertheless, I believed his congregation revered the godly spacious sanctuary of Fountain Street Church, with its rich stained-glass windows and ornate gold-tiled lobby. And with a very talented organist playing heavy classics as well as the traditional hymns, the parishioners could feel very comfortably entertained in the heretical atmosphere of Duncan's Sunday sermonizing.

How I looked forward to our long rambling lunches!—but not today. As soon as I sat down, Duncan demanded, "Why should Bill get a divorce?"

I knew, but I could not answer him. I finally realized that Duncan and I, and more importantly, Bill and I, were from different generations, with different views toward the sexes. I mean *basically* different, right down to our toes. Duncan, from his background, could not mentally reverse roles, could not view a woman as a human being with as much right to dominance as a man. Many comments he made brought this out. He talked about freedom in marriage; he didn't realize that society—at present—could not accept "freedom" for the woman as it did for the man; the man brings in the bacon, the woman tends the children, no matter that they both work or have other affairs. Reverse that role, and you raise havoc. Condemnation follows. Duncan found no value in parity, in working from the same base. It was unnecessary. I found it crucial. Crucial to building any worthwhile relationship between a man and a woman. Crucial to the raising of my daughter and all females. Lydia must understand she was an equal, in every way, to her brothers.

Bill and I needed to take the evening plane to New York for a Saturday noon meeting with a potential Albany TV manager, but Bill called me after lunch, complaining about an ear infection; he would try to make an early morning plane in time for the meeting.

When I called Bill from Chicago's O'Hare International Airport to let him know our Saturday meeting was canceled, he wasn't available. His mother coyly explained that he was at the Riegers' house—so coyly that I knew Sally was with him. After all my "advance" planning for a UHF television station weekend meeting, I was furious about his duplicity ... again. I scribbled in my diary on the plane:

> Where is the loyalty you demand of me? Where is the reciprocity? O, bee, where is thy sting? Had I been there, would you have acted thus? Could I have been invited to join in the fun? Now do you see how you have hurt ... so deep it won't go away? All those calls, all those promises are forgotten—or never meant. I want revenge, for having been screwed.

> ... But, why bother? There is much to enjoy elsewhere, much to be thankful for. Pay attention to the positive, the possible, the potential. ...

Fritz and his Yale friend, Mark English, were arriving from New Haven on Saturday for the afternoon Metropolitan Opera performance and dinner with us. Bill called Saturday morning and asked what our plans were for the day. After I told him the roster of guests at his apartment, he commented that it sounded like I had quite a crew there and asked if I would want him around too.

I answered, "Do what *you* want to do."

Bill said he was taking his mother on a color tour and would probably grab a plane later in the day.

I made plans to fly to Aspen because I would have to leave in a few days for the Omaha television meeting, which was set for 7:00 a.m. the next Saturday. I found out very quickly when calling Bill Fitzgerald and Gene Conley that the farming states started morning meetings at the crack of dawn (yes, before 7:00 a.m. during the week), and everyone showed up early, even on Saturday. Margre Durham had booked our Saturday meeting in the elegant and dignified HDR, Inc., boardroom at their new location on Indian Hills Drive. This was going to be our organizational meeting, and Woody assembled a wonderful crew—everyone but Woody, who told Bill that his participation would conflict with his role as head of the NU Foundation.

Bill and I met Friday night at the hotel. Little was said about the past weekend in New York City, and we retired early, knowing we had to be up before dawn. The phone rang about 3:30 a.m. I knew it was serious by the sound of Bill's voice: his mother had a heart attack. Bill got up, got dressed, and headed for the airport. I don't remember any discussion about our morning meeting.

As soon as the group arrived, I told them that Bill's mother had a heart attack and probably would not survive. I expected a sharp reaction when they realized he would not be attending the meeting, but they seemed unconcerned. Well, I was very concerned, because I had never run a UHF television organizational meeting before, and I wasn't prepared for this one. I wanted to cancel the meeting, but I could tell they were waiting for my presentation. I was scared, knowing they would be upset if I didn't make their morning worthwhile. These were business titans and community leaders of Omaha, eager to hear about the first new independent television station for Omaha. I couldn't wait for the meeting to be over, but there were many questions—all which I could answer because I had been doing most of the work with our

FCC lawyer, Reed Miller, in DC. They all seemed very satisfied with our first meeting. I couldn't believe it!

I called Bill from the phone in the HDR boardroom and asked, "How are you getting along?"

"As well as can be expected, I guess," Bill answered unenthusiastically, adding, "Sally's filing for a divorce … right in the middle of all this."

I thought to myself, *You can't plan heart attacks*, but I inquired politely, "What do you want me to do?"

"You'd better go back to Aspen to be with your kids.

What a discouraging phone call. Still in hiding, in death hiding. The more I dwelled on it, the unhappier I became. I'd felt so much a part of Bill's grieving in the morning before he left. His reaction over the phone was a tough blow to my sensibilities. In fact, I was amazed that I carried off the most important organizational meeting alone. Now I knew I could "go it alone." It was an exciting prospect. But financial success was not my ultimate goal; it was a means to an end. Money could allow time to organize my thoughts, plan my strategy, spend the time and energy to write it out.

I considered my involvement in TV ironic, since I disliked it for my kids. It seemed such a waste of life—the "boob tube" that it was. I didn't want to join TV viewers as a spectator; I wanted to control the medium as a player. I wanted to educate as I entertained, especially the very young. And I wanted my children to be players too. Would they agree? I left them on their own. First, I flew to Lansing, Michigan, for meetings at Young World and ACD, and then, later in the week, to New York City.

The Albany UHF TV-23 application, with a deadline of January 30, 1979, needed to be addressed in November. None of the written explanations or collation of documents was possible without the bank agreements and engineering contracts—both my responsibility, along with the pro forma and resumes of board members. Mannie Hannie was plowing through my two-inch-thick portfolio, still wavering, unable to commit to the $2 million loan commitment. I rushed around Albany, with our engineering consultant, to lease a suitable piece of land for our UHF television tower. Something needed to be cobbled together, knowing it could be, and probably would be, changed after the FCC made its determination. I signed up Fritz and Julian to help put it all together; Priscilla Morgan agreed to spend part of January helping us in Albany. Bill felt he could help us more by staying in New York City and tying down any loose ends.

In December 1978, I relished my first Aspen Christmas in my very own house, with all five of my children. It was glorious … and wild. It didn't matter that I would be leaving after the New Year to hole up in Albany for a month… or spending mornings in the KSPN studios and only joining the kids in the afternoons. Now they could ski all week and party every night; with three of them over twenty-one, they could belly up to the J-Bar without fear or favor. We all dressed in silly costumes—a local tradition on Christmas Day—to bomb down Aspen Mountain. The photo of them became my happiest Christmas card.

Chapter Seven

"THE YEAR THAT WAS"

…be willing to "sweep the floor"…

25ᵗʰ Reunion Smith College Class of '54 Standing: Joyce Hatton, Durinda Brownlee. Sitting: Ann Sargent, Michelle Florence.

Dad used to comment that 1971 was "the year that was": He bought new condos, one in Spring Lake and another in Pompano Beach, Florida; and a new forty-three-foot Hatteras. He took Mom on a fifty-two-day trip through the Far East, and then a nine-day voyage delivering the new Hatteras from the North Carolina shipyard to the Seaway Marina in Pompano Beach.

Well … 1979 was "the year that was" in my book. Three of my boys would be graduating two weeks apart, in May and June. And there would be other interesting events.

Our TV-23 team moved to Albany in early January, and the grind began. We holed up for weeks in a suburban motel that had an inner courtyard and large conference rooms.

My boys immediately took charge—the most self-controlled members of the group. Julio put us on a diet, believing that we had to watch our food intake if we were going to be able to work twelve-hour days until the end of the month. We started at 8:00 a.m., and ate nothing until 8:00 p.m. We were allowed caffeine drinks, but no alcohol, not even a beer, until evening.

Everyone we assembled had a unique role: Priscilla always saw the big picture, rearranging my mass of papers whenever necessary. She wasn't up to the boys' strenuous schedule, and when she felt we would make the deadline, she returned to the comfort of her apartment in the city. Fritz's typing pace kept me scurrying to keep the information and paper flowing. I never realized that it would take the physical talents of the boys to win this race. Because of Fritz's two decades of classical piano training, he was the fastest typist around. Both boys could type all day, and I didn't need to proofread any of it. They did that too. We took all the papers to New York City the weekend before the Tuesday, January 30, 1979, deadline. After Bill checked the financials and pro forma figures, I delivered the application to Reed Miller at Arnold and Porter, our FCC law firm in DC. It seems that in the excitement of the moment, I promised the boys 20 percent of my stake in the station if we won. They knew I couldn't add them as investors before filing. Would I keep my promise? Or even remember?

Two weeks later, I reminisced in my diary that we gave Steve Heater a 19 percent stock incentive if he turned KSPN-FM around in two years. He did. Here are my comments:

> But I still see the results six years later. Race made, he (Steve) hired a gung-ho sales manager who became general manager and a friend of all of us. When no equity appeared on the new manager's horizon, he left, and control returned to our newest stockholder (Steve). Pueblo dragged him and the station down, almost to irrecoverable disaster. Pueblo was sold, Aspen breathed fresh air, and now we're riding the crest. Up or over? I'd better decide fast.

On the way to Phoenix a few days later, I would learn that our China trip might become a reality. Talk about irony. I had been complaining in my diary that I never settle down, that I am very " … dilettantish, very spoiled, very uncommitted to my desire to explore, not geography, but the mind. When am I going to settle down to it? I keep thinking—when I get this done (Albany and Omaha) and get out of the Lansing biweekly tour. But they never seem to get done. Albany must be tracked, then Omaha; no one wants me to forget ACD or YW; KSPN and even KVMN are time consuming. ..."

I was dressing for Bill's and my once-a-decade golf game in Phoenix, when there was an interruption: champagne and fruit ... and a serious discussion about old Bill Marriott and his renewed interest in China. (Another project? Keep paddling. ...)

There was great excitement on Bill Seidman's part! He explained that things were moving ahead—to China on March 12th or 13th or? ...

I wanted to go now, not later. (Or, as Jule would relate in his favorite joke: "Zee excitement of zee momente vill bee lost.")

Watch the bumbling, the mess, the sorting out, the organizing—at which Bill was so adept. And, obviously, so was I.

"Sixteen-Year-Old Wins MC Scow Midwinter Regatta. FORT MYERS, FL— Brett Hatton, 16, sailing with his mother as crew, came on strong with two seconds and a first on the final day of racing to win this year's MC Scow Midwinters. Hatton was challenged early on in the series by Happy Fox of Grand Rapids, Michigan. ... Winds ranged from moderate to heavy for the five races sailed by the 22-boat fleet ..." (*Yachting* magazine, June 1979).

We needed the "heavy" wind, because most of the MC scow racers had no crew, so I could hang out, using the hiking straps, which helped Brett to keep the sail trimmed and the boat flat—both needed in order to sail a scow fast. We were a happy team.

Paul Eggert and Dale Edgerle invited Brett and me, and some other sailors, to follow them to Disney World, and we eagerly joined their parade. Paul Eggert was always fun, funny, and full of the devil, and we knew we'd all have a great adventure. It was marred by only one event: my jewelry case was stolen from my motel room in Orlando. All my jewelry was gone, except for my wedding rings and a five-link diamond and sapphire bracelet, which were hidden in our Aspen house. (I wouldn't have those much longer, either. The boys would feel sorry for a gal living down the road. She was kicked out of her house by drug-dealing boyfriends, and the boys invited her to stay at our house. She slept in my bedroom while I was traveling, and when I returned, all my jewelry was gone, and she was gone too.)

After a week of fun and fantasy in Florida, reality stared me in the face when I walked down our Mountain Laurel steps. Why did I start business projects anew? I had choices and felt fortunate to have them—look at it that way. Was my "libre" personality exposing itself to *me*? (Frustration.

Responsibility. Gratification. Justification. Fruition?) I felt so *dumb*—unable to concentrate on one subject long enough to trust my ideas about it. Work, yes; eclectic work; and talk, talk, but for what purpose? Rote communication, ultimately boring. I was so bored the night before in the J-Bar discussing the purchase of the Blue Victorian for KSPN's new studios. I *knew* my ideas—how about some others? With someone I respected and enjoyed an exchange?

Bill Seidman had proliferous thoughts. What a shame he couldn't organize them on paper. Would he ever try? Willpower. He didn't seem to have enough to be willing to be alone—independent—long enough to think a thought through to its logical conclusion. I wanted to do it—but was stuttering at each thought's inception. What else could I be doing? Forgetting?

I certainly stuttered … and so did Bill. After a week on the island of Eleuthera in the Bahamas, I commented in my diary: "So busy vacationing. Such an effort to find three workdays. Lots of sleep and exercise—a twelve-mile walk on the beach, tennis, snorkeling, motorbiking, moving from Harbor Island down to Potlatch. No time for contemplation."

Why? Time at breakfast to read papers or articles, or the booklet given to us at Club Med. (What a depressing feeling that place gave me! Las Vegas around the world, the sportive life.) Bill was going to write about the effects of inflation on the South American economies, drawing on his January experience. He never did.

Bill Seidman with his shell mobile

Bill made a mobile the night before we left. Vacations were not for contemplation. Not with Bill. Nor was any time with Bill meant for contemplation. He had his frenetic pace, his schedule, and I got pulled—inexorably—into it. Did I forgo my own existence, become part of his—like happens with marriage vows? I needed time alone, in my own house. I wasn't comfortable anymore in his apartment; in fact, I didn't like it.

But I was back in his New York City apartment for a necessary Albany TV-23 briefing the following week.

It was a beautiful sunny day in Aspen. Naturally, I had to work with a house full of kids, and I didn't work effectively with all of them around. I felt like I was running a youth hostel, and none of them were worried about my life view; they were too busy living their own lives. And trouble, real trouble, was brewing in Michigan.

Grand juries! Reading about them and dealing with them were two different experiences. When Bob Stocker, my Young World (which we now referred to simply as YW) lawyer, called to tell me that my company could be sued by the IRS, I thought immediately of the skepticism of the ACD directors. They used to laugh while insinuating that ACD's acceptance of YW's receivables was an accommodation to YW because "everyone" knew that most of them would never be collected. How would their view of the organization of a nonprofit jibe with mine? I hoped it wouldn't come up.

The next morning, April 4, 1979, Bob Stocker called again to relate that I was being subpoenaed, and he felt compelled to warn me that this could be a very sobering experience and that I shouldn't expect to walk in the afternoon of April 18 and be prepared to testify the next day. He warned me that I would need a personal lawyer, even though that lawyer could not accompany me into the courtroom. Bob explained that the grand jury was comprised of twenty-four well-meaning citizens who nevertheless followed the lead of the district attorney in all the proceedings. So the DA was the key, not the grand jury.

I asked Bob, "What if I can't remember, and say so?"

Bob replied, "If they think you're lying, they'll hold you for perjury."

Since I was the key witness, Bob also suggested that after I reviewed all the materials, I might want to invoke the Fifth Amendment. But that would imply I had something to hide, which I didn't. That is, not that I knew of—but how sophisticated would the grand jury be? How would they accept my view that the United States is in love with the concept of nonprofit? (More often stated by me as "Congress is having a love affair with nonprofits, and we might as well get on the bandwagon instead of hitting our heads against a brick wall, especially in the fields of education and child care.")

And it worked, although state employees had been skeptical right from the beginning, implying I was too smart, too wily, too business oriented, too greedy, to want to fritter away my time on penny-ante projects. Too greedy with my time, yes; with money, no. (But time was money, as I kept reminding people at the office.)

The public's attitude toward the education of the preschool child had infuriated me for years—especially the attitude of the fathers, who, more often than not, refused to think about education of children until those children had been educated enough to read and write. (And refused to pay for that early education—the "sandbox," as they used to tell me in the 1950s—certain that it required very little ability and therefore little pay.)

If the attitude of the young child reflected the attitude of the parent (no money, time, or effort need be put forth before the age of twelve or fourteen), so be it. No wonder public education is so demeaning: Who wants to be equal? One of many? The voice of the multitude? Mob rule? The tyranny of the majority?

On the other hand, who, if not us, will break the vicious circle of poverty and illiteracy and ignorance? Force the young child—nay, infant—to react? To stimulate these little ones' innate abilities?

And pay us to do it? Let us make money—i.e., *profit*—from educating children? Why that's done for love of humanity!

By Thursday, April 19, 1979, I was out of the woods. No more worries about nonprofit versus profit status with the IRS. The profit company, Young World, would be sold.

And when sold, how much should I contribute to others who had made it possible? Marge, Mary, Sue? Mary Jo? And Jule, the first investor?

And Bill Seidman? All his thought. All his planning. I'll never forget hiking up Hunter Creek to the meadow above, stopping for lunch, and listening to an entirely new, different approach to the resolution of my stock sale to Provincial House. It was July (or August) 1977. Bill's idea was ingenious and fair, and provided me with cash every month. No determination of cash value of my stock was necessary, and I remained tied to the fortunes of Young World until it was sold.

After our decision to sell, KinderCare showed up with a bona fide offer, rushing to beat their May 30, 1979, fiscal year-end deadline. I liked to work fast; it was an exciting prospect. And I finally would be free of YW. Free to pursue new opportunities.

The next weekend would be beautiful weather in the Rockies. How was

I going to use it? To live it? I wanted to spend the mornings writing and reading, but what about other work?

I had to go to Omaha on Monday, and that required preparation—phone calls!—ahead of time. I had to clean up Albany, but I thought I'd do that next week while working on Omaha. And KSPN needed serious thought—how quickly could we be prepared with plans, working drawings, so as not to waste time once we had the building?

I reminisced in my diary:

> How much time I've wasted! On politics! Grassroots. Ugh. I've put in my time there. Was that much necessary? All those hours at Republican HQ sorting out cards, making voting lists, not really being able to explain why I wanted to influence all those people.
>
> Who was I, at twenty-five years of age, to tell them how they should live, for whom they should vote? Did the Republican platform offer the best way? The so-called pursuit of excellence? It was as important to me then as it is now. Merit, not tenure. Saving voluntarily, not relying on social security. Big daddy Uncle Sam won't take care of you. You'll take care of yourself, and if you don't have the boots to be pulled up by the bootstraps, we'll find you the boots, not do the pulling. ...

The twenty-fifth reunion of Smith College's class of 1954 on May 18–20, 1979, was stuffed right before Fritz's graduation from Yale's new graduate School of Management (SOM). I wrote a few days later: "The Smith Alumnae College lectures reminded me of Jule's twenty-fifth reunion from Harvard College—or was it his twentieth from the "B" school (Harvard Business School)? The lecturers appeared either immature in their approach or downright demeaning in their assessment of our capabilities."

The Smith alums had set up panel discussions on careers in "Communications" and "Law/Politics." I was one of six asked to serve on the "Communications" panel. Nina Solomon Hyde was the star of our show, having been the fashion editor of the *Washington Post* for the past six years.

When the audience heard that I had five children and a stepson (four panelists had no children and the fifth had two), they questioned my ability and willingness to juggle a full-time career while caring for six kids. My tough answers—"yes, it is a very tough job"—created quite a buzz within the administration.

Most of the Smithies there were seeking advice on rekindling a career after twenty-five years as homemakers and soccer moms. They complained that their husbands wouldn't let them work after their children were born. Now the children had left, and, sadly, many of their high-powered husbands had too.

I told them, first, to be willing to "sweep the floor" and learn the "politics of the office." They were angry! Their Smith College professors didn't warn them to maintain their marketable skills, and they felt left behind … twenty-five years behind. Now the administrators were angry with me because they wanted the meetings to be positive and uplifting to a group of women who needed help. Did I help them? I would never know. I commented:

> As a result of my weekend, I find I carry more of the anger and fight resulting from my view of women's generally demeaning economic role in our society than my classmates. Few of the class of '54 work in management. Some are professionals, some creative, but few businesswomen.
>
> I didn't feel particularly accepted by classmates—admired or envied, maybe, but too strong, too tough to be enjoyed on such short acquaintance. Julio's comment last night that I was "always tough" underscored for me how little I like that accolade, especially because I felt Bill Seidman was so gross in his quick assessment of our new carpenter for the summer in Aspen. I thought Bill rude—and crude—because he didn't bother to think about how his remarks might affect Julio, who was a good friend of our new employee.
>
> To think I, too, am that way is so depressing. Can I possibly change? Brett complains, too, that I am so "positive" about my views—implying I leave little room for compromise or exchange of views. (*Dare* anyone disagree?) Why, oh why? Very politic, great if you're running for office. What am I running for? Or away from? Maybe Bill and I deserve each other—rough, tough, and running roughshod over others. *Ugh.*

Well, Fritz's graduation made my day! It was a relief to hear how well he was accepted by both classmates and faculty. I wrote this on his commencement concert program (Monday, May 21, 1979, 9:15 a.m.):

> Fritz's acceptance … is a joy to behold. Fritz seems forever happy, stable, and accepting of where and what and who he is. … And when a classmate said she now knew where he got his spirit, I was doubly proud, because his multitudinous talents are more similar to his papa's—music, wine, and languages, especially French. (During Fritz' first French class at Exeter, Fritz discovered *Blasé*, a word that Fritz felt

described his mother perfectly at the time. The name morphed into Blaze—which has stuck for over forty years.)

Antsy. But I took time with pen and paper on Friday, May 25, 1979, at 6:30 a.m., to explain:

Antsy. … I must leave in an hour to get my driver's license, so I can pick up a car in Denver at 1:00 p.m. to drive to New Mexico. And Lydia will have been waiting since 11:00 a.m. at the airport—but it's the best I can do with the airline schedules. I hope we have a happy time. It will take discipline on my part and on Bill's. He is being torn apart by guilt feelings toward his family. Since I won't let him off the hook, I am becoming the culprit. (Has he really put all of us in this position? *J'accuse!*)

Two days later, Bill's new 12,000-acre working cattle ranch in New Mexico had worked its magic on me. I reported in my diary:

In a daze. It's beautiful—warm, not hot, birds singing, insects buzzing but not bothering, people relaxed, informative, enjoyable.

A rainy climb, but a sunny ride. Lydia encompassing, experiencing, and wholly enjoying everybody and everything. Bill doing "his" thing—buying, planting, riding, partaking, seldom here, but enjoying it at a pace that would indicate weekly participation, not biannual (or triennial?).

Hidden, so many things hidden. Must I live this way? I, who am so open—or is it when it suits my fancy? This is someone else's place, not mine. Will I ever find a place of my own? To be free, not owned, bought, borrowed, or bossed? Why is this so important? Why should I care, if I can still live in my own way—using my own schedule, not someone else's? Can I imagine, believe that will ever happen, can happen, to anyone, not just me or my schedule, but anybody's? Are we creative in spite of it all? Concentrating on what is most important to us at the time? Not having that room, that island, that year, to use at our leisure?

There is a softness, a gentleness, a quietness that permeates the atmosphere at this ranch. Is it man-made or God made? Does it exist because the ranch—the land—was provided, or was it developed? How would Bill's kids do on someone else's ranch if "Pop-Pop" hadn't provided the capital, hadn't given them the wherewithal to make it work—time, money, encouragement? (I like them. I like their rebelliousness, but I worry that I burden them with our nebulous relationship. I wish I could get to know and enjoy them under different circumstances. That will never happen. Too many years have passed in these. ...)

To thine own self be true. To thine own self be honest. And be the best. Not to others, but to thyself. Then, ownership won't matter. Because you won't be owned—property might be owned, but not your humanity.

Back in Lansing, Michigan, many changes—good changes—were taking place at ACD and YW. I felt Marge Langworthy would succeed by herself, without her consultant (me) holding her hand. She could learn the legal end and the accounting end (which she did very well, I would find out the following year). The director's end Marge knew well. She could restructure, run good centers, train the staff, and expand the USDA's Child Care Food Program. I felt I must spend some time on the new rules and look for new ways to pay staff—and develop a pension plan for Marge.

On May 30, I commented in my diary: "It is hard to leave them, to become inactive, to pay no attention to the needs of the many, to ignore society. My ivory tower, can I exist in it? Or will I wither away from lack of activity (physical, not mental)?"

Who was I kidding? The next weekend was Julio's graduation. What a different experience from Fritz's in New Haven. Cambridge was home terrain, where I had visited many times with Jule for reunions and meetings. It was a rewarding experience, but fraught with emotion. Harvard was Grandpa Hatton's school and Dad's school—both the college and the business school—and Dad had a new wife.

Finally, the West Coast for Greg's graduation. Sunday, June 17, was graduation day for Adlai Stevenson College at the University of California at Santa Cruz. It was the only ceremony where I took notes from the keynote address, which was given by the provost, Joseph Silverman. And I couldn't decipher most of my notes upon review: "Dissidents ... Vietnam ... Civil War ... psychodrama ... confrontational hostility." But I liked this one: "Truth is a daughter of time."

Fritz was the first graduate to find a management position through our great connector, Priscilla Morgan, at the Lacoste School of the Arts, in the tiny hamlet of Lacoste in southern France. Priscilla Morgan's friend, art professor and artist Bernard Pfriem, founded the school in 1970. It was sponsored by Sarah Lawrence College. Lacoste had long been favored by artists for its extraordinary light and beautiful pastoral setting, which helped Pfriem persuade notable artists to come to Lacoste to teach and work. Fritz would be putting his new master's degree in Public and Private Management to its first test, and I was eager to see the results, as well as glorious Provence.

I returned to Aspen and plowed into the summer events that made the town so popular with its wealthy, artistic, and intellectual visitors.

The Design Conference in mid-June started the cultural parade.

Isamu Noguchi and Pussy Paepke in Design Conference tent

This year's Japanese theme would attract Priscilla Morgan's special friend, famous sculptor Isamu Noguchi. It was hard for me to assimilate all I learned that week—from Isamu and Susumu Shingu, from the lecture on Zen and the erotic movie *Realm of the Senses,* from the fashion parade of Issey Miyake, from the slides of Japanese gardens, from the Japanese winning TV commercials, and, finally from the discussion of China with Isamu and Elizabeth (Pussy) Paepke.

Shingu's short movie showing his wind sculptures was noteworthy, as much because of the filming—the cinematography—as the unusual wind sculptures he had placed throughout Japan. Wonderful windmills! And good for Bill's ranch. Susumu Shingu autographed a copy of his *Spider* book for me. (Oh … what tangled webs he weaves. …) I continue to enjoy the book, although I thought my grandchildren would prefer it.

After accompanying Fritz during the summers of 1975 and 1977 when he master-taped every concert at the Aspen Music Festival, I became accustomed to Sunday afternoons at the Tent—an imposing amphitheater designed by Bauhaus artist-architect Herbert Bayer. I didn't mind showing up alone on my bike because I usually found friends on the lawn with blankets, rugs, or sleeping bags. And some brought chairs or hors d'oeuvres or beer and wine or the Sunday *New York Times*. I skipped the chairs. It wasn't just hoi polloi on the lawn; Aspen's Hollywood residents often made an appearance too. But we all hoped to evade the brief summer afternoon showers that were typical in our mountainous setting. When it rained, I sometimes scurried inside and paid for a concert ticket.

I signed up for Mortimer Adler's Great Books series at the Aspen Institute and attended one of the new Executive Seminars, where I met successful business leaders from around the country. And they invited me to dinners and evening meetings. Sometimes the institute staff asked me to set up radio interviews with luminaries who were speaking or attending institute functions.

One of my favorite seminars featured Supreme Court Justice Harry Blackmun. Naturally, he was discussing *Roe v. Wade,* for which he had written the majority opinion in 1973. I was surprised by his defensive yet thoughtful posture. Although he was very low key while discussing it, he must have been shocked at the explosive public reactions to the court's decision, which was affirmed with a 7 to 2 majority vote. Since I applauded his decision, I didn't think he needed to defend it—just affirm it!

Other Executive Seminar readings included chapters from R. H. Tawney's *Equality* and Plato's *Republic.* I had never read anything written by Martin Luther King Jr., until we were assigned his "Letter from Birmingham City Jail," a call to arms based on biblical scriptures, with a sprinkling of Socrates: "To a degree academic freedom is a reality today because Socrates practiced civil disobedience." It was a powerfully written manifesto, commanding strong support from his black followers and the Christian-based coalition for human rights. I was so impressed with King's perceptive arguments; I felt the urge to go to law school and brush up on the Greek philosophers. (When would I have the chance to fulfill my dream?)

The Playwright's Conference later in the summer was good for me too; it made me feel comfortable in an arena I'd never explored, nor cared to. It was a way to tell a story, to entertain, to educate, to enhance life. It was a medium that required players, as well as the creator; staging a slice of life.

I've not wanted to do that; I've wanted to take it all in, sort it all out, write down my answers—essay style, not through plots, subplots, or dialogue, just exposition.

With President Jerry Ford, July 1979

President Jerry Ford arrived shortly after the Fourth of July, for an Aspen Institute event. I was eager to escort him around personally and direct the interviews. If I reminded Jerry that I had been Republican chairman of Ottawa County (a county with an 80 percent Republican vote), which, along with Kent County, comprised his old Fifth Congressional District in Michigan, he remembered me, but he appeared vague about my association with Bill Seidman and Phil Buchen.

When I returned to the KSPN studio to file reports after lunch, an emergency message came blaring across our police radio. Two hikers had been killed when they fell during a training session at a boys' mountain climbing camp in southwestern Colorado. I wasn't paying much attention until I thought I heard a name I recognized. I asked a reporter to follow up. I knew I was getting the information before the parents, and panicked about breaking the news to them. I had to be sure, as much as I didn't want to hear it. Yes, it was Danny Van Domelen, the strapping sixteen-year-old son of Nancy and Pete Van Domelen. Pete had been KSPN-FM's local lawyer from the time he moved to Aspen from Grand Rapids in the early 1970s. And Nancy was still running the Child Care Food Program for Colorado. And they were longtime personal friends from Grand Rapids. The news spread quickly to their family.

I waited overnight before calling on them. One of my kids asked me on the phone just before I left for their house what I would say at a time like this. I answered that I didn't know. And when I knew, I reported, "You don't say anything. You don't have to; and besides, I couldn't. But that was understood completely. Better than any words."

Pete met me in the driveway; we hugged, and I sobbed. Then I hugged Nancy's dad, and then Nancy, and then the rest of the family. I wrote that afternoon in my diary:

> Tragedy. How does one know it but through the death of a child? It is so unforgiving. Nancy commented that the ache would always be there, and added that, after the death of a partner, probably the grief can be alleviated by finding another person to love. And she reported that she was told she would have good times and bad times, and maybe time would help … but oh! how she would miss him.

About a month later, I walked into Pete's office carrying a wine labeled box, wishing him happy birthday. He reacted in such a delightfully surprised manner, almost teary, commenting that he hated birthdays, that I realized giving is most satisfying to the giver. He gave me a quick kiss, looked in the box, saw all the candy spread over the champagne, and went out to get me a chocolate candy kiss from his candy jar, which he knew I was replenishing. (I always eat candy in his office, and I had noticed the day before that it had been neglected this past month.) He said, "Have a kiss."

After we sat down, I, the client, sitting across from him at his desk, inquired how he was getting along. I tried in my diary to remember Pete's words, because he responded quickly and directly that he tried not to think about it, that, surely, it was a tragedy for Dan, but none of us can grieve for Dan; we grieve for ourselves. Pete found it a matter of discipline, because no one is immune from tragedy, and why should he think he was. Pete did not feel that he has had a tragic life, and he realized it could happen again. Pete said that it would be terrible if it did, but he knew it was possible, and he felt one thinks about it more, once it's happened. I reported in my diary that Pete confided, "I have my emotional times, and they just seem to come. But I don't have any trouble reminiscing about Dan; it may bring tears to my eyes, but it doesn't make me feel badly for having talked about him."

I told Pete that I had spent the last two mornings with Nancy and that she was getting some help in understanding through her study of astrology and parapsychology. I asked if this experience had any impact on his religious beliefs.

Pete answered, "No."

Pete explained that Nancy feels we are predestined; she has been interested in this field and has been reading books on the subject for about three years. Pete thought he might learn something from reading some of her books, because they sounded interesting, and he knew it had helped her to accept Danny's death. But Pete stated that he was not religious and never had been able to believe. He thought so much of life was coincidence, chance, that he couldn't predict what would happen.

I commented that I had not been "graced by God," that we are told that we believe "through the grace of God." He laughed and said he had been left out also. I talked about my visions when the children were born, how difficult it still was for me to accept what was revealed in them about the origin of the universe, how small and insignificant those revelations made me feel at the time. He agreed that Dan's death had made him look differently at life, at what was important to him, and also what a short time all of us spend living on this earth.

He said he realized that what was important was how one lived one's life, the style with which one reacted to events. He felt it was important how he dealt with Dan's death, how he faced up to living—almost Aristotelian in his comments about being able to look back and feel one has "lived the good life." I wished I had a tape recorder. He said it so well, and I had trouble remembering his phrases. It was a unique look at a man I obviously admired. He was more accepting of life than I could be. I felt I would have to think about it. Little did I know at the time that one day my family, too, would experience such a tragedy—the death of a child.

During one of the August Institute lectures, an elderly, sophisticated-looking gentleman asked me to dine with him and some friends from Chicago. Leo Guthman confided that he had been watching me all week and observed that I might benefit from a visit to his favorite plastic surgeon at Northwestern Memorial Hospital. He told me that I was very pretty, but I was starting to get a fat chin line. This problem was very easy to correct, he assured me, especially by a top surgeon like Dr. Norman Hugo. And he offered me residence in his exclusive high-rise apartment building for the week of surgery. I promised him I would think about it.

I knew he was right, and when I found out that Dr. Hugo was head of plastic surgery at the hospital, I called for an appointment. When could the doctor see me? Right away. I called Harriet Newman at her ACD La Grange office. Could she put me up in the house where she rented an upstairs room during the work week? She would ask Muriel. After some hesitancy, Muriel told her I could rent the room across the hall if Harriet was willing to share the bathroom. My best friend willing? Harriet was elated at the thought that we could spend a week together. And Harriet wanted to ask Dr. Hugo for advice too.

It was very early morning when Harriet dropped me off at Wesley Pavilion Hospital. After a thorough physical checkup, the nurses gave me sleeping pills, Valium, morphine, atropine, and Nembutal. Fly high! Since I was allergic to aspirin and had never taken mind-altering drugs, the pills took immediate effect. I felt great! Calm, happy, and compos mentis—I thought. I had no idea the extent of the surgery or how long it would take. I knew what Dr. Hugo suggested, and I agreed to it, trusting his judgment completely. He started cutting around my ears about 8:00 a.m. I could hear the cutting noise, but I couldn't feel it. Dr. Hugo talked to his assistant and me throughout the surgery. Dr. Hugo even showed me minute pieces of fat that he had cut from under my chin. This was becoming a lengthy operation! Yet, the first time I felt anything was around noon, when he stuck the Novocain needles into my upper lip. *Ouch!* Dr. Hugo laughed. He said they always save that until last, because, if they did it first, his patients probably would rebel. Once the lip was numb, Dr. Hugo shaved it very lightly and finished quickly.

I slept all afternoon, my entire head wrapped tightly in bandages. I knew poor Harriet would be shocked … and would dismiss any thought of plastic surgery after seeing me. The staff watched carefully for bleeding and expected me to be black-and-blue because I had my eyes done too. (For a second time, mainly to correct my scar and left-cheek sag from my car accident thirty years earlier.)

When I walked into Dr. Hugo's office three days later, his nurse called in the entire staff to look at me. They couldn't believe that I had so few black-and-blue spots from all the surgery. (I was probably ten to fifteen years younger than most of his other patients.)

My upper lip was another story. One week later, Leo Guthman insisted that I visit him to attend an art exhibit at one of his favorite clubs. The large scab across my upper lip was the only noticeable sign from surgery, and it was slowly peeling off in chunks. While we were having lunch, a large piece hung loose. I rushed to the bathroom and remained there until it fell off. I was so embarrassed, but Leo thought nothing of it; he said I looked young and beautiful, and my scabbed upper lip was not a distraction—to him.

I left the next day for Aspen with a clean upper lip. When my brother Gary stopped by my Aspen house a week later, I said nothing about my facelift, and he said nothing. When I asked him, weeks later, if I looked any different, he just said, "You looked well rested." I made the mistake of telling my kids about my facelift, and soon everyone knew about it. I loved the results and never regretted having it done at the young age of forty-six (well, almost forty-seven). I would be calling on Dr. Hugo again when he showed up in New York City a few years later as chairman of the department of plastic surgery at Columbia Presbyterian Hospital.

"Priscilla, we are going on the Concorde!" Priscilla Morgan and I shared early October birthdays, just four days apart, on October 6 and October 10. We hoped Bill would take us to Paris on the Concorde for our birthdays. Just one way; we'd find our own way home. Priscilla was eager to visit longtime famous friends in Paris, like the fashion designer Elsa Schiaparelli, and I was eager to see the boys before they left France in the late fall.

Bill said yes! Priscilla had helped both of us for years, but I was as shocked as Priscilla when Bill said he had made reservations for all three of us on the Concorde that week.

Ever since college physics classes, space travel intrigued me. One of the first books I remember reading after leaving the University of Michigan was Arthur C. Clarke's *The Exploration of Space*. But I was never a fan of "Star Trek" or science fiction. Much of what Clarke predicted in his writings turned out not to be fiction. With the development of the Concorde supersonic aircraft in the 1970s, I had high hopes of experiencing Mach 1 or Mach 2 at 50,000 to 60,000 feet of altitude—the closest I could come to achieving space travel.

Air France's special Concorde waiting room at New York's John F. Kennedy International Airport held all ninety-plus passengers comfortably while we snacked on hors d'oeuvres and consumed fine French wine and champagne. (It turned out to be the best part of the plane trip.)

When could we expect to break the sound barrier? At warmer sea level, much more speed is needed to break the sound barrier than at cooler high altitudes. Since the timing of the sonic boom would be relative to the speed at different altitudes, I never could find out when it would happen, and when it did, there was no sonic boom; it felt like the plane hit a small mogul on a snowy hill as it continued on its groomed path toward Paris.

Paris. Who wouldn't want to stay there? After eighteen hours of college French classes, I was ready to settle in. Not Bill. He rented a car, and we headed south.

We were exhausted by the time we located Fritz and Julio at the Lacoste art school. Accommodations around their tiny mountain village were sparse. But not the shops. I wrote: "Taste. Class. Yes, the French have it. Their hedonism offends us. Too much of a good thing. Dare we enjoy it? And, finally, how can they afford it?"

Oodles of petits magasins lined the sloping cobblestone streets in Lacoste. People shopped every day, sometimes twice a day. The charcuterie for meat; the marche de fromage for cheese. I ran across the cobblestones into a boulangerie and patisserie for my favorite croissants and brioches.

But the wines were a different story. I explained, "They were all delicious. Local wines bought in the supermarket cost less than one dollar, and never disappointed our developing palates. The best Châteauneuf-du-Pape cost five dollars, so we skipped it. The French must drink the best and send us the rest. Why they are so deserving puzzles us."

Fritz owned a car, a mini four-door Renault 5, Bill was ready to move on, so we packed up and we headed west toward the Pyrenees.

Tempe Reichardt had called Fritz from Marseille the day before we left. She was distraught. She had survived a midnight attack by French legionnaires who watched her get off a late train from Rome, and an assault by a huge black man in her hotel elevator at 2:00 a.m. The thought of being sold into white slavery was still on her mind.

Could we give her a ride? She was hoping to catch a train north to Dusseldorf, but she really just wanted to see family again—and we certainly considered ourselves family.

France/Spain Tour—From left: Tempe Reichardt & Fritz; Fritz & Joyce & Julio; Bill Seidman. October 1979.

Tempe would be taking us a little out of our way. Where? (We were heading south, toward Barcelona.) Could we go west first? Bill couldn't believe it. He had planned only a week in Europe, and Tempe was crowding his space. Quite literally. And more luggage crammed into a mini Renault.

After leaving Tempe in southern France, we drove south through the Pyrenees. They are not as high as the Rockies, but they seemed as high and as exhilarating.

In Barcelona on Sunday, October 14, I mused in my diary:

> Well, Bill has left. Life seems so foreshortened this week. At fifty-eight, he still cannot find time to travel, to not read American papers, news magazines, business articles carried in his briefcase. It will never be different. That is the realization. ...
>
> What shall I do? Run around Europe and write a diary? Enjoy the rest of the tour with Fritz and Julio like I did Pids (Lydia)? *Yes.* That I believe in. That is easy. It's after that. How am I providing for my future? Can I rely on someone else all my life? What do I owe my children? A home? An opportunity to travel? To race sailboats? To ski? To be together with me in my expensive village in the mountains?
>
> What do I owe my community? My country? My world? What do I want to give back? What best can I give back? What drives me to that desire? What motivates me—selfishness or altruism? It is important to know. We pass on to our children what we consider important, and I want them to feel their lives are meaningful, worthwhile, first to them, but, ultimately, to others. ...

We had terrible weather all the time we were in Barcelona. After our short stay, we headed back through Provence and on to Florence, Rome, the Amalfi Coast, and Tuscany, before returning to Provence once again. When we arrived in Aix-en-Provence, I exclaimed, "The colors of Provence!"

Fritz replied, "No, the *food*—oh, to get out of Italy!"

Breakfast in Italy had been a rude awakening. How could we bear ten days of Italian crusty, musty breakfast rolls when we could have had croissants and brioches that melted in our mouths?

Before we left France, I called Bill in New York City. It cost 176 francs ($44). And Bill wondered why I didn't call more often! But the call reminded me that I couldn't escape my responsibilities. I wanted to think about other things, not the radio or TV stations. Was it Bill's way of bringing me home?

He really was nice on the phone, saying he had taken care of everything for the moment; it certainly could wait a few more days. (I was hoping for a week. I wanted to see Cuenca, Madrid, Seville, and maybe Lisbon.)

November 1st. All Saints Day—a holiday in Spain and all of Europe. I liked the feeling in Madrid. Not even our first bad experience with a hotel changed that. After Fritz tried the phone and I tried the hot water (neither worked), we headed over to Fernando's apartment, only ten minutes away, for advice about a more suitable hotel.

Fernando's apartment was as exciting as I remembered it in 1963. Prints in the entryway, paintings covering almost every wall, antique musical instruments on one table, a collection of paperweights on another, and a rare book collection that should be the envy of every artist. Fernando's most recent paintings were hanging above his desks and on the easel in his studio. I really liked them.

His apartment was truly inspiring, not only to the young, like my kids, but also to me just as much. The effort to assemble his collections, the knowledge and taste required, was probably more appreciated by someone older, who understood the vagaries of time. Time wasted. (All those yacht club parties?)

The Spaniards loved art. It was everywhere. On the road to Madrid, we found large modern sculptures in the roadside parking areas. Buildings were adorned with frescoes and mosaics.

Fernando said Spanish TV was terrible, but he seemed to appear on it quite regularly. We viewed a tape of one of his full-hour interviews, and he looked good, intelligent and confident, discussing his subject. (Chinese art, I was told.) Fernando was also on Berlitz records. "I speak Spanish well," he told us the day we arrived, after a comment about it by one of the boys.

I asked why TV was so bad, "beneath contempt," and was told that the public was treated as if they were idiots; they were constantly talked down to. Why? Fernando said nepotism reigned, not competency. He found TV abominable all over Europe, except in Britain. (Perhaps I was working the wrong market.) But he said TV changed the countryside. Everyone stayed in at night and watched their TV (abominable as it was?). The masses. We watched a short movie (nine minutes) that Rafa had made about Fernando's work. Although it was well done, it was short for the subject. They explained that nine minutes was often the time slot that was available for shorts. It was shown on TV just prior to a showing of *A Clockwork Orange*, so it had a large audience.

Curious as to how this high-brow film would be accepted in the United States, I asked, "Are we interested enough in art? Artists? Their rationale? Their accomplishments? How many want to commit their lives to art? Music? Literature? Could they anyway? Do they have the talent, the money, the time, the energy? What are proper subjects for TV? Sports? Burlesque? Farce? Comedy? Travelogues? Politics? *Star Wars*?" Fernando is an intellectual but not a dilettante. The wide appeal, unfortunately, has to be to the dilettante side of humanity.

"To do many things well has been the problem," I told Fernando. "The ability to write, direct, produce shows that are notable and quotable does not seem to be an easily accomplished feat. I think it's because TV is new and government regulated. There is not—but there will be!—the multiplicity of channels available to allow programmers to sink or swim in the marketplace. More education at an earlier age, more channels, both should improve TV for future generations."

We rushed off to Cuenca the next morning. The city of Cuenca stands perched on a rock, dramatically separated from the surrounding mountains by two river gorges. The old part of the city is a natural fortress and has been used as such since Moorish times. The famous hanging houses that house the Museum of Spanish Abstract Art (Museo de Arte Abstracto Español) are typical examples of Cuencan Gothic folk architecture. I admired Fernando and his dedication to his museum masterpiece, commenting in my diary:

> The museum. *Fabuloso*, or some other equally hyped term. Magnifique. A tour de force. A splendid tribute to Fernando's good taste, perseverance, and money. Every painting is accorded its viewing space. The rooms are designed to take maximum advantage of the natural light, which comes through windows of varying sizes and angles—the windows opening to vistas of the gorge below, or to the city, the monastery, the canyon, or the hills beyond.

We left Cuenca on Sunday morning and hurried over to El Escorial for a quick afternoon visit before heading back to Madrid for the night. The boys found El Escorial a disappointment, and the road to Madrid was jammed bumper to bumper. They decided to go to Segovia, "only a half hour's drive north." Did we like it? I recorded my reaction in my diary the next day, on the TWA flight to New York City:

Segovia at night! A full moon on the forest floor, reflecting off the snow piled up on the curves near the top of the pass, about 6,000 feet. The aqueduct. The Alcazar. The Moorish cathedral. The Alcazar was built on a rock connected by a narrow spit of land to an adjoining hilltop. It was brightly lit, but it didn't detract from the moonlit countryside. ... The aqueduct was double arched through the center of town. It was unbelievably romantic.

After a month touring France, Italy, and Spain, I was stuffed with art and antiquities and still suffering jet lag the morning after arriving stateside. But I did not want to miss the breakfast fund-raiser for presidential candidate John Connally at "21," one of my favorite New York restaurants.

It was a rotten breakfast but good company—Press Secretary Brady and Bill Seidman—and, for me, an interesting speech, not having heard this candidate before. I liked some of his ideas on Congress, not the bureaucracy, being out of control. On fear of energy resources, Connally certainly proved to be right about the poisoning of the ocean from oil leaks or out-of-control nuclear energy installations.

On education, though, I thought Connally uneducated. He complained that our college graduates weren't prepared to do anything when they got their diplomas. Connally suggested we change the concept of public education in this country, because 50 percent of students had no more than a high school education. Therefore, "Artisans and other craftsmen should be treated with dignity, and high schools should have massive vocational programs so students would be prepared for jobs when they completed high school." I found these comments shortsighted, out of date, or, more likely, statements made with not much thought put into them. I'd had enough. ...

My surprise was my enjoyment in being back in the political fray. My knowledge was greater than before, but how could I use it effectively? I told Brady that I didn't like what Connally had to say about education, and Brady said, "Yes, we do need help in this area. How about helping us?" I told him that I was not prepared to tackle the policy toward the public school system in this country, but Connally was less so, and he was making noises that he thought the public wanted to hear.

I felt European schools were no example, so I philosophized in my diary:

What do we want? Another Renaissance? More artists, more GNP, expansion or contraction (quality, not quantity)? Material, ethereal?

It is touchy, because one can never get around what we are educating *for—what are our goals?* I don't want to enforce mine on others, but commonality is there. With thousands in our classrooms, how can it be otherwise?

Chapter Eight

"...IT'S IN THE PLAN."

We have different social systems. With you, it's
competition; for us, it's in the plan.
Cheng Bing, Chinese Provincial Leader
Guangdong Province, China. January 1980

Cheng Bing, Chinese Provincial Leader

While I was getting my education in Europe, Bill Seidman was getting visas for the Great Sky Land and Development Company's business venture in China.

Great Sky's chairman was Bill's friend, former Pennsylvania Senator Hugh Scott, a sagacious old China hand who collected art of the Tang Dynasty and authored a book on it in 1966 entitled, *The Golden Age of Chinese Art*. Senator Scott said that his trip to pre-Communist China in 1947 "aroused a love for the art of China, never to be quieted." Shortly after President Nixon visited China in 1972, Senator Scott led a delegation of three senators and their wives on a private three-week tour of China.

Bill set up the company in the spring of 1979, in Washington, DC, in the offices of the Washington Campus program on P Street. China's "narrow door to the west" (from an article in *Fortune* magazine in March 1979) was opening with the passage of China's new joint-venture law, and Bill hoped to take advantage of this opportunity.

Although Bill knew I was eager to go to China, I didn't pay much attention to Great Sky until Bill announced that his company finally had a bona fide invitation from the Guangzhou Provincial Government to come to Guangzhou (Canton) to plan a joint venture with the Guangdong Provincial Tourism Bureau. Two hotels, with a total of two thousand rooms, were to be built: one of Western design and one of Oriental design.

An invitation to the People's Republic of China (PRC) was not like most invitations, however. The China Travel Agency arranged everything for you, from arrival date, to plane or train tickets, to hotel and meeting rooms, to departure date. Bill warned me that I was not on the company's original list of participants, so he wasn't sure that I would get my visa in time to participate in the meetings, which were supposed to start on January 4, 1980. Since the visas would be distributed when the group arrived in Hong Kong (which was part of the British Empire until 1997), Bill suggested that we fly to Hong Kong, and I could wait there for my visa and train ticket to Guangzhou.

As predicted, my visa was not waiting for me in Hong Kong. When Bill and the other members of his group left Hong Kong for Guangzhou, I was disappointed and apprehensive—and now alone in a bustling commercial Oriental port. I told Bill I wanted to move to the posh Peninsula Hotel, where the concierge could help me work with the China Travel Agency.

"Three American Oceanographers," January 1980

My passport was sent into China, along with the passports of three American oceanographers who had just completed two weeks of exploration for Shell Oil Company in the South China Sea; they were invited unexpectedly to lecture in Guangzhou and Beijing. All of us had the funny feeling that we might have been tricked, never to see those passports again. But I had pals now—young professional oil engineers who wanted to see the sights as much as I did. We toured day and night, not sure how much time we would have to play in Hong Kong. After three days, we were told that our passports were being held for us at the China border, awaiting our arrival on a specified train. Such firm commitments made me nervous. I was chronically late. What if I missed the train on which I was scheduled? Would someone still greet me at the border, with my passport in hand?

When our train stopped at the border, the four of us felt like royalty. We were greeted immediately, given our passports, ushered through the immigration ritual, and served tea or beer by young waiters who hovered over us and attempted to teach us a few Chinese words, none of which I really learned because I didn't understand the tonalities of the Chinese language.

I finally arrived at the Tung Fang Hotel in Guangzhou, and was escorted to a huge restaurant on the top floor for a quick lunch. It was 2:00 p.m., and I was their only customer; I pointed to one Chinese dish on a menu that had English translations, changed my mind, and pointed to another. It was my first tangle with chopsticks, and, fortunately, no one was watching.

I walked down to a seventh-floor suite, to find an afternoon meeting already in progress. Thirteen people were crowded around a long narrow table in what was obviously someone's living room. It wasn't difficult to identify the players: the Chinese delegation of five, representing the Guangdong Provincial Travel and Tourism Administration Bureau, was lined up along one side of the table, all the men in identical blue cotton jackets, their leader wearing a blue worker's cap, and their pretty female interpreter in a lighter blue jacket with the same mandarin collar.

Our group, on the other hand, was a motley crew surrounding the other three sides of the table, with no particular order that I could discern. It consisted of Senator Hugh Scott; Bill Seidman from Great Sky; Francis Loetterle, senior vice president of Ramada Inns; Robert Jacobs and Juergen Bartels, also from Ramada Inns; Bryant Lemon, vice president of Rust Engineering Company; and our Chinese connection, an attractive Hong Kong-based

Chinese couple, Maria and Raymond Li, who also acted as secretary and interpreter.

A long, thorough explanation of the advantages of a worldwide computerized reservation system was being presented by Fran Loetterle, no doubt to justify the commission for this valuable service. He would stop politely about every other sentence, while the young Chinese interpreter translated it in a professional, deadpan manner. She was dispassionate when Fran was passionate, which forced Maria and Raymond Li to reinterpret in defense of his position. Fran's explanation went on for the remaining two hours of the meeting.

The previous day's session needed an explanation of floating interest rates. All the Western business practices that make up our "social system" were being explained carefully, painstakingly.

Cheng Bing, chief negotiator for the Chinese, with a very serious expression on his face, turned to me and confided quietly, "We have different social systems. With you, it's competition; for us, it's in the plan."

A seemingly simple explanation, but I would quickly learn that nothing with the Chinese was simple. Our half of this joint venture did all the work, from writing agreements that had to be rewritten and typed and translated between meetings (I had to type reports into the early morning light), to figuring costs and taxes that had to meet the guidelines of China's nebulous new joint-venture law, to presenting financing, all of which had to be summoned from Western sources (which I then realized was Bill Seidman's job).

Last but not least, I found out that only the Chinese dared eat and drink to their hearts' content. But eat together we all did … that very night. It was my first "banquet," with sixteen courses listed in Chinese on our individual menus. The secretary general of the province was the guest of honor, and our company played host. When the secretary general strode into the room, just like any Western politician, he had the same purposeful stride and smile, reminding me of Chancellor Schmidt. After shaking hands and greeting everyone, he went immediately to the table, a large round table with a wreath of yellow zinnias bordering the center portion.

Waitresses in short plain white jackets were pouring cognac, sweet wine, beer, or orange pop. Senator Hugh Scott offered the first toast, in a very formal manner. Everyone stood up, clicked glasses, splashing cognac out of the tiny cordial glasses, and said, *"Gom-bai!"* ("Bottoms up!) Cognac glasses were quickly refilled. Next, the secretary general offered a toast, also formal in the translation, and we stood again. Once more, cognac glasses were filled. The only gossipy comment was directed at me when I entered the room. Cheng Bing, still wearing his cap, observed drily, "I see that the other half of the Great Sky has appeared."

About those sixteen courses. How could I forget them? Snake soup, wild fox, wild goat, wild duck, tiny birds eggs that had spent a week buried in clay, and probably the mother birds cooked whole and eaten in their entirety, bones and all, like we eat smelt. Everyone served everyone else, not themselves. I smiled as my Chinese friend on my right dipped his jacket in his plate of food as he reached far into the middle of the table to serve me (all tables in China must be round), and our Chinese interpreter, Maria Li, swept across the wineglasses while serving soup to her dinner partners. And then, at the end, there were hot towels; we wiped faces, backs of necks, hands. Makeup? Dry complexions? They must exist only in the West.

The feast took its toll on Western stomachs by morning, but everyone managed to appear at 3:00 p.m., for more discussion of the services provided by the hotel management company. Before the Chinese delegation left, Cheng Bing very calmly announced, "Because all of you seem quite tired this afternoon, we would like to invite you to meet on Friday in more-pleasant, relaxed surroundings at the Hot Springs resort about eighty kilometers northeast of Guangzhou. Plan to stay overnight, so that we can meet in the evening also, if we desire."

Bill and I left quickly to catch an early concert at the Sun Yat-sen Memorial Hall. We were late. The hall was packed, but we were ushered, nevertheless, to the front row, where young Chinese photographers were occupying our seats. They scurried away, and, as I sat down, I felt a tap on my shoulder. Sitting in the second row were the three oceanographers who had accompanied me on the train from Hong Kong. Quite a coincidence in a city of four million inhabitants. And they told me that they had just returned from the Hot Springs resort where we were going the next morning. The one and only China Travel Agency plans for all foreigners, so I shouldn't have been surprised at our coincidental itineraries.

The evening concert was a conglomeration of Western entertainment: Spanish dances, Italian arias, American polkas, Russian ballet. The choices intrigued me, for I had no way of knowing what would appeal to the Chinese audience. And I couldn't tell from the applause—there wasn't any from the Chinese, just us foreigners clapping loudly in the first two rows. But the appeal was there; this was the third continuous week of performances with the hall filled to capacity.

We drove to the famous Hot Springs resort the following morning in a small bus, and we gathered for the afternoon meeting in a huge sunny room flanked by porches. An impressive painting, somewhat ethereal, covered most of the remaining wall. The ubiquitous teacups had been placed on a low table circled by overstuffed sofas and chairs. It was a welcome change from our hotel suite.

Afternoon meeting at Hot Springs, January 1980

At breakfast, our Chinese hosts announced their plan for the day: a walking tour of the important buildings (President Nixon slept here on one of his China visits), then a short tour by bus to the dam and hydroelectric station, then lunch, an afternoon meeting, and return to Guangzhou after supper.

The agenda for the afternoon meeting was a simple one from our point of view. It was a reading, with clarification when necessary, of a letter of agreement that Bill Seidman had composed earlier in the week. It was not long, only four or five typed pages, and not written in legal "whereas" language. But it was important to us that our Chinese co-venturers understood their obligations, as well as ours, and that became a major task for Maria and Raymond Li. They alone could hear the innuendos, and know the right time for further explanation or argument.

"Infrastructure Services" were not taken for granted by our side, for we were not prepared to pay for hotels constructed in a void. No space odyssey was contemplated, nor was it affordable. Sewers, drinking water, electricity, telephones, roads—not just lines to the site but main arteries to town—were of concern to us. Without them, no modern hotels could be built. Assurances were given by the Chinese, and reassurances. And we wanted to be convinced, we had to be convinced, for the survival of the project. But we had been living with too little infrastructure since arriving in Guangzhou to keep from doubting their ability to produce all the necessary services. (The décor of my hotel room was not enhanced by the foot-long rats that regularly appeared during the night in place of an electric vacuum cleaner.)

"Labor Costs" bore no relationship to those in the West but were not seriously debated, because no one knew the relationship between their productivity and their price. (And if they worked by "the plan," not by pay incentives, how productive would they be?)

...how productive would they be?

"Room Occupancy Guarantees" became a cause célèbre on both sides. As the afternoon wore on, the Chinese appeared eager to complete the negotiations on the letter of agreement so that Bill Seidman could take it to Hong Kong for review by potential lending institutions.

"Financing" was the last ingredient in our joint-venture recipe, but the most important. When we completed the reading and translation, at about 7:00 p.m., our Chinese hosts suggested dining before we returned to Guangzhou. We declined; we'd had a week of banquets, including lunch that day, and couldn't face one more. We retired to our rooms to pack.

Our translators, Raymond and Maria Li

Monday morning, we pulled together all the schedules that would accompany our letter of agreement. Bill was leaving early Tuesday for Hong Kong and needed two sets of completed documents for review with bankers and their legal staffs. Since most items were in order by Monday noon, I wanted to explore the downtown section of Guangzhou.

After I returned from an afternoon walk in one of the two parks that surrounded the hotel, I was shocked to find six workers milling around in my room. They appeared caught by surprise, too.

I demanded, "What do you want?"

One spoke up, "Oh, we're looking for your fuse box."

Six people to replace one fuse? After they left, I mentioned to my colleagues how odd it seemed, and one of them, who had worked for American intelligence in the Far East during World War II, announced casually, "They were probably bugging your room. I thought mine was bugged last June when I was here. They do it, I guess, to reassure themselves that you are legitimate. Do you have a Dictaphone?"

I answered, "Yes."

"Well, let's go down and check out your room."

He took apart my phone but noticed nothing amiss. Then he turned on my Dictaphone and carried it around the room, carefully checking the cold air registers near the ceiling. He heard nothing unusual but commented, "There are a lot of new sophisticated methods I don't know about, so I can't be sure. ..."

Just then, my clock went wild!

Late Tuesday evening, I received an enthusiastic phone call from Bill in Hong Kong. He reported, "Our agreement is the best yet to come out of China. Although the money market is tough, it's not impossible; but the banks need more time. We're going to meet again tomorrow, and, hopefully, we will have something concrete by Thursday morning, so I can return on the noon plane to Guangzhou."

I relayed the conversation to our negotiating team—and wondered if the other half of this joint venture had been listening.

On Thursday, Miss Lu, the Chinese interpreter, accompanied me to the airport to meet Bill's plane. She conversed easily in English, with lots of bounce and humor. She said her father was a doctor in Guangzhou, and she had learned English in local schools. "I've been interpreting for the Travel Bureau for three years, but this is the first time I've interpreted for this kind of business, with percentages, commissions, and floating interest rates, and I don't always understand what these words mean," she admitted.

Miss Lu expressed interest in my job, my "big titles," such as vice president. She said, "That's unusual for women in our country."

I promised to send her some books that discussed the changing roles of women in America.

As soon as Bill returned from the airport, he announced to our group, "The news from the banks is encouraging, but we will have to rework all of our figures to reflect the changes in the market and the availability of money, and a new schedule will have to be prepared and translated before we can meet with the Chinese."

The Chinese delegation informed us the next morning that they could not meet until evening. I was in a panic. Time was running out for our team members: some had to leave the next morning; others had to defer business commitments. I knew Bill was expecting me to stay, forewarning me, "You're going to have your hands full getting this agreement signed."

The Chinese were prompt, as usual, for the evening meeting, but for the first time, their leader, Cheng Bing, was missing. He had run every meeting for the past month, listening patiently to protracted explanations of the hotel management system, infrastructure, LIBOR (London Interbank Offering Rates), etc. Although noncommittal about the acceptance of our joint-venture contract by the central government in Beijing, he had committed months of his and his colleagues' time to the project. (But, as a veteran of the Long March, he may have viewed time from a different perspective.)

Cheng Bing's first assistant, whom we referred to as "the accountant," took charge of the meeting in his absence. He opened the session with a gracious apology for the delays in calling the meeting, and then announced, "We are eager to hear your report from the banks."

Bill put the notes from his bank meetings in front of him and began a long, carefully worded explanation of the potential financing terms and the deteriorating market situation. It seemed very clear to our side what could be expected from the financial community. But the Chinese spokesman said, "It is not acceptable financing. First, we must have a firm commitment; we must have assurances that the interest rate will not exceed LIBOR plus a half percent."

Bill explained again that the money market fluctuated, that we couldn't control events a year or two years hence. He reminded them that the price of gold had doubled since we began our negotiations, and we could no longer look to past events to predict the future. They remained adamant in their request for a firm commitment. The disgust on Bill's face was evident: How could he convince them that they were being treated equitably by the financial community? That they could expect no special favors? That they had to pay as much as, but no more than, anyone else seeking funds? Bill scribbled another note to me, warning me that I would have a tough slog through this group.

Sensing that we had hit an impasse, the Chinese delegates went into a huddle on their side of the table and emerged after a few minutes, offering a compromise: "We'll accept an interest rate that doesn't exceed LIBOR plus three-fourths of a percent."

Now it was our turn to confer in private, and we gathered together to hear Bill's proposal: "Let's accept the three-fourths over LIBOR, and tell them, if the loan is above that, we'll pay the difference."

It was becoming very clear to all of us that, unless the Chinese got their way, there wasn't going to be any joint venture.

When we agreed to a firm commitment of LIBOR plus three-fourths of a percent on the loan and promised them our half of the joint venture would absorb any costs above that percentage, the tone of the meeting changed immediately. Now there appeared an urgency on the part of the Chinese to conclude the negotiations and send us home. They explained they would need at least three weeks to put the letter of agreement in proper Chinese contractual form, but they assured us they would not change any of the basic agreements and would invite us back for the signing shortly after the Chinese New Year, which was February 16.

I was elated. We all were.

The Chinese suggested I go to the airport early in the morning and "take a chance" on getting a seat. I had to check out, beg to pay the bill in Hong Kong dollars because I couldn't get renminbi until I got to the airport in the morning. And I had to rewrite our agreement in triplicate, and in longhand, because our only typewriter was being used by our Chinese partners to type up their very lengthy contract.

We all assembled at about 1:30 a.m. to review and sign each other's contracts.

It was just as well that I was leaving because I had no voice left. Bill and I flew to Hong Kong the next morning and caught an afternoon flight to Hawaii. When we landed in Honolulu, I said I couldn't go on. ... I thought my eardrums would explode. Bill drove me to an emergency clinic nearby, and the doctor said that both ears were infected, plus I had pneumonia and laryngitis. The doctor said I couldn't fly for at least a week.

Bill owned a condo on Mokule'ia Beach on the north side of Oahu. It was one I had never seen but knew existed. Would it be available? After picking up some heavy antibiotics and sedatives, Bill drove me to the condo complex. Fortunately, his condo was vacant, but he couldn't stay more than a day.

Bill called my kids, who were living in our Aspen house, to let my family know that I had laryngitis and couldn't talk to them on the phone—not even a whisper. When Bill explained that the doctor ordered me to stay in Hawaii for at least a week, they did not believe him! They commented with their usual wry humor that it was just my excuse to spend a week in paradise. But I was so sick, sedated and dizzy, that I didn't care. Miraculously, my former neighbors from Grand Haven, Al and Marian Schuler, were vacationing for the winter in the same condo complex, and they later told me they checked on my progress every day.

Before I left Hawaii, I met a contractor who was in the process of somewhat similar negotiations with the Chinese in Shanghai. He looked tired and commented cynically, "In all likelihood, you will get a letter from the Chinese in about a month asking you to come back, not to sign documents as you think, but because they have about fifteen other things that they want renegotiated."

Bill and I continued to contact our potential joint-venture banks; I was expecting a positive letter from Mannie Hannie and Schroeder Bank. Ken Lipper of Salomon Brothers was calling foreign banks. I promised to call him and also call Pat Dooley at Chase Bank. Bill said he would call First National Bank of Chicago again. …

Bryant Lemon, Rust Engineering's representative in our joint-venture talks, wrote a report on June 3 about our China Hotel proposal. His conclusion:

> The result of the trip (in January to Canton) was that both parties of the JV agreed on a "letter of intent." The Guangdong Provincial authorities submitted it to Beijing, and we have heard that it was not approved. …
>
> Loetterle has been ready to return to Canton on two occasions during April and May, but has been put off by the Chinese both times. Presently, he is working through Raymond Li in Hong Kong and may be invited to Canton during June or July.
>
> … Finally, Loetterle reports that Seidman has probably found the $100 million needed and that Ramada and SKY have been working out an agreement. Also, the Chinese want the program to include all necessary infrastructures, which was not a requirement when we visited.
>
> All in all, it doesn't look too promising for the immediate future.

According to Pat Sullivan, Shape VP of Shape Asia, Guangzhou <u>now</u> is one of the four largest automobile manufacturing locations in China.Photo of Guangzhou courtesy of "Shape on the Roll", Summer 2017, Issue 84

Chapter Nine

PAIDEIA

Educate to live the good life, not to get a job.

Mortimer Adler
The Paideia Proposal, 1982

A new office. Glorius!

When I showed up from Hawaii, still weak and weary from Mao's revenge, I found my troops at KSPN eager to celebrate our ten-year anniversary on Valentine's Day—only a few weeks away. They would be planning a live broadcast from Aspen Mountain, complete with band, costumes, drinks, dancing. And I was eager to celebrate the fact that, after KSPN's ten years cooped up in the Jerome Hotel's "lower level," we were graduating to a new location: a large Victorian building on the north side of Main Street, only a few blocks west of the Jerome Hotel. I would have a glorious second-floor office with a large southern window overlooking the town and Ajax (Aspen Mountain).

The radio station's audience was growing too. According to the latest

Mediastat survey, KSPN enjoyed 73 percent of the entire listening market. And our big beautiful sales folders bragged about the size of the market:

KSPN-FM ... On Top of The Market. KSPN-FM, the 24-hour sound of contemporary music, news and information, serves Colorado's Roaring Fork Valley. From Aspen to Glenwood Springs, we reach a diverse and affluent audience. What makes KSPN-FM a smart advertising buy? Here are five solid reasons: ASPEN—SNOWMASS—BASALT—CARBONDALE—GLENWOOD SPRINGS.

My work with the BLM on KSPN's mountaintop land leases opened new avenues for translator and microwave transmission across the Rockies, not only for FM radio signals but also television. Ted Turner was using satellite transmission in Atlanta to send his low-power channel 17 signal (SuperStation WTBS) to cable system headends around the country, but I felt that we wouldn't be able to afford a satellite uplink for our small market. Even my radio pioneering compatriot, John Tyler, was forming a new radio network (Satellite Music Network [SMN]) that could transmit a variety of music formats via satellite to small radio stations across the nation. He called me from Dallas, hoping to sign up KSPN-FM for his new venture. We weren't interested; we were too big and too successful with our own unique format (we thought).

KSPN-FM crew, early 1980s Photo courtesy of Sue Ann Todhunter

By February, our Omaha UHF TV-15 application needed attention. Gene Conley had called me to report there were rumblings that professional broadcast investors were applying for the other Omaha UHF TV-43 frequency and would be beating us to FCC approval. None of us could believe that anyone would be interested in a frequency that high, with such a weak over-the-air signal. If they went on the air first, our second independent television station would be a disaster in such a small market. I wasn't willing to work on the Omaha application full time, nor was Bill Seidman, nor were any of our Omaha investors. And no one seemed to be tracking the legal bills from Arnold and Porter, our FCC attorneys. Bill had Phelps Dodge copper troubles to worry about, plus a new hip operation in April, and both of us had to work on the international banks if we were to see any real progress in our China joint-venture contracts. Omaha was getting lost in the mix.

Midge and Gary wanted a big summer bash at Gary's nine-acre estate on Spring Lake to celebrate Mom and Dad's fiftieth wedding anniversary. Gary surprised all of us when he bought the only landmark home in Spring Lake in 1977; it made front-page headlines in the *Grand Haven Tribune,* and local gossip was rife. (Who was this young kid, hardly out of college, buying the only trophy property left within the village? How could he afford it?)

The party date was early summer: June 20, 1980. Since Mom and Dad were courting in the Roaring Twenties, the theme was an obvious one. What was my long-distance assignment? Or, as it turned out, "our" assignment? First, the invitations and all the responses, sent to Mountain Laurel Drive in Aspen. And coming from all the kids, perhaps a skit too.

A poetic invitation was written by my gang of five. Julio then hand-printed the invitation on a fifteen-by-twenty-inch scroll. Copies were mailed in long tubes to hundreds of Mom and Dad's relatives and friends.

After Fritz's six years of practice at Yale directing and performing in shows, he was the natural choice to put together the "Roaring Twenties" skit. I had no idea what Fritz would produce, but I marveled at his classy authentic 1920s costumes, which were flown in from Brooks-Van Horn in New York City.

From left: Greg, Lydia, Fritz, Brett, Charline (Grammy) Hatton, Joyce, Julio

Drinks and dinner were served under a striped tent on the lawn. At dusk, the guests were ushered inside to the vestibule; they crowded around the grand piano to hear "The Saga of Tooter and Lyt."

"Tooter," Bill Seidman, and "Lyt"

From Fritz' program: "An operetta in one act ... delivered on the occasion of the celebration of the above-mentioned fiftieth wedding anniversary—June 20, 1980—during the course of a party at Gary and Vicki Verplank's, the likes of which would have made Jay Gatsby green with envy."

After the big party at Gary's house, I had to tackle a very prickly issue: my final departure as a consultant to the ACD and YW.

Marge Langworthy and ACD board members, July 1980

As the CEO of ACD for the past three years, Marge Langworthy had assembled her own handpicked board members, and they certainly felt no loyalty to me. Her lawyer, Doug Austin (who used to be a favorite of mine), was arguing vociferously with our brilliant Provincial House lawyer, Robert Stocker, about the future of ACD's association with YW. And Marge got what she wanted: the YW day care centers sold after six months. ACD would continue to manage the Child Care Food Program in Michigan, but both Harriet Newman's Illinois program and Nancy Van Domelen's Colorado programs might have to become independent non-profit businesses.

There would be a final meeting six months later, and then I would be gone … for good. Jeff Poorman didn't need my help selling the centers. He was young, bright, and brash, and he quickly sold the centers to Gerber, the popular baby food company with corporate offices and a factory in Fremont, Michigan, a small town north of Grand Rapids. We could have the centers back in five years if Gerber didn't like the day care business. (Gerber didn't, and they gave us back all the centers after five years. Jeff Poorman sold them again, one at a time, for more money than Gerber would have paid if they had fulfilled their land contract. I continued to get my share of the lease payments and sale of each asset. Thanks to Jeff, I had the best deal.)

July 1980 continued to be a very eventful month. First, it was the Republican National Convention in Detroit. I asked for press credentials for KSPN-FM. I was probably the only Colorado press person on our plane to Detroit who had the experience of actually being a delegate at a national GOP convention (in Miami, 1968).

Bill Seidman was working the crowd, hoping to put former President Ford in the vice presidential seat. Governor Ronald Reagan had won the primary vote, so he should have had the opportunity to pick his running mate. Well, Ford and his henchmen thought differently. Can you believe that President Ford wanted a copresidency with Henry Kissinger as secretary of state and Alan Greenspan as secretary of treasury?

And Ford almost got his wish. ... At the last minute, Ford released his demands, but Reagan was so pissed at his tactics that he picked almost an unknown to the convention for the second spot, former congressman from Texas and CIA director George Bush. I couldn't believe the apparent naiveté of the Ford staff.

From my report to KSPN-FM:

> The Reagan delegates are believers, not doubters. And they work and play hard; they don't waste time or energy second-guessing. They loved Rumsfeld's remark Monday night that President Carter "is naïve." But one can't help but wonder if they, too, aren't a little naïve. They seem *so* positive in their beliefs, as if they go through life accepting only what works for them. Can they learn from history, if they dismiss as rhetoric others' experiences? Does the intellect play much of a part in their lives?
>
> And where was the Republican intelligentsia at this convention? Kissinger let them down; brilliant Henry, the bureaucratic infighter, done in by his own machinations ... and his own lust for power ... and not deterred by Greenspan, who had his spot picked out at Treasury.
>
> (And where was) Bartlett, or Marsh, who as friends of Ford's, could have assumed more responsibility for helping Ford to make a decision?
>
> In the end, Ford, relying on his intuition, took the easy way out, thereby dumping his power-hungry advisors.
>
> Next, entered Bush at the eleventh hour, and one of the Reagan delegates asked, "Why doesn't he put on some weight so he'll look more presidential?" As I watched him speak Wednesday night at the convention, I thought he had put on weight during his long campaign—a

weightier stance, a weightier voice, and weightier convictions. He knew where *he* was—in second place. And Reagan kept him there!

The nominating process probably won the day, producing the optimum team for the Republican Party.

It will be interesting to see if the Democratic conventioneers do as well next month in New York City.

In my notes written while flying on the DC-10 heading back to Denver from Detroit after the convention, I noticed "a mood of euphoria" in the Colorado Republican delegation ... even with Bush as their vice presidential candidate. I wrote, "Just think, Reagan was making these delegates become pragmatic too."

I sat next to a retired army general from Winter Park and asked him what he thought about the Republican platform. "Well, our stand on ERA may have been a self-inflicted wound," he admitted.

But, personally, the general was strongly against the Equal Rights Amendment, especially the drafting of women, and he took great pains to explain why: First, he said that foreign governments would look with disdain at our country if we degraded our armed forces by admitting women to our ranks. In the past, only governments that were desperate and on the verge of collapse conscripted women. Second, he said that women were of little use in most service jobs. "We already have more women in the army than we can effectively use." He explained that women were not useful in backup positions to the front lines, because when the men needed a rest, the women couldn't come forward to take their places; therefore, they would just be "in the way."

I suggested that women might be good pilots.

He replied, "They'd have greater trouble ejecting from their craft."

(It was true that Mary Creason's older sister died in 1944 because she couldn't get the escape hatch open on the experimental plane she was testing—but maybe no one could.)

The general continued, "Besides, it's been proven that they don't stand up well as prisoners of war."

Welcome to my war of the 1980s.

The first to finish of the 274 boats in this year's 333-mile Chicago-Mackinac yacht race in mid-July was *Brassy*, a 61-foot C & C, skippered by Minor Keeler II. (Mike and his tiny whirling dervish of a wife, Mary Ann, were Jule's and my fun-loving friends from the 1960s.)

"It was a little rough out there," announced Bob Currier calmly, as the *Brassy* docked about 11:00 p.m., amid a throng of well-wishers and reporters. (Our family considered Bobbie the real skipper of *Brassy*.)

The boats it was really rough on, however, turned out to be the huge group—over 150 of them—that had come up the "slot," sailing the normal route between the Manitou Islands and Michigan's Leelanau peninsula.

"We did three death rolls on *Sleeping Bear* before Grey's Reef, and two more in the Straits of Mackinac," exclaimed Midge, who finished in third place in class I.

Death rolls? Midge had to explain: "First, *Sleeping Bear*'s chute was pulled dangerously to one side and then the other; then, the boat broached (lay over on its leeward side); after righting itself, the wind caught its sails again, and, with no steerage (I know, having been at the wheel when they broach), spun the boat into a jibing position, tipping it over to windward, with the spinnaker pole sticking straight down in the water—the so-called death roll, because if the boat has enough momentum going forward when this happens, all the rigging lets go." Back and forth, *Sleeping Bear* tossed out of control, the crew hanging on for their lives, until, finally, five death rolls later, the chute torn to shreds, the *Sleeping Bear* managed to set a storm chute and sail for the finish line at Mackinac Island, only three hours away.

After such a horrific Chicago-Mackinac race, I worried that Midge's tender *Sleeping Bear* sloop might not be competitive in future Mackinac races. I worried, too, because my boys were part of his crew.

But how wrong I was! In the Chicago-Mackinac race in 1982, Midge was first in his section, and second overall—in a fleet of three hundred sailboats.

The Sleeping Bear winning crew on Mackinac Island, July 1982 From left: Fritz Hatton, Dr. Karen Pierre, Pat Dennis, Bob Currier, Frank Whitton, Bari Johnson, Brett Hatton, Skipper Midge Verplank

Free at last … of Michigan work obligations, I moved on to New York City. Our Albany investors were expecting approval soon from the FCC for the license of Albany UHF TV-23; according to Reed Miller, our FCC legal counsel, we had the superior application. I would be the "designated driver" once again, responsible for putting the station on the air.

I camped out at Bill's apartment on East 67th Street, just a half block east of Central Park. With Bill's new hip keeping him off the jogging path, we started biking around the park. There were plenty of trails available—Central Park is fifty blocks long, from 59th Street on the south to 110th on the north. I quickly learned my way around and across the park, because Bill liked to bike up Broadway on Sunday, have breakfast, and make the late-morning service at Riverside Church. We would leave Central Park at 110th Street and bike up the hill past Columbia University, which was just south of the immense church on Broadway. World-renowned figures, like Martin Luther King Jr., had spoken from the pulpit. And my nemesis, Marion Wright Edelman of the Children's Defense Fund, spoke to the congregation about the need to provide quality health care to all children. (Who would disagree with that need? How you get there never seemed to me to be part of her equation.)

My radio, television, and microwave work required approvals by the FCC; I often made daily calls to Reed Miller or his associates at Arnold and Porter in Washington, DC. Perhaps a little education on my part at Columbia Law School might help our television station's bottom line by cutting down on our mounting legal bills for the development of the Albany UHF TV-23 station and the filing of the Omaha UHF TV-15 and Little Rock UHF TV-16 applications. And if I wanted to build that microwave transmission network for radio and television from west to east across the Continental Divide in Colorado (which had never been done before), who knew what legal hoops I might have to navigate to get there!

So … on September 4, 1980, I signed up for two courses at Columbia, one in the law school (a colloquium on human rights), and one in the graduate school of philosophy (a study of art and illusion, perception, and pictorial representation and metaphors). I wasn't sure the classes were going to help me with contracts, but they might help me with right thinking. I chose classes late in the day so that I could ride my bike back across the park before dark. As soon as class was over, I would hurry out to get a fast start down the hill from Columbia, enter the park at full speed, peddle like mad, and hope to get through the most dangerous northern bike paths without being followed. However, by late fall, the park was pitch-black by 6:00 p.m., and I had to commute to class by taxi from Bill's apartment.

My New York City boys urged me to buy a loft in SoHo. Now that Fritz was the acting director of operations at Christie's, he could afford a permanent location. The two of them went on the hunt. I paid little attention; I was on my own quest for independence.

John Gilmore, owner of Jerome Hotel, with local Aspenites
(I'm in the cowboy hat); Jerome Hotel, 1980s

John Gilmore, fresh from his recent divorce from Bobbie, had pulled me aside in his famous J-Bar during Aspen's Winterskol festivities to suggest that I get myself a good psychiatrist, warning me that I needed to get over my insidious infatuation with Bill Seidman: "You're hung up on Bill and that's going nowhere. It's preventing you from striking out and doing many new, better (?) things."

It may have been self-serving on John's part, but his parting shot (when I claimed a psychiatrist was too expensive) was "How much is your life worth?"

Although I didn't take John seriously, nevertheless, I called our great connector, Priscilla Morgan. Could she find me a really smart psychiatrist? Of course. She would call her old friend Hans, now mostly retired; Hans had counseled Robert Oppenheimer, the developer of the atom bomb. Wow.

People said there wasn't anyone smarter than Oppenheimer. I couldn't wait for my first appointment with Hans in New York City.

The doctor's office was near Priscilla and Bill's apartment building on 67th Street. Just a small, insignificant office, and Han's comments to me seemed insignificant, too, although I was being told what John predicted. According to my diary notes, Hans said my "easy way out"—to continue down the same path with Bill "as usual" was really not facing up to the fact that there was no future with Bill.

Hans explained, "Bill is not going to get a divorce, and the longer you stay in the present tenuous situation, the harder the fall will be when it comes, which it will, because it is building to that eventuality."

Also, Hans added that the person who does the getting out is the least hurt, so I'd better get moving. Hans was not sure I had the "emotional stability," which he then rephrased as "emotional maturity," to handle it when it does come.

Hans's comments sounded just like Duncan Littlefair's. I met with the doctor one more time, but he didn't think I needed him. I guess it was a compliment, of sorts. I was hoping for a magician, but, instead I got me.

But I got my loft; I got my independence. It was glorious. And it still is. The boys found a 3,500-square-foot third-floor loft on Broome Street, in a substantial building that was featured on the cover of *Loft Living* in 1977. The place needed work, but the basic needs could be met for me and all my family. Fritz could have his huge nine-foot Steinway concert grand piano. (And for an exorbitant fee, the piano could be moved to the third-floor loft. Fritz waited five months to save enough money for the move, and, when the movers showed up, they blocked off half of Broome Street, which in itself was quite a feat, because Broome Street was the main Manhattan route to the Holland Tunnel.)

Since the loft was close to New York University's campus, I checked into night classes in NYU's School of Film and Television. Guess who was lecturing! Our very own Albany TV-23 board member, movie director Arthur Penn. I signed up for the evening film class. Bill said he would like to attend too, when he was in town. I added his name but didn't think he would be much interested in dissecting the film angles of classics like *Citizen Kane*. Bill planned to come one evening with Paul Eggert, but the two of them got lost trying to find our classroom, and they rendezvoused in the corner bar instead. I'm not sure that wasn't Paul's original destination. (Paul was in town working on a new cable TV guide magazine and wanted Bill's help with introductions to captains in the industry. *Time* magazine had lost $5 million on a similar start-up, so Bill and I were not very enthusiastic about Paul's prospects for success.)

My Aspen house looked fantastic upon my return from New York City. Outside and in. I was not in much condition to clean house, so I was relieved to see the house looking neat but very "Aspen-y." Lots of plants do the trick every time.

Barbara Newman Luton, Bill Seidman, Harriet Newman. June 15, 1981

And what fun to see the Newman ladies. Barb and Liz are very classy gals, a tribute to their mom's interest and love during their developing years. They are full of pizzazz. I hope I can figure out a way for them to partake of the Design Conference without paying the $300 registration fee.

The Design Conference: We hardly partook at all, and when we did, it was not fruitful. The opening session was a disappointment because it was difficult to understand the speakers—their Italian accents were so pronounced. ... The evening was more rewarding: Bertolucci spoke clearly enough, slowly enough, and thoughtfully enough. (Bertolucci was infamous for the rape scene in his 1972 movie, *Last Tango in Paris*.)

The Italians filmed in a different context than Americans do, *and* they didn't have $40 million to spend on a film.

I asked Bertolucci, "Where do you get your ideas?"

"Everywhere. I got the idea for *Luna* from looking at the moon; I wanted to contrast its old face with that of a child. And I create as I go along; I enjoy contrasting one scene with the next."

I felt he weaved a picture together from many varied colored strands, or put the pieces of a puzzle together at the editing stage: it did not seem that he had a script written out ahead of time, more that he composed as he went along, juxtaposing one scene to another.

Former Grand Rapids International Designer and Aspen resident, Bob Blaich, at Design Conference

It was an interesting idea. ... I felt that Bertolucci filmed the way I thought—developing my ideas as I went along. I had not felt comfortable writing an entire outline first; I wasn't sure where the story was going to lead, or the speech, or life. Adjustment, flexibility—à la Plato perhaps, but was there any other way to live? To understand this so late in life was Harriet's and my fate; we had to discover it for ourselves. But we made sure it was taught to our children.

Was it worth teaching? Actually, we couldn't help but teach it to our kids. They would have gotten it by osmosis, but what about others? If I wanted to produce that script, I'd better weave the strands together, or collect the pieces that fit the puzzle. But when would I start?

Little did I realize that I had already started. I brought home to Aspen in the winter and spring of 1981 my law textbooks from my courses at Columbia Law School. Unbeknownst to me, my son found sample LSAT's (Law School Admission Tests) in the back of my books and decided to take all the tests. He couldn't believe how easy they were! He then announced that he planned to take the LSAT in the fall and needed all summer to study for it, especially since he had been out of college for a few years.

Wow! Adjustment? Flexibility? Needless to say, he dug in. All that energy concentrated on one goal. Yes, he studied for two months and then took the LSAT. And waited. ... Would he do well enough to get into a reputable school?

Rev. Dr. Duncan Littlefair Photo courtesy of Michael Grass

September 21, 1981, 9:00 a.m. Here are the notes in my diary from weekend meeting in Grand Rapids with Dr. Duncan Littlefair:

DUNCAN: You are so lucky; you're beautiful, smart, sexy, rich—and dumb.

JOYCE: Why?

DUNCAN: Because you have so much and yet are never satisfied.

JOYCE: I'm not?

DUNCAN: What are you doing in this town anyway … following him around like a wife?

JOYCE: I came for a wedding.

DUNCAN: Well, then, go take care of your wedding. You're better than that. Get out of here; stop acting like a wife.

DUNCAN: Our lives are 80 percent hypocrisy. We can't stand the truth. It's too painful.

Hardball. Bill and Duncan were playing it with me. And I wasn't prepared. I wilted like a flower. Fragile thing that I turned out to be. My life seemed petty, and I sank into the morass of self-indulgence; I felt sorry for me.

JOYCE: I don't like it when he lies to me.

DUNCAN: Then don't put yourself in a position where he has to. Don't act like a wife. You don't need that; you have just what a wife covets but can't have: to be desired—sexually—by her husband. Women are covetous. Terribly so. They want to possess the man they've given their love to. I could never let myself sleep with a woman. The next day she'd be calling. She'd want to continue the relationship. She'd want to own me. One-night stands are easy for men, but not women. Women want men to continue to desire them sexually, and when that is lost, women are devastated. Husbands lie to their wives to protect them from the pain of the truth. It's a hypocritical world, but it has to be. People couldn't stand the pain otherwise.

Our SoHo loft was a godsend in 1982. Lydia had transferred to Columbia University in January and moved into the loft. She rode the West Side subway from Canal Street all the way up Manhattan to Columbia University at 116th Street.

The kids fashioned a corner of the loft for me when I showed up, but they knew I would be moving west after I hired a general manager to launch the Albany television station. I liked having a New York office and mailing address and kids around to answer the phone.

Even Mom and Dad were eager to visit, although the stairs would prove a difficult climb for Dad, now that he was almost seventy-five. We could use the elevator, but it was time consuming to arrange for it every day, and we had to seek permission from our neighbors to go through their apartment to the elevator. *Ahh* ... loft living was still for the young at heart!

But who was worrying about the really young at heart?

After monitoring children's TV programs all spring on New York City's major television stations, I couldn't believe the lack of good programming offered up as daily fare. Old (really old) cartoons, over and over and over, *Sesame Street,* and someone had resurrected *Captain Kangaroo.*

What television needed for very young children was a supply of good storytellers—and good coaches, good moderators, good managers of people—very young people. They're most important because they're most impressionable; it is a lasting mark. Why were we so dumb? To eat our seed corn, or, rather, feed them fodder over the airwaves? Thank god, I've never trusted "them." (But should "they" trust me?)

Who had time to think creatively? After my lunch in DC with Bill Harris and his KidsPac, I wondered if anything of lasting value would develop.

The NIMH (National Institute of Mental Health) had a report on TV violence and its lasting impact on children. But I didn't bother to get that report. I knew advertisers wouldn't advertise if they didn't influence the reader or the viewer. No commercials, no television—pretty scary. If advertising can send you to market for Frothie's Beer, it can send John Hinckley to market for a gun. We knew advertising worked. In print or on videotape.

The problem was the preschool child. Before the era of TV, adults picked the reading material when they read to preschoolers. They didn't go to their lazy susan, push a button, and see which book popped out for bedtime consumption. And one read to children, or took them to the theater or cinema or library, on one's own schedule.

The requirements placed on adults to monitor children's TV viewing were unrealistic. What did the adult know about the fare available? Knowing a title (*Scooby-Doo*) didn't tell the adult the content, intent, or portent of a show. How often did adults force themselves to preview what children would be seeing? In many cases, it was an impossibility!

Was there really much difference between one's own TV and programs and one's own books? If our children were going to spend that much time hooked to the tube (up to four hours a day, with little indication anyone could do anything about it), we should give them the best education available in the world. After all, weren't we the richest country? And weren't our children our richest resource?

Dr. Mortimer J. Adler (1902–2001) Courtesy of David LaClaire

"Educate to live the good life, not to get a job," said (Mortimer) Adler. Okay, *Paideia*, explain to the average joe what Adler meant by "good life."

I was in the boob-tube business. Feeding stupid and foolish information for "living the good life." And how was I trying to improve it? Could I produce material as entertaining as this must be? No. *Because I hadn't done it..* According to PBS (Public Broadcasting System), we were unable to understand the complexity of international relations—or intrigue. How were we to go about teaching that to the uninitiated?

In the spring of 1982, mothers of very young children were coming into the world of work in record numbers, but it was a recent phenomenon. Their attitudes toward child care suffered jet lag. And the fathers, the majority of whom were brought up by nonworking mothers, suffered more, having been brought up in households dominated by working fathers. (Mom said Grandpa Secory made *all* the decisions.) Consequently, new parents had not had much experience equating good "quality" care of their young children with a dollar figure.

I felt the responsibility for good child care rested with the parents and not with the community or a community-appointed committee. A young child needs care—but it doesn't have to be a child care center to be quality; it doesn't even have to be the parents. But the parents must find the care they want and are willing to pay for. Local governmental bodies could be facilitators. Perhaps a place where caregivers could learn more about the education and care of very young children.

From my experience, caregivers would not take the time to attend classes at night, but they would be willing to bring their children—and those entrusted to them during the day—to a central location for entertainment or educational projects. Where would the money come from to teach the caregivers *and also* care for the children while the caregiver was receiving instruction? From the parents, but the community can help.

Since I wrote that last sentence after attending some community meetings in the lofty atmosphere of Aspen, I should have added that the AFDC program paid the tuition of the welfare families in Michigan's licensed day care homes and centers. And that dependence tripled during the twenty years I worked with Michigan's day care homes and centers.

Chapter Ten

MEGATRENDS

We are living in a time between eras.

John Naisbitt, *Megatrends*, 1982

KSPN-TV and FM Sales Manager, R. J. Gallagher and Joyce Hatton on Ajax Mountain

I would find no time over the next decade to worry about community in-volvement in preschool education, or "living the good life." My need for capital infusions into my multifarious entrepreneurial enterprises would consume all my time and energy.

By 1981, work on Albany's UHF TV-23 station was picking up steam. My first job was hiring a manager who knew the business. When I got through the first lengthy interview with a former manager of a large independent station who had his own personal agenda, I worried if there really would be any manager out there with good business sense.

We desperately needed an experienced manager. I had been looking at managers from independent stations, assuming a manager from one of the three network affiliates would not stoop to our level. Fortunately, our Washington, DC, stockholders knew that a piece of the action (station ownership) would attract some of the best and brightest, and they found Jim Boaz, the hard-driving manager of the Washington, DC, NBC affiliate, WRC TV-4.

Jim was perfect for this job: tough, exacting, and financially responsible with our limited resources. He joked that he was going to be the "free HBO" for the Albany market, loading up on classic movies and syndicated reruns. Jim knew (much better than I) the cost of live newscasts—he wouldn't be competing in that market. Jim brought in David Low, a well-respected, experienced broadcast sales manager, to organize the important sales component. On the financial end, my work for the FCC application process paid off. In February 1982, Mannie Hannie confirmed " ... its willingness to extend a $1,800,000 term loan and a $700,000 revolving credit to Albany TV-23, Inc."—that bank's first loan to an independent television station! But that wouldn't preclude the dreaded "cash calls."

We weren't having the luck with the Omaha TV-15 application that we had with Albany. Our extended filing deadlines found us competing with new applicants for both Omaha UHF TV-15 and Omaha UHF TV-42. It had been more than two years since we filed for Albany's UHF-23. Now we were no longer ahead of the curve in filing for UHF television stations in the top fifty markets. In fact, it looked like the Omaha channel 42 applicants could file first because they had less competition for their UHF TV-42 license. And I knew we wouldn't want to file second. Omaha was not a large enough market to support two new independent, nonaffiliated network television stations. Our legal costs with Arnold and Porter were mounting up as more applicants filed for the available licenses. And we were having a similar problem with Little Rock TV-16. When a local group filed against us, we knew we had to compromise, or leave.

No one continued to stay as far ahead of the curve as Ted Turner—in sailing or broadcasting. All my family knew his sailing capabilities; my kids called him "the mouth of the South." I knew his broadcasting prowess. He bought a defunct UHF TV station, and as an over-the-air station, he could microwave-link his signal to cable headends in the southeastern United States. Then, in 1976, he offered his station's signal nationwide via satellite. By 1979, the FCC gave the common carrier, Southern Satellite Systems, permission to microwave the WTBS signal directly to the satellite. And by 1980, no broadcast signal was necessary to microwave Turner's new twenty-four-hour cable-only news channel, Cable News Network (CNN), directly to a satellite.

Cross-ownership rules (owning both a radio and TV station in the same market) were in the crosshairs for low-power UHF television stations in 1980 and 1981. In the 1970s, after I found out that Ted Turner could send his low-power UHF TV-17 signal (SuperStation WTBS), and his Atlanta Braves baseball games, by satellite transmission to cable systems in all fifty states, I hoped the new rules promulgated for low-power UHF television stations wouldn't prevent KSPN-FM from also owning a low-power TV station in the tiny Aspen market.

In 1981 President Reagan's new FCC commissioners decided to eliminate all the cross-ownership rules for low-power television stations! And we could choose our own channel designation. I wanted channel 23; it seemed to be our lucky number.

I was raring to go, but I quickly found out my first adversary would be Steve Heater; he had no interest in Recreation Broadcasting Company owning a local television station that would be competing with KSPN-FM for broadcast commercials. Steve thought the Aspen community was way too small to support both our television and radio station. He remembered his sour Pueblo experience, where too many FM stations competed for too few dollars in a relatively small market.

Steve would be no natural supporter of mine, since I had replaced him as manager of KSPN-FM. And Steve was chairman of the board and owned more stock than I did. He could ignore my "fantasy" plans for distributing the signals via microwave to cable headends throughout the Rockies, emphasizing to the other stockholders my need for more capital contributions than he could, or would, make. Steve knew the local Canyon Cable manager wielded a heavy hand, controlling which local broadcast signals would be allowed on his precious cable channels—and ours would not be a "must carry" broadcast signal. We couldn't prove that viewers would be rushing to watch our old movies or syndicated reruns or live news or local ski reports. It would be a rocky road. ...

As soon as Recreation Broadcasting, Inc. (RBI) received approval for its low-power UHF TV-23 license, I forged ahead. I told my three loyal original stockholders—Bill Seidman, Allen Hunting, and Gary Verplank—that KSPN's television signal could soar (via microwave) across the Rockies all the way to Denver, where I knew our live ski reports would be eagerly received. And the Aspen panache captured a year-round audience of movie stars, rock stars, business moguls, and lovers of the classics in music and literature. (Who else could expect John Denver or Jimmy Buffet to stop by their radio studio? Or have their news reporters conduct interviews with former US presidents?)

Rocky Mountain cable systems along the route—TCI in Glenwood Springs, Heritage in Vail and Beaver Creek, and Summit County systems in Breckenridge, Copper Mountain, Keystone, and Arapahoe—could insert their own local news and commercials. No one contemplated using satellite uplinks in our small markets, the lease of a satellite transponder was prohibitively expensive.

Our tower on Red Mountain was interfacing with a translator tower down valley to carry our KSPN-FM signal into Glenwood Springs on a different frequency. I knew that the same towers could be used to microwave our television signals to the cable headends too. KSPN-FM sales brochures bragged that KSPN's signal was "on top of the market," serving Colorado's Roaring Fork valley from Aspen to Snowmass to Basalt to Carbondale to Glenwood Springs—where "visitors are attracted in growing numbers to the hot springs, as well as whitewater rafting, fishing, hunting, skiing, and wilderness pack trips." And KSPN-FM staffers wanted to build translator towers from Glenwood Springs to the Gore Valley, which serves Vail and Avon/Beaver Creek. These towers could microwave the television signal too.

I had to start from scratch with a television studio in our new location on Main Street. Move over, FM equipment, here we come. ... The battles with the entrenched FM staff became bitter, especially when I tangled with the sales force. My toughest and longest battles were over funding. I had few personal resources, but I did have some stockholders with deep pockets. Would they be willing to guarantee loans to lease the necessary equipment? I would have to put together more pro formas for local banks and hope the bankers would accept pro rata guarantees, because I knew my smart stockholders would never risk their total resources—much less divulge them. But I continued to forge ahead, lining up sources for new or used television equipment, hoping that I would receive bank approvals in time to install the mountain equipment before any major snowfalls, which could come as early as October.

When one of my sons announced that he and his longtime Aspen girlfriend wanted to be married on the same day in August that Albany's WXXA-TV 23 was planning its on-air opening celebration, I agonized over the decision. Where would my friend Bill Seidman go? He would choose to go to the Albany TV celebration. And I would want him to go. He was heading west in September, to his new appointment as dean of the business school at Arizona State University. His five-year commitment to Phelps Dodge was over, and he was eager to move on.

Bill Seidman was a born pedagogue. He was the driving force that created GVSU in the early 1960s and the Washington Campus program in the seventies. Bill knew the wily ways of Washington politics and influence. In his book, *Full Faith and Credit,* Bill wrote, "After President Ford had lost the 1976 election, I made a speech to the International Conference of Business School Deans explaining the importance of government to the bottom line of practically every business and criticizing business schools for ignoring its importance." They listened, and Bill ultimately signed up for his Washington Campus program an impressive list of fifteen schools, including Dartmouth, Cornell, Georgetown, Michigan, Indiana, Ohio State, Grand Valley State University, North Carolina, Texas, and University of California at Berkeley and Los Angeles.

Arizona State University was not on anyone's impressive list, especially Henry Kissinger, who surprised me by mocking businessmen in a speech that year in New York City, saying they "probably came from Arizona State." But Bill would be ready and would make his mark. What an organizer. He knew where to get the money—so important in the development of his fledgling institutions—and he knew which local Phoenix corporate boards or banks to occupy with his directorships.

Bill organized another event that fall: my fiftieth birthday party in October, in New York City. He called my New York clan and offered to pay for a party at the loft if they would do the legwork. My kids ... a party? The 1821 (eighteen-twenty-*fun*) aficionados?

Fritz lined up the most famous doorman in New York City, Gil Perez of Christie's. My artists created the invitation, and we all sweated out the guest list. SoHo was still off limits to New York's high society, and many of Priscilla Morgan's friends wouldn't think of venturing to Broome Street, even if Gil Perez would be opening the door for them. (They would then have to wait for a freight elevator or climb two flights of stairs, which seemed more like four flights because of the extremely high ceilings in factory loft buildings.)

No matter. The kids invited my old political friends and sailing buddies from the past twenty years. What a shock to see my political friend, Harry Calcott from Traverse City, who flew in, bedecked in full tuxedo, and Paul

Eggert, who rushed up from the Annapolis boat show on his Prevost bus, got lost in Lower Manhattan, stuck on the Brooklyn Bridge, and then had to back the bus down off the bridge! Paul was a little late, but he was handled well by Gil Perez, who double-parked his bus at the front door on Broome Street. (Brother Midge refused to leave the Annapolis boat show on Paul's bus, knowing it could be a risky adventure.)

Bill invited a Nobel Prize winner who still lived in SoHo, but he didn't come; the only no-show that I recall. The presents were too risqué to recall in print, except for the champagne, which all the kids lobbied for in advance. Fritz had his concert grand piano to accompany the musicians, and I'm not sure how or when the party ended. But Fritz said Gil stuck it out, rescuing the wayward out-of-town guests until the wee hours.

Yes, Bill, you organized a memorable event. Not sure all those guests were your favorites, however. All the more reason to thank you for the party.

My television projects were limping along by the fall of 1982. TV News would be different from radio news: radio was passive; TV was immediate. And that was just the tip of the iceberg.

What was happening every day to make this TV a reality? Money. And I was having problems with Intrawest Bank in Montrose. The bank hadn't received the financial statements of my stockholders, and they wanted 100 percent guarantees, joint and several, from each stockholder. I screamed, "No-o-o!" It was unfair; it would take too long to go back to each stockholder.

Finally, the bank agreed to go pro rata. I quickly sent money to equipment suppliers—wired $50,000 to Dyma Engineering and talked to ABS (Advanced Broadcast Solutions) about their $30,000-plus order. And I sweated out the programming orders. After dictating a telegram to MGM for four hundred movies, I studied the CNN II contract for Headline News, which was CNN's most popular half-hour program.

Our Victorian office building was abuzz. People complaining about being on top of one another, going crazy with the proximity—walls being built, desks arriving, salt everywhere. The kitchen was very useful to all, as predicted.

On November 9, 1982, I reported in my diary that the weather would be tough for the days our helicopter was scheduled.

"It will take only a day or two," said John Dady, our peripatetic engineer, who flew in helicopters around Colorado, installing radio and television tower equipment.

I didn't have much in the budget for installation. After reviewing our costs, which kept escalating as they always do, the leasing company warned me that I only had $15,000.

While watching Charles Kuralt read the national news with head bent, I decided we had to have a teleprompter—another $4,000 item for a single camera, or $6,000 for two. But it would be great for TV production and the ski and road reports.

Fortunately, we didn't need to pay for many new staff persons. I hired friends of the kids to handle the audio/video equipment. But the costs for tooling up were there, even if we were in a recession—or depression.

I needed to follow up with Glenwood Springs and Vail cable managers to get us on their systems, pronto. That would cost more money—again. Probably $20,000 for Glenwood, and $5,000 for Vail and Avon. And I had to follow up on national and regional sales, especially Glenwood sales.

My RBI stockholders deserved current reports and copies of bank guarantees. And I worried about Mannie Hannie's bank covenants for Albany TV-23—before manager Jim Boaz went to the bank. And lost in the mix, again, was Omaha TV-15.

And what about me? Could I see the forest for the trees? Did I have the wrong people in the wrong places? Account, account for each person, thing, project, idea, and be accountable. (To God?)

In 1982, Thanksgiving Day was more like Christmas—the multiplexer arrived, the TBCs (time base correctors) were in Denver, the satellite dish was on its way from New York. Our local cable operator, Canyon Cable, was prepared to string the satellite cable between our two buildings on Monday. We begged our local engineer, Dave Wright, (renamed by us "Dave Wrong") to find us some telephone cable so that we didn't have to pay to string it separately.

Ted Hartley showed up the night before. He arrived from Hollywood for the holiday weekend and became fascinated with the development of the TV station. He wanted to produce a TV documentary of my life as an entrepreneur. I told Ted what a pill Steve Heater had been and said I wished Steve would sell out to *somebody!* (Too bad Ted didn't marry actress Dina Merrill *before* 1989. The newlyweds resurrected RKO studios and began producing films, TV series, and Broadway shows.)

John Dady and the helicopter pilot were lost on the mountain the night before last. Most of us were not too concerned because Dady was somewhat of a loner and "disappeared" quite often. However, not with the helicopter pilot. They finished putting our transmitter and antenna in place on Red Mountain as the storm moved in and made it as far as Elephant Mountain (none of us ever heard of it). They put down because of the weather and spent the night. When it cleared at dawn, they appeared, none the worse for wear, at the Aspen airport. John's poor wife. And a few others in our employ who didn't know Dady's proclivities.

We put off KSPN-TV's opening date to Sunday, December 5. I invited all the stockholders, but I didn't get a confirmation that any of them would come.

What a weekend nightmare it was, starting on Thursday, December 2. John Dady called me in the morning, said he wasn't able to get our rebuilt STL (studio transmitter link) to work. He worried that we would have to get another STL. Everyone was ready to string Dady from his toes, but they would have to wait, because they needed him on the mountain.

Thursday evening, I flew to Denver to meet Bill Seidman, not knowing what the situation would be. I called Dady from Denver, and he gave me the bad news. "I can't get it to work. Tomorrow morning, beginning at 8:00 a.m., you and I will have to start calling around for an STL. You call Leasametrics in Denver at 8:00 a.m., and I'll call Farinon in California at 9:00 a.m., when they open."

It ruined my evening. I couldn't believe Bill wasn't more understanding of my predicament—and I wasn't interested in discussing Albany's problems; I had too many of my own to worry about.

Then he wanted to discuss personal finances and the house sale, and I wasn't much interested in that, either. I felt he treated me like a business partner rather than a friend.

"What expenses do you have on the house over the last four years?"

I kidded him about it, and he replied, "That's the way you have wanted it." And he probably was right.

But I said, "I don't think I have any equity left in the house, so why don't you just take it and forget the numbers? It's your money, and I want you to have it, because you need it to finance the Albany cash call."

Bill was furious; it reminded him of my attitude toward Jule when I was getting a divorce. I just wanted out—with no recriminations about money.

Yes, I wanted out of the house now, and I knew I hadn't earned any equity because I had borrowed my share from Bill to finance the TV stations.

Bill left for the airport at 8:00 a.m., and I called Leasametrics.

George Strickland answered, and responded to my inquiry by asking, "What's an STL?"

I responded by commenting, "I guess I'm not talking to the right person."

George called it a microwave link, and when he said no way could I get one on the right frequency in time, my hopes fell—and I thought, *What am I going to do with all those people Sunday night?*

He suggested that we try to fix the present STL.

Fortunately, Dady went ahead and called Farinon in California, and then asked me to talk to the domestic sales manager to see if we could get an entire new unit from them. To make a long story short, I decided to bring their lead engineer with the equipment. That way, we'd know it was right and installed correctly.

Farinon did send an engineer, just not the lead one. Bob Everett was plenty competent, and, thank God, healthy (lived on a sailboat in San Francisco Bay), because he had to climb the mountain to the transmitter at 8:00 a.m. Sunday morning—and it wasn't ready until 10:00 a.m., at which time we had audio without interference. We all whooped and hollered when our audio came through loud and *clear*. Little did I realize that the audio was still going to be our problem, because it was not sufficiently hooked up in the studio.

Well … KSPN-TV-23 did go "on air" on December 5! Not quite as planned. Missed the introduction because there was no audio for fifteen minutes. And then we went right into the movie. But the 350 people who showed up at Charlemagne's restaurant were so crammed in that they didn't miss a thing. (" … Why, you were only thirty seconds late!")

And from Mary Jo, the receptionist at Canyon Cable, the next day: "What a wonderful party! So many people! I've never been in Charlemagne! And my seventeen-year-old daughter had 'a little champagne' and confessed her whereabouts all the way home in the car. …"

And Mike Fitzgerald, our first advertiser: "Great party last night! Congratulations!"

By Monday morning, I had a dilly of a hang*over*—*over*served and *over*tired, and every time I looked at our tired signal (a sixty-cycle hum on CNN because of transformers near the cable, plus a bad receiver unit that I helped replace at midnight), my head pounded even more. We lost the audio going into the movie, which was late; and then lost the entire picture for about ten minutes. But from noon on, we stayed on air and on schedule, even if the picture was rotten on the cable. Our TV engineer, David Stewart, had not slept for seventy-two hours by Monday morning, so we sent him home for twenty-four hours.

I also realized on Monday morning that two-thirds of our studio equipment hadn't been hooked up. Well, the villain, I contended, was John Dady, who never took care of his end of the deal by letting the STL become the bugaboo that caused a three-day delay in getting the rest of the equipment ready and hooked up.

Two weeks later, December 19, 1982: *The Three Musketeers,* in color (actually, just one: red.) New A/V operators—Bob (the satellite man) and Dan (the night-flight man). Training on the job. *Ugh.* Frankly, the movie was probably so old that even David Stewart couldn't do much with it. Then it was black and white. Such a distraction! Especially with Tom Mines and another construction guy ("the engineer") in the background building new stairs. There was a lot of *work* ahead over Christmas vacation. ... I hoped my kids were prepared.

We made NBC-4 in Denver the previous Friday, with coverage of the Durant condominiums fire. We still were not doing local news. Not enough equipment or people to carry it out. And I had to get a cheap CG (character generator) because VideoText was having problems with the top of their line, and we wouldn't be receiving the other one until mid-January. Routing switcher and CG and other equipment were arriving via Federal Express the following day. Getting equipment at Christmastime in Aspen was a pain in the you know what. ...

Groundhog Day 1983: It was snowing, with storms backed up all the way to Tokyo. What has happened since December 19th? Lots. Money spent on TV? Lots. Fancy programming—bad cable reception. I blamed Canyon Cable. But where would I have been without them? We cost ourselves a month's revenues, but they cost us the second month's. We were almost there. Cleanup by the cable company was still needed in Snowmass and Red Mountain. I had a good signal at my house most of the time.

Finally, the radio and TV staffs were on the same team and working together. R. J. Gallagher was doing a great job as TV and FM sales manager. I commented in my diary:

What have I learned? The importance of the cable systems in the mountains. "Off air" means nothing. Getting on all the cable systems as cheaply as possible is all-important! Now I know the cost of programming and equipment and operating. Where do I go next? I still like the idea of Santa Barbara with full power—assuming the must-carry rule will still apply.

The Omaha TV-15 shareholders were furious with me because nothing was happening, and the A&P (Arnold and Porter) legal bills were enormous. I needed to write a letter for Bill Seidman's signature to Reed Miller. (Could I find their original estimate from last spring?) According to Reed's assistant, Betsy, they'd built a case and felt it was fiscally irresponsible not to pursue it. She claimed they cut her hours in the final billing, which I hadn't yet seen. While they were building our case for UHF channel 15, other applicants were stealing the show with their FCC filing *first* for channel 42. What a waste! For our Omaha stockholders. Who would have thought anyone would file for the weak over-the-air signal of UHF 42? We would quickly find out that with cable carriage, it wouldn't matter.

In 1982, John Naisbitt wrote *Megatrends.* His book was on the best-seller list for years. Naisbitt claimed we were moving from a managerial society to an entrepreneurial one. Certainly, that was happening in Aspen. We had organizers of new economic ventures all around us. They took the risks and rewards of opening new businesses; they had to manage their own employees—and suffer the consequences when they didn't! And wasn't that the way it should be? If TV-23 or KSPN radio failed to serve the needs of the Aspen community, then we didn't deserve to exist there.

I thought an editorial (on TV?) about the attitude of Aspenites would be appropriate. I began by quoting *Megatrends*:

Much has been said and written of late about our fair city and its inability to control the conduct of the working class—you know, those who wait on you, transport you, entertain you, what have you. We are blessed with beautiful surroundings and beautiful people. This should be a beautiful resort ... right? No, I think that's a wrong assumption.

Aspen is a community, not just a ski resort. Aspen has a history, having developed over the last century from a mining town to a skiing town in winter to a hiking and biking town in summer, and, yes, it's a dilettante's town, too.

Aspen can't be controlled by one company—as Keystone is. Nor one group (such as a resort association.)

And that's what makes Aspen so attractive to me—its diversity, uncertainty, and individuality.

And what about all those business failures we've been hearing about? Naisbitt reports there are 600,000 new companies created this year. That is six times as many companies being created every day—as compared to 90,000 thirty years ago. I can assure you there are more than six times as many new ventures here in Aspen now, in 1983, than there were in 1953 (when I first visited Aspen.)

Aspen, to me, is an exciting, lively place to be. We who live here, and those who visit, both must create the atmosphere that suits their needs. To quote futurist John Naisbitt once again: "We are restructuring America from an industrialized society to an informational society. We are living in a time between eras. It is a time of great change and uncertainty—we must make uncertainty our friend! It is a time of great opportunity and a fantastic time to be alive!"

Yes, I do believe I was living in a time between eras, but I'm not sure I thought it a fantastic time to be alive. And I hated filing, filing … yes, I hated it. And arguing about management styles with Cindy Chardonnay, our powerful and talented radio station manager. And being told by Bill Seidman not to pretend I was *the* expert on television when arguing with Albany TV's manager Jim Boaz. *Criticism.* Well, I'm told I'm good at that—so I got a little of my own medicine. And it turned my stomach as well as my mind.

I decided it was time for the next John Naisbitt editorial, and I warned myself, *Don't quote others. Don't get too specific.* Of course I did both; the Aspen Institute was an easy target:

Management of a city's growth, like management of your children's growth, may have serious philosophical implications. For who's to play the role of God and decide where, when, who, and how much growth?

We've tried Growth Management here in Aspen, with many Aspenites putting their oars in the muddied waters. And we've controlled some growth, but at what price? (Did we throw the baby out with the bathwater?)

Aspen Institute chairman, Robert Anderson, with
President Ford at Aspen Institute, 1979

Look at what's happened to the Aspen Institute: Back ten to fifteen years ago, Bob Anderson, head of Arco and donator of a half million dollars every year to his pet project—the Institute, wanted the Institute to grow and prosper here in Aspen. Plans were presented for new lodging facilities and conference halls by a multitude of developers over the past decade, but the city government turned them all down. Forget their rationale for a moment. Let's look at the results, for on this occasion the city's concerns about explosive growth backfired.

Did the Institute fail to grow? No, quite the opposite. It expanded its horizons worldwide, with conference centers, lodging facilities, or offices in Berlin, Japan, Hawaii, Washington, DC, New York City, and even here in Colorado, at Baca Grande.

Yes, it failed to grow in Aspen. In fact, if it had its way, the Aspen Institute for Humanistic Studies, founded more than thirty years ago in Aspen by Walter Paepke, would have packed up its library and art gallery and left Aspen entirely, so thoroughly disgusted was the Institute with the city's lack of cooperation or enthusiasm about their plans for development of the Institute property on the north edge of town. But, fortunately for the Aspen community, participants in its most popular and famous and lucrative program, the two-week-long

Executive Seminars, only wanted to study in Aspen. Somehow the ambience and the atmosphere of Aspen make long hours of Great Books study and discussion more palatable here than in the swampy summer setting near Washington, DC, or the dry desert air of Baca Grande.

In this new era filled with entrepreneurs instead of managers, maybe Growth Management Plans are outmoded concepts. Will our city fathers back the wave of the future and sail the uncharted seas with old Growth Management Plans? And risk losing another Aspen Institute, or maybe a Music Festival or a Design Conference? Who's to say?

A sobering best seller of the '70s entitled *The Limits of Growth* states, "The final most *elusive* and most important information we need deals with human values. ..."

AND I found that quote in an Aspen Institute essay on human growth. AND that essay was a result of several years of work on growth issues by the Aspen Institute in *Aspen* which culminated in a seminar of forty-five people from eight countries and thirty-three professions at the Aspen Institute in *Aspen* in July, 1977. Perhaps the Institute was remiss in not inviting Aspen's city fathers to participate in its discussion of "Growth, Values, and the Quality of Life."

Did anyone ever see or hear my "ivory tower" editorials? On TV or radio? I don't remember. I only remember being ordered to wear lots of eye makeup the first time I appeared on television in our studio. I really didn't know how to put on eye makeup, nor did I own any. I had worn cover-up creams after eye surgery, but that was all. My naturally heavy, dark eyebrows and lashes? They disappeared without makeup under the bright lights. My smart TV anchors moved me outdoors for speechmaking—and allowed me to walk around and punch air instead of desks.

Chapter Eleven

BREAKING GLASS

"My classmates could analyze, but I, thank God, could rhapsodize.
In business as in life, that's a far more precious thing."
Peter Barton's comments on Harvard Business School
classmates in his memoir written with Lawrence Shames,
Not Fade Away, 2002.

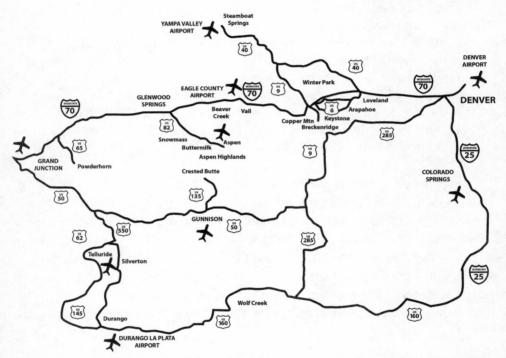

If I was going to find a microwave path to Denver, it was time for me to get organized and make the plan. First on my agenda, as always – money. Sell our Victorian office building. Next, I needed signed cable lease channel agreements all the way to Denver:

- Aspen/Snowmass—new contract with Kelly Bloomer
- Basalt/Rifle—Kelly Bloomer again
- Carbondale—ask Peggy deVilbiss

- Glenwood Springs—ask TCI
- Vail—ask Darwin Rader
- Rocky Mountain—check with Doug Lofland
- others off Castle Peak—check with Doug Lofland

Then the engineering. And it was so time consuming. Monday and Tuesday, all day Thursday, and Thursday night. But we had a plan and knowledge:

- about KVMT Vail—management/engineering/sites
- about topography—studios in Aspen to Smuggler Mountain to Red Mountain to Basalt Cable Headends to Lookout Mountain to Sunlight Peak to Castle Peak to Bellyache to Dowd (Upper and Lower) to Vail and Beaver Creek Studios
- about MDS (multipoint distribution system)
- about antennas
- about SMR (specialized mobile radio [two-way radios])
- about cellular

And who taught me? Our mountaintop engineer, Doug Lofland. And he taught me about computers too. ("Get yourself a personal computer—*now.*" I did.) But I missed Mortimer Adler. Not one evening did I have free. Bad planning. No time to read or write or exercise ... the things I enjoyed. Adjust my schedule; set aside time for my kids.

I may have been on a whirlwind tour finding mountaintop microwave sites crossing the Continental Divide to Denver, but my feat wouldn't be as productive as Peter Barton's.

We crossed paths in the topographical chart rooms in TCI's Englewood offices. (I was checking the Denver cable headend site on Mount Morrison at the request of United's engineering manager, Al Sharback.) Peter was curious why I was there, and I was curious why he cared. Who was he? This young, rambunctious kid who seemed just as irreverent and smart as his boss, John Malone—who was sitting in the room next door with his feet on a desk. (And by then, Malone could afford to, on his way to becoming one of the richest men in the United States.)

Peter was at the vortex of the cable business, on his own whirlwind tour " ... buying up everything in sight" according to his book, *Not Fade Away.* Buying up all those " ... mom-and-pop companies with ten thousand or twenty thousand subscribers; astonishingly, in the early 1980s, TCI was acquiring outfits like that at the rate of one every four days! ... It was an experience—a peak adrenaline rush ... It was extreme. It called for creativity and the testing of one's nerve, ... " Peter further reported in his book.

I should know. I had to deal with each one of them, the largest cable company being United Cable in Denver (soon to be part of TCI too). United Cable had 130,000 subscribers in the Denver suburbs in the early 1980s. I knew Peter wouldn't forget my quest: putting our Aspen-based television news and sports channel on Denver's cable systems. Why? Because he was nuts about skiing. He had been a hotdogging daredevil since his college days. I invited him to come visit us in Aspen. At any time.

When the major Denver television stations heard that KSPN-TV could bring the mountain skiing conditions live to their stations via microwave, I had a barrage of phone calls. First to call was Roger Ogden, general manager of KOA-TV (renamed KCNC in 1983). Roger really believed in local programming, as opposed to syndicated fare, and he wanted to buy microwave time on our system (before it was up and running). Instead, I wanted Roger to carry the advertising embedded in our "Ski and Road Reports," which would be carried live on KOA-TV's broadcast and cable channels.

After our meeting, Roger commented, "I envy the fact that you can be so entrepreneurial. ... Just do it! It took me a year of pro formas to get a satellite news feed approved."

Since Roger and his wife were interested in FM radio acquisitions, he seemed jealous of the fact that KSPN-FM would be putting its FM translators on prime broadcast sites like Vail's Castle Peak. But what a success Roger would become. (In 2007's *Broadcast and Cable* magazine, Roger was named Broadcaster of the Year, and reporter Paige Albiniak wrote: "Ogden believes that people and their creativity are the most important part of any media company's survival, and he has already made his mark as an innovator at Gannett.")

And Roger's wife, Ann Penny, did get her FM radio station—KYSL-FM, in Breckenridge, Colorado.

I had to forget my engineering acquisitions long enough to straighten out the shortfall created by my inept and inexperienced launch of our television station. The previous summer, I had hired a TV production manager who could teach us how to provide professional-quality local television commercials, but no one was buying—they weren't affordable in our tiny market. By comparison, our radio commercials were first-rate, quickly done, and inexpensive.

I agonized over my decision to fire the manager and his wife—both very competent and technologically savvy with all the TV equipment, which I was not. They had moved to Aspen from another state less than a year before. I'd found them a short-term rental—an old, picturesque mountain house in the most desirable location in Aspen, on Pitkin Green. The house had a natural trout pond and an attenuated winter shed with pasture for horses—all overlooking Ajax Mountain to the south.

The owners of the house planned to sell the property at some point in the future. They put a high price tag of $8 million on the three acres, which interested nobody. In the meantime, they were willing to rent the property, and that price tag was very reasonable ... as long as the occupants were willing to risk being kicked out on demand. I wanted to take over the rental as soon as my managers left town. And I was willing to risk the bad vibes that would be sent when my local staff discovered my intentions, good or bad as they may have seemed.

The house's long living room needed the open brick fireplace that filled a far wall. This was a true mountain house, with little insulation and large picture windows of thin single-pane glass. By converting two small ante-rooms to bedrooms, I created four separate bedrooms. I put two sofa beds in the living room—I was ready!—for family, friends, and relatives. And this would be my house, like my SoHo loft. But it was soon filled with people, horses, and trout.

With Michaela Crumley on Red Mountain, Aspen

My seamstress, Michaela Crumley, had three horses. (Only in Aspen do seamstresses own horses.) My shed and field accommodated three horses but no more. Wouldn't I like to ride the gentle one—in trade for boarding the horses? Of course I would.

Fly-fishing in pond on Pitkin Green, Aspen

My pond had very few trout, so … I stocked the pond in the late spring every year with five hundred trout, mainly rainbow, but some brown and golden trout, and, with fast-moving Hunter Creek feeding the fish every day, I watched the trout grow big and fat by fall. The first time Dad went fishing, he caught twenty-five trout. I always used a fly rod, but not Dad. He cast away and hauled them in. The pond would be a great attraction for fly-fishermen who wanted to bone up on their technique before tackling the overgrown trees and brush along the Roaring Fork River that flowed through the Aspen valley.

When Bill brought Federal Reserve Chairman Paul Volcker to stretch his fly-casting muscles, my television and radio personalities were duly impressed. At six foot eight, Paul probably tangled with the overhanging trees (including mine) quite often.

Peter Van Domelen and Bill Seidman showing off a trout

I needed to get to Denver as fast as I could, with microwave connections and leases in place on United Cable, Denver's largest cable system. United would bring along Mile Hi Cable, and, together, they controlled more than two hundred thousand Denver subscriber households. As Peter Barton liked to remind me, "Carriage is the name of the game." But my stockholders were paying dearly for it.

At 6:30 a.m., on Thursday, February 2, 1984, I wrote in my diary: "*On air* in Vail. Wow—a political nightmare, *and,* thus, *expensive*. Worth it—but time will have to show it."

By Sunday, I had calmed down: "Luxuriating—relaxing—sitting in the sun—calling all the kids I can find—reading *Mornings on Horseback*."

I hadn't written in either of my diaries for many months. Too bad. I enjoyed looking back at the current scenes.

We were on air in Vail, and successfully too, with a good TV picture and good news cut-ins for Vail. Our picture was great in Aspen too. I looked at *Moby Dick*. I remember seeing it with the kids the Saturday before Christmas 1982. The picture was bad—and probably so was the print. The multiplexer was a disaster.

Our staff was constantly increasing and changing. Over sixty now, with ten or eleven in Vail.

What was up with Bill? Not much. My ardor seemed to be waning. I seemed to be put off by his constancy to Sally. Now he claimed she was leaving Phoenix and going to Nantucket.

I asked Bill where he was going. "To my favorite pond."

Well, we shall see. … I thought.

Jule seemed very pleasant on the phone. I hoped he would find something to do more in tune with his many talents.

Even Boaz (according to Bill) was even tempered these days. I guessed the television station was making money. I hoped so. I didn't want to sell Boaz 1 percent of my WXXA-TV stock—but it was nice to have a little cash for a while. And the kids certainly eat it up.

On Sunday, February 19, 1984, I had my first serious skiing accident. And it happened because I had borrowed Lydia's skis, which didn't come off. Her bindings were set for her weight and strength, not mine. (And Lydia would be showing us her real strength that summer.)

Gary Verplank, Paul Kors, Jim Knox, Ralph Garlick, Mike
Toumajian, Joyce Hatton, Carl Reuterdahl, Dr. Dan Fox

I was showing off—doing what we called 360s on Aspen's Ruthie's Run—for brother Gary and seven of his buddies, who were using my house for a long weekend bash. I tore my rotator cuff, enough that my arm hung limp at my side. Didn't hurt at the time, but my arm didn't move, either, while I lay in the emergency room for three hours waiting for a doctor. Because I chose not to have it fixed, I would endure a long, painful recovery. And lose some mobility of the arm forever. But I thought the alternative worse: six months with my arm raised by a cast braced to my side, followed by months of painful therapy.

For the rest of the weekend fun, I suggested some ice fishing—so I could enjoy the show. ...

Bill Seidman, Paul Kors, Dick Kors

I recovered enough to join Bill Seidman a week later at the Wickenburg Inn, a popular inn and dude ranch northwest of Phoenix. The dinner honoring a tired President Ford seemed boring to me. People were fawning.

The next morning, I was more reflective:

Ah, business—and the personal, forever intertwined. Ford dinner, congressional campaign, money worries—personal and corporate. Bill's fortieth wedding anniversary coming up next week.

And the next evening, I felt burned. Bill had dropped me off at the airport before he picked up his wife, who was returning to Tempe earlier than planned. Speaking of "ceremonial shenanigans," I never convinced *Bill* of the twisted arrangement in which *he* chose to live. And I must love him, or why would I put up with his unceremonious dumping of me at the airport, knowing the planes to Denver were full and the weather was bad? My diary entry shows I hid it pretty well, I think:

Phoenix airport, February 26, 1984, 9:40 p.m. Sour. ... But—so what? Waiting—waiting for a plane to Denver. (Snowing there; besides, planes full.) One martini, six olives, thirty goldfish crackers. ... Enough. *Why? Yech!*

One of Bill's favorite comments to me was "You're a survivor." He must have believed it, because I didn't hear from him the next day. Would I *forget it?*

I was off to work in Vail on Saturday, for the Jimmy Heuga MS concert. My shoulder seemed better, but I returned to Aspen at 2:00 a.m., exhausted. Brett called for medical insurance—broken foot. The KSPN-TV news department called; they needed my car to cover the Glenwood Springs fire.

On Monday, I had a big day ahead, and little sleep because of my sore shoulder. My list was long. CNN was suing us in federal court over our contract. Our CNN audio and the movie's clarity both had to be fixed. The Vail FM signal had "cut out" problems. John Hellyer had questions about microwave paths. And I had to read White House Fellows material for my interviews coming up later in the month. (Interviewing potential White House Fellows candidates was another job appointment—courtesy of Bill Seidman.)

And I was told Ted Turner would be calling … la-di-da. Some day!

March 17, 1984; St. Patrick's Day. Fun at Highlands skiing with the KSPN crew. And my shoulder didn't bother me. Although I cruised all day, I fussed all evening in my new home on Pitkin Green. I liked the house—and almost liked the loneliness. I had a base, unlike New York City, which became home to some of my kids. And Michigan? It would be hard to go back. And to what? Memories. I hoped Jule could make a successful life there.

It was time for more investors. Who would have the interest? Wealthy people enamored of the Rocky Mountain lifestyle. Aspen and Vail were full of them, but they were movie stars or New Yorkers or Texans. Denver had ski enthusiasts like Peter Barton, who was giving me indications he wanted to be part of our venture. Peter didn't have cash to invest, but he had knowledge of the cable empire that was being assembled in Denver. He might want to join our RBI board.

I needed to produce new pro formas and explain the Malrite Act, which deregulated syndicated program exclusivity and distant signal carriage for the cable industry, as recently as June 1981. No wonder Peter Barton said cable system ownership was an opportunity not to be missed: "a goal that existed at the outer limits of our generation's possibilities."

Peter's support for my venture was helping me fight an uphill battle for new capital. When could we show the microwave connection to Denver? And its two hundred thousand cable subscribers? It would be coming. …

On Sunday, March 18, 1984, at 8:40 a.m., I reported in my diary:

Priorities! And what a snowstorm out the window.

(1) the overview (written)
(2) the backup (maps, etc.; contracts)
(3) the figures (pro formas)
(4) specifics (Malrite Act; CNN II; microwave licenses; boosters versus translators)

Done by 6:00 p.m.; exhausted.

On Sunday, April 1, I received an early morning phone call from L.A., where Brett was going to college. Brett heard on the national news that three men had been killed in a snowslide on Saturday at Aspen Highlands. Our radio ski report was odd from the Highlands. From my diary: "Even the Ski Corporation expressed condolences. The Highlands said nothing. *Weird.* ..."

I liked Sunday mornings and hated the pressure to go out, especially this morning to High Alpine in Snowmass. I was enjoying our Sunday morning program, *Sunday at the Symphony,* where we simulcast the MAA (Music Associates of Aspen) festival tapes airing on KSPN-FM radio with Rocky Mountain scenery videos broadcast on KSPN-TV 23 and channel 2 on the cable systems in Aspen, the Roaring Fork valley, and the Vail valley.

High Alpine turned out to be fun. It was snowing, but there was much camaraderie at the restaurant. Lots of KSPN staff—from Vail too. But the emphasis was on KSPN, not TV-2. How did it come about? Ah yes ... we had to learn what we could and could not do.

And the next morning, wishing I had money, I wrote in my diary: "Hate the wolves at the door!" *That* comment would come back to haunt me in less than a decade.

I now liked my new home. It accommodated a variety of guests. John Gilmore showed up after running twenty miles; he was tired and quiet. But his daughter, Tammy, and husband, Jimmy Hunting, were animated—and putting up well with Tammy's divorced Dad.

And Nancy Van Domelen looked happy in retirement. Her husband Pete looked handsome as usual—and was bawling me out for something. (CNN this time).

I was looking forward to Fritz's birthday party at our SoHo loft on Saturday. I hoped Bill Seidman would stay in New York City for the party.

Had a nice wine-y phone conversation with him. He seemed in the same condition.

My 1821 (eighteen-twenty-*fun*) aficionados were at it again. At the loft once more. Too bad the West Coast kids couldn't leave school—or afford to leave school—to join them for the celebration. And it was another penned invitation from our resident artists, Julio and Alison, in black and white for a black-tie affair. Fritz sang and played, Lydia planned and cooked, and I went along "for the ride" (with checkbook of course), but ended up as frazzled as everyone else. ... I found Fritz's Christie's associates most amusing—watching at 4:30 a.m., as they put the charm on Lydia's college roommates. And I enjoyed Jane and Allen Boorstein, who retired at a more reasonable hour.

Later that week, one of our "unflappable" employees celebrated her twenty-fifth birthday; it reminded me that my twenty-fifth birthday reflected a different generation. At twenty-five, I was tied down, with three babies, a full-time college schedule, a membership in the GOP State Central Committee, and a new nursery school, the first in West Michigan. Ah ... my first business venture.

Bill Seidman was returning to Aspen on Saturday. Would he be checking on one of his many business ventures? We watched KCWS-TV, channel 3, the new full-power indie TV station in Glenwood Springs. They were acting like KWGN (Denver's independent TV station). That was good for us, because they were not locally oriented but were redundant to other independent stations available on cable, such as WTBS. (Those would be prescient comments about KCWS. Bill and I hoped our other investors took note.)

After I dropped Bill off at the airport Sunday night, I picked up Brett and his sailing partner, Kathy, who were planning on a long spring break of nonstop fun. They went out Sunday night after 9:00 p.m., which set the pattern for the week. They skied and partied, and I worked. By Friday, I was exhausted, having gotten up every morning at 5:30 a.m.

No way could I keep up with Brett's young crowd, and I had Lydia moving in the next week for two months of altitude acclimatizing and serious mountain training before heading to the Russian Himalayas. I called Lydia in New York City and suggested she stop at 47th Street Photo and look at half-inch videotape cameras to take with her. I wanted her to learn how and what to shoot and how to put a program together. (Just not on the Russian Himalayas.)

On May 29, Lydia announced that she would be hiking up Mount Sopris with two experienced hikers. I wished I knew their experience. Why didn't I meet them first?

Most of May and June, I watched Lydia's athletic routine, not realizing how important it would become once she reached a base camp of 12,000 or 13,000 feet in Tajikistan. Ten-mile early morning runs up Independence Pass? The altitude at our house: 8,000 feet. (The altitude where the boys were training? Sea level. Being able to train at 8,000 feet would be Lydia's only advantage over three boys who were experienced mountain climbers.)

She won't climb every mountain, but Lydia Hatton just wants to climb one in the . . .

Soviet Union's Pamir range

By RICK KARLIN
Post staff writer

The mountains around Aspen and the 24,551-foot Pik Kommunisma in the Soviet Union are worlds apart.

But Lydia Hatton hopes to bridge that gap in a few weeks.

The 23-year-old Aspen woman was scheduled to leave New York on Sunday with expedition members Burton Ryan Jr, of Hempstead, N.Y., Burch Baylor of Darien, Conn.; and Andrew Ferguson, of Juneau, Alaska. The team was scheduled to climb Mt. Blanc in the French Alps this week.

After that warmup, they will travel first to Moscow, then to a Soviet-run base camp in the Pamir Mountains of Soviet Central Asia.

Hatton, in a recent phone interview with The Glenwood Post, said long-time friend Baylor asked her to join the climb after the team's original fourth member dropped out.

"He jokingly asked me if I wanted to go along. My first reaction was no way," she said.

While the others have climbed in the Himalayas and on Mt. McKinley, Hatton said

the trip will be her first major climb. Before leaving for New York, she trained with 10-mile runs in Aspen, climbing Mt. Sopris and practicing the use of sophisticated mountaineering equipment.

She said the Soviet government runs an active mountaineering program, and climbers from around the world are housed at the International Base Camp in the Pamirs.

"Mountaineers are given the highest respect in Russia," she said.

From the base camp, Hatton's team will be helicoptered to 16,500 feet. From there they will make a "4,000-foot rock climb" to a huge glacial plateau at 20,000 feet. Once across this stretch, pulling supply sleds behind them, they will climb on snow and ice to the summit.

She said avalanches will pose the greatest threat since the Pamir Range is prone to earthquakes. She was looking forward to "getting to the top and returning hale and hearty."

Hatton isn't the only Aspen representative going on the trip. She said the climbers will use Phoenix cross country skis, which are designed and manufactured in Aspen.

Lydia Hatton's bound for the U.S.S.R.

Courtesy of *Glenwood Post*

I had no experience mountain climbing, but I lived and worked in an industry that reveled in feats of glory by local climbers as well as mourned their tragic deaths. I remembered reporting Danny Van Domelen's accident in 1979, and the fatal sickness from oxygen deprivation of a prominent local doctor's twenty-six-year-old daughter. She was climbing in the Himalayas too, not far from the Pamir range where Lydia would be climbing. That doctor made sure our Lydia had every medicine possible for her climb up

Peak Kommunisma, the highest mountain in Tajikistan, at 24,590 feet, to be attempted without oxygen.

And, finally, I knew that a team of eight Russian female climbers— yes, all of them—had died in 1974 while climbing Peak Lenin, which was also in the Pamir range. All Russian women climbing teams were banned for fifteen years by the Russian government. The fact that Lydia was even allowed to go with her boyfriend and his two male partners was a surprise. And with no Alpine-climbing or high-altitude experience. But I didn't know that. I probably didn't want to know.

Not only would Lydia have the full complement of medicine, she would also have the best equipment and best clothes and best boots. It didn't start out that way. Lydia had rounded up used equipment, but it didn't take long for all of us to realize we couldn't tolerate even one tiny mistake. And Grandma and Grandpa Verplank stuffed her pockets full of cash. No one wanted her to go, and we all told her in our own crazy ways—including one of her brothers actually telling her she was crazy.

Lydia had explained to me before she left that the four of them wanted to climb Mont Blanc in the French Pyrenees because Lydia, especially, needed training crossing ice fields. That probably was true, but nothing short of canceling the climb would have satisfied me.

I did have the satisfaction that day of hearing that KCWS, the new full-power independent TV station in Glenwood Springs, went belly up—well almost, the fins were still flapping.

"They almost always wait too long," reported our lawyer, Pete Van Domelen.

When KCWS went off the air a week later, I knew I could get a cheap microwave unit, but I needed permission from TCI, the cable provider in Glenwood Springs. It wouldn't be the last time I needed permission from TCI.

Fourth of July was not a holiday if you were in the news business; I had to deliver an advertisement to the *Aspen Times* by 8:30 a.m. Then hurry to the office to deal with problems at our Vail studios. The Aspen Institute picnic in the afternoon would be a distraction—wandering around by myself. But what a lonely existence. Could I learn to live with it?

Two days later, I was looking forward to seeing my sailing family in Michigan. On the way to the airport, I hurried to the office to receive a message that our Vail KSPN-TV-2 manager had resigned, and I quickly accepted it, much to her surprise. Now my pace quickened; the plane was leaving the airport at 7:15 a.m., and it was home to the nest. Hoorah!

A week later, back in the saddle in Aspen, our mountain engineer, Doug Lofland, and I headed up the mountain at 5:00 a.m., by jeep and on foot, and arrived on the top of Castle Peak at 7:50 a.m. Our microwave equipment had taken a direct hit of lightning; the wires to our battery backup looked like they were soldered.

Early morning was wonderful in the mountains. Beautiful! There were flowers everywhere, especially fields of columbine. And mud. Yes, we got stuck, but Doug was, as usual, resourceful. That thin air at 11,500 feet made me think of Pids at a 12,000-foot *base* camp. (Only the *base* camp?) I felt I must go into the mountains early again; all that thin air cleansed the soul.

Keeping up with both my business and personal life that summer was confusing.

Ann, manager of the Vail television station, was gone—self-abnegation. Ralph, an A/V operator, was gone—fired. Daniel, an A/V operator, was gone—laid off. Business was exciting, nevertheless. I was working on Glenwood Springs, Summit County, and Denver microwave and cable connections.

Pids was in Moscow, or wherever she was supposed to be in the USSR; Bill Seidman was flying to Aspen from Washington, DC. Courtesy of Bill, I got my Albany WXXA-TV stock sold. *Malheureusement,* all the cash was swallowed up by RBI.

Fritz and Brett were racing on Uncle Midge's *Sleeping Bear,* from Port Huron to Mackinac Island. They came in *first* on corrected time! If they had the lack of wind brother Gary talked about, that would be good for Midge's tippy *Bear.*

On July 18, 1984, I received a card—finally—from Pids, but written (it said) on July 3. I wondered if they were at the base camp or climbing or what. ...

Fritz called the next week from New York City: he had a message from one of the mountain climbers, who had returned to New York to seek treatment for an arm fractured during a rock fall. Lydia was not climbing with them when it happened. Lydia's boyfriend, Burch, and the other male climber in their group were heading back up the mountain, again without Lydia. I was relieved that she was not climbing.

A few days later, I received another call from Fritz. The other climber with Burch told Fritz that Burch had to bring him down from 22,000 feet because of frostbitten toes. Now Burch was heading back up the mountain with Lydia. They didn't have much time left. They had to leave Russia within thirty days of their entry into the country.

On August 12, I heard from Lydia at 4:00 a.m., on Grandma and Grandpa Verplank's phone. She sounded great—like next door. She sounded strong, not husky voiced. She said, "I lost twelve pounds in three days at 20,000 feet. One loses six thousand calories a day at that altitude." Lydia said she was happy to be out of Russia, and so was I.

A four-page letter arrived from Lydia, written from Ireland's Aran Islands—"on the western edge of civilization"—with tough but colorful descriptions of her experience in the Pamirs:

> I am also indebted to Burch because, believe it or not, chivalry is not dead: he did come back for me. That is a gesture I'll remember … for the rest of my life—because I'll never *be* the same after going up to the extreme regions of the Pamir range, fighting every inch of the way to put the world under my feet. Headaches, yes; thirst, forever; sunburn under my chin; frost nip, of course; and eyeballs as big as my sunglasses shifting back and forth, back and forth, taking it all in, burning it in my brain.

Lydia probably would prefer that I quote from the more elegant introduction to her trip, written by Marianne Van Eenenaam, a talented correspondent writing for the *Muskegon Chronicle*, who interviewed Lydia and wrote a lengthy four-column article:

> "Time starts to take on geological dimensions when you're looking up at a 24,590-foot mountain peak. A feeling of excitement and fear grips you when you realize you are about to climb it…
>
> "…I'm learning as I go, but once you commit yourself to climbing, you have to keep moving." With Peak Kommunisma up in the clouds, the pair climbed over varying surfaces, very loose dirt, hard ice, an eight-mile-long plateau and almost vertical rock cliffs. "Climbing down that steep rock was one of the most terrifying experiences of my life. It was all ice, and we had to go backwards," she said…"

Lydia on ice wall of Peak Kommunisma in Russian Himalayas, July 1984

Written on a brass plaque on the door of the office of the dean at the Arizona State University's College of Business is *"Sine Emptore Nullum Negotium"*— "without a customer there is no business." I didn't need to be reminded by the dean, L. William Seidman. But Bill still sent me his *Phoenix Gazette* column, entitled, "Radio, TV, take it to the bank," on August 17, 1984.

I would be fighting all fall to accomplish that goal—customers! Who were my customers? Local and national advertisers. And what did they need? Cable subscribers! I commented in my diary on August 20:

My project is rather overwhelming:

(1) get microwave licenses and sites
(2) get contracts for Denver cable
(3) get moving on satellite channels
(4) get moving on channel 25 in Glenwood Springs
(5) get translator licenses in Vail valley
(6) sell TV advertising

And, most important … get some more money. Make a plan today. Therefore, no time to waste—writing in this diary.

Bill's last paragraph in his *Phoenix Gazette* article states, "It may be some time before other forms of entertainment-based communication systems change the pattern of recent years. If it does change, the man likely to change it is the newest shirt model with the eye patch, handsome Ted Turner of Cable News Network, SuperStation WTBS ... but more on this entrepreneurial great of the broadcast business at another time."

I was being called the "Ted Turner of Colorado" by some local broadcasters. But ... wait until I hit the front range and the Denver cable Goliaths.

My negotiations with United Cable were exciting. To them too. Jim Dovey, president of United Cable, and Bruce Smith, its marketing director, liked the idea of merging KSPN-TV's programming with their local origination channel's high school and college sports coverage and call-in talk shows. And they knew they could sell the channel to other cable systems in the region, because all cable systems were required to provide a local origination channel on their system.

Colorado Ski Country USA liked the plan also. They wanted more ski programs and ski reports on the cable systems in Colorado, and KSPN-TV was ready to go with both.

And John Hellyer loved it. It was his business—designing and installing microwave systems. Lynn and John had been helpful every step of the way ... eight microwave towers to Denver!

And I loved New York City in the fall at the loft with the kids. Seeing each one alone. And not with Bill. It seemed strange to be in NYC without him. But life goes on—and his interest had turned to his inheritance. I hated Tempe and his house there. Suburbia personified. And at his age. Mediocrity too. How did he stand it?

I realized that I ran a company in a fashionable resort area. But, more importantly, I ran a broadcast station—rather, *two* of them. I had to know how to program them, or I was in *big* trouble. I had to go to Vail right away for sales and programming of KSPN-TV. And then to United Cable in Denver on Tuesday. I needed more investors. I needed to sell the Victorian building. I was haunted by money worries.

Brett's transfer to the University of Colorado in Boulder for his last two years of college seemed perfect timing to claim in-state tuition, and I was thrilled to have him living at my house. But wait ... could anyone believe in-state tuition was refused to me, his mother? I, who had been a tax-paying Colorado resident for four years? With out-of-state tuition costing ten times more than in-state? My brother Gary suggested I contact Governor Lamm's younger brother, Tom Lamm, a Colorado attorney, who had attended the University of Michigan with Gary in the 1960s. I did.

State law dictated the results, as crazy as they were! Talk about a patriarchal society! Brett had lived with his father in Michigan in the past, and "fathers pay the bills." I was *furious*, because Brett had matriculated in California for the past year and visited me as well as his father, and no one knew who paid his college tuition. Tom Lamm suggested that Brett establish residency in Colorado, which took a full year. Tom insisted it was the fastest route for Brett. Even if I won the battle, by the time it was over, I'd have lost the war. So, yes, I lost. And I am still *furious*.

Holidays were often lonely times. But this year would be different. Lydia arrived in early December to work in television production. It was a pressing need. We were slowly developing our own programs—first, *Ski World with Andy Mill*, then *Two for the Road*, a classy production based on L.A.'s *Two on the Town*. It was written, produced, and directed by Tom Seidman, Bill's talented son, who normally worked in Hollywood, but spent months living at my house while producing more than a dozen shows. (Tom would get right to work, rising as early as 4:00 a.m. to be ready for a morning's shoot. I was duly impressed—with his concentration, focus, camera smarts, and writing ability—all the ingredients of good production stressed in our NYU film and television classes. And at minimal cost. What an education Tom provided!)

Fritz organized the New Year's Eve party that year, and, I am sure, the array of wine that appeared on my dining table. His very good friend from Exeter, a now quite pregnant Ellen Anderman Donaldson, arrived with her husband, Jim, carrying the dinner feast. Ellen's family lived in Denver and built an ultramodern vacation home on the lower slopes of Ajax in Aspen. I liked Fritz's New York City guest, Jim Crown, and his brother, Steve Crown too; they were fun and unassuming and bright. It was a refreshing view, knowing the Chicago-based Crown family owned the Aspen Ski Company, which dominated all resort activities throughout the Roaring Fork valley, from Aspen Mountain to Buttermilk to the huge Snowmass Village complex. Jim, one of seven children in the Crown family, would become the managing director of the Aspen Ski Company as well as other family businesses.

After dinner, I stopped at Memree and Perry Lewis's house. They had owned an Aspen home for years with Tom and Frannie Dittmer. The four of them made every New Year's Eve memorable. Their eclectic array of guests was always exciting, especially when they offered a date to squire me around for the all-night events downtown, where I could have provided the "dish" videos craved by television viewers—a sneak peek into the expensive private clubs where the rich or famous congregated. I watched wealthy businessmen escorting chic-looking ladies who were always conservatively dressed. (Elegant ivory long-sleeved silk shirts with pearls seemed to be the uniform one year.)

I was beginning to accumulate quite a guest list that month. Vicki Verplank's brother, Joe Bruhn, arrived from Michigan with his two sons. (The boys were marvelous.) And a friend showed up from Australia; I had to put him on a living room sofa. I complained to my diary: "Tired of so many people in my house. Work is all consuming. Would like some privacy!"

As they say, be careful what you wish for ... I soon changed my mind. On Friday, February 1, 1985, Brett drove buddies Eric, Mitch, Jed, and Jim from Boulder to Aspen to help us celebrate KSPN-FM's fifteenth "Blitzenbanger" birthday. We would need all the help we could find. The temperature on Aspen Mountain was 15° below zero Fahrenheit on Saturday morning, and the high in the afternoon was 15° above zero.. Lydia and Brett and their gang went skiing, but I didn't take any runs at all, except down the hill at 4:00 p.m. to hurry off to Keystone to race in a charity event the next day.

On Sunday, February 3, 1985 I reported:

Keystone. The ski race was nerve racking but exhilarating. I was very pleased with my skiing—and surprised I "held up" so well. Awards ceremony reminded me of old sailing days. Except here we had sixteen old "Olympians." Hank Kashiwa, a delight. Warm, charming, and a good coach.

Freezing day but warmer than Saturday. No food, drinks, or trips inside. ("You will ski better"—and I did.)

Met—thanks to Peter Crowley, my Sherpa—many potential advertisers, including my team partner, president of Bolle sunglasses, Steve Haber. And Miller Lite and Lowenbrau's Kevin... I need to do more of this.

Second-place team: Hank Kashiwa and Joyce Hatton Keystone, February 2–3, 1985

Yes, I did need to do more of that. But I probably would never match my second-place team award with Hank Kashiwa. Keystone resort and Lowenbrau were sponsoring the '85 Cystic Fibrosis Challenge. We had sixteen teams, with sixteen Olympians, each matched with amateurs—like me. They had no idea if I could ski at all. They knew I was president of RBI and KSPN-FM and TV, and therefore I "qualified."

It was a tight slalom elimination race, and only two teams could race at the same time. It seemed to take forever. I didn't fall—not once, not even during the final race, where Hank Kashiwa faced my other favorite Olympian, handsome Andy Mill, our Aspen star of KSPN-TV's first original production, *Ski with Andy Mill.* And, as I reported, Hank would not let me go inside at all. He said I was on a roll, and he didn't want me to warm up and slow down. I probably wouldn't have gone back out, it was so cold at the top of their hill—with the altitude at Keystone averaging a thousand feet higher than Aspen.

(Keystone and Breckenridge have a base elevation over 9,000 feet; Aspen valley is less than 8,000 feet. Both resorts have about the same 3,000 feet of vertical elevation. You don't want a beer before racing at an altitude of

12,000 feet; nor do you want Keystone boss, Jerry Jones, offering you a martini before an important meeting at his house at 11,000 feet. … Oh yes, brother Gary did accept his offer.)

I beat my opponent on Andy Mill's team, but my Olympian, Hank Kashiwa, lost to Andy. In that last race, the Olympian must win too. We were the last teams off the course. It was almost four hours since I climbed that first hill; I sprinted inside, hoping—hoping—I would make it.

When I returned to Aspen, I faced the same problems that had plagued me all year. How do we get our television sales up? When can we expect sales on Denver cable systems? And will I be forced to replace some of our best radio and TV personalities? Frank Eriksen, the funniest and most popular morning man we'd ever had on KSPN-FM, would be heading to San Francisco and probably taking his colleague, Jeffrey Schaub, our cocky, Ivy League-clad TV anchor, with him. We should be getting the Denver market soon. Too bad they won't wait for it.

Private Cable cover 1985 Courtesy of *Private Cable* Magazine

Satellite receive antennas on studio roof access AP Newswire service for both KSPN TV2 and FM radio station; Satcom 3R for ABC news network (radio); and Galaxy 1 for CNN Headline News programming (television).

Courtesy of *Private Cable* Magazine

Jack Cronin, a host of Aspen's annual spring wine party, is interviewed on the slopes.

My landlord, Jack Cronin Courtesy of *Private Cable* Magazine

Bill Seidman invited me to New York City the next week, telling me I needed some perspective on the situation. And he certainly gave me an amusing earful on the plane trip east. From my diary: " ... 'I am reintroducing you to the world of thinkers, intellects, etc.,' he said. Actually, he was reintroducing me to the world of finance, economics, etc. Not the arts; *his* idea of what is important—and, in the long run, it probably is partially my idea too, but not the main thrust, I sense. Obviously, I get nowhere when I *do* put my mind to it."

Our first stop in New York was the loft. The boys were eager to show us a new restaurant in Greenwich Village called Sip and See. Fritz insisted on buying the lobsters and even paying for the taxi fare—definitely now out of the womb. The dinner, with Bill in attendance, was energetic and fun and relaxed.

Not so the next night. We invited Priscilla Morgan to join us at the Bridge Café. Bill attempted to pay the bill, but his credit cards were denied because the waiter thought Bill didn't have a valid driver's license. Bill was very upset.

It was difficult for me to remember, or fully realize, that Bill was being vetted for a governmental position that required approval by the US Senate. And Senator Proxmire was giving him a hard time over the Equity Funding scandal. The FBI would spend almost six months checking out Bill's background before President Reagan's office announced his candidacy for chairman of the FDIC in July 1985. Bill didn't appreciate a minor restaurant employee deciding that he didn't have a valid *anything*.

And by June 1985, the *Denver Post* printed a happy picture of Bill and me dancing at a grand-opening party of the newly renovated Hotel Denver in Glenwood Springs.

Grand opening Hotel Denver in Glenwood Springs. The Denver Post, *June 6, 1985*

What a breakthrough on July 11, 1985! *Finally!* After years of begging for attention from the cable systems on the front range, it was hard to imagine such enthusiasm for our television station. And the excitement for KSPN, the Rocky Mountain SuperChannel, by both United Cable's president, Jim Dovey, and marketing manager, Bruce Smith, was palpable.

I spent the next day in Denver, meeting with United Cable, John Luhmann, Colorado Ski Country USA, John McGuire's firm (Aspen Business Center), top snow journalist Craig Altshul, among others, at Tabor Center's Vail Valley Days. We put together a marketing plan for the company, including billboards on I-25 and I-70 with United Cable, and joint advertising and public relations in the *Denver Post* and *Rocky Mountain News*. Bill Seidman flew in that evening for a weekend wedding and a company party in Vail, and a colorful balloon festival on Sunday morning in Snowmass.

I would run into Peter Barton often when I visited cable offices in Denver. One day, Peter pulled me aside and suggested that I create a joint venture with United Cable:

"Give them 20 percent and keep 80 percent."

There was no way United would settle for 20 percent, from my previous experience with joint ventures. Maybe one-third. But I loved the idea. It would guarantee carriage and coverage in an eleven-state regional mountain time zone. Peter had made brash statements about his successful negotiations for TCI, and I felt he knew best a cable owner's interest in a minority position in a joint venture. And he was right—about the interest. And I developed a serious interest in Peter Barton; I liked his can-do positive attitude and his rush to accomplish the tasks at hand. Peter wasn't much older than my eldest son, Fritz, but I was eager to have Peter join forces with our company as a board member and stockholder, which he quickly agreed to do.

United and Mile Hi signed an interconnect agreement on August 16, 1985. Now KSPN-TV would be on Mile Hi, without the extra microwave feed and expense.

I wrote in my diary, "Hoorah. If only we could get advertising sales up immediately. Gary is very upset with TV sales—but so am I. We have great potential for winter, but that doesn't get us through the fall. Money—and stock—must be given away. Maybe the whole company. Can Allen Hunting come to the rescue?"

It was hard to comprehend the changes that would be coming in the fall. Bill Seidman would be packing up and heading to Washington, DC. We spent a delightful weekend in October at the John Gardiner Tennis Ranch near Phoenix. I knew it would be our last outing in the west, and I expected a lonely fall existence without him.

But Lou Fox showed up in October to take over the reins as general sales manager of KSPN-TV. I breathed a sigh of relief and offered a room in my house until he could find housing for his family. And my fireplace was never without a roaring fire when Lou was around. His love and knowledge of sports programming was a godsend for our station—along with his hiring of young whiz-kid sportscaster, Drew Goodman.

As the winter ski season approached, the huge display ads in the Denver papers were striking, but there was no mention of Aspen or Vail, just the "Rockies":

"Pre- and Après-Ski TV. Only on KSPN, The New Rocky Mountain SuperChannel"

Lou Fox's sports programming was evident: "Get the edge on weekend sports viewing with KSPN's Big-Time College Football and Basketball and D.U. Pioneer Hockey action."

"KSPN—Fast Making Tracks across the Rockies!" The headline on another display ad. United Cable bragged, "When it comes to extensive television coverage of the Front Range, KSPN, the Rocky Mountain SuperChannel, is setting new track records."

When I was told there would be a family wedding at our loft on December 7, 1985, Pearl Harbor Day, I realized it would be a push in November to get ready for New York City and the start of the ski season, which typically was around Thanksgiving, but often much sooner if the wintry weather showed up in early November. Frazzled, I reported in my diary:

> Lou Fox is back; wedding plans, sales, investor's resolutions, Senator Armstrong, cable systems, programming, new morning anchor on the FM, new office. Cleaning up; getting ready for winter; worrying how to use the lift tickets on the front range.
>
>   Interesting fall. Surely needed Lou; yet, a lonely life. Bill ensconced in DC, unable to leave his wife of forty-plus years. Maybe I'll meet someone *free*, white, and twenty-one. It's that time of year.

For the rehearsal dinner on Friday night, Fritz was the only one who knew the routine at the Opera Club, but at least the rest of our extended family had memorized the dress code—especially the black tie for men. The Opera Club guests would be experiencing two sharply contrasting temporal and spatial environments, moving from the elegant location uptown and modern architecture ("…the second phase of the International Style") of the Metropolitan Opera House to our bare, high-ceilinged loft building in Lower Manhattan on Saturday night. And both settings would be filled with art.

The afternoon of the wedding day, I received a call at the loft from Bill Seidman. He was uptown with the Huntings, planning to show up for the wedding at the appointed evening hour. His voice was dark and husky. I knew something was terribly wrong. What was it?

"Bob Sproul died last night."

Oh no-o-o-o! I loved Bob Sproul. He may have been Bill's great friend since Harvard Law School, but he became mine too, the minute I met him and his sophisticated wife, Cara May, on the trails of Yosemite National Park in the early 1970s.

Hiking in Yosemite: From left: Robert Sproul Jr., Allen and Helen Hunting, and fellow hikers.

Jule and I hiked with the Seidmans, Huntings, and a group from the San Francisco Bay Area every summer until Jule and I divorced. I made certain that Bob Sproul hiked in front or behind me every year. Bob was a brilliant raconteur, and I was the most fortunate hiker of the bunch—hogging his space at every turn.

In September 1985, Bob sent an amusing letter to Allen and Helen Hunting, thanking them for sending him an impressive piece on Bill Seidman in Sunday's *New York Times*, adding that he "thought there wasn't enough emphasis on Joyce's role in all this."

On New Year's Eve, December 31, 1985, I had a long relaxing dinner at the home of Bill and Gretchen Gorog. I met Bill Gorog in 1974. Bill Seidman was bogged down with requests for interviews in the new Ford administration and asked me to entertain him for lunch. It was a memorable meeting for me. Bill Gorog announced at lunch, "I think everyone should get repotted once every five years, don't you?"

Bill Gorog was a technology wizard who developed LexisNexis in the 1960s. (And Bill Gorog would go on to pioneer the development of electronic banking and bill paying—a swipe of my credit card at a supermarket checkout stand always reminds me of him.)

Yes, Bill got repotted, working as executive director of President Ford's Council on International Economic Policy. And he would agree to invest in RBI too. That was an easy conquest, because he and Gretchen and their six children were investing in Aspen, building a modern new house on Red Mountain, directly above my Pitkin Green abode.

Even on New Year's Eve, listening to his great collection of Ella Fitzgerald records, Bill Gorog was very nice and always helpful when discussing business. Since Bill was my only local board member and so technologically proficient, I explained to him how I felt the communications landscape was changing. Satellite uplinks and transponders were becoming more affordable and could replace our long-distance microwave network to Denver.

But I must have been effusive that evening! The next day, I wrote:

> Talked too much about the satellite connection with TCI. It is exciting—but will it happen? All the changes necessary! Hopefully, will meet to discuss it next week—after the New Year's week.
>
> Eighty million dollars—blows me away. Or just a bargaining number? Hard to stay *up* so much of time. Wish my personal situation were more satisfying. Money. Companionship. Et cetera. However, my work is probably much more exciting than most. I have no other point of reference.

I was having a difficult time that spring balancing the potential for our television station with the reality of the present. … Working all the time and still not breaking even. I complained in my diary on March 2, 1986: " … May be on to something big. Too big for my present investors. Gary is very upset that I haven't turned the corner. The others are too, but he was always my great supporter. He has put in a bundle, and he is expanding his Shape business. … He will be here end of month."

Peter Barton had been pushing me for months to move on the uplink and the joint venture with United Cable. When Peter joined our RBI board, I was relieved to have someone on my side—someone so positive and optimistic about the future of our company. Peter blew into Aspen for his first meeting with me, took one look at our negative cash flow, and demanded I do something right away to stem the tide. In typical high-energy form, Peter suggested drastic actions: cut the television payroll, cancel contracts like the AP newswire, and withhold biweekly payroll liability payments.

I was shocked about withholding payroll tax, or any tax liabilities, and laughed it off—I had had too many years around Bill Seidman and his accounting firm. But I would find out to my horror that there were others in my accounting department who thought and acted differently.

I joked on April 2, 1986: "We are getting there—finally! Only need another $500,000, but then we should be on our way. ..."

On April 3, Albany WXXA-TV was sold for $11.6 million. And that was no joke. *Yes*, I should have held on to my stock. Tant pis! The Albany UHF television station was a great financial success and worth all the work. Happy investors, unlike Omaha. That was gone forever. And the UHF television market was not good anymore.

On April 4, I complained that I still needed investors, but our company had taken a new twist with TCI. The potential was great.

KSPN Program Director Frank Eriksen

Frank Eriksen was back as program director, bringing his knowledge and buddies with him. They would really kick ass. Was I busy.

And I was happy again by April 26. I thought we were going to make it. Cutting costs, and getting support from the cable industry, finally. "Carriage is the name of the game," said Barton, "and we have it, and we've paid for it!"

On Saturday, May 24, 1986, I spent four hours writing a report to my stockholders. They would be as shocked about the new developments with Peter Barton as I was at first blush.

Bill Seidman seemed to enjoy our ten-day trip to London and Edinburgh in April. He gave the impression that his desire to see me waned to about once a month—but for longer periods of time. We never got along the first day; he appeared hassled and not ready to enjoy our time together. But he had always been that way on long trips.

Bill didn't like being told that he might be living his life all wrong. Was it for the sake of the children? It was hard for all our children. How could they deal with it if they couldn't rationalize it?

When it came down to business risk, Peter Barton and I were rushing through life at a similar tempo, and that wasn't a satisfactory speed for some of my longtime investors. Allen Hunting was the first to complain: " … I'm not putting another nickel in this company until or unless we change the management."

I was sorry to lose Peter Barton's help on the Denver cable scene. Just when I really needed it. Peter's hard-charging boss, John Malone, president and CEO of TCI—the biggest cable operator in the world—sent Peter to Minneapolis to launch CVN (Cable Value Network), the first national home-shopping network. Peter said it was "an exercise in frenzy." But I felt Peter enjoyed the challenge. Wish I enjoyed mine more.

I had plans too—to build a cable superstation, beginning on September 15, on United Cable's channel 10. It was just a month away. Could we do it? Would we get Mile Hi's cooperation? Barton said, "Don't worry about it."

I did worry about it. We needed their facility before winter. We needed to add the microwave STL in Vail before winter. And then there was CPC, our new Colorado Production Company. Lydia Hatton helped to found it. Where could it go?

KSPN-TV, The Rocky Mountain SuperChannel, needed a signed contract—but with whom? Our new joint venture would be called KTV, Inc., but RBI and United Cable, along with TCI, couldn't agree on the very basic questions: It was no longer our 80 percent. Was it even our 51 percent? Who would control this joint venture? We needed a signed contract that gave us an opportunity to make money, not invest money.

The battle was just warming up. And my stockholders were paying the price for United and TCI's dallying—and why not dissemble? They weren't meeting my daily payroll. The longer they waited, the stronger their position. As Peter Barton continually reminded me, "The name of the game is *carriage.*"

"Regional Cable Channel Rising up in the Rockies," written by Mark Wolf, special to *Electronic Media*, November 17, 1986, was a more succinct explanation of my five-year struggle to develop the Rocky Mountain SuperChannel than I could ever produce. I had lived in the trees too long. And marketing director of United Cable, Bruce Smith, had comments in the lengthy, flattering, above-captioned article that were enlightening to both me and my stockholders. Here is an excerpt: " … 'We wanted our local origination channel to look more like a broadcasting channel,' said Bruce Smith, marketing director of United Cable. 'We had been talking to Colorado Ski Country USA about getting some skiing programming but Ms. Hatton already had the programming in place. We decided to buy into it. … '"

Really? Is that what *we* decided? Via Mark Wolf, Bruce Smith expounds more: "United plans to market the 'Super Channel' to other cable companies in Colorado, giving them an equity position in the channel. …"

According to Smith, United was giving them an "equity position in the channel." From *their* 49 percent? No one asked me, or my investors.

So how was this new SuperChannel going to make money—to pay for the "eight hop microwave relay system that cost more than $500,000 to construct"?

Mark Wolf explains further:

The Denver Interconnect, a joint venture of Mile-Hi and United, sells advertising on the Super Channel as well as national cable networks.

Mr. Smith has projected advertising revenues of close to $1 million in 1987 for the Super Channel. (An eight-person sales staff sells KSPN advertising in the Aspen-Vail area.) …

Mr. Smith was projecting million-dollar revenues, but KSPN's stockholders were not seeing a penny of it. Nor had our investors seen any signed contracts with any cable companies. And all sports contracts were being signed only by Lou Fox, general manager of KSPN-TV.

Who "we" were in the fall of 1986 was becoming a murky proposition. But United Cable was eager to tell the press they were our "business partner."

Denver Post radio and TV reporter Clark Secrest wrote "Brash Little KSPN Aims for Big Time as 'Superstation'":

> KSPN is in the process of becoming, if not yet a national superstation, one of regional nature. Being a superstation is principally a matter of wide program distribution, and KSPN already has taken one giant step in that direction: the use of eight mountaintop microwave towers to get its movies, reruns, outdoorsy features, ski and weather reports to United Cable's 145,000 suburban Denver homes. In the process, United became a business partner in the venture.
>
> KSPN's next priority is to sign up Mile Hi Cable, which operates within the Denver city limits and which would instantly add another 54,000 subscriber homes. From there, KSPN's Hatton, a former Midwest and New York business entrepreneur with previous television experience, envisions a lineup, via either microwave towers or satellite, up and down the Front Range from Albuquerque and Santa Fe to Cheyenne and beyond.
>
> Such an effort from so small a town as Aspen has never been attempted, and indeed no superstation of any size exists between Chicago and the West Coast. The ever-confident Hatton, in addition to touting her movie and rerun schedule, also cites the numbers of Front Range recreation enthusiasts who are vitally interested in the Aspen/Vail weather and year-round activities, matters to which KSPN pays close attention. "We're obviously providing a service people want," says Hatton. "I certainly think it's going to work, don't you?" Given KSPN's progress thus far, the little station that tried may indeed eventually prove that to be a superchannel you don't have to originate from New York, Chicago, or Atlanta.

In September, when United Cable moved KSPN-TV's signal from cable channel 25 to cable channel 10, United Cable also merged KSPN-TV with United's local origination channel. The move to channel 10 displaced the Denver independent, KDVR, which was forced to move to channel 31—the same number as its UHF broadcast frequency. I now knew we were on our way! United's cable channel 10 meant 145,000 suburban Denver homes! We now had a new business partner!

But, as they say, be careful what you wish for. ...

The move to uplinking was affordable and necessary. (Uplinks required so much power in 1986, we needed to build our uplink dish next to the electrical substation at the Airport Business Center.) But KSPN-TV's cash was in the microwave system.

The sale of KSPN-FM would solve our immediate cash problems. We had been disappointed with FM radio appraisals over the years, knowing Aspen was a special market that would appeal to the glamour-seeking investors. It did, finally, but not this time.

On New Year's Eve, at 6:30 p.m., we sold the FM. What a relief! We celebrated with the Gorogs at the Paradise Club, and then celebrated back home with Brett and Carla until 4:00 a.m.

Bill Seidman finally arrived late Friday night in yet another snowstorm. We had a good time with my kids over the weekend—but the Paradise Club party for FM and TV was *not* upbeat. Bill couldn't bear the heat and noise of the club.

My diary entry on Tuesday, January 20, 1987, in New Orleans, reflects little understanding of what we were about to do. But TV station manager Lou Fox certainly knew. Here's the report:

> Arrived last night in the French Quarter. Had a slow morning and moved to Hotel Provincial in early afternoon. Bill and I walked to the Hilton and convention center, after drinks at Two Sisters.
>
> Met with TV manager Lou Fox that night—what a downer! Lou was tired and ready to go back to Aspen. We gave him an important morning assignment, but he didn't want it. I had rewritten letters to syndicators, assigning all our KSPN-TV contracts to KTV, Inc., and I asked Lou to send them out. ...
>
> Great oysters at Felix's with former WXXA-TV sales manager David Low and his wife, Joan, and their new business partners. Then danced with them through the streets to great jazz until 2:00 a.m. Bill and I seemed to relax and enjoy the moment. We must be getting older and more appreciative of time. (And more accepting that what is, is?)

Thus concluded my diary entry. I was so-o-o-o busy, and yet, there I was, reflecting on it all. As for the uplink—I knew we'd find a spot. I couldn't believe the attitude of John McBride and others. His Aspen Business Center had the space, and he knew we needed it in order to have enough power.

They wanted to put Aspen on the national map—but not at their expense or inconvenience.

Launching satellite uplink at Aspen Business Center, with Lou Fox, TV general manager, and Rick Bralver, engineer.

Charles (Chub) Feeney was a man I was eager to see in the winter of 1987. Chub had been baseball's National League president for the previous seventeen years and knew the Seattle Mariners American League franchise was ripe for sale and could move to Denver. Chub was another successful roommate of Bill Seidman's from Dartmouth College, who, like Bill, joined the navy and attended law school after the war.

Bill called Chub at his home in San Francisco and explained KSPN-TV's interest in the Mariners, and I followed up with calls to Chub, making a plan to see him in New York City. Chub's family bought the New York Giants in the 1930s and moved the franchise to San Francisco in 1958. Owning and moving an American or National League franchise was not a novel idea to Chub. And he knew that we hoped to follow in the footsteps of Ted Turner, who launched his Atlanta Braves nationally a decade before by uplinking the games on his SuperStation WTBS.

I had not discussed Chub Feeney's participation with United Cable's leadership. I first wanted to have specific knowledge of the criteria required for ownership of a baseball team, although I had filed enough FCC radio and TV applications in the past two decades to understand basic community obligations of a national franchise.

When the *Rocky Mountain News* sports reporter, Norm Clarke, eager for baseball news at the start of the new season, jumped the gun by interviewing me for his April 12, 1987, Sunday sports section, I wasn't ready for a big-time announcement. I had no idea how United Cable would react to this new initiative on my part. I found out that Norm Clarke had also interviewed our general manager, Lou Fox, and United Cable's marketing manager, Bruce Smith, among others, *after* reading the four-column article in the paper! And I also found out why the *Rocky Mountain News* photographer was taking a picture of me in my favorite cowboy hat.

The bold headline in the Sunday sports section of the *Rocky Mountain News* read: "Local TV Station Owner Wants Mariners," with the subheading, "KSPN's Joyce Hatton Hopes to Bring Team to Denver."

The first paragraph read, "Television 'super channel' president Joyce Hatton of Aspen wants to become the Ted Turner of the Rockies and make the Seattle Mariners her Atlanta Braves."

Norm Clarke's explanation of our corporate structure must have been a result of his interview of Bruce Smith, because *United did not own 51 percent of KTV, Inc.—ever:*

Last fall, Hatton formed KTV, Inc., which is doing business as KSPN-TV. She is president of both. Fifty-one percent of KTV is owned by United Cable, Colorado's largest cable company. United hopes to sell shares to other area cable systems, using a Denver-based major league team as its programming crown jewel.

Bruce Smith, United's marketing manager, confirmed that KTV has its eye on the Mariners.

"It's just in the talk stage at this time, but nothing ventured, nothing gained," said Smith. "You've got to think big in order to be big."

Norm Clarke did a thorough job of explaining "regional" versus "superstation":

The operative word is regional. Commissioner Peter Ueberroth has declared war on cable superstations because they bombard other major and minor league markets. Ueberroth, in clamping down, has called them "blatantly unfair and against the rules."

"But KSPN would confine its broadcasts to an 11-state area through a variety of restrictions, including scrambled signals," said Hatton.

I was thrilled with the publicity for our new sports programming that would be uplinked to regional cable systems, which Clarke describes this way: " ... Once a low-power TV station, KSPN has made giant programming strides in the past year with sports packages that include Big Eight coverage, service academy football and World Cup skiing. On April 28, the channel will provide 10 hours of live coverage on the Denver Broncos' draft."

Clarke then emphasizes, "two major hurdles could dim Hatton's plans to put the Mariners under KSPN's umbrella."

Well, I knew one major hurdle: Ueberroth was opposed to any move out of Seattle, and that opposition would carry the day.

But the word was out about the possibility of a local Denver major league baseball team available on our sports network. (And they did show up in the early 1990s: the Colorado Rockies.) My deed was done!

Loyal Lou Fox brags in Clarke's article, " ... Hatton's claim to fame is that she can take something without a great deal of seed money, and with ingenuity and perseverance make something happen. She is in touch with a lot of movers and shakers."

Norm Clarke's last paragraph states, " … Her oldest son, Fritz Hatton, is the chief operating officer of Christie's auction house in New York City."

Later that month, I found the article posted prominently on Fritz's office wall at Christie's.

My power over KTV's future was slowly being stripped away. What would I do? In mid-April, I flew to Washington to see Bill Seidman—who was complaining too, about his mounting problems with FDIC failing banks. Bill had just experienced an "electronic" run (yes, in March 1987) on Texas's First Republic Bank. Bill predicted that the FDIC would own at least $7–8 billion of commercial real estate assets from defunct banks before it was over. I commented that he'd have at least ten times that amount to sell, and his organization was not set up to market it. … But I knew who could.

I also knew that I would need assurances from Bill Seidman that the FDIC could make a definite commitment to an auction with a high-powered firm like Christie's, which had a global reputation to protect. Bill quickly arranged a meeting for me on Friday, May 1, 1987, with Steven Seelig, Associate Director of Liquidation for the FDIC; Shannon Fairbanks, Chief of Staff of the Federal Home Loan Bank Board; and Lisa Miller, its Acting Director of Liquidation. Real estate and loan losses would be in the billions of dollars. The figures were staggering. After setting up another meeting in July with Lisa Miller, I headed to the West Coast for another Hatton wedding.

Newport Beach in May attracted all of the Hatton and Verplank clan. They knew it would be a festive outdoor event in a dramatic garden setting. My job was to find a unique location and a hot band for the rehearsal dinner. In Newport Beach, that was not a hard assignment.

On the morning of the wedding day, I was invited to play golf with Will Layman, the father of the bride. Will was shooting perfect pars on every hole, including the eighth hole, when we rode quickly past bridal scenery in the Laymans' garden. We didn't want to leave at the turn after nine holes as planned, not while Will was shooting perfect par! We pleaded for more time, and finally we made a deal to stop play when Will missed par. Well, that deal provided too much pressure, and we had to quit on the eleventh hole. But the perfect nine holes produced a very happy father of the bride. (And a very relieved mother of the groom.)

From Newport Beach, it was back to Aspen for me. To face the music.

Not quite what I'd planned either. I needed internal repairs right away and agreed to an operation in Denver on May 29.

Was I fiddling while Rome was burning? While I lay in a Denver hospital bed, United Cable's marketing director, Bruce Smith, was laying plans to direct the marketing of the Rocky Mountain SuperChannel from my office in Aspen. Bruce Smith arrived in Aspen on June 3, announcing he now was "in charge." But not paying the bills, of course.

I reported in my diary:

Saturday, June 13, 1987. Fifteenth day after surgery. Woke up early ... at least I slept all night. Getting energy back: Thursday in office for two hours—a little dizzy at first. Friday in office for two and a half hours, after one hour talking with Lou Fox at home, and able to cope much more easily, even with all the layoffs.

It is a beautiful day outside! And I am having trouble concentrating on anything—especially this diary. Why? I used to enjoy writing— ruminating. Have I nothing to say? Or too much to sort out in my life? Do I want to contain it in my head only?

So many things happening at the office. (What office? It's moving to Denver.) Will I have any control? (No.) Do I want to stay around with none? (No.)

Should I pursue my new idea for an auction channel? (Or one of Bill's? Not Bill's—no independence. ...)

Next weekend, I'll be in Michigan with Bill. Then—the next two weekends here, so I should have plenty of time to ruminate.

While I was off "ruminating," the KTV company pot was beginning to boil over ... We all knew the problem: United Cable wanted 51 percent ownership; my stockholders—all smart successful executives—were worried about their minority rights. They were refusing to give away control without some tough minority rights provisions in the contract. Only Bill Seidman stayed out of the battle. He had plenty of his own at the FDIC. But when I talked to Bill during a meeting in Peter Van Domelen's law office, Bill warned us, "Put this deal to bed!"

Two weeks later, my lawyer, Peter Van Domelen, suggested, "Write a chronology. Start a week ago Tuesday."

I did. After Dad's eightieth birthday party in Michigan, I returned to Denver via Minneapolis, with Fritz Hatton, who was eager to see Peter

Barton's new Cable Value Network (CVN), the first national home-shopping network.

Fritz Hatton, Laura Barton, and Peter Barton at Cable Value Network in Minneapolis

Peter Barton was an eager investor in RBI, and he also wanted us to "put it to bed." He didn't seem concerned that the deal wouldn't get done. After all, he was the real boss's "second banana," to quote Peter in regard to his boss, John Malone, who was in the process of buying United Cable.

In Denver, I met first with Bruce Smith, marketing director of United Cable and all-around factotum of KSPN-TV (now KTV, Inc.), and then with Jim Dovey, president of United Cable. We talked privately in their conference room. Jim started out by saying that United wanted to own "as much of KTV as it could" and also "wanted to run it, so would you please make plans to ease your way out of the picture."

I responded angrily to Jim's request, noting how blatant they were about running the company the last few months and realizing this had to be the result. I also said I wanted the company to be very successful (it was my investment too), so I would continue to provide whatever help or ideas I considered useful.

Jim said, "May I hear from you tomorrow?"

I said, "No. My investors are hard to reach, and I need to talk to them; it will probably be next week."

Jim asked me to come up with a plan for my leaving—and a timetable.

He assured me that my departure would be handled in a positive manner … amicably.

Before I met with Lisa Miller in Washington, DC, in July, 1987, I called Fritz at his Christie's office in New York City and told him I thought an auction by Christie's and a reputable New York commercial real estate company could resolve some of Bill's FDIC real estate problems.

Fritz' reaction was electric: "How did you know that Christie's was talking to Cushman & Wakefield?!" (Fritz had just returned from a Christie's meeting set up by then vice chairman Guy Hannen. Christie's had gone into the luxury residential real estate brokerage market, and Guy's new interest was in auctioning luxury commercial properties during this hot real estate market.) The timing of my call to Fritz had to be a coincidence; Fritz knew he hadn't mentioned the meeting to anyone in the family.

I promised Fritz that I could get cooperation from the FDIC if both Christie's and a commercial real estate partner with the reputation of a Cushman & Wakefield would consider the project. Fritz said he would look into it, but for now, Christie's was planning their first auction of luxury commercial real estate properties with Cushman & Wakefield in the spring of 1988.

Cushman & Wakefield's standing in the real estate community as the leading commercial real estate brokerage and advisory firm made it an ideal partner for Christie's, and its extensive network of sixty offices was ideally suited to support transactions of the FDIC's nationwide real estate properties. And, finally, Cushman & Wakefield thought that Christie's prestige and global marketing reach would make the commercial real estate auction process more acceptable to serious real estate investors.

After our meeting in July, Lisa Miller seemed very receptive to my ideas for an auction, as long as I had partners with proven track records, such as Christie's and Cushman & Wakefield.

Two week later, a letter arrived from Lisa Miller stating, "I offered to provide you with some insight concerning recent FSLIC sales so that you might better craft a written proposal. … Last year, FSLIC had net sales proceeds from real estate of $125 million. … Through June of this year, real estate sales proceeds exceeded $210 million."

Not only were the total real estate sales a drop in the bucket, the information provided did not advance my cause. I needed to see lists of unencumbered commercial real estate properties from the vast trove of real estate assets in their portfolio. Were these lists available?

Bill Seidman suggested I talk to Stuart Root, an attorney with and counsel to the Federal Home Loan Mortgage Corporation. Bill thought Stuart Root would become the next head of FSLIC (Federal Savings and Loan Insurance Corporation). I was eager to meet with Stuart before he took the job, and I arranged a meeting with him in September, at the Downtown Club in New York City, not far from our loft in SoHo.

The bombshell dropped Tuesday, August 4, 1987. *Splat!* ... We were sitting in the boardroom of United's headquarters in Denver. United's Jim Dovey seemed to be surrounded by a bevy of lawyers. I had brought only one to the meeting, my new Denver-based corporate attorney, John E. Moye, whom we, Recreation Broadcasting, had hired recently to negotiate this final deal.

"We want to unwind this transaction," Jim Dovey announced as an opener. Jim gave three reasons:
1. He had lost confidence in the relationship. ("It was a marriage that didn't work.")
2. United no longer was interested in the venture. ("We couldn't get the other cable systems interested.")
3. United wanted to limit their liabilities. ("We had no idea that KTV owed so much money.")

Guess what they really were saying: "Now that we have the equipment and the people and the contracts, we really don't need you." Peter Barton was my first call that fateful Tuesday, August 4, 1987. From his office at Cable Value Network in Minneapolis, Peter screamed,

"They *stole* our company!" He then asked, "Can you get back the microwave and uplink equipment?"

I reminded Peter, **"Carriage is the name of the game."**

Yes, they really were "stealing our company," as KSPN employee Kelly Butler remarked Friday morning. She would know, since she was working at United Cable in Denver, and kept track of all our program contracts and scheduling.

The next day, I asked Jim Dovey, "What will happen to our football contracts, like CSU versus CU, etc.?"

"Well, if KTV can't honor them, we would look at buying them and running the games on our system." (I found out that United Cable already had secret negotiations with TCI to develop a regional sports and lifestyle channel similar to KSPN, but decided to simply "dilute out" RBI's interest in KTV, Inc.)

My stockholders were furious! At me, at Peter Barton, at United Cable, at TCI. They knew we would have to sue United Cable. And so did I, and so did Peter Barton (who immediately resigned from KTV's Board), and so did United Cable's Jim Dovey and Bruce Smith.

Where was KSPN's ace in the hole, board member Peter Barton? TCI president John Malone's right-hand man, Peter had a reputation as a shrewd and sometimes vicious negotiator.

And United or TCI held all the cards: United's owner, Gene Schneider, would be sending both Jim Dovey and Bruce Smith to England in a few months to build a Denver-based cable company, United Global Communications, and Schneider would be selling United Cable to Malone's TCI. Peter was silent after his initial blast at United Cable. Why? Was he trying to repair the rift behind the scenes? Or preserve his job?

TCI's John Malone was still Peter's boss. Malone would be called the "Darth Vader of cable" because of his demands for excessive equity positions in cable programming services in return for carriage.

Had I relied too much on Peter's ability to control the cable crowd—and his boss? Of all people, Peter knew what was happening. Like Malone, Peter considered himself a superb negotiator. Peter had suggested we offer United Cable only 20 percent ownership of KSPN-TV two years ago! This joint venture was his idea! Now they had 100 percent. Some negotiation!

And some mess! Our staff (what was left of it) was in disarray: Kelly Butler was working at United Cable in Denver, on the program scheduling necessary to keep United Cable's channel 10 on the air (while taking United's orders—but not their pay). She looked to me for reimbursement until United had to take over (or lose her); other employees moved files to my storage shed on Pitkin Green, or sold leftover office and microwave equipment that had not been transferred to United's Denver studios.

I was amused by Shannon Leigh Luthy's expense bill of August 27, 1987, which read: " ... for mileage and expenses to help move KSPN-TV to *somewhere*. ..." United Cable continued to uplink our programs to all its cable affiliates, as if nothing had happened. They knew I wouldn't stop them; I needed a successful regional sports channel to prove the value of what was stolen from us. Oh ... what tangled webs we weave.

Sandy Mochary was a godsend. Sandy continued as my secretary, working out of my house, which became the new offices for KTV, Inc. Bill Seidman considered Sandy one of the most professional secretaries he knew, and he often told her he wished she'd come to Washington to work for him. But Sandy was a single mother with little Cassie to take care of. After Cassie's playpen was installed in my living room, I was ready to do battle.

In September 1987, United Cable hired the few remaining KTV employees, purportedly on a "temporary" basis.

Also in September, United Cable went about the business of systematically breaking contracts and license agreements that KTV had in place with numerous syndicators and distributors of programming, with United Cable substituting itself as the contracting party in place of KTV. In some cases, United Cable simply made what it termed a "minor change" to the programming contracts by striking out the name "KTV" and inserting the name "United Cable."

United also continued to use our equipment. United Cable's in-house counsel, Caren Press, was indeed quite troubled by this fact. She wrote the following to United executives:

> I spoke to our A/V operators today regarding the equipment that you thought United owned. ... They informed me that United does not own any equipment that has been used or that can be used, in connection with the company or its programming. The company has been using KTV's equipment thus far. This causes two problems. First, immediate arrangements must be made for the company to purchase new equipment. Second, the fact that the company has been using KTV's equipment does not help United's case *in the event that United is sued by Joyce Hatton or RBI.* [Italics mine.]

United Cable knew we were threatening to sue. I was being bombarded with letters from a new face at United Cable, owner Gene Schneider's son, Mark Schneider, a corporate lawyer and "Vice President, Corporate Development" of United Cable Television Corp., according to his letterhead signature block.

When Mark's letter dated September 10, 1987, started out, "The purpose of this letter is to memorialize the fact ..." I understood that I was about to become a victim of what they "proposed," and it would be up to me and my lawyer, John Moye, to "dispose."

Mark warned, "We have advised you that United is not willing to underwrite any financing of KTV because, as you have well understood, the financial success of KTV is a *function of cable carriage, not cash investment*."

A few paragraphs later, Mark's letter states the opposite requirement, *not* for *carriage* but *for cash*: "We have carefully weighed your implicit threats of litigation and firmly believe that: (a) United has satisfactorily complied with all obligations it has or may have to KTV or RBI or RBI shareholders, and that *KTV is functionally dead without further investment*. You will recall this was communicated to you on August 4, 1987; and …".

While I was being warned by Mark, United's marketing director, Bruce Smith, was writing on September 24, 1987, to Dan Smith, vice president of Mile Hi Cablevision (which had the other seventy thousand Denver subscribers), expressing Bruce's hopes that " … now that the ownership uncertainties have been resolved, KTV will be, *as first envisioned*, a cable-controlled entity."

My response to their proposal was a compromise on KTV's common stock ownership: dividing it equally between RBI, United, TCI, and ATC, with each willing to dilute up to 6 percent to be allocable to other cable operators in the Rocky Mountain region.

Mark Schneider responded: " … The main issue of difference between your letter and the interest level of ATC and TCI is that they think more equity will be required for carriage than 6 percent, i.e., the 20 percent level seems more workable. We will be in touch with you early the week after next to give you a fuller report on our progress. Our intention is to have things wrapped up one way or another by November 1."

My upcoming meeting at the Downtown Club with Stuart Root, scheduled for September 18, 1987, loomed larger than ever. Along with Bill Seidman's chairmanship of the FDIC, which insured the banks, an important position in the Savings & Loan (S & L) debacle would be the new directorship of FSLIC, which insured the thrifts. And Stuart Root would be named the acting director in less than a month.

Stu Root brought two young whiz kids with him to our meeting, but they seemed more interested in impressing Stu than me. And the one person who should have been at the meeting was Lewis Raneiri, who was home with pneumonia. Stu said Raneiri was "one of the best brains in the real estate market." Raneiri, considered the "godfather" of mortgage-backed securities (see the film *The Big Short*), had been ousted from Salomon Brothers, where he had been a vice chairman. Now Raneiri appeared interested in acquiring and operating financial services companies like S & L institutions.

Stu was willing to discuss in depth my global auction marketing company proposal, which did not identify major players, but he warned me, "Get an understanding of who controls the decisions re: this proposal. ... Selling real estate is a *very dirty* business. ... Time is marching on. ... You don't know what Christie's and Cushman & Wakefield are up to; you can't take a plan to FSLIC and say this is what we *may* do; you must line up the players now and present a concrete plan. You should ask to be considered by the S & Ls at the time they are putting their business plans together."

I asked Stu if we needed big players, and he responded, "Yes, you do need some in place."

Well, I knew who that had to be. ...

Bill Seidman was following my progress on the auction plan, for both FDIC and FSLIC properties, and invited me to the American Bankers' Association's annual convention in Dallas. All the bankers were looking forward to a major speech on Monday, October 19, 1987, by the new chairman of the Federal Reserve, Alan Greenspan, who was en route to Dallas that morning when the Dow Jones Industrial Average began to plummet.

The Dow's decline, twice as sharp as the 12 percent drop of 1929, remains the largest single-day loss in Dow history: down 508 points (22.61 percent). Panic broke out among the brokers and bankers.

Chairman Greenspan wouldn't be coming, and he'd have had trouble entering the building if he did. Bill hollered at me in the back of the room to run downstairs to the lower lobby and save him one of the pay telephones. I grabbed one quickly. Pandemonium set in around me as everyone started fighting over the remaining phones—about six pay phones in all—and about forty men (yes, all men) scrambled for access when a phone opened up. They were hollering for a phone, yelling over the phone, constrained and frustrated by the rudimentary pay telephone communications available.

Bill needed to get back to Washington as quickly as possible, but everyone else needed to get back too—to wherever. I made reservations to Denver; Bill, to Washington.

I turned around in Denver and made plane reservations to Michigan, because Grandma Hatton died on October 22, 1987. She was eighty-four years old. The funeral was Saturday, October 24, at St. John's Episcopal Church in Grand Haven. Fritz gave an endearing eulogy on behalf of our family. Here are some excerpts:

> All of us are here undoubtedly because Grandmere, or Grandma, or Mom, or Charline, touched our lives in one or many ways. In my case, the ink was indelible, and the best way I can offer tribute to Grandmere is to tell you some of the effect she had on me.

Charline Hatton with Bill (10), Julian (8), And Harry Hatton (5), circa 1935

While I resided at 1821 at the beginning (or eighteen-twenty-*fun* as it was later called), Grandma's house at 910 (Lake Avenue) was home away from home. Grandma, being widowed, took a tremendous interest in her grandchildren, and my siblings and I were fortunate to be the closest at hand. …

Grandma was a master at keeping my hands busy and clearly knew that model making would eventually wear off. She decided to press my interest in music by taking me to the symphony and the best recitals in Grand Rapids. It seems like I was five or six at the time. …

Whatever it was, Grandma supported me. In school, in music, in books, in ideas, in travel. I knew then, albeit less than I realize now, that she was helping many others too, and remember the breaks in our model building schedules that were caused by her Goodwill board meetings. Many years later, I stand in awe, understanding how remarkably unselfish she was and how thoroughly she devoted herself to helping others. This was partly her way of alleviating her loneliness and partly a way of venting her energies. Let us not forget that until the last decade, this was a lady who rarely drove less than seventy miles per hour, smoked like a fiend, and could not be without her *Early Times*, the name Greg gave to his yacht by way of indirect tribute.

Fritz put together a compendium of reminiscences of Grandma Hatton.. Here is mine:

To remember Grandma Hatton—where should I begin? She was a force to be reckoned with, from the day Fritz was born until the day Brett went off to prep school.

Because of proximity, 1821 was Grandma's project. Her job. Her factory. And she came with staff in tow: Lizzie the laundress, Harry the handyman, then A. D. and Janie. I provided assorted babysitters and au pair girls and Dean, but Grandma ruled the roost.

For a decade, Grandma drove the children to music and dance lessons. (Yes, even the boys took ballet.) The lessons were in Grand Rapids for Fritz, and Holland for Julian. It didn't matter to Grandma where she went, or how often; it was the teacher who was all-important.

When each of the children reached the ripe old age of eight, Grandma made sure that they received a full eight weeks of Interlochen Music Camp, and for as many—or as few—summers as each desired.

Not until much later did I appreciate how lucky I was! The children were well-nurtured and cultured by Grandma Hatton, and I was free to operate the nursery school and go back to college.

By December 1987, United Cable "proceeded to kill the KTV goose" (to quote my lawyer). United told all other cable companies that, together, they could form, without RBI's 49 percent ownership, the same type of business that had previously been conducted through "KSPN—the Rocky Mountain SuperChannel."

Mark Schneider wrote to Trygve Myhren (president of ATC) on December 23, 1987:

As we discussed the other night, attached is a proposed term sheet for a Rocky Mountain Sports/Lifestyle Regional Channel. We have been in touch with people in your organization describing the purpose of this venture and its financial needs.

... To summarize, United has found its former partners in the KTV effort to be unacceptable. It is our recommendation that we build off of the existing programming base created around United's Channel 10, including uplink, equipment personnel, and transponder, to create the new venture. TCI has given us conceptual agreement on this approach and my discussions with Bill Daniels indicate a likelihood of their participation.

Yes, it was likely that Bill Daniels would participate. On December 21, 1987, Kate Bulkley reported in the *Denver Business Journal*, "Daniels commits to stake in KTV." The article continues:

> United Cable Television Corp. has received a commitment from at least one local cable television company to invest in KTV, the so-called Rocky Mountain SuperChannel, ...
> Daniels & Associates, Inc., a local cable company and cable brokerage firm, has committed an unspecified amount to the channel. ...

It certainly was an unspecified amount to us, and it certainly was not committed to us, as we knew nothing about it! All fall, my lawyer, John Moye, and I had worked with United's Mark Schneider, hoping to make a deal that would have involved, as equal partners, RBI, United Cable, TCI, and ATC, with the last 20 percent divided up by cable operators along the front range.

The article gets more specific about Schneider and Daniels's interest in our channel: " ... 'It will be cash that will automatically turn into program-ming,' said Daniels ... 'It'll be substantial, but that'll be worked out when they figure out who's coming on board.'"

My acrimonious comment: "Not who *is* on board ...!"

Kate Buckley, the reporter for the *Denver Business Journal*, had no idea that KTV had been kicked out of the joint venture by United Cable on August 4, 1987! Her article continues:

> United Cable owns 49 percent of KTV, while Recreation Broadcasting retains 51 percent ownership. ..."

"From a philosophical side, we want to be a regional channel with proprietary programming and a regional flavor," said Dovey. "We will also have a heavy emphasis on sports where it makes sense. ..."

Whose "philosophical side"? How convenient for Mr. Dovey and his cable associates that my stockholders had invested five years of sweat and treasure to provide Mr. Dovey with his "regional channel with proprietary programming and a regional flavor"!

The article continues, "Possible sports programming includes collegiate basketball and football from the Big Eight Conference and the Western Athletic Conference. ..."

Possible? KSPN-TV's general manager Lou Fox had signed contracts in-house for the last year that were stolen by United Cable.

And Jim Dovey had a final wish, according to the article: "We'd love to get the Nuggets," added Dovey, saying, "the channel would be interested in the rights to any professional sports between Denver and Salt Lake City."

Well, if there was any debate about whose channel this would be, that was squelched by a letter sent to me two weeks later, dated January 4, 1988, from United Cable attorney Mark L. Schneider, (signed again: "Vice President, Corporate Development"), with a cc to John E. Moye, Esq., and Gary Verplank. The last paragraph stated:

> We must begin an orderly liquidation of KTV, payment of its outstanding liabilities, and dissolution of the company. We are prepared to assist however we can. Since United has been maintaining programming on Channel 10 since August, United will assume the Channel 10 liability for any transponder costs, equipment usage, personnel, etc. from the time KTV signed off in August.

What an amazing display of chutzpah!—gall, brazen nerve, effrontery, incredible guts, presumption plus arrogance—and total indifference to any business ethics! Our lawyer, John E. Moye, Esq., would become famous as the author of the "most definitive guide to the law of business organization available today"—the 880-page text *The Law of Business Organizations*, published in 2004. John is described by his Denver law firm, Moye White, as a "savvy businessman and expert on professional ethics and responsibility." Perhaps he was inspired to write the text to rid the world of the cable pirates developing in his backyard.

And that might include our own Peter Barton, who claimed in his memoir *Not Fade Away*, "Most managers counsel prudence and caution. At Liberty (Media), we urged just the opposite. We wanted our entrepreneurs to be bold almost to the point of recklessness. I had a personal credo that I also advised others to follow: 'Don't ask permission, just beg forgiveness.'"

Well … we would have to see if United Cable would be begging forgiveness. And would Peter get involved?

Since our corporate lawyer, John Moye, was not a litigator, I turned first to my favorite trial lawyer, Hal Sawyer, at Warner, Norcross, and Judd in Grand Rapids. Hal had served in Congress for eight years before deciding to leave in 1984, for health reasons. Hal did not know if I had a case worth litigating against giants in the cable industry; John Malone had gained industry clout by negotiating savvy deals with new cable channels, and the new cable channels were used to giving TCI equity stakes in return for access.

Hal thought I would need a good trial lawyer in Denver to help us decide if we should try the case—and where we should try the case: Aspen or Denver. And Hal thought a female lawyer's opinion might be helpful.

Did I? Not really. Not in a cow town like Denver, where the macho man was much revered. Peter Barton bragged about the small coterie of six brainy guys surrounding John Malone at TCI—yes, *guys*.

Although Hal didn't personally know any Denver litigators, he arranged one interview with a smart female litigator in Denver. I vaguely remember she knew a lot more than I did about the local legal landscape and the lack of acceptance of women as executives—especially in the rough-and-tumble negotiations with cable system operators. Sadly, I was too new at this litigation game to absorb her rationale. It was easier for me to hire a small Denver litigation firm, Holmes and Starr, who had an impressive public reputation in recent trials. Naturally, I wanted their star litigator, but I didn't get him.

And did I get the right venue for a trial? The subject would never come up again on my radar; someone, somewhere, had picked Denver over Aspen. Only time would tell. …

How much time was way beyond my imagination—and I had a litigator in the family. What games they would play! It could be an expensive lesson.

When Brett graduated in December from the University of Colorado, with a major in communications, the only job on his horizon would take him far from Aspen and Michigan—but the job certainly would allow him to use his natural talents.

Uncle Midge was sailing his newly built fifty-six-foot cruising ketch, *Oso Dormido,* (which he named after his racing boat, *Sleeping Bear,*) through the Lesser Antilles to Grenada. After Christmas, Midge hired Brett as the "bn"—the only permanent crew on board for the winter cruising season. Back then, we called any and all hired boat crew the "bns" (boat niggers—a term that is considered offensive today). Brett's older brother happily filled the "bn" role a decade earlier on *Sleeping Bear.*

Midge's new cruising boat slept six comfortably, but there were eight of us on board; Midge had his hands full. First, it was lessons in snorkeling, then scuba diving, then a tour of Brett's favorite haunts found on his trip sailing south to Grenada through the Grenadines.

And what was the most memorable experience for me? Needing a rescue by the boys while snorkeling in the fierce channel currents that flowed out to sea between the tiny uninhabited islands of the Tobago Cays. There were no hotels or restaurants in the Tobago Cays. Visitors had to arrive by boat—which made sailing in the Grenadines such a special treat. The number of moorings were limited too, so marine life could flourish.

I didn't realize how lucky we were to have had Midge's *Oso Dormido* fan the flames for ocean sailing once again. And my love of the sea seemed to have been inherited by all my clan. We would be back.

Lydia, Fritz, Brett, Joyce, Greg and Anne at Little Palm Island in the Grenadines

Chapter Twelve

FULL FAITH AND CREDIT

*The best-run auction firms today are in fact sophisticated marketing
organizations, supported by large administrative staffs, spending
their time packaging properties for sale and targeting buyers.*
Fritz Hatton, Senior Vice President, Christie's, 1988

Cover photo with Bill Seidman Source: National Journal, 21, May 27, 1989

A florid detail of the façade of the historic Audiffred building in San
Francisco graced the glossy cover of Christie's auction catalog of *Prime
Real Estate Investment Properties*, which, according to the opening page, were
"to be sold at auction on Thursday, March 24, 1988, at 11:00 a.m. precisely."
Exclusive sales agents were Cushman & Wakefield, Inc., with contact Earl
Reiss, and auctioneer was Christie's Realty International, Inc., with contact
Fritz Hatton.

I had to assume that no one could believe I had thought up the idea of combining Christie's with the FDIC and FSLIC in an auction of subprime properties in the daunting atmosphere of Christie's Park Avenue salesrooms. After all, it was my son, Fritz Hatton, Christie's Director of Operations, who was assigned by Christie's as their point man on this first project with Cushman & Wakefield (C&W).

When I suggested the auction process to Bill Seidman in April 1987, neither Fritz nor I knew we could be working together on this unique real estate asset liquidation program.

I knew Bill thought it was important to resolve the debacle facing him, but was I going to be someone's water boy once again?

I remembered what Stu Root had warned me about during our fall meeting in New York City: "Get an understanding of who controls the decisions re: your proposal."

But I also remembered Stu's other caution: "You don't know what C&W and Christie's are up to. ..."

Yes, I did know what C&W and Christie's were up to. Fritz told me they would use this first auction of "prime commercial properties" as their guinea pig for a future auction with the FDIC, and perhaps FSLIC, if FSLIC could get its act together. The results of this auction were key to Christie's and C&W's willingness to move ahead with the FDIC auction. Fritz described the sale in positive terms:

> ... We learned a great deal from this first sale and firmly believed that the mechanism we had devised, with some additional tinkering, would work well for the right kind of seller. The way to proceed seemed to be a sale on behalf of one or more motivated sellers with multiple properties to sell. *And we required a motivated seller because auction will not work unless reserve prices are reasonable in relation to appraised values.* [Italics mine.]

Well ... I had my work cut out for me! Fritz was leaving in April for Japan, where he had been invited to participate as best man at his good friend Tatsuo Okaya's elaborate Asian-style wedding. Tatsuo also invited other American friends and included me in his guest list. This was going to be my golden opportunity to meet with potential Japanese investors to determine their needs and interest in auctions of FDIC and FSLIC properties. (Bill Seidman had sent me a news clip in April 1987, suggesting that

Christie's should try Japanese investors, who were eagerly buying land-mark American properties.)

Fritz's articulate exposition of the auction process to a group of bankers explained the importance of targeting buyers:

> ... I would like to take a moment to debunk a few old-fashioned beliefs about auctioneering. The old-fashioned beliefs are (1) anyone can wield a gavel, and (2) auction is a method of last resort. The belief that anyone can wield a gavel is almost true, and I'd be happy to provide a few lessons during break, but the auction itself, in its modern form, is the culmination of thousands of hours of labor spent organizing and marketing the properties for sale. The actual auction or wielding of the gavel, one of the last events to occur in the marketing chain, merely determines the price, and whether the property is sold or not. The best-run auction firms today are in fact sophisticated marketing organizations, supported by large administrative staffs, spending almost all their time packaging properties for sale and *targeting buyers.* [Italics mine.]

I arrived in Tokyo in April of 1988 with a few of Tatsuo's American friends but without Fritz, who would be arriving two days before the wedding. Tatsuo arranged a crowded schedule of special events just for us, including a two-day tour of historic Kyoto, a formal tea in a family friend's palatial Japanese home, and a cultural evening with a very entertaining geisha. I did not know what to wear on any of these touristy occasions because my hosts were always men who dressed in severe banker business suits.

What a surprise to be treated as an American business executive by all the Japanese men. I did not meet any of their wives until the wedding day, but I did meet Tatsuo's bride-to-be and many of her girlfriends the day be-fore the wedding. One couldn't tell from their youthful activities that this was an arranged marriage by two of the wealthiest Japanese families. The girls invited me to their bachelorette parties, with extensive photo reviews of their childhood activities together. Their camaraderie reminded me of my sorority life at the University of Michigan. The girls did not appear to doubt the authority of Japanese men to control their lives or careers after marriage.

As soon as Fritz arrived at the Palace Hotel, he got down to business with me, discussing carefully the intricacies of the social custom of ex-changing personal cards at the wedding reception. How many would I need? Two hundred. What did a card say, and when was it presented? Now that was interesting: With one side in English, the other in Japanese, it would list my name and, most important, my title, President of Recreation Broadcasting Company, Inc., in Aspen, Colorado. I had to learn to say "how do you do" in Japanese, bow a little, and at the same time, offer my card—to the men only. And I would need business cards for my bank meetings that Tatsuo's family had arranged after the wedding ceremony. Tatsuo did not plan to leave on a honeymoon after the wedding; he planned to entertain his American guests as long as they remained in Japan.

The wedding day began very traditionally with a morning family ceremony that was an extravaganza to behold. It took hours to dress the bride in her heavy, ornate Japanese wedding kimonos and headgear. And the exhausted bride changed her clothes five times before the last evening reception was over. The protocol for the day was planned in detail for us, and we were happy to have time to rest, change clothes, and enjoy the park across the street with its cherry trees in bud prior to blossoming.

Tatsuo decision to designate Fritz as Western-style best man had occurred at the last minute. Fritz did not think there was an equivalent role in Asian weddings. At the wedding reception for two hundred guests in the Palace Hotel, the lead toast was given by Eiji Toyoda, a former neighbor and family friend in Nagoya and also the chairman of Toyota Motor Company. Eiji Toyoda was famous for developing the "just in time" manufacturing method that helped to make Toyota the third-largest car company in the world; he was considered the "Henry Ford of Japan" and was actively involved in the company through his nineties.

After hearing Mr. Toyoda speak, I understood why I was privileged to have prime-time meetings set up with representatives from Meiji Life Insurance Company, Mitsui Trust and Banking Company, and Mitsubishi Trust and Banking Corporation. My goal was to find out their level of interest in buying FDIC or FSLIC real estate assets. I met with all three companies shortly after the wedding; one said they bought nothing less than $100 million in appraised value; a second said they would consider real estate between $10 and 100 million; and the third said they would consider buying properties between $1 and 10 million in value. (Sort of like the three bears.)

The next morning, I experienced the 9:00 a.m. power-breakfast atmosphere in the Palace Hotel dining room. And it was powerful! Fully charged young Wall Street brokers were hungry to make deals happen at the height of the demand for American real estate. The pace was dizzying. With the strong yen leading the way, Tokyo was moving at twice the speed of New York City, consuming billions of dollars of America's trophy properties. Commercial Realtors like Coldwell Banker were concerned that Japanese investors would become the dominant force in America's commercial real estate marketplace.

And was I popular! When they saw "Aspen" on my card, they all wanted to know how best to contact the Aspen Skiing Company owners. Well, I could have told them (Jim Crown was Fritz's good friend), but, instead, I told them the company was not for sale and the owners did not need the money. ... No, there would be no motivated sellers.

Tatsuo insisted on taking Fritz and me to visit his favorite industries and the Hakone resort, which was famous for its stone hot springs baths—and I can attest that they were hot, hot, hot! Everywhere we went, we were showered with gifts, most very thoughtful, exquisite, and often representative of a company's products. Fritz reminded me that gift giving was a big thing in Japan—a sign of respect. Above a certain level, we in the West call them "bribes." Fritz said Westerners generally do not have the knowledge or sensitivity to exchange gifts with such a level of sophistication.

In the fall of 1987, Lydia complained about the lack of good television-related jobs on the East Coast. She thought about graduate school, and I suggested she apply only to first-tier schools—like Columbia, Yale, or Harvard—if she wanted to be taken seriously by the broadcast industry on the East Coast. When Lydia discovered that Harvard Business School no longer required the GMAT (General Management Admission Test) for admission, she forgot about applying anywhere else. And she had the good fortune to apply at a time when Harvard was making a firm commitment to equal opportunity and affirmative action; Harvard Business School had the resources to recruit women in such fields as organizational behavior and marketing, which were not traditionally taught at the business school. They accepted her with a caveat: she had to take a college-level accounting course and get a B (which the business school considered a passing grade). Lydia said, if admitted, she thought she would be the first student with a background in television production to be accepted at the Harvard "B" School.

So ... while Lydia was studying accounting in the summer of 1988, I was studying New York real estate law. Earl Reiss of Cushman & Wakefield liked to remind me that I didn't "know anything about real estate." He was right, and it didn't bother me until he announced that I would not get my commission (for putting this whole deal together!) on any auction sales unless I had a real estate license—and he put it in our first agreement:

> Payment of any commissions to me in accordance with this Agreement and the effectiveness of this Agreement is conditioned upon the following:
>
> (i) that I am licensed as a Real Estate broker or salesperson in the State of New York at the time of the commencement of marketing (first contact with potential bidders or customers) under the Agency Agreement; and
>
> (ii) that I am licensed at the time each payment is made to me hereunder.

But he also put into the agreement that "nothing is to preclude me from acting as a salesperson for an outside broker ... and for said outside broker to receive 1% commission ... in addition to fees I am otherwise entitled to under our Agreement." (I knew who might be interested in the Texas real estate: my old boss at Provincial House in Lansing, chairman of the board Otto Solomon. I would be calling him in the fall, as soon as Christie's catalogs were printed.)

C&W presented our first "Exclusive Sales Agency Agreement for the Offer at Auction of Various Properties" to the FDIC and FSLIC in July 1988. By September, all our agreements were signed. I was so proud and excited—it took little more than a year to bring my concept from inception to acceptance!

Christie's and C&W needed six months lead time to market the properties, requiring the first two months to work with the seller, whether FDIC or FSLIC, to assemble relevant information on the properties. FSLIC was turning out to be impossible—their information, according to Fritz, was sometimes lacking, contradictory, or just plain difficult to figure out. I worried that the auction might have to proceed without them.

Every time I stopped in Denver on my way to Aspen, our litigator, Jeff Reiman, would demand more and more RBI documents and correspondence, going back five, six, or seven years. Sandy Mochary was swamped with Jeff's requests for my personal files too, including all my *diaries* and my messy expense reports.

Jeff was preparing depositions for me, as well as for Gary, Jim Dovey, Bruce Smith, and Peter Barton, among others. But he hit a snag right away:

Both Jim Dovey and Bruce Smith were working in England, and they had no plans to return to the states in the immediate future, if ever.

By the summer of 1988, the Rocky Mountain SuperChannel on United Cable's channel 10 had morphed into Prime Sports Network, a joint venture between Bill Daniels and TCI. (Also in 1988, United Cable Television Corporation became a wholly owned subsidiary of a new company, a majority of which was owned by TCI.)

It didn't take John Malone's genius to realize the importance of owning (or stealing!) programming on his cable systems. And Peter Barton, his "second banana," as Peter liked to call himself, was returning to Denver from a successful launch of CVN in Minneapolis.

Every move TCI made was watched by our litigators. We needed to move fast before a jury would forget KTV or KSPN-TV or the Rocky Mountain SuperChannel." But the courts were moving at their own pace, and no one manipulated it better than TCI's aggressive lawyers. And with TCI's resources, there were plenty of lawyers and accountants to thwart all our poor (by comparison) litigator's initiatives.

TCI hired a forensic accountant to pore over a decade of my old personal and corporate accounts. By the time the accountant was done, he found me guilty of stealing $60,000 in salary from a corporate till (which one didn't seem to matter); the fact that I had more than $1.5 million in loans to the company didn't matter, either. It was crazy! But, for $200,000, one probably could find an accountant able to dream up any fabrication. Obviously, I was the one who needed Lydia's course in accounting. (And, yes, she passed it.)

Bill Seidman was loved by the media for his candor and his ability to explain in blunt layman's language (i.e., mine) the crux of a problem. Bill expounded on the roots of the S&L debacle in his book, *Full Faith and Credit:*

> The S&L crisis was born in the economic climate of the times. It was nurtured, however, in the fertile ground of politics as usual and the political mentality of "not on my watch." The system may have given rise to the crisis, but human beings, with all their faults, ultimately determined the scope of the debacle.
>
> The S&L mistakes resulted in the closing down of one-third of the industry, destroying the agency charged with promoting and insuring it, and costing the American taxpayers around $200 billion, plus interest on that amount, probably forever! No larger financial error appears to be recorded in history. And all because the use of the full

faith and credit of the US government was not treated with the respect and fear that must be accorded it.

C&W and Christie's demanded six months' marketing time from the FDIC for their Exclusive Sales Agreement—which seemed like a very long time to the FDIC, and a lifetime to Realtors waiting in the wings for their opportunity to sell the billions of assets accumulating from defunct banks and S&Ls. Both C&W and Christie's had benefited from their experience with the first auction in March 1988, and it was their experience and resources, combined, that made them a dynamic duo.

According to Fritz Hatton, C&W needed two months to create the due diligence materials; Christie's needed six weeks to produce and print the catalog—a well-designed product that would be the most widely distributed piece of information, setting the tone for the sale; the buyers needed two months or more to examine the properties—adequate time for the buyers was critical to their auction sale mechanism, as there were virtually no conditions under which a successful bidder could back out without losing a substantial deposit.

An extensive marketing campaign commenced ninety days before the sale, which was set for March 9, 1989.

The Washington Post – October 7, 1988:

"FDIC, FSLIC to Auction $100 Million in Property. On the block: buildings, hotels, shopping centers, warehouses, land and apartment complexes."— by Kirstin Downey

More than $100 million in real estate properties from failed banks and savings and loans will be auctioned in New York City early next year … "We've never done anything like this before," said Steven Seelig, associate director of the FDIC's liquidation division. "We're hoping to tap into the Cushman & Wakefield client base and Christie's client base. …"

Cushman & Wakefield approached the FDIC with the idea of the auction … Cushman & Wakefield was the big real estate player here. It agreed to market properties and sell them at auction on a strict commission basis—an attractive proposition for the agency. The FSLIC later decided to participate in the auction as well as a sort of pilot project.

(Obviously, I couldn't take credit publicly for any part of this venture—even though I had approached the FDIC with the auction idea in April 1987. With my business partner Bill Seidman head of the FDIC, and my son Fritz Hatton director of operations of Christie's, I was happy to remain in the background.)

Earl Reiss and Fritz Hatton had their hands full with FSLIC properties; organizing the properties for sale turned out to be an insurmountable task, and all the FSLIC real estate went off the auction block.

Did I have any idea what I was getting into with this project? Did Bill Seidman? Bill could control the FDIC, but FSLIC management was going to have to go, and Bill started working with newly elected President Bush's staff, and the Treasury Department, to design a rescue plan.

In his book, *Full Faith and Credit*, Bill states:

> The incoming Bush administration decided to remove the Federal Home Loan Bank Board as the insurer of the savings and loan industry and to transfer that function to the FDIC. ... Ultimately, the proposal meant that we could chalk up one of history's largest victories in the Washington turf wars. ... The proposed legislation also would create the Resolution Trust Corporation (RTC), which was designed to take over, dissect, bury, and dispense with the sick and dying S&Ls. Bringing this new monster to life was an experience that was a great, if not totally enjoyable, affair. ...

Would we be able to keep enough good properties in the auction to satisfy all the hard work of C&W's nationwide network of brokers? Properties were located in seven different regional markets. When potential bidders spotted a property they wanted, they could make a substantial offer and buy the property before the auction. However, commissions could be payable if the property went to contract after the initial thirty days of C&W's signed agreement with the FDIC.

I marveled at the marketing campaign designed by C&W and Christie's. Fritz explained that it had three major elements. First, was a direct mail campaign combining telemarketing with use of extensive proprietary lists to get the catalog into the hands of as many real estate investors as possible; almost the entire run of thirty thousand copies was distributed.

Otto Solomon received our slick catalog and agreed to look at properties in Texas. As a former builder, Otto had a keen eye for construction; he needed savvy local C&W brokers to show him properties, most of them located around Houston. I was happy with Otto's curiosity about Christie's auction technique. Otto was a master at bidding for big road contracts with the state of Michigan; he would definitely be showing up with his gold jewels on full display in Christie's hallowed showrooms on March 9, 1989, at 11:00 a.m. precisely.

"AUCTION REVISITED," was a flattering article by Susan Annin in *Investment Properties International*, in May 1989:

In its first international real estate auction, the Federal Deposit Insurance Corporation (FDIC) sold more than $40 million of its real estate holdings on March 9, 1989, at Christie's New York salesroom, 502 Park Avenue. The auction was a joint venture between Cushman & Wakefield, a leading business real estate firm, and Christie's, world-renowned auctioneers. ...

*Joyce (in front) observing the FDIC/Christie's/Cushman
& Wakefield auction, March 9, 1989*

... It appears that real estate auctions are about to have a resurrection. No longer will they be seen as a last ditch resort to dispose of distressed, obsolete, bankrupt properties by a crass caller before an unregulated, corrupt audience. The commercial real estate auctions of the 90's and the twenty-first century will assemble global buyers eager to purchase highly desirable real estate and real estate packages created by economic times. Auctioneers and brokers will work together

to assemble and market millions of dollars of properties. The FDIC/
Christie's/Cushman & Wakefield auction is a harbinger of this trend. ...

Fritz Hatton and Christopher Burge on podium

... According to Fritz Hatton, Senior Vice President at Christie's,
"Property owners have discovered that auctions are an efficient way
to sell real estate. Properties receive proper exposure and sales are
closed quickly. In addition, the bidding process offers buyers an equal
opportunity to make a profitable deal. ..."

The publicity for the auction was amazing! *USA Today* blazed a headline
the morning of the auction: **"Monets to Motels—Christie's Hosts FDIC
Auction."**

And Otto Solomon impressed everyone with his tough comments about
the state of real estate. (This was the same Edward "Otto" Solomon who, as
chairman of the board of Provincial House, almost two decades before, had
backed me up against the wall during our first board meeting and ham-
mered me with questions about my ability to juggle two jobs: taking care
of my five kids, plus running his new subsidiary, Young World, Inc. Otto
may have "roughed me up" at the time, but he still believed in me—enough
to invest $425,000 in FDIC property.) In the March 10 issue of the *New York
Post*, staff reporter Paul Thorp wrote:

"... According to those involved, it was a test that succeeded. "It was outstanding—and about time the government got off its dead ass to start putting the property back into the economy," said Edward Solomon, a wealthy Michigan road builder and developer who bought an unfinished office park in Houston for $425,000. The government's pre-auction estimate was that the office park might fetch as much as $1.2 million ...

After the lengthy legislative battle to create the Resolution Trust Corp (RTC), Fritz's final comment to the Banking and Law Institute's Thrift Assets Conference would be "fair warning"—as Christie's auctioneers say just before dropping the hammer for a sale: "... We hope that in creating the RTC, Congress has not made a mess of it by tying the FDIC's arms behind its back too tightly, and that we can return the mass of properties now in government hands to the private sector and the open market in a rapid and orderly manner."

Bill Seidman was at war with the administration, drafting the legislation for the new S&L plan; it was clear to Bill that the administration did not want the FDIC to run the RTC operation. Until the smoke cleared, it was impossible to plan future auctions. Besides, C&W was not happy with the FDIC's closure rate from our first auction; there was sloppiness in dealing with deliverable title. It was becoming apparent that this auction plan would not be cost effective for C&W in the future. For me, it was different. I didn't make a killing from my meager commission, but as the money drifted in, starting in May, I knew I would clear enough to keep me going until the next auction opportunity appeared on the horizon. But not nearly enough to pay my RBI bankers. That would require a successful jury trial or settlement. The date for that had not been established, but it couldn't come soon enough.

Grand River on left, Spring Lake on right, Lake Michigan in rear; Grand Haven on left, Ferrysburg on right, Spring Lake in front. Photo courtesy of Marge Beaver

When Brett called after the FDIC auction and calmly announced that he was planning a summer wedding, I was more than happy to get out of Washington.

I was eager to plan our first home wedding. Their chosen date was prime summertime, July 3, light until 10:00 p.m. on the western edge of the eastern daylight time zone. The venue had to be Aunt Vicki and Uncle Gary's waterfront home. With nine acres of lawn for parking and tenting, the hundreds of Spring Lake Yacht Club members who would show up by land or sea (invited or not) could enjoy this historic event: the first wedding in Spring Lake for one of Mom and Dad's eleven grandchildren!

Gary and Vicki Verplank, and Tony, Ashley, and Kyle, July 3, 1989

Fortunately for Vicki and Gary, the large wedding party, followed by a small flotilla of boats, could cruise across the lake to the yacht club for the reception. But what turned out to be most fortunate? The perfect weather!

The weather was perfect for dancing outside too. Once the rock band opened up, the drums reverberated up and down Spring Lake. My favorite dancing partner, Paulie Eggert, grabbed me, along with two little girls who stood by, looking eager to dance, and away we all went ... rocking the night away before half the guests had parked their cars or boats.

My friendship with Paul Eggert was something I always took for granted. He was part of my Spring Lake Yacht Club heritage. Whenever I happened to show up at a regatta or at the yacht club, Paul's buddies would kid him: "Here comes Eggie's hundred-pound bundle of fun."

At our Spring Lake Yacht Club soirees, Paul never bragged; he didn't have to. He was the E scow champion at the WMYA regattas for fifteen years, starting when he and his steady crew of three high school buddies were fifteen years old. Paul was fearless on the water; sailing on his ocean-rigged sloop in a solo Lake Michigan race, from Muskegon to Milwaukee to Chicago and back to Muskegon. Paul was the only sailor who flew a spinnaker and won the race by almost eight hours; he was home in bed when they handed out trophies.

Paul was really dyslexic, but he could fix anything, with or without tools. He had the naturally humorous personality that often emanates from someone very dyslexic—with the innate ability to make fun of himself. His stories just rolled off the line ... until the wee hours. No one at a yacht club party wanted him to leave, but Paul never wanted to leave, either. To my surprise, neither did I.

But I did leave in August—for Scandinavia with Lydia. I had accumulated United Airlines frequent flyer miles that had a fall deadline for use. I asked Lydia if she wanted to go to South America or Europe. I had the plane tickets but little cash. Lydia suggested we visit our former exchange student, Cecilia, in Stockholm.

We flew to Copenhagen and rented a car one way to Stockholm. We had to see Copenhagen's famous Tivoli Gardens before heading north to Bergen. Copenhagen should have reminded me of Berlin, which was a few hundred miles directly south, but Copenhagen seemed more like London—classier, less dogmatic. I wasn't worried about missing the bus, or boat, or Berlin Wall, which was already wobbling, but would stand for a few more months.

On the road to Oslo, it was easy to enjoy the massive beauty of the haystacks. Lydia loved them; I hardly noticed them. I was looking for Norwegian ski resorts—something that resembled my experience in the

Alpine architecture of Aspen or Vail. I imagined Viking chalets, but I saw old farmhouses and gently rolling hills. I forgot this was the land of cross-country skiing. With Norway's top mountain peak about 8,000 feet high (and Sweden's less than 7,000 feet), this was not like driving through the Rockies.

Happily, Lydia had a keen interest in the arts, just like her brothers. The huge sculpture park in Oslo got her attention. And the Millesgarden sculptures in Stockholm, on the small island of Lidingo, where Cecilia and handsome husband Anders lived with their two young children. I took pictures of three-year-old Gustav and toddler Fanny among Milles sculptures—reminding me of photos I took of our kids playing in the sculpture garden at the Museum of Modern Art in New York City in the 1960s.

I had not seen Cecilia since 1974, although Lydia had visited her five years prior to this visit, after climbing in the Russian Himalayas. It was so rewarding to know Cecilia's strong bilingual skills and nurse's training resulted in an important position flying European routes with SAS, Scandinavia's largest airline. Cecilia said that she was allowed to spend a lot of time at home with her children because of Sweden's flexible work schedules for new mothers. She could take a year off with each child and receive 80 percent of her normal pay, plus another six months off at less pay. And she got free medical care. However, Cecilia said most people opted for private supplemental insurance too.

The benefits for young parents in a small country like Sweden, with a population less than half the size of New York City, seemed surreal—something we would dream about here in the United States.

We planned a rendezvous soon, perhaps next summer at Lydia's upcoming wedding.

During the fall, I consulted in New York City with Earl Reiss of Cushman & Wakefield (C&W) and Fritz Hatton of Christie's, and met with new FDIC personnel in Washington, all of them hired by Bill Seidman for his burgeoning Resolution Trust Corp (RTC).

C&W agreed to present a new offer to the FDIC in December 1989. Their request of three months with an "exclusive agreement to act as agent for the sale of these real estate properties" fell on deaf ears. "Exclusive" was not going to be acceptable anymore. It was obvious to everyone at the FDIC and RTC that C&W and Christie's were the most experienced team for the job.

However, Congress wanted it bid out with "hiring points to the handicapped and minorities and to the performance of good works in the past, but very few points for past relevant experience in the field," according to Bill Seidman in *Full Faith and Credit*. Remember Fritz Hatton's "fair warning"?

At Christmastime, I rushed to Michigan to meet my first granddaughter. Brie would share a birthday with her uncle Julio. My first grandson, Nicholas ("Cole") Hatton was born last September in California.

While I was visiting with Mom and Dad in Spring Lake, I received a phone call from Donald Hannah. The name Hannah was well known to my Verplank family. Midge explained that the Great Lakes was full of tugboats and barges with the name "Hannah" printed in giant letters across their sides. Would this be the same Don Hannah? Yes.

Don Hannah said he wanted to diversify his corporate activities from the shipping business and international marketing, and he found rapid growth in the sales of real estate properties through the auction method. Don felt it was a growing trend and a definite opportunity for creative, innovative, and experienced entrepreneurs. He moved, in the late 1980s, from Chicago to Greenwich, Connecticut, to base his new company, USAuction, Inc., in Stamford, Connecticut. Don said that USAuction's national rollout plan began in earnest with a fast-paced assemblage of its team of experts and support staff, and he wanted to hire me as his global marketing and telecommunications consultant.

Before my meeting with Don Hannah took place, I received a phone call from Tom Whitehead in Washington, DC. (In the spring of 1974, Tom had secretly organized and led the effort to plan Vice President Ford's transition to the presidency.) Bill suggested Tom call me for help in forming a "global marketing company" to market the assets of the RTC and FDIC. From no jobs to two offers in one week! How would I work this out?

If Don Hannah talked about being creative, innovative, and an experienced entrepreneur, Clay T. ("Tom") Whitehead lived it. Tom had bachelor's and master's degrees in electrical engineering, and a PhD in management—all received from MIT in the 1960s. (This mirrored John Malone's educational career: bachelor's and master's degrees in electrical engineering, and a PhD in management earned in 1967. And both men bragged about the necessity of taking risks.)

I was going to get the education of a lifetime from Tom Whitehead and his sometimes partner (in my case), Henry Goldberg, of the Washington-based law firm Goldberg & Spector. Tom and Henry had worked on projects together for twenty years—from the time Tom created and ran the White House's first Office of Telecommunications Policy (OTP) in 1970. Henry served as general counsel to the OTP.

Tom crafted the Open Skies domestic satellite policy that allowed any qualified private company to launch communications satellites, rejecting the monopoly model for the technology. And then, in 1979, Tom formed a private company, Los Angeles-based Hughes Communications, to build the satellites. Tom's greatest achievement there was the Galaxy program of commercial communications satellites, which addressed the needs of a rapidly growing cable television market. (And where was I during this time? Building a microwave system that would be unnecessary once we could afford to pay for one of Tom's transponders!)

Tom left Hughes Communications in 1983, and spent the next two years laying the financial, technical, and political groundwork for a $180 million enterprise that became SES Astra, based in Luxembourg. Tom was criticized by some European politicians, who dismissed his proposed commercial satellite system as cultural imperialism—all to protect their government-run television channels. Tom forged ahead, and SES Astra, with the country of Luxembourg a major stakeholder, grew tremendously, with its programming beamed into millions of homes.

Henry Goldberg was known as Tom's "advocate and consigliore," but Henry had his own significant role in the revolution in telecommunications as new technologies and deregulation disrupted the established broadcasting and telephone industries. Henry was the leading lawyer in a copyright compromise that unleashed cable television. And building on his client base of new entrants and established players seeking flexibility under the FCC rules to introduce new technologies and services, Henry's law firm represented PanAmSat in developing a private competitive alternative to an international quasi-governmental satellite monopoly.

I would become familiar with their work because my new Washington-based office would be located in the lower level of Goldberg & Spector's beautiful office building at 19th and N Streets, in DC—the former home of President Theodore "Teddy" Roosevelt in the late nineteenth century. The early 1990s was the era of the fax machine, which was located in the room next to my office, and Goldberg & Spector's hundreds of pages of satellite leases would tie up the fax machines all night long.

Well … if I was going to have contracts with highfalutin lawyers in DC. and Connecticut, I needed a lawyer to represent me, one who would be reasonable but also responsible. I called my old college buddy, Bill Griffith, in Denver. Bill was curious about my work and quickly accepted my requests. I would fax him the contracts, and he would make the necessary changes and fax the contracts back. Bill was quick, fun, and no-nonsense. And he agreed to be my real estate broker in Colorado when I passed my Colorado real estate sales licensing test. (That association would turn out to be very beneficial for both of us.)

My first agreement was written by Henry Goldberg, the only principal who was also a lawyer. Henry and Tom Whitehead decided to call our new company Newport Partners. (Why? It sounded credible, I was told. With a litigator son living in Newport Beach, I thought it rang true.)

I liked the simple letter from Henry, written to me on January 30, 1990. It started out with a brief explanation of their plan: " … it makes sense to put in writing the essence of the agreement that we reached regarding Tom's and my plan to develop an interactive network to carry a televised auction of certain real estate parcels, savings and loan investment portfolios and/ or savings and loan institutions themselves, some of which are now being disposed of under the auspices of the RTC, FDIC, FADA, etc."

Henry then explained more specifically: " … what we have in mind is either our own stand-alone contractual televised auction event or an interactive television network component of a real estate auction event that has been developed by others, including the government agencies involved."

I agreed to work for them 25 percent of my time for one year, beginning January 15, 1990.

Next stop: Stamford, Connecticut. By the time I met with Donald Hannah at his offices on the ninth floor of a modern office building in Stamford, the entire floor was flooded with workers. I would be asked to fill the role of Senior Vice President of Government Sales—when we were submitting proposals to governmental entities. However, I would be retained as an independent contractor, not an employee, and I would devote 50 percent of my time to " … performing the work as set forth by Donald C. Hannah, President." I felt the compensation and commission were very fair. The term of my contract would be one year, beginning March 1, 1990.

I was off and running, and I would be running! I needed to find some living quarters in the Stamford area, or suffer the commute from the loft in SoHo. The trains and subway were very convenient for the reverse commute as long as I could face the dark, late-night subway rides through Harlem during the winter months.

Washington, DC was a different matter. I had to find temporary residential space immediately; no way could I afford a hotel. I found some residential rooms in downtown Georgetown, allowing me to ride my bike to work in DC. Soon I found a friend from Grand Rapids, Mime Stalland, who had moved from Minnesota to Georgetown after a recent divorce. Mime had a cute three-story townhouse tucked in a narrow lane not far from downtown. She was willing to let me rent the third floor for a short time. I was happy to have a beautiful home to enjoy, and a patio and garden filled with roses and bees—that liked me better than the roses.

My contract with USAuction may have specified a March 1 start date, but we were deep into our first RTC proposal by then. And we had contracted with Newport Partners as the telecommunications arm of USAuction for this huge international auction proposal. To quote Bill Seidman from *Full Faith and Credit* once again: "I made the decision to schedule an international auction to sell hundreds of millions in real estate in one record-setting and eye-catching transaction. The RTC would put on the world's biggest real estate auction and prove we could move with unaccustomed, ungovernment-like vigor and (we all hoped) attract more clients for our huge inventory."

Don Hannah moved with his accustomed vigor and put on the biggest show available. About ten USAuction personnel flew to Washington with four copies of inch-thick RTC proposals, catalogs, and boxes of videocassettes.

When the RTC announced the winner for this first giant international auction, I was shocked! And furious! No way could Gall, a small inexperienced auction company from Miami, handle the size and expense of this auction. I called Bill Seidman and told him the RTC had to reconsider their choice.

In his *draft* manuscript of *Full Faith and Credit,* Bill wrote:

As is often the case, the government people, moving in a new area and unfamiliar with auctions, turned to the private sector for advice. They seem to have received too much help in the design of the checklist from one of the potential bidders. From the RTC point system emerged an Auctioneer named *Gault* from Miami. His previous experience did not include auctioning any large pieces of property. *Gault* and his associate, the formidable Washington public relations firm of Hill &

Knowlton, seem to have overwhelmed our bureaucrats. A number of people, *including Joyce Hatton,* who had worked on a similar but much smaller auction at the FDIC, had warned us that there was no way on earth *Gault* could handle an international auction of large pieces of real estate. Cooke was informed, and asked to take a second look at his selection process. [Italics mine.]

[Note: In the published copy of Full Faith and Credit, my name was removed, and "Gault" was correctly spelled "Gall".]

In *Full Faith and Credit,* Bill continued:

Bill's assistant, David Cooke, pronounced himself satisfied that the process had been fair and efficient. ... The RTC went forward with the auction plan. But the RTC believed that Gall had failed to live up to his contractual commitments; he was supposed to invest $1 million in advertising and other preparations for the auction but never came up with the money. Cooke quickly came to the conclusion that the auction would flop. He asked for a delay, which was agreed to. When even the delay date was missed, we decided to cut our losses, cancel the auction, and take the criticism that we knew would come our way. The Congress once again accused us of incompetence and inefficiency.

I am sure Bill couldn't print the kind of incompetence I accused them of. ... But Bill further explains in the book, "Most important, when the government asks for bids, remember that the name of the bidders' game is to get inside the bidding operation and set it up to win."

That last part means, make sure you hire a "formidable" international public relations firm like Hill & Knowlton and not a regional firm. And make sure you find some minority status to hang your hat on.

No one was better at finding the minority inside track than Bill Seidman's bright Hispanic friend, Gary Trujillo, who graduated from Arizona State University in the early 1980s, during Bill's short tenure as Dean of the Arizona State University Business School. Bill became Gary's mentor, steering him away from accounting and finding him interviews with Wall Street firms. (Shortly after Gary accepted an offer from Salomon Brothers, he was confronted in the bathroom by his tough, cigar-smoking boss, John Gutfreund, who demanded, "Are you Bill Seidman's friend?" When Gary answered, "Yes, why?" Gutfreund replied, "Why in hell do you think you're here?")

In the fall of 1988, Gary enrolled in Harvard Business School and worked for Bill at the FDIC during summer break. They were fashioning the new legislation that created the RTC: FIRREA, the Financial Institutions Reform, Recovery, and Enforcement Act. Gary and his brilliant classmate, Gary A. Magnuson, prepared a case in the spring of 1990 for Harvard Business School, entitled, "L. William Seidman and the Resolution Trust Corporation." Lydia was in their graduating class and knew both of them, and she understood Gary Trujillo's abiding interest in "the Chairman," as Gary liked to call Bill.

After Harvard Business School graduation, Lydia was offered a position in the executive training program of NBC, on the fifty-first floor of Rockefeller Center in New York City.

But her first job? Planning a June wedding in Aspen. Colorado mountain towns are notoriously cold, wet, and muddy in the spring. A June 23 wedding date would need indoor and outdoor planning—just in case.

Sandy Mochary continued to run the office from my living room. Her main job was keeping track of everyone's sleeping and travel arrangements. Sandy had been in Aspen a long time—thank goodness. She knew safe places to eat, drink, and play. And shop. The kids took a picture of me on the front lawn, with an uncut fax that resembled a long white ribbon streaming in the wind. It was a busy week. ...

Gary Trujillo arrived from Phoenix on Friday morning, ambled into the house, and said, "Have you heard about the Chairman?"

"No."

Gary responded, "I don't know how he is, but I just heard that he fell off a horse at his ranch on Wednesday morning, and Tracy rushed him to the hospital in Santa Fe."

I begged Gary, "Please call the hospital and see if you can talk to Tracy." Bill's daughter, Tracy, ran the ranch. She was smart and tough, just like her Dad. She would be in control and wasn't talking to anyone, Gary said, especially the press.

But Gary called and quickly got through to Tracy. She explained that Bill had lost a lot of blood internally, and they feared he wouldn't make it.

I was crushed. And so-o-o alone in my grief. Few guests, I realized, knew of my close association with Bill. And those who did were preparing to partake in a long weekend celebratory feast.

And I intended to feast with them. No one in New Mexico wanted to hear from me. I asked Gary to ple-e-e-ease call again on Saturday morning. I knew he would; Gary wanted a positive report about his Chairman too.

Friday night, the groom's family hosted the dude ranch roundup.

With Michelle Myers Florence and Durinda Purkiss Brownlee, June 1990

This wasn't the usual rehearsal dinner limited to the bridal party; all out-of-town guests were invited, and some in town guests too. I had been wearing a favorite handmade beaver cowboy hat for decades in Aspen and would have felt right at home, but I thought a summer straw hat was more in keeping with the occasion.

And the weather? Warm! Mostly sunny. We canceled the indoor 6:00 p.m. Prince of Peace Chapel reservation Saturday morning.

We would be walking to the grounds of the Aspen Historical Society in town, not far from the Jerome Hotel, which had recently gone through one of its many makeovers. The hotel was authentic Aspen eclecticism ... especially the J-Bar. This was mostly a young crowd; no one would find seating provided for dinner, just thematic food bars in all four corners of the huge ballroom.

The grandchildren kept Grandma Verplank happy with her favorite old-fashioneds while she waited for the band to warm up. How she loved to dance. Too bad Dad never caught on. Fortunately, Mom had plenty of grandsons willing to swing with her at these festive family events—even at 8,000 feet of altitude.

I, on the other hand, couldn't keep up with my dancing partners. Bill Griffith could dance all night; as a champion squash player, Bill showed his athleticism on the dance floor. Off came my high heels, then my long chiffon scarf and wrap. When I finally got home, I found my hot tub filled with kids. They didn't need the hot tub. I did.

Gary Trujillo, left of Bill Seidman, at the FDIC offices, fall 1990

Bill Seidman's fall from the horse on his New Mexico ranch resulted in a broken pelvis and massive, life-threatening internal bleeding. His daughter, Tracy, who lived on the ranch, would not be in contact with me, and getting news about Bill proved difficult. I would have to rely on Gary Trujillo and others for any more updates, and I was overwhelmed with worry and frustration.

Bill pulled through, a tough sixty-nine-year-old fighter, and after three months of care and therapy, he was back at his FDIC offices, on crutches but in charge. I finally saw him again in the fall of 1990; he was sporting two canes and seemed uncomfortable facing me, even over a brief drink in the bar while his limo driver waited outside.

But I knew what to expect within a few days after the accident: My seamstress, the owner of the three horses boarded on my property, told me about her Dad's similar accident, and how it meant that there was no intimacy for him for the rest of his life. My old life with Bill was over.

During the six to nine months of recovery that followed, Bill was surrounded by his wife and family and staff, and I had little contact with him. Of course, he also knew that this was the end of an era, the end of our twenty-five years of intimate friendship, and he told me he wanted me to go on with my own life, to sail with Midge and Paul in Spain because that was what I loved. Over the course of two more decades, Bill continued to be my friend—available, encouraging, and loving in his own way. But his accident and the months that followed were a kind of growing up for me, a Peter Pan moment—I could look back at a wonderful past with Bill and know that it was time for a new future.

While I was home in Aspen during the winter, I received a surprise phone call from Peter Barton. Peter had moved back to Denver from Minneapolis, after selling TCI's Cable Value Network, and had started on his next successful project for John Malone: the launch of TCI spin-off Liberty Media. Peter had stood by and watched Bill Daniels and Mark Schneider and John Malone take our United Cable channel 10, the Rocky Mountain SuperChannel, and rename it Prime Sports Network.

Was the theft of our cable channel programming and equipment (and the resulting lawsuit) the precursor to Liberty Media's quest to " ... forge partnerships between the people who owned cable systems and the people who provided programming?"—to quote from *Not Fade Away*, Peter Barton's memoir written with Laurence Shames in 2002.

Peter goes on to explain:

These partnerships, we felt, would be of benefit to everyone. Cable operators needed varied and targeted content that wasn't available on free TV. Programmers needed start-up capital, and a guarantee that there would be outlets for their programs. Liberty made money—a lot of money, as it turned out—by *facilitating deals between the people with the ideas and the people with the wires.*

Often we invested in the resulting businesses. Thus, we ended up with significant equity stakes in CNN, the Discovery Channel, Black Entertainment Television, Home Shopping Network, Family Channel, MacNeil/Lehrer Productions, STARZ/!/ Encore, and Court TV, to name just a few. Through the nineties, the money snowballed. But the thing I'm proudest of about Liberty is only indirectly connected to its financial success.

What I'm proudest of is that the company became a sort of temple for entrepreneurs. *People trusted us enough to bring us their ideas.* If we believed in their smarts and their passion, we funded them and left them alone. I was privileged to be, among other things, a gatekeeper in this process. [All italics mine.]

Why was Peter Barton calling me now? It had been more than three years since the demise of KTV, Inc., the Rocky Mountain SuperChannel. Only now was I hearing from my former stockholder and chief negotiator—*my* gatekeeper, who believed in our smarts and our passion enough to invest with us and serve on our board.

What Peter had to say in his phone call made no sense to me. He inquired, "When are you going to settle this silly lawsuit?"

Silly lawsuit! What was really silly was his question, since no one on John Malone's team, including Peter, had indicated any willingness to settle. Which is exactly what I told Peter.

After Peter hung up, I called my lawyer, Jeff Reiman, and relayed my conversation with Peter. Jeff was very interested because he was preparing to depose Peter. Jeff wanted me at the deposition, but he ordered me to be silent and not comment on *anything.* Jeff explained that he planned to surprise Peter.

I looked forward to the deposition. I had always liked and trusted Peter and never understood his silence. But Jeff didn't trust him—ever.

Jeff's first question to Peter at the deposition: "Did you know that Joyce was taping your phone call about a settlement of the lawsuit?"

It did shock Peter, who looked at me in disbelief. And I was shocked too, knowing how ridiculous the idea was. (Taping a phone call from my home phone?) I was having a hard time staying composed and quiet—hardly my strong suits.

I don't remember any shocking revelations from that deposition, but the experience did have a lasting effect on Peter. He refused to talk with me about settlements or anything else—ever again. (Peter made a tidy fortune over the six years he was president of Liberty, with news reports estimating his worth at more than $70 million. During Peter's tenure in the 1990s, Liberty built a group of regional sports networks that merged with Fox Sports in 1995.)

Getting depositions from the main players of United Cable—James Dovey and Bruce Smith were both still working for TCI in the United Kingdom—became a major hurdle for our trial. When the trial was extended again and again by the district judge of Arapahoe County, our legal fees mounted by the day. And the United Cable (now TCI) legal bills had to be much more. We were approaching our fourth year of litigation, with no end in sight. That old saw, "Justice delayed is justice denied," was staring me in the face.

Our formidable foe was having his way with our assets too. By 1990, TCI had grown into the biggest cable firm in the nation, with 8.5 million subscribers, and Prime Sports Network was the largest regional sports network in the mountain time zone, covering eleven states. TCI and Bill Daniels were making money with Prime Sports Network. They could afford to litigate, while my stockholders were stuck paying all the bills for this "silly" lawsuit! All while TCI continued to use our equipment! No wonder my savvy hometown litigator, Hal Sawyer, questioned whether we should attempt a fight with the Goliath of the cable industry.

Six months after Gary Trujillo started Southwest Harvard Group (SHG) and brought in Gary Magnuson and Jess Valenzuela as partners, SHG won its first RTC contract. (The three of them missed the big auction debacle; the two Garys were still attending Harvard Business School at that time.)

Bill Seidman might have said that experience mattered in award-ing RTC contracts, but the SHG pioneers found out it didn't. In the *MBE* (*Minority-Business-Entrepreneur*) July/August 1995 article, "Destined to Be," Jeanie M. Barnett reported:

> "Being a 100 percent minority owned company was critical, but it certainly was not the deciding factor in our winning the deal," says Trujillo. "Our proposal was."
>
> " ... Years of experience means nothing," says Valenzuela. "When we started managing single-family-home assets, neither of us had ever done it before. But in 72 hours, we set up the systems, hired what it took, and understood the contract as if we'd been doing it for 15 years. ..."
>
> "Because we were a minority owned firm, and we did a good job, the RTC highlighted us as a success story," adds Trujillo. "Our question was, how were we going to leverage that?"

I found out in a hurry how one leverages one's minority position. USAuction had put everything necessary (and then some) into the contract applications of both the FDIC and the RTC, except minority executive participation. (As a female, I was considered a minority, but I wasn't the leader of the pack.)

Alone, USAuction got nowhere. Don Hannah looked for partners who had minority ownership. If he picked Newport Partners (yes, I controlled 51-plus percent), it wasn't quite enough to make a difference. He needed SHG, which was a majority Hispanic ownership at first, and then 100 percent Hispanic after its first year.

The third component needed was a national commercial real estate company, and none of them had minority ownership. The Binswanger Company was happy to climb on board with the advantage—the "bonus consideration"—given to its minority partner. I met with Binswanger Company executives in Philadelphia many times to acquaint them with the peculiarities of the FDIC and RTC solicitations.

One of the requirements in a 1991 FDIC solicitation for a nationwide auction of commercial properties valued at $500 million was the "historical relationship" of the partners. Well … we were a little weak in that area. Guess who won that contract! According to Harold Ellis Jr., president and CEO of Grubb & Ellis, "The Grubb & Ellis/Ross-Dove auction partnership was operational nationwide at the time the FDIC sought proposals to handle the project. …"

Grubb & Ellis claimed to be the largest full-service real estate firm in the country, with offices nationwide. And, to my knowledge, their joint venture didn't have any minority ownership. We would have to try again on a smaller $100 million regional proposal in Texas for the RTC. SHG had many offices in Texas—this solicitation would be right up our alley.

Jimmy Hunting, son of my longtime loyal RBI stockholders, Helen and Allen Hunting, lived in Aspen but invested around the world in a broad range of financial assets and commercial real estate properties. Jimmy called Sandy Mochary in the summer of 1991 and asked if I could help him buy the local Aspen Savings & Loan building from the RTC.

Of course I could, and so could Bill Griffith, my Colorado real estate broker, who offered to do the legal work for Jimmy—at little additional fee. Bill Griffith knew the commission was 3 percent, and he offered to split the fee with me. I insisted that Sandy be paid a modest fee from the total commission, not my half.

"Wasn't she working as *your* secretary?" Bill Griffith asked.

"No, she was working as *our* secretary," I replied, "and she kept the deal alive, because she knew all the players."

On December 19, 1991, the *Aspen Times Daily* headline read: "RTC's

Aspen Error Costs Taxpayers." The paper claimed the RTC had come close to selling the building several times since the thrift was declared insolvent on November 9, 1989, and a former bank president had made a higher, but rejected, offer a year earlier. (Jimmy Hunting paid $1.5 million cash. Who knows what contingencies existed with the other offers?) What really bothered the locals was the fact that Jimmy flipped the property the same day, selling it for $150,000 more than he paid for it. And sold it to a California real estate developer.

What should have bothered all the taxpayers was the $7 billion that had disappeared from the RTC's Denver office computers. The *Aspen Times Daily* reported, "The project appears fraught with waste, according to the (*Denver*) *Post*, and an independent auditor has been hired to investigate it."

Bill Seidman commented in *Full Faith and Credit*:

> The General Accounting Office was quick to highlight our problems. What else is an auditor for? They said our asset valuations were so uncertain that they could not provide an audited statement. Worse, in our Denver office we had closed down defunct S&Ls' computer systems without getting our own system properly on line, and about $7 billion worth of assets disappeared from our books, to be found again only after substantial accounting fees and a considerable amount of embarrassing publicity.

Bill's six-year term as chairman of the FDIC ended on October 16, 1991. *The Washington Post* featured an impressive picture and article about Bill's departure on the front page of the Business section:

> **"Clean-Up Man Leaves with Image Unstained"**, by Jerry Knight.
> ...Kissed by fate, Seidman took a job as a minor prince of the permanent bureaucracy and turned himself into the biggest frog in the banking pond.
> ...And in one of the most audacious turf acquisitions Washington has seen, Seidman managed to have the FDIC—and himself—put in charge of running the Resolution Trust Corp., the savings and loan cleanup agency. Many might have ducked the job of mucking out the S&L stables, but to Seidman, it meant increasing his army by 7,000 troops and adding to his resume: Chairman of the RTC, the largest financial institution in America.

…A master of the media, Seidman used prominent newspapers to float broad policy initiatives … and become so familiar a figure on television that he has been hired as a commentator on the Cable News and Business Channel (CNBC). Seidman's media success came not from co-opting but from candor. …

What was Bill going to be paid by CNBC? Sixty dollars per week. At age seventy, Bill Seidman would be looking for a job. But Bill knew the media exposure was priceless.

I knew something else was priceless. Bill Seidman, our only RBI stockholder who was also a lawyer, was no longer on the government's payroll, so he was now free to counsel us in our upcoming lawsuits. Bill had a conversation with Peter Barton on December 7, 1991. (Peter said that Malone [chairman of TCI] "needs to assess—and be briefed." Peter also said that he was personally nervous—worrying if it was wise to go in now to try to settle the lawsuit.) After reviewing Bill's conversation with Peter, I wrote the following letter to RBI Stockholders:

> … Please see enclosed billing and information about the United Cable lawsuit. At this time, I do not know if we are going to have the JAG (Judicial Arbiter Group, Inc.) settlement conference on January 2nd, as planned.
>
> Peter Barton called on Bill Seidman in Washington on December 7 to explore settlement talks. Since then, Bill has talked to Jeff Reiman and again Peter Barton, who insists on a "dollar figure" to present to the appropriate TCI leadership. Gary Verplank suggested we stick with our "bottom line" figure for the JAG conference … Bill Seidman has spent quite a bit of time this past week working on settlement talks. Let's hope they prove fruitful.
>
> Here's to a New Year filled with health, happiness, and $ucce$$! Happy Holidays!

The JAG conference was set for January 2, 1992, but I have no notes from it. The trial was *finally* set for the first week of February, only a month away. No one was ready to give anything away—yet. We had plowed through the muck too long to give in now. We had a room full of files—literally floor to ceiling—and more than a million dollars in legal bills before the trial even started! According to RBI's lawyer, Jeff Reiman, United Cable (TCI) was probably spending twice that amount.

United Cable's litigator, Spencer Dennison, a graduate of the University of Michigan Law School, put many experts to work, especially the forensic accountant who culled through my personal finances, going back to the early 1980s. Then they plowed through all my personal diaries—hundreds of pages—and noted every time I said I needed cash, which to them seemed to be all the time. (I was shocked to learn that once I mentioned the diaries in a deposition, they were fair game. ... Yikes!)

Bill Seidman wanted the lawsuit to be over, dreading the impact on me if we lost. But I was ready for battle; I just didn't know what I was getting into. (Duncan Littlefair said it was the "adventure within" that was worth pursuing. What was I doing here? Was my entrepreneurial spirit still in charge?)

I had work to do in Washington before I returned for the trial. The Texas Auction Group (a Binswanger Company/USAuction, Inc./Southwest Harvard Group joint venture) was waiting for their first BOA (basic ordering agreement) contract. This would be a huge commercial real estate auction in two Texas cities: Houston and San Antonio. I had worked for a year to put this together, and I didn't want to lose it now.

Just before I left Washington for Denver, the RTC notification of the BOA arrived in my office at Newport Partners. Rah! Our Texas Auction Group's application had been submitted on September 6, 1991, and the multimillion-dollar auctions were planned for late May of 1992.

I had worried for months about my court apparel. I wanted to look serious and professional, and *not* rich. This was not Washington, DC, nor was it New York City. It was not Aspen, either, where everyone was rich or retired. And all of the six potential jurors looked middle class, with jobs that would be severely impacted by a six-week trial. No one wanted to be there. Who was I to force them to sit for weeks listening to a tale about money? Money that all of the plaintiffs except me had in abundance. (Allen Hunting's family turned up in the Forbes 400.)

We noticed that the defendants, United Cable/TCI, had a team of special jury experts in the room. (I never miss *Bull*, a weekly CBS TV program featuring Bull and his team of special jury experts.) We, the plaintiffs, did not have any special jury experts. (I was asked to help make decisions about the jury pool, and, in retrospect, my suggestions were terrible.)

And we were a motley crew, mostly from out of state. I was the only plaintiff who lived in Colorado. It was quite the opposite for the defendants. This city was home base. Now who do you think the jury would be rooting for? My political brain sniffed trouble. No one was going to feel sorry for me; I lived in Aspen and Washington, DC, and New York City, and I was from Michigan. I was a female in a cow town—a dilettante in a cowboy hat, pretending to be a big-time operator. (One of my sons commented that we lost the trial the minute I walked into the jury room wearing my cowboy hat.) Our courthouse was in Arapahoe County, home to the largest cable companies in the nation—where some of the potential jurors had worked. Welcome aboard!

First on the agenda were opening statements. I thought both sides were well represented, although they presented quite different styles. United Cable's Spencer Dennison had that homespun, easygoing manner (typical University of Michigan training?); our litigator, Jeff Reiman, was the shark—on attack (Harvard Law School training?)

After opening statements, the plaintiffs would present their case. From Jeff Reiman's draft trial brief:

> Simply put, the evidence will show that in the fall of 1986, Recreation Broadcasting, Inc. (RBI), along with United Cable, created KSPN—The Rocky Mountain SuperChannel, a cable TV channel whose programming was available to cable systems throughout the Rocky Mountain region, featuring regional participatory and spectator sporting events.
>
> Yet, in the summer of 1987, after creating KSPN—The Rocky Mountain SuperChannel with RBI, United Cable stripped the business of all of its assets and then proceeded to use those very assets in the course of United Cable's 1988 formation (along with other, large cable companies) of Prime Sports Network (PSN). ...

One of the first witnesses called by Jeff Reiman was James Dovey, former president of United Cable Television-Colorado. In his testimony, Jim Dovey accused Bill Seidman, former chairman of the FDIC and RTC, of counseling me to conserve cash by not paying timely payroll taxes.

Well! Jeff Reiman got on the phone and called Bill Seidman in Washington, DC, and urged him to catch the next plane to Denver, which Bill did. By Friday afternoon, Bill was on the witness stand, staring down at James Dovey and emphatically denying that allegation. And Bill emphasized that he never told anyone, ever, to not pay their payroll taxes.

Those comments stirred the pot: Over the weekend, Bill met at Chicago's O'Hare Airport with TCI's top executives. They wanted out of this lawsuit ... after three days of trial. Bill felt that he could negotiate for our team and offered to accept a settlement for $4 million, subject to the approval of RBI's board.

Testimony in the courtroom continued all day Monday, with nothing said about the settlement offer to me. Jeff Reiman brought the offer to our attention after the court recessed for the day. Gary Verplank and I were the only two board members present.

Gary asked Jeff privately, "What's our upside?"

Jeff replied, "$25 million."

Gary asked me what I wanted to do. I said to Gary, "You and Allen Hunting are paying the legal bills, so you two should make the decision."

Gary conferred with Allen and told me that they decided to go for it. And then Gary asked me, "Are you going to hold this against me if we lose?"

"Absolutely not."

When Bill Seidman found out that the RBI board had turned down the $4 million settlement offer, he was livid. He felt that it was his reputation on the line. He had negotiated in good faith, and he was not supported by his board. Bill wanted nothing more to do with the lawsuit, including paying for it.

The next day, I didn't like the way the testimony was going. I commented to Fritz (who sat with me for the first few days of trial) that I couldn't believe how often Bruce Smith, United Cable's former marketing director, impeached himself.

Fritz observed, "Dovey did too, but less obviously. [It is] weakness of character ... he has been told to 'tow the party line' and has not been prepared to defend his deposition."

Bruce Smith and Jim Dovey testified over and over, "I don't remember"; or demanded, "How can you expect me to remember what happened five years ago?"; or explained, "I have been busy working for five years in the United Kingdom."

Obviously, someone in the courtroom was listening and sent me Art Buchwald's wildly funny weekly syndicated column entitled "Reagan's 18-Minute Gap", with Reagan crossed out and replaced with Dovey, and minute replaced with hour.

ART BUCHWALD

DOVEY's HOUR

~~Reagan's~~ 18-~~Minute~~ Gap

I t used to be that this nation's heroes said things like, "I only regret that I have but one life to lose for my country," or "We have just begun to fight," or "Give me liberty or give me death," or "Remember the Maine."

Nowadays all our heroes can come up with is, "I don't remember."

sandwich on toasted rye and a glass of buttermilk, and I had a cream cheese and smoked salmon on pumpernickel, with a bag of potato chips and iced tea. We sat at this back table against the wall that had a picture of Bette Davis and Humphrey Bogart. She was in a domino-print dress and he wore a

Art Buchwald begins: "It used to be that this nation's heroes said things like ... 'Give me liberty or give me death.' ... "

Then Buchwald descends into "... Nowadays all our heroes can come up with is, 'I don't remember.' ... 'Mr. President, did you know that Lieutenant Colonel North was going to lie to Congress?'... 'How could I know that when I didn't know anything?' ..."

Jim Dovey and Bruce Smith could lose their memories, but I couldn't. I was the plaintiff, arguing a cause that none of the defendants could remember existed. When Jeff Reiman called me as a witness, he wanted me to talk about my background in business. I probably would have been smarter to talk about becoming a grandmother four times over. I might have received more empathy from members of the jury.

I was cross-examined for days (it seemed like weeks) by Spencer Dennison. I was told later that Dennison placed three stenographers behind the courtroom wall to write down my entire testimony each day, then his team of experts would review the testimony overnight to be ready the next day with new questions. I was curious when the judge would ask them to stop.

The forensic accountant had huge exhibits showing the jury how I had taken money from KTV, Inc., as "salary," without accounting for it. (Well, let's see ... he accounted for it, so others must have too.)

United Cable agreed to invest $250,000 in KTV, Inc., in March 1997, but I think they invested it in their forensic accountant, instead ... because KTV, Inc. never received a penny from United Cable! I had invested more than a million dollars in RBI and KTV in the past decade, but the forensic accountant wanted $34,000 more. I found the accountant's work so convoluted that I couldn't follow his arguments. Finally, the judge suggested the lawyers find other witnesses to interrogate.

On March 10, 1992, District Court Judge Michael J, Watanabe published the Judgment of Recreation Broadcasting, Inc., v. United Cable Television of Colorado, Inc., et al.

We lost. On all counts. It took the jury only a few hours to render a decision—so quickly did they act that our team was not in the courtroom when the verdict was read. When we arrived, the jurors were standing outside the courtroom. One of the jurors was willing to talk to me. (Brave soul.) What were his reasons for this decision? He answered, "It was your diaries that convinced me you were undercapitalized. You were always short of cash. Always looking for money."

Jeff Reiman had been concerned with the instructions for the jury that the judge allowed—or, more importantly, didn't allow. Jeff and I listened to the judge describe the simple questions that he wanted the six jurors to decide. (Did we have enough capital? And so forth.)

The judge was merciless with Jeff and me. I just stood by in utter shock. The judge refused to use any of Jeff's basic questions. (Did they steal our idea? Our concept? Our microwave delivery system? Our company? Our sports programing contracts? And our equipment? And our trained staff? And so forth.) We had to lose if the judge's stupid questions were all that would be allowed in jury instructions after weeks of trial and years of preparation!

Jeff wanted to appeal. Gary and Allen didn't even want to think about another lawsuit. I agreed with Jeff about the need to appeal. That was not my decision to make, however. I did not then and do not now understand the judge's complete and outrageous control over jury instructions!

Driving to the airport, my litigator son said, "It's a crap shoot. It's business. You win some, you lose some. You go on and forget it."

When I walked into my Newport Partners office in DC, a few days later, my lawyer partner, Henry Goldberg, asked, "How did it go?"

I laughed and responded, "Well ... they offered to settle for $4 million. With an upside of $25 to $60 million, we refused to settle, *and* we lost."

"You refused to settle for $4 million!" exclaimed Henry. "My mantra is 'settle, settle, settle.'" Henry remarked that I didn't seem at all mad—or sad.

I commented, "The only way they can really win is to take away my spirit. It's business. You win some, and you lose some." (Guess where I got that good advice.)

I needed a permanent residence in DC to continue working on FDIC and RTC solicitations while they were still available. We all sensed they were winding down and soon would disappear, and my bankers would be haunting me to pay my ballooning debts from the lawsuits. When I checked out an advertisement for an apartment in Georgetown, I didn't expect to find a hilly private gated community with beautiful million-dollar townhomes built into the sloping hillsides. I would be looking at a lower level, which didn't seem low with its twelve-foot ceilings, wood-burning fireplace, and immense slate terrace overlooking three multimillion-dollar homes under construction at the base of the hill.

I loved it! And the landlady too, who greeted me warmly. She was eager to please, and so was I. A true Irish lass who never married, Maureen Murphy was quick to include me within her circle of friendly and famous neighbors. Maureen had a top job as an interior designer at the US Department of State and carried all the top clearances. My kids immediately decided she was a "spook," but she never revealed that side of her work to me.

In late June, a surprise visitor was sitting on my sofa when I returned home from work. Maureen probably let him in. It was my sailing friend, Paul Eggert, returning from Spain after sailing his fifty-four-foot sloop in tandem with brother Midge's fifty-six-foot ketch, from Puerto Rico to the Costa del Sol on Spain's southern coast. Midge and Paul were preparing for the Columbus 500 race (celebrating the five hundredth anniversary of Columbus's voyage to America) in November. They would be following the same route that Columbus sailed in 1492, starting from the port of Huelva in Spain, sailing southwest to the Madeira Islands, then south to the Canary Islands, and finally across the Atlantic to the tiny island of San Salvador in the Bahamas.

This year's birthday present would be coming from Midge. October 6 would be my sixtieth birthday, and it could be special! Midge invited me to sail from Puerto Banus on the Costa del Sol, around the Rock of Gibraltar to Cádiz, and take part in a preparatory race from Cádiz to Huelva, Spain—Columbus's port of departure for the New World.

I didn't accept Midge's invitation right away; I was worried about leaving Newport Partners for two weeks in the fall. My latest inspiration was beginning to develop with Cantor Fitzgerald, a financial services firm in New York City. It was always an adventure to visit their offices on the 101st to 105th floors of One World Trade Center, which was about a mile south of our loft on Broome Street—just a short bike ride away. Looking straight down from their 101st floor outer window always left me with a queasy stomach. I sensed this towering edifice was ready to tip over.

I proposed the plan to Cantor Fitzgerald:

...To attract the serious investors who are currently buying performing and nonperforming loans by sealed bids, our joint venture team plans to utilize a business-like and noneditorial auction methodology that would marry the best techniques of Wall Street and open outcry bidding.

...This marketing campaign will need to explain carefully and thoroughly a new technique—*electronic bidding* on Cantor Fitzgerald's Telerate system as well as their dial up service, Telerate Access Service, which allows the occasional information customer the use of his own personal computer for bidding. Also, this system, by itself, can serve as a worldwide billboard, advertising the FDIC assets 24 hours per day.

However, for those not so dispassionate number-crunching investors who may take that extra step or two before the gavel falls, our joint venture plan will include a live auction site where participants can bid in the traditional manner along with the telephonic bidding that will be displayed instantaneously on the worldwide electronic network.

Additionally, if the FDIC inventory is of sufficient size and importance, the auction day event can be made available to cable subscribers in the U.S. and satellite subscribers abroad.

The plan was enthusiastically received by the young Turks at Cantor Fitzgerald. They realized the possibilities for selling just about anything via electronic bidding. (We must have had eBay charging at our heels!)

Again, I was warned by Fritz Hatton—with his vast knowledge of Christie's older, more conservative clientele—that the older, more conservative executives of Cantor Fitzgerald probably wouldn't share my enthusiasm.

Chapter Thirteen

BON VOYAGE

"...a historically significant group crossing."
Midge Verplank describing the Columbus 500,
a 3,200 hundred-mile transatlantic race.

At the wheel of Egg Crate *racing in the Mediterranean Sea*

Bill Seidman stopped by my office to discuss my business future in August 1992. I was no longer working for USAuction; Don Hannah planned to move his Connecticut home and headquarters to Arizona. I continued to have my Newport Partners office in Henry Goldberg's handsome building, but I needed to have a steady income to support my lifestyle in DC.

My Aspen home and office would be closed by Sandy Mochary in October. Sandy was such a multitalented secretary that she quickly found other employment, but I now was dependent on Henry Goldberg's legal secretaries. I knew I needed to hit a home run for Newport Partners to deserve their time and attention.

I explained to Bill my concerns about the invitation from Midge. I couldn't afford to be gone for two weeks, although I knew Midge would be paying for my vacation. Bill encouraged me to go. He felt the trip would be good for me, saying there was nothing of importance in Washington that couldn't wait for my return.

I fully realized my life with Bill was over, and he was helping me to move on. Bill was beginning to become a sort of father figure—always willing to counsel me—and, in turn, I was happy to proof his speeches or edit his latest book or comment on his weekly CNBC broadcast, which I seldom missed.

SO...Off I went. Into a new world. I flew to Madrid, transferred to a smaller plane to Málaga, and greeted my welcoming party at noon the next day.

Midge arrived in a small car with two other passengers—Paul Eggert and Dave Weeks and the car became stuffed to capacity with my duffel bags, hats, and me. Midge already had six people on board his fifty-six-foot Whitby ketch, *Oso Dormido,* occupying all the staterooms, and that did not count me—and my luggage.

And guess what was docked right next to Midge, with no crew on board? Paul's fifty-four-foot Irwin sloop, *Egg Crate.* Midge explained that he didn't have room on his boat for the luggage, and Paul offered to store my stuff on *Egg Crate.* Paul also offered to "store" me, saying that he had no crew and needed me for the race from Cádiz to Huelva.

Wha-a-a-at? No crew coming?

"None."

Bon voyage. It was Paul's world that I would inhabit for the next two weeks. But I wasn't sure what my role would be. While I was sleeping in the afternoon, a lovely tall blonde accompanied Paul on a shopping trip for groceries for *Egg Crate*'s sail to Cádiz, with Gibraltar the first port of call. When we were assembling for dinner with Midge's crew, Paul insisted I ride with him to pick up not just the lovely tall blonde but also two other English ladies who were vacationing or working for the summer and fall in Puerto Banus. It seemed Paul had met them all in June, and they were happy to be invited for a dinner celebration. (Who would be their host? I never found out.) The three women crowded around Paul and Midge, and I was relegated to "family status" at the other end of the table with Midge's daughter, Melissa, her boyfriend, Warren, and Sue and Dave Weeks. My appearance on the scene appeared to be quite a downer for the tall blonde, who ignored me as best she could. (Was I just one more of Paul's admirers?)

After a few days of barhopping and outfitting the boat, I was eager to sail, but I was surprised when Paul immediately turned over the wheel and the navigation to me. That is, until I realized that the muscle jobs were hoisting the sails, especially the main, and throwing dock lines or dropping anchors. I knew how to read a compass and follow charts from two sessions of ground school when learning to fly back in the 1960s. At that point, we were on the cusp of GPS domination of all navigation. Still, Paul wanted me to learn how to use a sextant, because he had one on board and could teach me. I was not a patient student, though, because I wasn't planning any ocean sailing. Obviously, Paul had other ideas.

As we approached the marina tucked around the west side of Gibraltar, I developed knots in my stomach. With only two on board a fifty-four-foot sailboat, I had a difficult choice: dock (and talk to the dockmaster at the same time), or put out the fenders and throw and secure the lines. Paul made the decision. After checking our slip, Paul tied the fenders needed, lined up the boat, talked to Midge, talked to the dockmaster, and then handed me the VHF and ordered me to take the wheel—this done in complete silence while using hand signals. Paul's ultracool manner came naturally to him. He had sailed his whole life, often alone, beginning at age six. Paul couldn't stand to hear screaming by captains or crews from the stern or bow of a sailboat. Or the dock. Well, at least I didn't hit anything I wasn't supposed to.

Midge and his crew were eager to climb to the top of the Rock of Gibraltar and take the iconic picture, and so was I. We all trekked to the rock, and Melissa took the memorable photo of Midge, Paul, and me.

Midge, Joyce, Paul on top of Rock of Gibraltar

After leaving Gibraltar, I asked Paul if I could fish, because we were motoring to our next port. Paul wasn't happy to see a large fish gutted and filleted on his back deck, and if I wanted to keep a fish, I had to clean it. I wasn't quite ready for the big time. I had cleaned hundreds of trout caught in my pond in Aspen, but my first big catch turned into a bloody mess, flopping all around the deck until I could get enough 150-proof rum down its throat to quiet it down. I sat on the back deck with a hose, a razor-sharp curved knife, and the fish. Paul took pictures. Paul knew my Dad, the "old man of the sea," would be impressed. Not by the fish; by the fillets.

Next stop, the Puerto Sherry Marina in Santa Maria del Puerto, located slightly north of Cádiz (pronounced "Ca-dith" in Spain). I was the only member of our group used to the *th* pronunciation of many words, because of my association with Fernando Zobel, whom I assumed spoke classic Spanish. Now, every word in Spain with a *c* or *z* seemed to have a "lisp" sound: "gra-thee-us" for *gracias*, "I-bee-tha" for *Ibiza*, etc. Paul Eggert had a natural pronounced lisp, which distinctly enhanced his richly humorous stories. Paul was feeling right at home in Spain—and right at home in Sherry Marina, where the majority of yachts from all over the globe were assembling for the Columbus 500.

Santa Maria del Puerto had historic significance because the rich families of El Puerto de Santa Maria helped Christopher Columbus prepare for the voyage to the New World. It was here that the Santa Maria, the flagship of Columbus's three boats, was outfitted.

A welcoming reception in the Castle of San Marcos—used for centuries as the city hall—lent an air of authenticity and excitement for the gathering sailors.

Midge had shrouded in secrecy his plans for my birthday in one of Santa Maria's small outdoor cafés so endemic in Andalusia. Midge suggested we stop at a small, dumpy-looking café for a quick, late-afternoon glass of wine. I boggled over a display of hams, fowl, and fruits lining the long bar. Standing in the back of the dark café, almost hidden, were Midge's other guests for the evening: all his crew, plus a group of raucous sailors whom Midge and Paul had befriended while charting Columbus's path to the New World.

Paul had me park *Egg Crate* at the outer end of a T-shaped dock so that it would be easy for us to exit the marina on racing day. With only two on board, we wouldn't have to maneuver around a maze of boats to the starting line.

Which was just as well. … Midge's "bn", Gerardo, was up to his old tricks. He had promised to wake us at 7:00 a.m. for an 8:00 a.m. assembly gun for the race to Huelva, but, instead, he woke us at 7:45 a.m. by stomping on *Egg Crate*'s back deck.

Paul was furious. He jumped on the dock, ordered me to start the engine while he untied dock lines, and we were off to the races—quite literally. I grabbed the stopwatch and headed straight for the starting line. As soon as we were clear of the other boats, I turned into the wind so that Paul could hoist the main. We had good wind, but not too heavy, so I knew Paul would be unfurling the jenny (Genoa jib), which is a huge jib that tails back behind the mast if unfurled the whole way.

It looked like we were just going to make it to the line for the start. The timing was the same for me as an E scow start, and I had done hundreds of them in Michigan for four decades. Most of the other boats were hanging back, perhaps not as used to racing starts as Midge and Paul and I were.

Well, here goes. I looked at my stopwatch and yelled to Paul, "Five seconds! Four! Three! Two! One!" *Gun.*

Were we the first boat across the line? Wow! Were we excited!

Our excitement was short-lived. As we got out of range of the other boats, our jenny sail suddenly tore in half, and the shredded sail plunged into the sea. (It wouldn't be the only time, unfortunately.) We motored up the Odiel River and into Huelva, becoming the first boat to finish the race—or so thought the locals who greeted us. We needed to repair some of the rigging, so Paul got out the bosun chair. I grabbed my still camera, video camera, tools, and a line to reconnect the jenny halyard, and stuffed the cameras and tools in the side pockets of the bosun chair. Paul used the spinnaker halyard to tie the chair straps together (very carefully with double bowlines while I watched) and hoisted me up seventy-five feet with his self-tailing Barient winch.

What a view! I loved my first trip up the mast. My video camera captured all the sailboats maneuvering up the Odiel River. Then I used the still camera.

Oso Dormido *top photo;* Egg Crate *bottom photo*

I was more interested in taking pictures and videos than fixing the problem. Paul grumbled; he couldn't leave his post while I was sitting at the top of the mast, and it was cocktail hour. Paul was a fixer and certainly adventurous, but he had an irrational fear of heights (acrophobia); the first spreader up the mast was his limit.

At Huelva, I had to leave "Peter Pan". (My kids favorite name for Paul). If I wanted to have fun, I'd want to be around Paul. But that required distancing from the responsibilities that flowed into my daily life. Although Paul could be irreverent, his little indiscretions—and they were little—always seemed to get him in trouble.

I had to go back to work. The next port on Columbus's route was the island of Madeira, 400 miles southwest of Huelva in the Atlantic Ocean. I knew Paul had a new crew coming at Huelva. He begged me to come back when they reached the Canary Islands, which were 300 miles south of Madeira.

Son Fritz and brother Gary would be joining Midge in the Canaries; they signed up to sail in the final leg of the Columbus 500, a 3,200 hundred-mile transatlantic rally-race. (Midge called it a "historically significant group crossing.") The rally was slated to start from Gran Canaria in mid-November. They certainly wouldn't be expecting to see me.

I returned to Washington, DC, on Columbus Day, October 12, 1992. An appropriate arrival date, with my brain still in Spain. And no wonder that it was. I had no immediate solutions in my portfolio of work at Newport Partners that would defray the mounting bank debt I was accumulating since the loss of my five-year lawsuit in March. Midge had come to my aid, paying Old Kent Bank's interest bills during the litigation. Now it was up to me. Both Gary and Midge were being pressured by the bank to pay up or watch me face bankruptcy.

Bill Seidman wasn't going to rescue me, but he was willing to advise me, realizing better than anyone else that my government business career in Washington, DC, was over if I filed for bankruptcy. Bill was still mad that his settlement offer of $4 million from TCI was turned down by Allen Hunting and Gary, but I wasn't. I took the risk, and now I had to face the consequences. No matter what, I was not willing to let my brothers bail me out. And Bill knew that too.

I made the offer to Old Kent Bank that Bill suggested. The bank officers' reaction? They laughed at me. No way did they think I could raise $400,000 over the next five to seven years to pay them off. The bank insisted on a meeting with me and Gary in their offices in Grand Rapids. That was going to be interesting.

Not only was Gary a good customer of the bank, he also served on the board of the local branch. Why would they punish him for the sins of his sister? Why would they punish themselves? We were greeted warmly on the first floor of the bank and escorted to the executive offices on one of the upper floors. Now we were going to get down to business. They would be tough. Their dialogue was directed at Gary. Gary listened politely, but he was always unfailingly polite to everyone. He listened, really listened, and didn't interrupt. (Was Gary really my brother?) After listening, Gary said we would think about it, and then we left.

Why was I singled out as not capable of paying something back when I offered to do it? Old Kent Bank had nothing to lose. But they continued to insist that my brothers would have to pay, or I would face bankruptcy.

Bill Seidman was appalled at their intransigence. He said, "Forget them. They wrote you off five years ago. Don't pay them now, and don't pay their credit card that you have been using. They are punishing you, and you are taking their punishment. Don't file for bankruptcy now. It will take at least a year before it is effective. Work as long as you can at Newport Partners while you look for work outside the government sector. I will see if there is anything available at the Washington Campus. You are capable of running it, but you have to be computer literate, because the boss has to be able to answer e-mails without needing a secretary."

I might forget Old Kent Bank, but I couldn't forget the personal claims from my lawsuit that were not dischargeable by bankruptcy. When RBI agreed not to appeal its case, the cable companies agreed to drop their claims. That left my personal claim and a very large legal bill from our litigators for the six-week trial. I sensed that my team, always so loyal and responsible, would balk at the idea of paying the total amount, which was in six figures. More than a million dollars had been paid to them before the trial began in February.

I asked my Denver lawyer, Michael Abramovitz, to help me find a solution, which had to be arbitration. At least it would put off any payments for a year or more. Then we hired a Colorado bankruptcy attorney, Tom Quinn, to handle my bankruptcy filing and any personal claims against me. That might take two years. Now I was ready to go back to work.

Or was I?

I flew to Aspen the last weekend of October to organize my files and furniture. I had to be out of the house by November 1, 1992. In the summer, Gary checked out my large shed filled from floor to ceiling with lawsuit papers and files and recommended that we pitch them all, which we did. Luckily, Sandy kept some files in the house that could be needed for future litigation. Then I made huge lists for Sandy of everything to be shipped to the kids. I did not keep one piece of furniture. Where could I store it? Where would I be living? Maureen's house was fully furnished.

Fritz should have taken something; he'd paid my Aspen rent the last few months and provided me with a Visa Gold Card. But he was living in an apartment on Russian Hill in San Francisco. By the time he got one of his concert grand pianos in his living room, there wasn't much space for anything else. Nothing I had was worth sending two thousand miles to California, so it all went to Michigan or New York City or Boston.

Pictures, diaries, and personal files showed up at my doorstep in Georgetown, making no one happy. Maureen was in the design business at the State Department; her large house was filled with pictures, papers, samples, art books, design magazines, and rare antiques acquired in foreign assignments. We probably deserved each other.

If I was going to visit the Canary Islands, I had about two weeks to get the trip organized. I called the Travel Agents, my Aspen-based trusty travel organizers. I had to be one of their better customers, traveling over the past two decades the triangle from Aspen and Denver to Michigan and the East Coast—Boston, New York City, and Washington, DC. The Travel Agents kept track of my United Airlines "Mileage Plus" program and assured me I still had enough points for a round-trip ticket to Europe. And the Canary Islands? Yes.

I booked passage from Washington's Dulles International Airport to Gran Canaria Airport in Las Palmas, leaving November 6 and returning November 16, 1992.

The scene from the air as we approached Las Palmas was breathtaking. There were more than a hundred sailboats at the marina docks, lined up in rows, "Med-moored." (Mediterranean mooring: docking a boat "end-on" to a dock or pier, as opposed to lying up alongside. It is common practice in Europe, especially the Mediterranean.)

Las Palmas Marina, Canary Islands, November 7, 1992

Whatever inhibitions I harbored about my presence, they were gone the minute I landed. Paul picked me up at the airport, whisking me off in a rental car and away to the marina. It was a bustling international scene of flags, burgees, alphabets, and languages on both sides of *Egg Crate*.

Midge had *Oso Dormido* Med-moored about five boats away. He rushed over to say hello, shaking his head at me with a devilish smile.

When Paul's new crew arrived on board, they cringed at the mess in *Egg Crate's* bilge. They were not about to put up with the leftover hams from a wild transatlantic crossing. I watched Dick Riekse, a Grand Haven oral surgeon, deciding what to keep, which was probably nothing.

Midge and his crew had a different problem: they worried about no wind on the crossing, and needed to store a fifty-five-gallon drum of extra fuel oil. I hated to see that dangerous cargo on his deck. Lashing it down properly to the port side stays became a serious, time-consuming task.

The start of the race was at 1700 hours on November 15. Paul released his stern lines very early in the day.

Midge joked, "First time ever that Paul's leaving the dock before me."

However, Paul seemed to be having trouble lifting his anchor. A diving crew from the Spanish Navy was dispatched to the scene when many racing boats found their anchors or rodes (anchor lines) fouled by debris collected for centuries on the bottom of the ancient harbor.

Paul was not happy waiting his turn for the navy divers, commenting that his anchor was snagged on Columbus's garbage. Midge motored by, letting Paul see that he didn't have any trouble with a fouled anchor or lines.

It was a huge mess in a huge starting area. None of us could see the buoys or hear a starting gun. There were a hundred boats in the cruising division, which included both *Oso Dormido* and *Egg Crate*, and forty boats in the racing division. I had a hard time even locating the press boat, and when I did climb on board, I couldn't find *Oso Dormido* or *Egg Crate*. It was so-o-o-o frustrating; I never found either one. When I got back to the hotel, I didn't know that *Egg Crate* had to skip the starting area and head straight west to La Gomera.

Paul would arrive in San Salvador a few days after Midge's arrival on December 4. Both Midge and Paul could call during the race by patching into a landline from their single sideband (SSB) radios. I heard from Paul multiple times on his SSB when he wanted to vent his frustration over the permanent loss of his spinnaker only fifty-four hours into the race, and our Spring Lake Verplank family heard from Midge when he needed advice for a staph infection in his leg.

The *Grand Haven Tribune* reported:

Spring Lake sailor Midge Verplank and his crew of five recently completed a 3,200-mile race across the Atlantic Ocean in 18 days, 11 hours, beating Christopher Columbus' old record by two-and-a-half weeks (and finishing first in his division). ...

Also finishing ahead of the pack, but slowed by a torn spinnaker and a disturbing distress-call incident in the middle of the Atlantic was Paul Eggert of Grand Haven, who piloted his 54-foot sloop, *Egg Crate*, to a fifth place finish in his division and 18-20th overall.

Paul Eggert asked me to help him sail *Egg Crate* from Nassau, Bahamas to Fort Lauderdale, Florida, for repairs. But when? I had clients all along the southeastern coast of Florida who were interested in bidding on RTC or FDIC properties. I would have to juggle my meetings and auction dates, not to mention the weather reports, to make it possible. I flew from Fort Lauderdale to Nassau in early January to join Paul.

As we were crossing the Gulf Stream, we were hailed by a large, impressive looking US Coast Guard ship. They shouted through their bullhorn, "Where are you coming from?"

Paul answered, "The Bahamas."

The Coast Guard warned us that they were sending a boarding party. They knew that *Egg Crate* had not entered US waters in the past year. I was impressed with their knowledge, but Paul was worried. Would we pass the lengthy government inspection list?

I didn't know what to expect from a boarding party; neither did the Coast Guard officers and crew members know what to expect when they climbed aboard, guns at the ready. I was shocked!

They demanded in rough tones, "Where is the rest of your crew?"

They couldn't believe that two little old people were *it*. When they decided we weren't drug runners, they became very solicitous. One sneaked me a list of what they would be inspecting and told me to start writing our emergency plan. "Must be a written plan," he emphasized.

Another said that they would follow us into port in Fort Lauderdale and give us time at the ship's store to buy minor pieces of safety equipment.

And they did! I knew Paul would obey their orders to a T, since they were waiting for him on the dock. They checked everything off and quietly disappeared.

Whoa ... my first close call. I was a nervous wreck after docking in front of the US Coast Guard and too rattled to go to a business meeting—I thought.

I soon noticed that the high-powered principals at these meetings didn't care what I did in my spare time as long as I took care of their business in a timely and responsible manner. I scheduled flights to Miami from DC, on January 22, and back from Fort Lauderdale on February 3; then to West Palm Beach on February 18, to meet with First Boston about bids for Woodfield Country Club, then across the state to meet with a client of Jerry Wipperfurth's about RTC's Longboat Key properties; and then a flight back to DC on February 23.

I happened to return to Fort Lauderdale on Friday, March 12, 1993, the first day of an impending storm with possible tornadoes. I had been instructed by Paul to stay away from *Egg Crate* and find a motel room immediately. Paul was sailing his 16′ "MC" scow along with my brother Gary in the MC Scow Midwinter Regatta in the middle of the state, and the Spring Lake Yacht Club sailors were expecting the same storm. Everyone had heard that this was going to be a whopper. I begged our local motel owner to let me have his last room, just for the night. I didn't care if it was next to a shaky Coke machine; I only wanted to monitor the weather on TV. I assumed we'd be up all night (or until we lost power), because the tornadoes were supposed to hit at about 4:00 a.m.

I was monitoring what became known as the Storm of the Century, or the '93 Superstorm, with its reach stretching from Canada to Central America and continuing for three days. A total of 318 people perished in the storm.

Where was Midge? On *Oso Dormido*? In the Bahamas too? Yes, hiding in a protected harbor on Staniel Cay.

And where were Paul and Gary? Holed up on a swaying heavy Prevost bus with Paul's son, Chris, who had driven the bus from Michigan to Florida while towing a triple trailer filled with their MC scows. The winds would be "excessive," explained the race committee, who cleared the inland lake of all racing boats.

I had meetings set up the next week in South Florida with three different investor or Realtor groups, and everyone showed up as scheduled. Tough group!

Paul would not keep *Egg Crate* docked in Fort Lauderdale for the summer months; it was too expensive. He and Midge knew safe anchorages in the Bahamas, near Marsh Harbor, where they had previously parked their boats. And Paul hoped to find in Hope Town the same reliable caretaker who helped him in the past. I wanted to leave right away and catch up with Midge, because Lydia was expecting her first baby in late April, and the baby might come early.

I knew crossing the Gulf Stream was risky business. Since I was a new navigator, timing the entrance to the shallow banks north of Bimini during daylight hours was crucial. And knowing the wind and weather was part of my job. I was excited about my new role on *Egg Crate*.

So what went wrong? Paul complained that I couldn't stop talking (!) business on the phone. We needed to leave. The weather was good, and the winds light. We left anyway, with only Paul knowing I would be in a panic when we approached the banks and the rock at about 11:00 p.m. He was right. But we wiggled through, following a smaller boat until we hit the banks and the six-foot depths. As we were starting across the banks, I noticed on the chart that I would hit three-foot sandy bottoms to the south, but I would hit the rocks to the north. I headed south until we hit bottom, and then angled east at that point.

Paul suggested we anchor until dawn, when I would have an easy sail across the banks (while he slept). We drew five and a half feet, and most of our course would be at least six feet deep.

What a magical scene I faced at dawn—with the sun, barely peeking above the horizon, glistening across the still, flat water that surrounded us as far as the eye could see. I will never forget it. I have difficulty describing it; I felt transported into a fantasy land of sublime bliss. And I hadn't had even a cup of coffee.

We met Midge and his crew in the Abacos, and cruised the central Abaco islands, from Green Turtle Cay and Treasure Cay to Marsh Harbor, before heading to our appointed anchorages: Midge at Man-O-War Cay, and Paul in Hope Town Harbor on Elbow Cay.

I was happy to be working in Washington, but I knew it couldn't last. The opportunities for auctions and sales of RTC assets were fast drying up; the big investment and accounting firms were taking over and calling the shots. They didn't need me or the other small fry who had a chance to win regional bids two years ago. When I flew to California to help a client bid on a few small commercial real estate packages—in the $15 million range— we were outbid on all of them. I decided this job was no longer for me, or Newport Partners. And I was not ready to go to work for Coldwell Banker or any of the other national real estate firms.

Paul met me in San Francisco in early June. Fritz was still living on Russian Hill in San Francisco, in a sixth-floor apartment with a view westward of the Golden Gate Bridge.

Fritz asked Paul if he would like to go sailing under the bridge. I spoke up and said I wanted to go.

"It will be freezing out there," warned Fritz. "I wear long underwear and a heavy storm jacket and gloves, and bring my own inflatable life preserver—same kind as we wore for ocean sailing."

"Why is it so cold?" I inquired.

"It's June; the bay is cold. The Pacific is always cold, and the Farallon

Islands are thirty miles west of the Golden Gate Bridge. It will be a windy, wild ride."

Boy, was Fritz right about the Farallons! The stiff wind did not keep any of the boats from hoisting their spinnakers as we rounded the Farallons—a godforsaken group of rocks with birds stashed in every crevice of the jagged "sea stacks."

Because we were circling the islands, all the racing boats had to jibe their huge spinnakers as they turned. Jibing spinnakers in heavy air is always a risky proposition, and I worried that all of us were going to broach or lose a crew member in the rough seas.

Fritz at the wheel on San Francisco Bay

What a welcome to the Pacific. No—not very pacifying.

Fritz thought Paul would like the drive down the Pacific Coast Highway on California's Route 1, especially when he could drive the fabled Big Sur coastline. We rented a car and meandered in serendipitous fashion all the way. We stopped at Hearst Castle. Why? It was there—all ninety thousand feet of it; like a small shopping center. My favorite stop was Morro Bay. I liked the seaside's relaxed atmosphere, the local wildlife, and the birds (falcons?) perched on the bay's Morro Rock, a volcanic rock more than 500 feet high.

I returned to DC from Newport Beach, and Paul returned to Michigan. What was I to do? I interviewed with the Washington Campus staff and felt very inadequate for any job there. (I'd had a personal secretary for thirty years, and I wasn't qualified to be one.) I had no money and no social connections in DC. I lost most of my Beltway connections after I lost my best friend and mentor, Bill Seidman, and that was three years earlier.

After I flew to Michigan for the Fourth of July holiday, I told Paul that I had enrolled in a Beginning WordPerfect computer class in DC. Paul liked that idea, drove me back to DC in his jeep, and signed up too. Was this going to work? I typed fast; Paul was dyslexic and didn't type. Would it matter—if Paul learned the basic hardware of the computer, and I learned the basic software? He liked wiring; I liked writing. (Guess who would be installing the computers, weather printers, radars, and GPS systems on *Egg Crate*. But would I be using them?)

Our computer classes were held downtown on busy Connecticut Avenue. Nevertheless, Paul usually found a convenient place to park, no matter how crowded the circumstances. Paul wandered around the back of the buildings and picked a quiet corner marked Private Parking, and backed in his jeep. It took only a day or two for Paul to get a ticket on the jeep, which had a faux Michigan license plate labeled "BIG EGG" on the front bumper of the jeep. Paul's parking ticket was made out to "BIG EGG" as the only official license plate number. Paul continued to park in the back alleys and continued to receive tickets made out only to "BIG EGG." Only Paul could be so lucky. (One more of his little indiscretions—unplanned as it was.)

My office at Newport Partners needed to be closed. Except for a wall of photos, I had a typical lawyer-looking office—full of heavy, legal-size file boxes. I knew who would help me move the files to my apartment in Georgetown: Paul, who offered to drive me back to DC after a Spring Lake regatta.

I still had to face the Denver lawyers' arbitration committee, and worried about my lack of knowledge of the fast-changing cable industry. My Denver lawyer, Michael Abramovitz, said I didn't need to remember or review any files. Most had been pitched anyway. The date for the arbitration meeting was set for early 1994, and our former litigator, Jeff Reiman of Holmes and Starr, would be prepared to demand full payment from us—well more than $100,000. And Jeff certainly kept all his files.

What about my bankruptcy? A petition commencing a case under title 11 was filed on August 31, 1992, and an order of relief was entered under chapter 7. I still had to wait for the final order from the bankruptcy judge, which wouldn't come until next year. No matter what happened in my lawsuits, I planned to leave Washington, DC.

I traveled to New York City to confer with my great connector, Priscilla

Morgan. Lydia and baby Alexander showed up on her doorstep, too. They assumed I would be heading back to Michigan.

In front of Isamu Noguchi painting at Priscilla Morgan's apartment with Lydia, baby Alexander and Priscilla.

Maureen Murphy, Paul Eggert, and my brother Midge (once again) were surreptitiously organizing an event for my sixty-first birthday on October 6. Maureen's problem was figuring out how to clean out my apartment for the party. My large dining room table was packed full of files and file boxes from my Newport Partners office; I was in no rush to store them before October 6. Maureen kept insisting. I'm not sure where the files went, but every box survived my move out of DC.

When I saw the birthday dinner menu, I understood why Maureen wanted to use my apartment. The social hour was upstairs in her elegant living room with gleaming venetian plaster walls—the result of four coats of translucent marble dust applied with a fine steel blade over a period of many months by my artist son. The dinner was downstairs in my family room, with its utilitarian slate-and-marble floor. Baskets of large Maryland crabs, a local specialty, were passed around, and were they messy! But much appreciated. Maureen's idea, of course. Maureen was so much fun; all my family would miss her.

After the hurricane season was over in November, Midge and Paul were eager to move their boats to the Caribbean. We left our locations in the Abacos and headed south, first to Eleuthera, then to Georgetown in the Exumas. From there, we sailed down the east coast of Long Island, battling a storm and high waves all the way to Crooked Island. When we docked in conch heaven, the Turks and Caicos, Paul and I flew back to Michigan for Thanksgiving, and Midge continued on, taking advantage of an unusual following wind—all the way to Palmas del Mar on the east coast of Puerto Rico.

At Paul Eggert's cabin, December 1993

Paul's family always celebrated Thanksgiving at his cabin, but would his kids come this year? Should I leave? Or invite my kids? (They were best friends with Paul's kids.)

Life would be much more rustic at the cabin than at my mountain house on Pitkin Green in Aspen, because I really was in the country—living on the south branch of the Pere Marquette River, surrounded by 350 acres of private camping ground. I couldn't ride my bike or cross-country ski into town at the cabin. Or use a cell phone. Or watch TV. Small satellite dishes were on our horizon, and it wouldn't take long for Paul to figure out how to install one. And crossing Paul's private bridge (two three-foot-wide lanes separated by the flowing river below) was a sobering endeavor not to be taken lightly, and not to be taken ever by Paul's Prevost bus. Our first attempt to bring the bus near the cabin on the snowy dirt road was a disaster—Paul got stuck. It would be a long walk from the main road to the cabin when friends came to call.

If Paul left me alone at the cabin, I worried for my safety. Not so much from intruders, but from basic utilities that might go awry. If we lost power or heat or water, Paul could handle it easily; he had been around the cabin most of his life. I worried most about fire. After all, this was an authentic log cabin. And I had to rely on a landline for communication. (Where was my ham radio? Where was my car?)

I didn't have to worry long. Paul and I planned to leave after Christmas and not return until April. It was going to be an exciting sailing adventure on *Egg Crate*, which involved much of my family and would take us from the Turks and Caicos to the Netherlands Antilles off the South American coast. Paul realized I didn't understand what was involved, but he let me plan it anyway.

We flew to Provo (Providenciales) in the Turks and Caicos after Christmas. New Year's Eve was memorable, because it was the first time in almost two decades that I celebrated the night with someone special to me.

The next day, we needed to start across the Caicos Banks at high tide to get ahead of a front but Paul wouldn't wait for high tide. We left. And yes, we bounced off something (rock or post?) as we crossed the shallow banks.

Paul and I were going to split our nighttime schedules and plan to reach Puerto Plata on the north side of the Dominican Republic during daylight hours. However, we had the same following wind from the northwest that Midge had, only stronger and building. By the time I took over the helm in the middle of the night, we were cascading down the waves at ten knots—then eleven … then twelve and thirteen knots—unheard of on this fifty-four-foot sloop without a spinnaker flying. The stern of the boat was jerking back and forth more than usual. I blamed it on our wild ride; we were running straight downwind, preventer needed to keep us from jibing; I had my hands full. I was the navigator; I knew we were going to reach Puerto Plata before dawn; no way was I going to get help in the middle of the night in a large commercial port.

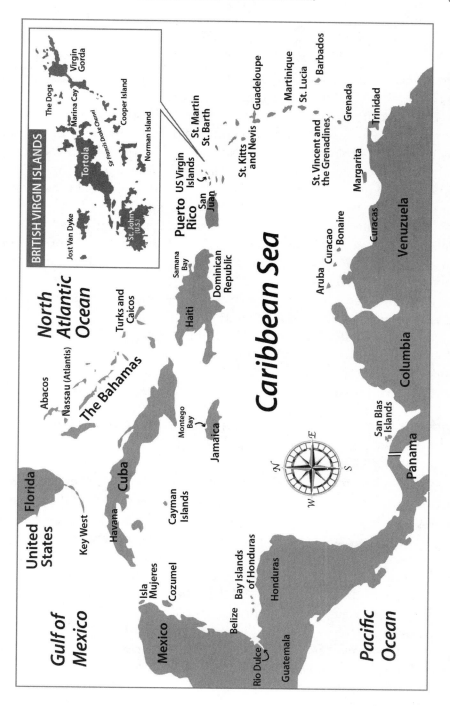

I checked our cruising book, Bruce Van Sant's *Gentleman's Guide to Passages South,* and read about Samana Bay—the Bali of the Caribbean. And mid-January was breeding time for the humpback whales. I changed course, knowing I had about another eighty miles before pulling into Samana Bay on the northeast coast of the Dominican Republic.

Paul woke up in Samana Bay. Not happy. Not knowing where he was, or why. It was so lush, so tropical, so calm and peaceful in the large protected bay, I was ready to park for a month. But I had set the schedule, and Mom and Dad would be waiting for us at Palmas del Mar within a week.

We sailed out of Samana Bay at dusk, Paul at the helm. I tried to sleep, but the bed started to rock softly from side to side.

We were moving quickly across the Mona Passage, and I cut the speed on the engine as we approached Boqueron Bay. I waited to approach the bay at first light before facing a blinding rising sun. I yelled to Paul through the open hatch, "Help me anchor!"

We had to replace the rudder in Boqueron Bay. I asked our mechanic, "Could we possibly have made it to Palmas del Mar?"

"No way. It fell off the skeg when I touched it."

"I think we damaged the rudder when we hit something on the Caicos Banks."

"Yes, that probably was it."

Sailing smoothly in the night lee off the southern coast of Puerto Rico had a calming effect on both of us. The bright lights of Ponce bounced off the water as we glided by.

Mom and Dad had visited Palmas often, but Dad had never been invited to go fishing on Midge's sailboat. *Oso Dormido*'s deck was not flush like *Egg Crate*'s, which had deck level openings to the side decks that allowed Dad to maneuver around easily. When Dad found out that he was invited to sail and fish on *Egg Crate* in the waters of the Caribbean from Palmas to Culebra to St. Thomas, he couldn't wait! He was ready. I didn't understand the need for all the gear that he brought on board, but I certainly was going to find out, particularly the fish fillet knives—long or short, curved or straight, all were extremely sharp.

Dad must have been talking to the local fishermen at Palmas, because he had all the right lures. He had no problem catching fish, especially large dorado.

Dad, 86, showing his filleting skills.

Paul and I said good-bye to everyone in St. Thomas and headed east for St. Martin and the Windward Islands. I had a schedule to keep; I promised two of my boys and their wives that we would pick them up in early February in St. Lucia and St. Vincent, and I promised Paul that we all would be dressed for the Mardi Gras celebration in Trinidad on February 15, 1994.

We breezed down the Leeward Islands, anchoring overnight in small harbors and picking up supplies as needed. We were eager to get to St. Lucia. I had to provision the boat for two weeks. We had plenty of seasick remedies on board, because Paul got seasick the first twelve to twenty-four hours at sea if it was the least bit rough. I didn't worry about my boys getting seasick, but I didn't know about the gals. Would I be sorry I picked these Windward Islands for our first *Egg Crate* cruise with my kids? I would soon find out.

Alison and Julio had a brief tour of mountainous St. Lucia when we drove from the airport to Rodney Bay. I showed them Marigot Bay, "the most beautiful bay in the Caribbean," according to author James Michener. We sailed down the St. Lucia coast, with the kids looking longingly at Marigot Bay; they wanted to stay. So did I, but I didn't allow enough time on the schedule. More importantly, I didn't allow time to wait for weather. The trade winds were consistently there, and powerful, but they took time getting used to. It was blowing when we headed south, somewhat protected in the lee of the island, but when we got out into the open ocean between St. Lucia and St. Vincent, the wind and waves picked up; I took the wheel, Paul shortened sail, and someone's only memory of the trip was "where's the bucket?"

We hoped Greg and Anne would be at the St. Vincent airport. After an overnight flight from Los Angeles to Barbados—4,000 miles, and a change to a regional airline that serviced the small airports in St. Vincent and the Grenadines, miraculously, they were right on time. Paul fixed a broken shaft, the kids sewed and taped the mainsail, and I passed around the sea-sick pills. Admiralty Bay on Bequia was not to be missed. With its beautiful natural harbor only nine miles south of St. Vincent, it was a must stop for every yacht. And the yachts all crowded in. (Watch the rodes! Especially after sunset.)

Next stop was the Tobago Keys Marine Park, a snorkeler's paradise—usually. I knew the kids liked snorkeling there in 1988 on Uncle Midge's *Oso Dormido*. But … how could I ever forget that scary strong current flushing me out to the open ocean?

We found moderate trade winds while sailing to Grenada's capital, St. George's. Still, all our artists on board seemed to prefer touring the mountains of Grenada, with its dense rain forests, rushing rivers, and frequent waterfalls. I assumed they were soaking up the scenery for their artistic endeavors.

On to Trinidad! And Carnival! The pièce de résistance?

We planned to cross the ninety nautical miles (about a hundred statute miles) from Grenada to Trinidad at night. Some of the crew downed enough seasick pills to keep them down until dawn.

It was clear and calm motoring into Trinidad's Gulf of Paria. Suddenly, the engine started to sputter and cough. When we looked over the side, we all cringed at the sight of a sea crowded with small, flesh-colored jellyfish. Paul knew the problem immediately: jellyfish in a through-hull intake fitting. Someone had to go swimming. Now. Paul knew who. (Had he done this before?) Paul grabbed a snorkel mask and fins and a small spear. He jumped over the side and disappeared under the boat. We watched with amazement. We were stalled in a busy channel entering the Gulf of Paria, hoping we hadn't lost our leader. Up popped Paul, spear in the air, jelly-fish dangling from it. He handed the spear to anyone who would touch it.

(Jellyfish tentacles can sting for hours after capture.) Paul climbed aboard, and we motored off again toward our marina at Port of Spain, the capital of Trinidad and Tobago.

Paul had been an active participant in Carnival for two years in the early 1990s, and his local friends were able to get us grandstand seats for the parade, which featured the famous native steel bands. We were given front row seats. As the bands marched toward us, their steel drums exploded in my ears! I looked at the toddlers sitting nearby and knew they must be ruining their ears forever. I plugged my ears. I couldn't stand the pounding of the drums. It was horrible. I wanted to escape.

When we headed into the crowded streets, I had trouble locating my kids. When one caught up with me, he announced quietly, "I just lost sixty dollars to a pickpocket."

"Don't you want to go after him?"

"No," he replied.

"Why not?"

"Because he's probably got knives and maybe a gun, and I don't have either."

I angrily looked around for the thieves. Suddenly... someone was behind me, grabbing the chain of my necklace, trying to jerk it over my head. (It looked like silver, but it was cheap tin.) He couldn't do it. That brazen maneuver infuriated the crowd of people surrounding us. A scuffle broke out. There were locals who knew the culprits and tackled them. It was one older guy and two or three small teenage boys. We slipped out of there.

By the next afternoon, we all were ready to leave Trinidad. Since the trade winds were blowing us straight west toward Margarita Island, the boys wanted to fly *Egg Crate*'s spinnaker. Both boys had flown spinnakers on Uncle Midge's racing sloop, *Sleeping Bear*. As they started to pull on the spinnaker halyard and tried to unfurl the twisted mess on deck, the wind filled the top of the spinnaker. Paul grabbed the ballooning sail, still twisted, watching it form an hourglass shape off the bow of the boat. They scrambled for the sheets to trim in the twisting sail and heard Paul shout, "Damn ... there goes my Rolex!"

It was dark when we approached Margarita Island—known for pearls, pirates, and earthly pleasures. We weren't looking for any of them. Dark was just the way we wanted it.

Paul had assured me and the kids that they wouldn't need visas to leave Margarita Island, because Paul had sailed there three years before and didn't need a visa. But the political scene in Venezuela was heating up, and now he wasn't sure. We decided not to check in with the authorities, for we would have had to list our crew.

Where could I anchor? We turned off our running lights after leaving the first bay we checked. My GPS equipment and binnacle lights were still shining brightly in the cockpit. Since I needed them to navigate, I asked for a large blanket to drape over me and the equipment. I could see a small inlet that would be legal for anchoring, but the depth wasn't indicated on my chart. We all were on edge. I don't remember if anyone slept.

We had a few days to find out the drill before the kids boarded their plane at Santiago Marino International Airport. And from what I was told later, they slipped into a crowded boarding line, holding their boarding passes in view. Nothing was asked, and nothing said. I was so-o-o relieved to see my kids leave. Paul and I took off too, sailing overnight for Puerto La Cruz, a favorite expat location for American sailors on the Venezuela coast. (Or so I thought; Paul had a detour in mind that absolutely delighted me.)

Dieter and Katrin Henzi on Stengah

Paul had stumbled on a quiet inlet while sailing to Puerto La Cruz from Margarita Island a few years earlier. This time we ventured in, totally alone, motor sailing and creeping along a marshy shoreline covered in thick high grasses. (Did Paul know where this was going?) As we neared the end of the long narrow inlet, we noticed our first and only sailboat, *Stengah,* carrying a Swiss flag; it was anchored for the night. When we found our own little hidden anchorage nearby, Paul motioned for the couple to stop by; thus began a monthlong friendship with Dieter and Katrin Henzi, on their way to Alaska via the Panama Canal.

We arrived in Puerto La Cruz the next evening and anchored offshore. When we entered the CMO marina in the morning, we were welcomed by a flood of people. My log was so waterlogged that I couldn't read all the services that were offered us, but I knew that expat sailors loved other expats!

On Sunday, February 27, my log read: "Sick from food till noon. Rest, Spanish lessons—do not leave the boat."

On Wednesday, we saw Dieter and Katrin. We arranged to talk every day at 8:50 a.m., on SSB radio. We traveled to Lecheria for a couple days to pick up diesel "permission slips" for the cheap rate (4.5 cents per liter)—"the national rate."

Dieter and Katrin showed up at Los Roques, and we both anchored off El Grande Roque. I caught two great fish—bonito and ojo gordo. After I caught the fish, I found out that I wasn't supposed to be fishing around Orchila Island, which was a Venezuelan military base. And if caught, their armed forces could have impounded our boat. No wonder the fishing was so good when we passed by the island.

While sailing to Dos Mosquises, I hit three coral heads *not* on our chart. I checked my GPS—both of them—and I took angles on islands. It was still blowing hard when *Marina Em* blew in from Las Aves and parked next to us. Tony McCleery invited us for coffee the next morning on *Marina Em*. He had fabulous mechanical systems, which he needed with a handicapped child on board. And retractable prison bars across all windows and hatches. Tony and I figured out that the GPS maps were about four miles off their printed coordinates. We both came up with the same figures, but Tony's sophisticated equipment would have been helpful to me before hitting the coral heads en route.

Dieter blew *Stengah's* horn early the next morning to wake us. Paul noticed our dinghy was gone. We stupidly left the dinghy in the water overnight instead of lifting it on the davits. We reported it to the Coast Guard and headed for Las Aves to join the Henzis. Paul was eager to get to Bonaire to buy a new dinghy.

We had a beautiful reach up the west coast of Bonaire, with full rig. After rounding up *Stengah,* we parked at Harbor Village marina to check out scuba certification.

Les and Freddie Fike from *Show Me* pulled up next to us and came aboard with stories of two round-the-world adventures. (We saw them on their sixty-five-foot Swan in Puerto Sherry in Spain preparing for the Columbus 500 race in 1992.) The Fikes' sailing experiences in Greenland were beyond belief—stuck in the ice for the winter, with their grandchildren on board. Tough sailors with a tough boat.

And then the great surprise: they saw our Achilles twelve-foot dinghy (they had one too), without the motor, on Las Aves last night. Seven "disreputable" looking fishermen were pulling it behind an old fishing boat.

Paul and I signed up for a five-day scuba certification, but Paul needed his Grand Haven stress test faxed to him before they would let him dive, so he got only four days.

What a scuba miscue I had the last morning of classes! I tried "buddy" breathing, but I placed Paul's mouthpiece upside down in my mouth. After swallowing half of the ocean, I shot up sixteen feet for air. But Simon Buckenridge had me right back down to complete the course and shake his hand (underwater) when the course was over.

Getting scuba certified with Bonaire Island instructor
Simon Buckenridge, spring 1994

Paul was eager to go back to the dive boat in the afternoon for a first dive on our own. Not me. I was apprehensive about diving so soon after my morning experience, and I became extremely dehydrated during the dive. It was hard for me to celebrate that evening. My jaws ached; my glands felt swollen; I couldn't abate my thirst. What was going on?

Monday morning, Paul and I biked to town to visit the immigration and travel offices. Bonaire was the first of the three "ABC" Netherlands Antilles islands (Aruba, Bonaire, and Curaçao) that we would visit, and it easily became my favorite. Imagine finding immense concentrations of marine life only fifteen feet from shore at fifteen feet of depth. The entire western shore of Bonaire, including the uninhabited island just offshore, Klein Bonaire, was a snorkeling and scuba diving paradise. And I tried to absorb it all in one week, but my head was not cooperating.

On Monday, we left at noon for Spanish Waters in Curaçao, about a fifty-mile sail west from Bonaire. I stood on the stern of *Egg Crate* and wondered if my head would stop spinning. *Ignore it*, I decided.

We rented a car Tuesday morning and drove up to Willemstad to find an impeller and check out the Curaçao Drydock. It was another tough day for me. The next day was a slight detour from reality to a doctor's office nearby. He told me I was okay: "Just take it easy, and have blood tests done as soon as you return to the states."

On Thursday and Friday, Paul and I worked on *Egg Crate*, knowing we were planning to haul it at the Curaçao Drydock soon.

On Saturday, I wrote:

Dizzy at 5:30 a.m. (same symptoms as Wednesday.). Read up on decompression sickness, and found I had classic symptoms. I called Simon in Bonaire at 9:00 a.m. He suggested I go to the hospital right away! I arrived at the emergency room at 11 a.m. All the Dutch trained staff surrounded me: ENT, interns, supervisors. They took X-rays, and drew arterial blood and venous blood (with oxygen level twice normal and carbon dioxide half normal).

The huge decompression chamber looked like a burial vault—and the "expert" who ran it looked like he had been pulled out of bed for this "emergency." I was truly frightened, wondering if I could get a "second opinion." The doctor stood over me while I wrestled with a small, cuffed brown bag. He ordered: "Brown bag it for a few days—and, remember, you aren't sixteen anymore."

Every service was completed as quickly as possible, with results in Dutch in hand. They did in two hours what Mayo Clinic does in two weeks. I received two bills: one from the hospital for $186.15, and a separate bill from the ear, nose, and throat specialist, Dr. Bierman, for $28.00. Before we left the hospital, I asked if I could call my dear friend, Dr. Dan Fox, an ear, nose, and throat specialist, who lived in Spring Lake, Michigan. The very efficient hospital staff connected me right away.

Dan said, "I want you to do an experiment that will tell me whether you have Ménière's disease or something else. I want you to turn your head from side to side, slowly, and tell me if you are affected in a specific location each time you move your head."

I was surprised to find out that if I tilted my head slightly to the right, the dizziness started. It only happened in that position.

Dan laughed and exclaimed, "You are lucky! You don't have Ménière's disease; you have labyrinthitis. It will take two to three months to cure, but staying away from salt, sugar, and caffeine will minimize the symptoms."

I walked carefully out of the hospital—and took his advice.

We spend a leisurely afternoon downtown in Punda, shopping and having a beer in the plaza. Our friends at Sarifundy took one look at me and decided Paul would need help laying up *Egg Crate,* and they started Sunday morning.

Two days later we left Spanish Waters for Willemstad and the dry-dock. The harbor entrance was picture perfect, with its quaint and colorful Dutch buildings, and floating fruit and veggie markets lining the docks. We coasted under an immense bridge on our way to the Curaçao Drydock.

Paul met Ralph Clay from Grand Rapids "on the hard." After three years living on his sailboat at the drydock, Ralph was a font of information about the drydock, his neighbors on the hard, Peter and Laura, and the town. He knew where to find everything, and he offered to take Paul and me to the airport and watch our boat all summer.

We were awakened at 7:30 a.m. by the drydock crew, who wanted to move the boat and haul immediately. They had only one hour before another big boat arrived to take our place. They moved us to crane number 17 of their 20 cranes, all of them 150 to 200 feet high. It was very impressive work; *Egg Crate* was placed on the travel lift and moved to the front of the dock.

Ralph invited us for a tour of Peter and Laura's cement sailboat, which they had stored on the hard at the drydock for the past six years—at eleven dollars per week. Paul and I hoped we could be more prompt with passage.

Chapter Fourteen

THE DOWRY

The Week That Was

*Midge, Paul, Kyle (on bowsprit), pregnant Judge, Joyce,
Ausma,— Mom and Dad (backs to camera).*

After our plane landed in Miami, Paul and I parted company. I rented a car, grabbed a sugar donut and a large cup of coffee, and headed across Alligator Alley, the long, lonely toll road crossing the Everglades in southern Florida. Mom and Dad were waiting at their La Peninsula condo on the Isles of Capri, and I hoped to surprise them with my early arrival.

I jumped out of the car when I pulled into their gated community. The world spun around me. I leaned on the car and waited. ... Uh-oh—it was "salt, sugar, and caffeine." I wasn't bothered while driving, and I made no stops. But what was I going to tell Mom and Dad about *labyrinthitis?* I could hardly pronounce the word, much less explain it. I walked slowly to the elevator. *Don't lean to the right. Smile, no hugs. Made it.*

I had to be careful walking along the breakwater, the docks, and the pool. And no tennis. I was in no hurry to return to Paul's cabin in Michigan; I would have months to worry about my new "labyrinthine" existence, and I didn't like being alone in the backwoods.

I flew back to Michigan and started looking for a small condominium. And a job. What about my current real estate broker's license in New York state? Were my three years of experience as a broker transferable? *Yes!* I needed a sales license first. That required mandatory classes for a week, followed by a test. Then another week of classes and the test for the broker's license.

I enrolled immediately in a real estate sales licensing class near the Eggert's former sixty-eight-acre shopping center in Benton Harbor. While attending class that week, I had time to sort through their personal bank guarantees (huge) and property tax obligations (also huge) for the shopping center. The shopping center's new owners turned out to be a pair of crooked lawyers, brothers Keith and Kenneth Mitan (with their own "Ma Barker" running the show), who were bankrupting more than one Michigan shopping center. Litigation was going to be messy and expensive. But it mattered. I believed the property would be very valuable because of its corner location at the intersection of US 31 and I-94: the major highway between Chicago and Detroit.

When I returned from Benton Harbor, I found a delightful spot on Spring Lake to hang my hat. All mine—with my own dock and boat-lift space. Thanks to Dad for the down payment (once more) and to Midge for the mortgage guarantees. My son Brett called it "condo bondage," and it certainly applied to me. I hated the silly rules concocted by the Yardarm condo board chairman and tried to ignore him whenever possible.

My condo had a second-floor loft that overlooked a twenty-foot-high living room with a grand view of Spring Lake. It was perfect for my home office. But I needed an official space too, where I could receive faxes and business mail. No one would take me seriously if I worked out of my home. Cell phones were few, fax machines were expensive, and commercial real estate deals required personal stamped and notarized signatures. Midge and Gary let me use a vacant second-floor office in one of the Verplank Dock Company's outer buildings.

I made courtesy calls on two of the largest Grand Rapids commercial brokerage houses. They weren't interested in my services. They probably felt I was too old and inexperienced to beat the bushes finding them new clients. Probably so. I was a new broker in Michigan, with my own office. I already had one potential client who needed to sell commercial real estate *now*. And I needed to get to work—if Paul's family would let me. They shared ownership in much of Paul's real estate.

Paul was in a peck of trouble. I could help him with a large array of real estate businesses, some inherited from his father. Paul owned properties in Lansing, the state capital; it was a place I knew well from years in politics and the child care business. I offered to use my new broker's license to sell or lease two of his small former franchised properties that had been boarded up and taken off the market. Both were good locations, but they were former gas stations; no bank would be writing a mortgage on that polluted property.

Stan Luben was Paul Eggert's property manager, talented bookkeeper, and president of the family holding company. And Stan managed well—representing our Western Michigan Dutch Reformed Church heritage: trustworthy, honest, hardworking, and loyal. (And Stan worked for Paul? Yes. For decades.)

Stan and I built signs that read For Sale or Lease, and we conducted open houses during the summer. One weekend, a young Chinese couple kept circling back around the north Lansing property. Surreptitiously, they stuffed a wad of cash in my coat pocket. I looked at them quizzically. They wanted me to keep it … *if* Paul would talk to them tomorrow. They needed Paul to negotiate a lease with an option to buy. All cash. Their relatives from New York's Chinatown were in Lansing on a mission to find a new business venture for one of their own. And they couldn't stay long.

I held the wad. It was a thousand dollars in small bills. One thousand dollars if Paul would venture out of his cabin! I begged him to come. I didn't hold out much hope that a deal would be made, but I clenched the bills, shocked that they would give them to me for a small favor. They knew, however, that there was another possible buyer about to make an offer, and they were taking no chances of not being first in line. Paul hesitated on the phone. I wanted to throttle him. Throw away a thousand dollars?! And perhaps the first deal in years for this "hot" property?

Paul showed up, and they "showed him the money." It was a great deal for everyone, including me. Nothing succeeds like $ucce$$. Not quite like doing business with the FDIC or RTC—or John Malone's TCI.

On May 9, 1994, I received a document from my bankruptcy lawyer, Thomas Quinn, that read: "The above-named debtor is released from all dischargeable debts."

What was not dischargeable were my personal debts in the lawsuit with TCI. I wrote a letter to Peter Barton, explaining that my bankruptcy lawyer, Tom Quinn, thought it very unusual that I was being sued once again by TCI under chapter 7 of the bankruptcy code. Peter did not answer me, but someone did, because, once again, "calmer minds prevailed": Tom Quinn settled the lawsuit with TCI's Spencer Dennison for $10,000—"$5,000 contemporaneous with execution of this Stipulation, and $5,000 on the earlier of December 23, 1994, or six months following execution of this Stipulation of Settlement."

What was not dischargeable by RBI was the final bill from Holmes and Starr, which was in six figures. I was called for a hearing with the Denver Lawyers Arbitration Committee in the summer of 1994. Who would testify at the hearing, other than I? Gary wanted to be there. Bill Seidman did not; Bill felt it was a lost cause (as did my litigator son), but, after much cajoling, Bill agreed to come.

It was a meeting I wish to forget. My testimony was ridiculous. I could no longer remember the information requested. Our former litigator from Holmes and Starr, Jeffrey Reiman, could remember. (He kept his files.) Jeff easily documented their hours and expenses from the six-week trial. I pleaded with Bill to "say something." What could Bill say that would have made a difference? Bill was a lawyer, and, like our current adversary, Jeff Reiman, had graduated from the highly esteemed Harvard Law School. Bill knew the lawyers were going to support one of their own. No matter how poor his performance. Gary also knew that he and Allen Hunting would be paying this huge bill.

Gary and Allen paid it promptly and didn't complain to me. They made the decision to turn down the $4 million settlement offer from TCI during the trial, but I made the mess that required a trial. I will be forever grateful to them.

During the summer months, Paul would invite me to crew for him on his MC scow whenever it was the least bit windy. Paul liked having a crew to balance the boat, lift leeboards, and trim the main, especially rounding a downwind buoy. I preferred crewing for Brett, but Brett took a crew only when it was really blowing; Brett had the strength and heft to sail most

MC races solo. Paul qualified for the MC Master class, which included all skippers over the age of fifty. As Paul's steady crew, we ended the season winning many MC Master trophies.

When I asked our good sailing friend, Skye Wickland, who was the best real estate lawyer in western Michigan, she replied, "Jon Anderson." Skye was a whiz of a paralegal, specializing in title research and other real estate matters at the Varnum law firm in Grand Rapids. Jon was her boss. His very pleasing personality masked a sharp, young, energetic mind that readily assessed problems and figured out quick solutions. And Paul had problems that needed quick solutions. Paul needed cash—lots of cash—to pay delinquent property taxes on the dilapidated Benton Harbor shopping center that had been thrust into bankruptcy by its new owners, the two embezzlers, Keith and Kenneth Mitan.. I knew Paul needed the best bankruptcy lawyers available in the state of Michigan to fight such wily lawyers, and he needed them now. And someone in Paul's organization found them ... in Detroit. Jay Welford was an expert in the areas of insolvency and bankruptcy—just what the doctor ordered for us. Jay would bring in as litigator his associate, Chris Cataldo, from their highly regarded Detroit law firm, Jaffe, Raitt, Heuer & Weiss.

However, other owners (who may not have known about the millions in bank guarantees) did not think the property was worth saving, and they asked the court to issue an injunction to stop the tax payment. Jon Anderson knew what had to be done—quickly. Jon drove fifty miles in one direction in the morning to complete a bank refinancing, then turned around to drive a hundred miles in the opposite direction during a long noon hour to complete a manufacturing facility closing—all papers signed an hour before the injunction was delivered. The delinquent taxes were paid; the deed was done.

Now it would be up to our Detroit bankruptcy attorneys, Jay Welford and Chris Cataldo, to win this bankruptcy case. And it would be up to me to sell the Benton Harbor shopping center—one more time!—for millions more than its mounting legal debts and family bank obligations.

The first person I called was Bill Seidman's longtime associate (and mine) in Washington, DC, Birge Watkins. Birge had been the director of the National Investor Outreach Program at the Resolution Trust Corporation (RTC). Trammell Crow, the giant commercial real estate firm, had recently hired him. Birge agreed to contact some of the larger firms around the country who specialized in shopping centers. I offered to pay Birge for his research time.

No one could have been more positive or enthusiastic about my project than Birge Watkins. He was a joy to work with. First, we had to price the center. Birge grew up in Grand Rapids and understood that local brokers in western Michigan would price the center much lower than brokers from big metropolitan cities like Chicago or Dallas. I didn't want Birge to know how low the local commercial brokers had valued the center. But I did want Birge to know that they put a high sales commission of 7 percent on the property, implying that its poor condition would make it a difficult sale.

Guess what price Birge suggested: $7.5 million. I gulped that suggestion down and said, "Let's give it a try."

Our first serious offer came in at $7.2 million, from a group in Toronto. (Birge, you were a saint.) The group would arrive in Michigan shortly to begin due diligence.

Well ... that offer woke up the other principals from Chicago who had been eyeing the center, hoping to get in with a price about half of the Toronto group's offer. The Chicagoans sat on the sidelines, watching the due diligence workers, assuming they wouldn't last in that long-forsaken corner of southwest Michigan. They didn't last long—just long enough to leave a strong impression of the new value attributable to sixty-eight acres of commercial real estate in a prime location. Our Detroit bankruptcy attorneys,

Jay Welford and Chris Cataldo, were impressed too, with the new value on the property they were hired to save for the Eggert family. How long would their battle continue? How long would Paul's?

Another knight in shining armor appeared on the scene just in time to rescue any miscues from my real estate forays. He was Paul Eggert's longtime accountant, Henry Bialik. I asked Henry to take over my sad-looking income tax account, and Henry realized it might not be so sad after all. I held a whopping capital loss from the loss of my five-year lawsuit, and that capital loss was not going away soon, if ever. But it also was not going to help defray my income tax from commissions or salaries. It was my "dowry" for some lucky man who needed it to defray his capital gains—his income from long-term investments.

Henry made certain that I documented carefully and completely all of my brokerage contracts, especially with Paul Eggert, knowing there could be challenges to my commission structure for leases or sales of his properties. Stan Luben could be relied upon to do the bookkeeping on my sales commissions and finder's fees for leases on the Lansing shopping center.

For the sale of some of the real estate properties bought in the 1950s by Paul's father, there would be huge gains realized because the properties probably had little basis and little debt. But. ...

Enter the Internal Revenue Code Section 1031—which provides a tax-deferred "like-kind exchange" of property *if* one follows specific rules. And one of the rules that could trip up some of Paul's property sales: the same taxpayer(s) who sell(s) the property must be the one(s) who buy(s) the new property.

(In 1994, Paul and two or three other investors were selling an old factory building that would provide Paul and the others with an ample capital gain. They were not a group who wanted to reinvest together; each one had his own reasons for needing the cash, and some had capital losses to balance the capital gains. I hoped Paul's group of owners would not consummate the sale until 1995.)

There were tremendous advantages for a commercial real estate broker who controlled both the selling and buying of property using the IRC Section 1031. The broker could receive a real estate commission on the sale and on the purchase. And the owner normally would be "trading up" to take full advantage of the tax savings—the 1031 exchange rules require the net market value and equity of the replacement property to be equal to or greater than the relinquished property.

For someone like me who was often late to the party, this was a challenge. I could never be late here with the IRS's strict deadlines. Never. It would be a scramble to identify three good properties for purchase in 45 days and close in 180 days. It was important to think ahead and anticipate the sales.

For years now, Paul had been creeping into divorce mode with his bright, vivacious wife. Paul was silent around me. He kept busy during the winter of 1995 at the Curaçao Drydock outfitting *Egg Crate*; it needed a lot of help after our hapless journey from St. Lucia to Isla Margarita with my kids the year before.

I spent about three weeks at a time during the winter at the Curaçao Drydock. Paul and Ed Bouwmeester, the manager of the drydock, became fast friends, and, whenever I arrived, Ed and his clever wife, Nettie, would invite us to their house for dinner and bridge games. Paul loved cards; I used to like to play in the 1950s, but once I started full-time work outside the home, I never wanted to take the time to play cards again. Nettie attempted to teach me something like "international bridge," assuring me that once I perfected the game, I could play bridge in any port in the Caribbean. Their three children, Marijn, Janneke, and Alex, were delightful. Paul and I hoped they would visit us in Michigan during the summer months.

When I returned from Curaçao in February, Stan Luben updated me in regard to our real estate business and bankruptcy lawsuit. I could rely on Stan to collect my 20 percent of a commission on a new lease in Lansing coming up on February 23. And Stan was tracking the marketing of the Bittersweet shopping center in Louisville with the center's long-standing property manager. Paul's father had bought the shopping center in the 1950s, and it was in need of serious repair. I urged Paul to sell it as fast as possible. It had little debt and would be a good candidate for an IRS 1031 exchange.

And, most important to me, Stan was following the leads of the two Chicago real estate developers who were showing renewed interested in the bankrupt Benton Harbor shopping center's sixty-eight acres. One of them was looking for a large retailer to take a major position at the center, something that had to be tied down to satisfy his investors. I admired his tenacity and hoped he could land an important tenant like Target.

There was not the usual jocularity from Paul Eggert in the summer of

1995. He was facing a long round of legal jockeying over his impending divorce—and I wanted no part of it, but I was part of it. My family knew I never wanted to marry again. Nevertheless, everyone knew that my marriage to Paul before the end of the year would be beneficial to both Paul and his wife. I needed to stay out of their way. And hope their smart lawyers could bring closure… this year.

In January 1996, I sent a lengthy letter to my children and extended family, from the Curaçao Drydock, explaining what I called "The Week That Was". Here are excerpts:

> I promised when I called on New Year's Day from Curaçao that I would write you about "the week that was" in Puerto Rico. … *So*, I've assembled some photos and a short (?) description of events leading up to the big day.
>
> Timing had become critical as the end of the year approached. Paul and I flew to San Juan on December 26, not sure what to bring with us. (Would we fly home the next week? Or fly on to Curaçao for a month?) Paul did his usual fast-paced pack-jam the morning of the 26th , but I was a wreck: clothes, house, office, family—*all* had to be attended to over Christmas weekend, plus boat supplies that I had put away for eight months.
>
> Grandma and Grandpa greeted us on the stern of the *Oso Dormido* when we arrived at 4:00 a.m. at the Palmas del Mar marina. Bad weather at O'Hare had ruined our flying schedule… We were all a touch bedraggled the next day, but Paul managed to find a fax machine and phone in a small alcove under two palm trees only ten feet from the boat. Riviera Yacht Charter owners Carlos and Terry set up shop for Paul so that he could continue to communicate with his lawyers and accountant in Michigan. Soon their fax was running out of paper … settlement discussions were becoming documents, and the modern-day fax divorce was becoming a reality before our eyes. After a week of *War of the Roses* repartee, calmer heads were prevailing.
>
> Then, by the morning of December 28, Paul announced, "It's not going to work." That was at 9:00 a.m. Paul's fax machine had crashed, a coconut had fallen on his head, and he had stepped in dog doo. Then, by 10:00 a.m., Paul's lawyers and others convinced him it was worth it to continue with the divorce process.
>
> At 11:00 a.m., Midge counseled Paul, "It'll get done. Calm down."

The lawyers had set a court date at 1:00 p.m., at the Ottawa County Court House in Grand Haven.

"Do you think your sister is going to be able to pull this off?" Paul demanded of Midge.

I was told that Midge, after some hesitation and a somewhat sheepish grin, told Paul, "Yes."

In the meantime, Gary's son, Kyle, and I had run off with Grandpa's golf cart, looking to upgrade our transportation into Humaçao.

When I arrived back at *Oso* with a Spanish-speaking chauffeur's limousine, Paul hopped in and told Midge, "Oh, boy, this is going to be a hell of a day!"

We were off to Humaçao to find a judge. ...

Paul's divorce was granted at 2:15 p.m. (Atlantic Standard Time-- one hour ahead of Eastern Standard Time). When the fax arrived from Grand Haven, Paul and I were sitting in Judge Lourdes chambers in Humaçao. Paul asked the judge if she could marry us that day. (I had told Paul earlier that I did not want to wait until the twenty-ninth, because that was Vicky and Gary's twenty-fifth wedding anniversary day.) The judge said she could do it immediately, but not after 5:00 p.m. at Palmas on Midge's sailboat, *Oso Dormido*, which I requested. However, after showing us pictures of her six-month-old twins (then seeing the La Claire picture of our clan), she offered to take down the necessary information and ask one of the other two judges if they would come to Palmas.

It was now 3:00 p.m. We set the wedding time for 5:20 p.m., and told our quite pregnant new judge that we would meet her at 5:00 p.m. at the Palmas Hotel to escort her to the boat, which was always hard to find in the huge marina.

We rounded up our chauffeur and asked him to find a floral shop and booze store in downtown Humaçao. When he stopped at the florist's, Paul called Midge to see if he still wanted to be his best man. Then Paul suggested to Midge that he invite "anyone who wanted to come" to show up at *Oso* at 5:30 p.m. And Paul honored my last request (!)—that Midge find some quarters for us off the boat for the night—to replace the bunk room we were occupying.

The florist wanted to take the entire afternoon to prepare appropriate wedding bouquets, so we helped ourselves to bunches of red roses and white carnations and two huge glass vases. We ran to a grocery store nearby and bought all of their champagne supply, which included two bottles that Fritz would not have pitched out, plus rum, Coke, wine, and beer.

It was now 4:15 p.m. I complained to Paul, "I'm going to be late for my own wedding!"

When we arrived at Oso, it was 4:30. Ausma and Midge had already cleaned up the boat, and Ausma was looking gorgeous, as usual, in a new sleeveless jumpsuit. Midge put on an appropriate sailing shirt (which barely passed approval by his very chic wife … or the groom.)

Midge obviously had parceled out the assignments at the time of Paul's call: Kyle and cousin Nils were to meet the seven-month pregnant judge at 5:00 p.m.; Gary was to find us a place for the night and a restaurant that would accommodate all of us for dinner following the ceremony. *And* he could not have been more successful at both. He found a beautiful villa overlooking the entire resort (which had ice, aspirin, and no phone), and an Italian café that provided a warm, cozy atmosphere.

As people arrived for the wedding, Paul plied them and *me* with drinks for fortification. After borrowing a shirt from Midge, Gerardo arranged a fifteen-minute bachelor party out under the two palm trees.

Why didn't we just get married quietly in Judge Lourdes's chambers? Well … with his usual foresight, Fritz had slipped me a small book for Christmas written by Miss Manners, a modern-day compendium of wedding etiquette. Now, the big no-no, according to Miss Manners, is a fake ceremony with an accompanying celebration— after the fact, so to speak. And we knew there was no way to keep this event quiet from my inquisitive family—unless we lied about it, which we were unwilling to do. Indeed, how fortunate we were to have so many of my family able to participate, especially Mom and Dad: at eighty-five and eighty-eight years of age, they didn't have to move more than thirty feet to get their only daughter down the aisle.

However, Miss Manners doesn't rule out future celebrations. Therefore, we intend to hold one for *all* of *our children*, when it is convenient for *you* to be in attendance…

Paul and I flew to Curaçao in early January of 1996. Paul was eager to work on Egg Crate so that we could sail to Jamaica to meet Fritz and his New York friends at Round Hill in Montego Bay in mid-February. Jamaica was 700 miles north of Curaçao across the vast Central Caribbean Sea. We needed to be prepared to sail a week or more at sea.

Probably the greatest blessing I inherited from my dad was my tough stomach. Not only had that trait carried me through five pregnancies with no morning sickness, it was about to carry me through the roughest ride of my life with no seasickness. My log tells the tale:

February 10, 1996. Paul and I left the Curaçao Drydock, leaving behind our ever-thoughtful Curaçao family—the Boumeesters: Ed, the manager of the drydock operations; Nettie, his wife; and their children, daughter Janneka, age sixteen, and two boys, Maryn and Alex, ages twelve and eight, who became very attached to Paul's dinghy, which, according to Ed, had one speed—fast. We hope to see them in the states in July.

"February 10, 2:30 p.m. Arrived at Santa Martabaai, Coral Cliffs, for an overnight stay in the very picturesque, quiet inlet to which Ed had introduced us on our first "trial run" sail in mid-January. It was a perfect location (twenty miles north of Willemstad and the Drydock) for our early departure to Aruba, shortening the distance from seventy-five nautical miles to fifty-five nautical miles.

February 12, 7:00 a.m. Finally! Left Curaçao, with the dawn's early light. Our weather fax showed a big H (high-pressure area) over the entire central Caribbean through the fifteenth—pleasant sailing weather for the entire week. We had been warned of "confused" seas just north of Aruba, where the North African western current intersects the current flowing northwest from the South American coast, but we didn't expect to experience the same waves off the northern tip of Curaçao. They were there—in great confusion—and with the twenty-five-to-thirty-knot southeast winds behind us, we rocked and rolled all the way to Aruba on a broad reach, averaging nine-plus knots. After almost two years in drydock, Paul's stomach didn't know what to do. Relieving the autopilot at the wheel seemed to be his quickest remedy, along with a Marazine washed down with Alka-Seltzer.

February 12, noon. Arrived at the southern tip of Aruba. Seas calmed down along the west coast, but winds were gusting up to thirty knots when we motored into Oranjestad harbor shortly after 1:00 p.m.

February 13, 6:45 a.m. Noticed a lull in the trade winds. I quickly jammed the boat in reverse and watched us (barely) clear the dock with our bowsprit.

February 13, 7:00 a.m. Off to Jamaica. Distance from Oranjestad to our first way point 40 miles southeast of Jamaica: 450 miles; distance to Montego Bay: 600 miles. That distance was of some concern to Mom and Dad (and maybe some of you). Guess who came to the rescue (!)

Uncle Midge, of course. No, he didn't offer to subject *his* bride to the rigors of the central Caribbean Sea, but he did insist on a twice daily SSB check on us, noting, very carefully, each time (he never missed) our coordinates (so much north and west), course (magnetic), wind speed, wind angle, and wave length, and then, and only then, could we digress to other matters. Paul seldom mentioned to Midge any problems with the boat. *What* problems? In chronological order, as I remember them. ...

February 13, 6:00 p.m. While routinely checking our fuel and water supply, Paul noticed that the water gauge registered 0 on both tanks. That's right ... we had not one drop ... 400 gallons pumped out of the bilge in one afternoon.

February 13, 7:00 p.m. About an hour after Paul announced there was no water in the tanks, the engine started to cough and sputter. Paul knew the problem was a dirty fuel filter (from bad diesel fuel bought in Venezuela), but he had only one small spare filter aboard. Paul refused to change filters, knowing we needed the engine later for the harbor(s) in Jamaica. Besides, we were averaging nine knots with no engine at the time, the wind having increased again by evening.

February 14, 11:30 a.m. During the morning, the wind increased (we were averaging ten knots with no engine), and the seas were building to more than ten feet and had yet to settle down. Suddenly, Paul noticed we were losing the largest batten (about twenty feet in the mainsail). When I came on watch at noon, I promised to try to keep the main full by steering more off the wind, *if* he promised not to try to rescue it in such heavy seas. He agreed.

February 14, 12:30 p.m. I heard a loud snap. The D shackle pin on the boom vang had broken in half. Paul got out of bed, put on his harness and life preserver, and, now sporting two whistles (we slept with one around our necks on long voyages), strapped himself to the mast and tied a temporary line to replace the shackle "until the seas calm down."

February 15, 12:30 a.m. By midnight of the fourteenth, the wind and seas began to calm down. So ... when I popped my head above deck shortly after midnight, Paul reported the twenty-foot batten was two-thirds out of its pocket and would need to be retrieved immediately, which would require my presence on deck. Can you imagine Paul's disappointment (and further frustration) when he dove for the batten as it slipped out of the pocket near the edge of the deck, and just missed it? But I was furious! If he fell overboard, there would be no way I would find him in the middle of the central Caribbean in the middle of a dark night, with no boat traffic nearby. (We'd seen only four or five freighters in three days.)

February 15, 3:00 p.m. Now to problem *solving*. Paul switched the fuel lines between the engine and the new generator, explaining, "The generator requires so much less diesel fuel than the engine, it might get by with a clogged filter." And in less than an hour, the engine was working well and at full power. But that didn't work for the generator. One of the two priming pumps to the generator was broken; therefore, Paul had to suck (literally!) the fuel into the filter, which he had just cleaned with paint thinner and replaced. "It took three of your chocolate valentine candies and two rums and Coke to clean my palate," he confided after emerging above deck.

February 15, 5:30 p.m. Paul showed me a very hazy outline of the Jamaican hills twelve miles to the west. Our estimated time of arrival at Port Antonio would be 9:30 p.m. (AST). Our Welsh electrician in Curaçao had sailed recently to Port Antonio and had warned us not to attempt entry into the harbor after dark.

February 15, 9:30 p.m. (8:30 p.m. EST in Jamaica). Off Port Antonio on the northeast coast of Jamaica. We looked for entrance lights to the harbor for one hour, and, not finding them to our liking, motored on toward Montego Bay, enjoying the quiet, flat water, the evening stars, and the music emanating from the beach.

February 16, 2:30 a.m. (EST). Off Ocho Rios. Paul stayed awake an extra half hour to see the lights and hear the music from the resort town of Ocho Rios, where his son, Josh, and daughter-in-law Michelle had honeymooned in October.

February 16, noon (EST). Two miles off Montego Bay. Having fussed over a desalinator for two days (one that had not been used in two years), Paul was very proud to have 400 gallons of fresh soft water in the tanks by the time we reached Montego Bay. I would be able to brush the fur off my teeth and shampoo the matted salty mess out of my hair before leaving the ship at the Montego Bay Yacht Club. Paul reported to Fritz, when we greeted him that evening at Round Hill, that I had spent four hours in the shower. I don't think he exaggerated one bit.

When we sailed into Montego Bay on February 16, 1996, I heard a plane circling overhead. It was a huge American Airlines jet in its final approach to the runway just off our port bow. The main runway of the Montego Bay airport ended at the water's edge. It was the most remarkable coincidence: After six days at sea, we met Fritz in flight over Montego Bay.

Round Hill turned out to be the perfect rendezvous with Fritz, who gave an impromptu "Fritz at the Ritz" concert during his brief stay. Fritz was a guest of longtime New York City friends, Roddy and Nazee Klotz.

Most of the villas at Round Hill had been owned by the same families for generations; the owners contributed to the local Hanover Parish charities with various fund-raising events. Our first evening, Paul and I participated in a silent charity auction, followed by dinner and dancing. Paul had been forced to grow a beard while crossing the central Caribbean Sea, and a sweet elderly lady came up to us on the dance floor and gushed over Paul's dancing ability and his handsome beard. (I liked it, too ... Hemingway-esque.)

A very British Nigel Pemberton invited us for dinner at his home in the Jamaican hills overlooking Montego Bay, and it became a cause célèbre because of the formality of the dinner scene. I still laugh at the thought of Paul's surprised look when Nigel's butler, cigar cutter in hand, grabbed the cigar from Paul's mouth and cleverly clipped the end of it. Nigel thought it was such fun to watch Paul's reactions (Paul was richly humorous and self-deprecating); Nigel insisted we stay far into the night for cognac and more cigars. ... Slight problem came up at that point—driving in Jamaica was on the left, English style, and Paul was dyslexic. When Fritz was around, he insisted on chauffeuring us to all events from the Montego Bay Yacht Club. That night, Fritz was not around, and Nigel had to find us safe passage back home.

The Montego Bay Yacht Club was one of the safer locations to park *Egg Crate* in Jamaica. Paul and I liked the location—far from Kingston on the northwestern coast. We didn't have much company at the marina, however. It was not a way station for cruising sailors. Not only was Jamaica in the hurricane zone, it was near no friendly country, sitting underneath Castro's Cuba. Haiti was 200 miles east of Montego Bay, Grand Cayman Island 200 miles west, and Curaçao almost 700 miles south.

So who would occupy a slip right across the dock from us? NZ Ship *Caniche* from Auckland, New Zealand. Paul had a playmate immediately; and I had a thoughtful tour director. Warren Tuohey had sailed across the Pacific with an all-male crew, and his wife, Marlene, joined him in the Caribbean. Marlene found the interesting places to visit, and then the two of us strategized, hoping to convince the boys to join us.

Feeding the very friendly hummingbirds

An especially difficult assignment was the bird sanctuary, where friendly hummingbirds could be fed out of the palms of our hands. Bamboo rafting down the Martha Brae River was an easier goal with the boys.

A local Montego Bay acting group wanted Paul to stop interrupting their play practice. They knew Paul would bring some humor to their rehearsals, which were held at Paul and Warren's Montego Bay Yacht Club bar, but the play must go on!

Guess who was entertaining the players and stage crew after opening night? Once the word got out that there was free food and booze on *Egg Crate*, Paul had to worry about a tippy, sinking ship. Paul kept warning the masses to spread out on the decks to distribute the weight. I hid in the galley, with many enthusiastic helpers, especially Nigel Pemberton, making gallons and gallons of fresh salad. I stayed clear of the crowded deck.

It was not a glamorous memory of a successful opening night.

Chapter Fifteen

MY ANGEL

Her ethereal being was beyond my comprehension.

"A Tribute to Lydia"

My brothers called me at the Montego Bay Yacht Club during the last week of March to report that Dad's surgery for his new knee was successful, but his recovery less so. Dad was in the intensive care unit of Grand Haven Hospital. Would I like to come home? Doctors were concerned that Dad, at age eighty-eight, was a little old to tackle such major surgery, but Dad had insisted, saying he did not want to live with so much pain in his bum knee.

By the time I arrived at Dad's bedside, he had started to heal, so I relaxed and headed to Brett's house in Spring Lake to say hello to his family.

Brett and Carla were entertaining childhood friends, D. J. and Barb

Edgerle. D.J., a budding young dentist, had moved his new practice from Maine back home to western Michigan. While parents congregated in the kitchen, I looked for Brie and Little Lydia, who, at ages six and four, were having an active conversation in the bathroom. Carla commented that they had just returned from a visit to the pediatrician; Little Lydia had a minor blood problem, and the doctor recommended some liquid iron.

I took a look at Little Lydia. My heart sank. I didn't want to know what I knew … from twenty years in the preschool business. Nor did I want Brett and Carla to know. Not yet. What could I do? I called my daughter Lydia in Boston; she had a pediatrician who had worked at Dana-Farber Cancer Institute. Lydia suggested I fax her the blood test results. I rushed to the Grand Haven Hospital late Friday afternoon to fax the blood test information to Lydia before she left her Continental Cablevision office in downtown Boston.

Lydia jumped into action immediately, suspecting the worst, crying privately on the phone from her Boston office, days before Little Lydia's diagnosis. Her pediatrician, hearing of my concerns (suspecting some type of leukemia because of the telltale circles around Little Lydia's eyes), offered to review Little Lydia's lab reports over the weekend. Lydia faxed the lab reports to his office Friday evening, and he called Saturday with his preliminary diagnosis: neuroblastoma. He urged us to get Lydia to a pediatric hematologist/oncologist. I didn't think one existed in western Michigan, but I liked the word *hematologist* better than *oncologist*.

For the next two days, we scrambled. … By Sunday morning, I was frantic enough to confide in Carla. We both started calling family friends and doctors for advice, and by late Sunday afternoon, our good friend, Dr. Dan Fox, returned both of our calls. On Sunday evening, he contacted a Muskegon oncologist who agreed to meet us early Monday morning before his other appointments.

Carla and I brought Lydia to the oncologist's office at Hackley Hospital early Monday morning. … That afternoon, Uncle Don Freeman returned my call from the previous weekend. He insisted I call directly Dr. Fahner, head of the pediatric hematology/oncology department in the new and luxurious Helen DeVos Children's Hospital in Grand Rapids, stressing that "Helen DeVos does not put her name on anything unless it is done right."

What a wondrous whirlwind reception we received! The minute we entered the pediatric hematology/oncology clinic, Little Lydia was whisked off to the playroom while the parents filled out forms and answered questions.

Nurses and social workers hovered around. ... I guessed they had heard the preliminary test results from Hackley. (Certainly, they could identify with those telltale marks around Little Lydia's eyes.)

Dr. Cornelius was very warm and gentle, but I could not believe how directly he reported the results: He suspected her cancer was, indeed, neuroblastoma, a rare cancer of the sympathetic nervous system that mainly affects children before the age of five. Dr. Cornelius outlined the necessary diagnostic surgery and tests, which would begin that very afternoon with Little Lydia's admittance to the ninth floor of DeVos Children's Hospital.

After the first week of surgery in April 1996, and the first round of chemotherapy, my family began to recover from the initial shock of such devastating news and began to prepare for a long six-month aggressive battle.

As word spread about Little Lydia's cancer, friends began to call with information that we felt compelled to explore, even though Carla and Brett were satisfied with their choice of protocols. Priscilla Newman, daughter of my best friend, Harriet Newman, suggested we talk to the head of pediatrics at New York's Memorial Sloan Kettering Cancer Center, Dr. O'Reilly. Although the N-6 protocol that Little Lydia was following had been developed at Sloan Kettering, Priscilla thought there might be newer experimental treatments that might work better. Priscilla had been the assistant to James Robinson when he was chairman at American Express, and he was the current chairman of the board at Sloan Kettering. We felt confident that Priscilla's contacts could provide us with the latest developments in the treatment of neuroblastoma. (Little did we realize that the research doctor Julio had interviewed the first week of April would be the same Dr. Cheung recommended by Dr. O'Reilly.)

After Little Lydia's second round of chemotherapy in early May at DeVos Children's Hospital, Carla and Brett called Dr. Cheung. He explained his new experimental protocol, N-7, and advocated its use for Little Lydia's particular type of neuroblastoma. Little Lydia would need to switch protocols immediately, or she would not "qualify" for this newest treatment. (That's right, the long arm of the federal government—in this case, the FDA—decides and designs all kinds of protocols.)

Where was Paul Eggert during this month of trials and tribulations? As soon as we knew Little Lydia's diagnosis, I called Paul at the Montego Bay Yacht Club and begged him to come home right away. Paul showed up the next evening at the DeVos Children's Hospital. The family was holding a meeting with Dr. Axtell, who was explaining that the protocol, N-6, had a 40 percent survival rate. Paul pulled up a chair next to me but did not utter a word. The scene must have been a daunting introduction to the serious decisions facing Brett and Carla.

Paul suggested that we have dinner outside the hospital surroundings, but Brett and Carla refused to leave Little Lydia's side, knowing she would be awake after an afternoon of surgery. Out the door slipped Paul, on a secret quest to find a really good restaurant in the neighborhood. A half hour later, Paul strode in, beaming, with arms full of huge takeout boxes filled with giant steaks and salads, along with "unnamed" refreshments. Leave it to Paul to relieve the tension and lift the spirits. Just what this doctor ordered.

At the end of May 1996, Brett wrote a thank-you letter to Mom and Dad. Here is an excerpt:

Dear Grandpa and Gram,

I'm sorry that I haven't seen more of you two since Grandpa's days in ICU at NOCH (North Ottawa Community Hospital). As you know, the times have become more challenging than ever before ... and I wish I could do something that could clearly convey how blessed we feel to have you guys in our corner of the ring for this battle.

We are leaving in two hours for Memorial Sloan Kettering Cancer Center in New York City, to get a second opinion. The doctor there invented the therapy regimen that Lydia is on now, and he has invented a new therapy that we may want to consider down the road a little way—after a few more rounds of chemotherapy. That option, if we deem it the strongest, would place us back in New York instead of Los Angeles, around August.

We are staying at the Ronald McDonald House a few blocks from the hospital. It is in a safe neighborhood a few blocks from Priscilla Newman's house on 73rd Street.

This is a very big week for us. The tests to be performed will show us if the chemotherapy is having a positive effect, as we hope, or let us know if we have to try something else. ...

We look forward to seeing you when we get home. Much love, and, Grandpa, stretch that knee. ...

Fritz and Julio and Julio's brilliant artistic wife, Alison Berry, stepped up to bat when Carla and Brett brought Little Lydia to New York City. Not only did they visit the Ronald McDonald House and take Little Lydia to dinner at nearby restaurants, but they endured the serious business at Sloan Kettering of donating platelets. They rounded up relatives and friends to donate platelets—a burdensome and scary proposition for the uninitiated, which included most of us. Charlie Hatton, a favorite cousin and charming young investment banker on Wall Street, willingly accepted the task of donating platelets. Wow! I will never forget viewing Charlie's black-and-blue arm—from shoulder to fingertips! (I have never had the experience of donating blood because I don't weigh enough to qualify for donating—but my sons have made up for my shortcoming, donating over and over again, especially Brett.)

Fritz flew home to celebrate the Fourth of July holiday with family and friends. After a morning of golf with his dad, Fritz joined our sailing crowd on Uncle Gary's large classic Chris Craft sea skiff, captained by his young son Kyle, for the mandatory viewing of the fireworks from the harbor in downtown Grand Haven. Fritz had invited Charlie and Shari Frutig's eldest daughter, Caren (yes, spelled with a C), to cruise with us. The Frutigs had been active members of the Spring Lake Yacht Club for almost two decades. (Charlie and brother Midge jointly owned a racing boat.) None of us had met Caren because she had been working on the East Coast for the past ten years. Like Fritz, Caren was home for the holidays. Was it fate that they met for this first date?

We knew it wouldn't be the last as we watched them snuggling on the back banquette of Gary's boat. The next night, Paulie (as Fritz called him) suggested we cruise to the BLT (Bear Lake Tavern) in North Muskegon for an early supper. Using Paulie's old, really old, speedboat to travel ten miles north on Lake Michigan at night could be a thrilling or chilling ride. At least Caren was a champion swimmer, having trained for the Junior Olympics when she was a young teenager. Yes, we all got along swimmingly.

Could it be true that our cosmopolitan Fritz, having worked halfway around the world, came home to meet his mate? And their next date? A mere three days later. In New York City.

Carla was kind to update friends and family on Little Lydia's progress as the family moved between Sloan Kettering in New York City, DeVos Children's Hospital in Grand Rapids, and their new condo on Spring Lake. After a discussion about Little Lydia's treatment and bone-marrow transplant, Carla described her courageous battle:

> I have saved the most important part for last. I wanted to highlight that Lydia's attitude during this fierce battle that we face has been incredible. She tells us that she has her very own angel watching over her and that she sees her from time to time. We believe her. She has an intuitive spiritual sense about her. Every day, she finds something positive to focus on. We believe that this battle is won (in part) with strong positive mental attitude and spiritual sense. She continues to amaze us with the strength and courage she displays. She charges ahead with great determination and seems fearless to us some days. She is a true inspiration to us and others around her. ...

And, obviously, also to Paul's daughter Amy, who was a close personal friend of Brett's. They grew up in the same neighborhood and attended elementary and secondary school together. And they both loved to sail. Brett may have been a trophy-laden sailor in his youth, but so was Amy. And Amy could race iceboats fearlessly as a young teenager, thanks to Daddy's tough example.

Amy was fearless in promoting her projects too. When she and her best friend, Cindy Parker, were cooking something from an East Grand Rapids cookbook called *After Grace,* which had been assembled and sold by a local East Grand Rapids group of women, they said, "What a great idea!"

They knew many people were asking how they could help Brett and Carla, and they felt the sale of a cookbook of homespun recipes would be a perfect solution. They also would have a plethora of art that flowed from talented Little Lydia's brush to fill the section dividers in the cookbook.

They named it *My Angel's Cookbook.* It opened with a page entitled, "A Tribute to Lydia." The first two paragraphs explain the title:

> This special collection of recipes, accumulated by family and friends, is dedicated to Lydia Elizabeth Hatton, the one who has made us all believe that angels do live among us.
>
> From the onset of Stage IV Neuroblastoma, a rare form of childhood cancer, in April of 1996, Lydia has enchanted anyone who will listen with stories about her Angel ... the Angel that speaks to her, guides her and comforts her ... when she's awake and when she's asleep ...

the Angel that is described in such vivid detail that we know that she carries an umbrella. ...

The cookbook committee: Amy Eggert, Cindy Parker, Susan Jerovsek, and Cammie Heatherington. With help from Lynne, Marlene, Sally, Holly, Sheila, One-to-One Marketing Services, Nancy Hatton, and Joyce Hatton.

What a tremendous effort was put forth by this enthusiastic committee to assemble almost six hundred recipes in six sections, from appetizers and beverages, to breakfast and brunch, to main dishes, side dishes, and salads—and to make the colorful choices of Little Lydia's whimsical artwork for the cookbook's front and back covers and the six section dividers.

Amy Eggert was also the catalyst for my first successful 1031 exchange. Amy's longtime beau, Spencer Barnes, worked at his family company, C. D. Barnes Associates, Inc., in Grand Rapids. They were general contractors, construction managers, and design builders. Spencer knew that Paul was looking for property to buy when the sale of the sixty-eight-acre shopping center closed. And timing would be crucial because of the strict IRC Section 1031 rules that require identification of one of three properties within 45 days and purchase within 180 days after the sale.

Spencer showed Paul and me photos of a handsomely designed modern office building that would fit the acreage that C. D. Barnes Associates owned at the busy corner of Spalding Avenue and Cascade Road, in the upscale neighborhood of Cascade Township. However, we couldn't just buy land; we had to have a building on it to meet our financial goals in the 1031 exchange. Time to make a decision was at hand.

We knew that the Louisville shopping center might sell before the sixty-eight-acre center. It would need a 1031 like-kind exchange property too.

But we couldn't get too far ahead of ourselves. When would Target Corporation make the crucial decision whether or not to lease property for a store on the sixty-eight acres? Jim Paul of JPA Real Estate worked for years on this project, knowing his financing for the shopping center would hinge on a Target contract.

And when would the Eggerts be free of the Mitans' madness? An FBI report would detail the scheming of the Mitans:

The defendants preyed on small business owners who were interested in selling. ... The defendants obtained a controlling interest in those businesses, failed to pay the agreed-on purchase price, then gutted the companies of existing assets. They diverted those assets into shell accounts so they could then further divert the funds for their own personal uses. The defendants would divert some of the target companies' funds to other targeted companies. The purpose of these payments was to keep the other companies alive by providing them with just enough money to pay their most pressing bills, and thereby staving off bankruptcy for a few more weeks. Within a few months, the companies were bankrupt, leaving rent, vendors, *creditors*, utilities, and *taxes unpaid*. [Italics mine.]

In the mid-1990s, Ken and Keith Mitan, both lawyers, were actively defrauding real estate owners across the state of Michigan. I don't know what route our lawyers, Jay Welford and Chris Cataldo of Jaffe, Raitt, Heuer & Weiss, pursued in ridding us of the Mitans, but they did it! Yes, the shopping center's original owners (Paul Eggert, et al.) would be forced to sell the center once again to pay off their creditors, especially banks and bankruptcy lawyers—whose legal bills were nearing the half-million-dollar mark. And Jay Welford was working diligently to maintain clear title for a sale. (Clouding the title was a favorite ploy of the Mitans.)

As the center's real estate broker, I needed to work diligently too, on the sale. I worried about my commitment of time and treasure to Lydia Elizabeth Hatton's complex therapy requirements.

In early December 1996, Carla Hatton wrote Richard and Helen DeVos to thank them:

[For] the incredible gift you have given to us and to this community through the Helen DeVos Children's Hospital. ...

Dr. Axtell and his staff agreed to take on this unprecedented project, to follow a new protocol under the direction of an out-of-state physician and participate in the critical communication between two medical teams who had never worked together. It was an enormous effort on their part.

We were pleased to hear Sloan Kettering's Dr. Cheung's assessment of Dr. Axtell and the Grand Rapids staff: "They have not missed a beat! All *i*'s are dotted and *t*'s crossed."

Also, I would like to thank you and the Amway Corporation for participating in the Corporate Angel Network. Lydia's treatment plan would not be possible without the gift the network has offered. We have flown on your Hawker jets with Jim and Doug and felt welcomed and comfortable. ...

May you and yours have a warm and wonderful holiday season. Your contributions are a blessing to all. We are so very grateful.

I offered to relieve Brett or Carla at Sloan Kettering whenever needed. The monitoring of Little Lydia's complicated therapy and comfort were difficult tasks when I filled in for Carla or Brett. Little Lydia didn't like it when her mom or dad wasn't there, and I was the only other family member available in New York City who understood the protocol well enough to be trusted alone with her. I was proud of her parents' trust of me, but I wasn't very confident of Little Lydia's trust. I couldn't fool her. She knew that her mom and dad understood her every whim, pain, or bored look, and I didn't.

Like Carla and Brett, I learned how important the Ronald McDonald House would become for my welfare as well as Little Lydia's. I moved between the hospital, the grocery, the pharmacy, and the Ronald McDonald House when I cared for Little Lydia at Sloan Kettering. Carla and/or Brett were usually present when Little Lydia was allowed to stay at the Ronald McDonald House. The activities provided by Ronald McDonald staff were sensitive to Little Lydia's needs at every stage of her illness, and lifelong friendships were established by Carla with staff members.

I spent part of January at Sloan Kettering and returned to Michigan in early February. I had meetings or hearings in Benton Harbor. We were moving forward slowly with Jim Paul's purchase of the sixty-eight acres.

We knew we would need to build out the Cascade property quickly after the Benton Harbor center's closing --and that purchase price would depend on the net sale proceeds. It was an exciting time to be the broker on both sides of this 1031 like-kind exchange.

After weeks of meetings and phone calls with Jim Paul and his company, JPA Real Estate, a purchase fax arrived on June 2, 1997. A week later, I met with Jay Welford, Jim Paul, Stan Luben, and Paul Eggert in an empty Benton Harbor office. I remember Jay Welford pushing Jim and Paul to stay until the deed was done. It was midnight, and Jim Paul was looking for a copy machine. Somehow, someone located one, and the papers were copied and signed. The purchase price made Paul Eggert very happy. He was ready to celebrate.

My children were pleased too, with our successful sale, but our battle to save Little Lydia kept everyone on edge. The doctors at Sloan Kettering sent her home in June; they refused to sanction any new protocols, but knew that Brett and Carla would explore all avenues available for a cure. St. Jude's could not help, but a Toronto doctor's experimental drug therapy sounded promising.

Brett's family headed for Toronto in my new "disco van," a high top seven-passenger sports van, with flashy lines of tiny bulbs above the windows and a rear leather seat that flattened into a queen-size bed. The TV and VCR and collection of children's movies stored in the high top's upper shelves kept Brie and Little Lydia busy on the road. The first experience with the Toronto doctor was encouraging—Little Lydia seemed to get some of her energy back. After a week, her energy waned again, and Brett and Carla decided to continue the therapy treatments at home in Spring Lake.

Little Lydia Elizabeth Hatton signing copies of My Angel's Cookbook at Spring Lake Yacht Club From left: Gary Verplank, Vicki Verplank, Little Lydia, Amy Eggert, Gabrielle (Brie) Hatton

Over the Fourth of July holiday, Little Lydia signed copies of her *My Angel's Cookbook* for the sailors who gathered around a table set up for the occasion by the cookbook committee. It would be her last outing at the Spring Lake Yacht Club. Little Lydia died on August 11, 1997, one day shy of her sixth birthday. The doctors finally confided that, indeed, Little Lydia was "N-myc amplified," but they knew we all (including them?) needed to have hope right up to the end.

What happened? ... I theorized in my diary:

> Scientifically curious I am, but not religious. But these signs—the cloud halo not around the sun but directly above us while we fly hundreds of balloons with messages for Lydia written all over them. And the butterfly, three days in a row, flying around our boat four miles out in Lake Michigan while we watch Brett skip the new Melges 24, named the *3 Lydias,* in a national regatta. ... And always her special angel. My next-door neighbor brought me a little white angel statue for my garden when Little Lydia died, and that angel has become very special for me, too. It has become a small shrine that I tend with loving care, sitting atop its own little table, surrounded by flowers and herbs. My agnosticism is being sorely tested. Why do I latch onto the signs that Little Lydia gave me? Her ethereal being is beyond my comprehension. So are my five children. If this had not happened, dragging out for almost eighteen months, how would I have known their staying power?

After Little Lydia's death, a beautiful large sailboat with an intriguing design painted on both sides of the hull had been delivered to the parking lot across the street from Brett's house in Spring Lake. It was a Melges 24 that had been ordered by Greg Hatton, who explained, "The idea for the Melges 24 came about as a means of giving Brett something fun to do after two really bad years."

The Melges 24 was the hot new boat, and a lot of sailors in Newport Beach and Southern California were buying them. Greg had the new boat delivered to Spring Lake by a good sailing friend, Eric Hood, and his crew from Zenda, Wisconsin, home of Melges Performance Sailboats.

The art for the boat was the product of another family artist, Anne Layman Hatton. The registration numbers on the bow were phony. The number on the port side was Little Lydia's date of birth. The number on the starboard bow was the day she passed away.

Greg explained that "The name *3 Lydias* came about by necessity. We wanted to name it *Lydia.* Then everyone asked which Lydia it was named after. So the problem was solved by naming the boat after all three Lydias."

The boat's first race was the Gay Regatta (Fruitport to Ferrysburg), on Spring Lake. Jule ("J. B." to our kids) was part of the crew.

The 3 Lydias artist, Anne Layman Hatton, enjoying the ride

Chapter Sixteen

BROKEN BARRIERS

Illicit international incidents.

Paul Eggert alone on Egg Crate

After the sale of the Benton Harbon shopping center, Paul signed an agreement with C.D. Barnes Associates for the purchase of property and an office building to be built at 5211 Cascade Road in Grand Rapids. According to the strict guidelines of the IRS 1031 exchange, Paul had to close on the new property within six months of the June sale of the shopping center.

And C. D. Barnes General Manager, Todd Oosting, had his work cut out for him too—constructing a beautiful office building, with the major work done by the closing deadline in December.

Todd's always pleasant manner with me (the broker representing the buyer) convinced me that the job would be in line, on track, and on time. And Paul wasn't worrying, either; he was thousands of miles away, in Curaçao for most of November.

5211 Cascade Road, Grand Rapids, Michigan

We closed on December 5, 1997. My broker commissions using the 1031 exchange for properties topped the half-million-dollar mark for the year.

I thought about the Old Kent Bank's attitude toward women in business; if they had been willing to wait for me to repay my RBI loan, they would have been paid back with interest. But bank officers insisted that I was not capable of earning enough money in a timely manner, and they forced me into bankruptcy in 1994. Only three years would they have had to wait. But again, this was western Michigan; it was still a patriarchal business community. But that was soon to change.

Paul and I rejoiced to see a beautiful healthy baby boy join Brett and Carla's household in December. We knew their whole family would want to join us on *Egg Crate* next month in Key West for the Melges 24 regatta. We would have to move fast to make this rendezvous possible.

Paul prepared *Egg Crate* in the fall for the long cruise from Curaçao to Aruba, Jamaica, the Cayman Islands, and up the Yucatán channel around the northwestern tip of Cuba to Key West. Castro's Cuba was still off limits to our cruising community.

Paul's trusty general manager, and all-around factotum, Stan Luben, took over my real estate obligations. Where would I have been without him? I had another 1031 exchange opportunity on the horizon with the sale of the Bittersweet shopping center in Louisville, and, lurking in the background, another lawsuit dealing with my real estate commissions on the past 1031 exchanges.

We left for Curaçao right after Christmas. We needed a third mate on *Egg Crate* if we were going to keep moving without waiting for weather windows. I located Mary Currier in Aruba, and we offered to fly her to Curaçao if she would sail with us to Key West. For decades, Mary's dad, Bob ("Os") Currier, was a terrific crew and cook on the Chicago and Port Huron Mackinac races. And Mary's older brother, Bob, was a renowned boat skipper on the ocean circuit. Mary would be tough, fun, and unafraid—it ran in her family blood, and she would be showing true colors soon.

Leaving Willemstad with Mary Currier

The minute we pulled out of the harbor at Willemstad, we were faced with thirty-five-knot trade winds and high waves.

Mary looked at me and asked, "Is this normal?"

I responded, "Yes."

We continued on to Aruba with little fanfare, but as soon as we passed the southern tip of Aruba, the seas went flat under the island's protection from the eastern trade winds. I turned the wheel over to Mary, feeling this was a good time for her to practice before we hit the heavy seas north of Aruba. We stopped briefly in Oranjestad for supplies. Mary took over again when we headed north for Jamaica. We both were wearing heavy weather gear, with our straps loosely wrapped around equipment on deck. Paul was below, storing the new supplies.

All of a sudden, we were *whammed* with a huge blast of wind, along with the usual square, confused waves that showed up once we cleared the island.

I could see we were going over, and I screamed (I am sure) at Mary to hang on to the wheel. I grabbed a deck post on the high side and watched

Mary, who was loosely strapped. The mainsail slammed onto the water, the lower rail underwater. Then, as fast as the boat broached, it righted itself. I yelled at Paul, down below, knowing he would be tossed around, along with anything not secured.

Paul came up laughing, saying he had never seen anything like what had just happened in the cabin. The tool shelves flew out and, just as quickly, flew back in place, including the tools! Paul stayed on deck and checked our straps. He tightened ours, and I insisted that he stay strapped in at all times too while working on the broken equipment on deck.

Smiling, Mary asked, "Does that happen all the time?"

"I hope not."

We had no major incidences (that I can remember) the rest of the sail to Jamaica. Having a third person on board to break up the twenty-four-hour schedule over the three or four days of sailing across the central Caribbean was an unaccustomed treat. We arrived at Port Antonio, on the northeastern coast of Jamaica, during daylight hours and pulled into a marina for repairs.

After stopping for a day in Grand Cayman Island, we moved on. We probably had 500 to 600 hundred miles of open water before reaching Key West. And a large storm was brewing in the Gulf Stream. The Yucatán current was powerful, and it could be leading the way as we raced north around the end of Cuba, but we needed to stay away from the Cuban countercurrent flowing west along the northern coast of Cuba. We would soon find out that we needed to stay away from Cuba, period.

When we pulled into Key West, we raced around town to find our families. All of them were camping in one huge house in downtown Key West. Fritz and his fiancée, Caren Frutig, would be stopping by to catch some of the action, and two other Melges 24 crew members, Chuck Simmons and David Fox, would be staying there too. And to keep all the little kids in tow, Lydia brought her nanny, Tiffany, and Tiffany's mother, who flew in from Green Bay to join the party.

Even Mom and Dad were there—thanks to Lydia, who flew from Boston to Tampa to drive Mom and Dad to Key West, a distance of almost 250 miles—and then, of course, Lydia had to drive them back (with four-year-old Alexander keeping Grandma Verplank company in his back car seat.) Only Lydia understood the time, the energy, and the money needed to make possible this long road trip for Mom and Dad at their advanced ages of eighty-seven and ninety. And only Paul understood how important it would be to find a dock for Mom and Dad (who used a walker) to board *Egg Crate* to watch the offshore races. No way could Dad climb in a small dinghy.

Where would Paul find a dock during race week? From the chatty guy moored next to us, who suggested we use the government breakwater. I would have to slip the boat into the protected side of the breakwater and hope we didn't get stopped or hemmed in by other spectator boats who might follow our lead. And *Egg Crate*'s sixty feet from bowsprit to stern davits would not be easy to maneuver around them. Oh boy—what was I getting into! …

Egg Crate had plenty of spectators aboard. David Fox's parents, Dr. Dan and Mary Fox, arrived to watch the Melges 24 races, along with the whole crew staying in the Key West house. Our location on the breakwater was the best around, because we were next to the harbor entrance, so we could enter and exit quickly. There were about seventy-five Melges 24s racing in the ocean off Key West, and their colorful spinnakers provided quite a spectacle.

The nightly gatherings were wild. A different bar or restaurant every night. Lydia let everyone know that she wanted *her* own boat! "All the work done to make this rendezvous possible was only for the boys! …" Everyone laughed at her rant, but I felt she was right. No one had worked harder to bring our sailing family together for Key West race week. And who could imagine that Michigan sailor Amy Eggert (who wasn't racing) and California sailor Chuck Simmons (who was) would meet and fall in love? Did we have a lifetime event unfolding on *Egg Crate*?

Greg had some final thoughts about their Melges 24: "The Melges circuit was very expensive. By the time we got the boat back to Newport Beach we decided to sell it. We owned it for ten months and blew a lot of money on the program. But we had a riot. Chuck Simmons met Amy Eggert on the campaign. We rented houses for family reunions. We had fun in Annapolis and DC. All in all, it was a great episode in our long and unique sailing life. The Melges 24. What a ride!"

After Key West race week, I flew home. I had to vacate my real estate office at the dock company, which everyone knew I wasn't using, and move all my files to the garage at our Yardarm condo. Relatives always made fun of my dozens of file boxes filled with pictures, videotapes, cassettes, films, diaries, and legal papers, but when I was sued in March for an excessive real estate commission on my 1031 exchanges, they were happy I had filed the backup papers to defend my position, which, happily, influenced the judge's decision.

It was time to look for commercial real estate for the upcoming 1031 exchange needed with the sale of the Bittersweet shopping center. We had time to shop, however, because we had some control over the closing timetable on the sale. I contacted Bill Bolling of Paramount Properties, Stan Wisinski's company in Grand Rapids, and Van Martin of Coldwell Bankers in Lansing. Stan Luben had many Realtor contacts too, after decades in the real estate business in western Michigan, but his contacts were not very eager to work with me if they were not the exclusive buyer's agent. I had to promise Stan that I would share my buyer's commission if they found an appropriate property that fit our strict 1031 exchange timetable. And that would happen in the near future.

When I returned to Florida, Paul found a cozy spot to park *Egg Crate* next to Diana and Bill Wipperfurth's condominium on Longboat Key. And next to their favorite hangout—the Buccaneer Bar and Grill. And, thankfully, they were there when disaster struck.

No one mentioned to us an important fact known to boat insurance companies: Tampa Bay is the lightning capital of the country, if not the world. Ah ... yes, there we were, just a few miles south of Tampa Bay, docked in a small marina with the highest stick around (seventy-five feet) and with a huge storm building over the central Gulf of Mexico pointing in our direction. I watched a hundred miles of lightning strikes lighting up the radar on the television screen in our master stateroom. I knew we were going to get hit. And I could see directly overhead through our giant hatch the top of the mast and the stays that surrounded the mast—backstays, sidestays, forestays. Paul fell asleep at about 11:30 p.m., while I was glued to the television network's radar screen; I had never seen a storm path like this: a hundred miles of solid supercell thunderstorms pointed at us.

Fifteen minutes later ... lightning struck the top of the mast like a bomb blast! First sparklers, then flames soared down every stay, circling the mast like a flaming tepee in an Indian raid.

I was so startled, I hit Paul and shouted, "Wake up! We're on fire! We took a direct hit."

Paul turned over in bed, looked up through the hatch at the mast, and replied, "I don't see anything."

The soaring flames were gone. I ran out to the main salon and looked at our radio and CD player. Their cabinets were scorched around the edges, the wires melted together. The heavenly welder had paid us a visit. The mast was charred at its base in the salon because of its interior wiring. The stay plates were charred around their bases on deck.

The electronics were gone—all antennas on mast and spreaders, three GPS, radar, autopilot, VHF and SSB radios and TV, DVD, and CD stereo systems with multiple speakers, all computers or cell phones plugged in, etc. The electrical system was burned out—and it wouldn't be the last time I experienced an electrical fire on a sailboat. Modern cruising sailboats were built more like the *Queen Mary* than the *Mayflower*.

I had recently purchased boat insurance, a requirement not in Paul's lexicon. I would have to call the insurance company and find a fax machine in the morning. Fortunately for us, Bill and Diana were still awake after midnight, sitting in their living room—probably watching the storm and *Egg Crate*'s sparkly fireworks display. Diana made me stay in their condominium. She knew I was scared of fire any place on the boat. The smell of burned wires was enough to scare anybody (except Paul). The next morning, I called the insurance company, and Paul checked out his favorite suppliers—sort of like Christmas for Paul. With a $6,000 deductible, our insurance company would suffer five times that amount to repair and replace the damages to *Egg Crate*'s electrical network from one bolt of lightning.

It was easy to leave Paul in charge of the smelly repairs and fly back to Michigan. I was in a work mode of ten days a month in Michigan, and it worked well for Stan Luben too. Stan and I reviewed our options for commercial real estate purchases. We liked the McKay Tower's downtown location, but not the old building; no wonder the price was low. The other office building on East 28th Street was a much better choice; it was quite new and handsomely designed, if slightly impractical, with two main entrances at opposite ends of the building. And the price and timing were right for our 1031 exchange needs.

Our race was a drifter most of the way to Key West. Our biggest competitors were the shrimp pots that dotted the shoreline as we approached Key West.

The race from Key West to Cuba had become an iffy proposition. The Tampa Bay to Havana race dated back to 1930, but it ended in 1959 with Castro's Cuban revolution. In the 1990s, Cuban Americans in Miami appeared to create problems for American sailors who wanted to race to Cuba. Nevertheless, the format for the Havana race was revived in 1996 by independent sailors from local clubs on the Florida coast. I knew of no problems reported by sailors who had to get clearance from immigration, agriculture, and customs. Of course, they could not bring back Cuban goods or spend money in Cuba. If we went, we understood that we were to say that we were "fully hosted" by Marina Hemingway (meaning that the normal fees for dockage and visas were waived).

The Race to Havana began on Palm Sunday, April 5, 1998, in the early evening, with a small group of experienced sailors. Gary, Vicki, Fritz, and Caren joined us for this exciting trip—my first opportunity to return to Havana since 1956! And we had a mystery guest join us who claimed he was bringing needed medical supplies to the island.

I knew *Egg Crate* was faster than most of the other sailboats, and no way did I want to arrive before dawn, which was possible sailing a course to Cuba that was about a hundred miles from Key West. It was overcast in the morning as we approached our destination. Our guest pilot was not half as experienced as Paul—searching for the "surf" which would identify the sand banks near the entrance. I didn't notice them, either, but Paul saw them immediately in the distance, and I slowed down until I could see down the channel to the marina. I straddled the two banks, using the high surf as a guide, and *Egg Crate* glided in to a cement dock that looked just like the breakwater at Key West.

We were one of the first boats to arrive, and our knowledgeable guest jumped off to greet the harbormaster as if he were the captain. At least he spoke Spanish. (I didn't understand any Spanish.) We were greeted in English and asked if we wanted to plug in to the nearest electrical outlet. That became a cause célèbre. We didn't have dockside cables of the right amperage. We plugged in anyway. I left all those decisions to Paul, along with the consequences that resulted. I knew our generator didn't like the meeting.

We parted with our itinerant guest. He had his own transportation, and we hired the local taxis. Every vehicle seemed ancient, but our drivers seemed very happy to have our business. Yes, American dollars would be just fine in payment. We took off to explore Havana. Fritz had the address of a wealthy Cuban friend's family home. We found it … we thought. It was being used as a day care school for young children. Fritz commented on the remains of the magnificent houses—the "palatial ruins." He felt the rich, wealthy Cubans brought the revolution on themselves; they "earned the revolution." To Fritz, it was "interesting to see the time capsule" and to see the Cuban countryside still so "bloody poor."

Caren added, "What a fabulous place it must have been in its heyday." Caren could see the potential in all the old structures ripe for "gentrification," and she hoped to return some day. (But her daughter beat her to it.)

We all wanted to have a double frozen daiquiri in Hemingway's bar, La Floridita, and most of us wanted to take the short drive out to Hemingway's country house and museum. Some of Hemingway's best-loved novels were written in a tiny square tower next to the main house. The museum was a valiant effort to protect books, papers, and memorabilia. The poverty that pervaded the countryside was evident in this historic place as well.

We raced back on Wednesday evening, April 8. None of us had any problems with any governmental officials.

However ... less than a week later, guess who was attempting another quick sail to Havana. Paul Eggert. I was visiting Mom and Dad at their condo in La Peninsula, just north of Marco Island, and I pleaded with Paul not to take his son, Chris, and girlfriend, Jennifer, across the Gulf Stream with a huge storm on the way. Paul said they had to go now because Jennifer had to return to Michigan at the end of the week to take important pedagogic exams. Paul knew that boating accidents often happen when sailors let their personal schedules override commonsense weather decisions. But he was a dad, his son wanted to see Cuba, and Jennifer, a neophyte sailor, had no idea what she might be facing (or, as it happened, not facing).

Off they sailed ... and quickly encountered high seas. Chris reported that he and his dad decided that Jennifer might never sail again if she faced the roily surf surrounding the entrance to Marina Hemingway. And Jennifer reported that she braced herself on the master stateroom bed as the boat rolled turbulently from side to side in the high surf. They docked in the same area as we had the week before, but they were told that their health exams would be "twenty dollars each," and there were other miscellaneous charges. They were on their own ... and only Jennifer understood any Spanish. She said Paul and Chris ordered food by pointing at the pictures but "everything ordered had eyes staring at them."

Now for the trip back to Key West. ... Bad weather, combined with bad luck, created a difficult situation: their main halyard broke, so no mainsail, and stuff in the bilge plugged the shaft, so no engine. With only the jib for power, the trip sailing back was long and arduous. Officials were put on notice. This was not going to be a quiet reentry. And, as soon as *Egg Crate* docked in Key West, Jen and Chris rushed to board their plane back to Michigan. Paul was left facing the music.

What would be my role? Find a lawyer who specialized in illicit international incidents. After all, I had friendly lawyers in Washington, DC. I called them and they referred me to a Washington law firm that had associates in Texas who handled minor embargo infringements. These lawyers loved people like Paul. What would be his penalty? (Embargo cases could be harsh. Some were up to ten years in prison.) And would the penalties be greater than the legal fees generated by the team of lawyers assigned to this case? Would they impound *Egg Crate*? Letters went back and forth. Charges were made. None of us understood what was happening. Who was talking to whom? Settlements were made. Penalties were paid. Lawyers' bills were debated. It ended, finally.

It was an expensive education. After all, the Trading with the Enemy Act was enacted in 1917.

Chapter Seventeen

TRUMPET VOLUNTARY?

Ghost of Gatsby... Art courtesy of Anne Layman Hatton

On June 1, 1998, the bold headline in the *Grand Haven Tribune* read: "DEVASTATING WINDS". According to *Tribune* writer Becky Vargo:

> They heard a noise that sounded like a tornado, or maybe a freight train. The wind had come up with gusto. Moments later that wind blasted through the Tri-Cities and Ottawa County at more than 120 miles per hour.
>
> The destruction left in its wake was like nothing anyone had seen in this area for years. Roofs were torn off buildings, condominiums

collapsed, trees were twisted and uprooted, boats were lifted right out of the water and wires were everywhere.

And where was I on Monday morning, June 1, 1998? Winding my way down Fruitport Road between a few downed tree limbs and underbrush, heading for the Grand Rapids airport. I had an early flight to San Francisco that I did not want to miss. Fritz was performing Tuesday night in a Noel Coward review at the elite Pacific-Union Club, a magnificent structure at the top of Nob Hill in San Francisco.

I didn't know that our MC sailboat was floating in the lake, having been blown off its dolly at the Spring Lake Yacht Club. Or that Brett and Carla's property had taken a direct hit.

I didn't know what had happened until I got to the airport in Grand Rapids. Paul said everyone was safe. He was on his way to the yacht club to rescue the MC. He joked that I couldn't lift anything anyway, saying, "Don't waste your plane ticket."

The musical event Tuesday evening was a very formal affair—white tie, to mimic the traditional Edwardian era, in the style of Noel Coward's high-class London clubs in the early 1930s. And tails would require me to buy a very proper long dress. Caren and I rushed around downtown San Francisco, shopping for a conservative, matronly gown befitting a sixty-five-year-old mother of the groom-to-be. We found one. My dress looked like something that Joan Crawford would have worn in the 1930s: long sleeves, high neck, fancy jeweled wide waistband, narrow long-skirted dinner gown. At least it would work for this occasion (and hasn't been worn since.)

Fritz sang a famous Noel Coward ballad, "I'll See You Again," and then the witty, fast-paced, "Mad Dogs and Englishmen," both while accompanying himself on the piano.

I would be very proud of Fritz's performance, but I felt he wasn't satisfied—too rushed, with not enough time to practice. His wedding was taking place next month in Grand Haven's tiny St. John's Episcopal Church. It would not be a tiny wedding reception, nor a tiny rehearsal dinner. I needed to hurry home to prepare for the rehearsal dinner, which would be just as elaborate as the wedding itself.

When I drove through Spring Lake and saw the uprooted trees lining both sides of the main street, I could have cried. All of my out-of-town children and their spouses would be shocked and disappointed to find their beautiful tree-lined village stripped almost bare; the wind shear sliced a narrow path down the main street, all the way to the cemetery on the eastern edge of town.

It would take a gargantuan effort to put our little community back together before the wedding on July 11. My assistant, Pat Young, who lived ten miles out of town, said her husband grabbed his heavy train saw and a partner and offered to help Spring Lake residents clear the trees and debris because "they were the hardest hit." The volunteer effort was amazing. We would be ready.

What is the most important ingredient for a successful party? (Or a successful radio station?) The music! Fritz and Caren could plan the music for a traditional Episcopal Church wedding. With Fritz's classical background, I expected the baroque. (In December 1952, his dad argued with the organist at the Presbyterian Church in Grand Haven, who contended, "Bach is not wedding music.") And Fritz's first choice for his wedding ceremony? Prelude and Fugue in C, BWV 531, by J. S. Bach (1685–1750).

I offered to find two bands for the Friday and Saturday night soirees. My wedding present to Fritz and Caren would be "the best dance band in Michigan" for the wedding reception, and an appropriate band for Friday night's Roaring Twenties rehearsal dinner party, which no one would want to miss. Our in-house artists designed clever invitations for the Roaring Twenties party. It was clear to all guests that they had better rustle through grandparent closets for the top hat or fringed skirt.

From left: Dorothy and Martin Johnson, Donald and Marlene Freeman

Everyone who was invited to the wedding did show up for the rehearsal dinner party in costume. Gary and Vicki's home, built in 1922 on nine "carefully tended" lakefront acres, would be the perfect palatial estate to represent an era of success and excess. With that in mind, our hosts for the evening, Gary and Midge, rounded up some rare antique cars and a photographer for the iconic picture.

It would be Dad's birthday on Friday, July 10, 1998. This was going to be a celebration at many levels! Dad would be ninety-one, and it would be Greg's birthday, too.

Where could I find a grand band that sounded like Glenn Miller, Benny Goodman, Tommy Dorsey, or Louie Armstrong? Right in the Tri-Cities! (When I was growing up, we used to dance at Fruitport Pavilion and sometimes Hyland Gardens or the Barn in Grand Haven.) All those bands and many, many more played at the Fruitport Pavilion and sometimes one of the other local dance halls. Bob Warnaar and Doug Baker kept the local bands organized during the 1970s and '80s. In 1998, I called Doug Baker, now in his eighties, and asked for his help. There happened to be a huge swing band, the Lakeshore Ensemble, that still played together for fun and entertainment. I hired them all. Since we would be outside in a giant tent, I did not worry about the sound reverberating off the walls. They played very danceable music—right out of the 1930s and '40s ... and even the '20s. At eighty-eight, Mom could still dance the Charleston, and her grandsons kept her busy.

Fritz's groomsmen excelled in their chosen fields—whether medicine, architecture, literature, or music—and their toasts at the rehearsal dinner amazed some of my dinner guests. My longtime New York friend and former business partner in TV and radio, Allen Boorstein, sat on my left (or often stood at our large round table), videotaping with a small professional camera throughout the evening toasts, and Don Lubbers, president of Grand Valley State University, sat on my right, commenting on each toast—or roast. When Jay Mead, a roommate of Fritz's at Yale and then a teacher of English literature in a private prep school, finished his oration, Don exploded with admiration, saying, "Where did these men come from?!"

I can't forget the in-law roast. What a warning to Caren from all four of her future sisters-in-law and Fritz's one brother-in-law. And it was a surprise! No wonder ... guess who got roasted. *Ouch.*

I haven't mentioned the weather because it was Michigan at its zenith—warm but not humid. And that would make the scene much more inviting, with white linen covered tables spread across the lawn instead of the parking lot of the Spring Lake Yacht Club.

My first view of the guests assembled in the nave of St. John's Episcopal Church was breathtaking. Tears flowed. I couldn't help it. This was where my children were baptized. Being here gave me the sense of going home.

Well ... theater in a small city like Grand Haven doesn't always go as planned. William Boyce's Trumpet Voluntary was a unique baroque piece for trumpet and keyboard—too difficult for our trumpet player to repeat, and the head usher, Braerton Carr Hatton, waited a touch too long to start the wedding party down the aisle. Suddenly the music stopped, and the trumpeter put down his trumpet. The bride waited. No music. Daddy and daughter marched down the aisle without music. And the show continued with the opening sentences of the Book of Common Prayer, page 423.

Now to the pièce de résistance: the "best band in Michigan." They were from Detroit. The band started to play as soon as the first guests arrived at the yacht club. Wow! What a blast! We danced until the band left in the early morning light.

I had to scramble after the hullabaloo created by a month of wedding festivities. We finally closed on the Louisville "Bittersweet" shopping center sale on July 1, which meant that my 1031 exchange timetable required an identification of three potential properties to purchase by Friday, August 14. We had eliminated the McKay Towers from our list in June, but we still liked the 6000 28th Street office building.

I listed it two days before the 1031 exchange deadline of August 14, 1998, and Paul closed on his "new" Bittersweet property on October 28, 1998.

Chapter Eighteen

THE CARIBBEAN 1500

...They cheerfully reported such mishaps as lost genoa halyards, a double wrapped spinnaker, a shredded mainsail, and loss of navigation lights, yet insisted they were having a wonderful time.
The 1999 Cal Fearon Memorial Award

Returning to the Bahamas in the winter of 1999 was not the exciting destination for us. We were looking forward to the Caribbean 1500 Rally in November; Paul's friend and Grand Haven native, Steve Black, convinced Paul to join the rally, which began in Chesapeake Bay after the hurricane season and ended 1,500 miles later in the British Virgin Islands.

However ... when I heard that there was a new marina being developed at the megaresort of Atlantis in the Bahamas, I explored the possibility that our little fifty-four-foot sailboat might be allowed to dock there. Yes, we could stay as long as we liked, and all of our guests (yes, *all* of them) could enjoy freely all the features and services of Atlantis.

Paul had been to Nassau many times on *Egg Crate,* but I knew he would ask me to navigate our route through Nassau Harbor and into the Atlantis marina. With some trepidation, I motored down the narrow entrance of the small landlocked marina. We were surrounded by a few megayachts ("up to 240 feet"), but there was plenty of room along the inner breakwater to park, if they would let me. I worried about turning around. I had no bow or stern thrusters; I needed to be prepared for a sudden dismissal.

Now Paul took charge; he suggested I pull along the breakwater and dock, which I did. Then, Paul asked the dockmaster for permission to stay there. Yes ... for now. It was the prime location—an unobstructed view of the enormous Atlantis complex. Paul and I could not believe our luck.

We became very popular very quickly. For good reason. The immense water park, the marine habitat, and the aquarium exhibits were so extensive and so unique, I couldn't wait to show our friends and family.

The Atlantis marina became home base for a month. Paul and I sailed first with Chris and Jennifer to Eleuthera Island, skipping the dreaded

Devil's Backbone passage to Harbor Island, and then took a ferry to Harbor Island—a picture perfect island with golf carts and pastel villas and pink beaches that were deservedly world famous.

When our next guests, Karen Pierre and Jim Piper, arrived at Atlantis, we had a hard time convincing them to leave the marina. After Karen and Jim returned to Michigan, Paul and I sailed to Freeport/Lucaya on Grand Bahama Island. Freeport had the only other international airport (Nassau being number one) in the Bahama Islands. Paul wanted to work on *Egg Crate* at a marina in Lucaya, and I wanted to fly home to catch up on business obligations.

Paul Eggert checking out the slide.

In mid-April, I flew to Miami to meet Caren and Fritz at the Biltmore in Coral Gables. "It's the wine *under* the table, not *on* it, that's important," whispered Fritz to me when I appeared at their table for dinner. (Since Fritz was the auctioneer for the large charity event, we got great *under*-the-table wines—none of which I could afford, *malheureusement*.) Then we hit South Beach on that warm tropical night. Streets and bars were jammed. The trendy, art deco atmosphere could have been SoHo or San Francisco.

I left for Freeport/Lucaya in the morning. *Egg Crate* was the cleanest I had seen it—ever. I wanted Paul's cleaning staff on board evermore. All for seventy dollars.

We had good weather crossing the Gulf Stream, but what a current! We aimed for Fort Lauderdale in order to hit Palm Beach. And we arrived with no chart for the harbor. After going aground on sand twice, we backtracked to find the Intracoastal Waterway and arrived at the PBYC (Palm Beach Yacht Club) anchorage an hour later. It was an impossible anchorage because of wind and current, and we would be forced to move.

The elegant lunch the next day at the PBYC with Os Currier and wife, Joan, was a culture shock for Paul. Blazers were a necessity. We spent the afternoon shopping for boat supplies and charts for the East Coast. Later, we biked all around Palm Beach, past the Breakers, the Lauder house, and Ocean Drive, and then up Worth Avenue to Taboo's, and on to Rinaldi's, the Colony, the Breakers, and Bradley's for dancing. (Yes, we danced on the bar at Bradley's and biked back across the bridge to *Egg Crate* at midnight.)

With Allen and Helen Hunting on their trawler, Stow Away

Allen Hunting and dogs picked us up promptly at 4:30 p.m. on Sunday. We toured their beach home, checked out their pristine forty-eight-foot trawler/cruiser, and enjoyed dinner at Old Port Yacht Club, which was Os Currier's favorite hangout, according to Allen.

Paul and I caught the 8:30 a.m. Flagler Bridge opening the next morning, and we headed north with good charts. It was 250 miles to Amelia Island. We sailed a hundred miles in twelve hours, but then things slowed down as we were forced to leave the Gulf Stream.

Of course, the wind picked up as we entered Fernandina Beach channel on Tuesday evening. We roared in between jetties, with twenty knots of wind, and asked for "local knowledge." A marina dockmaster asked where we were and our size, advising us to slow down but keep coming toward town.

The downtown marina made room (sixty-five feet for sixty-one feet of *Egg Crate*) on the breakwater. The current was going into the dock, the wind was going out, and the tides were seven to nine feet. (The dockmaster said the wind and current would cancel each other out, so plan on no wind or current.) The people on the dock clapped loudly after my hairy landing, and owners on surrounding boats came and shook my hand. I just shook, period. Paul made me a *big* drink—and one for himself too.

We planned to leave for Cumberland Island, to anchor in front of Greyfield Inn on Thursday, so we rented a car Wednesday morning, put our bikes in the back, and headed out to see all of Amelia Island. After we met one of the original Carnegie family founders of Cumberland Island back on our dock, we were excited to visit the island and dine at Greyfield Inn on Thursday.

Cumberland Island was my first look at the wondrous Georgia forests.

It was a most enjoyable day. I took pictures of the tiny, dilapidated chapel where John Kennedy Jr., was married in September 1996. His entourage used the Greyfield Inn, as well as the services of Fernandina Beach, for the wedding.

Paul and I were eager to prepare *Egg Crate* for the Caribbean 1500 Rally, starting in Hampton, Virginia, in a few weeks. On Friday, October 15, we pulled into Hilton Head, South Carolina, to wait out Hurricane Irene, which was pummeling South Florida. By Monday, Paul suggested we go as far as Harbor Town marina. We got fuel, and left about 1:00 p.m. No remnants of Hurricane Irene. We decided to continue to Charleston when we found a twenty-four-hour marina available. It was 1:00 a.m. when we arrived in Charleston Harbor—pitch-black, with few lighted buoys. After two hours of searching, we finally woke someone up at the marina, and he threw a beam of light on *Egg Crate*. It was 4:00 a.m.

The next day, I wanted to explore the USS *Yorktown,* the massive aircraft carrier built and commissioned during World War II. Its location was next to our marina. Paul and I biked to the gangplank and asked if we could bring our bikes on board. First, the official said no, but we pleaded with him, explaining that both of us had arthritic hips and couldn't walk the 900 feet of the flight deck. He relented ... then asked if we could walk the stairs for a tour of the bowels of the ship. Of course. Down, down, all the way to the monstrous engine room; the ship reached speeds of more than thirty nautical miles per hour during the heat of battle. One can only imagine the heat generated in the engine room, and the power needed to jockey the ship in positions to launch ninety airplanes. The complex construction of this floating factory built more than fifty years ago was difficult to comprehend—in a modern computerized world.

Paul knew I wanted to bike around downtown Charleston, but he was getting worried about reaching Hampton, Virginia, before November 1. (It was 285 nautical miles to Diamond Shoals at Cape Hatteras, and 117 nautical miles farther to Chesapeake Bay.) We compromised. I got a quick three-hour taste of the handsome architecture of the charming old South, and Paul got fuel and water for *Egg Crate*.

We were not planning to stop until we reached Hampton. I was at the wheel as we approached Cape Hatteras. It was an eerie feeling, knowing the wrecks that resulted from navigating too close to Diamond Shoals. It was dark, windy, and cold. So cold that I put on layer after layer of winter gear—gloves, hat, scarf, and over it all, my life preserver with safety straps. Paul was sleeping. I was sailing on my own, with only a reefed mainsail, having chosen a path that I considered safe. We had been at sea two days. We still had 117 nautical miles to go after we rounded the cape. I was chilled to the bone and miserable. ...

The downtown marina in Hampton was a lively scene when we appeared a day later. A neat and new-looking sailboat pulled in on our port side. And an affable owner hurried over to introduce himself as J. P. When Maureen Murphy showed up to join our crew, J. P. really loved her enthusiasm and her appreciation of his friendly manner. He nicknamed her "Mo." Then Bill Venhuizen arrived as our fourth crew, and J. P. was dutifully impressed, thinking, I am sure, that Paul and I had planned this assignation.

With J. P., we had a friend who would be checking in on SSB radio for as long as possible on our journey into the unknown (especially for J. P.). Yes, Paul and I were old salts compared with most of the sixty-plus sailors venturing into a 1,500-mile offshore journey. And, for the first time, I had a competent engineer, Bill Venhuizen, on board. Bill could keep repairing our rickety SSB fax/printer, as well as our electrical and electronic connections that would be key to our conversing with the fleet every morning during the race—not to mention tracking the eye of the fast-moving storm predicted to soon develop into a hurricane. (Hurricane Lenny, nicknamed "Wrong Way Lenny," traveled from the central Caribbean to the Atlantic in a west-to-east direction, which was unprecedented in the history of tropical record keeping.)

The fleet had an assigned hour every morning when they checked in on SSB radio and reported their positions (latitude and longitude). I started to give a detailed report on the weather every morning because I received printed weather reports on our SSB fax machine two or three times a day.

After the first three or four days at sea, the wind started to blow, and the seas started to rise. Maureen was at the wheel and turned around to face giant swells off the stern of the boat. She asked, "What's going on?"

I answered that it was a trough, which usually precedes a front and lasts a few hours. After another three days, the waves in the trough had swelled to twenty-five or thirty feet, and Maureen commented slyly, "About that trough that lasts three or four hours, ..."

Three or four days of wind gusting from thirty-five to forty-five knots began to take its toll on *Egg Crate*. Bill thought we were overcanvassed. The genoa halyard broke, sending the large jib into the ocean along the port side of the boat. Next, the spinnaker ended up with a double wrap. It was too windy to use it anyway. Finally, the mainsail, with no reefs in it, couldn't take the burden any longer and shredded before our eyes. But we had our engine, storm jib, and autopilot. Some of the smaller boats had worse problems; one had dismasted. With Hurricane Lenny approaching, United States Coast Guard rescue boats were dispatched from Puerto Rico.

We pulled into the marina in Spanish Town on Virgin Gorda, in the early evening at the end of the eighth day of the race. The boatyard was a flurry of activity, pulling boats as quickly as the lifts could work. We had two days to strip the boat of all sails and gear on deck and secure the lines to the finger docks. Paul worried about the wind and wave action tipping the side rails under the docks. The boat was a maze of crisscrossed lines.

Maureen and Bill hoped to catch one of the last planes to leave the island the morning of our third day. We found out later they both were successful; but where they landed, we never found out. The eye of the storm had passed thirty or forty miles south of us. The peak winds of 155 miles per hour were found in the southeastern quadrant of Hurricane Lenny. We were located in the northwestern part.

Paul and I were warned by the committee that we must attend the award ceremony. It is a good thing they told us; Paul probably would have skipped it. Why would he want to remember that race?

Paul's friend, Steve Black, the originator of the Caribbean 1500 Rally, was giving out a new award: The 1999 Cal Fearon Memorial Award:

"For their demonstration of the courage, determination, and persistence in the face of adversity that made Cal Fearon a cherished member of the cruising and rallying community ...

"The award this year goes to a boat that never let mechanical, electrical, or rigging problems interfere with their determination to have an enjoyable passage. ...

"It is a pleasure to present the 1999 Cal Fearon Award to Paul Eggert and Joyce Hatton of *Egg Crate*."

Chapter Nineteen

THE MILLENIUM

Yes, Peter Pan still dwelled among us. But Wendy wouldn't be back to cook for him or sail with him.

With Maureen Murphy, Raffles Hotel, Singapore, April 2000

William Grimes reported in *The New York Times* Travel section, on December 29, 1999:

IT'S a matter of record that humans cannot resist the primal urge to celebrate wildly when another year goes down the tubes. When it's a year, a century and a millennium all at once, mass madness takes hold, a frantic desire to greet the new dawn from an unusual vantage point. ...

At Foxy's Tamarind Bar, on the Great Harbour of Jost Van Dyke island in the British Virgin Islands, the owners are bracing for a flotilla of yachts and pleasure boats in 1999, based on inquiries that have been coming in for the last year. The harbor gets hundreds of boats on New

Year's under normal circumstances. "This time there could be 5,000 people," said Tessa Callwood, an owner of Foxy's. "There could be 10,000 people. We have no gates. ... "

Well! My brother, Gary Verplank, and his family had celebrated New Year's Eve for decades at their winter residence in Puerto Rico, but in the fall of 1999, Gary chartered a sixty-five-foot Irwin sailboat, with Captains Oliver and Sabine. Gary knew where every sailor in the Caribbean wanted to celebrate the millennial New Year's Eve. (Or "Old Year's Eve," as Foxy would say.)

Paul had to worry about rigging and sail repairs, or replacements, required on *Egg Crate* before he could fly home for the Christmas holidays. But Paul wasn't going to miss Foxy's this New Year's Eve, even if he had to motor over to Great Harbor. Nor was I. Even if I had to train for days to stay awake until dawn. (Paul was a late-night pro.)

I was thrilled that Gary and Vicki and their kids—Tony, Ashley, and Kyle, all in their twenties—would be meeting us at Foxy's. And Paul was happy to have on board Amy and Chris and their significant others.

Finally ... December 31, 1999: We arrived at Great Harbor too late to find an anchorage—especially for two rather large sailboats that needed plenty of scope. (It would not have mattered when we arrived in Great Harbor. We probably would have been crowded out by powerboaters who wouldn't care—or wouldn't know—if they hit us in the middle of the night.) We moved over to White Harbor and found anchorages. But we would have to travel to Foxy's in Great Harbor in our small dinghies around a point that faces the open ocean, which could make for a wet and rough ride while decked out in our party gear, especially at 3:00 or 4:00 a.m. And we wouldn't find any friendly cops who would keep the drunks at bay—or out of our bay.

The beach, the bars, the bandstands—all were jam-packed, with a sea of dinghies lining the shoreline. Paul and I stood in back of the stage, where we could enjoy the local fare and hear the music.

At about 2:30 a.m., some of our group wanted to leave Foxy's. That meant everyone had to leave. I was disappointed, but Paul said we could drop people off on their boats and then return to the party. Gary's family had their own dinghy, but we had a mixed crew on our dinghy when we approached *Egg Crate* in White Harbor. Paul dropped me off and said he would take the others back to Gary's boat.

Paul never returned before dawn. There I sat ... listening to their music and laughter for hours. I—the one who didn't want to leave the party at Foxy's. I harbored a big burn the next day.

Gary and his son Tony made matters worse with their comments: "You should have seen Paul. He was so funny. He was on a roll … you missed a great party."

And Paul's attitude? He slept all day.

The first week of the new millennium was not going well for me. After we stopped in St. Thomas for shopping and supplies, we planned to sail back to Palmas in Puerto Rico with Gary's chartered yacht, which was waiting in Charlotte Amalie Harbor. The trade winds were unusually strong out of the east; it was going to be a bumpy, fast ride. But, first, I had to exit our boat slip.

When I stepped behind the wheel, Paul's kids looked at their Dad with disbelief. "You're not going to let her back out! …"

Paul told them I did all the docking on *Egg Crate,* and he dismissed their concerns. I was still at the wheel when we caught up to Gary's boat, and I told Gary that Paul and his kids wanted to fly our large spinnaker, since we now had enough experienced sailors on board who could handle the lines. Gary thought it was too windy. So did I, but Paul wanted the kids to be happy, so up it went—and almost immediately upended *Egg Crate.*

"Head down!" the kids shouted.

Gary said he watched us in dismay, thinking we would broach. The boat spun around to windward, tipping as we spun, until the spinnaker lost air and *Egg Crate* flattened out. Down came the spinnaker.

When I docked *Egg Crate* in Palmas del Mar, I prepared to leave the boat so that I could run errands.

All the kids pitched in to help Paul wash the decks. As I was stepping around the mops, one of the kids asked me, "Why don't *you* help wash the deck?"

Paul never said a word. He knew who scrubbed the decks and who cooked the meals—and never the twain would meet. Off I went. I made a plane reservation home and arrived in time to celebrate Brett's birthday on January 9.

After Paul's family left Puerto Rico, Paul took off too, sailing *Egg Crate* alone, single-handed, for Key West, a thousand-mile voyage in the open Atlantic Ocean. Paul said he slept during the day, relying on other skippers to stay out of his way. ("That's the way the pros do it.") He sailed nonstop for almost a week, and when he reached Key West, he anchored and slept for days. I couldn't believe he would do something so foolish, so dangerous. Yes, Peter Pan still dwelled among us. But Wendy wouldn't be back to cook for him or sail with him.

I was eager to get back to work. Stan Luben had potential buyers for Paul's popular Popeye's franchise located on a busy corner in Grand Rapids. According to Stan, it was so-o-o popular because more chicken slipped out the back door than sold out the front. It would be another 1031 exchange property, because it had no debt and no mortgage.

On February 4, 2000, Gary's wife, Vicki Verplank, had the honor of introducing the man who would become the forty-third president of the United States, George W. Bush. At the GOP's annual Lincoln Day Dinner on the Grand Valley State University (GVSU) main campus in Allendale, Michigan, our family was so proud of Vicki. Her leadership experience as the president of the Spring Lake Village Council during the past two decades was evident in her controlled, smooth demeanor during her warm introduction of Governor Bush.

Mom and Dad celebrated their seventieth wedding anniversary on February 15, 2000. A colored photograph of them graced the front page of the *Grand Haven Daily Tribune.* They didn't look ninety. More like sixty. Dad told the reporter that "a little give and take kept their marriage strong for 70 years. ..."

Dad had plenty of opportunities to discuss my future with me while I took him to his weekly therapy sessions. He worried most about my living alone. Dad couldn't imagine life without Mom around, and he wanted to see me happy with a responsible mate who would care for me. He wasn't sure Paul Eggert was the man, but he was sure Bill Seidman never had been. Dad resented Bill's hypocritical ways—always assuming I would be the loser. I felt quite the opposite. I loved to learn, and Bill loved to teach. When Bill ran out of courses, Paul Eggert took over. And then, my eternal friend, Maureen Murphy, who never married, offered to teach me about the new "third world" order, courtesy of the U.S. State Department.

Maureen's itinerary for her spring trip to the Far East was so extensive, I fretted over the cost of my plane ticket—my major expense. Since Maureen would be traveling on United Airlines (and its Asian partners), I conferred with my favorite United agent, Bryan Carlson, and found a round-the-world ticket, good for one year, that allowed thirteen stops, as long as I didn't backtrack on my itinerary. Maureen would be traveling business or first class on long flights, but I would not pay the higher fees for upgrades.

Because I was going to so many third world countries for the first time, I needed shots, pills, and visas. That was a nightmare for Maureen too, because she had to feed me all the information I would need for each country and provide the applications for the visas, when necessary. Maureen had to turn her complicated itinerary over to the US State Department's not-so-efficient in house travel agency. She'd go crazy making sure it was accurate and upgrades to business or first class were approved in a timely manner. Maureen needed the unlimited luggage allowance in first or business class; not for her heavy, bulging briefcases but for my multiple suitcases, hat bags, and cameras. I truly was the bag lady. And with all that travel gear, I was beginning to limp noticeably from my degenerating left hip. Why she put up with me, I will never know!

Our first stopover was Tokyo. I learned my first lesson about the value of a diplomatic passport when we prepared to board the plane to Singapore. Since I was traveling with Maureen, I was upgraded to the same class as Maureen. And the first-class experience on an Asian airline like Singapore or Cathay Pacific was the pinnacle of service: gorgeous stewardesses in gorgeous uniforms serving a buffet of delicacies, champagne, and orchids. My kids always said I was Maureen's "cover," and I certainly felt privileged to fulfill that role.

Fritz Hatton was our source for fine hotels in the major cities in Asia. (When Fritz was head of operations for the Far East at Christie's, he often visited their many regional offices.) Fritz said our first choice in Singapore should be the iconic Raffles Hotel at 1 Beach Road. Was Raffles on the US State Department's approved list of hotels? It was. Did they have room for us? They did.

When we arrived at the airport gate in Singapore, we were greeted by US State Department employees who whisked us through a separate diplomatic arrival area, luggage in tow. No waiting in lines. No waiting for taxis. Someone at the State Department did expert advance work. Lucky me!

Off we sped to the Raffles Hotel. Its front entrance was magical—had I been transported back in time? The British Empire's indelible footprint was everywhere.

From Singapore, we flew to Colombo, the capital of Sri Lanka. All my advantages of an American *anything* disappeared, because the Sri Lankans were fighting a two-decade-long civil war. The Tamil Tigers controlled the northern part of the island and blew up government buildings the day of our visit.

Maureen warned me, "Stay out of the countryside. Stay away from all government buildings, including museums."

I was relieved to get out of Sri Lanka after a few days' stay.

Maureen's next assignment was Bangkok, but we planned to sneak away for a long weekend in Siem Reap, Kingdom of Cambodia, to view one of the wonders of the ancient world, Angkor Wat.

Angkor Wat Siem Reap, Cambodia

Maureen and I could not have picked a hotter time of year to explore the massive stone monuments. It was April. The sun was directly overhead. The temperature was easy to remember: 100°F during the day. The pool's water thermometer at our Raffles Hotel read 100°F too, and the famous Raffles bar gave us no relief, either, because there was no air conditioning in the hotel or the bar or the restaurants.

Now that we had seen an earthly model of the cosmic world at Angkor Wat, we were happy to return to Bangkok and our air-conditioned hotel. It was Easter Sunday. Maureen is an Irish Catholic. She knew where to go … all day long. After church services in the morning, we had to go to the Chatuchak Weekend Market.

From Bangkok, we journeyed to Calcutta, a city of thirty million or more. (Who's counting?) Not a city on any tourist's list. But I had a list. I wanted to experience Hindu religious ceremonies but not insult the believers. And I wanted to visit missionary Mother Teresa's home base. Both were possible, because the US consulate-general's office provided me with a driver and guide who spoke (I think) English.

My family asked me, "What made this trip special for you?" I wrote them in May of 2000:

My naiveté about the depth of the cultural and technical changes that have taken place in Asia, especially in the third world countries like Cambodia and India, is appalling. Why did I have to *go* there to know this? Others have commented to me that they know this is taking place, because they do business in Asia.

But I still didn't believe them. When I visited Japan in April 1988, Tokyo businessmen seemed smarter, more productive, and more inventive than their New York counterparts. (Breakfast meetings at the Palace Hotel just sizzled with excitement.) And when I spent a month in 1980 trying to do business with the Chinese government in the southern provinces, I expected little infrastructure and found none.

This trip was different. The world has been Americanized, right down to our five-year-old guide at the Angkor Wat ruins in the Cambodian countryside who demanded dollars, as well as the teenage punks at the Calcutta airport who grabbed our bags, loaded them into the consulate's van, and refused the Thai bahts offered instead of dollars.

Then there was the Internet, e-commerce, and wireless communications. My tourist guide in Calcutta (very much needed in a city of thirty million) led me through the muddy alleys to the important Hindu shrines, cell phone in hand. My e-mail was instantaneous, whether I was in Singapore or Siem Reap, Cambodia.

The alphabets on city signs in Colombo were a combination of English and Sanskrit or Arabic.

The billboards along the seven-mile stretch from the Calcutta airport to the heart of the city were in English only. But below the billboards lived millions of refugees from Muslim Bangladesh, in the most abject squalor imaginable. The contrast was stark and disgusting. The divide between rich and poor seemed insurmountable, and the "untouchables" were left untouched. ...

Before I used up my round-the-world ticket by returning to the United States in May, I tried to visit Ireland, but I couldn't make satisfactory arrangements when I left Calcutta, so I had to backtrack from the United States to Dublin. I was meeting my godchild, Lisa Brownlee, her mother's sister, Marily Wilson, and a large contingent of the Purkiss family for Lisa's cousin's wedding to a beautiful Irish lass.

With my godchild, Lisa Brownlee, touring Ireland in May 2000

I was enthralled by my visit, feeling a bond to the country of my children's Hatton heritage. Their great-grandfather, William Hatton, was born on a sixty-acre farm near Dublin in 1864. He emigrated to New York City in 1886 and moved to Grand Haven, Michigan, in 1910 to become general manager of the Eagle Leather Company.

I was still swooning, it seems, while I wrote this report of my visit to Ireland in May 2000:

Ireland—*First Impressions*:

<u>Green.</u> No wonder everything connected to the Irish is green. (What color is mist?) But those ruddy complexions … wind and water?

With Marily Purkiss Wilson, Dublin, Ireland, May 2000

Language. The Book of Kells and The Long Room in Trinity College. James Joyce. W. B. Yeats. I bought the most delightful book in the picturesque seaside village of Kinsale: photographs of the Irish countryside as described in the poetry of W. B. Yeats, accompanied by passages from the applicable poems. It's ethereal ... dreamy. (I never allow my mind to wander so freely. If I did, I believe that I, too, could write poetry. Need time more than concentration. And, if completed, I believe it should be very satisfying. Do I need to be in Ireland to capture that self-discipline?)

Kissing the Blarney Stone

Stories. How the Irish like company! They are so civilized. What would they do without their pubs? Pubs they can visit every day. A little Guinness to loosen the tongue. No wonder the country was poor until the communications revolution. The Internet was made for them. And are they using it well. The country is booming. Immigrants are needed to service the Irish worker, whose skills in literacy are in high demand by America's Silicon Valley industries.

People. I am pleased with my children's heritage from Loftus MacIl-hatton (?). They surely inherited the language skills...and the dramatics.

Food. Fabulous. Much better than any country I have ever visited, especially my own. I never had a bad meal or an upset stomach. Potatoes, every which way, with lamb or smoked salmon with homemade bread—that was my diet for a week.

Landscape. The countryside reminds me of trips to Bermuda, where each inch of that tiny island, viewed by tourists like me, looked like a landscaped fairy tale. Here, too, nary a billboard is found. Yes, I see this through the usual early morning or late afternoon heavy mist, but that only adds to the otherworldly charm of this beautiful island.

When I returned from Ireland, I was inspired to write a poem about "My Toddler Quinn"—my articulate two-year-old grandson.

My Toddler Quinn

Hard to navigate my mind,
Oh so many paths to find;
Every moment treasure chests
Baubles…
Bubbles…
Amid the wordfest.

Cuddly breath soothes and smothers:
Father, mother, sister, others.
Leave me *free!*
No bars, no twine envelop me,
Me, and my individuality.
See me *be!*

"My Toddler Quinn" in bumblebee costume

Our annual Coast Guard Festival's week of celebrations (always the first week of August) culminated on Saturday night with thousands of spectators lining the boardwalks and docks of Grand Haven's riverfront facing Dewey Hill. Boaters lined up neatly too, (many rafted together) in various floating craft that almost filled the Grand River channel. Speedboats marked "Police" roamed up and down the channel to keep a waterway open for emergencies and protect a safety zone in the channel directly in front of Dewey Hill.

We were waiting, while picnicking on Pronto Pups, gyros, beer, or booze. Everyone knew darkness arrived as late as ten o'clock in Michigan's eastern daylight time zone. We all knew too that, suddenly, patriotic music would blast from huge loudspeakers located across the channel on Dewey Hill, accompanied by the spectacular undulating colorful spray of Grand Haven's famous musical fountain. After that, the most powerful fireworks of the year would erupt on the huge Dewey Hill sand dune. Many of us had experienced how dangerous the situation could be when it was windy. Small fires or backfires of fireworks grew out of control quickly. Once they did, the whole grassy sand dune could burn out of control.

Controlling drunken skippers would keep the police craft running too. During one encounter, before our small speedboat stopped, I grabbed the wheel from my teenage nephew and his cousin.

The police asked if I had been at the wheel "a moment ago." I said I went below to use the head but quickly returned. They asked how long I had been a sailor or boater ("more than fifty years"), but they did not make me take any sobriety tests. The advantages of being a female sailor—in our patriarchal paradise.

Paul Eggert invited me to ride with him the next day, August 6, 2000, to a memorial service for Sally Roth at the Roth family's historic log-cabin cottage on Torch Lake. I was eager to let their only daughter, Sherry, know we wanted to honor her amazing sailing family, whom I had known and loved for the past fifty years. But I wasn't proud of my performance; I had a hard time holding back the tears once I hugged the grandchildren. But Paul seemed proud of me.

Paul was going to be busy for the next three weeks, preparing for his son Chris's wedding to Jennifer Kennedy. My brother Gary and his wife, Vicki, would be the hosts once more. Their home and expansive landscaped grounds provided a perfect romantic setting for a summer outdoor wedding. I did not feel I'd be very welcome in this setting, however, since Paul and I had parted ways six months earlier.

Before Chris and Jennifer's wedding day, Paul surprised me with an invitation to dine at his office condo. I was bemused by his announcement that "he" was cooking dinner. Perhaps he had an ulterior motive.

Paul offered to sign a new postnuptial agreement that would result in some major changes in our future travel plans. (No, the agreement wouldn't be post divorce ... just post wedding.)

First on Paul's agenda: A visit to the Annapolis boat show in October. Paul wanted to buy me a new powerboat. One that would replace his old speedboat that he promised his eldest son, Josh. I had little interest in his project until we arrived in Annapolis. There were "cuddy" cabins being displayed that represented a new dimension of the "speedboat" category. I was attracted to the Cobalt line of powerboats, with their rich-looking (oh ... oh) deep-blue painted walls. When I saw the Cobalt 293, there was no turning back. The layout of the cockpit and cabin, the mobility, the power, was more than I could have imagined. (It slept four, and had a head with sink and shower.) It was about thirty feet long and only eight wide. That meant we could trailer it behind Paul's Prevost bus … anywhere in the country. And that we planned to do. Paul ordered a new Cobalt and asked for delivery on Chesapeake Bay in the spring of 2001.

Second on Paul's agenda, but not to his liking: a new hip. It happened rather quickly. Paul noticed during the summer that his hip would lock up, and then he couldn't move … at all. I suggested a visit to my renowned orthopedic surgeon at Massachusetts General Hospital in Boston, Dr. William Harris. The list of innovations and developments in the Harris Orthopaedic Laboratory was mind-boggling, including the first implantation of highly cross-linked polyethylene in 1999 for total hip replacements. My first consultation with Dr. Harris in 1996 was suggested by Anthony and Lydia. Dr. Harris still wouldn't operate on my left hip, even though I limped noticeably, because it didn't hurt. He said pain usually drove his decision.

Paul and I sat in a crowded waiting room (always crowded) in Dr. Harris's office on Tuesday, October 10, 2000. After a lengthy wait, Paul's name was called. Paul stood up, but he didn't move. His hip locked up. Everyone was looking at Paul, standing still. Paul smiled at everyone and quipped, "You're probably wondering when I am going in." Everyone laughed. When the nurse approached, Paul's hip unlocked, and we limped in together. Dr. Harris didn't need convincing about Paul's condition, and he scheduled Paul for surgery a week after Thanksgiving.

Chapter Twenty

A PRODUCERS ACADEMY

"… as the nation's longest-serving university president,"

GVSU President Arend "Don" Lubbers and former President
Gerald Ford Photo courtesy of "The Lubbers Legacy"

Before I left Washington, DC, in 1993, I called on a prominent programming executive at PBS. On their national television stations, PBS had been running some classy documentaries like *The Civil War* by brothers Ken and Ric Burns. I asked her what she thought could be done to spread the wealth from the three dominating "third party" programming sources (WGBH in Boston, WNET in New York, and WETA in DC) to local PBS stations, such as WGVU-TV in Grand Rapids.

The PBS programming executive was blunt in her assessment. "Regional stations like WGVU-TV need to hire station managers who can attract the talent to do original programming."

Investing in talent can be a risky proposition. It's not like investing in buildings that carry your name on them for the next century. No one had been as effective and efficient over the past twenty-five years in finding money for Grand Valley State University (GVSU) projects as its energetic president, Arend D. ("Don") Lubbers.

In the mid-1990s, I asked Don for a tour of the GVSU Meijer Broadcasting Center in downtown Grand Rapids. It was a beautiful new building, with sparse broadcast equipment for its radio and television stations. The first concern of WGVU-TV's staff was the upcoming equipment expense for switching from analog to digital broadcasting, which was being mandated by the FCC within the next decade. Nonprofit PBS television and radio stations had to rely on charitable contributions and federal funds for their wobbly existence. WGVU-TV was tiptoeing into the on-air commercial advertising scene with minimal part-time "underwriting" staffs. (Original programming production required a lot of underwriting—and a lot of faith in the talent.)

However, WGVU-TV was licensed to a state university that existed to educate students (and faculty?) in all fields of endeavor. The university charged tuition for theater and music and speech and photography and film and television classes. (Ken and Ric Burns's father taught photography at GVSU from 1974 until 1993.)

I suggested a new department for the university: a "producer's academy," or some similar name. Naturally, I wanted Ken and Ric Burns to lend their names and their talents to the academy.

A talented writer, director, actor, and producer who knew GVSU well was Bill and Sally Seidman's son, Tom Seidman. After Tom graduated with a bachelor's degree in theater arts from Dartmouth, he attended the American Film Institute's elite Center for Advanced Film Studies in Los Angeles. In the 1980s, Tom worked as a DGA (Directors Guild of America) assistant director with famous filmmakers Robert Redford, Peter Weir, and Clint Eastwood. Tom also developed and produced for KSPN-TV the entertaining Aspen newsmagazine television series, *Two for the Road,* based on L.A.'s highly successful KCBS-TV magazine series, *2 On The Town*).

Tom showed some interest in my project but told me I needed to work in two areas simultaneously: the community of independent producers and the sources for potential funding. I asked Tom what he foresaw my role to be. Tom replied, "The grand overseer. The energy behind the project. The person who puts together the key people—the facilitator. ..."

By the late 1990s, I could see that teachers at all levels were transforming teaching venues from the classroom to the computer. We all watched exciting and brilliant teachers become the new actors in the information technology (IT) age—and their lectures were being produced and transmitted via the Internet. GVSU's professors, like the rest of the collegiate universe, were going to take advantage of the new IT learning opportunities.

On October 21, 1999, I sent President Lubbers a letter:

> Thank you for your interest, encouragement, and support for more locally produced quality programming at WGVU-TV and AM-FM. The TV and radio producers at WGVU were very enthusiastic supporters of the idea also, when I met with them two weeks ago.
>
> For TV, most of the prime-time programs originate at five major city PBS stations: Boston, New York, Philadelphia, Washington, DC, and Los Angeles. I see no reason why WGVU-TV 35 and TV 52 can't be the sixth. ...
>
> When I discussed that idea with Bill Seidman, he liked it so much that he encouraged me to put a committee together to influence the process and raise the necessary financing. *And* he said he would contribute financially to this project. His comments:
>
> (1) WGVU original productions would put Grand Valley State University "on the big map"—it would be the mouthpiece for the university nationally.
> (2) WGVU has $200 million of resources if all six stations were commercial (two TV and four radio).
> (3) Grand Rapids is "one of the richest cities."
> (4) Grand Rapids has the Van Andel Institute, the International Institute at the Seidman Business School, and similar resources for programming.
> (5) We would need a financial plan to make this work, and we could ask BDO Seidman or other local accounting firms to help us put this plan together. Local programs are already commercially based.
> (6) We *can* hire top talent.
> (7) GVSU will be a leader in the education of students in this field.
> (8) There is a greater need for original programming for the Web and interactive education and entertainment.

I had another meeting last week, with Casey Wondergem of Amway. I've known Casey since high school but have not talked to him for years. Certainly, I wasn't prepared for the totally negative reception

I received from him when I broached the subject of WGVU television staff and facilities assisting the Van Andel Institute in various ways. ...

Casey didn't think much of WGVU's current TV studios or producers, commenting that "Amway's own directors/producers have done incredible work. ..."

I asked about Dick DeVos's potential interest and participation in my idea, since Dick was on the GVSU board of directors. Casey's observation: "Dick has his hands full—in business with the Amway turnaround, in politics with his fight with the governor over charter schools, and at GVSU with his interest in moving the Nursing School downtown. He is working with Joyce Hecht on that project."

Finally, would you believe, Casey said, with no equivocation, "I see no fit here between the Van Andel Institute and what you are proposing. Maybe in four or five years, after we've had a chance to finish some of our build-out plans." All that, come February 2000, from Casey, the new Director of Public Affairs for the Van Andel Institute.

I plan to be home from our rally/race on November 16, 1999, and would like to contact you upon my return. I will be available by cell phone on the boat until I return to Spring Lake...

While in New York City, I met with a loft neighbor who had a PhD from the University of Michigan in media studies and communication. He had written and produced successful documentaries over the past twenty years and had ideas for my multimedia project. I planned a meeting with him in New York City in January for GVSU personnel and Bill Seidman. If people were going to fly to New York, I had to be prepared with a tight schedule and full agenda.

Bill Seidman suggested we use the University Club on West 54th Street for meetings and hotel rooms. That venue would be fun. I met Bill for lunch at the University Club many times in the past when he was being interviewed by reporters or entertaining business associates. The University Club had a rule in the dining room: no papers (showing) and no phones. (So how was the lovely female reporter from the *Wall Street Journal* going to take notes during her interview of Bill? Very discreetly. Her notepad was about two inches by three inches, if that, and she held it partially on her lap.)

Our meeting took place January 26, 2001. I was pleased to see Bill in a location that brought back fond memories—for both of us. Bill was gracious but businesslike in greeting John Gracki, the Associate Provost at GVSU, and Matt McLogan, Vice President for University Relations. I was unsure of their impression of my guest, who conceived a multimedia institute as a leadership organization that would not only ferment and produce future knowledge based materials, but an organization that would coordinate national and world-class projects that would distinguish GVSU and provide income for its efforts. Long distance learning, in its various forms, would be specifically addressed. His scope would range in form from broadcast (and narrowcast) materials to future interactive multimedia, which would exploit emerging tecnnology and the distribution opportunities involving both the Internet and the World Wide Web.

But his request for immediate payments from a state university sent his proposal into orbit, and information technology was moving so fast that I felt only the young could communicate its future.

Don Lubbers was planning to step down after thirty-one years as president of GVSU (" ... as the nation's longest-serving university president," according to *The Holland Sentinel* on September 12, 2000.) Don told me early last spring because because he had no idea how a new president might view our plans, and he wouldn't be around to guide the project. However, Don was quoted, in the same *Holland Sentinel* announcement, urging, " ... Grand Valley State University officials to expand academic offerings to keep pace with the growth of West Michigan. Lubbers recommended Monday that the Board of Control consider the creation of an honors college, a School of Pharmacy and *classes on the Internet* as part of its growth before he announced his plans to retire at the close of the academic year." [Italics mine.]

Bill was busy, too, with his many corporate board meetings and family commitments. Bill and I said good-bye the next day with the conviction, I believed, that if this project was going anywhere, I would need to find guidance from the next generation.

Chapter Twenty-one

THE ENTOURAGE

And the Blaze and the Prevost bus had to be there...

On the road...to the West Coast

There were a few important ingredients in Paul's and my new "post-nuptial" agreement that had me running in the winter of 2001. Since I would own 50 percent of any new property purchased through a 1031 exchange for the sale of the Popeye's franchise and would be the buyer's broker for its purchase, I couldn't move fast enough to see what was on the market in our price range.

Paul had insisted on a seven-figure sale price for his Popeye's franchise in Grand Rapids. I couldn't believe he wouldn't drop the price a few hundred thousand dollars. Paul was adamant about it; I thought he was being unreasonable. To get his funding, the minority buyer had to rely on government minority programs set up with Grand Rapids banks who made the final decisions.

Guess who won. Paul got his price, and I got a timetable for our next 1031 exchange. The clock started running the day we closed on the sale of

Popeye's. I had forty-five days to choose up to three properties—and six months to close.

Stan Luben worked on the sale of Popeye's for a year and asked many real estate agents to look for available properties in our price range. But Paul did not discuss our postnuptial agreement with Stan. I could be in a bind handling a real estate agent who found a good property that was not his listing, because I was the buyer's broker, and he wasn't. It came to a head when the Butternut shopping center in Holland was shown to us. The real estate agent who found the property was neither the listing agent nor the buyer's agent. Stan asked me to share my commission, because he had asked the agent to look for properties. After I heard how hard the agent worked for Stan finding the property, I split my commission with him. And with Paul too(!). I liked the agent's choice. And Paul knew I would work hard to make it a success.

Paul's hip was healing nicely, but he couldn't go sailing in the winter of 2001. Instead, Paul decided to paint the bottom of *Egg Crate*. When I visited the boatyard in Florida, Paul had rigged up a system under the boat where he leaned on one crutch while painting with his free hand. He loved working on his boats. And that included *my* new Cobalt power boat, which Paul named *Blaze*. He ordered all kinds of accessories, including the latest GPS equipment and radar, and an expanded bimini with full isinglass and screen enclosures—the latest air-conditioned tent. (Thinking of mosquitoes in Maine or sweltering anchorages on Lake Powell?) And then—without asking *me* (the owner of the new boat)—Paul switched "his" really old mortgage on "his" boat *Egg Crate* to a new 100 percent mortgage on "my boat" *Blaze*. Hmm. ...

I often joked about taking Paul to "Bali Ha'i" when we sailed into Samana Bay in the Caribbean. But would he want to see the real Bali? I had Continental airline tickets that were about to expire, and Jimmy Hunting had exclusive villas in Bali that were available for lease. I e-mailed Jimmy, not knowing if he was at his home in Aspen or Bali or Thailand. Jimmy was delighted to hear that I wanted to see his special project—a development now totaling twenty-five luxurious villas. Jimmy was sorry he couldn't be there to show us his beloved Bali, but he gifted us the use of his personal three-bedroom villa.

Paul and I were totally confused about our new surroundings upon arriving in busy downtown Seminyak in Bali—until we drove into our quiet gated community which featured traditional Balinese architecture. When the Villa Hotel's staff opened the back door to Jimmy's villa, we entered a tropical world of pleasure and beauty—rich tapestries filled the spacious great room that opened to an enclosed courtyard of lush natural gardens wrapped around an immense brightly tiled wading and swimming pool. A small Balinese style structure across the courtyard served as the third bedroom or private study.

Jimmy was addicted to surfing, a sport for which Bali was famous. However, surfing was not of interest to either Paul or me. The staff suggested we explore Bali's one-stop Adventure Tours.

Paul was going to be in his element. His first choice was the Cycling, Rafting, and Elephant Safari Ride Day Trip, advertised as:

"… Bali's best value for a day of action and excitement. Starting high in the mountains you will descend by bike through some of the islands most beautiful scenery, followed by a quick change into rafting gear and 1½ hours of fun filled action rafting on the spectacular Ayung River. After lunch, there is a short drive to the Elephant Safari Park, where your own elephant awaits you to take you on a 30 minute safari through the jungle. …"

We couldn't leave Bali without visiting the Bali Bird Park, which was also part of the adventure company's package. It was memorable—for magnificent botanical gardens as well as varieties of Indonesian parrots and other rare birds housed in a huge walk-in aviary. We brought home a coupon for a free week's vacation in a Bali hotel that expired in one year. I won it in a crazy promotion. It would be a honeymoon gift for Amy and Chuck at their fall wedding.

Paul and I were planning to cruise in the *Blaze* in the late spring of 2001, on Chesapeake Bay along the Eastern Shore. I contacted Maureen Murphy in Georgetown and asked her to join us. We needed a guide, and Maureen would turn out to be the best.

I knew St. Michaels by reputation only, but Maureen had friends with historic houses that had been lovingly preserved for centuries. From St. Michaels, we cruised south to Oxford, a major port for the ferries centuries ago.

Smith Island, where the natives had "relic" accents, was a long cruise down the Eastern Shore and required an overnight stay. The *Blaze* enjoyed a fast trip back up the middle of the bay, with Paul at the wheel and me glued to the GPS and radar so we didn't smash into the maze of boats and buoys that I was

tracking. *Whew!* At forty-five miles per hour, I had more of a workout than Paul, shouting directions over the roar of the powerful engines. We were a good match—and that was a true convenience!

Paul wanted to leave the Prevost bus and Cobalt trailer in Annapolis while we cruised up the East Coast to Maine. We told J. P. Smith we planned to call on him in Boothbay Harbor. But first I had to navigate out of Chesapeake Bay to the Atlantic Ocean. I needed specific navigation cards for each part of our journey. I was able to buy cards and charts that took us as far as Boston Harbor, but there was nothing available locally for the Maine coast. I would need to buy them in Boston.

Paul feeding Smith Island swan

Our route from Annapolis took us north about fifty nautical miles to the entrance of the Chesapeake and Delaware Canal. From Cape May to New York City was another 130 nautical miles. I knew that Paul would want to take the ocean route whenever possible, rather than any Intracoastal routes, because he could move fast—especially on the *Blaze*.

Before we left Annapolis, I called my nephew, Charlie Hatton, at his office near the twin towers in the World Trade Center (WTC) in Lower Manhattan. (Charlie's office had been in the WTC, but after the 1993 bombing in the garage under one of the WTC towers, his company took the precaution of moving from the iconic WTC to an office building across the street.)

Charlie was a sailor and knew his way around the waterways of New York City. I suggested that we pick him up at a dock in the Hudson River and cruise to his yacht club near Oyster Bay, Long Island. Fortunately, Charlie thought it would be fun, and he made it work.

The next morning, we suffered through our first rainstorm while sleeping on the *Blaze* at Charlie's yacht club in Oyster Bay. It poured inside the boat as well as outside. We were going nowhere. … I called Lydia and told her to wait for my call before driving to Newport, Rhode Island, from their home in Cohasset. When the weather started to clear around noon, Paul and I left Oyster Bay. After a few hours cruising up the middle of Long Island Sound, the wind picked up, and the waves began to build. I was in a panic, checking our GPS, bouncing around crashing waves, trying to locate a safe, nearby, navigable port. It was Stonington, Connecticut.

We had a short trip (thirty-five nautical miles) to our marina in Newport Harbor the next day. It would take Lydia and Alexander about the same amount of time to drive there from Cohasset.

Lydia couldn't believe the array of navigation tools I had accumulated for our trip. With the help of my GPS card, we cleared the bustling summer traffic in Newport Harbor and arrived in Martha's Vineyard in a few hours. We enjoyed touring the island before cruising to Nantucket Harbor, which was my favorite docking spot because our marina was in the center of town.

We split up, leaving Nantucket, and motored into Scituate Harbor before Lydia drove home to Cohasset. We waited for Lydia's clan to get organized before all five of us headed for Maine. From Boston to Boothbay Harbor was about a hundred-mile straight shot north-northeast.

The *Blaze* did not have the perfect bed-and-breakfast" setup at the dock in Boothbay Harbor. Far from it! In their crowded sleeping quarters, our three guests had a choice: fresh air or privacy. It didn't take long for them to decide that their Cohasset home was the best choice.

And Paul quickly left too, flying back to Annapolis to pick up his bus and boat trailer. Paul was ready to move on—to the West Coast. His daughter, Amy, was marrying her sailor beau, Chuck Simmons, in Newport Beach, California, in October. And the *Blaze* and the Prevost bus had to be there; they were part of Paul's entourage.

Chapter Twenty-Two

9/11/2001

... and how one remembers it....

Gabriel García Márquez
Living to Tell the Tale, 2003

We always seem to remember where we were when we hear about a shocking event. When the Japanese attacked our giant naval base in Pearl Harbor early Sunday morning, December 7, 1941, it was announced on our radio in the early afternoon. My dad brought us all into our living room on Jackson Street in Spring Lake, Michigan, to listen to live reports as they filtered in. I lay on the carpeted floor all afternoon in front of our radio, along with most of my family. Midge was ten, I was nine, and Gary was seventeen months old. The radio was housed in a large engraved wooden cabinet that was the centerpiece of our living room.

When President Kennedy was assassinated on Friday, November 22, 1963, I was sitting in our living room at 1821 Doris Avenue in Grand Haven, Michigan. Our four older boys were in school. Lydia, age three, and Brett, age ten months, were home with me. Someone, probably Jule, called me between 1:30 and 2:00 p.m., Eastern Standard Time, and told me to turn on the TV. At 2:00 p.m., Walter Cronkite, the nation's favorite news anchor, put down his dark-rimmed glasses and solemnly announced that President Kennedy was dead.

Where was I on September 11, 2001, when I heard that the twin towers of the World Trade Center (WTC) had been hit by hijacked planes? In a tiny news and coffee alcove adjoining the huge log-lined lobby of a Glacier Park lodge built on a former Indian reservation. Paul and I slept late in the somewhat primitive guest rooms that housed no modern communications. When we appeared in the lobby at 10:30 a.m., Mountain Time, we noticed guests gathered in small clusters around the lobby; most were crying.

I entered the coffee shop to ask the clerk why people seemed so upset.

He stared at me in amazement and said, "Don't you know what happened this morning?! Go in the bar and look at the TV!"

We were surprised to find the small bar open and crowded, and we glanced at the TV set behind the bar. Both towers were imploding! The video was streaming the collapse of the towers. (It was afternoon in New York City.) I grabbed my cell phone, which had a New York City area code, and called our loft on Broome Street—hardly a mile north of the twin towers.

"*How* did you get through?!" shouted a familiar husky voice. Julio and Alison were there! They were alive! They were too busy to talk!

But how my son remembered 9/11/2001. On Thursday, September 13, 2001, Julio sent us a lengthy email. Here are excerpts:

We're still in shock. Watched it all from our roof on West Broadway and Broome, one mile directly north, on an absolutely clear day without a cloud in the sky. Came back to SoHo from out of town Monday nite to take care of biz … Tuesday a.m. I was on the rowing machine, listening to my Walkman, when the DJ, at around 8:50 a.m., said something hit the WTC (World Trade Center). Dashed up to the roof … popped open the door to the roof, immediately squinted from the glare of the beautifully strong sunlight bouncing off the aluminum painted tarpaper (strange what a beautiful day it was), glanced up and WHAMMO!!!—there it was, right out of Hollywood, the big, gaping maw of a giant black gash in the middle of the north tower, surrounded by fire and black, black smoke. On the adjacent roof stood a neighbor. I cross the low bricks separating our roofs and he starts to talk. He says the low flying plane woke him up. He shows me the Polaroids he had taken moments ago after it hit.

The neighbor has set up an oversized watercolor pad and paints on the tarpaper and he's squatting, painting the twin towers and a few adjacent buildings. He looks up at me, shrugs and says, "What else can I do?" With ruler and pencil, he roughs in the WTC. "Hey, I got a telescope. Should I get it?" I say, "Sure. Why not?" He ducks down his fire escape to the window that leads into his loft on the top floor, and returns with the small yet powerful telescope on a tripod. We take turns looking into the black gash on the north side. There's a woman in the middle of the huge hole, standing on the lowest blown-out floor, standing alone, sometimes waving, right at the edge of the façade. She's surrounded by empty blackness, rising three or four stories above her and maybe five to ten feet on either side before the wrecked skin of the building starts a jagged outline that roughly imitates the contour of a large plane. Unbelievable. She's all alone. Then, next to her, another person appears momentarily and disappears into the blackness. "What is she doing there? How could she survive that?" asks my roofmate. We chatter on.

Smoke is billowing out of the west side of the north tower. The main hole where the jet went in is about two-thirds up the tower. Helicopters are circling high above. *Rescue that woman! Where is that skyscraper rescue technology? Float in a helium blimp with modified everything and pull those people out of there!*

I'm staring at the towers when, in the slice of sky that separates the two towers, I get a glimpse of a huge black silhouette. I feel the tingle of a positive thought: *A C-130 transport plane with fire retardant destined for the fire?* BOOM! Ball of flame, mushrooming red and orange. Ball of smoke, black, turning piss-yellow and gray, following the flames. Fire. Lots of it. *Holy shit, the other tower just got hit!* Among other thoughts and words, we realize that maybe it's not too safe up here on the roofs of these five-story buildings. We confer. We each have Walkman radios in one ear. The radio says there's another missing hijacked plane. *Hijacked? The hijackers must have flown them into the buildings. What if the next one kind of hits and kind of misses the burning towers and ricochets in SoHo?* These questions are bounced around by us. Soon the thought of moving is subsumed by adrenaline and the sense that I can't make sense out of going anywhere else.

We check on our woman. She's still there. She's moved off to the side and is leaning against some wreckage, still at the brink of the façade. My roofmate starts a fresh watercolor. In the new watercolor, both towers are burning. "Did you notice the shape of the hole in the north tower? It's just like the jet. You can see the angle it was at when it hit." I didn't notice, but then I look for it, and, sure enough, there's the silhouette of the jet, wing tip to wing tip.

Another person from the building I'm standing on shows up on the roof. "Oh my gods, I can't believe it's ...!" His words spew forth. He settles down. We introduce ourselves. He's from a small town north of Milan, Italy. He's young. He relaxes. He starts to chat ...

The woman in the middle of hell is still there. We say it's amazing. What a photo it would make, what a symbol. Nobody has a camera with a telephoto lens.

I go downstairs to check the TV for more info. Messages from relatives are on the answering machine. We return those. We're watching the tube when the south tower goes down. I race back up two flights to the roof. "Did you see it? Did you see it?" one roofmate shouts. "On TV. I can't believe it." We chatter about the usual stuff. ... "I never thought it would go down ... I didn't feel a thing, not a rumble. ..." People on the street are walking north, some smartly, others stopping to stare. People on the roofs around us are all reacting in different ways.

I look into the telescope. It's still aimed at our lady's ledge. She's still there. She's off to the right, leaning against a vertical piece of the façade, still facing us. *Hang in there, baby.* We notice the dim glare of fires behind existing glass windows below her. We gauge her chances. There's no smoke where she is, but the dull orange glare of fire can be seen in other floors below her, to the left and the right. The fires are not diminishing. Is there anything left of that sprinkler system?

Our roofmate has started watercolor number three. There is only one tower in this painting.

Oh shit, people are jumping from the remaining north tower. I turn around; I don't need to see this, ever. I look north, at the people in the street at Broome and West Broadway. Then the people in the street scream. I turn to see the north tower snapping at the level where the hole was. People in the street are running north. I don't remember hearing the roar and tear of steel; it's as if the spectacle was encased in a silent cocoon.

Expletives and awe erupt from our group. ... "I never thought that thing would fall ... and BOTH of them???" The huge plume of dust and smoke drifts toward Brooklyn and up the street level of West Broadway. The towers are gone. Both of them. Looking down West Broadway to where they once stood you could see the heat from the fires pushing up billowing smoke, the kind of conflagration that pumps heat and pushes smoke high into the air. But I can't see any flames.

The rest of the day ... seems uneventful. I run errands, make phone calls, listen to the mass media, etc. I try to get some regular work done. Impossible to concentrate. I head up to Sloan Kettering on 67th to give blood. I am O negative, the universal donor. The TV says they need blood. Barricades are up all along Houston Street, two blocks north of where we live on Broome. My street is a desert. No cars, few people. I ask one of the police officers at the barricade at Houston and Broadway if I can return home this way. He tells me, "No, not here; they're only letting people out, not in. I tell him I live here, etc.; he tells me to go way east and work my way home from the east side. Okay.

Julio on bike in Soho

I continue north on my bike. I cross 14th Street, and life is normal, except that it's like a huge traffic jam with lots of police everywhere and check points all over the place. I pass Beth Israel Hospital and notice a long line on the sidewalk. I check in with some volunteers with clipboards. One tells me that everyone is in line to give blood, but they can't take it right now, so leave your name and phone number, etc. I do. I imagine that the same scene exists at Sloan Kettering, so I abandon my plan to give blood today, turn around and work my way back home. On the way back, I pass blocks of vehicles mobilized for search and rescue and debris removal—twenty or more dump trucks, fifteen generators with high-powered halogen floodlights, a few dozen front-end loaders. Holy cow, the rapid mobilization of this armada of machinery is truly impressive.

Later that evening, we go down the street with our Tribeca friend to the Broome Street Bar. I feel the need for a large sudsy draught beer. "Sorry, we're closin' right now. They're declaring martial law down here. Got to get home." I assume this waiter is exaggerating. We go next door to the Cupping Room. They seat us but say the menu is limited. There are a few tables of people—families, buddies, etc. As I sip my sudsy Guinness, I feel like I'm in 1940 Paris when the Germans are about to start marching down the street. It's eerie.

I haven't been able to concentrate on my own work, but I have been able to work on this lengthy e-mail. It's one way to work through the jangled nerves. Hope everyone else is managing.

Stay in touch … Julian

(I remembered meeting with the young Turks of Cantor Fitzgerald on the 101st to 105th floor of the north tower of the World Trade Center during the summer and fall of 1992. They were very enthusiastic about my plan for auctions using electronic bidding on Cantor Fitzgerald's proprietary Telerate System. But the plan was shot down by older, more senior executives. When the plane hit the tower below Cantor Fitzgerald's 101st floor, over two-thirds of its workforce—658 employees—were lost, which was considerably more than any of the other World Trade Center tenants or the New York Police or New York Fire Departments. I would not know for months that the two men I knew had survived. They both had left the company shortly after our brief encounter in 1992.)

Life seemed to stand still after watching such tragic events. There were no commercial planes flying. All borders were closed. Paul and I were fortunate to have our passports with us because we planned to spend some time in British Columbia. But we didn't know if we would be allowed to cruise in Canadian waters at all. We left the Glacier Park lodge and turned in our rental car.

Park officials wouldn't let us bring our Prevost bus with boat and trailer into the park. And, besides, there was no way would I have tackled treacherous mountain roads in a seventy-foot rig. My turns at the wheel were restricted (by me) to the interstate highways.

When we reached the West Coast, we needed a place to leave the bus and trailer for a few weeks. We decided that Anacortes, Washington, which had a ferry terminal to the San Juan Islands, would be our best bet. Anacortes was less than a hundred miles north of Seattle but still in US waters, as were the San Juan Islands. We wanted to know that we could be cleared to cruise the Strait of Georgia. Fritz and Caren had chartered a sailboat on their honeymoon and sailed north for more than a hundred nautical miles up the Strait of Georgia to Desolation Sound. They loved the trip, encouraged us to go, and promised to visit us in the San Juan Islands with toddler Libby in tow.

The Canadian border officials were as wary as the US officers about our request so soon after 9/11. Our saving grace was our age. (But Paul did have a beard.) They warned us it was the end of the season and the marinas and parks in the Strait of Georgia would be closing the last week of September.

I wished to visit Victoria, the capital of British Columbia, and the Empress Hotel, which faced the harbor. We were told there would be little if any boat traffic because of 9/11, and we could park right along the breakwater and walk to the hotel and the Royal British Columbia Museum. I convinced Paul he would love the colonial-style Bengal Lounge in the Empress Hotel, and I could enjoy their curry buffet. Then we could experience afternoon tea while viewing the picturesque inner harbor, with the *Blaze* tied to the concrete breakwater. I experienced the afternoon tea. Paul checked out on the *Blaze.*

Paul and I hurried to Orcas Island to pick up Fritz and family, who were staying at the Rosario Resort. On our way to Vancouver Island, we followed some of the professional whale-watching boats and cruised down the Saanich Inlet to the docks at Butchart Gardens. It was a spectacular sight. On every lamppost along the docks hung heavily laden flowerpots. It was surprising to find in this northern latitude (almost 49 degrees) a Mediterranean-type climate that produced this botanical blaze of glorious colors.

We left Caren and Fritz and Libby at Orcas Island and headed up the Strait of Georgia. We didn't have much time, because the farther north we cruised, the earlier the camps would be closing for the winter. And we were determined to make it to Desolation Sound, which was more than a hundred miles north of Orcas Island. British Columbia tides and currents were very strong and dangerous. Tidal fluctuations ranged from six feet to twenty feet. Our powerful engines could be helpful in a tight situation, but swirling water seemed to be light as air, and we quickly learned to respect the narrows and the rapids, which were abundant, well known, and well marked.

Strait of Georgia—On way to Desolation Sound on the Blaze

We returned to Vancouver Harbor and parked in one of the city marinas. I was able to explore the Museum of Anthropology. The museum held one of the world's finest displays of First Nations art in a spectacular building overlooking the mountains and sea. But Paul was getting antsy. Amy's wedding was less than a month away.

On the morning of October 3, 2001, Paul and I pulled our seventy-foot rig off Napa Valley's historic Silverado Trail next to the lovely Luna Vineyards, a rustic estate surrounded by olive trees, poplar trees, and vineyards.

Fritz rushed out to greet us. It was crush day for Fritz and Caren's Arietta grapes. We couldn't believe it was going on today. (No one could predict the exact day grapes would be ready for harvest.) Fritz explained that thirty-two tons of cabernet franc, merlot, and syrah grapes were being pushed down into a destemmer. After destemming, the grapes would be crushed and pumped into stainless steel tanks, where they would remain for thirty days of fermentation and maceration before being transferred into new French oak barrels for aging for twenty months. Fritz said they would bottle this Arietta red wine the second summer after harvest.

Fritz couldn't leave his post, so Paul and I headed for St. Helena and a place to leave our rig. The tiny side streets of St. Helena wouldn't handle any turns of our bus and boat without stopping traffic.

We left in the morning for Newport Beach, joining the trucks on California's Interstate 5 that stretched the central valley for hundreds of miles. I was relieved to hear from Paul's daughter, Amy, that we were going to leave the bus and the boat in the Newport Dunes waterfront marina and RV park. I was a happy camper to camp out of the bus and out of the *Blaze* after our long two-month cross-country journey.

Amy Eggert and Chuck Simmons's wedding and reception in the

Newporter Hotel would be a "strolling walkway" from my room. Amy, the bride, was a champion scow sailor, along with her dad, at the Spring Lake Yacht Club. At least half of the Spring Lake Yacht Club membership showed up on my strolling walkway, or in one of the three Jacuzzis or swimming pools, or requesting a *Blaze* cruise of Newport Harbor.

After the wedding, Amy and Chuck flew to Bali. I worried that the hotel named on my winning ticket from our Bali visit last spring might not be to their liking. Nothing to fear, I found out—Bali was devoid of tourists because of 9/11. Amy and Chuck had their pick of the best hotels, and, when a beautiful little bundle showed up nine months later, we all knew the ritzy Ritz Carlton was the right choice.

It was time to go home to Michigan. We had one last destination for the *Blaze* on our route home. It had been suggested by Dad: Lake Powell—the second largest man-made reservoir in the United States. It was the end of October. Sunny and hot, hot, hot. And no shade. Anywhere. Again, there were few boaters because of 9/11. We tried to tour. It was too hot to go ashore. We finally retreated to our air-conditioned bus and the long drive home.

Chapter Twenty-three

NAVIGATING THE SEAS

From Belize and Bahamas to the North Sea and Mediterranean

On the way up Egg Crate's seventy-five-foot mast in the bosun's chair in the Bay Islands of Honduras

After two months on the road, it was time to pay attention to my new investment, our shopping center in Holland, Michigan. The strip mall looked tired. Not the supermarket, Family Fare, directly across our vast nine-acre parking lot: Family Fare shone brightly, and it might expand soon.

The strip mall side filled 50,000 square feet in the shopping center and needed a new façade, new roofs, and new tenants. Discount outlets were replacing specialty grocers. Our most promising new tenant would be Thai Palace, an authentic Thai restaurant with knowledgeable owners and chefs.

The Holland property was my only real estate investment with Paul Eggert. Stan Luben could manage Paul's other properties, which were located in more upscale urban locations. I wanted a say in managing this one. A fifty-fifty split of ownership and decision making could be a problem. Nevertheless, Paul seemed happy to let me make most of the major decisions.

Brother Midge also seemed happy to report a major decision that he had made. He'd just ordered a new sixty-six-foot Oyster sloop that would be built in England and ready for launch in June 2004. Midge sailed *Oso Dormido* from the Caribbean to Annapolis, and put it up for sale.

Midge was having some sad days in November, though. His eldest daughter, Lynn, had Down syndrome and suffered from various associated ailments all her young life. Lynn was fortunate to have loving care from Aunt Mart, Mom's older spinster sister, who treated Lynn as if she were her own only child, entertaining and educating Lynn for almost thirty years. Lynn died of cancer in November 2001. She was forty-two years old.

I kept a copy of my letter to Midge. An excerpt: "I just want to take this opportunity to tell you how wonderful you have been—caring for Lynn with Aunt Mart all these many years. Your stellar performance sets a marvelous example for my very extended family, and, needless to say, you always have been there for them, too. ..."

In the winter of 2002, Paul and I wanted to be there for Midge. He would be without his reliable *Oso Dormido* for the first time in fifteen years. We invited Midge to join us in Key West while we prepared *Egg Crate* for the long, tough journey to Belize and beyond. We would be fighting a strong Gulf Stream current when sailing west to Mexico, and then the Yucatán channel current all the way south to Belize City.

I couldn't believe Midge volunteered for our roller-coaster ride to Belize. He kept us on schedule ste-e-e-ering twenty of the sixty hours of our eventful trip from Key West to Isla Mujeres, a small island across from Cancún, off the Yucatán coast.

On our first morning at the Isla Mujeres Yacht Club, a smiling little dark woman in high-heeled sandals appeared at dockside. We needed to move off the gas dock; it was getting very windy. Mexican officials began to appear at our doorstep. Of course, the "captain" (yours truly) entertained them while Midge and Paul disappeared. After three different groups left, we still needed agriculture. "Too windy today. Wait until tomorrow."

Our weather fax looked good for an early departure on Friday, but a Rio Dulce regular warned me that evening in the grocery store that " ... schedules will kill you." He thought it would be too windy to sail south for at least a week. When he heard that we were determined to leave, he suggested we use only the main ship channel to Belize City. "The other ports are too dangerous to enter in this wind." Well ... the Belize ship channel was 200 nautical miles south, so we prepared for a night or two at sea.

During the second night at sea, we averaged only 1.4 knots over the ground, while tracking 8 to 9 knots over the water. Midge was very discouraged as dawn approached, seeing us dangerously close to Punta Herraro ("Point Horrors," Midge named it.) We were running very close hauled against the strong three-to-five-knot current and forty-knot winds.

Midge and Paul were both on watch as we flew by San Pedro Pass at Ambergris Caye, at about 2:00 a.m. With no current, *Egg Crate* sailed full speed ahead, averaging eight to nine knots. Dawn patrol provided me with a beautiful sight: two small islands with palm trees, one lighthouse, an easily identified red sea buoy, and gorgeous bright aquamarine-blue water. I entered Belize's eastern channel easily.

We arrived intact in the early afternoon on Ambergris Caye, and I creeped into the Belize Yacht Club dock, following a channel about six feet deep at high tide.

After days of muddy land activities and continuous evening celebrations, Midge departed. We sailed southeast across the Yucatán channel to Turneffe Island, eighteen miles away. My son Greg steered, Paul slept, and I navigated and worried about the narrow passage we must enter between the reefs to anchor near the Turneffe Island Lodge. (When I called the lodge, they told me to follow one of their dive boats through the cut.) We were enchanted by the place! Greg and Anne, with sister Tina and husband Tom Adams, wanted to stay for days at Turneffe Island before returning to Belize City to catch their plane back to California.

We had a week to clean and repair *Egg Crate* before Paul's son Josh and his wife, Michelle, arrived at San Pedro, but I had other plans for that week. Tikal, one of the largest archaeological sites of the Mayan civilization was close by—a little more than a hundred miles; the planes flew to Flores, Guatemala, the nearest modern city. I knew Paul would want to go too. His appetite for adventure was stronger than mine ... until he saw the really old single-engine plane that would be flying us across a hundred miles of thick jungle terrain.

As soon as we landed, we headed for our Hotel Isla de Flores. It may have seemed primitive (no radio, no TV, no telephones in the rooms), but it was rated number one in town. Tikal was forty miles away, in the middle of the jungle. No way would anyone be staying there. Our bus ride started in the morning. Tikal's immense size reminded me of Angkor Wat in Cambodia. The monumental architecture at the site dated back twenty centuries. It was overwhelming, impossible to enjoy in one short day, especially for two old people who needed new hips. Climbing the pyramids was an ordeal.

I preferred exploring the displays and books in the museum store. I realized that the Mayan culture permeated the lives of the indigenous people around us. Wherever we traveled in Central America, we were exposed to Mayan language, arts and crafts, design, architecture, mythology, and cuisine. Their primitive mythical designs sewn in the fabrics that I purchased in a Tikal "Tipical Store" are a constant reminder of our sailing adventures along the "Mayan Riviera."

I had become accustomed to biking on hard sand streets in Ambergris Caye, navigating through unmarked reefs—and, yes, avoiding their sharks-and-rays tourist sites.

Paul and I sensed we had better hire a guide with a boat to take Josh and Michelle swimming with the sharks and rays. I brought my good video equipment, believing that Josh and Michelle's two little preschoolers would be thrilled to see Mom and Dad swimming with the sharks. It was frightening to watch our guide sprinkle food around the boat to attract the sharks and rays. And when the guide felt there were enough specimens surrounding the boat, he jumped in. Next was Josh. Then Paul. Michelle watched. We encouraged her to go in—and, finally, she slipped over the side of the small boat. (Of course, I couldn't go in—I had to videotape the event.)

Paul and Josh looked like they were creating trouble, standing near the rays that hovered at the bottom of the shallow reef. Suddenly, a scre-e-e-eam from Michelle. She hightailed it to the ladder on the side of the boat. Up she bolted and flopped inside the boat. After it was over, Paul bragged, "The sharks are tamer than a pet dog."

Was I used to Paul's irreverent ways? Would Paul's minor indiscretions matter with the frontier mentality that pervaded Central American life? We were heading twenty-five miles up the Rio Dulce soon. With no guns on board. Stay tuned. ...

Our next guests on Ambergris Caye were world travelers. And experienced sailors. But they had never sailed the Yucatán coast or cruised the Rio Dulce. I wasn't sure if the movie on *Egg Crate* should be the wistful *Out of Africa* (we had the soundtrack on board) or the grungy *African Queen*.

Gary and Vicki Verplank arrived in San Pedro, ready to travel. We needed supplies for a month (just in case). Gallons of bottled water, skim milk, coffee, Coke, tonic, beer, wine, booze, and bug juice. The rest we could buy or catch as we headed south to the Rio Dulce River.

Although Paul and I had been sailing around the Belize islands for months, it was Gary and Vicki's reaction to their new landscape that delighted us so. They thought it a magnificent scene: the legendary outer barrier reef provided protection from the harsh winds and rough seas of the open ocean, while providing soft views of the natural topography untouched by human hands.

We entered the real world when we reached the mouth of the Rio Dulce. According to a PassageMaker article, "Pirates on the Rio Dulce," the US embassy in Guatemala warned:

> While violent criminal activity has been a problem in Guatemala for years, there has been a substantial increase in criminal violence in 2001, including numerous murders, rapes and armed assaults against foreigners. ... The embassy recommends that visitors 'exercise caution' in the Rio Dulce area: "Widespread illegal activities, such as narcotics smuggling, have increased insecurity in the remote area." According to the embassy, several U.S. citizens in Guatemala have been murdered, and none of their killers has been arrested.

We never carried guns aboard *Egg Crate*. Besides, we would have had to surrender them at the border; guns for gringos were illegal in Guatemala. We planned to take some precautions, nevertheless. We were told to stay in the main channel and keep moving. We were going to a well-known marina, Suzanna Laguna, the oldest in the Rio Dulce. Paul and I were so unfamiliar with the Spanish language that we couldn't order a hamburger at the restaurant in Livingston, the border port of entry to Guatemala. Gary saved the day. (All those winters in Spanish-speaking Puerto Rico?)

I was enthralled with the view on both sides of the river! I ran down to the salon and found the *Out of Africa* theme music. I turned on all the sound speakers full blast. As we passed the spectacular steep limestone cliffs dripping with tree branches, the dreamy music transported us to faraway jungles in Africa. No one wanted to cook breakfast; we might miss something. Finally, Gary and Vicki volunteered to go below and cook.

Paul and I reveled in the beauty of this legendary river ... so remote and so dangerous. But, in true tradition, Paul wanted to explore one of the tributaries, dense with foliage. He needed to launch the dinghy and lock the boat. This action was a no-no. We had communicated with no one except our marina. We had no other buddy-boat. We seemed alone on the river except for native dugout canoes.

We turned up the music on *Egg Crate,* locked all the hatches and doors, and took off in the dinghy. As we turned the corner to explore our chosen branch of the river, we discovered we were not alone at all! There was a huge dugout canoe filled with young school-age children, obviously on a "field trip." They were diving off the canoe and wading ashore. They stared at us in disbelief. And we cowered in our little dinghy (with a fast motor). They could have laughed at us, but they just stared, as if they had never seen a white man before. This was their world—their swimming hole—a river teeming and seething with life. And invaded by foreigners (who were secretly taking pictures—another no-no). We retreated to the safety of *Egg Crate* and continued on our way to our marina in Fronteras.

The marina manager waved warmly as we pulled into our slip. We felt safe and secure. The manager didn't mention that the yacht parked just a few slips away belonged to the couple killed the month before on the Rio Dulce. (Paul heard about it from another sailor in our marina.)

The marina had a wrap-around covered porch with a large bar in the center. It would be the perfect spot for breakfast for Paul. I had to learn the hard way that I couldn't drink the coffee. After the first morning, when my usually tough stomach started rebelling, a marina neighbor asked if I drank the coffee. I said yes. She explained that the water for their coffee was not brought to the boiling point to kill local bacteria, and I needed to make my own coffee with bottled water on *Egg Crate.* Paul didn't drink coffee and didn't get sick, and he loved their fried eggs and ham and bacon and sausage—and cold Cokes (no ice).

Before leaving the country, Vicki and Gary were eager to see Antigua, the ancient capital of Guatemala. We needed a minivan taxi to drive us there. Buses were the only public transportation; they were crowded with chickens, always dangerous, and dreadfully slow; our taxi took four hours, but a bus ride could take all day—if you got there at all.

Antigua was charming and civilized and safe. I wrote, "It is beautiful, surrounded by three volcanoes, and has an equally beautiful climate. The expats love it, because they can live well on little money."

The Casa Santo Domingo Hotel was recommended by Gary and Vicki. In early times, it had been the bastion of one of the grandest convents in the

Americas. Antigua was considered one of the best locations in Central America to learn Spanish. I couldn't wait to come back the following year.

Mom and Dad celebrating Dad's 95th birthday, July 10, 2002

It was time to plan a birthday bash for Dad's ninety-fifth birthday on July 10, 2002. Midge and Gary wanted it held at the Spring Lake Country Club ... easier for the growing ménage of children and grandchildren.

Carla Hatton had a small landscape company in Spring Lake; she became the major-domo, planning the décor for the large country club ballroom. It became a tremendous amount of work. About 150 guests were expected. And a band would be playing big-band dance music.

Neither Midge nor Gary had seen the ballroom in advance. When they brought Dad for the party, Dad couldn't believe his eyes. He was blown away. And so were Midge and Gary. Each of the twenty tables had centerpieces piled high with flowers and balloons that reached almost to the ceiling. It was a glorious sight! The country club staff asked permission to take photos for future use.

Dad welcomed all the guests with such genuine pleasure and ease, it was hard to accept the fact that he was ninety-five years old. And Mom, at ninety-two, still twirled around the dance floor.

Guests were asked to bring humorous memorabilia. Barbara Wipperfurth DeWitt's handwritten poster held the most childhood memories for me. (Barb was a month older than Midge and sixteen months older than me.) Some excerpts:

A heart full of memories are Mother, Dad, Toot, and Lydia, and the fun we had being their kids. As children and as adults, we think we had the best parents, best friends, and best neighborhood in the whole world. How blessed we all were and are. The memories are deep and wonderful and unimaginable to some people—our lifetime friendship. We remember:

--Ice cream made in the Verplanks' garage, with fresh cream Toot brought from the north.

--Christmas, when we ran back and forth to see what Santa had brought.

--Kunkel's Dock, where we learned to swim and where we made our ice-skating rink in winter.

--And roller skating on Kamper's Hill—*big!*

--Dad and Toot's poker club, and the men waiting for Toot to get home to play.

--Toot and Lydia and Mother and Dad in Chicago at a baseball game and then visiting a fortune teller who said they would each have another baby. The "ha ha" turned out to be two boys named Gary and Kurt.

--Grandpa Tony Verplank's and the Secory farm, where we loved to go because the Wipperfurth farm was in Wisconsin and too far to go very often.

--Memorial Day, the Fourth of July, and Labor Day picnics at the Bowen and Wells backyards.

Mom and Dad moved into Cote la Mer condominium 1-A in 1970, the year the large thirty-three-unit complex was completed. Dad loved to fish in Lake Michigan. He could park his fishing boat in one of the dozen slips that lined the docks in front of the condos. Mom could perch on their patio (with the Spring Lake Yacht Club directly across the lake) and watch her children and grandchildren race their sailboats on summer weekends. By the year 2002, Mom and Dad had developed lifelong friendships at Cote la Mer. They invited most of the condo association members to Dad's ninety-fifth birthday party. Only one problem: the flu was traveling through the Cote community, but no one wanted to miss this event.

Two days after the party, Dad commented that his cough was keeping him up at night. His faithful helper Carol suggested I take Dad to his doctors. They didn't like his symptoms and soon admitted him to the hospital. Dad joked that he had kissed too many ladies at his party.

Dad never complained about his health, but he did complain about his missing sons. Where were they? Both were traveling. Midge had trouble taking my call seriously. He had left Dad in good health the week before. I told him Dad was insistent. Dad wanted to see his boys! Dad sensed what I knew. One of the younger doctors took me aside and said Dad wasn't going to make it.

I turned to Dr. Dan Fox ("Foxy"), who has always been there when I'm flummoxed. This was not Foxy's resident hospital, but he came. He shook his head and said, "It doesn't look good."

Both of my brothers showed up and kept Mom company. She seemed to always be there. Toward the end of Dad's second week in the hospital, I arrived early one morning. Brett was sitting next to Dad's bed in the intensive care unit, really upset. He felt his grandpa had been given too much morphine. Brett knew all about morphine from his year in the hospital with Little Lydia. I didn't agree with Brett, but I said nothing.

After an hour or two, Dad woke up. I brought him lunch. He dutifully sat on the edge of the bed and let me feed him. Then Dad lay back down while a large group circled his bed to hear prayers from his popular Presbyterian minister, Reverend Dan Anderson. By three o'clock that afternoon, it was all over.

Dad's last words were "I love you all." I gave Dad a kiss, but I couldn't speak.

Monday night's *Grand Haven Tribune* ran a front-page headline: "Vernon Verplank Dies."

> The patriarch of a Tri-Cities business-minded family died Saturday. ... Verplank's father, Tony Verplank, went into business in 1908 by cutting ice out of Spring Lake. ... Today, the Verplank company has dock operations in Ferrysburg, Muskegon and Holland, and a fleet of trucks to serve the road building and construction industries. Vernon Verplank's sons, Midge and Gary, founded and operate Shape Corp. and several other local companies. His daughter, Joyce, started the first preschool in West Michigan and has gone on to develop several companies in Michigan, Illinois, and Colorado. ...

Keeping up with digital changes in lifestyle affecting office property required some changes in my brokerage activities. Our office building on busy 28th Street in Grand Rapids was not being used effectively. It needed one owner who could pull together the two disparate front entrances. We would be putting it up for sale in 2003. As an individual broker, I needed help getting the word out. My friends at Grubb & Ellis in Grand Rapids would be helping me once again.

Paul and I flew to Boston in October 2002. We were both visiting Dr. William Harris at Massachusetts General Hospital for our hip problems. His first hip operation with Dr. Harris in 2000 was so successful that Paul was ready to go back to have the other hip done. Dr. Harris scheduled Paul for his second hip surgery in November, less than two weeks before Thanksgiving, one of Paul's favorite holidays at his north woods cabin. We were asking for trouble.

My kids were upset with Dr. Harris. I was limping noticeably—and had been for a decade. Lydia begged him to operate. He said we could check my hip again in January when Paul returned to Boston for a checkup after his operation. Dr. Harris warned Lydia that pain drove his decisions on when to operate on patients, and I was "only seventy" and not in much pain. (His famous "lifetime" hip replacement truly needed to last a lifetime.)

Paul called Lydia's home in Cohasset to report that he had arrived at his cabin safely. The rest of his cabin report became available when I arrived in Spring Lake in early December. Poor Paul couldn't sleep; he couldn't move around easily inside the cabin; he couldn't move outside. He hurt. He was miserable. And he was not prepared to "rough it."

I thought of *Egg Crate* setting on the Rio Dulce in the jungles of Guatemala. When would Paul be ready to hoist a sail? I reported in my diary:

> We returned to Guatemala in January 2003. Paul had a new hip (and I was getting one in May), so we needed some experienced crew to keep us company for traveling around the Bay Islands of Honduras, back to Belize, and then to Puerto Aventuras, the largest marina in that part of the Caribbean, located directly west of Cozumel, on the Yucatan coast.

While our "experienced crew" from Spring Lake wended their way south to the Suzanna Laguna marina on the Rio Dulce, I attended a Spanish-language school in historic Antigua.

Paul was forced to ride the "chicken bus" from Antigua to Fronteras to work on *Egg Crate*. Paul said the bus was aptly named; he claimed to be well acquainted with the locals by the time he reached Fronteras, because the bus stopped in every small hamlet along the way, transporting more animals than people to markets. There couldn't have been much conversation, since Paul knew no Spanish (that I know of). Too bad, since his natural lisp would have replicated the Castilian Spanish spoken by Brett's godfather, Fernando Zobel.

The Spanish-language school I attended had a small campus with tiny cottages available for students to rent. I signed up for a week of lessons, which included all-day tours to Mayan archeological sites, native markets, Lake Atitlan, and the three volcanoes—one spewing fiery ash—that surrounded the city of Antigua.

A friendly expat from the States took me touring in the evening to her favorite local bars. One classic bar had a second floor where the local coffee czars (all men) were holding a meeting to decide the pricing for Central America's coffee growers. Their conversations soon heated up; shouting commenced. I suggested we leave. My friend laughed; she said that happened all the time. As the conversations cooled, one of the players came downstairs and joined us at the bar for a drink. (In New York City, economic decisions were made during the day on Wall Street. In Antigua, they were made during the evening in an elite bar.)

Our experienced crew had their own lifetime experiences just finding the Suzanna Laguna marina on the Rio Dulce. Stacie Stevens complained that they had to take a puddle jumper from Belize City to Punta Gorda and walk down to the waterfront to take a Scarab to Puerto Cortez, Honduras. Then she and Bill Venhuizen hired a driver to take them to Fronteras on the Rio Dulce, where, two hours later, they were dropped off at the river. They climbed into a big hollowed-out boat that reminded them of the *African Queen*, with its two hammocks hanging from the roof. Stacie said they had no clue where they were going in the twilight. Finally, the boat rounded a corner on the south side of the Rio Dulce, and they saw lights and Paulie sitting at the bar with the owner of the Suzanna Laguna marina.

Cash was king when cruising the northwest Caribbean. Before leaving the states, I would load up on small-denomination bills—especially one-dollar bills—and stuff the bulky envelopes in multiple locations around *Egg Crate*'s salon. The natives would paddle along *Egg Crate*'s hull in small rowboats or dugout canoes, grab the lifelines, and hawk their local fish, eggs, crafts, or jewelry. (They had to explain to me that their eggs would keep a month if we turned them every day and did not refrigerate them—ever. I bought a few dozen eggs at a time in a large flat carton. We flipped them often but not daily. And they kept for weeks.)

We were eager to be off to the more civilized Bay Islands of Honduras, an English-speaking group of islands a short distance north of the Honduran coast.

Utila, the smallest of the three major islands in the Bay Islands, lay about 20 miles north of the Honduran coast and about 120 nautical miles from the mouth of the Rio Dulce. When we arrived, we were not impressed by the ugly commercial buildings that hugged the flat shoreline of the small harbor. After stopping overnight to check in with Honduran customs and immigration, we sailed another twenty nautical miles northeast to Roatan, the largest and most populated island in the archipelago.

Safety was our main concern. No big city or isolated anchorages for us. We found the Roatan Yacht Club near French Harbor and anchored around other boats. It was a short dinghy ride to the main dock, but a long climb up steep wooden stairs to the main clubhouse. My bad hip and Paul's new hip were sorely tested. I was happy I wore my dressy straw hat and long pants when I viewed the other guests—most were properly British in garb and manner, as if waiting for afternoon tea. They frowned at Stacie's skimpy cover-up. But retreating down all those steps was not an option for any of us.

I admired a wealthy young Honduran who was very understanding about the plight of his people. He was organizing hospital airlifts and clinics for poor Hondurans on the three main Bay Islands. An American medical volunteer was working with him on the project. (Their presence reminded me that my assistant, Pat Young, was also volunteering that month to help American doctors in Guatemala.)

A peppy, professional scuba-diving production crew was showing clips from their shark video shoots earlier in the week. Some of the divers offered to take us swimming and chumming with sharks. Their videos teemed with sharks—so many that it was hard to find the divers among the sharks! No way were we going swimming or snorkeling or diving in the Bay Islands after that viewing.

My experience in Guanaja, the most remote and enchanting of the three larger islands, will be etched in my memory forever. We didn't have much choice about anchorages. There were very few cruising sailboats—and few people—and no roads. We anchored near a hilly shore on the southeast side of the island.

A storm was brewing from the west, not leaving Paul much time to winch me up our seventy-five-foot mast to fix the broken equipment at the top of the mast. Bill offered to help Paul winch me up in the bosun's chair, which Paul tied very carefully to the main halyard (always using his trusty bowline knot). Up I went, faster than usual; Bill was eager to get me up there quickly.

One final pull by Bill. (I was already at the top of the mast.) *No!* That final pull jerked the halyard cable out of the pulley and wedged it into the top side of the mast—with all my weight wedging the cable farther into the mast.

I tried to lift my body up to loosen the strain on the halyard cable. But I was sitting at the top and couldn't find any lines that could lift me higher. I fixed the equipment on the mast while Paul tried to find a way to take my weight off the main halyard cable. First, he sent up more tools, using the spinnaker halyard to hoist up the equipment—tools I would need if I could get my weight off the main halyard. Paul decided that I must move my bosun's chair from the main halyard to the spinnaker halyard. I needed strong pliers to loosen bolts on the shackle. And I needed a big, heavy screwdriver to slide under the main halyard's cable to jerk it loose and lift it back on the pulley.

At this point, I had been at the top more than two hours. My arms were getting tired. It was starting to rain. (Paul said he was embarrassed that they hid under the bimini canvas while I was struggling at the top of the mast in the rain.)

The sky was getting black to the west. It was after 6:00 p.m. (Would I be up all night? What about the lightning?) I had to conserve energy. I dropped my arms and shook my hands. I had bolted the spinnaker halyard to my bosun's chair and had to unscrew the bolt on the main halyard. With one arm pulling my weight off of the bosun's chair, I used my other arm to unfasten the bolt on the main halyard.

I wasn't done. But I rested anyway. I was getting used to the rain. I jammed the heavy screwdriver under the wedged cable and pulled it loose enough to slide it over onto the pulley. It was 7:00 p.m. and almost dark. My arms shook from exhaustion. (Probably from fear too. ...) The mainsail halyard rode down with me, rolling smoothly through its pulley at the top of the mast.

Bill and Stacie had to leave from the Belize City airport on February 20, 2003. Paul and I were eager to head north from Ambergris Caye to explore the Yucatán coast we had missed on our windy trip to Belize harbor in the winter of 2002. The big touristy island of Cozumel was more than 150 nautical miles north of Ambergris Caye. It became our first destination. With the help of the strong Yucatán current, we could sail fast if the wind didn't stare us in the face.

We sailed along Cozumel's west coast at dusk. I found out the hard way that Cozumel (like Barbados) just doesn't have any friendly protected anchorages. We tried anchoring in a few places, but it was too deep; the anchors wouldn't hold.

Puerto Aventuras, a dream of a marina only fifteen miles west of

Cozumel, became our new destination. We parked along the quay, not knowing if we would be kicked out the next morning.

Egg Crate on the quay in Puerto Aventuras

We were welcomed with open arms. Not only could we stay there, we could also unload our bikes and lock them on the concrete dock next to *Egg Crate.* Then we could ride our bikes to the boutique shopping area, the dolphin pools, or wherever the maze of walkways was paved.

We never had one bit of surge in six days. And guess the price for all this: $17 per day—yes, the total bill for our week was $102.

Paul and I had a fast sail riding the Yucatán current all the way to Key West. I was eager to fly home from Key West to get back to work. I had a major hip operation coming up in May. Paul visited friends in Fort Myer's Beach before hauling the boat once again at Lighthouse Boat Yard. It was a chore he seemed to enjoy.

By the time of my journey to Massachusetts General Hospital, my renowned surgeon, Dr. William Harris, had recently retired. After all those years visiting Dr. Harris, I was forced to choose one of his three protégés. Someone said that Dr. Dennis Burke was nice—if I could get past his tough but oh-so-efficient head scheduler, Liz.

Lydia was prepared for my two-week visit; I would be her third hip replacement patient in three years. And Dr. Burke also had his own team. His favorite anesthesiologist became my favorite too; he kept me numb for almost twenty-four hours. After three days in my happy morphine daze, Lydia picked me up and drove me to Cohasset.

I enjoyed two weeks with Alexander, toddler Claire, and their lovable Portuguese water dog, Buster, When I returned to Michigan, I moved into a hospital bed in Mom's living room at Cote la Mer. Paul could visit from my corner condo next door.

I was accumulating condos; I bought the corner condo when it became available in 2000 so our Verplank family could care for Mom and Dad—both in their nineties. It was the prime ground-floor location on the east end of the condominium complex, with the most windows and morning light. (Not quite Paul's request, since he didn't like to see the sun before ten or eleven in the morning.)

Before I left for Boston in early May, I hired an experienced residential renovator to remove the wall between the kitchen and living room of my Cote condo. The lake was fifteen feet in front of my patio doors, but the kitchen view was blocked by the wall. I wanted that wall gone.

And the wall was on its way when I returned from Boston. If I hadn't been in Mom's condo on a hospital bed, I would have been gone too. Some angry Cote la Mer Association board members knocked on the door of my corner condo while Paul was sleeping in the big back bedroom. Paul didn't answer. The board members walked in and bustled about the construction area. When they wandered to the back bedroom and peered at Paul, that was it. Paul dressed, left, and vowed never to live in my Cote la Mer condo. (Would he keep his promise?)

The Cote board members were vicious that summer. Poor Mom, a widow less than a year, was ninety-three years old. She had been lovingly cared for by Dad and their friends at Cote la Mer for decades. She couldn't understand why the Cote board was so upset with me.

I wrote the Cote board a four-page handwritten letter explaining that my very reputable builder had gotten the proper building and plumbing permits before starting the renovation. Still, the Cote board refused to meet with me; they stated that I needed their permission before starting this project. They demanded I return the wall to its previous status. "With the same wallpaper?"

"Yes," a Cote board member replied.

I asked my architect to speak at our condominium association's annual meeting, held once a year in June. The Cote board hired a lawyer and warned me that my representative would not be allowed to speak at the meeting, because the issue now was a litigious problem.

And they enforced their admonition, with older condo members at the annual meeting shouting at me from the rear of the room, "Sit down!" And I did, because Mom was present and visibly shaken.

It was a tough summer. Since the board refused to meet with me, I finished the renovation and delivered a glowing letter to the Cote board from my plumbing inspector stating that all thirty-three lakefront condos should do a similar renovation. The building inspector signed off too, complimenting my builder on a job well done.

Nothing I said satisfied the board. I had not asked permission *before* doing this renovation and I *therefore* must be punished. The battle was joined in court. It was going to be expensive. Again. Paul wanted no part of it. He had enough experience with the Michigan judicial system to sour him for life. But I had a son who was a seasoned litigator. He commented early on that the litigation might cost $50,000, but the unique spacious lakefront views of the renovated condo would be worth $50,000 more. This litigation could go on for years ... but would Paul?

Fall was a great time to visit New York. The weather was sunny and cool, and the energy of the city was exciting. I was ready to go back to work, and it seemed such an easy thing to do when I was around all my old business partners. Did I want to work selling real estate in the Caribbean? Or acting as Shape's broker in Gary's quest for property in Texas or Mexico? I planned to talk with Gary again about it.

The Boorsteins invited me to join them at an attractive Basque restaurant called Marichu on East 46th Street. When I arrived, I was surprised to find Bill Seidman there with his latest "friend," or at least his new business partner, Jackie Pace. Bill reminded me that Jackie and I had met during our P Street days in DC, when Jackie, a lawyer, was an FDIC speechwriter for Bill. Jackie was involving Bill in her new business venture: buying Caribbean island banks. They claimed the banks were not a tax dodge... But my kids thought their scheme was not only unethical but also not immune to Congress' legislative tentacles.

We had a heated argument about the Iraq war at our Marichu table. Allen Boorstein was disgusted with President Bush for starting a "stupid" war in Iraq. Bill Seidman was not. I asked Bill why; and his one word answer was "oil." Bill would not elaborate; he was not about to get in an argument with his good friend and host for the evening, Allen Boorstein.

Paul and I had promised our only daughters, Amy and Lydia, that we would return to the Bahamas during the spring of 2004. The shining Atlantis was the goal, but we all wanted to see and enjoy Harbor Island's famous pink beaches too—if I could navigate the dreaded Devil's Backbone approach into the bay.

The weather was not as predicted on February 12, 2004, when we left Key West. With twenty-knot winds out of the east, we slugged it out slowly against the waves building along the Gulf Stream. Bad weather and bad planning kept us holed up in Chub Cay for three days, with no Internet and no telephone. We finally arrived at the Atlantis Marina on February 20. During the next month of sailing trials and tribulations Paul, neverthe-less, maintained his usual wry, sometimes ironic, self-deprecating humor. Everyone loved reading Paul's stories, which he always sent from my com-puter, using caps only. Carla Hatton wrote: "Paul's stories always put a smile on my face." Here is part of Paul's rendition of our tour, written from Harbor Island after all of our guests had flown back to the States:

DEAR AMY AND CHUCK,

THANKS FOR ALL MY GREAT PICTURES ON THE CD WITH MORE THAN 550 AWARD-WINNING PHOTOS. ALSO, BLACK DOCKING LINES, NEW DINK [dinghy] LIFTING LINES…

WE ARE NOW BACK IN HARBOR ISLAND, IN THE SAME SLIP AND SAME WIND. THE GUY IN THE CEMETERY IS STILL ABOVE GROUND.

ATLANTIS IS BUSIER THAN EVER. WE FOUND A POOL, WITH JUST SCREAMING LITTLE GIRLS, THAT ONLY MOTHERS OR SITTERS USE… WON TEN DOLLARS AT THE CASINO WHILE JOYCE TRIED ON BATHING SUITS FOR TWO HOURS WITH LYDIA.

WE PARKED AT A REALLY FANCY MARINA, THE LYFORD CAY CLUB, AT THE WEST END OF NEW PROVIDENCE ISLAND, WHERE THEY HAD THREE PAGES OF RULES. EVEN HAD TO TUCK YOUR SHIRT IN AT ALL TIMES! COULD NOT EAT AT ANY OF THEIR RESTAURANTS WITHOUT A SPONSOR. AGENT 007 LIVES HERE. HE WOULD HAVE SPONSORED US, BUT HE WAS GONE.

WE WERE BY FAR THE SHORTEST MAST IN THE HARBOR.
A 160-FOOT SLOOP HAD TO KEEP A RED LIGHT ON TOP OF ITS
MAST SO AIRCRAFT WOULD NOT HIT IT...

After waiting seven days for the weather to clear at Valentine's Marina on Harbor Island, we got a favorable weather report for Monday. We backed off the dock, in low, low tide, with the sun at our back as we approached the Devil's Backbone. I followed A-1's tracks on the Garmin GPS exactly, while communicating with Paul at the wheel, using all four walkie-talkies.

We turned the corner into the main stretch of beach along the Devil's Backbone. Out of the blue—*wham!* The washcloths and shampoo bottles flew off the shower rack, the refrigerator door flew open, breaking a balsamic vinegar bottle on the white carpet, thirty spices spilled out on top of the vinegar, my favorite automatic toilet slipped off its hinges, the bikes slid three feet forward along the lifeline, Paul draped over the radar, and, thank goodness, I had my thick life preserver on, or I would have been crushed against the mast.

The boat bounced back. Paul pulled the throttle in reverse. We sat. We looked around. We still were right on A-1's GPS track (pilot for Devil's Backbone). We still couldn't see the coral reef we had hit. The boat rolled from side to side in the surf, mixing the broken glass and vinegar into the spices on the kitchen floor.

We inched forward and cleared the reefs along the beach. Now we didn't know how far out to go around Bridge Point. The book said to watch for the "rather indistinct coral ridges'" that would be to our starboard.

Beep! Beep! Beep! ...—I counted seven of them. Our savior: the fast ferry from Nassau. It was heading straight at us. It rounded the point and wanted to pass. We stopped, not knowing which way to go. I called them on the VHF radio. They didn't answer—there was no time. They veered to our starboard and whooshed by at thirty knots. *Egg Crate* pitched, but now had a clear path around the point. We followed the fast ferry tracks out until it quickly faded. We threaded the reefs slowly past Bridge Point. Paul was really anxious now. He just wanted this over. He saw the destruction below. He was willing to go through Spanish Wells, knowing how shallow the water was along the outside route at low tide. We glided into port with eight feet of depth under us the whole way. Carpets got scrubbed and toilets got rehinged. And lunch got served.

We continued past Little Egg Island, the last island to windward. With thirty-five nautical miles to go to Nassau, the wind built through the afternoon: twenty knots, twenty-five knots, and thirty-knot gusts out of the north, backing to the northwest. We agreed that Paul couldn't take the mainsail down before we entered Nassau Harbor. It was too rough. I checked the chart for the third time. The entrance was at an angle of 150 degrees, and the wind had backed to 330 degrees, which put it exactly behind the boat. I hated watching Paul steer closer and closer to the buoy at the entrance; I felt we were going to need more room to head up and come about before driving straight downwind.

All of a sudden, Paul exclaimed, "I'm going in!"

Paul had taken the preventer off (which kept us from jibing downwind), thinking that we had plans to come about. He shouted, "I think we can make it at this angle! I'll sail across the entrance to the Nassau shoreline, and we'll turn into the wind there. Watch the waves behind me!" (When *Egg Crate* slid down big breaking waves, the waves tended to pitch the boat totally out of control.)

I yelled, "Here comes another one! You're heading down! Head up!"

"I can't—much! I have to stay clear of the inner breakwater! Watch the waves!"

Paul headed for a group of small boats anchored in the shallow water near the western shore. "Take the wheel!" he commanded. "Head into the wind before we run aground!"

Nassau Harbor's average depth was thirty-five to forty feet. I glanced at our depth. "Ten feet! I'm turning her now!"

We put out two anchors in our favorite spot, near the yoga camp in front of Club Med, with a magnificent view of the Atlantis skyline. It was a great vacation—the kind a senior citizen always looks forward to. ...

On Monday, April 12, 2004, from Fort Myers Beach, Florida, I reported in my diary:

This will be my last communiqué from *Egg Crate*. (Really??) And I certainly am leaving with fresh memories of horrific weather. This morning's storm produced a sixty-three-knot gust of wind that left Paul wondering if the boat was going to blow over before we blew into the bridge at Big Carlos Pass. ...

When I think about it now, I realize that I was probably safer from tornadoes in the bay waters on our 55,000-pound sailboat than I would have been in a high-rise apartment on the beach.

For the future? I like the Venezuelan coast. At least there, the trade winds are steady, if strong. The water is warm. The latitude is under twelve degrees north—below the hurricane zone. And the only place where we took a direct hit of lightning—28,000 volts—was just sixty miles north of here, four years ago. According to our insurers, the Tampa area is the lightning capital of the world. But I don't need our insurers to tell me that.

As soon as I returned to Spring Lake, Midge announced that the commissioning of his long awaited 66' Oyster sloop, "Sundowner" would take place mid-June. And yes, Paul and I would be invited to sail on its maiden voyage from Ipswich, England, on the North Sea to the island of Mallorca on the Mediterranean Sea.

I couldn't believe that Paul Eggert agreed to sign the purchase agreement (PA) for the sale of the 6000 28th Street building before our six-week sailing trip abroad. Now I really needed to move fast. I e-mailed local brokers and my three favorite commercial real estate companies: Grubb & Ellis in Grand Rapids, Coldwell Banker in Lansing, and Woodland Realty in Holland. I told them that Paul had signed the PA for the sale of 6000 28th Street, and the closing would be—most likely—July 29, 2004. That meant I had to find a like-kind exchange property in the $4-5 million range by September 10.

Paul and I arrived in Ipswich on June 19, 2004. Oyster Yachts rigged their sailboats in Ipswich after the hulls were constructed in Southampton. Midge, Paul, nephew Kyle Verplank, and I were all waiting for Lydia and family to arrive from Paris to have the celebratory dinner launching Sundowner. Lydia explained they had to take the train to London and then rent a car to drive to Ipswich, which was like Boston—every road a curve and every intersection a rotary, except the driving was on the left.

Midge's new sixty-six-foot Oyster sloop, Sundowner, was first-rate in every way. All major sails and winches were operated by pushing a button. We did have a nice tippy boat when all the sails were up. And it was fast! The fifteen-foot dinghy hung out on both sides of the stern, even though the boat had an eighteen-foot beam. The bow thruster motors were so powerful that they knocked out the computer if used at the same time. (No navigating while landing the boat. ...)

I was assured by Midge's new captain that we still were planning to leave in two days for Guernsey, about a twenty-four-hour trip. We would have a full house for that part of the trip, because an Oyster engineer would be sailing with us to Guernsey. Our Norwegian friend, Truls, was arriving soon and would be sailing as far as Lisbon, Portugal, before flying back to Norway on June 30.

I struggled to learn the new computer, GPS, radar, and chart-plotter interfaces. Fortunately for me, the chart plotter and radar combo were the same as ours on the *Blaze,* and the SSB weather fax was similar to ours on *Egg Crate.*

For practice, our Oyster computer expert let me chart our course to Lisbon, which was almost 800 miles. From Guernsey, we would sail across the Bay of Biscay, about 340 miles to the northwestern tip of Spain. We'd stop in one or two ports that Truls suggested on the Spanish Atlantic coast, and then Truls would disembark in Lisbon.

After Lydia returned to Boston, she called Uncle Midge and asked if we were still afloat. (Unfortunately, Grandma Verplank, age ninety-four, thought we were not, and called Lydia in a panic.) We had developed four major deck leaks through the chain plates on four of the six stays of the mast as soon as we hit the rough, angry English Channel current; the salt water poured in over the crew's bunks on the port side, destroying everything in its path.

We motored into Ocean Village Marina in the Southampton harbor at 3:30 a.m., and were rudely awakened at 8:00 a.m. by a crew from Southampton Yacht Services (SYS)—the crew (!) who built *Sundowner.* The news was not good: one to two weeks for repairs.

Truls left at noon for Norway. We were sad to see him leave, but he said England was his backyard, and he did not need to see it again. Kyle picked up travel books on England and Scotland, and Midge and Paul picked up our touring car at Hertz. Kyle and I were not sure we trusted dyslexic Paulie driving on the left, but someone had to spell Midge on this tour. The response from my California sons was typical.

From the sailor: "Hoeee thit!! Paulie sucking down a Kent in one hand, rum and Coke (no ice) in the other, knee on the wheel, driving on the wrong side of the road. … The thought of it all is too horrific to imagine. Good luck with the repairs, and I hope King Richard is picking up your hotel rooms."

From Fritz, who had spent six months in England, working for British-based auction house, Christie's: "*Blaze*—great opportunity to do some touring in merry olde England. Leave Paulie in the pubs if he resists, and get some culture in Bath (phone Michael and Daphne Broadbent—01 ...). Exeter (the most beautiful English cathedral), the north coast of Devon, etc., etc. ..."

I sent my kids the last update—hopefully!—before leaving England for the Channel Islands on July first. I felt we accomplished all that Fritz suggested in the week on the road: Uncle Midge dutifully completed a long tour of Oxford University's historic campus, complaining that he learned one thing—two hours was the maximum time he could walk on a "walking tour." And Paulie preferred the train ride when we reached Blenheim Castle. And my wish to see *Macbeth* at Stratford-on-Avon's Royal Shakespeare Theatre sent Paulie, Kyle, and Uncle Midge back to our fifteenth-century hotel for a nap. But ... the rockin' nightspot, Chicago, woke everyone up for dancin' until the wee hours—two nights in a row. No one wanted to leave Stratford, but Fritz said we shouldn't miss Bath or the Exeter Cathedral, so we hopped in our comfortably slow diesel Land Rover station wagon. The men liked the Roman baths, and I loved the impressive Exeter Cathedral. Paulie and Kyle joined me for the Evensong service, looking impressive in their navy blazers.

And, *yes*, Uncle Midge did all the driving—and never at night and never after even one beer.

We had a nasty sail crossing the English Channel on Saturday, with gale-force winds, strong currents, and sloppy seas. I could not help but think of the thousands of men on D-day, June 6, 1944, crossing a rough English Channel. (I remembered the black headlines in our *Grand Haven Tribune* announcing, "D-DAY!!") A Guernsey construction worker told me that the five years of German occupation during World War II was very rough on the local populace. Jersey, the southernmost of all the Channel Islands, was only twelve miles off the western coast of France.

There was a water festival in Guernsey, along the huge breakwater that lined the main street of St. Peter Port Harbor. Fortunately, it was at high tide. The largest marinas have locks because the tide is twenty-five feet! It was an amazing sight to see sand and rocks at low tide outside the marina walls. And we had fireworks. On *our* Fourth of July.

We planned to sail nonstop to Puerto Banus in Spain, which was over 1,000 miles from Guernsey. What would our Mediterranean scene be like, with the summer at its zenith and the wars in the Mideast sizzling?

Our Mediterranean port, Puerto Banus, was a quiet scene when we arrived in the fall of 1992, and the majority of the yachts parked there were owned by Arabs. This time, I arrived at the peak of the summer boating season, but the Arabs no longer appeared as the dominant tribe on the grandiose boat circuit. After 9/11, the Mediterranean Sea had become a busy waterway for our ships.

When we left Puerto Banus, heading east along the Spanish coast toward the Balearic Islands, I was shocked to see a huge aircraft carrier in the distance, approaching us. My trusty binoculars soon saw the American flag flying. We had been warned that our American flag might not be a welcome sight in many ports of the Mediterranean. But we hoisted it proudly for the US Navy as the vessel cruised by.

On to Mallorca, the largest and most famous island of the Balearic archipelago. Midge loved Mallorca. Why? "It's a beautiful island with wonderful architecture, fantastic restaurants and stores, and a narrow-gauge railway that winds its way from Palma across the central plains, through mountains and tunnels, to the northern city of Sóller. No one should miss the train ride." Since we were staying for a week before flying home to Michigan, I tried out the train, the buses, the restaurants, and even agreed to go shopping with Midge and Paul. (They knew I hated to shop.) I found a silk pantsuit right away, but the pants were too long. No problem—have a cappuccino next door, and return in a half hour. I wore my new outfit the last evening in Mallorca, in one more special restaurant chosen by Midge, our designated *Sundowner* tour director.

Chapter Twenty-four

THE JOURNEY TO "FURTHUR"

"Furthur" is a combination of the words "further" and "future"... They say the best thing about the future is that it arrives only one day at a time. This universal truth ensures the richness of the journey to "points further."

Musings on "Furthur," 2005

Checking out Mary Lanka's art work on the transom of
Furthur *Nanny Cay, British Virgin Islalnds*

As soon as Paul and I returned from Mallorca, I faced a slew of "due diligence" problems that had to be negotiated immediately. I was the broker, not the owner, not the manager; but it was my job, nevertheless, to work out the answers with Jon Anderson at the Varnum law firm. Jon was always upbeat, a joy to work with, and fast. We agreed to do most of the repairs, which were minor, or credit the buyer when he offered to do them. I was relieved when the buyer put off the closing of the 6000 28th Street building until August 31, 2004.

Paul had seen depressed on the *Sundowner* voyage, missing his Spring Lake summertime sailing festivities. No way was he going to miss live televised coverage of the 2004 Summer Olympics, which were being held in Athens in August. Once again, I was on my own—whether caring for grandchildren or potential 1031 business opportunities.

When the operating agreements for our new LLC needed attention in the fall, Paul left town to work on his daughter Amy's new California home. And when I told Paul that we would have a triple closing of new 1031 properties in late October, Paul decided to extend his trip for another ten days—flying from California to Florida to work on *Egg Crate*. But he promised to return home in time to sign the closing documents… What was he trying to prove? !

Whatever Paul thought of me (if he did think of me at all), it was not a role I relished. After the 1031 documents and operating agreements were prepared for the closings, I left town. It happened to be the same day that Paul returned from Florida.

I was planning to spend weeks writing this memoir at a "shack with a view" (a hunting cabin) on my son's property in upstate New York. Well … my plans for writing lasted about two weeks.

I left to visit Lydia and her family. It was almost turkey time for the Pilgrims, who had landed at Plymouth Rock almost four centuries ago. (Plymouth was a half-hour drive from Lydia's house in Cohasset.) However, that visit was cut short too, when the stork arrived early in Napa Valley, California.

I returned to Spring Lake in early December. Mom looked beautiful and frail. Something was wrong with her stomach, but the doctors weren't saying what. The previous winter, Midge had taken Mom on a strenuous boating trip through the Strait of Magellan around the southern tip of South America—quite a feat for a ninety-three-year-old lady. And the voyage had seemed to take its toll on Mom's health. At family gatherings before Christmas, Mom announced that she wasn't going to be around much longer. We feared she was right.

And I feared Paul was not going to be around much longer, either. Paul had complained to friends that I was never around. He had moved to his office condo in Ferrysburg. (Once again.)

Midge and I took Mom to the hospital for a checkup at Christmastime. Gary and Vicki and their kids were vacationing in Australia. After a few days of tests, Mom's doctor took Midge and me outside Mom's room and told us there was nothing more that could be done. We should take Mom home. The doctor would set up hospice care. Realizing for the first time the finality of his statement, I began to cry. The doctor gave me a big hug, and

I sobbed on his shoulder. Midge knew it was time to call Gary. When we found Gary, he wanted to return home immediately.

I didn't understand hospice care. Carol Knutsen had taken care of Mom and Dad for years and had continued to care for Mom after Dad died in 2002. She wouldn't abandon Mom, nor would I. We set up the hospital bed in Mom's living room and dismissed hospice care. When Gary and Vicki arrived from Australia, Vicki took charge of my large Cote living room and transformed it into a warm receiving room for friends and family.

Paul had moved permanently to his condo in Ferrysburg but needed to stop by our Yardarm condo to pick up mail. Paul always expected me to have his mail and multitude of magazines neatly sorted in separate piles on the second-floor steps of the Yardarm condo. He called me at Mom's condo, asking about his mail. (He didn't know that I had not been home at our Yardarm condo for weeks. And why didn't he look in the mailbox?)

Mom died on Sunday, January 16, 2005. She was almost ninety-five years old. Her obituary stated:

> ...She is one of the gifted few to experience all the remarkable transformations of the 20th century during her long life. A legendary beauty, she retained her athletic good looks into her nineties. ...
>
> Married to Vernon Verplank for 72 years, the two shared a wonderful life together, traveling to exotic places around the world from the Arctic Circle to the South Pacific... Mrs. Verplank played a supportive role when her husband embarked on community projects, including the construction of a new Presbyterian Church in Spring Lake and new Spring Lake Yacht Club.
>
> Most important to her throughout her life were her husband and family. Mrs. Verplank is survived by her three children. ... She is survived by twelve grandchildren. ... Also, twelve great-grandchildren. ...

Timing is everything, as I would find out to both my delight and sorrow. In the spring of 2005, I sold Mom and Dad's Florida condominium and my Yardarm condominium on Spring Lake—both at the height of the real estate bubble. In the summer, I bought a Boston whaler that Lydia named *Blazette*, which I parked in Dad's slip at Coté La Mer.

Ahh … yes, I now owned two Coté La Mer condos and one giant lawsuit circling my unilateral decision to remove the inner wall between the kitchen and the living room of my corner unit. And I had the support of the Spring Lake building and plumbing inspectors, who granted building permits on the property before I started the renovations. In the end, their support won the day. They said that there would be no improvement if I was forced to replace the missing wall. So, $50,000 in legal fees later, I won. And so did all the future Coté La Mer condo owners—many who would follow my lead and knock out their inner walls.

In the fall, after Paul filed for divorce, I bought Midge's fifty-six-foot Whitby ketch, *Oso Dormido,* which we renamed *Furthur.*

The boys explained that *Furthur* was "The world's most storied bus. If there can be a bus more famous than Sooper Fly's Smokin' Green Spartan. (Paul Eggert's bus.) The owner of *Furthur* during its immortal final run in the 1960s was Ken Kesey (author of *One Flew Over the Cuckoo's Nest*— later an Academy Award winning movie starring Jack Nicholson as Nurse Ratched's nemesis). You can see already how a journey to points further, as well as the journey into the future, are appropriate for *both* the boat *and* this very exciting new chapter in Mom's life. ..."

Furthur also became known as "The Bus to Never-Never Land." ... Well, I spent ten years riding with Peter Pan. Was I ready to get off that bus? And miss the opportunity to be the owner of my very own sailboat?

Obviously, no. It was an exhilarating experience! After scratching for adequate crew for a month, I left Annapolis on November 2, 2005, on *Furthur*'s maiden voyage to the British Virgin Islands (BVI's). Bill Venhuizen knew the boat, having crewed for Midge when they brought the boat from the Caribbean to Annapolis two years before, and Mike Pumphrey knew engines better than anyone on the boat or in the marinas—as well he should, having built the engines for his winning hydroplanes. My professional (that means paid) captain was Tom Braun, the youngest of the crew, at thirty-five years of age. I was the oldest, and I was the navigator. I learned to trust no one to navigate for me after a close call with a freighter during our first night sailing down Chesapeake Bay.

We enjoyed a peaceful week at sea, with cases of Gosling's rum and ginger beer. (Captain Tom was not drinking; he was working.) We cleared customs and immigration on Tortola's West End and proceeded to our next port, Nanny Cay, where Midge and Michel Picot (his new captain on *Sundowner*) were waiting to fend off at the gas dock, knowing who would be at the wheel.

Slowly, I approached the dock. A big push on the bow thruster—"Too long!" shouted Bill. "Short blasts ... save the batteries ... stick the bow in the dock ... use the thruster!"—*But* the dock crew and my three able throwers saved the day, and made the landing look quite respectable.

We had to leave in three days for the Bitter End marina on Virgin Gorda, because Bill and playmate Stacie had four days to see the BVIs. We sailed at noon. The wind was howling twenty to twenty-five knots, and the seas were five to six feet. Well ... after battening down the hatches and everything else as we motored straight into the seas, I went below to store the cameras. Then ... *Wham! Wham!* Back and forth wobbled the boat. Mike moved the shaft a quarter inch and demanded we return immediately to Nanny Cay.

Mike was right. Big damage. The cutlass bearing was shot—and we could have lost the "stuffing box," which would have caused water to rush in. Mike had lined up a boat to tow us and also take us right to the lifts to be hauled.

And *Furthur* was hauled November 24, 2005. She would be launched in early January and, hopefully, would be healthy for years to come.

I was having a good time with my newfound freedom from Paul's schedules. Lydia encouraged me to join them at Loon Mountain in New Hampshire for the Thanksgiving holiday. I hadn't tried to ski since my hip operation in May 2003, so Lydia treated me like a beginner—leading me down gentle sloping hills. It was easy with the newly designed short rental skis and my patient instructor.

From Boston, I traveled to New York City. It was time for my last four days of continuing education classes for my New York State real estate broker's license. After fifteen years as a broker, I no longer would be required to take classes. Too bad, because I enjoyed most of the teachers who volunteered for this "good citizen" assignment. My last instructor was a top assistant to Donald Trump, the brazenly successful real estate tycoon. She was hilarious. Such passion for her job. She paced back and forth across the classroom floor, pounding her fists in the air, reminding us, "this is war!" All while discussing her process for locating land and air rights necessary for new Trump projects in crowded cityscapes. (*Yes*, history does repeat itself.)

Most of the winter of 2006 was consumed with my desire to restore *Furthur*.

Launching Further *with John, Michel, and Midge*

I ordered a new bimini that could be fully enclosed. (It was the best feature on Paul's *Egg Crate*.) The galley needed counter space and a clear view of the entertainment center's new TV. Michel's friend, John—also from Canada—was, like Michel, a superb cabinetmaker. He would spend many months rebuilding the salon and the galley—probably his first galley redesigned by the cook. (Because I never got seasick, I was always the cook when our sailboats thrashed through rough seas.)

While sailing on *Furthur* in the spring, Maureen Murphy asked me to join her on a short jaunt to Panama, where she would be working on the ambassador's residence. I was pleased to be included in her entourage, along with her Hillandale neighbor, Sharon Goldsmith. (No neophyte in Latin America, Sharon was coordinating university graduate-level studies in many Latin American countries, just not Panama.) I warned Maureen that I did not speak or understand Spanish. (That's right … that week in Antigua, Guatemala, studying Spanish was wasted on me unless I was reading the newspaper.)

But a trip up the Panama Canal was not to be missed. It would be homage to Dad! Why? When I interviewed Dad in 1995 (he was eighty-eight), he remembered everything about the boats he owned and the places he explored. What a prodigious memory!

"Look at our world map. We have visited every continent except Antarctica," Dad would brag while pointing to the different colored pins, each color representing a separate voyage.

Dad's world map

When I asked Dad which trip was his favorite, he replied unequivocally, "The Panama Canal." Too bad Dad wouldn't be here to know that I, too, would be traveling the Panama Canal.

Most Panamanians I met in our hotel didn't speak English. Nevertheless, the US State Department provided all the travel services. The drivers, who were also my guides, spoke English and acted as my interpreters, negotiators, aides-de-camp, or "advance men," as needed.

Since Maureen was busy during daytime hours, Sharon and I decided to tour the Panama Canal. Our lead driver and event organizer, Katia, escorted us to the boarding platform of our passenger ship.

"Please let me introduce Hernan, the captain of your ship today," offered Katia.

Hernan quickly led Sharon and me up the passerelle of his ninety-two-foot vessel before the other three hundred passengers arrived by bus from their mammoth cruise ship, which was too big to go through the locks. Sharon and I grabbed a prime table near the pilothouse. After the ship pulled away from the dock and the pilot was installed (necessary on all commercial vessels for the entire voyage through the locks), Hernan motioned for me to come into the pilothouse. Sharon was not around at the time, so I slipped through the lifelines and entered the small pilothouse.

Hernan and Miguel, the pilot, were the only two in charge of the vessel.

Miguel spoke excellent English. I told Miguel that when I was a teenager, my dad took me along on a 450-foot freighter that was transporting coal to the Verplank docks from Lake Erie ports. As we approached the Straits of Mackinac, the captain let me steer through the straits—and I left an expensive snake trail behind the ship.

I was wearing a new Oyster regatta shirt that Midge had bought for me during the Oyster sailing races in the BVI's the previous week. Hernan asked me if I sailed too. I told him that I lived on my sailboat during the winter in the BVI's.

He said, "Good. You can steer here too, through the Panama Canal."

The pilot, Miguel, laughed and paid no attention. I got behind the wheel, and Hernan left the pilothouse so that I would have to steer. Hernan would return every once in a while, grab the wheel, and steer to one side of the canal.

"Why?" I asked Miguel.

"There is a big 950-foot container ship around the next bend, coming our way, and we need to move over."

We were twenty-one feet wide. I didn't know how wide the big ships were; I only knew they were less than a hundred feet, because they were going through the locks. (There were locks in each direction.) We gave them plenty of room.

At the wheel of the ninety-two-foot passenger ship in the Panama Canal

The Miraflores three sets of locks

As we approached the first set of locks, Hernan took over. The Miraflores locks were three separate locks in a row. We went through each lock with two other commercial passenger ships our size, one rafted next to us. In front of us were two or sometimes three new private yachts of about forty to sixty feet, and no sailboats and no trawlers. Because of the currents, the small yachts were having trouble staying away from the filthy walls of the locks. Across from us, heading in the opposite direction, a container ship was being assisted by full-sized train engines running on tracks the length of the locks. The ships did not tie to the locks; they tied only to the engines.

I kidded Miguel that he didn't do anything but watch Hernan. He replied with a laugh, "With Hernan, you don't have to do anything. He is the best."

I took stills and videos of the entire trip from the pilothouse, using my new digital Nikon Cool Pix camera. It tells the rest of the story. Sharon said I could have had an interesting evening if I wanted it.

Before leaving Panama, I had my own passion I hoped to satisfy. I was surprised by joy! (With apologies to *Surprised by Joy* author, C. S. Lewis.)

Like most female sailors in the Caribbean, I admired the intricately hand-stitched and geometrically designed fabrics, called "molas," which were worn as blouses by all the Kuna Indian women of the San Blas Islands, an archipelago of three hundred small islands near the Panama coast south of Colón. I'd wanted to sail there for the past decade, but I couldn't find anyone who wanted to venture in a dangerous part of the Caribbean just to visit the San Blas Islanders. Most sailors who stopped there were on their way through the Panama Canal to the Pacific Ocean.

I suggested to Maureen and Sharon that we fly to the San Blas Islands for a long weekend. But Maureen could not change her plane reservations, and Sharon would not travel by dugout canoe. They went to the rain forest; I explored the San Blas Islands—alone. Maureen believed that Katia would find a safe place for me in the archipelago.

Katia found only two resorts. The newer one was full, so I was left with the Dolphin Lodge. And Katia told me there was a big problem with the lodge: there was no landing strip on that island. I would need to travel, with all my luggage and new digital camera, by dugout canoe from Mamitupo, the nearest island with a landing strip.

I wrote my family a detailed report upon my return to civilization:

Katia insisted that I memorize "Mamitupo"—over and over, on the road to the local regional airport, because my small Aeroperlas plane made a stop at Playon Chico first, and many other islands after Mamitupo.

We left the Panama City airport promptly at 6:00 a.m. About forty-five minutes later, a helpful passenger escorted me back into my seat near the cockpit of the plane when we made an unscheduled stop after Playon Chico. (I had asked the copilot of our old Twin Otter, "Is this Mamitupo?" He had nodded yes.)

Each island stop took about five minutes; each flight, about ten minutes. As an old pilot of small planes, I was impressed with the pilot's ability to maneuver in and out of the skimpy landing strips half hidden by early morning mist. Kuna Indians were boarding on one island and getting off on the next, as long as there was room on the plane.

I noticed that Katia's printed travel schedule said that my returning flight from Mamitupo back to Panama City (only one flight a day) would be an hour later than the delivery flight each morning. Well ... the Kunas knew better. When the plane stopped to drop off passengers, they were on the runway, ready to hop on, because they knew that the plane was not coming back later. (And I found out the hard way: I missed the morning plane back to Panama City and was forced to stay at Dolphin Lodge an extra day, much to my delight.)

"Hat-chon?" asked Geronimo. (Yes, that really was his name—Chief Geronimo.)

I nodded and pointed to my bags: two backpacks and a small suitcase. Katia made me buy a second backpack for bottled water—four quarts—a large pack of travel Kleenex, and bug spray. It was the start of an eight-month rainy season, so I stuffed the other backpack with a lightweight slicker, umbrella, and one pair of shoes—kivas that could stay wet all the time. An alarm clock, matches, and underwater flashlight were stowed already in the backpack.

We climbed into an immense dugout canoe with a small motor on the stern. The canoe carried ten people comfortably.

There was one other large canoe tied to old tree posts along the dock, and then many tiny canoes, some with sails, most with only paddles, lined up on the sandy beach. Father, mother, baby, and toddler climbed into a small canoe next to us, and father started paddling. I looked at a small island well protected by a chain of reefs.

A San Blas Island sailboat

"That's the community island," explained Geronimo. "We don't have towns, just communities."

The Dolphin Lodge was farther away, on a tiny island that housed only the resort and work buildings surrounding it. As we approached the dock, we could watch workers paddling their small dugout canoes between the islands.

Playtime in the San Blas Islands

After breakfast with Chief Geronimo, the Kuna women asked him to find out what foods I did not like.

"I like most everything."

"Octopus?" Of course. "Chard?" Naturally. "Langouste?" Yes. I found out langoustes and giant crabs were specialties of the Kuna Indian kitchen.

"Coffee?"

No! I had learned—while sailing on the Rio Dulce in Guatemala—not to drink native coffee. (The next morning, I donated one quart of my precious water to the kitchen for a pot of delicious Panamanian coffee.)

I asked Geronimo if I could use his computer to send a message to my family.

"Five dollars for fifteen minutes," warned the chief.

Geronimo and a young assistant watched every word I typed and kept track of every minute spent on their one available contact with the outside world. Their phone worked through their Internet connection. (Living on a sailboat in the Caribbean, I should have learned from them.)

Next, I agreed to visit the community island before lunch. Just the two of us. The other guests were swimming or enjoying private time. And they all spoke Spanish, except the pretty transplant nurse from Canada who arrived on my plane that morning. But she could rely on a boyfriend, a successful young Australian Lebanese who was the CEO of a Colón Free Trade Zone company.

The Kuna Indian women were extremely shy and polite during my negotiations (through Geronimo) for their beautiful molas. I did not bring much cash, so I tried to figure out quickly what were typical Kuna designs—designs they wore, not what they thought might appeal to a tourist like me. They wore mainly geometric designs, and once in a while, a mythological figure was stitched in the middle of a mola maze.

For my kids, I bought padded mitts of such painstaking workmanship that I doubt they will be worn at the stove or grill ... but hang forever on their kitchen walls.

After lunch, Ildefonso, our afternoon guide, packed snorkel equipment, seven plastic chairs, and our personal refreshments in the bow of his dugout canoe. We cruised far from the lodge and the community island to a tiny isle with a shallow sandy beach.

Their snorkel equipment looked antique. The first mask I tried was too small. Ildefonso tried to stretch the strap. It broke. He threw the mask on the beach, where it kept company with the scraps of rubber sandals littered in every direction. The next mask he tightened, grabbed a snorkel, and shoved it under my strap. I wandered off for two hours, swimming without a leak from mask or snorkel. Black sea urchins lined the sandy bottom in five feet of water. I couldn't believe that the carefree little Kuna children swimming nearby knew not to touch them. (They did.)

After our swim, the chairs were lifted from the beach into two or three feet of water so that everyone could sit, drink beer and wine, and enjoy the warm water.

Two Canadians perched in the chairs, water lapping up to their chins, and reached out to grasp the beers from Ildefonso's assistant, who ran back and forth from shore with a seemingly endless supply.

The more serious Canadian told me he was volunteering in Bolivia as the controller of a Montreal charitable foundation. "We all owe something to our communities," he explained.

"Don't you miss your children and grandchildren?"

"I see them three or four times a year. ... I can't sit around Montreal just to see my grandchildren. They don't need me."

The other Canadian worked in Panama and was showing his friend first the San Blas Islands, then the Pacific beaches, and, finally, the mountains in northern Panama. He teetered back and forth in his chair, beer in hand, gesturing to Ildefonso that he did not want to leave this beach anytime soon. (No, he did not make it to dinner that evening. ...)

Our Argentine doctor and his wife appeared to live well. They were obviously happy, if slightly oversized, which didn't seem to bother either of them. Always in their bathing suits at breakfast and lunch, they were pleased just to sit, relax, and enjoy our warm watery drinking hole.

Returning to our tiny island resort, with the lovers and Canadians

And then we have the lovers. Young, attractive, and no-nonsense. We discussed his Muslim beliefs. ("I will only marry a Muslim.")

Her reaction: "And I could never marry a Muslim."

"Would either of you change your minds or your faith?" I inquired. "No."

"Do you pray often?" I asked him.

"Yes, in my own way. I pray many times a day, quietly and alone."

"What about 9/11?" I ventured.

A shocking answer from her: "You had it coming. After the way the United States has treated other countries, especially Latin America, you should have expected it."

Wow. From Edmonton, Canada. Well educated, well traveled, in her twenties. No friend of the United States. Yet she was my friend that day and that evening and the next day. And his special friend too.

The ugly American … and the only one staying at the Dolphin Lodge that weekend.

By evening, my upper lip was puffed up, and my nose burned. And I had open sores between my toes. Out came the Zovirax and anti-you-know-what for the feet. I realized that was the end of my snorkeling or going barefoot.

I wanted a hot shower. There was a single water pipe coming into my hut. Temperature? Same as the ocean. Cool for washing hair, but otherwise bearable, when water was available, which was not all the time. As we say in the BVI's, they were on "island time."

Our resort had electricity from a generator. The one ceiling lightbulb over my bed went on automatically at dusk if I was in residence. If I was at dinner, a kerosene lamp mysteriously appeared next to one of my three beds. Lights and lamps were turned off at about 8:30 p.m. The larger community island next to us had no electricity—and there was no activity after dusk. The Kuna Indians slept in hammocks. I tried the hammock on my porch only once: I couldn't move around or sit in it. I couldn't read or see the ocean; I fell trying to extricate myself from it. I'm not Kuna.

The young Indian boys working at the lodge wanted to learn English using my large illustrated book, which was written in Spanish and English, describing their Indian culture and history. I loaned one of the boys my reading glasses. I was impressed with their eagerness to learn.

And when they understood that I owned a large sailboat, they insisted that I bring my big sailboat to their island so they could be guides for visitors to all the San Blas Islands, using my boat. ("No, no, I do not want to have a commercial charter service," I kept telling Ildefonso. But he was adamant, as were the other boys, and they wouldn't let the idea go.)

The Indian women, always dressed in their colorful molas and beaded leggings and armbands, were so warm and so loving to me that I felt guilty leaving them. I knew I could teach their children, I could sail their islands, and I could promote their welfare.

There were kisses and hugs all around when I left. I will miss them. They brought me such joy!

Who will run the ship after Chief Geronimo? He lamented the fact that he is sixty-seven years old. Now you know that is *old*.

How long would it take for me to realize I had to go back to work—and get off the bus? The day my divorce would be final? Would I be making a business deal with Paul that left me with no security and little income? And major investments necessary to preserve and develop my only asset?

I conferred with the three people I most trusted about finances: Bill Seidman and my brothers, Midge and Gary. Bill said I should diversify my holdings instead of pouring all my assets into one real estate deal. I laughed. Did I have a choice? I would need to work if I didn't want to live on the meager earnings of my investment income—investments that could be risky too. Bill didn't argue with me.

I turned to my brothers. I asked them to back me up if I got into trouble, because I did not have enough assets to weather any storm if I invested all my money in one commercial real estate property. It was the summer of 2006. The real estate market was soaring. Appraisals were peaking. My entrepreneurial spirit was burning.

Finally, my divorce was granted on October 24, 2006. I was a happy camper—very excited about plans for a jazzy new sports bar and major renovations on the strip side of my 100,000-square-foot shopping center, which now was 100 percent mine. I had agreed to buy Paul's 50 percent after a lengthy appraisal process, which took place during the spring, summer, and fall of 2006. Paul still wasn't satisfied with the final appraisal, insisting he would be back in court in 2007 with new numbers after our divorce.

I flew to the BVIs in January 2007. Sailing on *Furthur* took on a new dimension: not only were my kids too busy to join me, I was also too busy. When a major electrical fire erupted in the nav (navigation) station of my cabin, I realized it would take months to repair. I moved the boat from the Bitter End Yacht Club to an inexpensive marina on Tortola for repairs, and headed back home to face Paul Eggert in court once again.

The judge asked Paul's original appraiser of the real estate if he was satisfied with the original value established in 2006. He was. The judge refused to hear Paul's new appraisals from the reputable firm, Coldwell Banker, which would have raised the value another million dollars. It was February 2007.

It didn't take long for Maureen Murphy to convince me to join her once again on her latest assignment to Australia. After my glorious experience in Panama, I was ready to go. I had much encouragement to go from Fritz and Caren, who, with baby Libby in tow, had spent three weeks in Australia in 2001. They loved the country.

Although the spectacular opera house in Sydney Harbor was first on Fritz's list, he recommended a visit to the famous Barossa Valley wine country north of Adelaide in South Australia. That proved to be a very worthwhile suggestion. I needed help designing and equipping my fancy new sports bar that was being constructed in the Holland shopping center. And no one was more prepared than top interior designer Maureen to ferret out unique artifacts on this journey. We found a handsome rough-hewn wooden bar on a wine tasting tour, and I hoped to replicate it for my sports bar. (Be careful what you wish for. ...)

Blazers Sports Pub and Bistro opened on Wednesday, October 24, 2007, one year after my divorce.

It also was opening night of the major league World Series. We were packed! And guess what team was making its first National League World Series appearance? The Colorado Rockies—two decades after the *Rocky Mountain News* sports section headlined, *"KSPN's Joyce Hatton hopes to bring team to Denver"* (April 12, 1987). Unfortunately for Blazers, it was a short World Series; the hot Boston Red Sox won a second World Series in four seasons, sweeping away the Colorado Rockies in four games.

From left: Butternut Event Center, Blazers Spots Pub and Bistro

Patrick Revere of the *Holland Sentinel* reported the next day: **"Hot Wing Sports Bar Opens on North Side":**

A limited number of northend eateries and the lack of a true sports bar in the Holland area were the compelling reasons behind the development of Blazers Sports Pub. ...

Blazers has six high-definition, large screen televisions and sports programming packages through Charter Cable and DirecTV. ...

Blazers, and the adjoining Event Centre, an entertainment venue and banquet hall that seats 250 people, are owned by Joyce Hatton. A commercial real estate broker, Hatton said she invested more than $1.5 million in the two locations. ...

The bar wraps around a bistro-style restaurant that serves starters...

A primary feature in Blazers' barroom was inspired by a bar top Hatton saw during a wine tasting tour in southeastern Australia.

"We found two oak trees that were dead about a year," explained General Contractor Bill Venhuizen. "We got them right out of Waukazoo Woods about four miles from here, and we cut them to make more than 60 feet of the bar. We had to pin them together with metal braces to prevent them from warping and build up about a quarter-inch of lacquer on it. It's just beautiful."

The restaurant employs more than 50 people...

Two weeks after we opened Blazers and the Butternut Event Centre, I was on my way to Boston's Massachusetts General Hospital for a second hip operation. I didn't want to go, but I had serious back problems during the summer. Midge insisted I keep my scheduled appointment and stay at his home when I returned from Boston.

We had planned a grand opening for Blazers and the Butternut Event Centre on Thanksgiving eve—one of the most popular bar nights of the year. Gary told me it was so crowded that the lines were three deep surrounding the bar, waiting for drinks. I was lying in my hospital bed in Midge's living room, fuming that Midge wouldn't let me join the party.

That wasn't the only situation I was fuming about. A county-wide referendum from 1976 banned the sale of beer and wine on Sunday from 2:00 a.m. to midnight.

What did our Sunday NFL football TV spectators do? They headed south across the Allegan County line to watch football games and drink beer. The picturesque lakeside village of Saugatuck was their favorite rendezvous.

So what did I do? What did other retailers and restaurant owners do? In the spring of 2008, we held an organizational meeting to weigh our options. We had four: File petitions in the village, township, city, or county. Our shopping center was located in Holland Charter Township, which was more populated than the city of Holland. I wasn't willing to join the county-wide group until I believed they had a chance to file the forty thousand signatures necessary to place a proposal on the November 4, 2008, ballot. We needed about four thousand signatures in the township—a number I felt we could accomplish in a timely fashion. Brett VanderKamp, owner and developer of New Holland Brewing Company, convinced me to file petitions for both township and county.

The summer months of 2008 were spent organizing our "Say Yes to Sunday" door-to-door campaigns in Holland Township, while the county committee members solicited at fairs, festivals, parades, and supermarkets in the rest of the county.

I could not believe what happened! I received this letter on August 29, 2008, from the Holland Charter Township clerk (after we had submitted *four thousand* signatures of Holland Township registered voters to his office):

> My office has completed the process of validating the signatures of the circulators and the individuals who signed on the petitions you submitted to our office. After completing this process there was a total of 2,908 valid signatures. This did not meet the required number of 3,694 valid signatures to put this proposal on the November 4, 2008, ballot. Therefore, I cannot certify this proposal to place it on the ballot. ...

However, the Ottawa County Clerk validated *forty thousand* signatures to put the *county-wide* proposal on the November 4, 2008, ballot! Whoopee!

What happened? I was told the clerk validated *only* the signatures of the four thousand *circulators* of petitions (who had to be registered voters of state of Michigan), not the forty thousand signatures of the individuals who signed the petitions (and had to be registered voters of Ottawa County).

How did this happen? The Ottawa County "Say Yes to Sunday" campaign chairman, Jim Storey, an eight-year veteran Hearing Commissioner for the Michigan Liquor Control Commission (1999–2007), was the magician politician. Every campaign needs one.

The Sunday beer and wine ballot would pass easily on November 4, 2008. Blazers and our other wine and beer retailers in the shopping center, including the Family Fare supermarket, could sell beer and wine starting Sunday, November 16, 2008.

But we all were late to the party. Blazers customers started to disappear with the heavy layoffs in all of Holland's north side industries in the spring of 2008, and by summer, most of the original Blazers' staff were gone. In September, I hired a successful catering company to manage Blazers and the Butternut Event Centre. The new manager did not want any interference from me—no Monday morning quarterbacking. She intended to bring in her own chef and advisors; her tough style seemed perfect to weather the storm.

Midge was aware that I wanted to sail on his new eighty-two-foot Oyster sloop, and I wiggled a late invitation in October to join him and his crew in Lisbon, Portugal. We would be sailing 400 miles southwest to the Island of Madeira, and from there, 300 miles south to the Canary Islands.

My sailboat, *Furthur,* was "on the hard" (in drydock) in the BVIs, having been put up for sale almost a year before.

I returned to Michigan in late October to witness a chaotic business scene. Everywhere. Our local banks were demanding money. Or foreclosing, forcing friends out of business and their homes. Gary and Midge were in the automotive business (and GM and Chrysler were going bankrupt). They were also in the shipping and trucking and asphalt business. No one was immune.

Verplank Dock Company Hundredth Anniversary, 2008 With Gary and Midge Verplank

When I heard that Bill Seidman would be speaking at Grand Valley State University about the banking crisis, I asked Dottie Johnson, a GVSU board member and local friend, if I could attend. She said, "It's full."

I texted Bill and told him I needed an invitation. Bill texted back, "I will get you in. Just come." And when I arrived, Dottie invited me to sit with the board members in the front row.

Bill was as sharp as ever during his discussion with Grand Rapids community leaders about the banking crisis. And he knew I wanted to meet and drive him to his CNBC commentary appointment in the campus broadcasting studios after his lecture. Bill was still the born pedagogue, loving his work.

Don Lubbers, former president of Grand Valley State University, was Bill's chauffeur for the day and invited me to accompany them to Bill's scheduled appointments.

Bill Seidman preparing to broadcast on CNBC at Meijer Broadcast Center, October 2008

It was fun to catch up with Bill, whom I still considered my best friend; we planned a meeting in May to discuss my book. Bill said he would be resigning from most of his company board directorships in the spring and would have more time for recreational activities. He liked to brag that he rode his bike for ten or eleven miles every day and always wanted to compare his bike-riding mileage with mine, which he surmised was always less than his. Smart man.

I couldn't believe the negativity of our bankers in regard to the future of the Michigan economy. Our small local banks were taking a beating, and they were taking their customers with them.

The timing of the appraisal, in October 2006, of the value of what would be my only asset from my divorce—the 100,000-square-foot Holland shopping center—could not have been worse: Midge kidded me about it, sending me charts from JPMorgan Chase that demonstrated the rise (the bubble in 2006) and fall (the crash in 2008) of US commercial real estate. As Midge commented, "The charts show the sad tale. If you had better timing and your divorce was in 2009 (instead of 2006), the center's value would have been a few million dollars less. ..."

Fortunately, people still had to eat; our Family Fare supermarket buzzed along on even keel. And our popular Thai Palace restaurant brought in family members to help out during the recession. It was going to be a long haul to recoup my losses from the build-out of the strip side of the shopping center, especially Blazers and the Butternut Event Centre. Changes would be coming.

April 29, 2009, was Bill Seidman's birthday. I called his cell phone, left a funny message, and waited for him to call me back. I was curious if he knew that I was planning to write about our long-standing affair in my memoir. (Bill would caution me, "Don't publish it until I am dead.")

After my divorce, I often turned to Bill for advice. He was always there when I called, always willing to talk, to think, to discuss my concerns. It probably was his abiding interest in people that kept him anchored to his weekly CNBC commentary for almost two decades.

On May 13, at about 2:00 p.m., I was working at my desk in the living room, with the television on silent mode, when a "Breaking News" strip rolled across the CNBC-TV screen, with a simple message: "L. William Seidman is dead." May 13 was also Paul Eggert's birthday.

My good friend, Don Lubbers, was the first to call. ... Tom and Harriet Newman's brilliant daughter, Sara Newman Clarke, soon called from California, asking, "Are you okay?" And my kids all checked in when they heard the news.

I couldn't believe Bill was gone. I had the same reaction when I lost Dad—visibly gone, but virtually always there ... my anchors to windward.

The New York Times obituary the next morning stated:

> L. William Seidman, a plain talking accountant whose credibility and unflinching stance in political skirmishes helped him transform the unglamorous job of chief banking regulator into one of the most powerful positions in Washington, died Wednesday in Albuquerque. ...

The *Grand Rapids Press* had a bold front-page headline: **"Ex-FDIC chief left his mark. L. William "Bill" Seidman, 88, remembered for local, world impact."**

Matt Becker, partner in the BDO Seidman office in Grand Rapids, commented in the *Grand Rapids Press*, "Bill was a true champion for the entrepreneur, and Grand Rapids and the entire business community will miss him greatly."

No matter. Bill said, "I'm not too great a believer in legacies. My father used to say, 'Put your hand in that bucket of water, and then take it out. Do you see where anything's been there? That's the way life is.'"

Chapter Twenty-five

"THAT'S LIFE…"

*That's life (that's life), that's what all the people say / You're ridin'
high in April, Shot down in May / But I know I'm gonna change
that tune / When I'm back on top, back on top in June
I've been a puppet, a pauper, a pirate, a poet, a pawn, and a king / I've been
up and down and over and out and I know one thing / Each time I find
myself flat on my face / I pick myself up and get back in the race…*

Song written by Dean Kay and Kelly Gordon (1963),
(and popularized by Frank Sinatra)
© Bibo Music Publishing, Inc.

By the summer of 2009, changes were a necessity. I sold *Furthur*. I sold *Blazette*. I sold my renovated corner condo at Coté La Mer. I turned over ownership of the shopping center to Midge. Blazers was closed by the catering company, and the space was used to expand the Butternut Event Centre for more catering opportunities. I continued as a real estate broker in New York and Michigan, but it was not a job—especially in the depressed atmosphere surrounding commercial real estate.

Now I could devote time to finishing my book. Did I have the discipline to do it? Or would I be swallowed up in my grandmother role in life? No, my children wouldn't allow that. (As they liked to remind me, I had a three-day limit to my visits.)

I was in no mood to write my story. Fortunately, Maureen Murphy rescued me once again, this time with an invitation to join her in South Africa after the New Year. It was going to be a complicated itinerary, because the South African ambassador had two primary residences: one in Pretoria, north of Johannesburg, ("Joburg") and one in Capetown, at the southern tip of the African continent. And the residence of the consul general in Mozambique needed attention also. I was excited about all the new safari locations that were bubbling up en route.

Our Southern Sun Hotel in Maputo was beautifully situated right on the beach of the Indian Ocean, with a Portuguese-speaking security guard always in view, standing at the steps leading to the beach. (Mozambique was a Portuguese colony until it became independent in the 1970s.) South Africa might be an emerging market, but Mozambique was definitely a poor third world country.

After much exploring by phone for a weekend safari reservation at Kruger Park, a savvy American foreign service worker (with his surgeon wife in tow, working on the AIDS problem in Mozambique) called the travel agency at the American embassy in Pretoria and found us a great safari deal that had been discounted because of last-minute booking.

We did see all the "Big Five" (lion, elephant, water buffalo, rhino, leopard) in the first twenty-four hours, with a private guide at the wheel of our large Land Rover. It was an experience not to be missed! And all was quickly photographed by Maureen, a much more artistic and proficient photographer than I. (Fortunately, Maureen forgot her camera and had to use mine.) I sent picture books to my grandchildren of each animal or bird that Maureen photographed during our three-day adventure in Kruger Park.

On to South Africa. ...

Apartheid didn't work in America, and it now had all but disappeared in South Africa. There probably would be no white political leadership again in the country.

All the white communities in Pretoria and Joburg, from middle class to wealthy, were gated, with electric barbed wires fencing them in. Even the immense new eighteen-hole golf course community development being constructed on the north side of Joburg was fenced in—with high electric barbed-wire posts.

And what about the luxurious, elegant Tuscan villa in Pretoria that housed Maureen and me for four nights? It was located only one block from the American and British ambassadors' residences, among others. High concrete walls (with the barbed electric wiring sitting on top of every wall) enclosed all the private residences or villas or bed-and-breakfasts in this exclusive Waterkloof Ridge suburb.

Cape Town and the Western Cape—the best of South Africa—we left for last. Maureen took a week's vacation for the Cape Town visit, and we tried to do it all ... perched in our secure nest at the American ambassador's residence in the hilly Bishops Court section of Cape Town. We enjoyed the amazing and exciting native art on all the walls in the ambassador's residence.

Ifa Lethu

The art was collected by the Ifa Lethu Foundation, to celebrate native heritage by repatriating works of art taken out of the country during the "struggle-era." Fortunately, the art was not removed from the ambassador's home and returned to local museums until the day we left Cape Town.

I was not about to drive on the left, but Maureen assured me she was used to driving in Ireland and England. We rented a small car and had it delivered to the ambassador's residence. Maureen was an excellent speedy driver, maneuvering around all the roundabouts while I counted exits on the GPS screen. The GPS let me put in "lat-longs" for destinations. It surprised me when the Petite Ferme, a must-see Wineland's restaurant, gave us our directions in latitude and longitude. South African wine country is almost as beautiful as Napa Valley, with roses planted at the end of each row of vines in the dry hilly locations of a very windy and mountainous Winelands.

The Winelands

Then it was on to the cable car at Table Mountain, where there was a sign at the top warning us that if the horn blew, it was time to hurry back to the cable car to be transported down ASAP. This was a very windy peninsula!

Cape Point, South Africa: "Baboons are dangerous"

As we were climbing to see the Cape Point lighthouse, a visitor walking down warned me, "You are so little, you will blow away at the top!" With the warm Indian Ocean current meeting the cold Antarctic current running up the Atlantic side, it was a boiling rage of wind and water hitting rocky Cape Point. Finally, we hit the scenic beaches along both coasts—from the warm Indian Ocean to the cold Atlantic.

What an education I experienced—of wine, emerging markets, third world economies, Islam versus Christianity versus Judaism versus Zulu voodoo. And what will be the future for South Africa? Will there be a democracy with 10 percent whites and 90 percent blacks? Will there be any whites left in South Africa? It was not a very encouraging picture.

After more than thirty years in the US State Department, Maureen Murphy decided it was time to retire. She was planning a last trip to Bern, Switzerland, in the winter of 2011. Did I want to go? Of course. Could we go to Zermatt? And see the Matterhorn?

The Einstein Museum in Bern, Switzerland

I forgot that Albert Einstein was living in Bern in 1905 when he developed his special theory of relativity, which led to his famous formula: $E = mc^2$ (where E = energy, m = mass, and c = speed of light – $186,000^2$ mi/sec.). It changed old perceptions of space and time. When I discovered the Einstein Museum in downtown Bern, my dedication to exploring it took every free moment for the week we visited the city. The exhibits were detailed, showing experiments that Einstein used to demonstrate the expansion or contraction of time and space.

My interest in physics and electronics has been a high-speed chase during my lifetime. Just understanding the magnitude of Einstein's discoveries could be a lifelong adventure. From the force of the atom bomb to the reach of the electronic global network, Einstein's work continues to envelop our lives.

Our scary journey up the steep mountainside into the famous ski resort, Zermatt, was a thrilling experience for me— even though I had traveled by train across the Colorado Rockies for decades. And Zermatt had the perfect Swiss mountain village architecture portrayed in every modern American ski resort poster. (Think Vail.) This was ski country and this was February, the heart of the winter ski season. But we weren't skiing.

I loaned Maureen a vest and scarf, and she bravely accompanied me on the highest open-air cog railway in Europe—up the Gornergrat to the Kulm Hotel at the summit (3,089 meters). The train dropped off skiers along the way, while Maureen photographed the Matterhorn in all its glory.

The Matterhorn

During the summers of 2011 and 2012, Midge was planning to invite friends and family to cruise on *Sundowner* in the Mediterranean Sea. And I was working once again in the political arena. Mitt Romney was running for president, and I would do whatever I could to see that he didn't make the same foreign policy mistakes as his Dad, Governor George Romney, who was my favorite presidential candidate during the 1960s.

When Maureen Murphy invited me to visit her in Florida in February 2012, I brought along my computer to e-mail Mitt Romney supporters every day for a week, encouraging them to campaign for Romney before the very early Michigan primary day of February 28. Like his father in the 1960s, Mitt Romney was having trouble garnering support from Michigan conservatives.

After Mitt Romney's primary win in Michigan, I returned home to a new campaign—a disincorporation of our Village of Spring Lake. It needed to be absorbed by the Township of Spring Lake, which was six times its size. (In Michigan, a village is part of a township; its citizens pay the same township taxes as other residents in the township. But if the village is incorporated, villagers also pay village taxes. City dwellers do not pay township taxes.)

My former business partner from Lansing, Jeff Poorman, a governmental tax expert, had stopped by my condo in January to express his dismay that I would put up with the double taxation. The rationale defied description, and the township's tax attorney agreed.

In a front-page article of the *Grand Haven Tribune* on March 22, 2012, Mark Brooky reported:

> **"Villager Readies Petitions**—SL voters will be asked to sign a petition seeking a merger of Township and Village. There couldn't be a better opportunity than now for the village to dissolve into the township, according to Spring Lake Village resident Joyce Verplank Hatton.
>
> Hatton and the dozen or more people she said are ready to help with the grassroots effort may be out knocking on doors as soon as this weekend with petitions to get that issue on the village's Aug. 7 ballot.
>
> She said the 11.6 mills annually taxed to village property owners for village services are unnecessary, and the village should end its search for a new manager before spending any more money or time on it.
>
> "This is crazy to have two full bureaucracies right next to each other," Hatton said, pointing to the Spring Lake Township offices less than a block away from Spring Lake Village Hall.
>
> "We only need one manager at $80,000 (a year)," she said. "We don't need two managers across the street from each other, literally, at $80,000 apiece."

Circulating petitions with grandson, Chris Hatton, May 2012

By Monday, May 7, 2012, *Grand Haven Tribune* reporter Marie Havenga announced in another front-page headline: **"Merger Petition Proceeds**—A petition drive aimed at asking voters to determine the question of dissolving the village—has crossed the finish line."

Yes, with 349 signatures! (Only 306 needed.)

And my nephew, Kyle Verplank, and his wife, Samantha, were part of the core consolidation group. Kyle said that residents would need to decide for themselves if the financial benefits outweighed potential loss of services—such as leaf pickup and rubbish day.

I was ready to go into details on how merging the municipalities could work ... when, out of the blue, a devious village council member brazenly announced that Spring Lake was a *charter* village (one of the few in the state), and so the General Law Village Act of 1895 did not apply. And because the Home Rule Village Act of 1909 made no provision for dissolution of a village, and the Spring Lake charter did not provide authority for such an action, the language on the petitions was wrong.

So ... less than a week after our petitions were filed and accepted by both the clerk of Spring Lake Township and the county election commissioners, our village council members initiated legal proceedings to challenge the validity of the petitions for disincorporation of the village.

Michigan Circuit Court judge, Jon Van Allsburg, threw out our petitions. I screamed that the right to petition was part of the first amendment! But, it appeared, the right to petition was not possible until the Spring Lake Charter Village Council amended its charter.

We would be back.

After the loss of my bruising petition battle, cruising in Croatia, with its wealth of Roman architecture, appeared at the top of my agenda in June. And brother Midge did not disappoint me. He told me to come early in June and stay late. Midge planned to sail north along the Dalmatian coast, but arranged an all-day bus tour of Dubrovnik, "the Pearl of the Adriatic," the day I arrived.

Our busload of tourists divided up into groups, depending on our interests and abilities. When I realized that I couldn't climb the high steps to walk around the outer walls of the city as Midge suggested, I joined two vibrant Swedish gals who wanted to explore Dubrovnik's gleaming marble walks lined with baroque artifacts and architecture. The convivial atmosphere in the streets captured our attention, and we soon were joining some local restaurateurs, sampling native delicacies and wines at their outdoor café.

With Maria Wallberg and Katarina Olofsson

That event consumed the rest of the afternoon. After returning to the boat, I invited my Swedish friends to tour *Sundowner* and join Midge and me for cocktails. They were eager to share adventures of their busy family lives in northern Sweden, and I was happy to make new faithful Facebook friends.

Our weather in mid-June was cool, but that never bothered Midge's Norwegian guests, Truls or Kika. If we were at anchor, they would start their day diving off the stern of *Sundowner*. I watched with apprehension. Our latitude was 45 degrees north—the same as Montreal or Minneapolis. The Adriatic Sea was cold. And Truls was eighty years old. But they had a home in Norway on the North Sea. Now that was *really* cold.

I had other interests. The shoreline was awash in history going back centuries. I had never seen anything like it.

Pula Harbor and Roman amphitheater

When we approached the harbor of Pula on the Istrian peninsula, we could view the first-century Roman amphitheater in the distance—in the heart of the city. It would be a five-minute walk from the marina. I put on my hiking shoes and headed for the amphitheater. It was so immense that I couldn't capture its size in a photograph.

My last port on *Sundowner* was Rovinj, the star attraction of Istria.

It was visible from a great distance. The tower of St. Euphemia's basilica, modeled after St. Mark's bell tower in Venice, stood high on the hill at the tip of the small peninsula that encapsulated the town of Rovinj. The tower was surrounded by colorful Venetian villas and shops crowding together on the steep sloping hillside.

Rovinj's active fishing fleet filled the public piers of the busy waterfront. Midge docked *Sundowner* stern first at the end of a long private concrete dock.

Sundowner *Med-moored in Rovinj*

With no pilings or finger piers on the dock, Med-mooring was required once again. It could be a dangerous maneuver; the anchor line stretching off the bow of a large sailboat could trip up small boats passing by, and our wobbly passerelle could trip up *Sundowner*'s guests stopping by.

After Truls and Kika departed for Norway, Midge ferreted out a restaurant in a bizarre location on Rovinj's hilly terrain overlooking the harbor.

It was perched on a rocky ledge that jutted out over the sea below. The views from our seaside table were daunting—but the most unique setting was taking place as the tide went out: A group of waiters were grabbing portable tables and chairs, carrying them down steep stone steps, and placing them on huge flat rocks that lined the shore. Then the waiters reappeared with fresh linens, wineglasses, plates, and silverware. Next, the guests (the actors?) arrived on cue. Midge and I watched in disbelief. What a performance.

And what a remarkable young nation-state! Croatia became an independent entity only two decades ago. Its ancient Roman heritage tied the country to Western Europe and culture, which was evident when Croatia joined the European Union in 2013.

Photo by Peter Sensor

A jeroboam of Arietta Napa Valley red wine, vintage 1998, was setting on the bar in Midge's spacious living room on December 23, 2012. It was inscribed, "To the Unsinkable Blaze, Gramatolla, Jo-Jo, on her 80th Birthday!"

Midge was expecting more than a hundred guests, and twenty-two of them would be my immediate family. My birthday was October 6—not a convenient time of year to celebrate, since most of my grandchildren would be in schools or colleges across the United States. But they all showed up at Christmastime for the iconic picture, crowding around the fireplace along with Midge, the venerable godfather to them all.

The e-mail invitation to the party, a cartoon depicting me in my ancient cowboy hat, riding a bucking horse on the "quick sands of time" while swinging a bottle of bubbly "Youth," was a collaboration of Julio and Greg's wife, Anne Layman Hatton. The invitation read, "Holiday Cheer and Birthday Celebration –(*80 is the new 60*)."

Family picture at eightieth birthday party, 2012 Photo by Peter Sensor

Where was I at sixty? On October 6, 1992? At my birthday party in Cádiz, Spain. Where was I living? In Washington, DC, or New York City or Aspen, Colorado. Where was I working? At Newport Partners, on 19th and N Streets in Washington, DC. And where was I headed? I did not know.

Did I know in 2012? I hoped to finish a memoir. With forty file boxes strewn all over my condo and garage, I couldn't move until it was done. And I kept getting distracted by my consuming interests in politics and early childhood education—for all preschoolers, *not just the poor*, whether sponsored at the national, state, or local level.

After a Spring Lake Board of Education member resigned in October 2012, I applied for the position on the school board. The Spring Lake board members would be considering new bond issues in 2013 to address the school district's needs in the areas of technology, transportation, and infrastructure. Except for Governor Snyder's new statewide Great Start Readiness Program—a pre-K educational day care program for four-year-olds who qualified by meeting special criteria like "low income," "single parent," or "family history of abuse"—Spring Lake school officials seemed to show little interest in pre-K or early 5's classes in their public elementary schools. I wanted all preschoolers, rich and poor together, to be given the opportunity of education.

On December 3, 2012, I submitted my resumes to the Spring Lake Board of Education. Two days later, I received a quick reply from the Spring Lake

Public Schools Superintendent. He explained that " …the board chose to prioritize those who have recent and substantial experience volunteering in some capacity for the school."

That explanation reminded me of the opposition to my appointment in 1974 as director of the Office of Child Development at Health, Education and Welfare. The nominee also would head the White House's Children's Bureau, and that made the job a presidential appointment. My recommendation for the appointment came from the National Association for Private Schools. (That meant "for-profit" or "charter" schools.)

Ron Cordray reported on the front page of the *Grand Rapids Press* in May 1974: **"Ford's Choice Denied Appointment":**

> … The Grand Rapids Association for Preschool Education said those in the profession "are very, very concerned because she hasn't been trained. This is a specialized field." … HEW said the criteria for director of the Office of Child Development "ideally" required a background in either the delivery of health programs for children, the child welfare sector, or in pre-school education of children. …
>
> A spokesman for the Office of Child Development commented that the position requires "nerves of steel and the constitution of an ox." The office has been vacant for two years.
>
> But Mrs. Hatton—a former candidate for the State Board of Education and long active in Michigan's Republican Party—won't be occupying it.

As described earlier, in 1976, two years after I was denied the appointment, I created the nonprofit Association for Child Development to launch the USDA's first computerized statewide Child Care Food Program in the nation in three states—Michigan, Illinois, and Colorado. By 2012, more than fifty thousand preschoolers were participating daily in the ACD's child care food programs in Michigan and Illinois.

During the Christmas holidays and my eightieth birthday festivities, all my children and grandchildren took the opportunity to visit with Jule at his assisted living center in Grand Haven Township. Jule was eighty-five and not well. The kids called their dad J. B., as did his wife, Nancy. The grandkids called him Grandpa J. B.

I would try to visit Jule once every week or two, depending on Nancy's schedule; Nancy preferred I visit when she was busy working or traveling.

Our out-of-town kids felt badly that they lived so far away on both coasts, and they encouraged me to visit Jule when he liked company. Fritz kept his Dad stocked with DVDs of his favorite operas, and when I played them for him (with the audio blasting away the way he liked it), Jule's tiny neighbor lady with dementia would hear the music, walk in, sit down silently, and listen for hours.

As the summer progressed, we knew that Jule would not make it to another Christmas. He died on Thursday, September 5, 2013.

Sara Newman Clarke, the youngest of Harriet and Tom Newman's four girls, was the first to e-mail me. She had been one of the first to call when Bill Seidman died four years earlier. I saved her e-mail. She should be writing this book; I treasure her thoughts. Here is what Sara wrote:

> Weighing in … with heavy heart but with a raft of gratitude for what we have shared in our lives. Our family's history and identity are bound to yours in my mind. And though I felt often intimidated by J. B., he is nonetheless one of the cords in a complex, richly textured shroud that envelopes an era. So we continue on, and I am mindful about working harder to steer again toward you all as "grown-ups."

Our resident wordsmith wrote and delivered the eulogy. Here are excerpts:

> The last time I was in this church was the first week in August. … And we got to hear some great ideas and suggestions from this pulpit about tolerance. And I was sitting right over there thinking about my dad, because if J. B. Hatton was nothing else, the man was tolerant of others.
>
> How could he not be? Just take a look around you at the cast of characters that are his family.
>
> How many people in this room could glide through raising the wild bunch that raged for more than thirty years at 1821 Doris Avenue? J. B. did it—with wit and humor.
>
> How many people could hold forth in a dining room of six hardheaded kids, all yelling at the same time; the youngest, standing on his chair to recite another life story starting with the words, "Each time"; while his seventy-five-year-old mother quietly requested another bourbon by simply perching the empty cocktail glass on top of her head? …
>
> …It was a madhouse of energy and creativity on top of that sand dune overlooking Lake Michigan. And J. B. Hatton just sat back and

smiled at his creation—because all of that energy and creativity was, after all, just a reflection of the man himself.

J. B. Hatton was a classic: a man of arts, letters, theater, and music…

Behind it all was a very quiet mandate to all of us. Go to the best schools. Excell at what you do. But more than anything else, do what you love. …

… The greatest gift my father gave me: The love and confidence in children to let them chart their own course in life, no matter how rocky that may turn out to be. He had such incredible faith in all of us, and for that, I'm eternally grateful.

Greg's heartfelt eulogy for his dad made me reflect on the mandate that his dad gave to me when I was his new bride, barely twenty years old, in December 1952: "Go to the best schools. Excell at what you do. But more than anything else, do what you love…"

Jule wanted me to go to the best schools too. He suggested I transfer to the University of Chicago, where they had a special program that let me skip the bachelor's degree and receive a master's degree in three years.

Jule certainly believed in Mortimer Adler's *Paideia Proposal*—that "education is never completed in school or higher institutions of learning, but is a lifelong process of maturity for all citizens."

In our modern world of information technology (IT), Adler's long-held beliefs still ring true today: " … a system oriented primarily for vocational training has as its objective the training of slaves, not free men, and … the only preparation necessary for vocational work is *to learn how to learn, since many skilled jobs would be disappearing.*" [Italics mine.]

Shape Corporation Quarterly, Summer 2013

Gary and Midge Verplank's entrepreneurial spirit helped to provide more than forty years of innovative engineering solutions as Shape Corporation facilities circled the globe, from Mexico to Japan, China, Thailand, India, and Europe. And the Verplank Dock Company's enterprises dotted the lakeshore along with the Shape factories; they served an array of industries, including automotive, office furniture, medical, trucking, and road construction. Gary is CEO of Shape Corporation, and, while Midge is not actively managing the Verplank Dock Company, he keeps Gary company in the boardrooms as they control the global expansion of their privately held family organization. They place great emphasis on leadership training, innovation, continuing education, and community involvement.

Our Verplank family was saddened and shocked when Gary's wife, Victoria Bruhn Verplank, died of cancer on May 1, 2014. At sixty-nine years of age, she was the youngest of our generation and seemed the most robust. Vicki had a tremendous talent for interior design, drawing, and painting. She left an indelible stamp of art and designs in the lobbies, hallways, and conference rooms of Shape Corporation's many local facilities. And she left her mark, too, on the Village of Spring Lake, restoring historic buildings during her fourteen years of service on the Spring Lake Village Council, followed by five years as village president.

My best friend for more than sixty years, Harriet Newman, died on September 18, 2014, and her husband, Tom, died three months later. She was ninety-one; he was almost ninety-four. I had to face the reality that my close friends were rapidly disappearing. Would the next generation come to my rescue with a new project?

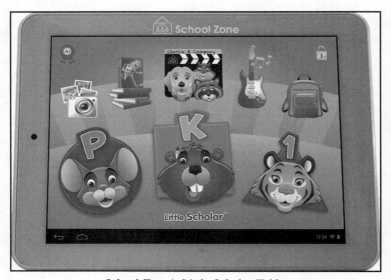

School Zone's Little Scholar Tablet

In December 2014, I read an article in the *Grand Haven Tribune* that mentioned School Zone Publishing Company's successful introduction of their first learning tablet for kids. The Little Scholar tablet was rated the best new product for preschoolers by *Tech and Learning* magazine.

I bought School Zone supplies forty years ago for my Young World child care centers. Their workbooks, toys, games, and flash cards were developed by longtime educators Dr. James Hoffman and wife Joan Hoffman. The Little Scholar tablet was developed by their son, Jonathan Hoffman, who spearheaded School Zone's leap into the electronic universe. The company's expertise in educational development of at-home learning materials specifically for preschoolers gave them an advantage over competing kid-tablet pioneers.

However, the best part of this story was a chance meeting a week later at my neighborhood grocery store. I recognized an attractive elementary school administrator whose parents had been close friends of my parents. (Small towns do have their advantages.)

I asked Sue Fuller if she still was consulting at the Muskegon Area Intermediate School District.

"Yes," she answered hesitantly.

"Well, I have a new idea to explore with you." I explained my concept for a pilot program. I needed to start small. I had no choice; I had to prove the pilot project's value before I could find ample funding for it. This would be a program structured for day care home providers in similar fashion to my successful USDA Child Care Food Program, still sponsored (forty years later) in Michigan and Illinois by the Association for Child Development (ACD).

One of the items funded in this year's state budget was Governor Rick Snyder's targeted investment in early literacy. According to State Senator Geoff Hansen, "Michigan's children, parents, and teachers deserve additional tools to improve Michigan's early literacy system."

My press release explained that "the additional tools" were what this Little Scholars Pilot Program was all about. I felt the key to success in teaching IT programs to preschool children was teaching the teacher (the day care home provider) how to use the tools. It was critical to train the providers *first*, because many of them revealed that they had never used a computer or smartphone. The tablets were loaded with two hundred or more apps—most were educational for preschoolers, starting as young as two or three years old, and required no Internet connection.

Sue Fuller quickly found the basic ingredients that made the pilot program possible: The Muskegon Area Intermediate School District and a regional nonprofit organization, Pathways, Michigan. They provided information and manpower necessary to identify the 172 licensed day care home providers in Muskegon County who might be interested in the Little Scholar training program for the thousands of preschoolers in their care. And, finally, to make the pilot program a reality, my brothers, Midge and Gary Verplank, provided the funds for the tablets and headphones.

The day care home providers' reactions after the first set of meetings in May 2015 were electric! They rushed up after the sessions, giving me hugs and thanking me for thinking of them. One commented that this was the first time in her twenty years as a licensed day care home provider that anyone had given her any training or free educational materials.

At a training session in February 2016, an owner of multiple private day care centers wrote, "I've wanted to use technology at my center. I was undecided on what to purchase, either a tablet or a laptop. This was a god-send! It encompasses everything appropriate for early learners. I am very appreciative for this opportunity. Thank you so much!"

THE GRAND RAPIDS PRESS, Tuesday, Oct. 13, 1964 • 7

Would Tackle Dropouts Early

LANSING (UPI)—Republican candidate for the State Board of Education Mrs. Joyce Hatton Monday said that the problem of school dropouts needs to be attacked at the pre-school level.

Speaking at the Lansing Women's Republican Club, Mrs. Hatton, of Grand Haven, said that nursery school programs and training should be encouraged at the state level in the culturally deprived areas of the state where, she says, many children enter school from kindergarten seriously retarded.

"It is, therefore, necessary that we begin an approach early enough to stimulate children to the benefits of the educational opportunities available to them in Michigan," Mrs. Hatton said.

Attack Dropout Problem Early, GOP Candidate Says

The time and place to attack the problem of school dropouts is in the nursery school, before the child enters kindergarten, Mrs. Joyce Hatton of Grand Haven, Republican candidate for the State Board of Education, said here Monday.

Speaking at a luncheon meeting of the Ingham County Republican Women's Club, Mrs. Hatton, the mother of six children, said nursery school training programs should be encouraged by the state, particularly in "culturally deprived areas of the state."

"Many children come to school seriously retarded when they enter kindergarten," she said. "It is therefore necessary that we begin an approach early enough to stimulate children to the benefits of the educational opportunities available to them in Michigan."

The wife of a Grand Haven businessman, Mrs. Hatton has operated a community nursery school for eight years. She is a member of Gov. Romney's Citizens Committee on Higher Education and has served on the board of directors of the Grand Haven unit of the League of Women Voters.

She is a candidate for a four-year term on the new State Board of Education.

"Would Tackle Dropouts Early," the Grand Rapids Press,
Tuesday, October 13, 1964 (Does history repeat itself?)

Chapter Twenty-six

CONCIERGE SERVICES

...Read your "Rules and Procedures"...

NO Village TAXES!

The Village of Spring Lake has one-sixth the population and acreage of Spring Lake Township. And the Township is experiencing explosive growth with its twenty-six miles of scenic land bordering Lake Michigan, Spring Lake, and the Grand River.

As I explained when I petitioned for disincorporation of Spring Lake Charter Village in the spring of 2012, our village is part of the township, and its residents pay the same township taxes as other township residents who do not live in the village. But villagers also pay village taxes—thus the very unfair and unnecessary double taxation. If the village government did not exist, village residents would receive the *same* services offered to township residents.

Only some villagers want to be taxed for "concierge" services, such as extra police protection, faster snow removal, curbside leaf pickup, down-town landscaping, etc. However, the power to tax is almighty, therefore the Spring Lake Village Council taxes all village residents and businesses. Those taxes support *administrative* salaries approaching a million dollars.

My campaign in 2016 for President of Spring Lake Village had one theme, "NO village TAXES. I won with a plurality in a three way race on November 8, 2016.

Then reality set in. All of the Spring Lake Village Council members at their first November meeting were plotting with the Village Manager to adopt her outrageous severance package if the village disincorpo-rated. And to further obstruct any action I might take in 2017 to fulfill my campaign promise, the council also planned to vote at their final meeting in December, 2016, to adopt a new nine-page *"Rules and Procedures"* resolution that would strip the new president—me—of almost all customary executive privileges enumerated in our village charter. I was to be a figurehead only.

What was I to do? I asked my personal attorney for help. He sug-gested I hire the respected municipal attorney from the Varnum law firm who represented the city of East Grand Rapids, Cascade Township, and other Michigan communities. Though the attorney was very busy, he was intrigued by my quest for disincorporation of the village (something that had never been done in Michigan), and he agreed to represent me.

My municipal attorney couldn't believe the cabal that was formed in November and December by the Village Attorney and Village Manager.

I was sworn in as President of Spring Lake Charter Village on January 3, 2017. The next day I called the Village Attorney to discuss village business. He warned me, "I can't speak to you. Read your *'Rules and Procedures'*. You need permission of the Village Manager to talk to me."

And later in the spring when I asked pernission to confer with our Village Attorney about the disincorporation community meeting, the Village Manager replied, "You just waste their time. Hire your own lawyer."

Varnum's labor attorney looked at the severance package requested by the village manager and informed me that *no severance contract* was allowed by our Village charter. He provided me with a written scholarly opinion which the new council members refused to read— ever. Or pay for. Yes, I paid personally for all my village legal services.

Shortly after I was sworn in, a wealthy village resident announced he was organizing a Citizens Committee to "examine all aspects of the potential dissolution of the village and make available a detailed summary of its findings". (The charter stated that I, the President, could appoint citizens committees. But a first organizational meeting was held before I knew it existed.)

The Citizens Committee depended on the Village Manager, Treasurer, and Attorney for all their agendas, resource information, marketing materials, and meeting rooms. The financial information the Citizens Committee received from the Treasurer described a dark dystopian picture of civic disruption if disincorporation happened: the result would be a "disaster"; village parks, police, and maintenance services would wither or disappear; residents "may lose proximity to Spring Lake and the Grand River"; the Spring Lake Yacht Club property might be sold to "some community near Detroit".

I asked the Chairman of the Citizens Committee if he had considered the auditor's annual report (which showed a net position for governmental activities of seven million dollars, with more than a million in cash), and he answered "no". The Village Treasurer did not show the Citizens Chairman or anyone on his committee any balance sheets from the auditor's report.

Although the Citizens Committee was against amending the charter to allow for the right to petition for disincorporation, they encouraged the Village Council to allow citizens a vote on amending the charter. Why? The Citizens chairman told the Council to "properly fund a public awareness and education campaign", stressing over and over to Council members that they _must control the message_.

For the two community meetings in June, 2017, the Village Manager distributed hundreds of pamphlets showing the Treasurer's most convoluted financial information imaginable and describing in detail the dire debt payment options, especially the sale of important parks and equipment and property and buildings OR assessments of taxes to cover the debts. As the only speaker for disincorporation on the panel for the meeting, I was never shown the pamphlets before the meeting.

Who paid for this marketing spree? The Village taxpayers whose money I was trying to save. Who authorized these wasteful expenditures? Not me! The Village Manager and Council members assured the public that thousands and thousands of dollars must be spent to save our little village.

And finally, on August 9, 2017, the day after the vote was held to amend the Village charter, the bold headline in the local newspaper blasted: DISINCORPORATION IS DEAD.

So what went wrong? In the era of "fake news", it is still the message and *who controls it*.

Yale University historian, Timothy Snyder, recently published a tiny book, *"On Tyranny"*, with the subtitle, *"Twenty Lessons from the Twentieth Century"*. I liked them all, but two lessons are most relevant here:

No. 5: **"Remember professional ethics."** Snyder explains: "When political leaders set a negative example, professional commitments to just practice become more important. It is hard to subvert a rule-of-law state without lawyers, or to hold show trials without judges. Authoritarians need obedient civil servants, and concentration camp directors seek businessmen interested in cheap labor."

No. 10: **"Believe in truth."** Snyder explains: To abandon facts is to abandon freedom. If nothing is true, then no one can criticize power, because there is no basis upon which to do so. If nothing is true, then all is spectacle. The biggest wallet pays for the most blinding lights."

EPILOGUE

So … what will be next? What will be important to know or do in my ninth decade of life? I remembered Dr. Duncan Littlefair's advice to me after he retired from the ministry: "The greatest adventure in life will be the adventure within."

How will I come to terms with the fact that I will never know how I came to exist? Does the search go on?

I have reflected on this: I'm busy. I have been in the midst of a village controversy… and I'm in my ninth decade. But I'm still excited to be part of the journey—not sitting below decks, but hand on the tiller, happy to feel the wind on my face.

" 'Tis not too late to seek a newer world," says Tennyson.

"For my purpose holds

"To sail beyond the sunset, and the baths of all the western stars…

"To strive, to seek, to find, and not to yield."

My interest in the adventure within and without continues. And my interest in education. Especially my own.

Sanctuary, with Dr. Duncan Littlefair at the pulpit. in Fountain Street Church, 1970s Photo by Michael Grass

The following excerpt is from Dr. Duncan Littlefair's sermon "The Trouble with Being Civilized" (1977):

We have to find our way out of the Christian dilemma. We did emerge from that animal stage into something else, a higher animal. You can't wait until you die. That's a terrible waste! And you can't go on repressing and denying. Repression and sublimation are not enough.

The only way is that we understand. That we go back and really try to understand who we are in our totality as an animal, as a beautiful animal, a human animal but beautiful, so that we can accept ourselves. Not deny ourselves. Not deny our Self. Accept our Self. And express our Self.

We didn't fall from Paradise. It's been a long long journey. A marvelous journey. An unbelievable journey! From the darkness of unconsciousness into the brilliant light of reason. From those murky swamps from which we crawled to space ships to the stars. A long long journey from that original animal form to the human beings that we are.

Acknowledgements

W hat would I have done without Niki Hansen? Niki educated me in the ways of WordPerfect for the past two years. She copied, re-searched, and confirmed sources to reproduce hundreds of images and file all of them on Excel. I am and will be forever grateful.

Jay Mead, a Yale roommate of my eldest son, Fritz Hatton, offered to edit my book. His knowledge of the English language and literature has been invaluable.

Arend D. ("Don") Lubbers, former President of Grand Valley State University, read the first lengthy version of my manuscript-- all 700 pages-- and encouraged me to publish this book. As did my artist son, Julian Hatton III.

My daughter, Lydia Stansbury Hatton, suggested the title: *Breaking Glass - Broken Barriers.*

Joyce and Niki Hansen celebrate at the Village Baker in Spring Lake, Michigan